For him I won again
The Ausonian realm and reign,
Rome and Parthenope;
And all the land was mine
From the summits of Apennine
To the shores of either sea.

~Henry Wadsworth Longfellow (1807–1882 C.E.)

The Eternal City

The Last of the Romans: V

The Eternal City

A NOVEL OF BELISARIUS

WILLIAM HAVELOCK

First edition May 2024

Book cover design by Dusan Markovic
Maps by Daniel Kogosov "Zalezsky"

ISBN: 978-1-7379808-6-5 (hardcover)
ISBN: 978-1-7379808-7-2 (paperback)
ASIN: B0CVPPWN5P (ebook)

www.havelockbooks.com

For Mukai, who dared me to see the world.

CHARACTERS

Adalfuns	A Gothic chieftain in Messana
Aetius	Long-dead general of the Western Roman Empire, Attila's nemesis
Agathias	Former slave to the Imperial Palace, and now servant to Varus
Agila	A Visigothic warlord, close to Theudis, rival to Indulf
Aigan	An officer of the Hun foederati, succeeds Simmas
Alexander	Varus' young son
al-Harith	Ghassanid king, brother of Mariya
Aliya	Handmaiden to Mariya
Amalasuntha	Queen regent of the Ostrogoths in Italy, murdered under mysterious circumstances
Anastasius	Deceased Roman emperor of Varus' youth
Andronicus	A resident of Constantinople, a religious zealot
Antalas	Mauri chieftain, leader of the Frexenses
Antonina	Young Roman aristocrat, daughter of Basilius, wife of Belisarius
Arareiks	An Ostrogothic champion
Archelaus	A former excubitor and leader of the Thracian Army, killed in trial by combat
Ascum	Alani ballista commander, serves the Cappadocian Army
Athalaric	Dead king of the Ostrogoths, grandson of Theodoric, only child of Amalasuntha
Attila	Long-dead Khagan of the Hunnic Empire
Auria	A princess among the Mauri, wife of Troglita
Aya	An Egyptian slave to the Imperial Palace in Constantinople
Azarethes	Commander of all Persian armies
Baduarius	Ostrogoth, tribune of Belisarius' spearmen, slain at
Badwila	Septem
Basilius	An Ostrogoth chieftain, ruler of Panormus
	Former East Roman consul, comrade to Justin Liberius. Died of old age

Belisarius	Roman general, husband to Antonina, and paramount Imperial military leader
Bessas	Armenian, leads Belisarius' cataphracts
Cassiodorus	Justinian's priest and religious official
Cephalas	Greek, former spearman of the Thracian Army, aide to Varus
Chanaranges	Personal excubitor to Justinian
Dagisthaeus	Ostrogoth, brother of Baduarius, a deceased tribune under Belisarius
Domnicus	An elderly general in Egypt
Fastida	A deceased chief amongst the Gepids
Fulcaris	Centurion within the Herulian foederati
Gelimer	Usurper of the Vandal Throne
Germanus	Justinian's cousin, general of the Thracian Army
Gibamund	Nephew of Gelimer
Godilas	Deceased general of the East Roman armies, and a close friend to Justin
Gratian	One of Solomon's centurions
Gunderic	A respected warlord of the Vandal armies
Hakhamanish	The magus, a priest of the Zoroastrian religion
Hermogenes	Imperial minister and legate in the Persian War
Hilda	Illegitimate member of the Vandal royal family
Hilderic	Former king of the Vandals
Hormisdas	The Catholic Pope in Rome
Hypatius	The eldest nephew of Emperor Anastasius
Ildico	Attila's final bride
Indulf	Ostrogothic chieftain
Irilar	A Herulian recruit, cousin to Fulcaris
Isaacius	A Jewish soldier in the Thracian Army, killed in battle against the Avars
Jabalah	King of the Ghassanids, killed at Thannuris
Jamila	Handmaiden to Mariya
Joannina	Daughter of Belisarius and Antonina
John	Belisarius' second-in-command
Justin	Deceased Roman emperor, former master of Varus and Samur

Justinian	Roman emperor, husband to Theodora
Kavadh	Shahanshah of the Persian Empire
Kazrig	Khan of the Avars
Khingila	Warlord of the Hephthalites, slain at Dara
Khosrow	Heir to the Persian Throne
Leo	Long-dead Pope, met with Attila
Liberius	A senior advisor to the Emperor
Magnetius	A chariot racing champion
Marcellus	Lord of the excubitores
Marcian	Latin centurion, second-in-command to Solomon
Mariya	Princess of the Ghassanids, wife of Varus
Mundus	Tribune of the Thracian Army, Germanus' second-in-command
Narses	Theodora's chief spy and advisor
Nepotian	A wealthy Roman senator, and Solomon's father
Nzamba	An Aksumite spearman
Odoacer	Ostrogoth who overthrew the last Western Roman Emperor
Opilio	Centurion of the Herulian foederati, slain at Dara
Patroklus	Trainer of Green Chariot Racers
Paulus	The Roman emperor's minister of the treasury
Perenus	An exiled Lazic prince, and Varus' second-in-command
Perozes	Persian noble and general
Petrus	An aged Roman priest
Phocas	Personal guard to Hermogenes
Pompeius	A nephew of Emperor Anastasius
Probus	A nephew of Emperor Anastasius
Procopius	Imperial scribe and historian
Rosamund	A captured Gepid pagan and healer
Samur	Formerly a Herulian slave to Justin, Varus' only sibling
Sembrouthes	Commander of Aksumites guarding Princess Mariya
Sergius	Latin centurion under Belisarius
Shaush	Prince of the Avars, eldest son of Kazrig, slain in battle against Belisarius

Simmas	A commander of the Hun foederati, slain at Callinicum
Sindual	New centurion of the Herulian foederati
Sinnion	An officer in the Hun foederati, succeeds Sunicas
Sittas	A Roman general in Armenia
Solomon	A young Roman aristocrat and komes, son of Nepotian
Sunicas	A leader of the Hun foederati, slain at Callinicum
Symeon	A spearman of the Thracian Army
Theodora	Roman Empress, wife of Justinian
Theodoric	Late hero-king of all the Goths
Theudis	Regent for the Visigoths in Hispania
Thurimuth	An Alemanni, first-spear centurion in the Thracian Army
Tiberius	Hypatius' young son
Tribonian	The Roman emperor's minister of laws
Troglita	A centurion in the Thracian Army
Tzazon	Brother of Gelimer, and general of the Vandal armies
Uliaris	A Frank, leader of Belisarius' bodyguards
Valerian	A centurion in the Roman Empire's eastern provinces
Varus	The narrator, a Herulian, and leader of the joint foederati under Belisarius
Vitalius	A youth of the Imperial household
Wazeba	An Aksumite spearman
Wisimar	A young warrior among the Vandals
Xerxes	Persian prince and commander of the Immortals
Zenobia	Varus' daughter

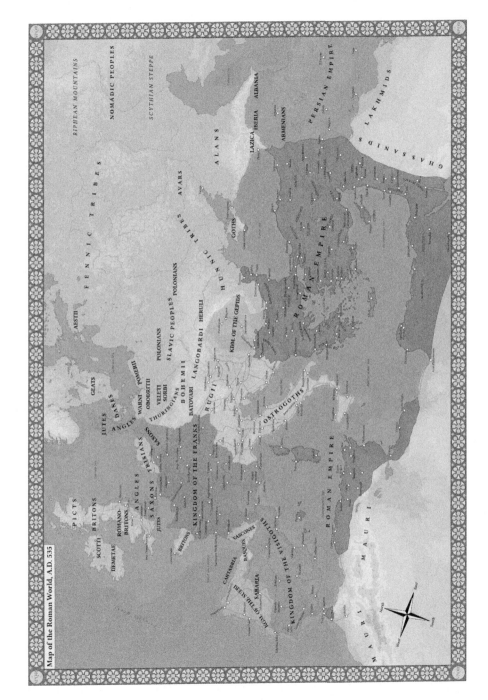

Map of the Roman World, A.D. 535

Map of the Italian Penninsula, A.D. 535

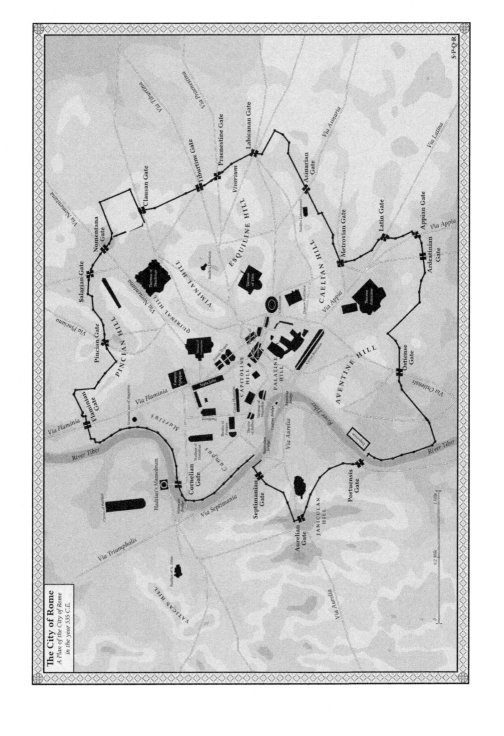

The City of Rome
A Plan of the City of Rome
in the year 535 C.E.

SPQR

Gates and Roads

Nomentana Gate · Via Nomentana
Clausan Gate
Salarian Gate
Pincian Gate · Via Pinciana
Flaminian Gate · Via Flaminia
Cornelian Gate
Septimianian Gate · Via Septimania
Aurelian Gate · Via Aurelia
Portuensis Gate
Tiburtine Gate · Via Tiburtina
Praenestine Gate · Via Praenestina
Labicanan Gate
Asinarian Gate · Via Asinaria
Metrovian Gate
Latin Gate · Via Latina
Appian Gate · Via Appia
Ardeatinian Gate
Ostiense Gate · Via Ostiensis

Hills

PINCIAN HILL
QUIRINAL HILL
VIMINAL HILL
ESQUILINE HILL
CAELIAN HILL
CAPITOLINE HILL
PALATINE HILL
AVENTINE HILL
JANICULAN HILL
VATICAN HILL

River Tiber
Campus Martius

Baths of Diocletian
Baths of Titus
Baths of Caracalla
Hadrian's Mausoleum

Via Flaminia
Via Triumphalis
Via Appia
Via Latina
Via Ostiensis

PROLOGUE:
THE BONDSERVANT

Life was its own private hell, as far as the bondservant knew. Not merely for its suffering, which was as plentiful as it was demeaning. No, this unhappy wisdom was born from the pointlessness of such drudgery, where the endless bowing and scrubbing neither improved his station in life nor fostered a sense of fulfillment or purpose. While warriors rode out and carved their names with the glories of their deeds, the bondservant remained behind, scraping pots and cleaning shit.

But the bondservant would not be contented with such a life. Better to be hanged or boiled or torn to a thousand pieces—anything to escape the futility of meaningless repetition. For the bondservant had given life to yet another plot that would see him freed far from these brutes and their knotted whips.

It would be better than last time. His maneuvers had worked perfectly, bringing the devil's powder to the lips of the old king. He loathed the rulers and their show of power, finding their claims of superiority repugnant. Those men voided their bowels all the same as the lowest slave, their status afforded merely by their birth or capacity for violence over weaker men.

In his hubris, the old king had fallen victim to the bondservant's machinations, the blame for his corrupted chalice falling upon some ill-fated girl. Gnarled fingers grasped at an unbreathing throat, and the bondservant privately rejoiced as the old man choked his last breath, ridding the world of his stench.

Yet the bondservant lacked the vision for what came next. No matter, for none who survived the old king would have ever suspected that a cowering and stunted man such as the bondservant could have toppled mountains. He would simply strike again.

This time, however, the bondservant would be prepared. Pilfering pouches from the new king's great hoard of treasure, the bondservant would gallop far into the distance, entering lands unknown to those who had conquered and enslaved his people. This time, the bondservant had the means and the unbreaking will to see this young hero fall. All he required was the appropriate moment to strike. And that time, through numbing patience, had finally come to pass.

"May all the gods curse you, oh king," the bondservant whispered as the hero passed by.

The young king appeared so proud atop his horse. Wielding his father's sword and leading a host that numbered in the tens of thousands, the hero likely had no doubt that he would emerge victorious, a shining example of his honored father. Yet the bondservant knew otherwise, for there was more than blood coursing through the monarch's veins.

THE GREAT SILENCE OF GOD

As a slave, I believed that life bends towards justice, and good fortune. Now, with my beard turned gray and knees creaking, such naivete has long departed my worldview. Though I have little doubt that those of the ancient Empire did live in some sort of magical land of peace and plenty, those of us now living are condemned to eke out our survival upon barren rocks populated by brigands and murderers. As the unyielding wheel of fate rolls ever forward, all the promise of youth has been ground into dust, leaving behind but a solitary, forbidding truth.

Life is pain. Bitter, lonely, excruciating pain. Its trials may be weathered with others and temporarily alleviated by passing fancies of love or hedonism, yet such pleasures are as evanescent as the morning dew of early spring: departing within hours of the rising sun, revealing all the suffering and loss that all who walk this earth must bear. Life is pain, and eventually, it must be felt in isolation. God help me. God help us all.

But most of all, God help Belisarius. A man who gave everything and suffered much. Even today, I doubt that my general had a single vanity that he lusted after, with no gold and glory to twist his loyalty or degrade his soul. Nothing, of course, except his wife Antonina, for whom all manner of sense was abandoned, and no cost was too great.

Belisarius did not love Antonina. It was far worse—he worshipped her. Such adulation may have been pleasing to the proud woman, once my classmate: Antonina wanted to be a queen. Yet Belisarius took joy in the simplicity of a camp and the solemn peace of duties performed well, and for that reason alone, there were never two people as dissimilar, and the tug of opposing loyalties deprived my lord of every happiness that he had mustered in this life.

To me, and perhaps to Belisarius, God turned a silent ear, no matter our prayers. Far too many friends had died, and those who survive have been maimed in body or in mind. Although the priests today profess certainty that the fabric of my soul has been washed clean of the blemishes of war, the truth remains that we had been forced to commit unspeakable sins in the name of Justinian. All was forgiven in service of the divine emperor, whose soul is guided by Christ our Savior—so they proclaim. I trust in their judgment, but when I turn to faith, I find no peace in the path I have chosen.

Clerks recount with glee the Triumph of Belisarius. Procopius most of all, with the Emperor's chief scribe insisting that the ceremony had been at once a jubilant display of Roman glory and Justinian's wit. Such stories must be tempting for those who were not present, for even those who lined Constantinople's streets merely saw a procession of unfathomable wealth against a backdrop of the Empire's most decorated living warriors. They witnessed all the splendor that traipsed alongside victory, but none of the evil that skulked in Constantinople's government, avaricious for even more bounty than Belisarius had acquired from Carthage. From Procopius' writings, one might believe that the Triumph honored the sacrifices of Belisarius, temporarily relegating him to the posture of a living god amongst a sea of bent-backed and diseased mortals.

There is no truth to such claims. I should know, for I saw firsthand how Justinian transformed an ancient Roman rite into a festival of self-advancement, gaining the awe of a mob that had recently bayed for his blood. The weeks after the Triumphal march saw Constantinople's populace begging not to overthrow their Emperor, but for Belisarius to lead the Imperial armies across the sea, to avenge the distant Amalasuntha and reclaim Rome with a single thrust of the blade.

In all my years before or since, I have never seen a more masterful display of politic. Justinian had turned a little-known Gothic queen's murder into a necessary quest to restore Roman honor.

And I loathed him for it.

God knows how often Rosamund insisted that I discard my oaths and seek freedom, while others doubtless counseled Belisarius to do the same. Why follow an emperor who thought only of glory? Why struggle beneath the jeweled heel of a man who considered his servants as little more than tools to shape and carve a rough-hewn world to his liking? Often, I had no answer. But honor, as always, kept Justinian's regime in order—though the weaker man inside of me insisted that all kingdoms are ruled by similar creatures.

Whether or not that distressing thought was true, my servant Rosamund's increasingly angry pleas that I escape with my household for the north tugged ever harder at my desires. Toward freedom and away from the den of thieves that had become Constantinople. To a simpler life, and a more honest one. After Papua and Septem, I had little thirst for blood and required no further glory to secure my place in the Empire. So why did I remain in my duties?

Honor, yes, but not only that. As always, I lacked the will to strike out into that vast unknown. I had a wife and two young children, a burgeoning household of servants and former soldiers, and hundreds who would call me lord and execute my will. And, in turn, I held the trust of two figures whose worries engulfed my own and that I dared not betray.

"Theodora and Belisarius need me," I insisted. "I cannot abandon them now. Especially not now."

"Then when?" Rosamund exclaimed. "You promised me that you were finished with the Romans."

"I know," I murmured. "And I'm sorry."

There were few people living who were comfortable speaking to me thus, regardless of our privacy of a stone-walled room overlooking the Forum of Constantine. Yet Rosamund held no reserve, spitting venom at Justinian's greed and my meek willingness to follow along. Two floors from the dust-strewn streets, we two discussed our futures amidst soft carpets and marble busts. These were quarters fit for a wealthy senator, whose use Theodora had gifted after my return from the Pillars of Herakles, although my family resided within the Imperial Palace.

"I have heard apologies many times." Rosamund groaned. "And it seems like I must suffer them many more."

We were a week past Belisarius' Triumph, and Constantinople's population had swelled. Many thousands had their purses temporarily fattened at the general's expense, spurring a rush of purchases of rich foods, soft silks, glass, pottery, and even several of the buildings in the city's poorer quarters that had been depopulated after the great riots.

The city was still bereft of mass entertainment—Justinian had not outlawed chariot racing after the riots, though organized teams such as the Greens and Blues were strictly prohibited, with their surviving leaders rotting in the sweltering desert mines of Palestina Secunda.

Though the Ghassanids had carved a comfortable home in the region, my wife Mariya shivered when she learned the fates of the lead chariot racers in a meeting with Theodora: two years choking on sand and gravel, gnawing on rotting leather sandal straps to ease hunger pangs, with few surviving the ordeal. With no sporting events in the Hippodrome for distraction, Constantinople instead filled the theaters each night, then overcrowded taverns and brothels, with an equal mix of travelers and city dwellers alike. Though drunken brawls were inevitable, it was reassuring to see Constantinople prospering, the memory of charred buildings and heaps of split corpses slowly fading into history.

Procopius tallied the cost of such donated silver at a full twenty centenaria, or the weight of ten burly warriors. Afterward, Belisarius had offered donations of ten centenaria to the Patriarch, several churches in the Empire's inland provinces, and a handsome payment to the under-construction Hagia Sophia.

Procopius wrung his hands at such baffling sums, yet Belisarius brushed any accusations of extravagance aside. I doubt the general ever cared much for wealth, and even if he did, his portion of the Vandal treasure left him comfortably able to afford those costs. And from the expense, tens of thousands feasted at banquets in Constantinople's streets, while Justinian bubbled with glee at the execution of his will.

Yet few of us in the army's leadership were happy. Marcellus worried over the lack of recruitment in simple spearmen and honored excubitores alike, grimacing at stiff joints and arthritic fingers at each of the weekly meetings he hosted in the palace. Bessas fretted over a shortage of heavy horse, while Ascum complained both of a need for new ballistae and ten thousand pots of naphtha to replenish his stores. They and many others grumbled at Justinian's declaration of war as they nursed battered bodies and fatigued souls.

Though Belisarius was not among the complainants, neither did he appear eager at the prospect of another war, fresh from the loss of his boyhood friend John and the dishonor brought by his wife's tryst with the soldier Sergius.

The only man who outright cheered Justinian's announcement was Gunderic, although even the boisterous Vandal giant voiced caution at the task ahead. "Skewering an Ostrogoth in single combat will be little more than crushing an ant," he insisted. "I'm more worried about their numbers, though. A million ants can take down a great beast, if given the proper motivation."

"A half million men might be an overestimation, but not by much," I replied, recounting what limited information Narses' spies had been able to garner from the Gothic army. "Mostly farmers with fire-hardened staves, but Theodahad's chieftains can call upon a hundred thousand warriors, all trained and armed in the style of Theodoric."

Gunderic beamed. "Perhaps one of those cockless milk drinkers will be man enough to kill me?"

"Not likely," grunted Wisimar, a centurion within the Vandal foederati. "Italy's harvests have been poor, and their valleys flooded with disease. More likely you'll fall from hunger, shivering and shitting yourself."

Though the Vandals prided themselves in their dark humor to the point of vanity, it left me with little relief. "If what Indulf says is even partially true about the Gothic forces, we should not tread carelessly. Baduarius was an Ostrogoth, after all, and he was Belisarius' greatest fighter."

Gunderic's head bobbed in a rare gesture of respect. "Aye, indeed he was. But he learned how to take a man's life fighting Rome's enemies, not Theodoric's. And Indulf is a slithering worm, feasting on dung and lies. If such creatures are called warriors in Italy, perhaps Belisarius' fifteen thousand men will be plenty to pluck Theodahad from his throne, eh?"

"The Ostrogoths haven't fought a real war in over a generation," added Wisimar. "Theoderic was a great warrior in his youth but did little in our lifetimes. While the Vandals and Romans soaked the earth in blood, the Goths have only gotten fat."

"Perhaps," I said, drawing playful smirks from the two Vandals. "But they are many, and we are few. And, whether Justinian would admit it, the Goths have made Italy their home for a half century, and I wonder whether the Italian farmers and merchants would see us as kinsmen."

Curiously, both Liberius and Father Petrus were of a similar disposition to Gunderic, voicing cautious excitement during a private meeting in a palace antechamber. True, they possessed none of Justinian's yearning for power, or the look of lust that spread across the Emperor's face when he declared his intentions for war, yet they both attempted to stoke support for the venture.

"I wasn't sure if I would ever return to Italy alive," Father Petrus said. "A blessing, surely. God has afforded Justinian and Belisarius the opportunity to triumph over foes as towering as Goliath."

"They did not fall with a bloodless sling to the head, Father," I grumbled. "But through death and suffering."

Liberius sighed. "I know your disappointment, Varus. The path ahead is certainly the one I would not have prepared, risking much on a single throw of the dice. But an army hardened by deprivation and hard-won victory—and we have our dromons, besides. Petrus is right. This is an opportunity that is hard to fathom, despite all of our hopes and plans."

I shook my head, wanting to roar with indignation. Why was the sheer difficulty of the coming invasion so consistently ignored by its partisans? "Our spearmen are at half strength from flux and wounds, and our horses will need a season of fattening to return to form," I pointed out. "I need a thousand new spears, and a hundred thousand fletched arrows, and still-uncounted sets of ringmail. And this is only for the foederati, not counting the vast bulk of our cataphracts, ballistae, and thousands of horsemen and spearmen to wield it all."

"Then it shall be your responsibility to train and lead them as Belisarius' second," Liberius said simply. "Don't just complain; issue commands. Even to me, if you think my feeble body might be of appropriate use. But between Empress Theodora and General Belisarius, the entire Empire will bow to your will."

Father Petrus raised a hand in supplication. "We know the difficulty, Varus," he said, adding a lighter tone to Liberius' goading. "None doubt the complexity or the strain placed upon you. But we all swore an oath to Justin. That dream has never been closer, thanks to you and those few others who have sacrificed so much."

It seemed hopeless. I lacked the words to explain to the two older men all that boiled within me, simmering just beneath the skin like some untended cook pot. Yet their insistence brought me to shame, and their calling my oath into question left me feeling brittle. Perhaps my greatest frustration, however, was the realization that I was trapped, with no path forward other than headlong into a Gothic shield wall.

Stoppering my fountain of reluctance and doubt, I offered only one final regret.

"For every day I have spent with Mariya, I have spent twenty on campaign," I said. "My children don't know me. I am like a thief in my own house, treated like an interloper. How do I explain to them that my oath calls me away again, for many months, or even years?"

"Though I am surly, I do not think myself cruel," Liberius said. "I've already spoken with Mariya. She and your children will accompany you on the campaign."

My eyes widened. "But... but what of Pella? The estate, the household? And the children! The risk of travel—"

"All shall be taken care of," Liberius interrupted. "The Ostrogoths lack warships, and your family will remain safe with Belisarius' retinue and the army's baggage train. Your estate in Pella shall be managed by those Mariya trusts, until you are able to return."

I considered this. Though his forethought did help lift my emotions from worry to tentative enthusiasm, I still nursed doubt. "Lord, why did you not tell me?"

"You are a busy man!" Liberius exclaimed. "Besides, I thought you would be grateful. I once was a teacher in the palace, after all— *your* teacher, no less—and I thought that your children might do with a good bit of learning at my side. Your daughter, at least, until your son comes of age." He smiled, but only briefly. "I must confess, however... there is one fact that concerns me."

I frowned. "Lord?"

"It is concerning," Liberius spoke slowly, "that Justinian was so quick to heed Indulf's pleas. Indeed, it is equally worrisome that none of your officers questioned this earlier. I may be able to make arrangements for your family, Varus, but I cannot do all your thinking for you."

My head swam from the abrupt shift. "Lord," I began, "I can only assume that Indulf and Justinian had spoken prior to the Triumph. It's disconcerting that Indulf has such influence, true, but I doubt Justinian's intentions have changed at all."

Liberius frowned. "Don't be a fool, Varus. Indulf demands war against his own countrymen, traitors though they may be, and our Emperor accedes like a sow in heat. You think this is sheer coincidence? Whenever such actions align, and so neatly, it is only prudent to ask oneself *why*."

"What Liberius means," Petrus interjected, "is that you must not be rash in your preparations. Guard your thoughts and keep them from all save those you trust deeply. We were concerned with spies in Carthage, and I can guarantee you that such dishonorable creatures now skulk in Constantinople as well. As for Indulf and the Emperor, none but they knows what words were exchanged between the two of them, or why the Emperor kept his plans secret from even his wife. What we do know is that Justin's great dream is now within our grasp, though the danger ahead will be dire."

"Speak little, and listen much," Liberius agreed. "And inform me of what you hear. Your entire life has led to this opportunity, Varus. The Ostrogoths are divided and unprepared in a manner that shall not happen again in Justinian's lifetime."

Disagreement was fruitless, that much was clear. So I surrendered to their will, rife with self-pity and a boiling frustration against the Emperor, who bound my choices and condemned me onward. I could not satisfy everyone: Rosamund's dream would be placed aside so that Justin's might be fulfilled.

At least, I reckoned, Liberius had had the insight to ensure what changes he could to alleviate my conscience. Mariya and my children sailing to war at my side—the thought alone seemed selfish. Yet if Mariya had concurred and their security could be vouchsafed... I could not argue for them to remain in Pella. I was a husband and father as much as a soldier, and selfish though it may have been, I wanted my family at my side.

Many weeks would be spent organizing this expedition under Belisarius. Massive coils of flaxen rope were hauled onto ships, while barrels of nails, thousands of staves, and a small city's worth of split logs were loaded by oxen alongside spears, freshly fletched arrows, long spathas and shorter daggers, ridged iron helmets, and a wide array of mail and lamellar chest pieces. Despite Narses' warnings of my dwindling golden hoard, I made further purchases, doubling the tents for field encampments and personally repairing the wares of Fulcaris' Herulian foederati. Food, water, wine, horses, and beasts had to be selected and ordered for embarkation, although they would not be loaded until the final days before our voyage to Italy.

Though Samur insisted upon independence, I also spent a hundred golden aurei on his behalf: importing Hunnic bows and ordering a fresh set of shoes for all their ponies, with the hopes that this would incentivize more Huns to flock to Belisarius' banner as mercenaries. Many of the Hunnic veterans had accepted Belisarius' offer to depart the Roman Army with honor and a portion of the Vandal spoils.

Yet for each discharge, two new, eager Huns were sworn into the foederati, acknowledging Sinnion and Aigan as their overlords. Samur could never be expected to serve as the acknowledged ruler of the Empire's Huns in the same manner as Sunicas or Simmas, yet Sinnion and Aigan deferred to Samur's instinct in all things, leaving the result the same.

And still there remained an impossibly long list of preparations to be made. A hundred meetings, split between Belisarius' expeditionary officers, Marcellus' excubitores, Theodora's private briefings, and nightly discussions with my household of how to manage the increased burden of Mariya and the children, both at sea and on land.

Though Rosamund executed my will and Cephalas executed most orders amongst a burgeoning staff of many dozens, Agathias proved a welcome addition by alleviating the clerical burdens expected of my office. Where Cephalas was illiterate and Rosamund disdained writing her thoughts, loyal Agathias tabulated daily developments and the mounting burden of expenses. Procopius huffed at young Agathias' presence, insisting that the youth's services would be inferior to those of his own staff.

Though I could not see it in the suffocating despair of the time, I had plenty of reason for optimism. Hundreds of attendants, clerks, servants, and warriors would respond to my call. More, the Empire's unmatched dromons ensured mastery over the Adriatic, Ionian, and Tyrrhenian Seas, guaranteeing safe transit for men and supplies between Constantinople, Carthage, and wherever Belisarius intended to engage the Ostrogoths on land. Our army was considerably wealthier than it had been immediately after the Nika Riots, with ample silver ensuring nourished bodies and deftly forged iron in each veteran's weapons and armor. That largesse extended to my household—I had a loving wife and two healthy children, and had comfortably rewarded my followers beyond their expectations or hopes. All told, we lived well. For a time, at least.

Through it all, however, ill omens clouded any advantages. I had struggled leading a thousand men at Septem, and drew little confidence at the prospect of instilling command over the thousands of Belisarius' forces as his second. Our navy was unmatched, true, but wars are won on land, and the Goths outnumbered us twenty to one without calling upon their levies. Even after bribing unblooded youngsters and greedy veterans to pick up the Imperial sword and banner, Belisarius' forces would be woefully under-manned for the invasion, with early tallies suggesting the force would be smaller than those he commanded in Mesopotamia or Carthage.

Both Hakhamanish and Theudis predicted my present course. Outwardly, I had long scoffed at their so-called portents: Theudis was no more than a manipulator and Hakhamanish a quack with a skill for fire trickery. Any prophecies I wrote off as self-fulfilling. I was a warrior—of course my future was one soaked in death. The Ostrogoths were a centuries-old enemy of the Roman people who occupied our sacred soil—of course Justinian would exploit weakness and deliver war to that tribe. From such logic, I drew comfort, dismissing both men as enemies who sought nothing other than to do me harm.

Yet, in the black void of night, their voices filled my ears all the same. They do so even today, worse than ever.

Outwardly, I made promises to serve with honor, and to strive for the long-awaited return of the Eternal City to the Emperor's bosom. Inwardly, however, I prayed. I begged God to alter Justinian's course, allowing his battered and exhausted forces to stay home. Both prostrate in a church and in private thoughts in palace meetings, I beseeched my Savior for the peace that had been tantalizingly close until the Triumph.

But God was silent. Justinian was not. And so, we sharpened our spears and readied for the carnage to come. In focusing upon our enemy in Italy, however, I neglected the threats residing far closer, slithering through Constantinople's streets and infecting the palace itself.

THE ZEALOT

It was a day that began little different from so many others. Waking well before dawn, I slipped away from a sleeping Mariya, pressing a kiss upon her forehead before escaping into an adjoining room. After returning to her quarters in the palace, Mariya insisted that both of our children should never be far—whether her fears were from ill memories of the riots or a healthy distrust of the palace's safety, I did not know. Nevertheless, we still retained rooms in a building near the Forum of Constantine, now primarily used by an aloof Antonina.

I crept across the floor, taking padding footsteps so that the iron nails within my boots would not disturb Zenobia and Alexander in the nearby rooms. The Imperial Palace never truly slept, but within my household, only Rosamund awoke ahead of me before sunrise— usually far earlier, for she rarely spent her nights in the palace, preferring the freedom of the building reserved for my household. Though I had begged Rosamund to take a guard from the Aksumites or my foederati on her route in the still-pitch hours of night's end, she had only shrugged and grinned.

"The gods watch over me in this latrine pit," she said. "And I know how to protect myself if confronted by a drunken lecher."

I shook my head, but my retort was weak. "Drunks and perverts don't worry me so much as the cruel and the cunning. You are free to do as you wish, but I would prefer you take an escort."

"Perhaps next time," she'd said dismissively, suggesting nothing of the sort would occur.

Even for the most mundane of tasks, Rosamund accompanied me to all meetings in the palace and ventures in or around the city walls. When privacy dictated discretion, she waited patiently as I entered an enclosed palace room, ready to instruct on my next appointment or duty. Sembrouthes occasionally joined us, yet the burly Aksumite warrior clearly loathed to be separated from Mariya and frequently dismissed himself to station himself by her side.

"This city is full of cutthroats and rapists," Sembrouthes had once muttered. "I'll be happy when Mariya and the children leave."

After our experience with the riots, it was hard to disagree. "Your desire shall manifest soon enough," I had told him, "although I doubt Italy will be easier on your anxiety."

That morning did not bring a day I had been yearning for, its timetable populated with meetings from sunrise to sunset. Rosamund did not complain, although I could tell of her desire to rush into the open air and mix with Perenus and the foederati, as they moved free from the trappings of Imperial rite. Nor did I, for I did appreciate the ability to rest my weary and wound-riddled body, staying mostly seated for the day.

Yet occasionally I grew restless, finding my mind wandering during a tedious account from one minister or another on our preparations for war, and wished to shed my duties and spar with wooden swords amongst friends. Alas, since the conclusion of the Nika Riots, most battles at the palace were fought with words and wit, and only rarely with dexterity and strength.

It was at one of a hundred war councils that my mind wandered into happier dreams of listless freedom, separated from the grinding responsibilities of power and dependents. In my first years in the army, I believed that generals and legates spent hours fashioning battle strategy, with every moment spent positioning each banda, inquiring upon the numbers and tendencies of the enemy. While such gatherings certainly exist, by the Vandal War, I realized that most meetings of military leadership were instead stuffed with clerical reports and tallies of goods stacked for campaign transport or in depots for later procurement.

Worse, time was given to ministers lecturing on the religious nature of our endeavor, and how we must seek signs of God's favor against pagans, heretics, and apostates. Between incense-scented priests and soft, ink-blotted clerks, it seemed Belisarius' senior officers were as likely to die from crushing boredom as from any Gothic axe.

Even so, I should have known better than to allow my eyes to glaze and mind to grow numb. Yet on this occasion I did, and as one of Procopius' underlings droned on about acquiring hardened cheese for the journey to Italy, I conjured thoughts of more carefree times with Isaacius and Perenus. As I shuffled absently in my seat, lost in my reverie, I too late realized I was being addressed directly.

"Do we bore you, tribune?"

This from Paulus, a man who, despite seeding the discontent that had fomented the Nika Riots, still retained favor with the Emperor.

Jolting upright, I shook my head. "Apologies, minister."

"Accepted," Paulus continued. "I was begging to know whether you have considered our proposal for resupply in Italy?"

"I..."

"That decision can wait for another day," Belisarius interjected, saving my pathetic answer and frowning at Paulus. "I promise you, Varus intimately understands the perils of undercooked bread and a violent stomach."

Paulus bowed his head ever so slightly. "I shall inform the Emperor. Be wary, however, for we have just a few weeks remaining until Constantinople shall be parted from your happy presence."

"Noted." Belisarius' frown twisted into disgust. "Before we part today, I want to know how the Emperor would have us proceed into Ostrogothic territory. Each of you has presented proposals, yet somehow we still lack direction about what we are going to do."

How true it was. Justinian had made his wishes abundantly clear in the Hippodrome, yet offered no instruction as to how that dream might be achieved. That unhappy duty was left to Belisarius, although the general made no decision without first consulting with ministers and commanders alike. Sitting stiffly in his chain, Belisarius' once-athletic face and sharp jaw appeared swollen and bedraggled, a coarse beard covering bloodless cheeks. As he had done in Carthage, Belisarius made few public appearances and disdained meetings, although never to the point of shirking duty. In a matter of months, he seemed to have aged a decade.

Nor did Belisarius now express his characteristic warmth. I did not fear him, but neither did I feel at ease in his presence as when he had been at Antonina's arm or peering over maps with John into the darkest hours of night. Since returning to Constantinople, I had seen the general on only a half dozen occasions, and never alone, communicating by a flurry of couriers. Among such requests were demands that his attending officers craft a strategy to seize Italy from the Ostrogoths, leading me to prod each of Belisarius' veteran officers for their input.

"I'd go by land," Germanus began. "Ride to Naissus, and then push hard for Salona. Theodahad lacks the ships to resupply the Dalmatian coastline, while we have both dromons and direct roads to Constantinople. Within a half year, we could control everything through the ruins of Aquileia and have unchecked passage into Italy."

It was a notion with merit, and one I personally favored. The Epirote provinces were closer, with firm land blessedly beneath our boots. Alas, this plan was also riddled with faults.

"Too slow," Bessas replied. "Even if you conquer Dalmatia, you'll give the Ostrogoths in Italy a half year to prepare. You'll be tired and sick crossing into Italy, and they'll be better organized and far more numerous around Ravenna."

"Then by sea?" suggested Ascum. "Storm Apulia and roll up the peninsula like an old carpet."

"That might work," I countered, "but you'd be vulnerable." Ascum scowled at my words as I privately prayed against another sea voyage. "There are few landing points to shelter our landing craft,"

I went on, "and a wary Gothic force could toss us back into the sea before we have sufficient strength to build defenses."

Liberius chuckled. "Neither sea, nor land. Surely then we'll strap ourselves to birds and fly all the way to Rome."

"No."

The fledgling discussion halted, with even Liberius limiting his tongue. Thirty heads turned toward a haggard Belisarius, deferring to the victor of impossible battles in Africa and Mesopotamia.

"We'll do both," Belisarius ordered. "Land and sea. Can this be done?"

None dared answer, for the request was as complicated as it was pragmatic. Soon, Belisarius turned to me, his cold eyes prodding for an answer.

"Lord, we would need twenty thousand men for the landing in Italy, not including sailors," I began, scratching crude number markings onto a vellum canvas before me. Having met with the planners of both strategies, I could recite the needed requests from memory, while knowing full well their costs were excessive. "And another fifteen thousand to wrest Salona from the Goths. As it stands, we only have men for one strategy."

"Correction," Belisarius said, "we will have limited soldiers regardless of the choices we make here. The Emperor will spare me fifteen thousand men, and any dromon able to float. It is far from ideal, but the Emperor has made his wishes plain."

Mundus snorted, his teeth clenched as he sat in silence, prompting Paulus to narrow his eyes at the grizzled tribune. "Something bothering you, Mundus?"

"Suicide, for one," Mundus snapped. "All of you know that I'd happily die in a battle of the Emperor's choosing. I didn't join the army for feather beds and sweet fruits. But it's pure fucking insanity to rush fifteen thousand men against a hundred thousand screaming Goths that are defending their homes. We need more support; the fact is plain."

Such criticism of the Emperor sent Marcellus reeling, but he offered no resistance or correction. No one else spoke, until, frowning, Perenus bobbed his head deferentially. "Might we recruit more foederati?" he suggested. "Huns? Or Gepids?"

"Please try," Belisarius said. "I'll pay their wages from my own hand. But the Emperor will not allow any more men to be stripped from the provinces to staff this war, nor provide the weapons or gold for additional men."

Without further explanation, Belisarius rose from his chair. He reached toward his belt, withdrew a strip of rolled parchment from a courier's tube, and tossed it toward the center of the table. As Belisarius' second, and one of the few in the room capable of reading the Imperial languages, I grasped for the scroll and smoothed it to read aloud, feeling both awkward and uncertain at the theater playing out in the war council.

"These are the words of Justinian, Caesar Augustus," I began. "In preparation for the conflict against Theodahad and the rogue kingdom of Ostrogoths, I name Flavius Belisarius, my servant, as Strategos Autokrator, serving as both magister militum and legate of the Roman armies."

"Nothing we didn't know before," Valerian said. "Congratulations, Strategos. You have to be the first person to hold that post in many years."

"Godilas held it, before he died," I added. "But it's a rare honor."

Ascum groaned. "Keep reading, Varus. Let us see what honor earns us."

After the pleasantries, Justinian's words reaffirmed Belisarius' diminutive numbers. The Emperor argued that, despite tribute from the Vandal conquest, conditions of the Eternal Peace strained the Imperial Treasury. More, the Empire's borders had already been stripped of as many spearmen as possible, and thus Justinian contended that there were no more men to spare. Fifteen thousand men were all that Belisarius could call upon—less than those he had taken against Gelimer in Africa. Belisarius would not be prevented from bolstering his household guard through recruiting unbloodied boys and foreign fighters, but not even the limitanei would be allowed to fill the considerable gaps in our ranks.

These pronouncements were unsurprising, for the Emperor had thrust Belisarius' armies into such predicaments before. Dara. Callinicum. Ad Decimum. Tricamarum, Septem. Yet rage boiled in my chest as I recited the words. The routine of being out-manned and undersupplied had grown tiresome over the years, and I found it difficult to not be resentful.

In that, it seemed, I was not alone. "You might get a taste for suicide after all, Mundus," Ascum spat. "Justinian cloaks Belisarius in honor and then sends us all into a pile of dung in search of gold nuggets."

Marcellus rose, scraping the legs of his bench along the stone floor. "That is not the Emperor's desire! The army is short on men, that much is true. But we still need to protect against a dozen tribes along the Ister, even while keeping the peace in our new prefecture in Africa."

Ascum rose to meet Marcellus, the corners of his flame-shriveled face twitching as he spoke. "True or not, your Emperor just fucked us bloody. All because he's jealous of Belisarius' success."

Although many had opinions on the Emperor's temperament, none could—and none yet can—state for certain what secrets were locked away in his mind. Whispers of Justinian's jealousy at Belisarius' success were first seeded by Antonina well before his ascension to the throne of Caesar, after the general was chastised rather than rewarded for his bloody victories in Tauris.

Judging by the later actions of Hermogenes, the onetime Imperial legate during the Persian war, I believe there is substance to those rumors, more than even the most salacious gossip would disclose at the time. Though I was loath to admit it in my youth, I now understand that Justinian did have a rare talent and vision to build greatness atop ashes, yet his abilities could not forestall such works from the poison of suspicion. And, as Ascum rightly had it, the greatest target of Justinian's jealous ire was the same general who had made his dreams manifest—Belisarius.

Marcellus slammed a fist onto the table. "Shut your mouth!"

With that, any modicum of order evaporated. Some, like Perenus and Aigan, rose in defense of the resentful Ascum. Others, including Germanus and Paulus, protested against the veiled disloyalty against Justinian, particularly a mere three years since the Riots nearly cost us all our lives. Mindful of my position, I said nothing, although God knows my heart lay square with Ascum's sense of abandonment. Instead, clutching the parchment that bore the Emperor's words, I merely kept a watchful eye upon Belisarius' face, wondering whether Justinian really would send thousands on a reckless mission out of jealousy.

Awkward on his feet, Ascum surged toward Marcellus, his acid tongue launching a tirade of frustrated curses at Justinian's intransigence. Within heartbeats, the war council erupted into a melee. There was no true danger: as Justinian's excubitores, only Marcellus and I carried weapons in the palace, and I knew that even in anger, Marcellus would never dishonor himself by drawing a blade against an unarmed foe.

Regardless, officers grabbed at collars and roared indignity, violent shoves sending bodies crashing into furniture. For men who had fought and bled together in a half dozen battles, an onlooker would think us either drunk or under the weight of a blood feud to be brawling thus. Germanus and I both attempted to keep peace, although by holding Ascum and Perenus at bay, I earned myself an accidental elbow to the rib cage.

The flurry of limbs afforded little time to respond, yet I found two men who did not engage in the fray. One was Belisarius, scowling but silent as Ascum and Marcellus tore at one another, and the other was Liberius, who buried his face in his hand with a slow shake of disapproval. And it was one of these two who brought the brawl to a halt.

"Cease!" Belisarius bellowed, his tone unusually harsh.

Many, including me, flinched. The press of men dissolved,

drawing away from the others at the general's order, some with more grace than others. The Hunnic officer Aigan, attempting to detach himself from a grapple with Mundus, caught his furs on a bench and went stumbling toward the head of the table, where his massive body collided with Belisarius. The general managed not to tumble to the ground himself, but the damage was done.

The room grew silent, and I cannot remember daring to even breathe as my unblinking eyes trained upon Belisarius' furious gaze. It was an accident, yes, but Aigan's toppling over was both formally unacceptable and culturally horrifying; any officer yielding even an accidental dishonor to a strategos would be viewed as both insubordinate and treacherous.

"Lord, forgive me!" Aigan begged, flinging himself prostrate at Belisarius' feet. "An accident, Lord, I swear on every god worshipped in the Empire."

After a single breath, Belisarius crouched, wrapped his hands about Aigan's shoulders, and lifted him to his feet, brushing a layer of dust from the Hunnic horseman's black furs as he did. Aigan said nothing; head bowed, he made to return to his knees.

Belisarius stopped him, gesturing for Aigan to remain upright. "It was Sunicas that told me that Huns do not kneel to any but other Huns, and only those fit to lead," he observed. "He was a man who died so that others may live... even those who hated his people."

Any remnant of hostility was smothered at the mention of Sunicas' name. Belisarius rarely discussed the Hunnic leader's sacrifice, where he, his brother Simmas, and a small cadre of Hun riders held a ravenous Persian enemy at bay while thousands of Belisarius' forces escaped the Callinicum battlefield. I had witnessed a Persian warrior spear the life from Sunicas, then chop head from body before tossing the lot gleefully into the Euphrates River. Samur had wailed at the death of his surrogate father, and I still struggle to comprehend the enormity of Sunicas' martyrdom. I had become no stranger to death, nor expressed particular fear that I might find my end at the edge of an enemy blade, yet the Huns had fulfilled their duty beyond any sacred or fraternal oath.

"Just as Sunicas sacrificed himself so that many of you gathered here might survive," Belisarius continued, "I hope that all of you know that I would do the same to save your lives."

"Of course, Strategos!" Aigan rasped.

Marcellus nodded. "A fact well-known to us all."

Belisarius raised a hand for quiet as others added their voices in support. "God and all the apostles know that I do not relish war in Italy. I dreamed of glory in Rome once, many years ago, when our room was a bit fuller with friends now departed."

Stepping away from his bench, Belisarius began to pace around the table. As stiff legs hobbled within my reach, I considered nodding or shouting my support, yet found myself too numbed by the others' solemnity. With the little I had seen of Belisarius since Carthage, I had not witnessed such emotion from him, or even so many words. All but paralyzed, I barely turned my head for fear of disrupting the moment. This was the general I knew well, fleeting though his return may have been, and I would not miss it.

Stopping near an upturned stool, Belisarius swept his cloak aside and bent to return the seat to its proper position. "I pray to God, but I fear death," he continued. "I would give anything for my little Joannina to live a blissful life, one where her father's chair is never left empty by duty or injury. I would like to be a good parent, yet find it nearly impossible given my responsibility, and I hate myself nightly for it. I am her father, as I am the father of thousands in the army, who place their hopes of survival and happiness upon me all the same."

"And we love you for it, Strategos!" boomed Bessas.

"No doubt, we do," Marcellus agreed, echoed by Ascum and a half dozen others.

Belisarius offered a weak smile, the glimmer of happiness too brief. "I lost much in Carthage, as have so many of you in our battles together. All I wanted was to take my wife and child into the mountains of my childhood, exchange my weapons for farmer's tools, and grow fat and happy. I want that kind of peace for all of you—on the bones of Christ, I swear it. But the army is commanded to Italy, and if duty calls me to that fate, I would see the task done well, and with minimal suffering. Not just for our men, but for the Romans and Goths who inhabit the Ostrogoth kingdom."

"Your will, Lord," Aigan said. "But I must ask… why such mercy? Theodahad would show us none. He slew his own queen, and her child who would be his king."

"Because." Belisarius' speech was clipped, pressured. "Just as we want nothing to do with this war, neither do the farmers and townsfolk who find themselves under Theodahad's dominion. I am no fool, and will not sacrifice my men's safety for an enemy. But if we show those of Italy and Illyria peace and order, show them that they, too, might be able to reap crops and raise children in a land of peace and justice, our fight might be a blessedly brief one."

Belisarius had shown a similarly gentle nature in Mesopotamia and Carthage, yet this posture still came as a surprise, antithetical to all military doctrine of Rome's past, from Marius to the present day. Even Godilas insisted that war, as terrible and regretful as it was, must be fought with an unrestrained malice toward one's enemy, lest their cruelty overpower your lenience.

Belisarius was of an entirely unique mind in disallowing violence unless it was first initiated by an enemy, and generally avoiding burdening locals with unpaid board when we occupied their territory. Such restraint was preached adoringly by priests like Petrus, yet drew the ire of many a training officer—something I can personally attest to from my time under Archelaus' command. Few in Belisarius' ranks would appreciate the general's rationale, and fewer still would relish yet another sacrifice to a foreign land and an exceedingly numerous enemy.

So none reacted to the end of Belisarius' speech. Indeed, it was unclear, at least to me, that a reaction was desired—yet within heartbeats I felt Liberius' gaze fall upon me. Without so much as a nod or a smile in my direction, his will was evident, and I was confronted with a choice: leave the army and return to my family as I had long desired or embrace my fate as Belisarius' second, and lead thousands to conquest in long-lost Italy. Either way, there could be no further half measures, only a full commitment to one life or another.

"Your will is my own, Belisarius!" I cried, instinctively throwing up a salute. "We shall return Italy to the Empire, and all will know peace!"

For this, I won a weak smile from Belisarius and a tacit nod from Liberius. Others swiftly followed my example, all memory of enmity evaporated. Ascum and Marcellus shuffled uncomfortably, muttering apologies to one another.

Rosamund had always lectured me that magic exists in this world, that it bends to the whims of those with great destinies, but I was loath to give credence to such superstition. Yet in that moment, it was hard to deny that Belisarius had a supernatural ability to bolster confidence and maintain order amongst his men. Of all those I have met before or after, Belisarius alone emitted an aura of calm that seemed to assuage my deepest worries, as if the man's very soul could lift concerns from my shoulders and leave me with peace, however temporary.

Yet despite the officers' newfound agreement, there was no great elation at Belisarius' conviction, nor even so much as contentment; even Marcellus had privately voiced disagreement with the Empire's grand desires. There was no thrill of forthcoming adventure, nor even the prospect of boundless spoils as had been taken from the Vandals. All that unified us was a common brotherhood, with Belisarius at its head, and perhaps that was enough. God knows, I still harbored my own private pangs of worry, yet hearing Belisarius' own struggles somehow dulled the sting of reluctance.

"I am grateful to all of you for sharing my burdens, for I do not deserve it," Belisarius declared as the voices quieted, lowering his head in a bow. "As a last announcement, I am raising additional officers to command staff. Vacancies remain, but I have selected a leader for my bucellarii, as well as a temporary replacement for the Thracians while Troglita is stationed in Carthage. I leave it to you to welcome them."

Once again, Belisarius withdrew a scrolled parchment from his belt and tossed it at the center of our table before striding for the exit. I rose, hoping to ask Belisarius for a meeting before he left, yet was stymied by the other officers.

"Tell us what it says, Varus!" Perenus grinned, tossing the furled scroll to me.

"You can read it for yourself," I replied, catching it. "Why ask me?"

"I *could,*" Perenus replied, "but poorly. Reading's despicable work. A job for poets, clerks, and kings."

"And ministers, dear Perenus," Liberius added, his silence finally broken. "If you had to read through one of the campaign's supply ledgers, you'd understand the true meaning of suffering. Digging latrines is lovely work by comparison."

"It's not the digging latrines that's the problem, Minister," Ascum said with a smirk. "It's cleaning them. A duty I've found myself in more often than not."

I unknotted the scroll's leather ribbon and unfurled the parchment to find a litany of names and titles—promotions, and many of them. The fortunes of men from each of the Empire's armies had been considerably raised: Some were destined to join Belisarius, while others would staff new postings in Carthage, Mauretania, and Mesopotamia. Most names I did not recognize, yet as I scanned through the document, I found one that brought me to gasp.

Marcellus scowled. "Well?"

"The lord Mundus, for his many years of faithful service, is named general of the Thracian Army, and magister militum per Illyricum," I said, my words drawing to a hush as I spoke the title. "It is by the will of Justinian, Caesar Augustus, that Mundus will command the landward assault to liberate Illyria and its long-lost provincial capital of Salona. Absent Lord Troglita, who is an emissary to Tribune Solomon in Carthage, I appoint Constantinianus as the Thracian Army's Tribune and second-in-command."

"Gods!" Ascum beamed.

Mundus grew pale, his weathered face somehow softer. "Me, a general..." he murmured. "Lord of the army..."

"And a damned good one too!" Perenus shouted.

Marcellus clapped Mundus on the back, but the newly minted general still frowned in skeptical sobriety. "But what of you, Germanus?"

Sounds of joy halted as Germanus, who had been interim commander of Mundus' new army, rose from his chair. Even Mundus' happy bewilderment shifted to awkwardness as the grizzled man crossed his arms, grinning sheepishly. Germanus, however, beamed at the pronouncement, nodding to Liberius. Privately, I questioned this newcomer Constantinianus—the name held no repute amongst the Thracians, good or ill, that I knew of, nor was he a veteran of the Vandal War. This was not an ill omen by itself, yet I worried. Was Mundus being set up to be plied with an Imperial lackey with little martial skill—or worse, a sycophant who intended to spy on the Thracian Army for Justinian? The practice was well-known amongst military officers; I served as Theodora's own confidant in Belisarius' army.

Still, whatever misgivings I or others might have expressed of Constantinianus, a pronouncement from Germanus stopped all other thoughts.

"I'm transferring," he declared. "Unless the Emperor has children of his own, he requires a designated heir. I am to assume that happy post."

At that statement, even I gawked in silence. It was exciting to see Mundus raised to the hallowed rank of general, and ultimately unsurprising given his two decades of soldiering and success as Germanus' second. But Germanus... Justinian's heir? Strictly by bloodline, I supposed it was logical enough—the two were cousins and were rumored to be on friendlier terms—yet such a direct, intimate connection between the two had never broached my mind. Where Justinian was bookish and insatiable for glory, Germanus possessed an air of caution that made him popular amongst the Thracian spearmen.

"Well, fuck my hole." Ascum cackled. "Be careful, lads, this one might dress himself in purple soon enough."

"God willing, Justinian will outlive me by many years." Germanus betrayed no hint of flippancy. "I will still retain my rank, and will be Belisarius' liaison in the capital. I will be able to advocate for your needs directly with the Emperor's ministers each day."

"A blessing, surely," I answered at last, while the other officers seemed still agape.

And it was, in a way. I trusted Germanus, who never placed personal interests above the betterment of his men. But at the same time, the news placed Theodora's position in question, even if Germanus was only informally Justinian's heir. The Empire looked upon women with even the slimmest designs on power as blights upon the natural order, after all.

Centuries ago, one such woman included the Palmyrene Zenobia, after whom my own daughter draws her namesake. No army had ever willingly backed the sole claim of an Augusta, nor would an Imperial court peacefully abandon the claims of a designated male heir for an Emperor's consort—even if the male heir was neither a natural-born or adopted son. No, ambitious women were at best cast aside like overworn garments, at worst slain by one catspaw or another.

Then again, the Empire had never been ruled by one such as Theodora. She was a woman unlike any who had preceded her, and it was impossible to know for certain what her future held. My oath nagged weightily as I gazed upon Germanus' unassuming smile, knowing full well what dangers his advancement threw upon Theodora.

What could Liberius be thinking? I wondered.

Answers would not soon arrive. Though I lived in the palace for nearly all my childhood, it is only in the baleful experience of old age that I can truly discern the motives of Liberius and Justinian, and see the truth as they saw it: Theodora remained childless after years of marriage. Though far from old, Theodora could not be said then to have retained the youth of her more carefree years: In those days, I would presume Theodora to have been in her mid-thirties, her face just beginning to show lines of worry after serving more than a decade as a senior figure, first under the aged Justin, and now as Augusta alongside Justinian. She retained all the raw strength that enthralled so many, as much as the first day I encountered her in the Hippodrome, yet still she lacked the greatest source of political power that Roman empresses could draw upon: children born from the Caesar Augustus. And though I knew of women who had borne babes at Theodora's age and older, it was exceedingly rare for such children to be the firstborn, and Theodora herself had vaguely hinted at her barrenness.

Yet Justinian was said to love his wife far more than yearn for a son, and as an anxious and suspicious man—as Belisarius knew all too well—the Emperor must have held a love for Theodora that eclipsed the sun itself to choose her over a younger bride eager to bring him an heir. For all his faults, I do not doubt it for the briefest moment, for Justinian remained enamored with my mistress until his dying day. And for such a childless augustus, Germanus—loyal, beloved, and battle-tested—was a natural choice of heir.

Absent Belisarius, the gathering dispersed as officers hurried to their tasks or gathered around an animated Germanus. Even Liberius joined the fray, standing aloof as he monitored the heir with an expressionless face. It felt improper to leave, yet with no opportunity to converse with Belisarius, I was eager to escape yet another military gathering. Only Perenus noticed my movements toward the exit, and flailed an arm to catch my attention.

"Varus." His voice was low as he drew me aside, darting a glance toward the unsuspecting gaggle of officers. "I need your advice."

I chuckled, curious at his uncharacteristically somber tone. "Christ save us, but whatever it is, your concerns must be serious to ask me."

Again, Perenus' eyes darted about until, satisfied that there were no eavesdroppers, he whispered his intrigue. "Hereka is pregnant."

Though I attempted to mirror Perenus' gravity, a broad grin

slipped across my face. "Congratulations, you rogue! To think—Perenus a father!"

"Not so loud, you oaf!" Perenus' eyes went wide. "It's still early, and I'm in a bind."

"A bind? How so?"

"Well, this wasn't something I planned—but then again, not something I resisted either." Perenus blushed. "We still aren't married."

I chuckled again. "You wouldn't be the first bridegroom with a babe already coming on the wedding day."

"I can't just *do* that, Varus," Perenus hissed, again stealing a glance nearby.

At that, I was truly puzzled. "Marry her? It's not like it's hard! Just pay a drunken village priest a few coppers, and you'll be wed three times over."

"If only it were that easy." Perenus set his jaw. "Hereka's father could not prevent her from leaving with me—something about Vandal women living freely—but if he discovers his unwed daughter pregnant without his blessing... he'll geld me."

That threat, at least, made more sense. "And you believe he would not approve of you if you sought his blessing?"

"The Vandals don't know me well—at least, not beyond the drinking." Perenus winked, then sobered. "But anyone short of a famous warrior would be unworthy of a chieftain's daughter. I'm no layabout, but I'm hardly an Alexander either. So what in the deepest hell am I going to do?"

Again, despite Perenus' insistent secrecy, I laughed. Children out of wedlock might be distasteful to the Roman elite, but was common enough amongst the Empire's soldiers. And Perenus, lacking the shame and instinctive modesty that had grown pervasive in Roman society, was hardly a prude, yet the current subject visibly bothered him.

"There's nothing funny here!" Perenus rolled his eyes. "What should I do?"

My mirth melted, and I thought of how Justin would handle such a predicament. "You seem to care for her, no? More than as a camp companion, I mean."

"Deeply," Perenus replied, his voice a hush. "She won't show it, but I can tell that Hereka worries about her father's disappointment as much as I do. I would spare her that, as much as I can."

"Then the choice is a simple one." I shrugged. "Grab your armor, meet her father, and tell him that you're going to marry his daughter. He should respect your directness, and doesn't need to know of the pregnancy until the marriage is well established, besides."

Perenus nodded, but his face was drawn. "Thrasa's as likely to club me to death as embrace me as a son," he muttered. "Directness be damned. The man is a typical Vandal, worshipping manic strength, and little else except his daughter. Even with my promotion, it was difficult enough to keep him from strangling me in my sleep in our last months of Carthage. Someone powerful would need to join the union to satisfy his sense of honor."

It was a small matter, yet Perenus spoke truthfully. Under Roman law, Thrasa was within his rights to thrash Perenus bloody for impregnating his daughter outside of marriage, although I doubt the Vandal chieftain knew or cared for such legal trappings. No, undoubtedly Perenus was right, and he would deal with the matter in the Vandal way: challenging Perenus in a pointless duel to the death. Still, I knew that even amongst the Vandals, such vengeance could be stifled with the correct application of influence and prestige. This was a lesson I learned at Justin's feet long ago, when he, too, had to address the worldly cares of the many soldiers who called him lord prior to his ascension to the throne of Caesar.

So, to spare Perenus such a confrontation, and save Hereka from choosing to honor her father or her lover, I elected for a third option.

"Marcellus!" I called. The lord of excubitores peeled himself from Germanus' gathering to amble over. "You still need recommendations for men to join the sentinels?" I asked as he drew to my side.

Marcellus grunted. "Dozens, as long as they're competent and loyal. I would even pay to equip them, so long as they can take an order."

I nodded. "Then Perenus is your man. Belisarius will need him to command the foederati against the Goths, but there is not a soldier I would trust more to safeguard the Emperor."

Perenus' eyes drew wide at the brazen recommendation. Joining the excubitores would not only add to his respectable income as a leader of multiple bandae of foederati, but would confer unrivaled status as a member of Rome's elite band of warriors.

Marcellus scratched at his jaw, stubble forming against a normally clean-shaven chin, and nodded.

"I've seen you fight," he said. "But more than that, I trust Varus' judgment. I will recommend your name to the Emperor, if you would like to join our brotherhood. God knows we will need you in the years ahead."

"He will not disappoint you," I replied, leaving Perenus open-mouthed and dumbstruck. "But he requires your permission to marry after taking the white cloak. Does the Emperor still grant permission to marry?"

Marcellus' mouth twitched—a gesture that signaled disgust in most men, yet was perhaps the closest thing to a smile the dour komes excubitorum would betray. "Indeed he does, although the Emperor has not officiated such ceremonies since the first year of his reign. I doubt there will be any problems obtaining permission, but the cost of the affair will be Perenus' to absorb."

"Gladly, Lord." Perenus beamed.

Marcellus nodded. "It is concluded, then. Varus and Chanaranges will explain your duties, but the oath-taking will occur as soon as I can gather a quorum of the brothers. Be sure this is what you want, Perenus, for the oath is for life, and few of our number die old men on feather beds."

With our exchange ended, Marcellus returned to Germanus' still-excitable gathering, and I, at last, moved toward the room's exit. Perenus halted my progress once more, however, placing a hand upon my shoulder and gripping hard the iron and leather armor.

There was no casual mischief in his face, only an awe-struck contentment. For a heartbeat, I believed that he might embrace me, but he merely patted me on the shoulder. "I don't know how to thank you, Varus. Me, a brother of the excubitores…"

"Thank me by keeping me alive in Italy," I countered. "And save me time today. Go to the officers not invited to this meeting, and tell them of Belisarius' words. Give them the option to leave the army with honor and wealth. Particularly Xerxes, for this fight is not his to bear."

"Very well, but you know he will refuse," Perenus pointed out. "They all will, really, if *you* insist upon going."

Smiling, I sighed. "Inevitably. Nonetheless, I must allow them the ability to choose. Now let me escape this place before Paulus or one of the other bureaucrats make my life more complicated than it already is."

Nearly forgotten along the walls of the room, I shuddered as Procopius locked eyes with mine. He motioned in my direction, doubtlessly ferrying one of a thousand missives that the Emperor's secretary crafted each day. Even today, the sight of ink-smudged fingers returns my mind to Procopius—a man who, if nothing else, was dedicated to his work in a fashion that was commendable amongst clerks. Yet I found his entreaties brought little more than headaches. His tasks were at once onerous and mundane, things that the simplest prefect could address in a few minutes yet which Procopius insisted fill the days of Belisarius and myself.

But Perenus, ever at the ready, intercepted Procopius' progress, allowing me to escape into blissfully cooler air and a hoped-for freedom that the day's logistical tasks were completed.

At first, I cherished the temporary relief. There is a childlike joy in eliminating the planned burdens of the day, and I intended to rush back to my family for some excursion or another. Even after weeks of being reunited with them, my two children still looked upon me as a foreign presence, a stranger tolerated by their beloved mother.

Alexander was still too young to resist my entreaties, yet broke into fits of angry tears if I held him for too long.

Zenobia, however, eyed me curiously in our private moments together, scowling with an unsettling skepticism for a girl not yet three. She shed few tears in my presence, and had recently begun to offer sly smiles and sheepish hugs when prompted. This was something I intended to build upon, God willing.

But giddiness would soon shift to rage. And it all began when I discovered Rosamund missing, her usual perch in the hall adjoining my meeting vacant.

THE RESURRECTION
OF CASSIODORUS

The white-haired Gepid woman? She left for the market." The palace guardsman leaned on his spear with a yawn. "She said she would return soon, before your work would conclude."

"How long ago was this?"

The guardsman shrugged. "An hour, maybe two? I'm not in the habit of keeping schedules for barbarian women."

I frowned. "That barbarian woman has saved at least a hundred Roman lives after battle."

At that, the man bobbed his head, perhaps aware that his words had drawn the irritation of a senior officer. Still, I felt a sudden urge to lash out at the young man. "Stand straight with your spear upright, or are you so feeble that you require a walking stick?"

"No, Lord!" He snapped to attention, immediately shifting his gaze to the opposite wall save a quick glance at my own eyes to ensure I was not displeased.

In my years of service, I'd allowed far worse abuse to melt about me, but something about the man's jab at Rosamund overruled my restraint. "Have you accompanied a campaign, soldier?"

"I have not had the honor, Lord!"

"And the Nika Riots?" I pressed. "I do not remember your presence when we defended the Emperor against the mob."

"No, Lord!" the man replied.

I moved two paces closer, my chin perhaps a hand length from his own. At that distance I guessed the lad was little more than eighteen years—a man, but one with little experience of the world. Undeserving of punishment, but also old enough to be chastised for insulting those who bled for Justinian's Empire.

"That Gepid woman killed men to save the Emperor and Empress, in the very throne room where ten thousand Greens almost overthrew the Empire. She fought, when a fair number of the palace guards pissed their trousers and ran away. What gives you the right to pass judgment on her?"

His eyes widened. "Lord, I... I offer apologies, a thousand apologies. I did not know."

"Correct," I barked. "You know nothing. So assume nothing, if you wish to remain in the Emperor's service."

"Yes, Lord!" the man replied. "Apologies again, Lord!"

Though I detected a light tremor in the lad's foot, he stood straighter, not crumpling against the pressure even as he swallowed hard, and I decided not to push further—humiliation is a poor teacher of the young, and I myself had balked under the cruelties of older men at his age.

"Good," I concluded. "Show respect to yourself and to others, and you will advance. Make no more foolish comments, or I shall hear of it."

Not waiting for a response, I turned toward the hallway's length and navigated for the nearest staircase. The hardened tips of my boots rang out against the marble floor, yet the din of dozens of voices all around muffled the disruption. I hurried, fearing an unwanted social entanglement would waylay me, offering only gruff acknowledgment to excubitores, nodding as I passed. Within moments, I emerged from the palace, eyes burning from the sudden rush of light against the palace's interior gloom.

Though it was odd that Rosamund would leave and not return, true worry had not yet set in. After the annihilation of the social gangs supported by the Greens and Blues, Constantinople had become, for the most part, blissfully free of rampant crime, although the occasional sins of theft and murder remained unsurprising to residents. Likewise, Rosamund possessed a streak of independence that I'd grown used to, and though she eschewed my guardsmen as companions in her city travels, there was little risk that she might be violently accosted in daylight. She had traversed the city alone countless times, and I assumed she would be perfectly safe.

I was wrong. I lacked the wisdom to recognize a new foe, one who was far more resourceful and infinitely more dangerous than any chariot mob. And, unfortunately, it was one I had disregarded entirely.

Passing through the palace gates, I found Constantinople's streets bare enough that the echoes of each footstep drew uncomfortably loud. Even the Hippodrome held little activity, for with chariot racing halted and its more ardent supporters burnt to ash, few occasions called for the use of the cleaned and rebuilt testament to Roman games. Besides an occasional beggar, there was little noise whatsoever, and it was not until I reached the Forum of Constantine that the cacophony of activity rose in curious harmony with the pungent odors of life, altogether evoking the Constantinople of my childhood.

There were a great many merchants, with several stalls hosting a Roman dekarchos or centurion as they haggled over the costs of a freshly forged dagger, iron-lined greaves, or even collections of waterskins that had to be frequently replaced due to leaks and tears. I recognized none present, although the bustling atmosphere further eased my anxieties as I scanned the stalls and side streets for Rosamund.

Yet above the barking of merchants and clatter of feet arose a piercing cry: exhortations to Christ the Redeemer. Reverberating at once a lustful joy and seething hatred, these cries to the Savior were a sound that once had been foreign to Constantinople's populace, yet now, and since our return from Carthage, were all too familiar. For weeks, I ignored such a rabble as nothing more than the ravings of young men and older boys caught in the fervor of village priests and self-proclaimed prophets. Brimming with words of apocalypse and salvation, these men held sway in the distant provincial towns of the wild hills of Moesia or the desert wastes of Egypt, and found little audience amongst the urban masses of Constantinople. They were easy enough to ignore as a passing nuisance, born of boredom and faith.

Until I saw her. Her white hair, so characteristic of the pagan Gepids, left her easily identifiable against a sea of Greek and Latin bodies, their hooded cloaks stained with all manner of unwashed filth. Black linen and darkened leather, so painstakingly cared for, were besmirched with horse dung. Rosamund used a forearm to shield her head against the flying detritus, but globules burrowed into her disheveled mane. From behind her limited protection, Rosamund spat defiance at her tormentors.

"This makes you feel powerful?" she screamed in accented Greek. "You're all worms! And you'll roast in the hell that your priests love to lecture about."

Though I rushed toward Rosamund, I was too distant to prevent what happened next. An older man, his pate hairless except for a few stray silver strands, plucked a loose stone from the gutter. Spitting toward Rosamund, he whipped back his arm, the stone too large to be comfortably gripped by a meaty fist. I burst into full sprint, my eyes fixed upon the swinging arm and its missile.

I reached Rosamund just as the stone was released. It was a weak throw, sluggishly tossed from a soft arm and an improper grip that robbed the stone of force. Yet as it connected with Rosamund's skull, a staccato thud left little doubt of the damage wrought. A gash opened above her left eye, a stream of blood pooling from the fresh wound, and she shrieked, drawing a hand to the injury.

Only a heartbeat behind her, I drew my blade, its honed edge rattling against its leather-and-iron scabbard. Whether the balding man detected the threat behind him I cannot be certain, although he did not flinch at the telltale wisp of sharp metal. One of his colleagues, a much younger man with a wispy beard and mud-stained robes, eyed the armor-clad attacker behind his friend and mouthed a warning, although it was far too late in coming. I was a warrior, trained by killers to snatch the lives of my victims before they could mount any defense, and I wanted nothing more than to unleash pain on Rosamund's tormentors.

But despite years of rashness, I was not a fool. Rather than stab into the man's unprotected spine, I turned my sword and swung hard toward the man's head, so that the flat of the blade smacked into his pate. It connected with a thud, sending the man into a crumpled heap before he could turn around and discern his attacker.

"Order!" I yelled. "In the name of Emperor Justinian, cease your wrath!"

Normally, a shout accompanied by an expensively attired and armed man would render even the most inebriated vagabond at attention. Now, however, Rosamund's tormentors only hissed with anger. Several pointed, while others gathered stones, and one younger man rushed forward to lift the bald man to his feet.

"What gives you the authority to strike Brother Andronicus?" the younger man sneered.

With an eye on a quivering Rosamund, I snarled a response. "I am an excubitor. What gives you the right to assault my servant?"

"Because she is a pagan whore!" the bald man Andronicus screeched, his eyes unfixed and legs unsteady as he leaned on his savior's arm. "She was about to invoke spells on Christians!"

The younger man nodded vigorously. "These Gepids worship trees and copulate naked under the stars. Christ abhors such creatures, and our master commands us to strike against the enemies of our Christian empire."

"What is it that you hate most?" Rosamund seethed, cradling her bloodied eye. "That I'm a barbarian, a pagan, or just a woman?"

I did not allow these dozen men in their stained and frayed clothing to offer a response. Instead, with my naked blade glinting in dim beams of light, I shuffled toward Rosamund, shifting the sword's point to any who might defy my passage. None did, and I soon lifted Rosamund to her feet, careful to keep watch over the gathering.

"Neither the Emperor nor Empress would condone such violence," I roared. "Who gives you authority to gather and disrupt the common peace?"

Still holding Andronicus aloft, the younger man smiled. "You must not know the Emperor as well as you say, excubitor Varus Veridicus. But you, too, have the look of a steppe warrior, so perhaps you share the Gepid witch's predilections?"

A knot strained my throat at such intimate recognition. Though I was a wealthy citizen and high-ranking officer, I lacked the popular glory of Belisarius or the austere imperium of Theodora, and generally could move anonymously even when ensconced within my excubitores' armor. Some merchant citizens surely knew who I was, for a great deal of silver coins of my household purse had been spent to outfit and equip my men.

Yet the calm sureness of the man took me aback. He lacked any measure of size, for he stood but a finger length taller than Rosamund, with none of the musculature of the plow fields or dockyards, yet he expressed unbridled confidence all the same.

I forced a scowl to mask my surprise. "And what is *your* name, citizen?"

"None that you would know, if that is your intention," he replied, his sickly smile fixed below his unblinking eyes. "My name is Philip, and I am but a humble student of Cassiodorus, beloved of God and entrusted by Emperor Justinian to rid Roman lands of sin."

I felt a chortle slip through my tight lips. "Cassiodorus? That old lecher took a rotten vegetable to the face in the Hippodrome. I grant you this one opportunity to leave in peace, or I shall summon the Emperor's guardsmen to wrap you in chains."

Andronicus, still dazed, laughed. "He doesn't know!"

"Unsurprising," Philip replied. "The august Emperor would not share our designs with his sort."

"Kill them, Varus!" Rosamund hissed in Heruli, a hand pressed about her eye. "If not now, they will make you regret such mercy."

Philip smiled again, raising a free hand in mock surrender. "I do not need to understand your tongue to absorb your intent. You have routed us for now, and we shall leave, but know that even tribunes shall be punished for harming holy Roman men."

"Enough blather." I waved at the lot with my sword. "All of you, back to the sties you call home!"

At first, none rushed to obey my command. Several glowered, while others turned toward a staggering Andronicus. However, the older man whispered to Philip, who called for the gathering to disperse. With little more than a grunt of acceptance, the dozen fanatics professing allegiance to Cassiodorus filtered from the forum. Only then, with a few lingering merchants scurrying from Constantinople's streets, did Rosamund trade her defiance for pain.

"You should have flayed those bastards," she muttered, her unmarked right eye welling with tears as she gingerly pawed at the left.

Sheathing my sword, I knelt close, keeping my arm wrapped tight around her body. Rosamund twitched and sobbed, howling in fury as she kept her face hidden. Her hair and jerkin were odorous with blood and dung, mixing with the smell of the fragrant roots that she ground into powder before washing into a repulsive aroma not unlike the acrid stench of death. Nevertheless, I showed no sign of revulsion, worrying only that she, essentially a member of my family, had been gravely hurt.

"How bad?" I whispered.

Even before she replied, I knew the outcome would be poor. I had seen too many similar wounds on the battlefield and could predict their prognosis with a morbid accuracy. Her words were unsurprising.

"I can't see," she sobbed. "I can't see out of this eye. The bastard's stone struck me cleanly."

"We will attend to it immediately." I forced my voice to stay even, despite burgeoning worry.

"A half-blind healer. What a pathetic joke." Rosamund winced, keeping a hand tight over the injury. "I shouldn't have provoked them."

Unencumbered by my sword, I lifted Rosamund from the ground, cradling her back and legs as I held her tight to my armored chest. She was hardly a burden, as diminutive as she was, yet still I exerted considerable effort to keep my gait even and her body level. She pressed her uninjured cheek into my chest, pale skin unflinching against the cold iron of my chest plate. The few who remained in the forum stole glances amidst their trading, yet other than a wary glance to detect possible threats, I cared little for prying eyes. Instead, walking beside the road back to the Imperial Palace, I allowed myself fleeting glances at Rosamund's face, finding little other than bloodied fingers.

"You'll be just fine," I whispered, desperate to sound helpful. "I've seen men suffer far worse on the battlefield and recover fully within a fortnight. You'll see."

"Varus the truth-teller," Rosamund said sadly, almost mocking me. "You have never been a good liar. It is amazing that you have survived amidst these Romans for so long."

I chuckled. "Sometimes, I marvel at that myself. But I have you to thank for cheating death many times. So I need you to heal quickly." Through a grimace, Rosamund offered a weak smile, which I returned. "My children depend on it," I added.

Granted easy access back into the palace, I secured a private room for Rosamund's care. Though I voiced words of encouragement, privately my anxieties boiled into helplessness. As I barked orders for a healer to be summoned, I realized how much I depended upon my Gepid servant for even the simplest salves for cuts or headaches. Even in her pain, Rosamund reserved enough contempt for the first gray-bearded healer to request another, regardless of the man's status as the personal physician of the Imperial family.

"I've soothed the pains of three emperors, and this pagan witch would place herself above me!" the old physician complained.

I nodded but did not defy Rosamund's orders. "Save yourself the trouble, then. We will find another."

"Cephalas," Rosamund croaked. "Find Cephalas. He's observed

me care for others. He'll need Agathias, though—for a hale set of arms."

"As you wish," I replied. I dismissed the physician, who retreated with a flurry of curses, and sent a palace courier to seek Cephalas.

"Hot water, in the meantime," Rosamund added, biting her lip as her nose wrinkled in pain. "And clean linen, to wash the wound. Something freshly laundered and free of city filth."

Ever nearby, palace slaves rushed to Rosamund's room upon my summoning. A grubby-faced boy soaked in Rosamund's request for Cephalas and Agathias, sprinting down a marble staircase and out onto the city's streets mere moments after receiving his instructions. Others fulfilled simpler tasks—fetching a pot of water that had been simmering on a palace stove in anticipation of a later meal, clean rags, even a skin of sour wine. Preferring to retain my wits, I declined that last offering, though Rosamund accepted a hearty swallow. And still another slave, unbeknownst to me, ventured to the highest levels of the palace, retrieving one I did not expect to attend to Rosamund's plight.

Absent her usual gaggle of courtiers and ladies, Theodora moved brusquely through an adjoining hallway and hailed me from afar. Still adorned in her court raiment, pearls danced along her ears and throat as she approached, followed only by a small collection of servants. Even with paint and kohl layering her face and a towering diadem dominating her tightly bound hair, Theodora's face was plainly human, lined as it was with worry.

"An attack?" she asked, stopping outside of Rosamund's door, lightly panting from her efforts.

I kneeled, only for Theodora to grab my collar and curtly raise me to my feet. As her icy fingers brushed my skin, I peered directly into her olive eyes. Theodora had surprised me before, yet seeing her glide about the slaves' quarters, inspecting the health of my servant, left me equally in gratitude and suspicion of her. I doubt that any other member of the Imperial household would descend into the palace's stifling bowels, willingly or no.

"You should not be here, Augusta," I murmured.

"No time for that," Theodora insisted. "Speak plainly, and tell me what has transpired."

"As you command. A gang of religious fanatics cornered and attacked Rosamund—perhaps a dozen."

"So not a riot." Theodora allowed the briefest flash of relief to break her frown. "Is there anything I can do?"

"Pray for healing, although Rosamund is a pagan," I replied, yielding no look of distaste from Theodora. "Her attackers claimed a blessing from the Emperor, and that they took direction from Cassiodorus. I thought Cassiodorus was banished from court?"

Instantly, Theodora returned to her gaze of worry. "He was, but wormed his way back by appealing to the Emperor. Even I cannot convince Justinian to purge that bloated boil."

"So, it's all true?" I asked. "The Emperor grants these roving preachers immunity, and they may molest Roman citizens as they please?"

Theodora's eyes closed as she let out a thin stream of air from her pursed lips. "Justinian only ever meets with Cassiodorus' messengers. I know they've spoken of purging the city of pagans and apostates, but I admit I only ever took it for foolish prattle. I shall speak with my husband… but I worry that I do not have his ear on this issue."

"Pagans and apostates," I echoed. Those like Rosamund, in other words, who shied away from the Christian God for ancestral deities, or anyone who maintained beliefs in Christ that were contrary to the teachings of the Pope in Rome or the Patriarch in Constantinople. Though small minorities in most cities, such nonbelievers represented sizeable populations in hinterland provinces.

Major cities like Constantinople and Antioch formally banned such creatures, though rarely carried out these bans in practice. Instead, practitioners of the pagan and apostate faiths mixed with Jews, Zoroastrians, and all manner of foreign worshippers of the northern steppes or eastern deserts. I knew all too well that these groups had little favor with the Imperial government, but rarely did the Emperor seek to assault peaceable citizens who offered no harm to commerce or order.

"Why now?" I asked. "The Empire is mostly Christian already. What good does brutalizing chunks of the population do for the Emperor?"

Theodora closed her eyes again. "Keep your voice low, Varus," she urged in a hushed tone. "Especially here, and especially before me. From what little I know, Cassiodorus has convinced my husband that the Empire's many calamities are evidence of God's disfavor on a land that brokers idol worship and heresy."

"Augusta—"

"Varus, Cassiodorus includes me in their number," she hissed. "Because of Jakob, I presume. Wherever he may have found his authority, Cassiodorus cannot yet strike at a member of the Imperial household, nor any of my direct retainers, but Jakob's followers have been hassled and beaten just as Rosamund was. I shall do what I can, but I require your assistance for as long as you are in Constantinople."

"Always," I replied. "But how?"

"Justinian wanted to speak with you even before this incident, although about what I cannot know," she began. "You must keep me informed of the attitudes of the people in the meantime. If Cassiodorus' reach is truly beyond a dedicated core of fanatics, I would know of it before there is a threat of uprising."

"I shall do so. Discreetly," I added. "But surely Narses has tentacles throughout all the city's docks and brothels? I doubt what my household finds will surpass his informants, whoever they may be."

Theodora's voice fell ever fainter. "I am not certain that Narses remains mine to command," she admitted.

I never liked Narses. Perhaps it is prejudice, for eunuchs were ever a source of derision amongst the warrior class. Perhaps it was Narses' affinity for perfumes, and soft silks, and rich food—gluttonous and vain, even by the accounts of the patrician class. Regardless of the cause, Narses' character galled me, though I never questioned his loyalty. Until then, he had appeared like me, an unmovable creature of Theodora's, willing to fight and even die for her will. The thought that the spymaster had switched loyalties was more than simply unsettling. Indeed, though I had faced death enough times to recognize danger, Theodora's confession kindled more fear than I had known in many a battle. Narses was both unpredictable and dangerous, and not an enemy I longed for.

"He has the Emperor's ear now, and while Justinian allows me to govern in most things, he is still Augustus. Even the most honored empress will never be viewed with the same deference as the weakest emperor, and for my husband's faults, he is a capable man."

As Theodora finished her warning, a rustling sounded from the nearby set of marble stairs. Cephalas' voice echoed along the walls, requesting entry to the palace on orders from an excubitor. With their access swiftly approved, Cephalas and Agathias hustled from the hallway's far end, and not alone—a yellow-cloaked Sembrouthes and an armored Xerxes followed closely behind.

"Just because we have survived riots and war does not mean threats to our survival have vanished," Theodora whispered. "With power comes enemies, and I wield more power than most. I fear you're the only person I can trust."

She did not wait for a response, but raised a jeweled hand to lightly pat my bearded cheek. In a fluid motion, Theodora gathered her gown and slipped into Rosamund's room, offering a few muffled condolences that were returned in kind. Only heartbeats later, the Empress removed herself into the hallway and disappeared into its warren, leaving me in the company of my panting companions.

"Cephalas," I began, giving the men time to regain composure. "Rosamund will instruct you on what you must do to heal her. Agathias, you will assist. Follow Rosamund's instructions, and commit the lesson to memory."

"Of course, Varus," Cephalas said. "But why me?"

I shook my head. "Rosamund doesn't trust the Imperial physicians, and you've toiled closely alongside her. It's not ideal, but you've a steady hand, and she trusts you."

Though solemn, Cephalas straightened at the compliment, then hoisted a bucket of warm water at his feet as he issued his own instructions. "Agathias, take Rosamund's healing box from Xerxes. I'll carry the water, but we'll need as much light as can be mustered."

"Of course," I said, calling for a nearby servant.

A younger boy appeared, eyes wide as he recognized one of our party. "Agathias! You truly are free!"

"Yes, but there's no time to discuss that now," Agathias replied, his face visibly reddening in the dim light. "Fetch as many tapers and lanterns as can be safely hoisted in the room. We will talk later."

Beaming, the slave boy darted away, summoning assistance.

"An old friend of yours?" I asked Agathias.

"A kitchen scullion who took my place after I was freed." Agathias followed Cephalas into Rosamund's rooms before I could inquire further.

Sembrouthes did not allow silence to linger. "You should have let me come with you!"

"What happened?" Xerxes interjected. "The slave told us only that you had been attacked, and Rosamund injured."

I offered what little information I could, and in hushed tones. Theodora's warning for discretion had left me paranoid of eavesdropping palace slaves at nearby, unseen peepholes—I should know, for such a task had fallen to me many a time in my youth, loathsome as I found such spycraft.

Both men reacted with scorn at the actions of Cassiodorus' cabal, yet I left out any details of Theodora's personal concerns. Neither asked why the Empress attended to such a relatively trivial matter as the injury of a citizen, nor did I offer any explanation. Truthfully, Theodora's concern—and her admitted lack of control over such a resurgent threat—left me uneasy. The Empress was, after all, a person who effectively controlled the Roman government. No petitioner who sought Justinian's favor would not also send private inquests to beseech the Empress' aid. And she spoke true—Justinian adored her, the woman who defied tens of thousands of rioters when all others demanded abdication and defeat.

So why would he keep Cassiodorus' trust, knowing this would only imperil his beloved?

It was a puzzle, one that only added to the burgeoning stack of questions haunting a scheming court. There was the curious death of Legate Hermogenes that, while officially a suicide, left faint clues that murder was a more likely contributor to the disagreeable man's end. There was Justinian's insistence upon war with the Ostrogoths, for even with the murder of Amalasuntha, invading the Italian peninsula carried terrible risk to an overextended, under-strength, and exhausted Roman Army.

And all these predicaments, the uncertainty and instability around me, compounded my own personal questions—doubts of the great gifts I had received through the course of my life, frustration at the stubborn reluctance of Liberius or Father Petrus to yield their purpose or meaning. Though battlefield victory had made me a powerful man, I possessed no means to unravel the most irksome knots that brought worry to my sleep and doubt to my heart.

Of course, I said nothing of this to Sembrouthes or Xerxes at the time. There was nothing they could do to allay my fears—that power resided only within Liberius, and perhaps Petrus and Theodora. Instead, I remarked on my concerns of the rise in banditry amongst Cassiodorus' zealots, and insisted that none in my household would walk Constantinople's streets without an armed entourage.

Sembrouthes agreed. "That includes you, stubborn ass."

I nodded. "You're right, as always. We might need to request more men from Aksum to distribute the burden, or task some of Perenus' foederati to double or triple our guards."

"I will send messages to al-Harith's court today," Sembrouthes said, visibly pleased. "They will forward our request past the Red Sea to Aksum."

"Perenus wouldn't balk at sending a few Herulians under Sindual, either," Xerxes added. "But does this mean you will not be commanding them directly?"

I shook my head. "As Belisarius' second, I'll have a smaller detachment of men, but my task is to give guidance to the strategos."

Xerxes nodded, his face impassive. "Where shall I go, Varus?"

Even with Theodora's warning and Rosamund's pain lingering on my heart, I chuckled. "With me, to help beat some discipline into the army as a senior officer." Xerxes' face broke into a grin before I added, "If you would like, that is."

He offered a sweeping bow. "I suppose I would—although nobody knows how I shall succeed. You Romans bray like jackals in victory, but moan constantly at the slightest defeat!"

"Jokes aside," Sembrouthes interjected. "The invasion of Italy, the murder of a Gothic queen, and now unrest in Constantinople... There's much at risk, and we don't understand where the threat is even coming from. The slightest setback could set the Emperor against his people once more, and I'm not sure we could prevail in another uprising."

Gesturing for silence, I nodded and replied with a hushed whisper. "I know. This time, from here forward, I promise to obey your restrictions, Sembrouthes. All of us will. But all we can do is follow orders, and the truth."

"And if the truth and our orders are not allies?" Xerxes countered. "In Persia, anything not born of truth and light is evil, regardless of our intentions later on."

I suppressed a grimace, for Xerxes' words brought flashes of Hakhamanish from my memory. Even with years separating me from my encounter with the magus, his curse sang in my memory as if the words had just been spoken. But, I reasoned internally, if I and the Roman Empire were destined to ruin, why had we just reclaimed Carthage and preserved Justinian's government from an innumerable mob? No, his mystical predictions defied logic. Yet in the gloom of the palace, logic made a poor shield against a jabbing imagination.

"We follow orders and defend each other," I answered. "That's all that can be done. And I'll be damned if I don't live up to the epithet that the foederati granted to me in the Triumph."

More light chuckles, interspersed with moans of muffled pain from within the chamber. As Sembrouthes and Xerxes traded tension for ease, I realized all at once how weary I now felt. Not physically, for no muscles complained of taxation, and only a few long-healed wounds offered noticeable aches. No, my fatigue was a swirl of emotion and thought, and I desperately wanted the day to end. Though it was still daylight, I pledged to return to Mariya's bed and crash into a heap as soon as Rosamund's recovery was certain, shutting myself away from the world. Sleep, and the absence of a thousand questions for friends and foes, would cure all.

My plans were not long for this world, however. It was Sembrouthes who first detected the interloper. Xerxes and I stiffened a heartbeat later, sensing armored footsteps drawing ever closer. As the new arrival came into view, I recognized the excubitor Chanaranges, and I knew that the day's woes were far from over.

"Varus, the Emperor wants to see you," Chanaranges announced. "Now."

THE LAW AND ORDER OF
JUSTINIAN

I'll follow." Sembrouthes was first to respond, instinctively grasping the air where the spear that had been seized upon his arrival at the palace normally resided.

Xerxes nodded. "As will I."

"No," Chanaranges said shortly. "The Emperor asked for Varus alone."

Sembrouthes began to complain but halted as I patted his shoulder. "The Emperor shall not wait on his excubitores," I said, nodding to Chanaranges. "Take me to him, brother."

Both of my friends reluctantly obeyed, remaining outside Rosamund's door. I followed Chanaranges, who led me to nearby stairs and toward the palace's highest levels. Only then, away from the maze of rooms and endless opportunities for prying eyes, did I dare seek Chanaranges' advice.

"I cannot assume why our Emperor would seek me out with the day's business completed," I ventured.

"The Emperor did not seem pleased," Chanaranges admitted. "I wish it were not so, but nor would I wish you to attend him unawares. Narses informed him of a scuffle at Constantine's Forum."

"Narses," I muttered, uncaring that my distaste for the man was palpable.

"Not a creature I would willingly share cups with," Chanaranges agreed. "Although every ruler needs a spymaster, and his competence in that unsavory craft seems… unquestionable."

"As it was when he served Theodora," I replied, again not disguising the venom in my tone. While I never held Narses as a friend and found his profession both dishonorable and disagreeable, I still counted him an ally in our shared allegiance to Theodora: A golden signet ring bearing Theodora's name and Imperial seal was nestled safely in a leather pouch at my belt, and its sole brother occupied Narses' pudgy thumb. But now, based upon Chanaranges' insight and Theodora's worry, I wondered how long Narses had held the Emperor's ear, just as I worried at how a man like Cassiodorus could retain Imperial favor.

Regardless, I held no enmity for Chanaranges himself. I never knew him as anything other than an honorable man and an exemplary excubitor, carved from the same bedrock as Marcellus or even Justin himself. Both Marcellus and Chanaranges were raised to such hallowed recognition by Justin, yet where Marcellus filled Justin's vacancy as komes excubitorum, Chanaranges was assigned as the personal bodyguard of Justinian.

Hailing from one of the Empire's desert provinces, Chanaranges' naturally darkened skin seemed always burned and peeling, and in rare meetings with other excubitores, I found him rubbing against sunburn. Though only forty years old at most, he seemed to have aged a decade or more as Justinian's excubitor, yet he never complained openly. Amidst all the ill tidings that swirled about me, I gave silent thanks that Theodora afforded me an extended leash to grow a family and retain an element of privacy, for Justinian clearly did not yield the same to Chanaranges.

"We're attending his private quarters today, not court," Chanaranges explained as we ascended to the highest level.

"A private audience?" I muttered. "Must be serious."

"Rare enough." Chanaranges kept his pace steady as he reached the final staircase.

By this moment, I had no need for Chanaranges to direct me to the Emperor's secluded rooms away from the court. The topmost rooms of the palace were well known to me, having spent countless hours serving my dominus after his ascension to the throne of caesar. In recent years, however, I had only visited the palace apex twice—once during the chaotic final stand of Justinian's government against a howling mob, and before that, in my final audience with Justin.

The latter memory burned with nostalgia, for though I had been poor, life had been far simpler as a freshly forged centurion. More, at that time, Justin as well as Godilas still lived, bearing the impossible weight of government while providing rare opportunities to me that others would have killed for. My final meeting with Justin seemed as fresh as ever, and the pain of not knowing his final bequest was as sharp as the day I learned of Justin's demise.

Come back from Cherson, and I'll tell you everything. I promise.

Still equipped with my weapons as an excubitor, I grazed my fingers over the pommel of Justin's dragon-hilted sword. Now, it was another who occupied my dominus' Imperial quarters, yet to me, those rooms would always have deeply personal significance.

Justinian, however, cared little for Justin's heritage or the customs of the past. Justin's trophies and keepsakes from past battles had been replaced by bright frescoes of Christ's life, and the relatively simple curtains and wardrobe that my dominus had preferred had been swapped for sweeping displays of violet and gold.

Amidst the gaudiness, Justinian added a truly colossal map of the known world, painted mosaics that covered the entire floor of his private meeting rooms with sapphire waters, vast deserts, and nigh-impenetrable forests of Europa's interior, the details of every mountain and stream that a banda or merchant caravan might confront in their journeys dwarfing even Justin's renderings of the Empire and its many enemies. In every way, Justinian's quarters mirrored the grandiosity of his personality, which I did not know from direct conversation, but could see manifest in his decrees that had reshaped the Empire for better or worse.

Nearing the final entryway to Justinian's offices, I spied Theodora exiting our intended room. Her face bore none of the confidence that she wielded in court, traded instead for flushed cheeks and tired eyes. She bit her lower lip, her kohl-lined lids now seeming almost unfriendly as they widened for a moment upon my gaze.

Be careful, she mouthed inaudibly.

Aware of the four passive yet vigilant excubitores standing on either side of the Emperor's door, all I could do was offer a light nod. Chanaranges and I waited respectfully for Theodora to take her leave before continuing onward, with the four excubitores pushing on the double doors, one per each ponderous wooden panel.

Chanaranges motioned toward the door, a finger over his lips. "Be on your best behavior. No outbursts, if you wish to keep your hide."

I could not tell if this was a pithy attempt at a joke or earnest advice, but I nodded all the same, and proceeded into the interior. Incense billowed from the enclosed chambers, rendering me light-headed and setting my eyes watering. Other than burning wicks, my senses were assaulted by a rushing sound from inside the walls: a racket that would terrify a Roman plebeian unfamiliar with city life, but which I knew was only the flow of water, channeled from the nearby aqueduct directly into the Emperor's private residence. Here, even heated water was available for Justinian's private use, while most in the city depended upon massive, lukewarm, and often unkempt public baths. All the wealth of so many nations under Roman thrall allowed Justinian and his most treasured retinue to live like gods, and Justinian cared little to disguise it.

"Tribune Varus," Justinian called. "Come closer so we might talk."

Like Theodora, he was adorned in all the trappings of Imperial majesty. His body was wrapped in rich linen colored with purple dyes from the rocky shores of Tyre and belted with silks whose gold embroidery displayed various titles and honorifics afforded to emperors of the past. Curiously, even while in this private chamber, Justinian retained his crown and all the torques, rings, chains, and gems usually intended for public ceremony. While Theodora, and Justin before her, took pains to show regality in court, both gleefully removed all uncomfortable ornaments once in the privacy of their chambers and away from any but their most intimate oath sworn retainers. Yet Justinian remained as expensive as ever.

As I drew closer to the Emperor, the smell of incense grew stronger, snaking through my nostrils and turning every breath into a struggle. Justinian stood before a burning brazier and a great cross, yet the frankincense seemed to emanate from his very robes as much as the religious offering. Justinian's gold-crowned head disguised a thinning hairline, while his face and throat were freshly shaven against the rising preferences of bearded Roman spearmen. Though certainly not plump, Justinian's naked chin bore early evidence of a rich diet and no physical exertion, its already weak and receding lines growing soft and exacerbating a receding jawline. Though he had been a military officer decades prior, few would imagine such a body had once served against the Empire's enemies along the Ister.

I approached, urging away a sneeze with a quick cuff of my armored forearm. Though incense had been common enough in Justin's court, Justinian's excessive love for the fragrance irritated my eyes and tickled my nose. "Highness, you summoned me?"

Justinian smirked as he bobbed his head once, as if I were some exotic creature imported from the distant jungles far beyond the already-distant kingdom of Aksum. A different man might have been perturbed, but all I felt was mild relief that my emperor did not demand my head for wrath against Cassiodorus' servants.

"I have heard of your negotiations with the Franks," he said. "And I meant to speak with you about it sooner. Aptly done, excubitor."

The compliment was absent any hint of sarcasm or scorn. Animosity would not have been unexpected, yet instead, Justinian chose to leave me both uncomfortable and uncertain of how to appease my monarch without simpering or appearing too callous. Sorely lacking the required quick wit, I opted for truth.

"Augustus, the success lies mainly at Liberius' feet," I admitted, then added as my thoughts shifted briefly to Uliaris, "And the good fortune of one of Belisarius' bucellarii."

"Nonsense," Justinian countered. "You took a would-be enemy, transformed them into an ally, and convinced them to absorb the brunt of the risk against Theudis. More importantly, though, you've placed both Gothic kingdoms on alert of a Frankish invasion—critical for the success of our current enterprise."

Justinian's compliments were unpredictable. I would have been better prepared if he had greeted me with bluster, shouting threats. Instead, I only coughed against the brazier's fumes and wondered why he had truly summoned me to his presence. "Critical?"

Justinian beamed. "Oh, yes, excubitor. Wars are expensive, and prone to maiming and death. Far better the Franks take some of Theodahad's attention than we face the full brunt of the Ostrogoth armies, wouldn't you say?"

"Highness—"

"It's an obvious answer, I know," Justinian interrupted. "Tell me of Theudis' warlords, as well as the young Frankish prince you came to terms with—Butilinus, if Procopius' notes can be trusted."

Again, the exchange was not what I expected, but I was happy enough to oblige. I recounted all that I could remember of Theudis and Theudesgel, of Agila and Butilinus, of their mannerisms in diplomacy and stratagems in combat. He even inquired about Indulf and the Ostrogoths, asking about their prowess and trustworthiness as fighters. As I spoke, Justinian interrupted frequently, nodding and moving his mouth as if to practice foreign Gothic and Frankish words.

I have little doubt that Justinian prospected similar answers from Liberius shortly after our return, yet still he listened and engaged with me like a young boy hearing a new tale. He did not balk at my account of Indulf's torture of Agila's young relative, nor at the hundreds of examples of cruelty in our seizure of Septem—if anything, it only seemed to make him hunger for knowledge of these foreign peoples all the more. Above all, his greatest interest lay within the predicament of each tribe's lands, noting the strategic isolation of the Visigoths or the bloody yearnings of the Frankish tribes. Only after I completed my tales did he seek my opinion on more recent matters.

"Do you believe Belisarius is prepared to take Italy from the Goths for me?"

Though I loathed the invasion order, I did not hesitate. "Yes, Highness."

"Very good," Justinian answered. "But permit me to rephrase the question. Belisarius possesses the skill for winning a campaign based upon his success against Gelimer. But does he want to?"

I stammered; I did not know what to say. Bereft of warmth or friendship, Justinian stood before me unblinking and unmoving, barely even breathing. There were half-true answers I could impart to ease the Emperor's mind, and those more forthright that would leave him on edge. Though I cared little to ease Justinian's worries, I opted for prudence.

"Few men lust for war, Highness, and those who do are not worthy of trust. Belisarius is a man who longs for the simplicity of peace, and the ability to sleep absent the nightmares of death and worry."

Justinian's gaze was unchanged. "Narses tells me your men have dubbed you Varus Veridicus," he said, elongating each syllable of my epithet. "Liberius insists the honor is well-deserved. I will need of your honest leadership in the months ahead, excubitor. So, I ask you again, but bluntly: Would Belisarius ever seek his own glory and abandon me?"

My eyes widened. "Never, Highness. Even under the torturer's knife, he would not forsake you."

Justinian pursed his lips. "Thank you, excubitor. A final question on this matter, however."

I bowed my head. "I am your servant, Highness."

"Will the army serve my will in Italy?"

A truly honest answer was no. Our veterans, rich from Vandal gold and extensive back pay from the Imperial coffers, had no immediate need for plunder. Nor did Justinian possess that unnamable quality that garnered boundless love from his men—Belisarius did, and Justin before him, and perhaps even I had a bit of it in me after the war with Persia. But Justinian did not share the travails of the troops, nursing swollen feet from endless marching or the fear of painful and lingering death by a savage enemy. He was Augustus; he enthralled powerful citizens such as Belisarius and Theodora but was viewed with indifference at best by Rome's armies. If he had abandoned the palace during the Nika Riots, few would have mourned his departure and subsequent ignominy.

"You command the loyalty of the armies, Highness," I reasoned, cuffing at a layer of sweat on my brow. "I've led men from a dozen tribes against terrible foes. If they did not balk then, they will not now."

As Justinian considered my answer, I added all that I dared as a barb. "Even if we are outnumbered, on a distant shore, and fighting a stronger enemy on their home soil."

At last, Justinian smiled. "Italy is not the Goths' true home, Varus. Even Amalasuntha understood this, before her throat was cut. But I understand your point, and it is why I inquired about Butilinus and the Franks."

Again, I bowed, for the gesture seemed to please Justinian. "Of course, Highness. But my agreement with the Franks was merely to recognize their dominion over the Alemanni, not to request allied units to fight Theodahad's armies along the Alps. Even if we dispatched an emissary now, we might not know an answer for three months at minimum, and closer to half a year without fair winds."

"I know." Justinian's grin broadened. "That's why I dispatched ambassadors before you returned from Carthage."

Again, he left me grasping for a response. Even educated by Liberius, having observed Imperial governors and ministers grapple with one another in all manner of debate and argument, I was left disarmed by Justinian's skill for rhetoric. Worse, he seemed aware of his superiority and relished my surprise. For the entry of the Franks into the war, even if only to distract small sections of the Gothic army, was as welcome as it was momentous.

"As I said, your alliance with the Franks may prove invaluable in the months to come. Battles are not won with swords and blood alone, but with meticulous planning and logistics. Be sure your strategos understands this well, for I do not wish to hear further grumblings from our soldiers that Justinian cares nothing for their lives or asks for the impossible."

I bowed deeply, though the movement only worsened the stinging of my eyes as my face bisected a smoky plume. "Gratitude, Highness. Your will shall be done."

Justinian waited several heartbeats before signaling that my prostration should end. I yearned to depart, feeling strangely vulnerable despite the Emperor's compliments and confession that he labored to ease our campaign, even if only peripherally. Somehow, I felt used, a crude tool in the hands of someone far craftier in court politics than I—and someone who, despite his words, seemed to care little for my well-being.

Justinian watched me glance toward the door. "One final piece to discuss."

My spirits dropped, my legs stiff and sluggish. "Of course, Highness."

"I have heard whispers that you assaulted a priest earlier today in the Forum," Justinian murmured. "Is there truth in this?"

Alarmed, I stumbled directly into my self-defense. "I—I did not realize he was a priest, Highness. And he hurled stones at my servant, a free woman and Roman citizen."

Justinian nodded, more to acknowledge my statement than to show empathy. "He shall be punished for breaking my peace. But so will you, Varus."

"Highness?" I choked.

"From all that is reported of your deeds, you are a reliable and humble servant," Justinian went on. "But you struck one of my priests, without my leave to do so. Cassiodorus will be informed of my decision, and I shall confer with him regarding your punishment."

My skin flushed. "Highness, he would have killed my servant had I not interfered."

The Emperor scowled. "I have labored for years on our laws, done the hard work of placing into writing all the precedent of the tangled web of Roman custom, and I will see those laws followed. If this priest did as you say, I shall sit in judgment of him. But striking a Christian priest carries a grave penalty, excubitor. Be thankful that I intend to spare you any lasting physical harm."

There was nothing to say. Inwardly I raged, eyeing this small man so assured of his position. Not long ago, he was a near-friendless figure of scorn and ridicule, fearful of blood and unpopular for a predisposition to execute plebeians with little legal recourse. In a way, the entire situation felt ridiculous, like some sort of theater performance, with Justinian in the role of spurned monarch. He was possessed of deadly intent, however, and all he would allow was meek acceptance.

"I understand, Augustus."

"That is all I ask," he replied. "What I intend to make our people understand is that justice is the firm and continuous desire to render to everyone that which is his due. Excubitor or slave, law governs all. Without it, we are nothing more than steppe savages."

As quickly as our exchange had begun, it was over. Justinian turned away, shuffling toward a looming stack of parchment that lined a nearby text. He did not sit, but plucked one and delved into its contents, stamped with the regalia of his hallowed office. The room's incense continued to befuddle my senses, making me all but desperate for escape, yet I could only do so once the Emperor dismissed me.

"You shall hear of your debt to the Roman state on the morrow," Justinian remarked, not looking up from his scrolls. "And along with your future lawful decision-making, I expect you to remain steadfast in your loyalty to me while in Italy. Regardless of what your mistress, or your strategos, might decide is in their best interests."

I saluted, met by a casual wave of the Emperor's hand—dismissed.

Whether from the incense or the Emperor's maneuvering, my body felt unclean after the exchange. Relief washed over my skin after departing his suffocating offices, and in the fresher air of the hallway, I paused for a moment to fill my lungs and toss a nod to

Chanaranges and my brethren in white cloaks, before descending to the palace's lower levels.

Uneasy in my mind and on my feet, my thoughts flitted about aimlessly as I arrived at Rosamund's temporary chambers. Along with Xerxes and Sembrouthes, I found Perenus with ten Herulian foederati now standing watch—all unarmed, of course, yet even a child could understand their intention to guard what lay just beyond the closed door.

"Theodora sent a slave to inform me of what had occurred, and to order me to bring guards into the palace," Perenus explained.

Still befuddled by Justinian, I frowned. "Guards? For how long? Does she expect an attack on the palace?"

Even if Cassiodorus multiplied his numbers by three, he had no reason to assault Justinian. More importantly, Belisarius' armies were stationed within fifty miles of the city and had demonstrated an unquestioned willingness to purge Constantinople of an unwanted mob.

Perenus shrugged. "Theodora's slave didn't reveal her thoughts, but I don't believe she's concerned about a battle in the city. But I've seen Cassiodorus' minions in the streets since we returned from Carthage—they multiply like lice. No concern if they were holy men like Petrus, but these ones... their talk is far more antagonistic."

Nodding, Xerxes whispered to me in Persian. "If the Emperor supports religious mobs in his streets, he's doing so to gain influence. But Justinian's gain will be the loss of any with a differing point of view."

"I know," I replied in my own weary Persian. "Keep vigilant, and protect our household and retainers."

All I could report from the meeting was Justinian's inferred patronage of Cassiodorus, as well as the undefined punishment I would face for my crimes. The latter declaration drew their protests, but I simply lacked the stamina to engage further.

"We will know more tomorrow," I reasoned, "and I expect the penalty will be something minor, like a fine. But for now, I'm exhausted. If Perenus and the Heruli will stand guard at Theodora's invitation, there is little else we can do today."

None pressed further, and I did not squander my final opportunity to end the unhappy day. After rapping my knuckles against Rosamund's door, I gained entry to what was a relatively calm scene: Agathias preparing a concoction of foreign herbs and roots that Cephalas would administer to a prone Rosamund. Her skin had been cleaned, and her injured eye bound tight with clean linen, all dung or blood wiped from her face and hair. As I grazed her hand, her unbound eye flittered behind its thin lids, yet she did not stir to consciousness.

"We gave Rosamund an elixir from her own instructions," Cephalas explained. "She will likely sleep for a day and a night, based upon her explanation."

Then there truly was nothing more to be done. "Make sure someone stays nearby, day and night," I told him. "I'm leaving the palace for Mariya, but fetch me immediately if the situation changes."

I departed with Xerxes and Sembrouthes, allowing Perenus and his detachment of Herulians to guard Rosamund's doorway. We exited the palace to mostly empty streets and the earliest smattering of showers overhead. Normally, such cleansing water would be most welcome against the filth of Constantinople's streets, but the nagging threat of rust on our armor—and the suspicious calm of the night— warranted a brisk retreat. We moved at a light jog, our metal clinking with each step. Before reaching safety, we passed again through the Forum of Constantine. Few traders kept their stalls open through the rain; the only large congregation was yet another band of Cassiodorus' followers.

"More this time," Sembrouthes warned. "A lot more."

I never saw Cassiodorus present at these meetings—indeed, I had not lain eyes upon the disgraced religious minister since his ignominious fall after the Nika Riots. Instead, his cronies normally gathered crowds of fifty or sixty—rarely more, and rarely for a greater duration than an hour. Yet now, the mob swelled to at least several hundred, with the Forum's guardsmen showing little willingness to disburse the gathering. After all, there was no law in Justinian's compendium against large groups in public, provided that all members remained orderly and free of violence.

Though none called to us, our presence was easily noted, even at a distance of a full fifty paces: Several black-garbed followers winnowed through the crowd to capture a glimpse of us three, and I recognized Philip in their number. He stepped forward from the mob and raised a hand in mock greeting.

"Ignore them," I muttered to Sembrouthes and Xerxes. "They will not follow us."

Mercifully, I was correct. After escaping the Forum, we soon reached my property. I sent Xerxes to request further Herulian guards from Fulcaris before ascending to higher floors myself. In the interim, Sembrouthes would remain behind, stationing his existing Aksumites around both the front and alley entrances until Herulian reinforcements could be procured. Satisfied and overwhelmed, I retreated to my bedroom, pleased at the sound of Zenobia playing with one of Mariya's servants—that, at least, meant the day would not be entirely filled with ill tidings.

My relief was short-lived; I heard weeping well before opening my door. It was inconsolable, the sound of a wounded animal, racked with an unusual, alien pain. Placing a hand on my hilt, I gently nudged the door open, only to find Mariya sitting inside on a bench, a sobbing Antonina at her side. Her face was haggard, powders and paints streaming down her cheeks, as she turned and recognized me.

"Varus!" Antonina cried. "Belisarius is bringing charges against me!"

BURNING

Though a youth of slavery has trained me for patience, I am nevertheless limited in how many troubles I am willing to absorb at a given time. Between Theodora's warnings, Rosamund's assault, Narses' caution of my diminishing hoard, and Justinian's conniving, I wanted little more than isolation and sleep. Perhaps my understanding was further frayed by the sheer surprise of Antonina's pronouncement, for although Belisarius was within his legal right to banish his adulterous wife from his household, there had been little warning that he would do so. This announcement placed Antonina in terrible danger of poverty and disgrace—and, as I was Antonina's assumed patron and protector, this left me with one more burden to bear.

Yet it could wait. I wanted to explode in frustration, to cast even Mariya from my rooms, bar the doors, and sleep, not waking even to eat. It was only sheer discipline keeping me civil. I swallowed my anger, but even silent pleas from Mariya could not convince me to lend an ear to Antonina's grief.

"Give me a moment, Lady," I murmured to my wife.

She frowned. "Varus!"

Antonina wailed again, burying her face into manicured hands, leaning slightly on my wife for support. Mariya's tired eyes glared at me, but all I could do was dismiss myself and retreat to the building's lower levels. Jamila, one of Mariya's handmaidens, bowed her head as I passed.

"A cup of wine, please," I asked. "And a plate of whatever food is easily available. Doesn't matter what it is."

Hearing another wail above me, I escaped to a small open atrium in the building's center, settling atop a marble bench alongside a half-filled pool. It was humid—uncomfortably so—but the drizzle had subsided and removed the threat of rust to my armor long enough for me to stay out of doors. Jamila soon returned with my fare, and I sat alone, popping overripe grapes into my mouth between swirls of wine. Sticky juices mingled first at the corners of my mouth and soon into my beard, mixing with beads of sweat that formed from the thick air.

Since the first time Mariya had entranced me during her betrothal to Solomon, I had taken considerable pains to further her happiness—and God knows she had done the same for me, as evidenced by her exertions to free me from Hermogenes' wrath over Marcian's death. So why did I leave her so abruptly with Antonina like that, with so little cause or justification? As an old man, I can now understand how the foolish inexperience of youth invites these problems, avoidable in the moment yet with consequences that reverberate for days or even years to come. At the time, however, I simply did not care what the consequences might be. I would like to say I possessed some excuse, that the mental burdens of serving competing masters, or the physical dread of yet another war, had filled my cup of worries to overflowing—but that would be a lie. Instead of heeding long-dead Godilas' insistence upon reason over rashness, I had surrendered to my anger. And, if only for an hour, it felt wonderful.

At the conclusion of that hour, I realized that my flippancy was a mistake.

"Varus?"

Rather than send a servant to fetch me, Mariya had ventured to the atrium herself. Her features were lined with displeasure as she approached, and as she drew to my side, she grimaced. By then my face and body were drenched in sweat; I must have reeked.

"Why are you behaving this way?" she chided. "Antonina could use male friendship, a steady listener to speak through the emotions she feels now."

"I owe her nothing!" I shot back, too late regretting the magnitude of anger that slipped out. "She tormented my brother and me for years when we bore collars on our throats, but *now* she seeks my support? My protection?"

"You still owe her your courtesy, Varus," Mariya said, her voice low and full of a frustration I rarely saw. "At the very least. All that requires is your ear."

I sighed. "Mariya, she's guilty. I was there, and saw it for myself. And because of that, she's placing you, me, and our children in peril of angering Belisarius if we protect her further. Belisarius did nothing to deserve this."

Mariya did not respond. Instead, gathering her crimson stola, she left my side and seized a perch three paces distant. Her eyes focused upon the atrium's columns, her silence a far more shaming jab than any tirade or argument. I felt compelled to speak further, even as I sensed the ground beneath my argument churning and giving way like wet sand.

"Antonina betrayed us," I continued. "Belisarius somehow blames me for it, for he rarely speaks to me outside of couriers and written commands. Theodora insists that I inform her of developments, while Justinian is distrustful of everyone and demands that I strike against Belisarius and the others if they speak against him. Antonina did wrong, so why should I suffer from it?"

Mariya's eyes closed, her head shaking lightly. "It is because she did wrong that she needs your help. All you must do is listen."

Tiny droplets of rain thrummed against the marble, spattering against the small pool at the atrium's center. Brushing off beads of condensation that formed on her forearm, Mariya motioned to return inside before adding, "When you did wrong, others took time to listen to you."

God in his infinite mercy, but the shame I felt. Mariya did not need to scream or rage, for such actions were utterly foreign to her nature. Silent disappointment was enough to render Mariya's verdict that, in her eyes, I was an unfeeling hypocrite. I waited but a few moments more until, when I was assured that Mariya had left, I went back into the enclosed rooms, seeking rags and fresh clothing to sweep away caking sweat and replace the damp garments that had borne me through the tumultuous day. After dressing quickly, I again climbed steps toward Mariya and Antonina, and opened the door.

Antonina knew precious little, although what information she gleaned from her denouncement was damning enough. Per Antonina's account, Bessas delivered a scroll sealed with a waxen image of Belisarius' wolf. As she spoke, Mariya rose and handed me the document, etched in the clean and elegant script that I had come to know flowed from Belisarius' own hand. Bessas gave no further instructions, but the message itself was plain.

"He isn't seeking my death, but he's casting me out from his household," Antonina summarized, fat tears further smudging her already-ruined powders. "I'm to be returned my dowry of fifty solidi, plus a mule to bear my clothing."

"Is this more than you thought, or less?" I asked.

Antonina let out a sob. "I don't know. It's ruinous, either way. And I don't know what to do."

"You can stay here as long as you desire," Mariya said soothingly. "Correct, Varus?"

A knot formed in my throat, but I nodded. "Of course."

Another sob followed as Antonina sank into the bed. Mariya plucked strands of hair from Antonina's face and gently rubbed her shoulder, leaving me feeling both useless and awkward. Still, though, I was determined to regain Mariya's good opinion.

"Lady, what do you really want?"

"What do you mean?" Antonina said, her voice muffled against the feather-stuffed mattress.

Sucking in a deep breath, I calmed my rising frustrations and reluctance. "If God could grant your heart's desire, what would you wish for? What do you want from Belisarius?"

The sobbing stopped. Antonina's expression grew solemn, almost angry, possessed of the defiance I had known in our years in Liberius' classroom. "My wish is that I had never met Sergius," she said softly. "But short of that, I would want Belisarius to forgive me. Anything else, and I'll die alone and disgraced."

I frowned. "Why?"

"Did you not listen on our voyage from Carthage?!" Antonina snarled. "I never stopped loving him. But between duty and me, the Emperor will always take the greater portion of his heart. You don't know him like I do."

"No, I don't." Her words pricked at the rising doubt I felt about Belisarius' trust in me. "Perhaps I never knew him well. I am not John."

Antonina shuddered as if splashed with icy water. She fixed her eyes upon mine, something that she never would have deigned to do in our youth together. Her cheeks seemed bloated beneath blotchy and dark-rimmed eyes that suggested a lack of sleep as much as the terrible fear she must have felt. Despite it all, a scowl carved itself across Antonina's features. Though I found Antonina's presence in my household a difficulty, and her many needs downright annoying, shame nevertheless smoldered across my body. I had dishonored myself by speaking ill of Belisarius before his wife—even if Antonina herself had been the author of her own embarrassment. I ardently wished to erase that outburst from memory.

Curiously, despite everything, Antonina seemed protective of her husband's reputation. She allowed the scowl to linger for a few moments until, with a sigh, her features returned to a mournful look.

"He doesn't blame you for what happened," Antonina muttered. "For John's death, anyway. But Belisarius is not nearly the fool you suggest to blame you for my sins. He will come around, if you are patient enough to forgive his pride."

Her words might have seemed soothing to one not present to hear their inflection. Indeed, perhaps I should have been reassured that all would be well, and that my friend would eventually return to me, as she suggested. But instead, the bite of her response struck with all the force of a Vandal dagger, rendering me stupefied.

It was only through Mariya's deft maneuvering that the conversation continued. "Do you think Varus might be able to speak to your husband, and reason with him?"

Antonina shook her head violently. "No. That would only humiliate Belisarius further. It seems I must seek relief where I can, and however I can." Antonina's face began to well with tears once more. "I don't want to lose my child, Varus!"

"You won't!" Mariya wrapped her arms around Antonina. "Joannina is a sweet girl, and her father would never deprive her of her mother."

"It's Roman law, against an *adulteress*," Antonina said. "If he casts me aside, I'm going to kill myself. I shall tie a stone to my feet and jump into the Golden Horn." Her sobs grew thicker, making her nearly incomprehensible. "At least then, I won't be a burden to anyone anymore."

"Stop talking like that!" I leapt to my feet, shrugging away previous embarrassment. "How dare you think of leaving your daughter without a mother!"

More weeping. Antonina, normally haughty, had crumbled before me like a stale crust of bread. No retorts or snorts of disgust. Whatever I had once been to her, little better than a worm, she now had no visible disdain for me. Only sadness. And in that moment, I believed that Antonina fully regretted her dalliance.

"Don't worry, Varus," Antonina said resignedly. "I don't intend on surrendering immediately."

I could have pried further, but Antonina seemed to have no additional information to add, and I did yearn for the solace of isolation. "Let me think this over," I said, which drew a contented look from Mariya. I allowed both women to remain in our quarters and searched for an empty room, collapsing on a small lectus with my boots dragging along the floor. My mind instantly went blank, and not even the discomfort of the too-small perch could disrupt my slumber.

I awoke to a prodding in my shoulder. Moaning, I kept my eyes closed, my body straining from even the slightest movement as I thirsted for sleep. But the prodding, such a tiny thing, continued. Rolling my head in the direction of the intruder, I pried my lids open.

It was Zenobia. Little Zenobia, my adventurous daughter, not three years of age but full of chatter and bravado. She flashed a toothy grin, her tiny hands reaching to my collar as she pulled herself onto the lectus. Curling into a ball, she lay her head upon my chest, placing her thumb in her mouth. Lifting my head to look at her, I found a tangled mop of hair beaming behind pronounced dimples.

God and the apostles, but even then, Zenobia resembled her mother as if copied from stone and animated to life. While her younger brother wailed for food and attention, Zenobia rarely complained— something even her nursemaids noted was unusual for a babe. When we had just returned to Constantinople from Mesopotamia, Jamila cautioned that such calm might warn of a simple mind, yet now, nearing three years of age, Zenobia displayed a cleverness that suggested otherwise. Outwardly stern and quiet to strangers, Zenobia basked in her mother's love, and had even warmed up to me in the months we'd shared daily contact. She had not done so right away; at first, I was merely another armored intruder to her house. But this was a start, and a lovely one.

Following Zenobia was another pattering of steps, but far too rapid for any child or adult. Haeva, the young dog gifted to me by the Visigoth Agila at the end of our fight for Septem, half ran and half stumbled toward the lectus, unbalanced atop her growing body. Bumping into a wooden table leg, a wet dog nose sniffed first near Zenobia's dangling feet and later near my face.

Still cradling Zenobia, I lowered an arm from the lectus near the floor, blindly searching for the dog's head. Soon I found a fuzzy ear, and Haeva halted her fidgeting as she leaned into my offer for a vigorous scratch, groaning in canine delight. Eventually I withdrew my hand, and Haeva skittered back to the hallway and toward the rooms of Tiberius and Alexander, leaving Zenobia as the sole occupant of my attentions.

"What is it, anaticula?" I asked, referring to her as my little duckling. "Tired from playing with Tiberius?"

Zenobia shook her head, her eyes locked on mine as the point of her chin dug into my ribs. "Pater, Uncle is here," Zenobia said, drawing each word with deliberation. "He is arguing."

"Samur? Arguing?" I cleared my throat and struggling to a sitting position. "Is everything safe?"

Zenobia nodded, her chin digging further into my chest. "A stranger. Uncle is angry. I don't like that, and I'm hungry."

"Don't worry, anaticula," I replied. "Let's see what your uncle is angry about, and I will find you some honey. Would you like that?"

"With fruit." Zenobia grinned slyly.

"Honey with fruit," I said, surrendering to her demand.

Wrapping an arm around her tiny waist, I rose from my makeshift bed and lifted Zenobia onto my hip. She was small for her age—again favoring her mother's disposition—with thin limbs and a black mane that seemed to mask her face. It was a mundane moment, sharing an interlude with my daughter, but it left me incomparably happier— relieved, even, for it was a sign that, despite the time spent apart, my children might still come to love me.

Opening the door to the adjoining hallway, I could hear Samur's voice rattling through the floorboards and all the way up two flights of stairs. Zenobia was correct: There was no denying Samur's anger at the unrecognized intruder. Squirming on my hip, Zenobia looked again at me.

"Why is Uncle angry?"

I smiled, shaking my head. "I don't know, anaticula. But it will be well, I promise. Let's fetch your treat."

As we paced down the stairs, Samur's protestations grew clearer. "Last opportunity. Leave now, or I'll peel back any fuzz remaining on your bald pate. You won't need a barber for the rest of your life."

An icy voice replied. "You think your gang of heathens frighten me?"

"I do," Samur answered. "With as much as you talk, I do."

I hurried down the last steps, my ponderous boots easily alerting those on the ground level of my approach. Their arguing ceased as I appeared, Zenobia still on my hip. In my absence, the entrance to my home had become crowded, stuffed on the one side with a detachment of Samur's Huns, Sembrouthes' Aksumites, and Xerxes, already baring his curved steel, and on the other with hooded figures, some bearing the crosses and garb of village priests, others with clubs and mattocks. At the center stood Samur and the older bald man I'd struck earlier, both staring at my arrival. Neither Mariya nor Antonina were present, although I spied Aya, another of Mariya's servants, hovering in the background.

"Go to Aya, Zenobia," I whispered. "Ask for honey and fruit. Your pater needs to address these men."

The bald man, who I had heard called Andronicus, opened his mouth, but Samur stomped his foot. "If you wag your tongue in front of my niece, I'll cut it out, root and stem."

Zenobia ran to Aya, who lifted my daughter into the air and rushed toward the kitchen in the bowels of the building. Though I knew I must eventually confront Cassiodorus' thugs, I did not expect them so soon, or within my own house. That indicated a level of courage, or at least enough foolishness, that they would evoke further violence without much prodding. And while I trusted the Huns unquestioningly with the security of my household, I feared how their crass manner would complicate the situation further. I could not be seen as meek before these scurrilous priests, yet at the same time, only an idiot courts one disaster so soon after another.

With Zenobia safely out of earshot, I bared my teeth at the priests, fixing my face in a look of rage.

"What in the hottest hell is the meaning of this intrusion?!"

Andronicus puffed his chest. "Lord Varus—"

"You enter my home without invitation, and with weapons?!" I roared. "Give me one reason I should not have Xerxes cut you into ten thousand squirming pieces. Even Justinian's laws permit me to do violence to brigands attacking my home, and Zhayedan are artists with blades."

"This one is quite fat," Xerxes snarled. "Ten thousand might become twenty before the day is over."

Andronicus bobbed his head in mock obeisance and gestured for his two dozen or so followers to lower their crude weapons. With his order followed, he then pressed two bare palms together in supplication.

"Lord Varus, I am not come here to inflict violence upon you."

I scoffed. "You have a hilarious method of purveying peace, then."

"You did strike me earlier, Lord Varus. And I am a priest." Andronicus smiled, not allowing time for a retort. "But my God is a forgiving God—as is yours, from what Cassiodorus has been told. And Cassiodorus would alleviate the painful lash of justice for those willing to repent."

I shrugged, making a deliberate show of indifference. "The Emperor weighs my crimes, not some mob."

"This we know well!" a second voice called, one that I recognized as Andronicus' assistant, the younger Philip. "You struck a priest, which is the sin of wrath. For that, only the great and wise Justinian has the power to pardon you."

I sighed. "Stop prattling. If you're not here for me, then why are you here at all?"

Andronicus' mouth split into a vast grin, revealing gaps in his teeth like fallen warriors in the shield wall. "The Gepid Rosamund. You know her well."

Samur tensed, his gloved fist gripping the pommel of his sheathed sword. "Give me the word, Varus."

"Two minutes' work," Sembrouthes added, lowering his spear toward the nearest of Cassiodorus' men.

My heart swelled at their willingness to fight for me, but I quickly cringed, knowing how such direct violence might beget only more penalties sought against me.

"No blood," I commanded, fixed upon Andronicus. "Speak."

"Cassiodorus is entrusted with the great burden of purging this land of sin," Andronicus began. "For too long, pagans and apostates have corrupted our Empire's soul. They must be eliminated, or God will destroy us all."

"And your Gepid servant," Philip added, "is famous amongst the armies for her skill—*alleged* skill—in healing. But she is a notorious witch. However, if she converts to our faith, and recognizes Cassiodorus as the man who led her to Christ, she shall face no punishment."

Andronicus stretched out both arms in a broad embrace of air. "And we shall rejoice! For in Rosamund's conversion, the many pagans she inspires shall see the inevitable triumph of our Lord."

It was an impossible offer that Rosamund would resist with every morsel of her vitality. Indeed, perhaps Cassiodorus knew this, only intending to appear loving and forgiving with the option that she convert so that his secondary penalty would not be seen as cruel. Or perhaps he did not, and the offer was genuine. Regardless, the exchange was everything that Rosamund loathed about Roman culture—the uncompromising extortion or conquest of others who do not conform to Roman desires. Rosamund reviled men such as Andronicus, which left room for only one response.

"And if Rosamund refuses?" I asked. "What will happen then?"

Andronicus' hands fell slowly to his side, his smile replaced by animated sadness. "Then her soul shall burn for the rest of time, and beyond."

"Sinnion!" Samur yelled, and the Hunnic chieftain's men drew their blades in swift reply. "What say you?"

I glared at Samur. "Do not antagonize them," I ordered, the Hunnic words spilling from my tongue like hoofbeats. "We just want them to leave."

"Burning? A fantastic idea!" Sinnion boomed in Greek, not hearing my pleas. "Out of practice amongst my people, but lively in the time of Attila and Bleda." He turned to one of his fur-clad warriors. "Chelchal! Fetch an iron rod, and heat it over the cooking fire."

As the Hun Chelchal sprinted to fulfill Sinnion's demand, Andronicus protested, appealing for peace.

"Lord Varus, we beg you to speak with your Gepid servant and urge her to see reason. But if she will not... Cassiodorus may be satisfied with an alternative."

It was an opening. An opportunity to quell hostilities and extract peace from sure conflict.

"Such as?"

Andronicus shook his head. "I cannot know his wise mind. But he is a man who loves peace and would see bloodshed averted."

He babbled and protested for several minutes more, backed by interjections from Philip and others under his sway. They all insisted that we surrender to Cassiodorus' wisdom, especially given that I and the greater portion of my men were Christians as well. Some further appealed to my sense of loyalty to Justinian, who sanctioned their behavior. Samur, for his part, countered every suggestion with a scoff or a jape, ignoring my angry glances. And amidst the arguing, Haeva stumbled from the heights of the building down to the main landing, barking maniacally in her half-puppy, half-war-dog yelp.

Any hope that I had of an amicable conclusion died as Chelchal returned, white-hot iron firestick in hand. Though menacing, it was not nearly as searing hot as a freshly forged blade from a blacksmith, for Chelchal had precious little time to find and heat his instrument. Nevertheless, Andronicus eyed the weapon with caution, taking a step back as the Hun returned to his place behind Samur and Sinnion.

"The penalty for witchcraft is death, Lord Varus," Andronicus concluded. "And I would spare your servant that pain, which would condemn her in the eyes of God and his flock for all time. Repentance is our goal, to which the Gepid woman need only obey, and swear fealty to Christ and His priests."

There was no stopping the Huns from replying to direct provocation. Though I was slow to caution Sinnion and Samur, they would not have had ears to hear me after Andronicus' threats.

"Death?" Sinnion yelled, seizing the firestick's handle from

Chelchal's grasp. "Men like you do not get to pass sentence upon people like us!" Brandishing his weapon, he lifted the still-heated firestick's tip to his own cheek. "In Attila's time, Hun warriors marked their kills by burning lines on their cheeks. It also removed the need to groom beards—wise, especially when butchering Romans on campaign!"

It was a light touch, no longer than a heartbeat, but a thin welt had formed along Sinnion's cheek. The sizzling of flesh lingered in the room, but the Hun chieftain did not seek aid for the injury. If anything, he delighted at the display.

"Now, which of you will honor this scar with your blood?" Sinnion hissed. "Perhaps we should resume Attila's tradition this night!"

Andronicus' mouth dropped open, a look of horror spreading across his face. "Madness..."

"Pagan filth!" one of Andronicus' followers spat.

"Oh, aye!" Sinnion replied. "But before your cockless masters find me to punish my heresy, I'll have already cut your throats and galloped fifty miles distant. Now, end your business here, or my men's faces will all have many layers of markings."

Andronicus motioned to argue, but Philip laid a hand upon the older man's shoulder. "Cassiodorus will have your answer on the morrow, Lord Varus. I suggest you demonstrate greater understanding in his presence than you have with ours."

"Get moving, worm!" Samur answered for me, edging forward.

"Yes," I concluded, stepping beside Samur to prevent a sudden scuffle. "You men are not welcome here. Do not return."

With a wave of his hand, Andronicus bade my enemies retreat, and they clambered away, evaporating the tension in the room in less than a minute. In their place was a great void, with men returning weapons to scabbards and looking nervously to me. Sinnion returned the firestick to Chelchal, running a gentle finger over his fresh wound.

"Go put the iron in a water bucket," Sinnion instructed.

"I've heard that Attila would scar the faces of his oath sworn as a badge of honor, but I believed it tales for children," Samur said.

Sinnion shrugged. "It was real enough, but has not been practiced since Valamir defeated Attila's heir at Bassianae. After that battle, the Hunnic tribes scattered to the winds, and there was no recognized leader to grant face-brands."

Fleeting curiosity piqued a desire to hear more of such tales, but there was no time. Instead, I brought the men's attention back to our present enemies. Offering Haeva another pat to her head, I turned to my task.

"Sinnion, I would appreciate your Huns guarding the door," I suggested, careful to show deference to the chieftain before his men despite my superior rank. "Some might return to set the building alight."

"Not while I breathe." Sinnion nodded. "We will do so."

Twenty Huns filed out of the room, leaving behind Samur, Xerxes, Sembrouthes, and Mariya's Aksumites. "Sembrouthes, have your men rest while we have Sinnion. We might need all of you later, and I'd rather you were fresh."

"I won't decline some sleep," Sembrouthes said. "Wake me if a changing of the guard is needed."

Soon, the Aksumites, too, departed the room, leaving it eerily quiet. Samur let out a deep sigh, and he slouched, rubbing the chafing skin along the hem of his armor.

"When did you return to Constantinople?" I asked. "How did you know to seek me out?"

"I had just returned with the Hun foederati on recruitment when we found Xerxes rushing through the streets," Samur explained. "He told me of your need, and rather than leave Xerxes to seek out Fulcaris and the Heruli to aid you, I took that responsibility upon myself."

Xerxes nodded. "Sometimes, good fortune is more favorable than the greatest of skill. The Ahura Mazda saw our need and joined Samur to our cause."

Samur gave a smile arched with skepticism. "Did you really strike that priest, Varus?"

"With the flat of my blade only, just as he was about to smash Rosamund's skull."

Samur snorted. "And of course, the Romans find you in the wrong. So both of you are facing charges?"

I nodded meekly. "I'd put Rosamund on a fast horse and send her far away if I could, but she's in no condition to move. The mob might have put out her eye."

"Bastards," Samur snarled.

"What do you wish to do about your own punishment?" Xerxes asked me. "There is no honor in their claims against you. I could kill them all, if it would help matters."

I choked with surprise and shook my head. "No, too messy. And I'm not sure what my punishment would even be, or if it would be worsened by Rosamund's lack of repentance."

Samur looked upon Xerxes with a bemused grin. "Not that I don't appreciate your gesture, but why are you willing to take that much risk upon yourself?

"I still owe Varus a life," Xerxes replied. "Zhayedan are not known to run from a debt."

I shrugged, unresolved fatigue beginning to creep again through my body as the final rays of sun slipped from view. "You saved my life in Africa multiple times."

Xerxes shook his head. "It isn't enough, Varus. And besides, where else might I go where I would not suffer from poison or hunger?"

He spoke with the characteristic Persian penchant for honesty, yet his words struck me as odd all the same. I heard them long ago, under far different circumstances, my vision still clouded by the shroud of youth. In the forests of Moesia, when I pried a Gepid girl from a burning hut a few days north of the Ister.

I wondered: *Am I merely a collector of the discarded and the disdained?* It might have been a Christian virtue, had most of my foundlings not been pagans and disbelievers. Xerxes intended his loyalty to raise my spirits, yet I grew melancholy as my thoughts drifted back to Rosamund, who bore so many identities in the service of the Empire. Healer and servant. Pagan and witch. A woman and an accent-addled foreigner. How much longer would she bear the trappings of Roman society before leaving my service? I would never force her to remain, yet I did not know how I could function without her. Even more than my wife or any soldier above or beneath me, I depended upon Rosamund for all things—often for life itself, as my recovery after Dara and Ad Decimum proved.

"Just keep watch over our household, both of you," I instructed Samur and Xerxes. "Both Theodora and Belisarius have warned me of powerful enemies, including those we might not yet see. Both here and anywhere we might travel. Cassiodorus is but an unforeseen threat, although thankfully has few soldiers under his thrall."

"Don't disregard his strength just because it lacks spears and blades," Xerxes cautioned. "Priests have power over men, and your Constantinople is just as vulnerable to their message as any other land I've seen."

Samur nodded. "Well said, and too true."

At that, the noise of pattering feet echoed from the floorboards: Zenobia, bearing a clay jar of honey and a full sprig of grapes, giggled as she ran from an angry Jamila.

"Get back here, you little jinniyya!" Jamila hissed.

Zenobia was not waylaid, and weaved between furniture to escape Jamila's grasp. Spying Samur, she scrambled behind his legs, cradling the pot of honey and beaming at Jamila from behind her new protector. Another set of footsteps sounded from the staircase, and Mariya rushed in, too, scanning the room for any sign of threat.

Jamila turned first to Mariya, then to me, bowing her head low. "Lord, I apologize. I tried to keep her under control, but when she gets an idea in her head, she becomes as untamable as the wind."

Despite the lingering tension of Andronicus' threats, I laughed. "Do not worry, Jamila. The intruders are gone."

Spying Zenobia behind the arch of his legs, Samur bent over and, with a single swoop, pried the clay pot from Zenobia's sticky grasp.

"Uncle, give it back!" Zenobia wailed, grabbing at her stolen prize. When it proved out of reach, she balled a tiny fist and smacked Samur hard on his thigh.

"Zenobia!" Mariya chided.

Samur grinned and knelt so that he met Zenobia's level. "When I was a child, we traded for what we wanted. I will trade this honey pot for two grapes. Do you agree?" He brought dirty fingers to her jaw, pinching at the distinctive point that she shared with her mother. Then, unstopping the honey jar, he sniffed at the contents inside.

"Mmm," Samur hummed. "What do you think?"

After consideration, Zenobia nodded, plucking two grapes from her sprig and handing them to Samur, who dipped them into the honey before plopping them in Zenobia's mouth. Seeing her delight, he laughed. "The most important lesson I learned, however," he continued, "is that when you work together to solve a problem—the rewards are far sweeter than struggling alone. Do you understand?"

Zenobia nodded, a drop of juice from the grape sliding out of the corner of her mouth. Samur handed her the open clay pot and rose to standing, nodding to Mariya. "Keep watch, for I think Xerxes is correct. The sooner we all leave Constantinople, the better."

Zenobia tugged on Samur's leg, offering him a grape. He accepted the gift, allowing Zenobia to offer another to Xerxes, and a third to me. Soon, Jamila returned, scowling at my daughter.

"Zenobia, back upstairs. Alexander is asleep, but Tiberius asks for you. Both of you should rest your heads soon."

After Zenobia departed, I revealed the full extent of the day's events to Samur and Mariya. Neither were pleased, reinforcing Samur's warning.

"I can visit Theodora in the palace," Mariya offered. "She must be able to protect you from these men. You sacrifice so much for her."

"Not this time," I said. "All we can do is wait for Justinian's messenger on the morrow, and see if Cassiodorus really will make an appearance. If there is a true threat to anyone's safety, we will take preemptive action. But we must be patient. Justinian would not have allowed me continued access to my blades in his presence if he felt me a threat."

"Perhaps not you, but he would not hesitate to send Rosamund to a pyre," Samur grumbled.

"That will not happen," I promised. "But we must wait for more information. Tomorrow will give us our answers."

And so it did. And those answers were ruinous.

ULTIMATUM

A s promised, Justinian's courier arrived early the following morning. He was some middling lawyer, a younger man and former favorite of Tribonian who had not been purged along with his master upon Justinian's reforms after the Nika Riots. A servant notified me of his arrival, and I readied myself to greet this unwelcome guest.

"Lord Varus." Dressed in soft white robes with a heavy golden chain, he strode confidently into my household. "My name is Simplicius, and I bear the unhappy duty of informing you of the Emperor's recommendation to rehabilitate your crimes."

He pursed his lips in perhaps the least-sincere display of empathy I have ever witnessed, and unstrapped a leather satchel from his shoulder, which he unknotted to withdraw a scroll. It was small, little bigger than the size of a fist, but sealed in wax stamped in the image of the Emperor. He further urged me to inspect the document to satisfy its authenticity, but there was little need. Plucking Aetius' dagger from my belt, I cut open the wax and unfurled the message, finding Procopius' careful script denoting Justinian's command.

Varus, Tribune of the Romans, is charged with wrath and assault of an ordained and trusted citizen-priest. By law, he may attest such charges in a formal proceeding, with a maximum penalty of ten years in the Imperial dungeon. If Tribune Varus should willingly admit to his crimes, the Emperor Justinian is willing to commute punishment to ten lashes with a common Roman scourge, the sentence to be executed in the Bovis Forum for public view. Tribune Varus' decision in this matter is required by dusk on the day of receipt of this message.

Justinian's name was scratched below the pronouncement, perhaps the only word that he had scribbled himself. Even with Procopius' clerical assistance, however, the words were uniquely Justinian's, both in their legal tenor as much as their implied threats. As this was a civil rather than a military matter, I had no recourse for a trial by combat, and a public trial with one of Justinian's lawyers as my arbiter was guaranteed to be unfavorable to my fortunes. Ten years in an Imperial dungeon... this was a death pronouncement as much as if Justinian insisted that I hang from the gallows, for what few men do not starve on the rotten and meager rations almost always fall perilously ill within a year. As young and healthy warriors, Xerxes and I had survived several weeks in the dungeons of Barbalissus and Antioch, and even that brief interlude made my body feel ancient and brittle.

In this, Justinian sealed my decision, just as he likely wanted the situation to unfold: seek a mild but public punishment for a valuable commander and thereby demonstrate his status as a fair sovereign who gave no undue favors to cronies. It was all theater, as much as any work of long-dead Aeschylus, for I was certain within the roots of my soul that Justinian would not allow his favorites to suffer, even privately. With me, however, Justinian could offer Constantinople's citizens the blood of a warrior who had dared to question a religious leader, regardless of circumstances.

With a curt nod, I dismissed Justinian's creature, who left with a more honest look of unhappiness that he would not then bear my answer back to the palace.

"Unthinkable!" Mariya screamed as she read the letter. "Moronic!"

My eyes widened as I urged discretion. "Even here, keep care of your criticism of Justinian."

"Or what, he might flog me too?" Mariya yelled. "At least then we'll match our stripes. My father would never punish his most loyal supporters this way!"

I lacked the stamina to argue, so I shrugged. "He is the emperor, Mariya. What would you have me do? Risk a decade in prison, and probably death?"

"Do something! Anything!" she replied, a single tear falling from a corner of her eye and staining her meticulously applied cosmetics. "What good is being some Roman lord if you cannot bend the rules a few times?"

"Loyalty comes with sacrifice," I insisted.

"Sacrifice be damned!" Mariya shrieked. "Your emperor takes my husband away for a year, perhaps two, and I say nothing. He does it again when I'm caring for our little child, but against the howling Vandals—and again, I say nothing. And now he would take away what life I have built for us once more, so that we might slog on overcrowded ships and death-strewn battlefields of Italy? And all the while, beat you for keeping order in the street?"

"That will only be for a brief time," I replied, an obvious lie. "And we will be together and safe, all of us."

It was a piteously weak counter, and guilt surged like bile in my throat. Until now, Mariya received the news of her accompaniment with me to Italy with an austere grace—pleased with her family being reunited but resigned that her utopia in Pella must come to an end. She had made occasional comments about missing her work in caring for the Empire's crippled veterans and penniless orphans, delighting in what happiness could be offered through providing nourishing food and opportunities for the children to play and the men to work within the bounds of their condition. I placed blame upon Justinian for tearing Mariya from her hard-won purpose, but I knew that it was my own intransigence, as much as any Imperial decree, that kept me with the army—something that Rosamund had repeatedly scolded me for.

My guilt was magnified by the relief I felt knowing the costs of operating Pella might diminish, for I had little appetite to force her to reduce expenses otherwise. She had been the daughter of one of the wealthiest kings of Asia and husband to a man who had inherited his own fortune of gold, and I did not wish to trouble her mind with the reality that my household was slowly, but certainly, becoming financially unsustainable.

Mariya balled a fist, her manicured nails digging rents into soft skin as she shook her head. "I was so happy in Pella, Varus. And after you returned, I thought my heart might burst. I was useful to others, and free, and with everything I dreamed of when my father first said I would be married off to the Romans. But now that is all gone, and for what?!"

Crossing my arms, I turned my gaze to the ground. "I know you were reluctant to leave Pella, Mariya, but it will still be there for you when we return. Liberius promised."

Mariya shook her head, closing her eyes as she bit lightly against her lower lip. "Rosamund whispered in my ear, Varus. She warned me against trusting Liberius or Petrus. I know you love them, and it is obvious they care for you, but it seems clear to me that they are using you just as much as Theodora or Justinian is."

"Not true," I argued. "Liberius would never ask me to do anything against my will, and Petrus cares only for the souls of me and those dear to me."

Mariya sighed. "Sweet, trusting Varus."

Her tone, so disingenuous, was disconcerting. "What do you mean?"

"Liberius is not some kindly grandfather, Varus. He has his own ambitions, including his designs for you," Mariya replied. "The same as Rosamund, or Samur, or anyone else all want things from you."

The jab was too much. For a heartbeat, I forgot myself. "The same as *you*, Mariya?"

Mariya's face darkened. "I have done everything you have asked of me, Varus. I am the only one who tries to keep our family safe and together!"

She was correct, of course. Whether by oath or the tug of friendship or a simple lust for adventure, my campaigns had taken me about the known world. My children hardly knew me, and I had been parted from my wife for more days than not. Mariya was not wrong to glare hot fury at my insinuation that she alone had pursued some selfish aim, and by her strained voice, I could tell that I had hurt her.

"I just meant—"

"It doesn't matter." Mariya was resigned. "I just want to go home, with you and our children. I hate Constantinople," she added.

"I sensed as much," I replied. "And once this ordeal with Rosamund and Cassiodorus is over, we can leave."

Mariya's nose twitched at my claim. At first, I believed it was out of hatred for Cassiodorus, though was soon proven wrong. "Why couldn't Rosamund just keep her mouth shut?"

"It was she who was attacked," I replied, a bit stunned. "Not the other way around."

"But she goaded her attackers and made things worse," Mariya said. "Made things worse for *you*, because she knew you would come protect her."

Our conversation had taken a dangerous and most unwelcome turn. To my knowledge, Mariya knew nothing of my prior tryst with Rosamund, engaged years ago when Mariya had first arrived in Constantinople, but the edge to her words bore hints of jealousy, or so I thought. Did she suspect something?

"Perhaps you are right," I said, as evenly as I could. "But if I surrender my servant to those worms, I lose face. We lose face, Mariya."

Mariya nodded, but pressed just a hair further. "For as much affection as Rosamund shows you, I only wish that she would be more mindful to keep you safe."

None of my childhood lessons with Justin's teachers had prepared me for diplomacy with my wife. Every answer I searched for seemed dishonest, or likely to inflame further anger. So, rather than reach, I again opted for honesty. "Mariya, you alone have my love. But I also trust Rosamund without reservation. She would do nothing deliberate to harm me, or you, or the children."

"I know you do," Mariya mumbled, yielding a weak smile.

Stepping closer, she rose atop her toes to plant a kiss upon my cheek, sending her perfumes washing over me, enchanting my senses as much as she did our first meeting. "I know your heart, and have nothing to fear."

And although she did not, guilt struck hard in this clash with Mariya. There was little that I did not share with my wife. Indeed, I trusted her with my secrets and fears more than anyone, even Samur. But I could never speak the words to admit that, in a night of drunkenness prior to my dispatch to Cherson, Rosamund and I had shared one another. There was no regret, nor indeed reason for guilt, for it happened long before Mariya and I were coupled, but still, it was a rare piece of my story that I had declined to share with my wife, fearing that it might place everything that I had grown comfortable with in jeopardy. In that moment, I yearned to confess, for the omitted truth only added to the strains upon my mind.

But, at least in this, I could not reveal the truth. "You have nothing to fear, carissima," I said, returning her kiss. "Not ever."

Mariya smiled, but the pleasure was short-lived as she grazed my back with a finger. "Not even love can save us from Justinian and Theodora's desires, it seems. I will make certain that our children and I will have everything needed for Italy."

"It is only temporary, I promise."

Mariya's eyes closed as she shook her head. "Let us pray it is so."

Soon thereafter, I readied myself for a return to the Imperial Palace to proffer my response to Justinian's summons. With Cephalas or Agathias remaining with Rosamund in the palace's interior, it was the Aksumite Wazeba who assisted me with my weapons and armor.

"Excubitor?" Wazeba asked, referring to the set of interlocking lamellar that I owned, then gesturing to the other. "Or custom?"

"Excubitor, with all my weapons," I answered. "If the Emperor's ministers want to flog me in a forum, I intend to remind them of my service."

Wazeba nodded. "Do you think they will require it today?"

"No idea," I replied. "But if Justinian is intent on extracting pain from me, I'd rather he get it over with."

Wazeba helped secure each piece of armor before handing me each weapon, one after the other. To either hip of my iron-studded belt, I attached my scabbarded sword and the Scythian axe, and stashed my dagger along the belt buckle. Wazeba further attached Khingila's bow and a quiver of arrows along my back before handing me an ouroboros-crested shield. He even lay the white wolf pelt along my shoulders, securing it with a thin iron chain against my neck. I did not procure a spear, for it would add little to my presence and be cumbersome in the palace's confines, but even without it I felt somehow safer, more complete. Perhaps Hakhamanish was correct, in his way.

"Let's be done with this," I grumbled.

Samur wanted to accompany my procession, although I resisted such an extensive show of aggression.

"Justinian won't risk angering a hundred armored Hun foederati," he insisted.

I declined. "Perhaps not, but it would infuriate him all the more. Besides, the court would balk at the presence of Huns in the palace and would not look favorably upon me."

"Hypocrites," Samur scoffed. "The Huns are good enough to have their bodies torn apart in the Empire's battles, but not worthy to share the same air as its nobility."

Thankfully, Samur obeyed my wishes, although only after I confirmed that a half dozen Aksumites would serve as my retinue. Though not deemed culturally superior to Huns in a substantial manner, the Aksumites were still formal allies of Justinian, and, as they'd been a regular presence along palatial grounds throughout the riots, would not draw excessive consternation—at least no more than a heavily armed and armored freedman parading in the Emperor's presence, at any rate. I stole a kiss from Mariya and a brief embrace with the children, and escaped onto Constantinople's streets.

Flanked by Sembrouthes and Wazeba, I weaved through back alleys to avoid any of the city's fora. Even in the impoverished and rat-strewn lanes, I could hear the chanting of Cassiodorus' men, seeming emboldened by their recent victories. As before, the sky was overcast, although no moisture fell from the heavens as we meandered toward the palace.

Our indirect path took us toward the Hagia Sophia. Thanks to an army of Egyptian and Cypriot laborers, tremendous progress had been made within the preceding months of reconstruction, with the church foundations and support walls now sprouting from the ground as if the greediest of vines. Though Theodora had been overgenerous in allocating funds from my own hoard to pay for much of the building's cost, I had yet to visit the site beyond a passing observation.

"I've heard some of the palace guards say that it will be the largest building ever constructed," Sembrouthes marveled.

"Not possible," I countered. "The Hippodrome covers a far greater expanse, let alone the Colosseum in Rome and the pyramids of Egypt—as I've heard tell, anyway. But if Justinian's plans are to be believed, it will be a dome of light."

Though the massive church had begun to take shape, there was still little to see for those of us who had limited knowledge of the architectural plan. One day, I told myself, I would visit when the building was closer to completion, both to see whether my involuntary donation had been well spent, as well as whether it could truly live up to the vision of Justin and so many others. I ardently wished it to be so.

Skirting the construction's edge, we had only two hundred paces left to reach the main entrance to the palace. The duty guards seemed both unperturbed of my presence yet clearly anticipated my arrival, with the lead spearman walking forward to greet me. As he did, I noted that no excubitores were present at the outer gate—not unprecedented, but still unusual in the aftermath of the riots.

"Tribune Varus, you will follow me to your designated room," the lead spearman said. Looking toward Sembrouthes, he added, "And your followers will need to wait outside or return to their barracks."

That, again, was unusual; previously, the only measures taken against the Aksumites was to disarm them prior to granting admission. "The Aksumite kingdom is our ally, soldier," I replied. "Sembrouthes is an honored guest of the court."

The spearman raised a hand in deference. "I mean no offense to you or Aksum, Tribune. But I have orders that you, and only you, shall be directed to the intended meeting place."

Each word raised an internal alarm that danger was imminent. I choked down the desire to flee, forcing an uncompromising glare upon the lesser-ranked man.

"You have your orders that you must follow, as do we all," I said. "But surely you would allow our Aksumite friends to visit their wounded friend? Surely that is permitted, given that there are no public ceremonies scheduled."

Growing outwardly uncertain, I could tell that the watch commander wanted to decline the request. I certainly would have if I were him, and such orders came from an Imperial minister. But he also risked my wrath where, stained as it might be in the view of Justinian, I could condemn the man to a ghastly existence on some distant and near-inhospitable frontier.

"Very well, but all their arms must be seized until they depart the palace," the guard ceded.

The Aksumites lined up to hand over spears, shields, swords, and daggers, with the process taking some time to check each man for hidden blades. While his kinsmen occupied the guards' attention, Sembrouthes leaned to me with a whisper. "What is your plan? I cannot protect you if I do not know where you are."

"No plan, but at least you will be in the palace with Rosamund," I said. "Besides, if Justinian intended to kill me, I doubt he would allow me to enter armed into his quarters, excubitor or no."

Soon, we entered the palace, accompanied by a half dozen guardsmen who flanked my unarmed entourage. The added escort irked me, implying a lack of trust in my decision-making and vaguely threatening violence if I did not comply. Though it was no fault of the guardsmen, I still resolved to make their task far more difficult. As they directed me up one flight of stairs and steered farther up another, I turned from my course and headed down a different hallway.

"Tribune, your audience awaits upstairs," the leader of the guards said formally.

Doubtless, it was an awkward affair for those guardsmen. I held high position in the Empire, and against fears that I might be perceived as immodest, I had acquired a reputation as an honored warrior in Belisarius' armies. In different circumstances, such guardsmen would never treat me with anything other than honor and friendship.

"Whoever it is can wait a moment more, for I did not set a specific time for our meeting," I countered. "I would find my servant, wounded and in the palace's care."

The leader of the guards stamped his spear on uncovered marble. "Tribune, my responsibility is to bring you to your meeting—"

"Which you shall do!" I interrupted. "Only give me a moment's time—not long, I promise."

Even with five accomplices, there was little the guard commander could do but accede to my whim. "Very well," he said. "But briefly. And," he added, "you are going in the wrong direction."

"What do you mean?" Sembrouthes' muscled neck and arms tensed.

The guard commander nodded. "You seek the Gepid? She was moved down below, to the quarters of palace slaves."

"Preposterous," I all but snarled. "Why?"

The guard raised a hand in deference. "It was not my decision, Lord. I merely know she has been moved. As she is facing a severe punishment, she was deemed unfit to enjoy palace comforts."

"Tell me who did this," I insisted. "Cassiodorus?"

"I honestly do not know, Lord," the guardsman replied, "but at least she is not in a dungeon. That was her other option. I will show you were she was taken."

I did not require any assistance, however. Yes, the palace's underground was a vast network linking hundreds of rooms and various hidden passages into Constantinople, but I knew them well, and there were few enough places where Rosamund might be placed without attracting attention, resistance, or an opportunity to escape. It was odd, thinking Rosamund a prisoner: although no bars prevented her departure, I doubted that Justinian's guards would allow her free passage from the palace's walls while her sentence and fate lay undetermined.

The guard called from behind me, struggling to maintain a clear tone as he rushed forward in full armor. "Lord Varus, if you would allow me—"

"I know my way around the palace, soldier," I shot back. "Far better than you or your men ever will."

At that, there was no further interruption or delay. Downward we trod, following torches that grew fewer and farther between the farther we trailed into the palace's depths. In the gloom, I could hear dozens of bodies humming with activity, from washerwomen to kitchen scullions to those entrusted with cleaning and scraping night-soil from ornately decorated chamber pots—neither a glorious task nor a mindless one, for a slave that scratched the pot's gold leaf or bent its silver decorations would easily be subject to banishment or worse, as I well knew from an incalculable number of mornings as a younger child. I saw few slaves venture along the hallways, but I knew instinctively that the palace and its walls were alive.

After perhaps a few hundred paces of plunging into the palace's heart, I turned onto a too-familiar hallway and found a man sitting on a stool. An arm propped up a long-haired head, moving little and seemingly disinterested with his surroundings. He was unlikely to be a slave or a freed servant, for none sworn to Imperial service would sit so idly and so carefree in public.

As I accelerated my pace, the man's head turned toward me, his features masked in gloom. Still, despite the darkness, I knew every wrinkle and crack of that stone enclosure, as well as every room that lined that servants' hallway. Immediately I knew Rosamund was housed behind the door to the man's left. I could not suppress a laugh.

The man shuffled behind me. "Varus?"

"Nothing," I responded. "It's just the room that Samur and I shared in bondage to Justin."

And a sensible selection it was. Small enough to prohibit more than two or three children from sleeping on the room's floor, but wide and deep enough to signal special favor to its occupants. Even in my earliest years, I recognized the privilege that Justin conferred upon Samur and me, but I knew nothing of why, or that there was more to come. In many ways, returning to that room teased at unresolved frustrations at Justin's untimely passing.

"Is that you, Varus?" a familiar Heruli voice called.

"Yes," I answered, drawing close to a torch mounted upon a nearby wall. "Sindual?"

"Indeed," came his reply. "Fulcaris ordered me here to relieve Perenus, but Marcellus prohibited me from bringing a full detachment of our foederati into the slave quarters. I volunteered to stay alone as Rosamund's friend. Cephalas and Agathias too, although they're inside."

My eyes widened. "Rosamund still requires care?"

Sindual placed a hand on his lips, beckoning me closer. I complied, leaning close to hear hushed Heruli words. "She's as hale as she can be, given the circumstances. Cephalas and Agathias are inside as protection." He craned his neck to peer beyond me. "Is that Sembrouthes with you?"

"Yes," I answered.

Sindual shook his head. "The guards will make the Aksumites leave. I don't understand what's transpiring beyond Perenus' limited knowledge, Lord, but Justinian's men are treating us like criminals."

"In their eyes, we are criminals," I muttered. "Keep watch. I will leave the Aksumites to assist you as I try to rectify this matter. But thank you for your loyalty."

Another vigorous shake of Sindual's head followed. "It is nothing, Lord. A great many of my men in the foederati owe Rosamund their lives."

I clapped Sindual on the shoulder before turning to the door. It seemed entirely too small, that portal into my childhood, its worn wooden panels and rusted iron hinges identical to my memory. The guard captain again sought my attention but did not press further when Sindual and Sembrouthes collectively blocked his way. Instead, I pushed the door open with a creak, revealing Agathias' dark-rimmed and exhausted eyes on the other side.

"Varus! Thank God!"

Agathias propped open the door just wide enough for my entry before slamming it shut once more. As added security, he jammed a wooden wedge into the bottom of the door, although I doubt it would have done more than annoy a palace guardsman for a few moments.

"Narses' men expelled us from the upper floors," Agathias whispered. "Perenus resisted, but we were outnumbered, and they all carried weapons."

"Narses?" I echoed. Then this truly had been Justinian's will. "You did well to keep Rosamund safe," I said to Agathias.

"But how long must we stay here, Varus?" Cephalas interjected. "They gave little explanation for the move, and even less regarding why they're allowing us independence instead of imprisonment."

"Cassiodorus is waiting to see what I will do about my own punishment," I explained. "But until then, they dare not harm Rosamund."

Cephalas groaned. He had never been one for uncertainty, meticulously planning each day per Rosamund's instructions and the needs of my household and warriors. But I dared not tell a falsehood to reassure his anxious mind—there was far too much at risk with poorly understood enemies whispering into the Emperor's ear. Cephalas started to explain the progress made with Rosamund's treatment when her wispy voice brought all conversation to a halt.

"Cephalas, Agathias." Her words, from where she lay upon a coarse straw mat, were barely a whisper. "Please let me speak with Varus alone. Just a moment is all I need."

Both immediately obeyed, unblocking the doorway and shuffling into the gloom. Absent the others, I gained a closer view of her thin limbs and small frame where she rested upon a coarse blanket. Though the room was illuminated by only a half dozen tapers, Rosamund's skin seemed even paler than normal, and perhaps waxy against the flickering candlelight. Her filth-strewn clothes from the prior day had been substituted for a body-length woolen shift, coupled with a scarf preferred amongst the more modest plebeian women that populated the Empire's towns and cities. After our years together, I could not imagine a more unfitting garment for Rosamund, who appeared happier in mail and leather that conformed to her slight frame. Many layers of thick linen bandages were wrapped tightly around the injured side of her face, obscuring her injured eye and emitting a faint, earthy scent—likely some concoction or another that Agathias had prepared upon Rosamund's instruction. In all our time together, I had never seen Rosamund this frail. It terrified me.

"You seem angry, Varus," she said. Even her voice was devoid of its characteristic fire.

I flared my nostrils, not caring to counter her observation. "They tossed you down here like some slave, despite all that you've done for the Empire."

"I do not mind it so much," Rosamund remarked lightly. "I feel far safer in the company of servants and slaves than I do with that nest of snakes in the Imperial court."

"You have far more patience than I, then," I said. "Funny, but this is the room that Samur and I shared for many years under Justin's thrall."

Rosamund smiled, flashing her teeth. "Here? You might as well have been Varus the princeling in a room like this—yet you complained so."

I laughed, rearranging the weapons along my belt so that I could sit more easily at Rosamund's side. She attempted to lift her body to face me but winced at the effort and fell back to her prone position. A light whimper escaped her lips, but she neither complained nor begrudged her limitations. With what little range of motion she had, Rosamund reached out a hand. Instinctively, I placed it within my own, yearning to comfort my friend no matter my guilty misgivings from that morning with Mariya.

"Cephalas and Agathias tried, but the eye is useless now," Rosamund said. "I'm doomed to stumble about, useless to the world."

"No!" I insisted, gripping her fingers firmly. "You are a warrior, the same as any of our foederati, marked with scars from battle."

"That's generous of you." Rosamund smiled sadly. "Help me remove these bandages."

Releasing her hand, I scanned the wrappings. "Are you sure that is wise?"

She shrugged. "By now, the bandages serve no purpose, now that the wound is cleaned and stitches are not required."

I would have preferred leaving the linen alone but had no will to resist Rosamund's request. Rising again to my feet, I leaned toward Rosamund's head, prying off my gloves and placing them in an empty pouch along my belt. With both hands, I traced the interwoven bandages along the length of her face, searching for a knot or endpoint to unbind the wrappings. Fumbling about, I failed in my early attempts and eventually elected to cut the linen loose.

"Hold still," I commanded. Drawing my dagger, I gently dug its honed point between the linen's folds, guiding it with my fingertips and careful to saw away from Rosamund's face. Agathias had performed his duties well; the wrappings were tight and took more effort than expected to undo, but eventually the severed linen fell away in clumps on each side of her face. Heart pounding, I beheld the true extent of Rosamund's injuries.

Her eyelids, though ringed with vivid bruises, were still able to open. Her upper eye socket had a deep rend where the stone found its target, carving a thin valley through her brow—that, at least, seemed to be healing, though it would scar. But the injured eye itself, where there had once been a deep green iris ringed by a malevolent yellow, there was now only a veil of white. I did not know what to say. Even one not acquainted with the healing arts could tell Rosamund's fate: the eye was blind, or at least mostly so.

She knew it, too. "Place a lit candle in front of my face," she whispered.

Again I deferred to her wishes. I plucked a candle from the wall, grasping the wax with my thumb and forefinger so that molten droplets would not hit my skin or her own, and held the flame aloft, staying a full pace from her eye. She placed a hand over the uninjured side of her face, leaving the clouded orb open.

"Anything?" I asked.

"Just shadows." Rosamund sniffed. "Shadows and darkness."

And then she wept. From pain, frustration, fear, or rage, none but Rosamund can know. Likely all at once. There was nothing I could say to change the outcome, nor any amount of gold to bargain for the return of Rosamund's sight. True, it could have been far worse, for she still retained full sight in the other. But icy logic is not what human emotions are made of, and Rosamund found no solace in the outcome. She grasped my hand, squeezing hard as she shut her eyes tight, sending tears streaming down her cheeks.

"I cannot serve you with one eye," she moaned, her voice still little more than a whisper. "What use am I? Just a bumbling, clumsy leech."

"No!" I insisted. "You are my friend, Rosamund, perhaps the best I have. And even with one eye, you are still far more skillful than any other quacks and surgeons that stalk the army."

She laughed between sobs. "That's true. But the threshold there is painfully low."

I reached out to brush the injured eye. There was no reason, and I cannot recall why I did it. It just seemed proper, for I yearned to offer some modicum of comfort to Rosamund. In our years together, she had asked for little, nothing excessive or indulgent, so perhaps in witnessing such desperate sadness, my instinct was to offer what pitifully little I could. Her lids closed, allowing me to brush away tears stuck to thick lashes, and she offered a smile in gratitude.

I was not able to linger for long. A pounding rattled the doorframe, with an unwelcoming voice sounding from the other side. "Tribune,

I must insist you come with me at once."

"Go," Rosamund said. "Come find me later, if there is time."

I still had not told her of the terrible threats she faced. Though irresponsible of me not to, I could not bring myself to stack greater weight upon her already-burdened mind. She would rage at Cassiodorus' insistence at her conversion—that much was evident, without even asking. So I neglected to press further, leaving her with comfort rather than the truth.

"Rest well," I told her, "for I will need you soon enough."

Reassembling my equipment and unbarring the door once more, I stole a final glance around my childhood room before levying a nod to Rosamund. Unlatching the door, I quickly swapped positions with Cephalas and Agathias, instructing them to remain with Rosamund until the situation grew safer.

"Not a problem," Cephalas said. "I'm comfortable enough shitting in a bucket and eating moldy bread—I served under Archelaus the same as you."

At that, Agathias grew pale, drawing a laugh from Cephalas and myself alike. "Don't worry," I reassured him. "I will have fresh clothes and nourishment brought to you. As for your bucket, bribe a slave into providing occasional assistance."

Plucking two silver denarii from a pouch at my belt, I slid the coins into Agathias' grasp before shutting the door behind me. Visibly perturbed, the palace guardsman directed me back toward the closest stairwell, forcing me to leave Sembrouthes and Sindual behind.

"Don't start fights, but keep a close watch," I instructed. "I will find you as soon as my business is completed."

By then, I had exhausted the patience of my armed guides. We parted from the Aksumites and ascended multiple flights of marble stairs, passing by other guardsmen or an occasional excubitor as we drew closer to the more privileged rooms of the Imperial Palace. The building seemed oddly vacant given Justinian's usual penchant for lengthy visits from supplicants, diplomats, and merchants, with no foreign guests and few petitioners seeking an audience with the

Emperor. Of course, a careful ear could detect light rustling behind the walls of one room or another, but I saw few slaves or servants as I proceeded to my destination. And they performed their duty well — to remain unseen unless the situation warranted the presence of a lowborn bondservant or a wild barbarian hailing from the endless northern expanses.

On the palace's main floor, just before rising to greater heights on the next marble staircase, a voice called out to me. My guide groaned and accelerated his pace, but he had little authority to prevent me from returning the greeting.

"We are already lagging behind schedule," he said as I sought to find the source of the voice.

"Not mine," I countered. "No details were provided to me beforehand. We can wait another moment." I spied a friendly face. "The man is an elderly priest, after all."

Father Petrus rushed into view. "Varus!" he called, straining his already rasping voice. "I've been looking everywhere for you. Liberius is petitioning the Emperor as I speak. Do not antagonize Cassiodorus!"

I paused, not used to seeing him move faster than a brisk walk. "Father?"

"Justinian has granted Cassiodorus the right to determine punishment for you and Rosamund, within the bounds of law," Petrus panted. "Varus, did you truly strike a priest?"

I nodded, gritting my teeth. "I did not know he was one at the time, Father, and he was about to kill Rosamund with a stone. All I did was stun him. There should be no lasting injury."

Petrus placed a hand on me to steady himself, leaning his slight weight on my frame. Then, throwing an eye to the guardsman, he switched from Greek to Latin. "It is as I thought," he whispered, "but that makes no difference to what you will face. Is there any possible way that Rosamund could be convinced to accede to Cassiodorus' demands?"

"No," I replied in the same tongue. "She has rebuffed me a

hundred times since we met, and that is as her friend. To a Roman minister and one as Cassiodorus, she would rather burn in hell."

"That could be her fate, Varus!" Petrus hissed. "Even Liberius is having difficulty with Justinian. Cassiodorus has a hold over the Emperor that is far more dangerous than any other we have faced. Even Hermogenes."

It was unsettling, but I still did not understand the extensive concern. "I have already spoken with Justinian, and will settle this unhappy affair soon. But Cassiodorus has no spearmen, and no friends outside of Justinian. Before the Nika Riots, he was just another fat old man gorged with power and wealth."

"You may characterize what Cassiodorus once was—what he has become is something else entirely," Petrus said. "Just tread carefully."

"I will, Father, but I won't allow him to treat my friends and oathsworn like vermin," I replied. "This nuisance has gone on long enough."

Petrus was clearly unhappy but had no further time to press the issue. The leader of the guards coughed loudly to gain my attention and huddled close to prevent any further distraction from sending me off course, making me protest such childish treatment. Though he and his men backed a respectful distance away, they formed a crude square to accomplish their intended goal.

After parting from Father Petrus, my progress was otherwise uneventful. Each sculpture or fresco I passed was etched into my memory—even now, decades later, I can still picture those busts less frequently cleaned of dust or the frescoes whose paint had been improperly applied, and have no doubt of their exact location in the palace today—and thus the ambience of the Emperor's residence did not awe me like it would any plebeian and a fair number of the provincial aristocracy. Instead, my mind was trained more upon the potential threat that might lie around each hallway bend, for Roman history is not absent tales of assassins, cutthroats, and poisoners, even within palace walls. Beyond such immediate fears, I took little heed of where we were going until we had already arrived.

"In here," the leader of the guards ordered me. "Your guest shall be with you imminently."

I stepped inside. As the door clicked shut behind me, I found myself in a smaller audience chamber on the palace's upper floor, used occasionally by Justinian to receive private audiences from prefects and governors. By palatial standards, it was a modest room, adorned with only a modicum of gold leaf and a small array of simpler columns in the Greek style that had long fallen out of fashion. There were no priceless sculptures or intricately detailed maps of the known world, only an oval wooden table with places for perhaps one dozen visitors. As I was the first to enter the room, I had no idea who I was expected to meet, or truly even what the terms of such a clandestine discussion might be.

The wait was brief. A knock at the door forewarned of another entrant, although the guards announced no name or title. Instead, all that greeted me was a mess of thinning gray hair and beard, a gaunt face whose loose skin hinted at a lifetime of gluttony until recently, and dirt-matted robes belted at the waist with a frayed flaxen cord. The man nearly resembled a sort of particularly disheveled Father Petrus, except where Petrus was thin to the point of frailty, the man before me still carried a small pouch of flesh that rested just above the improvised belt. One would easily confuse him for another village priest, drunk on God and wine amongst a sea of the illiterate, the superstitious, and the pagan, yet this fellow carried himself with a cold dignity that betrayed unquestionable confidence. Underneath the theater of poverty and deprivation, he also possessed a strikingly familiar face.

"Lord Varus," he said, hobbling toward a bench on the opposite side of the table. "Thank you for meeting with me. May I sit?"

At once, I abandoned Petrus' warning to tread carefully. I should have listened, but all I wanted to do was impale this insipid fellow on the edge of my sword and watch him wriggle as he begged forgiveness. "I do not command you, Lord Cassiodorus. You may sit where you please, it makes no matter to me."

"You have my thanks," he replied, his thin lips guarding a mouth with multiple missing teeth. "Shall we begin?"

"You can begin by explaining why your men assaulted my servant and stormed their way into my house," I growled. "The last time I faced down men with clubs and hooks in Constantinople's streets, they all ended up in a pool of their own blood in the Hippodrome."

Cassiodorus grimaced. "You have my apologies, Lord Varus. My followers are ardent, but perhaps… overeager in their desire to serve our Lord."

Shuffling in his seat, Cassiodorus rested two gnarled hands upon the room's table. There were no rings or jeweled chains, nor any of the trappings of office that I remembered from my previous encounter in the Emperor's Box during Perenus' final chariot race. They were filthy hands, whose fingers seemed more familiar with carving soil than brushing against the precious pages of the written word or praying for the souls of Constantinople's denizens. Cassiodorus' body was far thinner than I remembered, with loose skin hanging limply about his upper arms and jowls. Small sores along his hands also suggested chronic pain, yet another affliction for a man who by all accounts had been a famous glutton in the palace kitchens. Yet, the figure who stood before me resembled little of the pampered, obese cretin.

I scoffed. "That is no answer, Minister. Why do your men stalk the streets and disrupt Justinian's peace?"

Cassiodorus sighed, another thin smile on his weathered lips. "As you likely know, I was not always the godliest of men. Oh, I knew the Testaments as if engraved in my very soul and could recite passages as well as any patriarch, and I told myself that thrice-daily prayers and outward protestations of faith were enough to earn God's favor as I surrounded myself with luxury."

"I remember that well," I said. "And some plebeian threw rotten vegetables at your face, just as the riots began."

Cassiodorus' smile broadened. "That he did. God gave me the blessing of chastisement, and an opportunity to redeem my soul. And so, I eschew the trappings of kings and princes and spread the message of God's love amongst our growing collection of poor and hungry believers. And believe me, Lord Varus, they are so very many."

He offered little enough that I could not guess, although whether the outward protestation of faith was a ruse or a heartfelt gesture, I could not say. Given the state of the man's haggard body, I believed him honest, in his own way.

But I also did not care. Dressed in eastern silks or coarse mountain wool, Cassiodorus was the leader who brought pain onto many, and was a direct threat to Theodora. Then and now, I find him a hypocrite, dressing zealous faith in honeyed words laced with intimidation.

"What do you truly want, Minister?" I said shortly. "For your purported transformation, all I can tell that you are doing is hiding from most of Justinian's court and stirring a rabble of idiots and malcontents to hassle the residents of Constantinople."

Cassiodorus bowed his head, eyes closed, and offered his hands in supplication to God. "It is not what I want, Tribune, but what God insists of me."

"You find virtue in inflicting suffering upon those less powerful than you, just because they are pagan?" I snorted. "That is not the God of peace that I know."

Cassiodorus' eyes opened, but his hands remained outstretched. "You are a poor student of the Scriptures. Our God is a wrathful, avenging God."

"Spoken without a hint of arrogance," I shot back.

Cassiodorus' hands finally closed together into a single clap. "I do not blame you for your misconceptions, nor for your animosity to me. The faithful tell me that you are an ardent follower of our Savior, though you keep company with heretics and follow that Latin priest Petrus. God may cast misfortune upon you for such poor choices, but you may yet be redeemed for your faith."

Perhaps Cassiodorus' strategy was to provoke my raw annoyance until I yielded. If so, it was working, for by this point I did not wish to entertain such discussion any further. I was willing to stay only to bargain for Rosamund's safety and freedom, not to simper at the feet of such a vile and self-serving creature. Perhaps that was why Petrus warned me against my own instincts, but again, I was foolish enough to cast aside his sage wisdom. Only in my own twilight do I recognize the bait Cassiodorus dangled for me.

"I ask again," I said, "what do you really want? Your men attacked my servant with no provocation, so whichever punishment you may seek for her I shall pursue against your own."

Cassiodorus laughed. "Paganism is its own heinous sin, and is compounded when those dark magics are turned against the Godfearing. Rosamund's provocation is far worse than any other imaginable, I fear, for she cursed the followers of Christ. As you well know, that is amongst the gravest of sins, whose perpetrator might suffer searing punishment."

"You have no proof," I pointed out. "While Rosamund's injuries attest to her tale."

Cassiodorus paused. "You may not believe me, but I have no wish to consider you an enemy. Aside from Rosamund, and those pagans and heretics who carry your banners into battle, you and I are of the same allegiance."

I snorted again, but Cassiodorus continued without any sign of irritation. "But I shall do what I must to serve God. Even if that means performing acts that are otherwise repulsive or antagonistic. I take no pleasure in your servant's pain, but such inconveniences are but the tiniest blip of the eternal torments that await her. Her conversion will guarantee her a blessed place at the side of our Redeemer, and shall encourage many hundreds to follow her example. All I require is her baptism."

"And if she refuses?"

Cassiodorus' eyes closed as he shook his head. "Unfortunate indeed. If she refuses, then she shall receive a foretaste of the hell that she is so apt to take into her bosom."

"Eat shit and die," I spat. "You make a grievous mistake by keeping Rosamund prisoner. She has friends, minister, far more powerful than you can imagine."

"Oh, my imagination is vast." Cassiodorus smiled as his eyes narrowed. "You speak of the heathens, murderers, and rapists that follow you in the army. Strength of arms may instill fear in many that you are used to dealing with, but it is as a children's plaything to me."

Despite his threats and boasts, I still did not fear Cassiodorus. I had led thousands, veterans of the Empire's wars against the Avars, Persians, Hephthalites, Vandals, and even the Visigoths. Our foes brandished all manner of arms to pierce and slash, and I did not recognize Cassiodorus' feeble thrusts. Godilas and Justin reared me to be a leader of warriors, and I was well equipped to meet the threat of a mob made of bored youths following a greedy old lecher.

"Let us be done with this," I said. "What is your price for Rosamund's freedom? My childhood was surrounded by men like you. I know well the glow in your eyes around gold."

Cassiodorus offered a curt nod. "I have my price, although it pains me to trade an opportunity to liberate the Gepid's immortal soul for earthly gains. But I must, if God's flock is to grow."

"So name your price and be done with it."

"No, no." Cassiodorus shook his head like a teacher disappointed in his pupil. "You will know my price when the time is proper. And when that moment comes, you will pay anything, even your own life, if I ask for it."

"Raving lunatic," I spat. "I accept the Emperor's justice against me, for that is within his authority. But much sooner than later, I will make sure that you face your own judgment."

Cassiodorus nodded with a smirk, ignoring my threat. "Her moment comes soon, so you do not have long to wait."

"When?"

Another sympathetic nod. "Sometime after your own punishment, Lord Varus—and I shall tell the Emperor you accept his merciful commutation. Perhaps soon, perhaps a year from now. The greatest lesson the Lord has passed to me is patience, and I have learned well. When the time comes, you will wish you had paid greater respect to one you deem decrepit and corrupt. I certainly used to be, but God hardened my resolve for greater things."

With that, our meeting drew to a close. There were no promises of friendship, nor any idle talk expected even of those rivals who were outwardly friendly to others they would rather see riven with a blade. Unwilling to wait for Cassiodorus to shuffle across the floor and away to his secret quarters in the city, I stormed out first, not stopping to acknowledge the guardsmen or excubitores who saluted or nodded as I passed. Instead, I descended into the palace's lowest levels for a quick rejoinder before departing for safer rooms away from Justinian's minions.

"Any problems?" Sembrouthes whispered.

"No," I replied, brushing aside Cassiodorus' flamboyant threats. "Stay with Sindual until I can get Perenus and Fulcaris' men access to the palace once more. The only danger to us is being found alone— otherwise, all these fools can do is rave and froth at the mouth."

After Sembrouthes' acknowledgment, I departed, believing my business was done. It was not until later that I recognized Cassiodorus' victory, and that the silent blows he struck would do far greater damage than any battle I had yet faced.

FORUM OF THE
BRAZEN BULL

Two mornings later, few in my household were particularly concerned with recent inconveniences. Cassiodorus' mob had been proven powerless against Samur's Huns, and though Justinian's pronouncement of my guilt was disconcerting, the intended punishment—the public flogging—was more embarrassing than truly worrisome. Soon, it would all pass, like a cloyingly vibrant bad dream, especially when Rosamund's sentence would be similarly commuted or abandoned outright.

Or so we thought.

My punishment had been scheduled an hour before the sun's zenith—in this, at least, Justinian had demonstrated thoughtful mercy, for the entire procession would complete prior to the worst of the day's sun. Though spring was only just emerging after the frigid slumber of winter, Constantinople's paved streets and open fora could be uncomfortably warm even on relatively cool days, their countless stones absorbing the sun's heat indiscriminately.

Mariya still grated at my acceptance of the penalty, and insisted that I seek dispensation from Theodora, but I shrugged such pleas aside. If Theodora could spare me pain in this matter, she would have already done so, and well before my appointed hour in the forum. Frankly, I simply did not understand the concern that others saw in my punishment—after all, men are chastised regularly in the army, and with far more than ten lashes.

True, I did not *desire* the feel of a scourge tearing into my skin, and fully believed that the common people would point and mock, yet those concerns were petty in my mind. The lictor's whip would not bite worse than a Persian arrow, and the common people held little love for a Herulian anyway. A childhood of public disdain had hardened me against what the people might believe, and as long as I had the resources to protect my family and see my household well supplied, my soul was armored against the fleeting mockery of the hundreds who bore witness to my judgment.

My resignation had only been reinforced by a visit from Liberius and Petrus on the previous evening, with both men visibly weary from extensive days petitioning Justinian. Though Liberius' words did not surprise me, the weightiness of defeat certainly did.

"Justinian will not be moved, Varus, though I did all that I could," he said. "Your punishment has less to do with you, and more to do with demonstrating power to his subjects."

"Power?" I asked. "He is emperor. What more could he need, especially after all that has transpired? None has greater authority than he."

Liberius sighed. "You were a fair student, Varus, but you still have so much to learn. Power does not come from titles, but from a willingness of the masses to be led. From Alexandria to Singidunum, men toast Belisarius for plucking victory from the maw of death, while foreign ambassadors and provincial governors alike seek Theodora's blessing for anything that would benefit from the Imperial seal. Men even gossip that Theodora exerts power beyond Justinian's grasp, noted by her favor bestowed upon the eastern clergyman Jakob Baradaeus."

"Jakob does not instigate mobs," I mumbled. "Only a difference of opinion."

Liberius rolled his eyes. "And therein lies the problem, no? This creature of Theodora's holds an opinion counter to the Emperor's design for a Christian empire. And in my years, I have rarely known emperors to clap joyfully when disagreed with."

"But—"

"But nothing." Liberius stopped me short with a wave of his hand. "Justinian has vision and unsurpassed ambition, but it is as if he is being squeezed by two immense and unbreakable stones. Justinian loves his wife above all things and needs Belisarius to achieve his most longed-for desires but resents both for seizing what he perceives as his glory."

"But Belisarius loathes glory," I replied. "And Theodora only wishes to help the people. Neither are braggarts, let alone usurpers."

"It does not matter." Now it was Petrus who intervened, smiling weakly. "The Emperor feels slighted, Varus, and regardless of the cause, that makes it a dangerous time for all of us. Cassiodorus fuels that resentment, whispering that Justinian alone can restore the Empire to God's grace. I beg you, exercise restraint against Cassiodorus, and leave your punishment with your honor and discipline intact."

"I will." Even as I said it, I remained skeptical of Liberius' pronouncement. Alas, as both men well knew, I was headstrong and naïve, even unto the morning of my public disgrace.

My punishment had been meticulously planned. For the ceremony, Justinian had resurrected the use of lictores, or attendants to the Emperor and his civil magistrates, to fulfill legal proceedings. Though the profession had fallen out of use upon the collapse of the Western Empire, in favor of Imperial soldiers or limitanei to execute justice, the memory of the lictor was engraved in many a sculpture or fresco in Constantinople, giving Justinian ample inspiration for their resurrection.

Justinian commanded twenty-four freshly appointed lictores, all male Roman citizens of strong build and adorned with a more old-fashioned toga of the age of Augustus. Often retired soldiers, each man hailed from the plebeian class by Roman custom, and carried a fasces as a symbol of their authority to fulfill Imperial decrees. The fasces was a cumbersome and impractical weapon, little more than smoothed sticks of equal length bound in a cylinder and topped with an axe head, yet even today the denizens of Constantinople knew its power.

I was to arrive unarmored, and any weapons could be transferred to a follower or held in trust by a lictor until the ceremony's completion. A medicus would be within earshot, although Rosamund, as a defendant to a separate crime, was disallowed to me. Most of all, the proceedings would be public—a warning to all present that even those who held the Emperor's trust were subject to the same laws and restrictions as the dirtiest and tattered plebeian. It seemed somehow humorous to me that the whole display was necessary, for certainly the outcome of the Nika Riots had demonstrated Justinian's boundless desire to enforce discipline and order. For the place, Justinian had selected the Forum of Bovis, that infamous gathering place of the Empire's more unscrupulous residents.

The Forum of Bovis, or the Forum of the Ox, was a lesser trading square that housed a great many workshops for common professions—tanners, lesser blacksmiths, weavers, and the like. Located near Constantinople's southwestern coastline, it also contained vast warehouses for goods hauled from ships entering the city's harbors, and nightly became a congregation point for sailors seeking an evening of drunkenness or debauchery.

Though it received its name for the massive bronze ox that adorned the forum's center, it was more popularly and infamously known as Constantinople's square for punishment and execution. The worst offenders were neither hanged nor burned at a pyre, but locked inside the ox's hollow stomach and heated over a rising bonfire. It was a slow death, and not one easily forgotten by spectators—indeed, perhaps the horror thrust upon the witnesses was the very reason for broiling traitors and mutineers alive in the first place.

Thankfully, such punishment far exceeded my own crimes. Ten lashes was nothing, I reasoned. Archelaus had inflicted far worse. It would make for little more than an uncomfortable month of healing, by which time we would be preparing to depart for Italy.

This gave Mariya no comfort as she stroked the bare skin of my back, muttering frustrations at Cassiodorus, Justinian, Theodora, and just about anyone else who inconvenienced our household. Mariya could not accept that the issue was resolved, regardless of how many times we rehashed the argument.

"Loyalty is only worthwhile if it is repaid in kind," Mariya bit out. "If Theodora is going to abandon you, is there any hope of appealing to Rosamund? Perhaps if she converts, we can arrange for your deliverance as well as hers."

Unlike with Cassiodorus, I now managed to contain the ire that boiled in my stomach. "Rosamund has earned my trust a thousand times over. I would never ask her to do such a thing if it were against her will."

"But this whole situation is because of her!" Mariya cried. "Surely she would understand that—"

"No!" I yelled. "Enough. Justinian will mark my skin and we will be done with this. In a few months, it will be little more than a fleeting memory. One brief exchange with the lictores, and all will be forgotten."

Mariya flinched as I spoke, and she only slowly turned to gaze at me, her lips pursed and her dark eyes leering upon me. It was as unfamiliar a look as I could have imagined upon my wife's face, and one that rendered me helpless and wordless. I was easily twice Mariya's size, a grown man, but as it dawned on me just how much my outburst had upset her, I again felt a helpless boy in Anastasius' court.

"As always, you act without considering me," Mariya said, her words quivering with anger. "If that monkey Cassiodorus whips you in a public square, do you think *I* will be spared any grief? Any shame? That your *children* will be? This is more than what you claim it is, Varus. It is not some nick of the razor that will patch up in due time."

I winced, but my mind was unchanged. "Mariya, if I accept Justinian's judgment, the issue will be put to rest," I explained. "I broke the law, and the punishment is a mild one. In a month, we will be far away from this den of thieves. It will be over, I promise you."

"Of course it won't be over!" Mariya said. "How can you not see it? This is only the beginning, Varus. Do you truly believe that

Rosamund's attack was an accident?!"

"It was," I insisted. "You weren't there to see—"

Mariya rolled her eyes, as if I were being willfully naïve. "Cassiodorus is just another courtier, Varus. He craves power and needs money, and he uses Jesus to achieve it. You are an easy target to acquire both."

I still did not follow Mariya's reasoning. "I am a sworn warrior of the excubitores. Hardly an easy target for some pudgy priest to bully around."

"And yet," Mariya said, "here we are." She stayed silent a moment. "In one action, Cassiodorus attacks Theodora's trusted servant and shows his power by forcing an excubitor to accept the lash like a common criminal. And all because *you* prove so useful as a common target. I guarantee that he will not be satisfied with a few stripes upon your back."

Mariya's insights, while sensible, seemed pointless to my circumstance. Perhaps Cassiodorus' crowd had attacked Rosamund intentionally to bait me into acting as a pawn—what did that change now? Embarrassment flamed into frustration. "I have no choice, Mariya!"

"There's always a choice!" Mariya yelled. "Push Theodora to support you. Bribe one of Cassiodorus' men. Pay spies to find Cassiodorus' men breaking laws." She paused again, squeezing her eyes shut. "Do *something* other than just lie back and wait for your enemies to tear you apart!"

The whole exchange felt horribly, utterly wrong. I had rarely seen her so angry, and never at me. Still, my mind was unchanged. "I gave my word to the Emperor. My oaths demand that I see this through."

"Men!" Mariya bellowed. She clenched her fists, only to slump in defeat. "Blind obedience is for little boys," she said, her voice now hollow. "Do what you must. But I promise you, Cassiodorus will not settle for a brief display of repentance. There's more than God in that man's dreams. And it will be Rosamund that gives him an excuse to put us all in danger."

That last jab pushed too far. "I owe Rosamund my life! You ask me to not be weak, not to be manipulated, but how would the world see me if I abandoned my oldest servant like some worn-out belt just to save my reputation?"

Mariya softened. "I did not say to toss her aside, Varus. But she brought this calamity upon us by goading Cassiodorus' followers. If she were to convert—"

"Rosamund will never convert to Christianity," I interrupted. "Believe me, I've tried."

Mariya's frustration turned to curiosity. "Have you?"

Truthfully, not with any vigor, though I was unwilling to admit that to my wife. "Yes."

"Then ask more firmly," Mariya said. "Anyone can see that she dotes on you, regardless of what you claim. Some even wonder—"

"She doesn't dote on me!" I shot back, slamming my hands together with each syllable. "I've told you before. She is a loyal friend and nothing more."

Sighing, Mariya's defenses finally dropped entirely. She would not meet my gaze, and when she spoke it was with the softest tone. "I know, and I believe you."

"You should!" I shot back, unconvinced.

"I do," Mariya replied, albeit with the same resignation. "I just don't want you to lose everything—your standing, our *family's* standing—because Rosamund is too proud to act differently in Constantinople. She has paid good service to me too, you know, but I would never let anyone jeopardize my children or my husband."

The argument faded without resolution. In hindsight, I do not blame Mariya. I was a trusting fool, believing that a woven nest of oaths and honor kept the Empire moving onward. I desperately wanted to believe so, though in my twilight years, such naivete is long absent in my sensibilities.

As preparations were made to see Justinian's will executed and Cassiodorus' thirst sated, Sembrouthes and his men remained in the palace, for I could discern no avenue to substitute the Aksumites for any Hun, Heruli, or Vandal detachment. Instead, I leaned upon Xerxes as my temporary bodyguard and escort, although I did not believe the extent of his talents would be required on our sojourn to the Bovis Forum. He readied himself well before sunrise, his shimmering scales a clear message of wealth and skill in the arms secured along his belt. Samur entered my building just after dawn, accompanied by yet another dozen Huns under Sinnion's co-chieftain Aigan.

"We could always fillet Cassiodorus' men and send any guards running with piss down their legs," Samur joked, although likely not entirely a jibe.

I rolled my eyes. "No, Justinian asks for comparatively little. Let's keep from committing treason for another day."

"You will have nothing to be concerned with, Varus," Xerxes added. "I have scheduled a bit of a surprise for your lictores."

"Perenus? Fulcaris?" I asked.

Xerxes shot me a mischievous grin. "Gunderic. I thought the Heruli a bit too civilized for such an occasion, and Belisarius approved their armed entry into Constantinople in preparation for the voyage to Italy. When I explained the dangers you faced to him, Gunderic threatened to cut the manhood from anyone who would lay a weapon upon you."

"He means it, too." I laughed. "Keep them in good order, but make their point known."

Not long thereafter, the hour of my appointment drew nigh. Mariya led three children—two my own, and the third a curiously burly four-year-old Tiberius—to each receive a brief embrace before my departure. Little Alexander wailed, Tiberius smiled sheepishly. Only Zenobia returned the gesture, her thin sticks of arms squeezing my neck after I raised her from the floor. Returning Zenobia to Jamila, I offered a kiss to Mariya, which was returned in kind with as forceful a passion as I had ever experienced.

"If this goes poorly, there is no dishonor in refusing Justinian," Mariya whispered into my ear.

"It will be perfectly fine." Any further debate felt pointless.

Mariya bit her lip as if struggling to suppress some condemnation. Her eyes shut tight, her jaw clenched.

"This is wrong, Varus," Mariya whispered.

That final warning spawned irritability within me. "We've talked about this—"

"That doesn't make your way of thinking correct," Mariya whispered back. "But your mind is made up. Just promise me that you'll keep some measure of caution around those creatures."

It was the world's easiest promise to make. I was a lord, and a commander of warriors. This brief episode of Justinian's law might be inconvenient, and even temporarily humiliating before the city's residents, but it would pass soon enough. And, thereafter, all would be as it was before Rosamund's attack, albeit with fresh scars along my back.

"Of course," I whispered back, stealing another kiss.

I departed with Xerxes, Samur, and Aigan's Huns. Lacking my armor, I felt almost naked, and significantly smaller. Instead, I bore only the excubitor's cloak with a shirt and trousers of dyed black linen. However, though I left my broader arsenal safely stored with Mariya, I did not leave without my sword. Besides that, the only other tokens I bore were Mariya's pendant, Petrus' bronze cross, and Theodora's gold signet ring. The pendant and cross I buried beneath my shirt, but the ring I wore proudly upon the smallest finger of my shield arm, hopeful that someone might recognize it as the rarest symbol of the Empress' favor. In that little gesture, I signaled my disregard for the severity or solemnity of Justinian's event.

Thus, at the center of my armed formation, I strode confidently toward the Forum of Bovis, remarking again at the relative emptiness of Constantinople's streets and stalls. It was a fair distance to that Forum, taking our small party perhaps an hour to traverse the freshly swept stones, drawing curious eyes from small groups of onlookers haggling at one stall or another.

"Must be intimidating, seeing Huns stroll about Constantinople's streets in full armor," Samur said in Heruli.

"You would too, if you were them," I answered in the same language. "Attila threatened to burn Constantinople to the ground. He would have, too, if he had not been distracted by the Western Romans."

Samur yielded a muted smile. "Sometimes I wish Attila really had destroyed the Empire, and all the patricians in it. What a world that would have created."

"Too late to know now."

Privately, I wondered about where the two of us might be had the Hunnic conqueror fulfilled his destiny. It was a sobering thought, but not one worth dwelling upon, for though the Huns retained incredible martial ability, they remained fragmented into a thousand clans and tribes along the northern wastes, separated from the Empire by vast distances and equally vicious tribes who had no love for the onetime followers of Attila.

My teachers had once spoken in hushed tones that a united Hun army might still fulfill Attila's dream, for such a united mass of skilled warriors would have no peer. God intervened, however, and blessedly the Empire's most terrible enemies remained scattered and divided—likely forever. All that remained close to Constantinople were the foederati, and such men were far closer to Roman citizens than any wild plains rider.

Nearing our destination, the noise from the Bovis Forum stood in contrast to the otherwise depopulated city. In the alleys nearest the forum, boys carried baskets of fruit and jars of honey, while butchers shouted descriptions of various cuts of seasoned meat that could be heated and readied within moments to the customer's liking. Despite Justinian's dislike for lascivious behavior, a great many prostitutes weaved between stalls and grasped at potential customers, their perfumes mixing with the odors of meat, piss, dung, and pungent sweat.

"At least Justinian still listens to Theodora about some points," Samur said, pointing out one such woman as she paused from caressing a would-be customer to ogle the Huns as we proceeded.

"Aye," I replied. "She did insist upon safety for women, even those who sell their bodies."

"They sell their bodies no less than us." Samur grinned. "And prostitutes usually don't slay their customers. Perhaps you have a reason to dislike them?"

"No..." I fumbled. "They just..."

"Aren't Christian?" Samur teased. "Wasn't one of Jesus' companions a prostitute? I never paid enough attention to be certain."

"That's different," I insisted, tiring of the conversation amidst greater threats around us. "Christ forgave the sins of everyone, prostitutes included."

"And you shouldn't?" Samur's smile widened. "He who is without sin, cast the first stone! Until then, let prostitutes earn coin, I say."

Before we could filter into the forum, a horn blared notes from its far edge: staccato and orderly, telling of a military formation on the march. I recognized the sound instinctively, having heard it a thousand times over the past years—a thousand times a thousand, it seemed.

"Gunderic is here," Xerxes said. "I will go to him and make sure they behave."

I nodded, and Xerxes escaped into the crowd. While many stared and gaped at the Huns as we passed, none dared stand too close, nor impede our progress. With Samur as our leader, we entered the Forum just as the last of the Vandal foederati took position on the forum's southern edge, opposite a massive wooden stage erected for the public punishments. Its timbers were freshly cut, for this section of Constantinople bore the worst of the pitiless fires that consumed the city after the riots.

"Vandali Justiniani," Gunderic's voice soared, his accented Latin betraying his heritage. "Halt!"

"Here we go," Samur yelled back to me, his voice piercing through the crowd.

Finally, Samur and I emerged into the Bovis Forum, gaining a clear view of the massed foederati and the opponents they stared upon. Gunderic had assembled no fewer than four hundred men—a full banda—and they all shone with freshly polished armor and brightly painted shields. Their devices comprised mostly Justinian's eagle or Chi-Rho, but the officers stubbornly adhered to the bent-cross of Arian Vandal heritage; both Gunderic and Wisimar carried that emblem, with the former wielding a massive bulwark that seemed half again as large as a typical Roman shield. Such sigils must have infuriated Cassiodorus' followers, who decried the Arian faith of the Goths and Vandals as nothing short of devil-inspired heresy.

And there were many of them. Far more than I anticipated. Far, far more than I ever thought would bite from Cassiodorus' corrupted fruit, but now here they were. Two, perhaps three thousand, crowded about the platform in a swirling mass, outfitted in the garb of poor farmers and weary tradesmen alike. Their eyes were full of a lust that I had seen many times before, but only on the precipice of battle.

"Jesus," I muttered.

"Not likely to help you here," Samur joked. "I bet there are a lot more of them praying than us, so the Savior's ears will be well worn out before we have our say."

At that point, I had no instruction other than to await the Emperor's request to approach the platform. Seeing nothing, I directed our small detachment toward the Vandals, with Gunderic raising an arm in welcome.

"Spoiling for a fight, Varus?" Gunderic beamed. "Not a cock amongst these chickens, I'd wager."

"No fighting today, God willing," I replied. "But I am glad you are here."

Gunderic stepped closer, giving me a hard smack on the shoulder. "I expect you to come and baby me when I inevitably anger one of these shit-eaters. But if they get violent, this gathering will end very quickly."

The odd boast, usually from the younger of Cassiodorus' ranks, rang out. Others voiced their own wishes for our deaths, or for our suffering in eternal brimstone. The Vandals, most of whom spoke only poor Latin, laughed merrily at the display, but none returned a crude gesture or even unsheathed a blade. To do so would mean combat, and a direct violation of Justinian's peace, when Gunderic's duty was merely to intimidate. And despite our adversaries' bluster, Gunderic performed his task well.

At the center of the forum stood the massive brass bull. Holes had been carved into its body at various points, big enough to easily peer into the bull's innards, but small enough that only the tiniest birds could flit within. Their purpose was as simple as it was cruel—the condemned would feel the tantalizing breeze of fresh air, with safety but two paces distant, but unreachable. It also afforded onlookers with a clear view of the burning body, roasting alive, and an outlet for the screams of torment and weeping for mercy. Cassiodorus' men kept a full ten paces distant, giving the bull an ominous aura of fear, though it stayed empty.

We did not have long to wait. Cassiodorus was not visible on the dais, nor Justinian, nor any Imperial minister, although a dozen Imperial guardsmen were arrayed along the platform's twin entrances to prevent the mob from rushing up—there, at least, good order remained. In absence of the dignitaries, a rising swell of noise deafened all attempts at conversation, leaving me to stand silently by Gunderic as we deferred all action.

Until a second horn boomed through the forum: now with long, sonorous notes more familiar amongst the limitanei, warning of intruding tribal war bands along the border. I'd heard them before at Singidunum and again along the walls of Dara but was puzzled at their presence in Constantinople, until my companion guided my gaze.

"There." Gunderic pointed at a glistening mass filing in from where I'd entered not moments ago. Emblazoned in the Emperor's sigils, they were bedecked in coarse armor, cheap iron sheets wrapped atop studded leather. But there was a vast array of them—perhaps another thousand in neat rows that parted the crowd and advanced into the forum's opening. Some ascended to the dais, while others formed a ring around the bronze bull.

"City watch," I explained to Gunderic.

He spat. "How in Pluto's stinking arsehole did my men lose to you people in Africa?"

I could not help but smile. "Be careful with the pagan gods, some might hear."

"I hope they do," he replied.

Even outnumbering Gunderic's forces more than two to one, the city watch was a pathetic display of strength. But it was not meant as such, for no fighting would likely be required; all that Justinian needed was their massed presence to shame me into good behavior. The watch's presence blunted the effect that the Vandal foederati would have upon the proceedings, limiting my ability to control a bloodthirsty crowd.

A rolling horn blared again, calling the city watch to order. If Archelaus had been present, he would have pissed himself laughing at the display, for those guardsmen were arrayed in ragged order and poor physique. Nevertheless, their faces remained blank, struck with cold dignity as their horn blared again, and again, and again.

Finally, as its last notes died across the overflowing forum, a dozen guardsmen rushed onto the dais, followed swiftly by dark-robed priests. Immediately, I noticed Andronicus, his balding pate and cocksure grin greeting the crowd with outstretched arms.

"Children!" Andronicus cried. "Children! The Emperor has heard your pleas. Through the resplendent Justinian, God will return to the Empire's heart!"

An eruption of cheers followed, and Andronicus, though moving with stiff solemnity, seemed to fight a pleased smile at the sound. Men and women fought to out-yell one another in praise of Cassiodorus and invoking God's favor, with children bouncing upon shoulders for closer views of Cassiodorus' honored disciple. Eventually, after a considerable delay, the shouting subsided to a murmur, allowing Andronicus to continue.

"Emperor Justinian, in his divinely inspired wisdom, has reformed the tangled web of Roman law into a godly codex. Judicious and fair, the Emperor and his lictores have found multiple citizens guilty of crimes of various severity. Justinian, the great and magnanimous Justinian, grants Cassiodorus the authority to carry out approved sentences upon today's criminals."

There was less cheering this time, for bureaucratic talk of law and order rarely inspires passion in the masses. And why should it? They lived barely three meals from starvation, an illness away from permanent poverty or infirmity. Upon Andronicus' pronouncement, however, loaves of bread and freshly picked apples were tossed into the crowd, generating a preferred response.

"Justinian Augustus!" called one voice, and then another. The cries were uneven, echoed at random and never gaining a singular voice, but the overall effect was clear enough.

Andronicus nodded. "Cassiodorus' followers accept the Emperor's charge with great solemnity, but equal purpose. For although Christ calls for mercy where possible, those who break the laws of Caesar and violate the sanctity of God must pay for their crimes. We begin today with an episode of treason. A traitor so vile, so self-serving, that he would see thousands of Godfearing Romans dead for his personal gain. Such barbarity cannot run unchecked in God's Empire!"

As a chorus of hisses and fury confirmed Andronicus' declaration, a team of fasces-wielding lictores emerged from the forum's alley. Between them they hauled a man, his arms and legs each hoisted above the ground by an individual lictor.

"What are these cunts getting at?" Gunderic asked.

I shrugged. "No idea. I was told I alone would be scourged today."

"If I'm to stay here all afternoon, I'll need to find a latrine soon enough." Gunderic groaned. "Could use a wineskin and a brothel too. Your countryside forts have little to be desired."

Rather than join Andronicus upon the raised platform, the condemned was hauled toward the bull. Several lictores, unencumbered by the limbs of the captive, rushed forward to unlock and open the bull's hollow stomach. Others directed a train of palace slaves adjacent to the display, each slave hauling stacks of split logs and kindling: plenty to burn a great fire and more than enough to roast a man alive. Yet more slaves stacked the unlit fuel into place, nestling logs within a stone-lined firepit positioned beneath the bull's belly.

I pitied the condemned. Though I have seen men and women die in innumerable and horrifyingly creative ways, I had no desire to witness the torturous Brazen Bull in use. Both Gunderic and Xerxes remained impassive throughout the display, although other Vandals' brows furrowed at the ancient procession of punishment against the vilest of offenses. It was only then, as the logs were being positioned and the condemned readied to be ingested by the bull, that the man's face turned toward my direction. Swollen eyes widened, and the man gained a newfound vigor as he struggled against the lictores' grasp.

"Gunderic, they are starving our people!" he screamed. "The women and children die with bloated bellies and threadbare clothes. Do not help them erase the Vandals from this life!"

Shooting a look toward Gunderic, I found the Vandal chieftain as stony as before. "You know him?"

"Not well," Gunderic muttered. "His name is Tulga. A distant cousin of Gelimer, who followed Ammatas into Ad Decimum."

"Gunderic!" Tulga cried again, but was bashed in the mouth by the shaft of the fasces.

Atop the dais, Andronicus raised his hands again. "This man, this Vandal, conspired to kill Justinian's appointed leader in Carthage. A crime, after his people were shown leniency upon their defeat!"

Some within the crowd tossed stray vegetables at Tulga, though none threw stones; the risk of striking a lictor was too grave, and the penalty for such an error could be the loss of a hand or worse. Most were content to spit at the affirmed traitor, wishing hellfire and torment.

Wisimar shuffled toward Gunderic, nodding to me in recognition. "This is not the way warriors should die."

"Vandals are not petty cutthroats or traitors," Gunderic answered impassively. "We follow the strongest, and Belisarius earned his dominion over us. Tulga disgraces our heritage."

"So say these Romans," Wisimar hissed. "I doubt there is a breath of truth to it."

Andronicus raised an arm for silence, followed by the clattering of spears and shields amongst the city watch. "Tulga of the Vandal people, you have been chained and hauled from Carthage to Constantinople. As a Roman subject, you are found guilty of the unforgiveable crime of treason. Your sentence is the Brazen Bull, the only punishment fit for such disgusting creatures."

Tulga did not wail, nor jerk against his captors. Instead, covered in greasy dirt and layered with bleeding sores, he allowed the lictores to raise him into the bull, which was sealed and locked from the outside. Then, he turned about in his bronze prison, peering out of the open slits. Again, he found Gunderic, but kept silent. The crowd's fervor rose as Andronicus fetched a lit torch from the platform, handing it to the chief lictor.

"Go, Roman, and fulfill your duty!"

Thousands of voices screamed in a concoction of rage and delight as the open flame trailed down a wooden staircase and over to the bull. Tulga's face followed that procession, but he stayed silent. The lead lictor said nothing as he lowered the torch into the firepit, thrusting the flames toward faster-burning kindling. As the flame caught, the lictor tossed the torch fully into the flames, backing away several paces to avoid the swell of heat.

"I will not beg!" Tulga shouted. "You sacks of sheep shit have no dominion over me! I honor my father, and my father's father, and all the Vandals who came before!"

This riled the crowd further but gained no response from Andronicus or the lictores. As for the fire, at first, there was no change. The wood, likely young and wet from recent rains, bubbled and steamed as the flames spread. As the crowd jeered and chanted, a single yellow flame rose from its berth and licked the bull's underside. Steam gave way to a blaze, covering much of the bull's stomach.

It took time—perhaps five minutes, perhaps less—but eventually, Tulga groaned in pain, still facing Gunderic as he maneuvered in the bull to move away from the sweltering floor. Flames danced higher and broader, simmering the air about the bronze bull and forcing Tulga to rasp and cough as he struggled for air. Affirmed in their duty, the lictores backed farther away from the device.

And then, the first scream. It was a lone call, involuntary, and bereft of force. But the pain was true, and desperate. Andronicus lifted his nose as he basked in his victory, while others clapped and roared approval for their Lord.

"Justinian! Justinian! Justinian!"

Then the screams continued. Initially guttural, they transformed into a keening howl, more fitting a beast than a man. Through it all, the bull did not offer reprieve, with its heat billowing farther out into the square. Upon a chance wind, a whiff of burning flesh flooded my nostrils, accompanied by a smoke-filled heat. Samur gritted his teeth at the display, but like Gunderic, made no maneuver to intervene.

"This is no death for a warrior," Wisimar snarled, his arms tensing where he stood alongside Gunderic.

"No, it is not." Gunderic yielded his first note of dissent. "But you will watch all the same."

"Gunderic!!" Tulga screamed, his voice cracking against the rising fire. "Gunderic, save us!"

I leaned closer to the Vandal giant. "You can leave, Gunderic. There is no reason for you to witness this."

"There is every reason," he grunted. I did not push further.

Tulga thrashed against his cage. Hair caught to flame, and blisters formed along exposed limbs. Tattered linen followed close behind, smoldering over the man's body until it was severed at the seams. The stench of burning fat grew more pungent as Tulga's screams melted into primal agony. No Vandals moved, nor threatened to draw blades, all merely watched as their kinsman finally fell, a hulking and unrecognizable mass.

"Belisarius commands us," Gunderic muttered, seemingly to

himself. "He earned that right through conquest."

Neither Wisimar nor I responded. Thankfully, the screeching of death subsided as Tulga fell motionless inside the bull. Slaves rushed forward to throw buckets of water to douse the flames, causing the liquid to sizzle and burn away as it slapped the glow of exposed bronze. After a time, the heat, too, fell away, and the lictores unbarred the bull's entrance and withdrew the condemned inside. All I could see was a charred torso, and I muttered a prayer that Tulga's soul might know a reprieve.

"Roman citizens!" Andronicus cried. "The traitor is in hell. But more crimes must be addressed, per the Emperor's instructions!"

"This is sick," Samur muttered.

"Quiet!" Xerxes said through his teeth. "We are nearly finished. Just wait a bit longer."

Andronicus spoke again, droning about Justinian's sagacity and glory in the restoration of the Empire. At first I listened, but halfway through the address, a black-hooded follower of Cassiodorus approached within two paces.

"Lord Varus, I wish we could have met again under happier circumstances," the figure said, lowering his hood. "It is time for you to come with me."

I recognized him as Philip, Andronicus' younger follower, and a clear leader of sorts amongst the mob. "On the dais?"

Philip nodded. "It will not take long. And then this unhappiness shall be in the past."

Gunderic glowered, leaning over the diminutive priest. "He does not go alone."

"Warrior, this is not your decision to make," Philip replied, though he shrank away from Gunderic's looming shadow.

"Varus does not walk alone," Gunderic repeated. "You priests are supposed to be educated, but perhaps you do not understand my words."

At Xerxes' signal, Wisimar and a half dozen Vandals took formation around Gunderic. Again, none drew weapons, for that would have been in violation of the Emperor's peace, condemning all of us as outlaws and brigands. If Philip understood the Vandals' restraint, I doubt he was willing to gamble his life on pressing the matter.

"A few of you may walk to the platform," he conceded, "but not join at the top."

Gunderic nodded, signaling for Wisimar to accompany me with a dozen men. Xerxes joined my guards, as did Samur, but Gunderic remained with the banda. "Someone needs to keep them in line, otherwise there will be a yard of dead Romans."

We made rapid progress to the platform. By that moment, all I desired was an end to the pageantry, removing myself and those I loved from these rabid dogs. Samur, however, remained as tense as ever, standing shoulder to shoulder with me as we scanned the crowd for any warning of aggression. None came, for between the Vandals and the Huns, not even the faith-drunk crowds were inebriated enough to commit suicide upon our blades. Philip walked two paces before us as he parted the crowds, content to afford me room to move freely.

Reaching beneath my shirt's collar, I plucked the golden dragon free, lifting its chain from about my neck. "Return this to me when the punishment is over," I whispered, handing it to Samur.

"Gladly." He placed it safely in a pouch at his belt.

We reached our destination quickly, with the city watch signaling my guards to remain behind. Xerxes and Samur protested, but again Philip interjected himself.

"I allowed you to accompany Varus through the mob, and now I ask you the courtesy of honoring your word of noninterference," he said, as though lecturing a petulant child.

I nodded to both my companions. "Wait for me. This will take but a few minutes."

Leaving them upon the forum's stones, I ascended the platform, towering over the thousands of onlookers below. At such heights, the lingering stench of the bull nearly overpowered my senses. I stifled a cough, lest I show any weakness. Trailing Philip, I approached Andronicus, who nodded with a knowing smile.

"Citizens! Behold, a proud excubitor, the tribune Varus!" Andronicus yelled. "An honored soldier of the Emperor's valiant armies, but also a man who struck an ordained priest of the Christian faith!"

A chorus of furious threats roiled the crowd, words invoking violence upon essentially all parts of my body and soul. I acknowledged none, although silently thanked God that rotten food was not hurled toward me and stared blankly upon the far edge of the forum. Andronicus continued, and while I nearly allowed the man's voice to fade as my attention wavered, his next words were unexpected. For the crowd, they were as intoxicating as any wine.

"For such punishment, the Emperor Justinian requests that Cassiodorus, our shepherd, oversee Lord Varus' sentence."

Men and women alike erupted in cheers, gasps, and a palpable eagerness to lay eyes upon the man himself—he who was so rarely seen, and not in public since the conclusion of the Triumph. As if on cue, a man at the edge of the platform threw back a ponderous hood, revealing the weathered face and gray hair of Justinian's minister of religion. Leaning upon an iron-reinforced stick, Cassiodorus hobbled atop wooden stairs and lurched toward the center stage, awash in praise and requests for salvation. He halted near Andronicus, nodding to his disciple, who rushed away to allow his master sole access to the thousands of followers.

"Children!" Cassiodorus rasped, struggling to speak over the swirling cacophony. "Children, hear my words!"

Within heartbeats, the forum hushed. A few creaks and giggles lingered, but the Bovis Forum had fallen eerily quiet despite the crush of bodies near the dais. Cassiodorus took his time, breathing steadily—presumably laboring to produce words to the frenzied masses, though a more cynical onlooker would see him as merely heightening the drama of the moment.

"I am a sinner, my friends, a sinner so vile," he crooned.

And a quack, I thought. *Who pissed himself at the start of the riots.*

A muffled resistance formed. "No!" cried the crowd.

"Yes!" Cassiodorus answered, clutching his chest. "I hoarded wealth, stuffed myself to the point of gluttony, and rose to incredible heights of authority by using the name of God. I admit it!"

Leaning against his cane once more, Cassiodorus shuffled a few paces away. It was a clever display, making him appear every bit the kindly grandfather, slowed by age and reliant upon a walking stick. Most of it was a lie, I guessed, for Cassiodorus appeared hale enough to walk unassisted, and I knew the man to be of an aggressive character. Internally, I forced down a boiling rage, resisting the urge to snap my fingers and send Gunderic's Vandals on a rampage that would fill the forum in a marsh of blood. Yet all I could do was stand and watch — for I had not been informed of the specifics of the proceedings, let alone that Cassiodorus would subject me to such theatrics.

"And God punished me! For my pride, my sloth, my envy, and yes, my blasphemy," Cassiodorus continued. "My body was pressed into the smoldering fires of poverty and deprivation, but my soul emerged purer and more resilient than ever. For God is like a blacksmith, forging and reshaping lives to meet his wisdom and to receive his undeserved mercy."

Abruptly, he pivoted to face me. "My sins make Lord Varus' appear insignificant. God forgave me!" Cassiodorus paused for cheers, which came in waves. "But," he went on, gesturing in my direction, "but God required my penitence. Since that day, when I lay humiliated and broken, I have committed myself to following the gospel of our Savior, and to lead other sinners to salvation. And to my dying breath, we shall not cease in our devotions!"

Halting but three paces distant from me, Cassiodorus paused for an extended time. Then, turning back to the crowd, he concluded his speech.

"Lord Varus is a hero. A vaunted excubitor, slayer of Fastida and Khingila, and a stalwart in our faith. I do not hate him for his crimes, but shower him with love."

Silently, I prayed that a gull might swoop down at that very moment and plaster white shit on Cassiodorus' bald head. No doubt, he would have cried that, in fact, dung was a favorable sign from God, but still, it would have amused me enough to make up for the feigned divine favor. Cassiodorus was no Solomon, no hateful lifelong enemy of mine, but I loathed that insipid creature all the same.

Opening an arm, Cassiodorus scooped me into an awkward embrace before I had time to understand his intentions. He stood more than a head shorter than me, and struggled to wrap his arm even to my shoulder, but the gesture was visible all the same. "And because I love Lord Varus as my brother in Christ, I must offer him the opportunity for penitence. The noble and glorious Justinian granted me oversight of Lord Varus' opportunity for redemption. Ten lashes in this ancient forum, and his soul shall be cleansed of the sins by which he stands accused."

Several lictores paced toward the center of the platform. A broad podium was placed in plain view of the crowd, its top as broad as a man's outstretched arms and its base weighted with a ball of lead. Their task completed, they retreated ten paces back, instructing a team of slaves to position a weapon rack on the far edge of the platform. I could see at least two flagrum, each equipped with two ox-hide appendages intended to lash a wide expanse of flesh with a single crack. Blessedly, no metal was embedded into the scourge to rip and tear until the ribs emerge: every Christian knew of Jesus' suffering at the hands of the scourge and the pain wrought by the metal edges, and so I muttered a prayer of thanks for that small mercy.

Andronicus emerged again, joining Cassiodorus. Unfurling a scroll, he pretended to read, although it was clear its words were memorized. "Varus the Herulian, Tribune of the Romans, you have been summoned for penitence to the Forum of Bovis. As a Roman subject, you are found guilty of striking a blessed and ordained priest of the one true religion. Your sentence is ten lashes with the scourge, per the judgment of Emperor Justinian."

The lictores drew close, gesturing me toward the podium. "Lord, if you would please remove your shirt," one chubbier man asked, his voice as deferential as a palace slave's. "Forgive us for what we must do."

This was the moment I had prepared for a hundred times over, imagined endlessly, wondering how my body would respond to the whip and the baying crowd alike. I had anticipated the revulsion I felt for Cassiodorus' men, and a lesser degree of resentment to the ungrateful mob that cried for my blood, but otherwise the ritual did not jostle my confidence. What did surprise me, however, was the discomfort I felt as I found the eyes of Xerxes, Gunderic, and dozens of Vandals, their faces fixed in stern glares. Whether my punishment was deserved or not, I was at least guilty of bringing my friends to this place, subjecting them to the dangers of the mob, all because I was not clever enough to avoid Justinian's justice or Cassiodorus' prying fingers.

Regardless of the embarrassment I felt, the lictor appeared far more terrified of me. And no wonder—I doubt they had ever chastised an excubitor, let alone one who held patronage from a living empress. But of all the offal present, I felt no enmity to him, nor his fellow lictores, who symbolized order in Constantine's city. I nodded to the man, pulling my shirt from my head, and exposing my torso. "Do your duty, lictor."

Another lictor joined his colleague, his brow furrowed. His words tumbled forth with an equal measure of fear and excitement. "Tribune, would you prefer straps to hold your arms against the podium? To prevent... prevent flinching?"

Firm your mind, a voice rumbled inside my head. *Show no fear.*

The voice belonged to Godilas, though I could not place when or if he'd ever said those precise words to me. Godilas had often lectured on the necessity of showing a stony face to the world, regardless of what emotion might churn in the heart, but I had been a poor student of the subject, often reprimanded by Godilas for the rashness that stems from anger. Now, however, I saw the wisdom of his spectral lesson. Cassiodorus' men wanted fear. If I wavered or appeared incapable of accepting Justinian's punishment, then their victory would be complete.

"No," I roared defiantly. "Leave me."

Thus unbound, I moved, shirtless, toward the podium. Cassiodorus hobbled close, caressing the bronze cross at my throat with a mangled and dirt-encrusted finger. "God forgive you."

Taking a deep breath, I reached out toward the opposite edge of the podium, gripping hard until both of my palms flushed white. Though large, the pedestal was not nearly wide or tall enough to support my frame, although it still gave me something to grip and bear the coming pain.

I recalled the two men who had been flogged and eventually hanged in Singidunum for cowardice against the Gepids. I knew I must not show fear, nor beg for reprieve—that would only incense the torturer against weakness and would unman me as a warrior of Justinian's court. Nor should I tense my body against the lash, for many a misbehaving warrior has suffered graver injuries still by straining his muscles against the blows.

Most of all, however, I had to mind my jaw. Even the most fearless brute of a warrior would flinch against the bite of a whip, and a careless one might bite clean through his tongue in so doing; it was not rare to find common spearmen with scarred, shortened tongues, struggling to swallow food and choking on wine as a result of such unfortunate impulse. That, I believed, would be a far worse fate than a few stripes of the whip—forced to meander through life, dribbling food and speaking sloppily as a drunkard.

Fortunately, the chubbier lictor helped safeguard me. He plucked a sort of small cylinder from his belt, thin leather strips wrapped tightly around its wooden form.

"Bite down, Lord," he muttered, offering it to me. "To keep from gnashing your tongue."

While I had publicly rejected straps for my body, I happily accepted the block. Grunting my gratitude, I relaxed enough to lodge the block between my jaws, confident that I would at least keep my tongue and all of my teeth when the day was concluded. The taste of it was bitter, but the surface had thankfully been smoothed so no slivers of wood might stick in my flesh. Returning my hand to the podium, I gripped hard and waited. Two lictores plucked the flagrum from their holsters, unfurling the leather thongs and giving a crack upon air to gain appropriate measure of the weapon.

Andronicus finally gave the signal. "Lictores, perform your duty!"

Calm, I thought internally. *Calm. Breathe.* And, dutifully, I sought divine protection. *Christ, who suffered unjustly, see me through this pain.*

I would not show fear. I could not. Not if I wished to remain a man in the eyes of the mob and a worthy leader before Gunderic's Vandals. My stomach quivered as my ears tracked the thrum of the lictor's boots, awaiting the fateful moment when my pain would begin. I could feel sweat beading across my back, chilling my flesh as a light breeze rolled through the forum. I might have shivered had the stench of burning hair not wafted from the bull at just the correct moment, stilling my body with disgust.

One lictor—I am not certain who—sucked in a stream of air. I could feel the planks beneath my feet move as he reared back, readying the strike. Again, I forced myself still, and glared toward Cassiodorus.

Within moments, I heard the hiss of leather.

"One!" a herd of sonorous voices rang out.

I will not boast and claim the pain was insignificant. It was not. Though I could not see the strike, the leather burned against the thin layer of skin above my spine and ribs, and I could feel welts forming. Though far from the stabbing pains of battlefield wounds, it hurt.

Not so bad, I thought. *Breathe. Calm. This is nothing.*

I could still feel an uneasiness in my gut, reinforced by a hot trickle along the skin of my back. Initially, my mind trained itself upon that fresh wound, absorbing each throb of pain that rippled across my body. I felt nothing else—not sore muscles, nor long-healed injuries, nor even the chill. Pain dominated my mind.

Until, that is, the chanting began.

At first, I thought it was Cassiodorus' crowd, along the far edge of the forum. It seemed like a childish taunt, jeering at the chastisement of a wealthy Roman officer. As I looked up, however, the second lash scoured my skin, and I saw the true origin of the chant.

"Two!" the Vandals cried, led by a jubilant Gunderic.

After pronouncing the Latin number, the Vandals slammed the rims of their shields twice against the forum's dressed stone, their clatter a short but deafening boom. That second lick stung, but Gunderic's taunting roar was enough distraction to dull the pain.

Despite myself, and despite the wooden block between my teeth, I choked on a laugh. Somehow, Gunderic had made this exhibition of Roman justice into both a game and a jibe. The chants continued, with the shield-bashing increasing in number and on par with the lictores' count. Even Cassiodorus' fawning supporters lessened their noise, which only goaded the Vandals into their game all the more.

"Three!"

The stinging worsened, though less than I had expected. It doubtless would have been worse alone, with only the jeers and curses of Cassiodorus' acolytes to accompany me. Oddly, my thoughts fluttered to Christ as the lictor prepared the fourth blow — how could anyone possessing mortal flesh accept the measure of punishment that He had, and that so many others had, in the early Empire? To be scourged and crucified, possibly taking days to die, shivering in pain and thirst... No, ten lashes was nothing next to the scourging that Petrus lectured about, when Jesus was put through terrible trials.

"Four!"

Calm. Calm! I thought privately, even as I was unable to keep from grinning at the Vandals. They hooted in rapturous approval as I accepted each lash with mere grunts, and the smile found my face easily, though I feared to laugh amidst Cassiodorus' thugs; joy in such a moment would have been equally as harmful as fear, and would give the priests cause to demand more punishment for an unrepentant sinner. Instead, I accepted the blows as meekly as I could, forcing myself to wonder again how anyone with a longer sentence and more lashes to bear could keep their wits about them.

By the fourth blow, thin streams of blood ran down my back, their hot stream uncomfortable against my torn skin. Each blow pained me more than the last, yet Gunderic's cheers slaked the worst of the suffering with a peculiar sense of humor. By the fifth blow, even Andronicus seemed confused about how to proceed.

"Five!"

"Not so bad," I mumbled to myself—though my lips moved, helping to numb the pain as Gunderic's encouragement rattled through my ears, I made no sound aloud. *Half finished*, I kept thinking. *It is already half finished.* The punishment truly was nothing to fear.

Cassiodorus, on the other hand, was unwilling to allow me to complete my sentence so easily. Raising an arm, he stayed the lictores' movements and turned to face the crowd. "Penitence requires more from Lord Varus," he called. "He shall take the remaining blows as a child."

Initially, I could not understand his intention. After a nod from Cassiodorus, however, it soon became clear, when the chief lictor approached with wary deference to make the demand known to me. "Lord, if you would unknot your trousers."

"Lictor?" I mumbled around the block in my teeth, certain I had misheard.

"You will take the last five lashes to your buttocks," he explained, albeit with a note of trepidation quivering in his voice. "Please unknot your trousers, and allow them to fall to the ground."

Turning, I glared at Cassiodorus. This was not required to slake Justinian's demands and felt particularly cruel given the context of my offense. Not that I was prudish, for life in the army leaves one exposed to all manner of nudity and compromising situations. My embarrassment came more from the fact that Cassiodorus ordered me about like a misbehaving child—and that, I realized, was exactly his intention.

"Do you disagree, Lord Varus?" Cassiodorus asked sweetly. "Are you too weak to continue?"

"Arrogant bastard," I said, grateful the block would muffle the words.

Instinctively, I glanced toward the Vandal formation—afraid, I must admit, to unman myself in their eyes. When I found Gunderic, however, he was offering a salute. Yet beside him I spied a new face, one that was grim and serious beneath a soaring white plume.

"Just five more!" a familiar voice yelled. "That's nothing for you! You stood against Shaush in Tauris! Against Khingila, and Gelimer! Show them what a Roman man truly is!"

The voice came from Belisarius. Standing beside Gunderic, his heavy lamellar armor contrasting against the lighter mail of the Vandal banda, the Roman strategos mirrored Gunderic's salute. Then, catching my gaze, Belisarius leaned to mutter something to Gunderic, who nodded.

"Varus Veridicus!" he boomed. Gunderic's call was taken up by four hundred Vandal throats, who pounded their shields all the more vigorously into the ground. Lacking a shield, Belisarius clapped his hands to the rhythm, chanting with the foederati.

"Tribune?" the lictor asked, peering at me.

"Lord Varus?" Cassiodorus beamed, appearing to believe me beaten. "I am a patient man, but the Emperor's business cannot wait."

I withdrew the bit from my mouth. "One moment," I replied, oddly at peace.

Unstrapping my belt, I allowed my empty scabbard to fall to the ground as gently as possible. I then unknotted the ties that held my trousers aloft until they, too, were loosed. As I dropped my trousers, I spat onto the ground, conjuring a mild taunt and placing my hands upon the podium's edges.

It was a humiliating experience, to be stripped naked and beaten like a naughty child, but Belisarius' chanting calmed me. There was no misunderstanding the situation—Cassiodorus' flogging alone was not having the effect he had desired, and this last gambit was intended to break me.

But it would not. Not with the voices of my men goading

me onward, numbing the pain at my back. This was nothing. Not compared to Christ, who accepted torture for the salvation of others. Not even against my prior battle injuries. No, this was only a slight wound to my pride, and nothing more.

"Continue, lictor," I called in Latin. "Best to not keep the Emperor waiting."

With that, I stuck the block back in my jaw, and for the first time, I witnessed a flicker of doubt flash across Cassiodorus' face. It was little enough, an instinctive bite upon his lower lip, yet the minister soon composed himself. "Continue!"

The lictores obeyed, striking hard against my buttocks—not as hard as they'd lashed my back, but a stinging blow nevertheless. Worse, even, as the whip now dug into fattier sections of flesh than my muscled back. I grimaced, baring teeth at Cassiodorus, but gave no other sign of pain.

"Six!" the Vandals cried in between their recurring chants of my name and epithet. Again I laughed, nearly allowing the wooden block to slide from my jaw. Again, the pain seemed blunted by Gunderic's example, and my resolve bolstered by Belisarius' calm presence.

"Seven!"

God, the pain of the seventh blow nearly brought me to spit out the block. The whip had caught me at the fold between my arse and my thigh, biting deep into my skin. I grunted louder, eager to show no evidence of the pain I felt. *Keep calm, for your children, for Mariya…*

"Eight!"

I flared my nostrils at Cassiodorus, wishing to seem careless as I accepted the whip. The eighth lash did not have nearly as bad an effect as the seventh, though the stripe along my upper thigh stung mightily.

"Nine!"

One more, I thought, the stinging burning despite the Vandal cheers. *One more, one more, one more…*

"Ten!"

"Varus Veridicus!"

"Finished, Tribune," the leader of the lictores called to me. "You may dress and return to the forum."

Another nod, first to the lictores, and later to Cassiodorus. Blood leaked from my back and buttocks, with every shift of muscle underneath torn skin a minor agony. Still, I spit the block from my mouth and returned it to its prior owner, then slipped on my trousers and shirt, caring little that the bloodstains would ruin the linen forever.

Relief washed over me like the frigid waters of the Ister in winter. It was done. I had taken Cassiodorus' worst and emerged no less a man from the trial. I had been stripped and beaten before the mob. I had been cut in ways that would make sitting or sleeping difficult for a month or more, yes—but the punishment was over. I had fulfilled my debt to the Emperor, made better from the encouragement of Belisarius and the playful cheers of so many Vandals. I had kept my honor as a warrior, and as a keeper of oaths. Whatever social taunting I might suffer was temporary; for all the grave threats that Mariya had feared, none had come to pass. Lightness perfused my body, churning over and around a heart filled with gratitude.

"Thank you, Lord," I mumbled. "Thank you for guiding me through this."

With a pained grunt, I strapped my belt around my waist once again before pacing my way off the dais. Only a few plebeians dared to hassle me upon my first steps away, and none once I was reunited with Samur.

"Pox-scarred bastards," Samur growled. "They'll pay dearly for this."

"Not today," I managed, exhausted. "Let's get back to Gunderic and leave. It stinks here."

Samur nodded, spreading my order to Xerxes and the Huns. We carved through the crowd, which was already disinterested in the scourged Roman officer now that Cassiodorus and Andronicus had retaken the center of the platform. We found Gunderic not long thereafter, nodding his approval.

"Took the beating like a man, you did." He grinned.

"Indeed." This from Belisarius, who still stood at Gunderic's side. "Although I wish you would have sought my support beforehand. I would have liked to assist you, however I could."

Beneath his helmet, his visage was little changed from our prior gatherings at the palace's war councils. An exhausted set of black-rimmed eyes framed a pale face whose beard, though still carved to Roman military custom, was noticeably unkempt. Still, his armor was immaculate, and he seemed to take renewed vigor from his white-plumed helm.

"I apologize, Lord," I responded. "I thought you would be too busy to concern yourself with such trifles."

Belisarius shook his head. "Your worries are not trifles to me, Varus. In the future, seek me out immediately if you have any problems, and I shall do the same."

"As you wish, Lord." I couldn't help myself; I beamed, my spirits soaring despite the burning pain along my back. These were words I'd longed to hear, and I drank them in over and over in my mind. It might appear little, but the gesture gave me hope that Belisarius might return to a modicum of his old self—at least toward me.

"Of course," Belisarius added, a note of teasing in his voice, "do try not to start fights with priests in the future."

I had barely begun my reply when the city watch horn blared again. My vision instinctively flitted back to the stage, where I spied Cassiodorus seeking quiet amongst the masses once more. From the corner of my eye, I spotted clusters of yellow robes moving along the forum's edges, and with great, painful effort, I pivoted to gain a greater view. Few in the Empire favored such bright yellow clothes, let alone military men—as these must be, to judge by their emblems.

Squinting, I spotted yet another yellow tunic, with no fewer than six others behind him at the forum's far entrance, closest to the Imperial Palace. Their darker skin contrasted against the fairer Greeks, and I suddenly realized. The Aksumites had arrived but were struggling to gain entry to the forum—prohibited, it seemed, by the city watch, who denied even Sembrouthes entry when he wriggled to the front of their formation.

"Why are the Aksumites here?" I whispered.

Belisarius shrugged, following my arm as I pointed out Sembrouthes. "Are they not supposed to be?"

All the world seemed to freeze in place. In an instant, any hope of a peaceful resolution died. Despair, as gripping as I any I had known along the plains of Tauris, slithered through my veins. "No."

"Children!" Cassiodorus called. "We have one more criminal. One whose crimes dwarf even the sin of treason."

"Samur, take your men and gain Sembrouthes access to the forum," I stammered. "Find out where Rosamund is."

"Right," Samur replied. "Aigan, with me!"

They sprinted away, weaving between the press of humanity. Meanwhile, I peered through the crowd, seeking any sign of what Cassiodorus' next maneuver might be. He gave me little time to act. With a wave of his hand, Cassiodorus prompted the lictores to action, with a team of six marching toward a smaller alley linking with the forum. Using their fasces, the lictores carved their way to a nearby cart, using two slaves to drive its wheels forward. I saw a burly sack wriggle atop the cart's storage bay, and began walking to intercept.

Until Xerxes stopped me, grasping carefully at my shoulder. "No, Varus. Whatever it is, we cannot stop it now."

"He's correct." Belisarius now. "We must be patient."

Between the bloody pain along my back and the surging dread in my gut, I groaned in anger. But I listened, for Belisarius' patience was well formed. There was nothing I could do until we learned more of Cassiodorus' intentions. Though the cart took only a few minutes to pass from the entrance of the forum to the platform, it seemed an eternity in hell. Time slowed further as a team of a dozen slaves lifted the cart over wooden stairs and onto the dais, placing ponderous stones behind its wheels to prevent it rolling away.

"For too long," Cassiodorus droned, "pagans have enslaved this land to their superstition, sacrificing children to the maw of their gods and copulating beneath the stars. Their numbers remain vast throughout our Empire, joined by the heretics under Baradaeus," he added. "God would forgive them all such heinous transgressions, but our most ancient religious laws dictate the punishment for an unrepentant witch."

Dread clutched my heart. I knew what would come next, knew it to the root of my soul, yet prayed nonetheless that the heretic that Cassiodorus spoke of was someone else. Anyone else. Someone not beholden to me.

"Burn them!" an onlooker called, his chant carried by a hundred others nearby. "Burn them!"

Cassiodorus nodded sadly. "Though we have begged her to receive the Lord's boundless grace, she spits upon such mercy. Bring us the condemned!"

Somehow, the forum seemed more crowded than before, overflowing with children and adults alike in a frenzied push to be closer to Justinian's personal priest and minister. I knew what would come next, and felt like my heart and stomach would slip from my body from the mortal dread reverberating through my body. My eyes welled, but I did not know why, for it was not sadness that consumed me.

"No," I muttered to no one. "Don't."

"Carry the witch to the cleansing fire!" Cassiodorus called.

Four lictores entrusted their fasces to colleagues before hauling the cart's wrapped bundle aloft. Walking down the platform stairs, they wormed their way toward the Brazen Bull, pausing before its open hatch. By then, the metal had cooled back to its original appearance, with one lictor using a bare hand to test the bull's locking hinge. His partners tore at the cloth atop the bundle, revealing a mass of bone-white hair underneath.

"You are all cowards!" Rosamund spat, her arms shaking. "Vermin! Offal! The gods will curse you all for this!"

Rosamund bared her teeth, prepared to levy further condemnation to Cassiodorus' followers. Yet she was silenced by a backhand from

Andronicus, smacking her mouth. Dazed, Rosamund wavered on her feet, her eyes temporarily unfixed as blood trickled onto her lip. She appeared uncharacteristically frail, drained of the impudence and vigor that had seen her through many long nights on campaign. It was a frailty that I had not seen in her since Moesia, when a different band of destroyers had come to annihilate Rosamund's family village. Since then, the perpetrator of that raid had been slain in a trial by combat, allowing me to wash any guilt I felt clean from my mind. Now, however, all that evil resurfaced, goaded by the knowledge that I had forced this life upon Rosamund. Even if she wanted to, she never had a chance to become Roman, and now the mob would torture her for that grave sin.

"No!!" I screamed, reaching for my blade.

An arm across my chest halted me—Gunderic. "Varus!" he hissed. "If you draw your blade, she dies. We must free her without violence."

Belisarius, too, placed himself before me, casting occasional glances at the lictores' movements.

"God!" I screamed inanely. I struggled against Gunderic's grip, a useless effort in my weakened condition. All I could do was watch and pray the theater would end and return all to safety and comfort.

Mariya had been correct: This entire affair was utterly, incomparably wrong. All I loved would pay for Cassiodorus' ambition.

For his part, Belisarius sprinted to the dais. Three bucellarii emerged on cue from the Vandal banda, shoving plebeians about to reach their oath lord, but Belisarius did not shrink from the press of potentially hostile zealots. Once he reached the line of city guardsmen, he removed his helmet and gestured wildly to the platform, visibly furious at the guards' intransigence. And I stood back, apart. There was nothing I could do, nor did I have even a notion of what I might do differently.

"Bastards!!" Rosamund screamed, recomposing herself after the slap. "Let me go, or your children will die screaming in pools of blood! Your nailed god will not protect you from what comes!"

Andronicus attempted another smack, but this time, Rosamund anticipated the blow. Instead, with a jerk backward, she forced the lictor that held her arms to stumble, so that Andronicus' fingertips only grazed her cheek.

"Some man you are!" Rosamund snarled. "All you're good for is hitting captive women. Badly, too."

Andronicus paused for a moment. Then, as a broad grin carved across his face, Andronicus beckoned the lictor to follow. Rosamund struggled, but though she jerked against her captor, the lictor's unwavering grip ground against her wrists, bringing her to howl with pain.

Satisfied, Andronicus paced toward the center of the dais. Then, stepping beside Cassiodorus, Andronicus beckoned for silence with a great sweep of his arm. Again Rosamund struggled, yet this time a blow to the back of the head silenced her from leveling another curse. As Rosamund hung in the lictor's grip, I tensed my arms, instinctively stepping closer to Cassiodorus' men even as I knew all the city guard tracked my movements.

"Patience," Belisarius pleaded, turning to me as I drew beside him. "You won't do her any good by getting yourself killed in a manic charge."

Patience was not a virtue I often ascribed to. "How long do you wish me to wait? Until after they bleed her white?!"

Despite my tirade, Belisarius remained calm. "Until an opportunity presents itself," he said, so only I could hear. "Cassiodorus did not time Rosamund's punishment without thought. He's doing this because he knows you're watching."

Belisarius was correct, I knew. Yet the truth left me feeling only more helpless. Even as Rosamund revived from her daze, her eyes tracking me amongst the crowd, there was nothing I could do. Not even as she mouthed desperate pleas, begging me to act.

"Varus..."

The mob swirled to a frenzy. Had I deigned to scream, I am not certain that Rosamund would have heard me. Instead, I waited, wishing death upon Cassiodorus' men as I held Rosamund's stare.

"Rosamund, of the Moesian Gepids, you are brought here condemned of unrepentant witchcraft," Andronicus shouted. "As a Roman subject, you are sentenced to death. What say you?"

Andronicus motioned for silence, which fell only reluctantly due to the more drunken tongues in the gleeful audience. Again, Rosamund quivered, even as her face contorted with resentment. "Only the gods can claim my life. And they will come for you soon, worm."

Andronicus laughed. "Unrepentant to the end. There is only one adequate punishment for witches in Justinian's empire!" A gnarled finger pointed toward the metal beast in the forum's center, still stinking of cooked meat. "The Brazen Bull! Burn in hell, witch!"

I retched. Samur snatched at my collar, keeping me upright, though stepping away from any projectile from my mouth. Nothing emerged, though my legs buckled. My men must have assumed the sudden weakness a consequence of flogging, though I knew the truth. I did not have the stomach watch Rosamund burn to death, screaming.

The crowd roared and hissed, noises of delight mixing with vicious hatred at Rosamund's squirming. Rosamund, however, spat defiance. "You think you're righteous?! One day soon, a conqueror will come and destroy all of you. And women like me will laugh atop your ashes!"

Andronicus leveled a fleshy finger at Rosamund. "Roman citizens, cast this witch into oblivion!"

Where Tulga entered the bull with acceptance, Rosamund kicked and screamed with each breath. She hadn't much strength, though, and the lictores had little trouble forcing her inside the metal beast and securing its lock. Within its belly, she jostled about, as if searching for an escape, but found only the small holes to peer upon the safely distant crowd. It was then that her eyes reconnected with my own, where I stood still restrained by Gunderic, praying that Belisarius would intercede.

"Varus!!" Rosamund wailed, her fear unbridled and utterly foreign.

Finally, Belisarius slipped past the city watch and rose to the dais, but this garnered only muted interest from Andronicus. Cassiodorus, meanwhile, essentially ignored the strategos, ending any forlorn hope I had for relief. Near Cassiodorus, the chief lictor acquired a freshly lit torch, and despite Belisarius placing his body firmly in his path, the far larger lictor easily weaved onto the forum's stones and toward the Brazen Bull.

"No!" Rosamund wailed. "No! No! No! Nehalennia, Mother, save me!"

I recognized the name of Rosamund's goddess, one of the highest in her pantheon. Despite her pleas, the heavens did not part, nor did the forum quake and rumble, other than the steady slapping of thousands of feet upon the stone roadway. Rosamund's screams became all but unintelligible as she switched to the Gepid tongue, invoking the goddess again, the god Tuisto, and all manner of pagan deities as she gazed upon the smoke-blackened skies.

"Release me, Gunderic!" I roared. "Now, or by God I will peel the skin from your face."

At last, he did so, muttering apologies that I could not hear as I sprinted toward the platform's stairs. Later, I would learn that Gunderic and Xerxes rushed closely behind, jostling a fair number of onlookers and drunkards, but no memory of this remains to me. Nor did I feel the lingering pain of the scourge, or even my boots smacking against the stone floor. All I sensed was a fresh heat emanating from beneath the bull, and the screaming. In so many ways, it was the same keening wail that corrupts my dreams, and does so to this day. Only now, it took the form of my name.

"Varus!!" Rosamund wailed. "Don't let them take me! No!"

An officer amongst the guardsman signaled for me to halt, but I smashed their ranks aside with little more than a forceful shoulder. Gunderic was correct in his assessment—such men made for poor fighters, especially if their pathetic wall could be broken by a single angry and wounded man not deigning to raise his weapons. Hauling myself back to the platform, I caught a glimpse of the flames just beginning to rise but not yet licking the bronze enclosure.

"Cassiodorus!" I roared.

"Varus!!" Rosamund called again, her scream turning to pain. "Mother! Mother, no!"

My heart seemed not to beat as I sprinted over to the hobbling priest. "Cassiodorus!"

As I drew close, a team of city guards intercepted me, with one driving a fist into my gut and sending the wind from my lungs. I doubled over, fell to my knees, but still I crawled toward the priest, only five paces distant now.

"Cassiodorus!" Belisarius yelled along the edge of the dais. "End this now!"

But Cassiodorus only had attention for me. "Lift him," he said, gesturing for the guardsmen. "He will do me no harm."

Two guardsmen held me upright, their arms locked under my armpits. "Cassiodorus," I rasped. "End this. Please."

Cassiodorus shrugged. "She had her chance. Why should I defy the Emperor's law?"

Winded, wounded, and swimming in frustrated rage, I suddenly understood what that bastard wanted to hear. "I beg you," I wheezed. "I will do anything."

A broad smile etched across his weathered face. "Half your spoils from Carthage."

Amidst the screaming, and the cheers, I heard Mariya's voice. Devastated. Betrayed by a husband too proud to admit that he was wrong. In an instant, Cassiodorus would leave my children's future in doubt, steal away everything my wife had built, rob me of what I had suffered for, through year after year of brutal campaigns— plunder that would keep my household functioning, my warriors fed and armored, and my mind placed at ease that all would be well.

Cassiodorus might only have asked for half of my spoils, but what he achieved was no less than shunting me into impoverishment.

"Done," I answered, struck at the cost as if by an Avar arrow. It was financially ruinous, but required. There was no other way. I would find a way to live with the loss.

"And your estate at Pella." Cassiodorus smiled, his eyes glinting like polished iron. "The houses, the port, all the goods inside… everything."

I snapped upright. "Pella?"

Cassiodorus' grin widened, somehow, revealing his overlarge teeth. "We can bargain if you like, Lord Varus, if you feel there is time. But my followers are many, and in need of resources."

Never in all my years had I felt so utterly routed. Cassiodorus beamed upon me as if he were a parent doting over a child, doubtless to reinforce his public reputation as a penitent and a forgiving man. I hated him. Every speck, every mote of dust, every whiff of sweat that trailed from his unfitting, frayed garments. My chest tensed at the need to do violence to such a vile creature, to tear out his liver and stuff it forcefully down a bloodied throat.

But he had routed me. Completely, and without reservation. Rosamund's screams filled the forum as Cassiodorus fixed upon me, unblinking, a single hand outstretched as if asking for a spare crust of bread. In a stroke, Cassiodorus had taken not just my wealth, but the only home that was legally mine, and Mariya's.

"Well?"

"I accept!" I yelled. "Please!!"

He nodded, raising his arm to the crowd. "Lictores, cease! The Emperor grants reprieve."

Shuffling to me, he leaned close. "You would do well to hurry. The lictores are proficient at starting fires, but less so at putting them out."

"Bastard," I mumbled.

He laughed. After struggling free, I leapt from the platform onto the ground, followed closely behind by Belisarius. My feet stung from the impact, for we fell from the height of a man, but somehow, I found the strength to dash ever forward. Most citizens parted from my path, while a few were pushed aside, but soon a clearing opened as the bull's heat wrapped me in an uncomfortable embrace.

"Buckets!" I yelled. "Where are the buckets?"

"Here!" Belisarius panted, finding a stack of filled buckets positioned to prevent an uncontrolled spread of flame, but no slaves to wield them.

"We're coming, Rosamund!" I called. "Just a minute more!"

Belisarius and I both hauled two full buckets at a time, struggling to keep our gait lest the precious liquid spill onto the stones. A single youth offered assistance, positioning buckets closer to the flames as we formed a team to combat the blaze. The smell of burning flesh again filled my nostrils, but I forced my concentration to the task before me, my mind empty. As I tossed the contents of my pails into the fire, an angry steam rose from the blaze, but the heat was little changed. Belisarius followed my example, sweat dripping from his brow.

"Too slow!" I yelled. "We need more!"

"Behind you!" Gunderic bellowed, tossing four full buckets into the fire.

Xerxes added a further two, and with that, the fires seemed to weaken, at least, though they did not die out completely. Hissing steam flew all around the bull, sheening us all in sweat. Xerxes and Belisarius ran for more buckets, tossing an occasional pail onto the heated underside of the bronze bull, yet the disconcerting absence of screams caused me to freeze.

"Gunderic, we need to get the lock open!" I yelled.

He nodded, pivoting to face two nearby lictores. "You! Give me two of those great big sticks!"

The lictor huffed indignation. "You mean the fasces? Those are sacred instruments of Roman—"

"I do not care if they fucked your mother AND your father!" Gunderic boomed. "Hand them over, now!"

Justinian would be furious at such surrender, but they obeyed. They did not have to, and should not have, for the fasces truly were sacred to Roman heritage. But Gunderic prevailed, tossing me one of the axe-topped staves and pointing to the lock. "You smash at it, and

I'll try to pry the lock apart with the axe head."

Though the flames fell considerably as Belisarius and Xerxes added further buckets, the blaze was still lit, and the gushing steam threatened to sear our exposed skin. But Gunderic hardly grunted as the heat scoured his wrists, and so I followed his example. Gunderic jammed the iron point of his fasces between a narrow opening along the lock's bars and leaned into the wooden staff, firm, but careful to keep it from snapping. As he did, I hefted my own fasces and leveled it square to the iron bars, then pulled back and swung hard.

No success. My axe head glanced off, the latch still intact. "It's been exposed to flame, so it must be weak!" Gunderic called. "Keep going!"

He pulled, and I struck again, and again, each blow sending further sparks into the diminishing flames. Though the lock warped, it did not break, causing panic to wriggle in my gut.

"Hurry!"

"Move!" a voice shouted behind me. "I found a hammer!"

Samur pushed his way forward, followed behind by Aigan's Huns and an exhausted team of Aksumites. Lifting his stolen hammer high in the air, Samur swung wildly and struck the lock with all the might his arm could muster. Again, the lock bent but did not yield. Samur bashed again but reeled back as the edge of his cloak spread from the pyre's flames. It was easily doused, but I took Samur's place as I swung my fasces a final time.

It snapped open, falling into the smoldering fire. Gunderic knocked aside the latch's severed pieces with his axe head, then pushed the bull's door open with the fasces' iron point. As the door opened, I threw aside my own borrowed weapon, coughing through a thick mist of smoke and steam as I searched for my friend.

"Rosamund!"

Nothing. Leaning further, I brushed a hand against the bull's steam-filled entrance. It was hot, uncomfortably so, but did not burn. Gripping the bull, I leaned further into the open stomach, sipping what air I could.

"Rosamund!"

With my eyes watering from the veil of smoke and steam, I could see little more than the end of my own nose. I rose to my toes, plunging my head and shoulders further into the bull, struggling to reach for anything, and, sputtering, rasped a final call. *"Rosamund!"*

At first, I saw nothing amidst the smoke. Then, suddenly, a hand shot through the choking shroud, and its fingers squeezed my arm. Jumping back in surprise, I traced those fingers back to their torso, releasing Rosamund from her nook. Though I could not yet discern her face, I heard her hack a painful wheeze, and as I released her into the open air, the weight of her body fell upon me fully, with no strength to support itself.

Returning my heels to the forum's stones, I gently positioned Rosamund into my arms, just as I had done after her prior assault by Andronicus. Stepping a dozen paces from the bull, I found her body blackened with soot and traced with burns, her clothes intact but pocked with holes and charred at the hems. Her white hair, that well-known trait of the Gepids, was shriveled in places and singed in others, with the disheveled remainder as dry as autumn straw. Her face, still layered in unhealed bruises, formed small ash-blackened cracks along her cheeks, leaving her roughened lips and swollen tongue grasping for moisture as she rasped smoke from her body.

"Samur, water!" I yelled. My brother stole a waterskin from a nearby Hun and ripped off its stopper. Slowly, Samur tipped the open skin to Rosamund's lips, sending dark grime puddling from her face and onto her torn clothes. She coughed again, shaking her head violently.

"Wait," she scratched.

With that, she spluttered for some time until, the impulse contained, she nodded for the water. Samur granted only a few brief swallows at a time, tossing an occasional spray of lukewarm liquid along Rosamund's body. She felt hot in my grasp, unsurprisingly, but to my great relief did not appear burnt to the point of amputation, or even severe blistering. Undeniably, however, she was in a great deal of pain.

"Don't let them..." Rosamund begged, her voice quavering. "Don't let them take me, Varus..."

"It's over," I promised, glaring at an approaching drunken spectator. The man, lightly bearded and bearing a youthful face, seemed to consider challenging me through an excess of wine or the goading of his comrades, though sense eventually caused him to back away.

Rosamund moaned. "It hurts..."

"I know." I softly shushed her, deaf to the mob that had been deprived its latest victim. "I've got you. All will be well."

Samur approached, joined by Gunderic, Belisarius, and enough Vandals to discourage even the most inebriated onlooker from encouraging further violence. Belisarius' eyes went wide with disbelief as he scanned Rosamund's body before throwing a disgusted glance toward the dais.

"I'm taking Rosamund back to Mariya," I growled to my followers.

Samur nodded, his eyes dancing about the crowd as he searched for attackers amongst the confused and still-riled mass. "What of Cassiodorus? He will not care?"

"I have paid my debt to that devil," I answered. "In time, he shall do the same for me."

And so, still weak and bleeding, I carried Rosamund from the Brazen Bull, cursing Constantine and even God himself for allowing such evil as the Bovis Forum to exist. In a single stroke, Cassiodorus had punished his enemies, placed himself as Justinian's undoubted confidante, and gained considerable wealth. It left me bereft, confused, and, in so many ways, rudderless.

For there was nothing I could do but hope and pray that God still heard me. For at that time, it did not seem He did.

SOLOMON, SAVIOR
OF CARTHAGE

Rosamund's screams rattled the walls of my home. Initially, it was a coarse moan, as if a corpse had thrown off its shroud and come to torment the living. Days later, the screams became more clearly born of a live human soul, though still just as piercing. Throughout all those first weeks, however, the one common factor was that, whether after the lightest doze or the deepest slumber, Rosamund would wake screaming. Weeping. Pleading.

That first night, sore and shivering from my wounds, I woke amidst total darkness to the sound. Sembrouthes explained Rosamund's predicament but reassured me that the Aksumite Wazeba would calm her fears, help her silence her screams.

"No." I slipped into the hall, lifting the nearest torch from its iron handle. "This is my responsibility."

Upon cracking open the door to Rosamund's chamber, my nostrils were infused with the acrid reek of sickness. Mixed into the aroma were pungent wafts of boiled wine—a favorite of Rosamund's and therefore of Agathias'—in cleaning broken skin. Few Romans swore by this method, with some in Justinian's court insisting the practice utterly pagan, though many highborn Christians were not above its use when they or their children suffered grievous injury. Rosamund had insisted that the wine, boiled and properly applied, prevented rot in the flesh, and for that, I did not begrudge Agathias for the offensive odor that pervaded the darkened room.

And then the scream. A scream to cease the heart's beating.

"No!!" Rosamund screeched. "Let me go!"

Nocking my torch along a bronze holster, I rustled into the room. "Who allowed the room to grow dark? More light!"

"Let.... me... go!"

Rosamund struggled to rise but only managed to sit upright before falling, useless, onto her bed. The sheet beneath her was spotted with blood, evidence of the small cuts along her body, as well as blistered fingertips that had torn and bled after her futile attempt to scrabble out of the Brazen Bull. She shivered as if freezing, though stilled as her eyes fixed upon me, framed by torchlight.

"Varus..." Rosamund groaned. "I thought—"

"They can't get you." I sat beside her. "Not anymore. There are a hundred men patrolling the streets outside our building, day and night."

Rosamund's eyes shut slowly, almost painfully. "When I doze, I can smell that demon. I can hear..."

But whatever Rosamund could hear, she did not say. Instead, shivering once more, she scratched at the blanket with blistered hands, pressing fingerprints of blood onto the cloth. Desperately wishing that she would cease, I drew the blanket about her more closely, my body brushing hers.

"Why..." she rasped, but her words ended on a choke. Finding a water cup nearby, I raised it toward her cracked lips, and, once refreshed, she turned her fury upon me. "Why would they do this to me? After all I have done for them—"

"Because." I, too, was enraged at Rosamund's injuries, yet I was equally ashamed by the loss of Pella and the bulk of my coin. My anger and frustration seeped out of me in every direction, at every moment. "They are evil men. Just as you have said all along."

And just as Mariya warned me, I added to myself. But I had been too stupid to see what Cassiodorus was capable of.

Rosamund seethed, gritting her teeth between spasms of pain. "They're going to suffer, Varus. All of them!"

Though fearsome, her rage was quickly extinguished, sapped as she was after her day of torment. As she lay back, resting, possibly sleeping, I sat with her, careful to watch the candles, maintaining the flickering light well through the night's darkness. Eventually, spent, I retired to my chambers, thoughts awash in the thorns of my predicament. I had to protect myself, and my dependents. I had to raise money, or at least foster some sort of patronage to pay my expenses until I could secure more plunder—hopefully soon. But, try as I did to think through my worries, I found no solutions.

And as my mind blurred at the precipice of dreaming, loathing clouded my judgment. Not merely for an avaricious Cassiodorus or an unquenchable Justinian. No, I hated myself. For despite the tremendous blessings received throughout my younger years, I had pissed away a vast quantity of my good fortune. My wife was a princess of a rich tribe—how in God's name would I keep her in comfort, and a burgeoning household fed and sheltered besides?

Sleep brought no solace. Not for several nights. Numbers danced in my mind, crowned by the burnished faces of dozens of long-dead emperors. Blood mixed with coin as I awoke in the night, chest burning, fearful that in the coming days my life would be utterly and completely altered for the worse. And on more than one occasion, my dreams turned to my first year with Rosamund.

I insist that you understand, such thoughts were not desired. Yet still the dreams came after long nights spent by Rosamund's bedside. Her soft, pale skin had been unblemished by fire, while wiry fingers grasped at the leather knot of my belt. In those dreams, I awoke to flushed skin and confused desire, believing myself going mad. In the days after the forum, Mariya questioned neither my silence nor my dishonest excuse that a sore back left me desiring only solace and a simple routine.

I would be remiss not to acknowledge the extensive aid I had received in those days—both for my benefit and in sharing vigil over Rosamund. Agathias was a constant visitor, employing other servants to fetch medicines from the city's merchants before applying them to Rosamund's wounds himself. Samur was another, particularly willing to sit through the long sleepless nights that had begun to sap my strength.

Still residing as a guest of my house, Antonina called upon Rosamund one week after the forum, I learned—the steady chattering of her voice was plenty audible behind a closed door. She remained for an hour or so, talking and talking, though I cannot recall hearing Rosamund's response to any of Antonina's inquiries. It seemed my old classmate had held a conversation unto herself, though she pretended the visit was a splendid one.

"Not that I'm not grateful," I began, greeting Antonina as she departed Rosamund's room, "but I never saw you as someone to sit over a sickbed."

"Rosamund is my friend!" Antonina countered, her brows furrowed. "We spent plenty of time together in Africa. Am I not permitted to worry about her?"

I shivered awkwardly. "Of course you are. It's just—"

"Good, then." Antonina was plainly uninterested in my reply, showing a hint of her former haughtiness. "I'll return tomorrow too, if that pleases you."

Rosamund had many visitors, though appeared to engage with few. One conspicuous holdout was Mariya, who hardly seemed willing to even discuss her household's wounded Gepid servant. Upon being questioned at her absence, my wife only rolled her eyes.

"I did warn you, Varus. And with Rosamund incapacitated, I have much to see to in this household."

She was right—yet the jab still stung, especially as I had not yet shared with her the extent of my losses. It was shameful, to conceal such a rupture to our way of life, and yet I convinced myself it would be premature; no paperwork had yet been drawn, after all, and besides Cassiodorus, none but I was party to that verbal oath.

"Still, your visit might make her happy," I prompted.

"You have half the army visiting Rosamund," Mariya continued, irritated. "And to be honest, I don't think she enjoys the company."

Again, Mariya's tone made me feel small, battered to the ground. "They are her friends, Mariya. Her fellows. Of course she enjoys their company."

"Rosamund is not like any of your other *fellows*," Mariya replied icily. Then, sighing, she shook her head. "That was ungraceful of me. I don't mind you comforting your friend, Varus. And I pray for Rosamund's recovery. I truly do. But I cannot just visit her as if all is well and pretend that I can forgive her for causing our house so much grief."

"I understand." I felt miserable, happy only to conclude the encounter.

Rosamund rarely spoke those first few days. Speaking appeared to extract its own measure of pain, triggering extensive and even bloody fits that only a chilled draught of honeyed water could alleviate. I spent a fortune on shaved ice from the palace—money I no longer really had, but I simply could not be bothered to balance the ledger. All I wanted to do, from the bottom of my soul, was help. Not just because she was my friend or my most trusted and most tenured servant, but because I felt guilty for her horrifying ordeal. Perhaps if I had listened to Rosamund, to one of her many entreaties, and left the Empire long ago, she and I and so many of us would have lived happier lives. Alas, age yields only wisdom to understand the past, not the power to change it. All I am left with is unfulfilled promises. And regrets.

"You're doing all you can," Belisarius offered, when I confided in him my guilt. "The world is a vast place, full of evil intent. You cannot control everything. But you can martial your will to make things better, as soon as you are able to."

"She would have been better off in Moesia," I muttered.

Belisarius shrugged. "You can't know that, Varus. Besides, you've shown her more kindness than most war captives ever see—sold into slavery in the mines, or the fields, or the comfort of some fat lord's bed. Stop blaming yourself for what you cannot change and find ways to improve the things you can."

My visits with Belisarius had been helping to break up the glumness that permeated my household, and to give me a sense of rhythm in my days as my back healed from its lashing and the army continued its preparations for Italy. Still, outside of a few hours' training and preparation, the bulk of my day was spent in my temporary home, protected by a dense array of veterans more than willing to butcher an angry priest.

Visitors were frequent—not just to Rosamund, but to me, with Perenus, Fulcaris, and Gunderic each offering their aid in my feud against Cassiodorus. I did consider using their muscle to renege in my promise, but ultimately I lacked the courage to do so. Nothing favorable could come from breaking my word, for it was that promise that had saved my friend's life, and its rupture could endanger us all once again. More than that, I dared not anger God through grievous falseness, regardless of the circumstances. The bargain had been struck.

Few visitors, however, were as steadfast in their duties as Sembrouthes. He had always been indefatigable, but now I doubted he slept more than a few hours each night; he certainly never rested more than a single shift of guard duty around the house. Samur's Huns and Gunderic's Vandals patrolled in force, but it was Sembrouthes who stalked the halls day and night, weary but unwilling to sleep. When I insisted on his need to relax, the taciturn Aksumite burst into apologies.

"It is my fault, Varus." Sembrouthes was all but groveling at my feet. "I should have stopped them."

"The lictores?" I asked.

He nodded. "They came with Justinian's guards, insisting they had the right to take Rosamund. I scuffled with them, but they overpowered me."

"Your men were unarmed!" I sighed. "Besides, if you had broken a few skulls, Marcellus would have been honor-bound to send the excubitores to destroy you. And I would now be mourning the death of a friend as well as the near execution of another."

Sembrouthes nodded and insisted that he agreed, but as the days passed, his behavior did not change. Mariya cautioned me to allow the proud warrior to grieve in his own way, recalling a stubborn streak that even she could not break as a girl.

"He believes only in perfect discipline," she explained. "One time I swiped a few silvers and escaped from my father's palace, looking for sweets from a traveling merchant. My father buckled over laughing when he heard—mostly since I overpaid for my treat a dozen times over—but Sembrouthes near killed himself from the humiliation of neglecting to watch me more closely. He refused food for three days, took great exertions every night after the completion of his guard duties... by the following morning, he'd nearly collapsed. Only when my father threatened to imprison him did he finally rest."

I rubbed my jaw. "That's exactly my worry."

Mariya shook her head. "His pride is wounded, but he will survive. Let him feel that he is performing his duty to your satisfaction once more, and he will relax in turn."

I listened and did as she bade, keenly aware in the meantime that my own pride had taken a grievous blow.

Finally, I could bear the secret no longer. It took me three days to admit my losses to Mariya, but when I did, I was thorough and forthright, recounting Cassiodorus' price for Rosamund's freedom and the state of our finances. Truthfully, I did not fully know the status of my wealth, for Narses retained the accounts as I drew against the ledger for one expense or another. We would not be poor, I told her, but neither would we be like Crassus. We simply had to adopt greater prudence in household spending to avoid a more dire problem—or so I hoped, at least.

When she spoke at last, Mariya's voice was faint, almost girlish. "Can you petition Theodora?"

"No," I answered. "I dare not risk Cassiodorus' wrath so soon. The more distance we place between us and Constantinople, the safer we shall be."

Mariya nodded, a tiny tear streaking through her kohl. "And Pella?"

My head sank low. "No longer ours."

Mariya sat, unblinking, as occasional tears further blotched black lines along her cheeks. She wept, I knew, not only for the loss, but because she had been correct all along—Cassiodorus had likely planned his seizure of Pella, possibly since I had returned from Carthage. I was a pathetically easy target—so much so that my wife had warned multiple times of the terrible danger I had waded into, and now I had proven her powerless to change my will. Swiftly, her shock transmuted into anger, and as Mariya glared at me, I wanted nothing other than to hide in some dark room, far away. I would have happily taken twenty more lashes to avoid confronting my wife in such distress.

"I told you, Varus," Mariya seethed. "I told you!"

I had never seen her so changed so suddenly. All serenity was wiped away, replaced by raw disgust: for the Empire, for me, for Rosamund... likely for all of us, and more. But I, surely, was the worst offender, for I had stumbled into a trap that Mariya had cautioned against multiple times.

Again, I allowed frustration to overtake sense. "I know, Mariya. But realistically, what could I have done?"

"Leave this hell!" Mariya screamed. "Roar at her the same way you do to your spearmen. Make Rosamund *obey*."

"Mariya, one day we can buy it back—"

"Stop!" Mariya cried, balling her fists as her entire body shivered in rage. "Just stop!!"

In that moment, twenty lashes would have been nothing—I would have accepted a hundred twenty if it meant I could take back my failure. Instead, I had subjected Mariya to the same uncertainties that plagued so many in the Empire—instability, and the looming, if still distant, threat of destitution. I attempted to lay a hand upon Mariya's back as she buried her face into her hands, but she refused my touch. I sat beside her for some indeterminate time, attempting yet failing to assemble the proper collection of words in my mind that would right the situation. Eventually, Mariya calmed enough to sit upright, her eyes swollen, her tears mixed with dark kohl.

"I understand, Varus," she said, her words a resigned drone. "You don't need to give me false hope. *This* is my life now."

"This?"

"The life of a dependent," she muttered. "With little purpose."

"That isn't true!" I moved closer. "The expedition will need you, Mariya—so many men, and women, and children. There will be people for you to help. Perhaps even more than Pella!"

"Perhaps," Mariya granted. "But who will pay for it all?"

There was no helpful answer. A born princess, Mariya never knew the uncertainty of deprivation. Wealth was a tool, not a mythic aspiration, but something to procure one of an infinite number of fleeting desires. Not that even I, with my humble beginnings, truly understood poverty, for Justin had provided well for my brother and I in our early days and beyond. But I knew enough of the meanness of a life of scarcity to feel apprehension at the thought of my dwindling purse, as well as my wife's unhappiness at it all.

"I..." My guts twisted, a flutter of bile in my throat. "I will find a way. I promise."

Mariya sighed. "No more promises, Varus. All they create is disappointment."

I shivered involuntarily as Mariya rose from her seat and retreated out into the hallway. I did not see her again until the following day—calmer, and even outwardly happy, though bereft of some spark, the carefree yet motivated will she usually possessed, and the vitality that came with it. Even when Mariya offered a peck upon my cheek as I passed, it lacked the usual ardor I had come to know from her in our years of marriage. And for that, I hated myself.

When away from Rosamund or Mariya, I found myself curiously alone, left to heal and think on my own. I did spend time with the children—chunky Alexander, fearless Zenobia, and the somber, quiet Tiberius. Often, Joannina joined in their play, providing Antonina with rare unencumbered happiness and keeping the servants on alert for misplaced toys and children sneaking from their beds. Though my skin still stretched in pain with sitting or lifting, I pretended not to notice the pain as I joined in on the children's games, allowing them to chase me about the upper floors as if a wild beast to be hunted or sneaking them treats from the underground kitchen.

Only Zenobia seemed unfearful of my presence, although all grew more comfortable as we passed hours together or alongside one of the women. In a peculiar manner, Cassiodorus' punishment had afforded me one gift: precious time with the children. For that, at least, I am grateful, even to this day.

Of all I saw of the children that week, it is Tiberius who stands out the most in my aged memory. A year older than Zenobia, his speech at the time was abashed, though I eventually discovered he possessed a broad vocabulary and an unencumbered speaking voice. Lanky for his age, Tiberius played with the other children reluctantly, although he seemed upset when not asked to join in their games. At times, I wondered how much he remembered of his horrifying tenure in the Hippodrome as his father played the part of false emperor, but I convinced myself that such memories would have blurred, even disappeared, due to the lad's age. It was a notion I might well have believed, had my own dreams not been haunted by screams of my earliest years amongst the Heruli.

It was the third afternoon after my punishment that I remember most distinctly, for that was my first true interaction with young Tiberius without my children, or their mother, there with me. I was sitting on a couch along the building's upper floor, wincing and hissing as Agathias applied a poultice to my scourged back.

"The concoction is Rosamund's recipe, I promise," he said.

"I trust you," I replied. "But it stinks, and it stings."

Groaning as he rubbed the balm onto what felt like thick, not-quite-healed scabs, I did not notice Tiberius slink into the room. Agathias did, however.

"Tiberius, should you be here?" he asked, accidentally pressing the linen rag too firmly onto my back.

I winced. "Mind yourself!"

"Apologies, Lord." Agathias withdrew hastily. "But we are

probably finished for now. I should reapply this tomorrow, and each afternoon until the scabs fully form."

"And if I refuse?"

Agathias shrugged. "Rosamund did not say. But I imagine your flesh might rot, so there's that."

I chuckled and gave Agathias permission to depart. Tiberius, however, remained where he was, his discerning eyes fixed upon my naked back as he pursed his lips. Alone with the lad, I did not know what to say—my guardianship over the son of the dead Hypatius still left me uneasy, particularly due to my dishonesty to Theodora regarding the boy's identity: She believed Tiberius an orphaned foundling rather than the scion of Justinian's erstwhile enemy. Xerxes knew of Tiberius' parentage, and likely Perenus too, but neither they nor anyone else had ever pried too closely. Mariya had a wide reputation as a caregiver for poor children, after all, yet both she and I worried over whether someone might guess at the lad's identity in later life. Thankfully, Tiberius little resembled his portly father, both in appearance, as well as with a serious and introspective demeanor, even at so young an age.

"No need to worry about me," I said, searching to defeat the silence between us. "The cuts do not hurt."

"Why did they do that to you?" the boy asked. "Those men who came to the house with clubs."

"Only God truly knows," I answered, for I could hardly air out my deficiencies as a husband to Mariya and a protector to Rosamund. "But they will not trouble you any further."

Tiberius nodded meekly. "But why were they allowed to do this?" he pressed. "Did you do something wrong?"

I decided to simplify my explanation to fit within a child's mind. "A priest was attacking Rosamund, and I struck him. You like Rosamund, yes?"

Tiberius nodded. "Before she got hurt, she would sit and talk to me. She would tell me stories and let me listen." He smiled to himself. "I don't always like to talk, but I love stories."

So simple. So straightforward, lacking in guile or wit. Tiberius had witnessed his fair share of horror, yet he could still enjoy childlike pleasures, still venture these innocent questions into the Empire's affairs. Tiberius was no Samur, that was certain, for Samur had long been a suspicious, private creature—even before his torture by Solomon's thugs, even as a boy. Tiberius was a good lad, and one whose presence pleased me, despite whatever loathing I felt for his slain father Hypatius. It still felt dishonest and unclean to conceal his parentage. Though I reasoned it had been necessary to keep my family safe, the twinge of guilt I felt for the ruse keeping Tiberius safe now only added to the devastation I felt I'd wrought upon everyone around me—my friends, my brother, my wife, my wards.

But that was neither the child's fault nor his concern, at least not now. I banished the thoughts from my head. "Why don't you like to talk, Tiberius? Does something bother you?" I asked.

He shook his head. "I just like to listen." He paused. "And… sometimes I worry that others might poke fun at what I want to say."

"Why would they do that, Tiberius?" I wondered aloud, genuinely curious. "All we want is for you to feel happy and safe."

Tiberius nodded but seemed unconfident of his reply. "Because I might say awkward things. Zenobia and Joannina aren't able to talk to me when I ask them things, and the adults seem worried."

Furrowing my brow, I gestured for Tiberius to sit next to me, and as he did, I wrapped an arm around the boy, resisting my own feeling of awkwardness at such an intimate display to one who did not share my blood. But then it became clear that Tiberius sorely needed such reassurance, and there were few better capable of providing it than me. "What are you worried about saying? What are your friends not willing to speak with you about?"

Tiberius pursed his lips, chewing the inside of his cheek. He kept his eyes cast away from me, but he did not resist my presence, and leaned back into my arm.

"Tiberius, will you answer me?" I asked softly.

"Others do not answer my questions about my mother and father," he mumbled at last. "Zenobia and Joannina know their parents, but I do not know mine. Only that they went to heaven."

I nearly choked. It felt as if I were listening to my younger self, desperately seeking the words to express a longing that was never sated. "I know very well how you feel, Tiberius."

"You did not know your mother or father?"

"Neither Samur nor I did," I replied. "We do not know their names. Only that they were Heruli."

Tiberius shifted in his seat, his eyes finally meeting my own. "Did it make you sad when you were little?"

"Yes," I answered. "It makes me sad to this day."

Though his own face was blank, Tiberius seemed to be fighting a noxious brew of doubt as he studied mine, biting his lip. "Did you know my father, or my mother?"

"I... came across your father many years ago," I replied, struggling to remain impassive. "And not as a friend."

Tiberius offered a light nod, his disappointment palpable. "Can you tell me about him?"

I swallowed my guilt. "One day, I will. But not now. For now, the most important thing is to know that your parents loved you with everything they possessed."

Another nod, albeit slower and even less satisfied. Hearing those words tumble from my lips, I felt chilled, as if struck by a shard of the coldest ice, so easily did they spill out. Was this how Justin felt, when he offered the same incomplete comfort to me so many times in my early years? I held all of Tiberius' answers but dared not share them, for I knew that if others discovered the truth, it would mean the boy's death—perhaps even my own, for not even Theodora would brook the maturation of a rival to Justinian's throne, let alone one who had better ancestral claim, and until recently, even the preference of the mob. Hypatius made me take Tiberius to save his son from the inevitable slaughter of the Hippodrome, but in so doing condemned us to a lifetime of worry for assassin's blades.

I yearned to give the boy a notion of comfort, but I could not bear to lie to him outright, nor did I wish to burden him with the fear that came with the truth—let alone the risk to my own family. One day, I promised myself, I would pluck Hypatius' ring from its hiding place amongst Mariya's jewels, give it to my ward, and explain all, but not this day. Not for many a day ahead.

Instead, we sat together. Though returned to silence, Tiberius seemed to take comfort in my attentions, leaning his slight weight against my arm despite the pungent odor of Agathias' healing salve slathered across my naked back.

Then, a pattering along the outside hallway floor interrupted our repose. The door, which had not been latched shut, slowly opened, with first a plodding nose and then an overexcited Haeva, who clumsily bounded into the room. Crashing into my legs, she pressed her muzzle into my knee, insisting upon attention. I responded in kind, scratching her head and ears as she wagged and panted with frenetic enthusiasm. Tiberius giggled and extended his own hand to meet the pup's delighted licks.

"Do you enjoy playing with Haeva?" I asked.

He nodded, continuing to scratch one of the dog's ears, yet did not pluck himself from my arm, staying silent all the while.

"Perhaps you would like to train her with Cephalas?" I offered. "Haeva will be coming with us to Italy, and we can't have her urinating where she pleases, nor yapping and lunging at every passerby, can we?"

"No, not at all." Tiberius nodded again as he broke into a toothy smile. We sat there for a time, taking turns stroking Haeva's thick yet cropped fur. Any guilt over withholding information from Tiberius evaporated as I listened to the boy laugh—a noise that eventually drew the attention of Zenobia, who stormed into the room and plopped herself at my unencumbered side as two of Mariya's maids bustled in after her. I waved the children off to return to play, leaving me to complete my healing session in solitude.

Later, I summoned Sembrouthes, who still labored ceaselessly from his self-induced punishment.

"I want you and Xerxes to train Tiberius how to fight," I told him.

"Now?" Sembrouthes asked. "The lad cannot be older than five years old."

"Were you much older when you began?"

Sembrouthes shook his head. "Not by much, I suppose."

"He's inquisitive, far beyond his years," I continued. "He will not grow with a fabled family name to support his rise, so he must distinguish himself through arms and education. I will speak with Mariya regarding the latter, for that will benefit Zenobia as well, but as for the weapons training, he will learn from you and Xerxes. In time, my son will join him, but not for a few more years."

"You honor me," Sembrouthes said. "I will train your ward as best as I know in the tradition of my people."

I grinned. "Then they will be passable, at least. Godilas beat Samur and I into warriors, so perhaps your pupils will become their own leaders one day."

So it was that in my respite, I ate, I stole what little sleep would come from a pained back and buttocks, and I embraced time with my children, wife, and household. Only rarely was my reprieve from duties interrupted, with requests from the palace about some inane subject or task. A pleasant note from Theodora waxed extensively about her well-wishes for my and Rosamund's recovery, with a single line insisting upon a private meeting as soon as I could return to the palace.

Simultaneously, Liberius' courier delivered a note absent any niceties, instead bearing a warning of continued risk to me and my estate despite satisfying Cassiodorus' thirst for my gold. Then, of course, there were the visits from others such as Perenus and Fulcaris, who kept their tones hushed and uncomfortable when asking about my flogging or Rosamund's belayed execution.

"I should have been there," Perenus muttered bitterly.

"There was nothing anyone could have done," I responded. "And if the punishment were worse, I needed you to be untarnished from my punishment."

"I won't let it happen again," Perenus replied. Both he and Fulcaris sat with Rosamund for a time, yet she lacked the stamina for extensive conversation and seemed to prefer solace as she lay on her bed, taking in the cool breezes that swept from the sea and into her open window. Two weeks after surviving the bull, the worst of her burns had begun to heal, and the prior injury to her head improved markedly, but it would be several weeks before her body was hale enough to walk.

Her mind, I feared, would never be the same.

Toward the end of my leave, polite yet urgent requests for support emerged from the palace. Theodora's couriers requested notice of my availability, while both Procopius and Narses demanded updates on the seaborne army's readiness. Narses appended a separate note reminding me of the state of my household finances and the free transfer of Pella to Cassiodorus, which I disregarded. Little good would come from belaboring what I already knew.

But my obligations to the army could not be similarly swept away. Belisarius wrote to voice his sympathies and that he would shoulder my burdens as tribune until my recovery—a welcome message, although delivered once again by Bessas.

"We only have two months until the expedition," he explained. "Belisarius hardly sleeps. He wants to see you but cannot leave the palace or the barracks for now."

There was plenty of reason in Belisarius' excuse, but I knew the real deterrent of his visits was Antonina. She still resided within my household, after all, living under the threat of divorce, condemned to exist as merely a comfortable patrician rather than the wife of the most powerful warlord since Aetius. Against Rosamund's near execution, my own spiral into penury, and the burgeoning task of preparing an exhausted and under-manned army for expedition to hostile Italy, Antonina's drama factored little into my thinking.

Instead, I simply continued to do whatever Mariya requested for her friend—and, honestly, I did wish to see my old classmate comfortable and her daughter happy and carefree—but there were limits of the cost to my attentions I could bear. For now, I listened to Bessas' excuses for Belisarius, waving them aside with acceptance so that the Armenian could offer what proved to be a happier announcement.

"Also" —Bessas grinned— "Belisarius asked me to procure you a new horse. A Nisean, just as before."

I was genuinely surprised. "Why? How?"

"Our trade routes with Persia made the task somewhat easier," he explained. "The strategos himself covered the cost outright, for a yearling. One of my riders will break him in, because I know you have no skill at this."

"None at all," I agreed. "And you have my thanks. But… if I am to be honest, Bessas, I did believe that my mounted duties were a thing of the past."

Bessas shook his head. "As Belisarius' second, you cannot *walk* hundreds of miles on the campaign ahead, now can you? The men and officers must see you at all times, on the march or on the battlefield. These are Belisarius' very words," he added.

I nodded, grateful. "If those are Belisarius' words, then this is Varus' acceptance."

"Good," Bessas replied. "And while we all understand your need to heal, many in the palace would benefit from your return when possible. Can I tell Belisarius that you shall return soon?"

"Tomorrow," I promised.

The next day, my scabbed back felt aflame with itching as I readied for my return to the palace. The responsibilities of preparing me fell to Agathias, for with Rosamund mending, Cephalas had taken over the burdens of my household's daily operations. It was not a task he had much success in—where Rosamund was meticulous and memorized the finest detail of food purchases to dispensations of captured Vandal treasure to my men, Cephalas jumbled and mixed his responsibilities with a hopeless forgetfulness. Mariya reminded Cephalas of forgotten duties gently enough, though it was clear she nursed a private smoldering annoyance.

"We need more help," she insisted to me. "Cephalas has no skill in running a household."

I agreed, though felt the urge to defend my friend. "He just needs more time to learn."

"And while you spare unlimited time and patience on an illiterate, one-armed man," Mariya grumbled, "the rest of us suffer and look slovenly to the Imperial court."

"All will be well when Rosamund recovers," I insisted, earning a wordless scowl.

While Cephalas was easily flustered by his many mishaps, Agathias soaked in knowledge like the immense cave sponges in the coastal caves of the Euxine Sea. This flustered Cephalas further—not from petty jealousy, but likely more from self-deprecation. Agathias assumed the easier healing tasks normally taken by Rosamund, while delivering my scribbled messages to army leaders and warehouse officials alike. When I insisted that such extended duties were not required of him, Agathias only grinned, insisting it was a pleasure as much as a responsibility. Though freed from Imperial bondage, he nevertheless pursued tasks with the same passion and desire to please as when I first met him. In many ways, as a former slave myself, I understand the cause of that desire.

One week after the forum, fully dressed and armored, I first stopped in Rosamund's room, ignoring the uncomfortable stretching of the skin along my back. By then, she was capable of sitting, with the small burnt patches of skin scabbed over in what would eventually become thick scars. She drank a thistle tea throughout the day for nagging pain, and another powder unknown to me that had been ground by Agathias for more restful sleep. She had also cut away the bulk of her hair, with the remainder reaching only to her shoulders.

"A fine change." I grinned, nodding at her shorn locks.

Rosamund smiled—perhaps the first time I had seen since the Bovis Forum—though her eyelids lingered half open. "The ends of my hair were singed, and parts were burned. Agathias cut as much off as needed."

An eavesdropper might believe Rosamund's tone purely practical, as if her new appearance were done out of necessity alone. But I knew her well, better than any man or woman alive, and she did seem pleased with herself. Though still young—no older than twenty-six— the ravages from two assaults, the incipient scars, and the shortened hair made Rosamund appear suddenly older. Less carefree, certainly, but somehow wiser, too. In an odd way, she seemed almost like a younger version of Liberius.

"It suits you," I replied. "Is there anything I can provide for you?"

Her smile faded. "No. Just peace." She clutched at a blanket and shivered. "Actually, there is one favor I would ask."

"Name it. Anything at all."

Rosamund twisted in bed, whimpering as a section of burned skin rubbed against the mat. "Can you... limit my visitors?"

"Of course." I made for the door—my presence offered no benefit to Rosamund's recovery, after all.

"Not you," Rosamund amended, stopping me but wincing with the effort. "Or Agathias. Or the guards. Everyone else, though... I don't want to see anyone else, at least for now."

There was no joy in her voice. No longing for camaraderie that I had known in our early years together. It was unsurprising, of course, though I lacked guidance on how to interact with a more withdrawn, sullen Rosamund. "You won't be bothered until you've recovered, I promise."

Rosamund nodded in gratitude as she snatched at a clay cup, even as her fingers were obviously too weak to hold it. I stepped beside her, placing my hand beneath hers, and guided the liquid to her lips. I knew not what to say, but I desired to encourage her, or at least garner a laugh. But I had no strategy for either.

"Is your strength returning?" I asked at last.

"If it were, then *I* would be applying the healing salve to your back," she muttered, rolling her eyes. "Agathias is eager but has all the grace of a drunken hippopotamus."

"He's learning." I smiled. "But that isn't truly an answer to my question."

Rosamund plucked at the thin blanket that covered much of her body. Though she was still modest about her appearance, her legs lay bare, presumably too tender for even the touch of cloth, laced with angry welts as they were. Her skin, normally translucent and lined with sapphire veins, had reddened to an angry hue.

"I hurt constantly," she complained in Heruli. "My skin cracks, and my joints ache. My head swims with pain, and the urge to vomit never appears far. But even that is preferable to sleep. When I dream, I feel the hands of Cassiodorus' men, pawing on my body as they put me in that beast."

Breathing heavily, her face contorted into the sort of pained rage that I had seen in the aftermath of many battles far distant. "What kind of monster would torture and kill in such a way?"

I shook my head. "I have no excuses, Rosamund."

"I didn't do anything!" Rosamund yelled, her words ringing against stone. "Nothing!"

"I know—"

"No, you don't!" Rosamund seethed, straining her voice. "They call me witch or barbarian or a cunt. But they would do unspeakable things to satisfy their god." She spat toward the floor, drawing another wince. "A god who relishes pain. This is the one god you Christians mew about?!"

Drawing a chair, I sat by her bedside and snatched her hand once more. "Rosamund, if I would have known—"

"*If you would have known,*" Rosamund mocked. "If your fucking emperor commanded you to put me in that bull tonight, you would have it done before the moon's zenith."

I squeezed her hand. Rosamund's ire was too much, especially after a week of rows with Mariya. "No, Rosamund. Not today, not ever."

Rosamund shuddered and clenched hard against my arm, showing that surprising strength once more from her small fingers. Yet, soon enough, she lay back upon her cushion, spent.

But not entirely—for then, I saw in her raw hatred, tinged with a glimmer of fear. "They will all suffer for this."

Rosamund's eyes fixed upon mine as she swore her vow. This was a gaze I had witnessed only once before, when her same, judging eyes demanded that I stand against the grievous sins of Archelaus.

"On my oath, they will," I swore.

I did not—could not—explain to her how costly her freedom had already been. Both in body and in purse, I had been humiliated before Cassiodorus' zealots. Varus, a lord of misfit warriors and a widely traveled excubitor, forced to beg for the mercy of a filth-stained priest. Not that hearing the cost would have slaked Rosamund's fury, anyway—if anything, it might have incensed her further. But I told myself I simply did not wish to add to Rosamund's worries. A broken body is more than enough to mind.

"They will all die screaming," she continued. "What is coming for those bastards is far worse than what any man is capable of."

Her words unsettled me. "What do you mean? Have you seen something?"

"No," she replied. "Just a sense of foreboding. The gods will not allow such awful men to dance unopposed in the streets, after all. Something terrible is coming, Varus, and it will consume all their souls more completely than the hottest funeral pyre. Hotter than that torture device they would consign me to. I cannot say what, but I feel it coming. And I fear it more than anything we've yet faced."

I shuddered, though whether from the sight of her extensive injuries or hearing the eerie invocations to her gods, I cannot say. To this day, the thought of Rosamund's pagan deities sends me grasping for a cross—though I well know they are mere figments of tribal superstition, and could barely name two of them besides. There is only one true God—so it is said, taught, preached, and so, too, do I believe. But there is something else in the world, for I have seen evidence of that too.

I did not know then, but I would find much later, that Rosamund's warning was correct. Far more correct than she could fathom.

But that comes later. In that moment, I merely bent down, offering Rosamund as gentle an embrace as I could muster, which she returned in kind. As further proof that I was unrepelled by her injury, I pecked a kiss atop her head and insisted that she rest while Cephalas prepared the household for its journey. She chuckled but surrendered to my will, though not without grumbling that she would have to fix a thousand mistakes after resuming her post. With that, we shared our farewells, and I departed for the palace.

Alongside Sembrouthes, I took six Aksumites as an escort. Xerxes, too, volunteered to join us, which I declined.

"They might not allow you entry," I explained. "And instead, I'd rather you visit Uliaris." As our departure loomed, the roving Frank had been tugging at the back of my mind, for I had neither seen nor heard of him in quite some time. "I doubt Belisarius gave him instructions on our departure, and we'll need to pluck him from whatever winesink or whorehouse he's stumbled into and ready him for Italy."

Xerxes shrugged. "I can try, but who knows Uliaris' mind. He will never be well in the head until Belisarius forgives him for John's death."

"Well, do what you can. We owe Uliaris a great deal for driving off Theudis from Septem, and I would keep him from an inglorious death choking on his own vomit."

Xerxes agreed, albeit reluctantly. I knew he loathed such tasks—pampering and coaxing a near-suicidal warrior to rejoin his comrades was beneath a leader of Zhayedan—but I also knew that he would not fail. Of all the men and women I have ever met, Xerxes embraced perfection unlike any other. He never compromised in his duty, and he was staunchly loyal—evidenced by, among other things, how quickly he had become a close friend.

With Xerxes disappearing into the city in search of Uliaris, my retinue and I proceeded on our way. We passed small gatherings of Cassiodorus' zealots, who despite their spirited declarations of faith against heretics and apostates, stayed well clear of us. More the better, for though I swore blood vengeance against Cassiodorus, I had little doubt that the Emperor would condemn me to a further ten lashes for any further infractions against the gathering of rabid priests. As we passed through the Forum of Constantine, however, I did spot a familiar face—the same younger man who offered aid in dousing Rosamund's pyre. I knew him enough to place him with a glance, but this time, passing more slowly, I gained a clearer view at his face, and I all but stopped in my tracks.

It was impossible. A ghost, or a demon perhaps, but not a man of flesh and blood. In that moment, my legs took root onto the paved stones, and my hand rushed instinctively to my hilt.

"Isaacius?" I whispered, frantically searching in vain for the specter.

"Who?" Sembrouthes asked. "An enemy?"

I paused for a time, although I cannot say for how long. Though I struggled to recall the features of my long-dead comrade's face, to the depths of my soul I had no doubt it was him that I laid eyes upon in that moment. But as quickly as the figure swept into view, he was gone. Grabbing the bronze cross at my throat, I muttered a prayer, hoping that an evil spirit had not been dispatched from the underworld to torment me further—and, equally, that I was not falling into madness.

"Nothing," I eventually replied. "Let's keep going, before trouble brews."

It only took a few minutes of a brisk pace to reach the palace gates. Unlike in the week prior, we gained easy access, with my only encumbrance being the throbbing ache as my shirt and armor chafed against healing flesh. Ignoring the pain, I traveled first to a war council planned amongst Belisarius' most senior officers, leaving Sembrouthes in an adjoining hallway. Two excubitores nodded to me as I entered Belisarius' offices, their heads bowed a heartbeat longer than normal—a sign I received as reassurance of my place in the hallowed brotherhood despite my chastisement.

"Ah, Varus," Belisarius bellowed upon my entry. "Excellent to see you returned. Are you well enough to join us, though?"

"Well enough to spill ink and stare at parchment like you bunch of clerks," I shot back, beaming. Though I found the labor of campaign preparation tedious, it still felt liberating to be returned to Belisarius' men.

There were far fewer officers present at this meeting than at recent gatherings. Aside from the strategos, a dour Mundus propped his chin up with an arm upon a nearby table, flanked by a much younger man I had not yet met. Ascum was there, gorging upon a basket of plump grapes, while Bessas fanned himself with an empty courier's tube as sweat pooled along his brow. Joining them as leader of the combined foederati was Perenus, bedecked in the freshly polished armor and white cloak of an excubitor.

"Mundus conducted the ceremony while you recuperated," Perenus explained, gesturing to his new garb with a grin. "But I know I have you to thank."

Conspicuously, the table held no Gunderic, nor Samur, nor Indulf, nor any of the rising officers like Valerian or Fulcaris. It made the room seem emptier, as if haunted by the spirits of our friends long-dead on Tauris, in Mesopotamia, or along the coasts of Africa. There was only one reason for such an intimate meeting—mistrust. The inclusion of a stranger seemed ill advised, but my caution was alleviated after Mundus introduced his companion.

"This is Constantinianus," Mundus said, slapping his much younger comrade on his back. "My second for the land invasion, with Troglita still in Carthage. He's Theodora's cousin, by some distant uncle."

Like Solomon, I recalled Justinian's appointment of Constantinianus to senior leadership in the Thracian Army. I could only plead with God that Constantinianus would show better judgment, or at least more selflessness, than my longtime enemy.

"A distant relative," Constantinianus corrected. "My grandmother was sister to Theodora's mother. I had not met the Empress until after she was wed. She was kind enough to pay for my training, and my position in Moesia."

"Terrible place, Moesia," Perenus grumbled. "Wet, cold, with bad food and grubby people."

"That it is." Constantinianus laughed. "But it is home, for now."

Until that point, I had not known Theodora retained any extended family. Not that I necessarily would have, for the Empress never mentioned anything of her childhood or lineage in our meetings. There was little reason to doubt Constantinianus' story—his entry to the palace was proof enough that he possessed the Empress' blessing. Nevertheless, the younger man left me uneasy, both from his unknown strength of connection to Theodora, and even more from his considerable youth. If Constantinianus was chosen for leadership due solely to his scant connection to the Empress' bloodline, Mundus' Thracian forces might face considerable hardship in the battles to come.

"Have you seen much fighting in Moesia?" I pried. "Years ago, several of us clashed with the Gepids, but you would have been too young to serve at that time."

"Some," Constantinianus said, retreating into his bench with a slouch. "Not nearly as much as you. I know I would not be your ideal selection as second in the army, Lord Varus, but I can write, and I've trained extensively with the Moesian governor's weapons master. I will not shirk from my responsibilities to Mundus."

Constantinianus' self-deprecation took me aback. "I have no doubt, Constantinianus. Just promise me that you will keep my old centurion alive, and whole."

"Done!" He grinned, straightening in his seat with a newfound confidence.

The business of Belisarius' gathering began mundanely enough. Ponderous lists contained drafts for provisions by land, to support Mundus' invasion of Illyria, and by sea, for Belisarius' larger force venturing by sea. Other maps detailed intended meeting points, where ships and caravans following both armies' progression could place goods in predetermined depots. Of course, Mundus grumbled at the need for not only more men and horses, but bows, wagons, swords, waterskins, nails and rope, and every other tool of camp life.

"We're attacking a larger force, with garrisoned and provisioned defenses, with the scrapings of the Imperial economy." Mundus groaned. "Not having enough men is difficult enough, but lacking supplies—"

"There is nothing further we can do," Belisarius interjected. "Although I will confer with the Emperor, and with Narses. Eventually, they will see our need for greater support, but we must fulfill our duty until that day."

It was a topic that had arisen often enough that the likely answer needed not be spoken. Though Justinian lusted for Italy's return to the Empire, he was loath for Belisarius to receive the glory for such an achievement. If Belisarius conquered a foothold but struggled to gain dominance against the Ostrogoths, it would afford Justinian with an opportunity to swoop into the Italian provinces with a different favorite and claim the heart of the long-dead Western Empire. If a few hundred or even a few thousand Roman soldiers should suffer and die in the interim, that was little matter to him. Narses, by this point, had likely planted the scheme in the Emperor's mind.

However, that nagging worry was not the grimmest consideration of that day. Belisarius plucked a stiff vellum scroll from his heap and showed its text to all of us. Although only Constantinianus and I were fully literate, Belisarius' solemn face spoke well enough of its tidings, and he shifted our focus to future impediments.

"Solomon sent a treasure fleet to Constantinople, yielding a full dozen gold talents as tribute to the Emperor," Belisarius began. "Solomon claims his reorganization of conquered territory is proceeding far more expeditiously than could be anticipated, with tax revenue flooding into Carthage and Hippo."

"Twelve talents?" I muttered, then asked, "How is that possible? We took the Vandal treasure after Gelimer's surrender."

"It's possible through theft," Perenus pointed out. "Solomon must be bleeding Carthage white."

Belisarius nodded. "In recognition of his talents, and in securing defenses in Africa, Sardinia, and the Balearics, the Emperor is naming Solomon a prefect, as well as magister militum per Africam."

"There's definitely no God if that git can be the civil and military authority of the African provinces." Ascum scowled.

Belisarius sighed. "Normally, I would hope that Solomon's capabilities are genuine. There does appear to be plenty of truth attesting to his competence, for garrison commanders report little crime and plenty of construction of new barracks and fortifications."

I eyed the scroll in Belisarius' hands. "But?"

"But," Belisarius continued, "we have received other, more private messages from Carthage. Liberius and I have met privately about their contents, and believe them genuine. Troglita writes to us in a cipher, just as Caesar once did to his officers."

Belisarius handed Troglita's vellum to Constantinianus, followed by an additional parchment of fresher lines—the translation. Glancing first at Troglita's text, then at the deciphered message, he read aloud.

"There is peace, but revolt is imminent. Its leaders are unknown but high-ranking. Solomon is unwilling to listen. I can trust a small contingent of soldiers here, but most are loyal to local lords. I do not know if I will be able to maintain order."

Bessas whistled. "Not good."

"No," I agreed. "Troglita is not one to exaggerate. If he says there is danger, it is far worse than the letter reveals."

Belisarius' council faded to silence. Few of us believed Solomon would be a new Augustus, true, but the stark danger implied in Troglita's note ran counter to the recurring messages of progress, orderliness, and most recently, free-flowing tribute to replenish Justinian's coffers. Still—revolt, so soon after Carthage's conquest? Even with enemy spies wormed into the crevices of the Carthaginian palace, it was difficult to comprehend. Belisarius obliterated the Vandal government, so who remained to challenge Roman authority?

"We will change the seaborne invasion plan," Belisarius declared. "Instead of taking Brundisium and Barium, we will seize Sicily."

I, too, could not help but whistle at such an abrupt but sweeping alteration to months of planning. "Sicily will be easier to capture but will completely separate our forces from Mundus," I put in. "It also leaves us facing the same problem that we have now in capturing a beachhead on the Italian mainland and splitting Theodahad's armies."

"Mundus will still possess a clear land route back to Constantinople," Belisarius replied. "While Sicily will give us a firmer launching point if Carthage requires aid. Justinian will be furious if the city is overrun."

"Of course." Bessas grunted. "But that's Prefect Solomon's problem," he said, emphasizing each syllable of the freshly granted title.

Belisarius closed his eyes as he exhaled a weighty breath. "In addition to gaining a new title and permanent status to govern our new African prefecture, Solomon is granted the hand of Justinian's niece, Praejecta, in marriage. She sails for Carthage tomorrow, with a fleet of six dromons as an escort."

Mundus chuckled. "And on this life of ours continues, with dung floating atop the churning waves."

"Unless we send Varus to pluck away Justinian's little niece," Ascum said with a cackle. "It worked last time... although Justinian might snip his manhood for stealing this bride."

I crumpled a small wad of parchment and tossed it at Ascum's head. He ducked, still chortling. Belisarius, however, was less than pleased.

"If Troglita believes a revolt is possible, we must prepare accordingly," he said. "If Carthage is threatened, the Emperor would insist our voyage pivot to secure the city, and his niece."

Sighing, I nodded. "It will be done, Lord. When would you have the armies depart?"

Belisarius shrugged. "What say you, Ascum?"

"Given the longer voyage, and more aggressive invasion plan to take Sicily, Campania, Calabria, and Apulia, we could not leave until the equinox," Ascum reasoned, now serious once again. "But we'll need to select an invasion point, at least for our fleet to gather."

Belisarius nodded. "Five weeks, then. Not much longer than we anticipated. As for our initial conquest, that decision is Varus' to make."

Though I'd anticipated Belisarius would place such a burden upon me, I had no ready answer. Before he perished after Tricamarum, it would have been John who'd make the offer. And based on what I'd seen of the man, he would have known every port and supply line mapped in his mind, dictating minute shore landings across the Sicilian expanse. By contrast, all I had at my disposal were Liberius' teachings and a vengeful Indulf. It was my knowledge of the latter that affirmed my strategy.

"Syracuse," I said, pointing to the ancient city upon a splayed map. "It's on the eastward side of the island, and therefore more prone to surprise from an attack by sea from Constantinople. Theodahad's men will expect us to attack Lilybaeum or Panormus from Carthage due to the shorter lines of attack, so they'll have those sites garrisoned, and the other cities less so."

A fabled city, more ancient than Rome. A place that had spawned all manner of legendary Greeks, and a gateway between Italian and Greek culture. A city that I had visited once before, albeit briefly, and found to be a place of relative plenty. And though it was small, a place I believed Mariya might enjoy, or where she might at least temporarily forget her losses. In this, I was naively hopeful.

Constantinianus frowned. "How do you know that Syracuse would readily fall? If it resists for more than a week or two, your men will be bottled up on a narrow patch of land, easy pickings for Gothic war bands."

I nodded, having at least prepared for that. "We have Indulf and the Ostrogothic foederati, who swore blood vengeance against Theodahad. Indulf gained us access to Syracuse once, and will be able to do so again, either through bribery or stealth."

"Sensible," Belisarius confirmed. "Make sure Indulf is prepared for his role. If he performs well, I will convince the Emperor to name him military commander of the city and its ports. He will grow richer than all of us within two years."

It was done. There were an unending array of errands to complete, but by acknowledging Troglita's warning, Belisarius committed to the final plan for our insane, suicidal invasion of broader Italy. However this unfolded would be a tale spoken with hushed tongues in all of Constantinople's taverns and brothels, a course to set the Empire's dwindling forces forth to determine the fate of us all. And it would, by God, ignite the greatest war mankind had ever known.

THE JUDGMENT
OF ANTONINA

B ut the war was not the only battle waged by Belisarius. And after
ending my business with the diminutive war council, I discovered
just what effect the business with Antonina would continue to have
upon my life.

Even with Justinian's patronage of Cassiodorus and his band of
zealots, it was nevertheless Theodora whose attention was prized
by any Roman citizen or foreign merchant seeking favor from the
Imperial court, and I was no different. I found her absent Justinian
in the Imperial great hall, surrounded by a collection of silk-laden
Roman ladies and a line of petitioners ambling for position for the
Empress' attentions.

Surprisingly, I spotted Narses standing behind her chair, his rotund
body unmistakable despite every attempt to hide in the shadows of a
vast marble column. Unfortunately for me, Narses possessed a keen
eye to discern all who entered Theodora's presence, he detected me
within moments of reaching the Empress' queue. Departing his post,
he slinked across the hall to intercept me.

"Theodora wishes to speak with you privately," Narses whispered,
cupping jeweled fingers about his mouth to hinder eavesdroppers.
"And it behooves you to find other sources of income soon. Justin
intended for Pella to be an opportunity to replenish your inherited
fortune over time."

I groaned. "I know, Narses."

"Do you, Varus?" he hissed. "You can sneer and scoff at me all you wish, even though I have only *ever* attempted to aid you. But you can only maintain your current household expenditures for another year—if that. Within two, you surely will be dependent upon the Emperor's largesse, which is not boundless these days."

"Yet bountiful enough for you to seize two gold talents for the Hagia Sophia," I muttered.

Narses shook his head. "You need to learn quickly, Varus. I take and do nothing. The Emperor and Empress ask, and I obey. The sooner you recognize this, the easier your life will become. Honesty bears little fruit, but unscrupulous loyalty is a bountiful tree."

Not pausing for my reply, Narses departed for his prior perch, where he leaned into Theodora's ear. She nodded at his whispers, the pearl-encrusted diadem dancing atop her head, and after concluding an audience with her latest petitioner, summoned a nearby white-cloaked excubitor.

"Petitions are concluded for this day," the soldier bellowed. "Return on the morrow, and the Empress Theodora shall hear your pleas."

There were groans and muttering, but all turned to depart the Empress' presence. The shuffling of a hundred individuals took several minutes, for many were crippled or bore infirmities that made each step laborious. After the final elderly patrician escaped beyond the ponderous hall doors, Theodora rose from her throne.

"All others, leave me that I might speak with Varus alone."

Those remaining—excubitores, slaves, and even Narses—rushed to obey her command. As always, I had little doubt that interlopers lurked inside the nooks behind select walls, but there was nothing to be done—and Theodora, who had even greater reason than me to fear an unfriendly spy, still beckoned to me with a swipe of her hand. It was not lost upon me that Narses, too, had been dismissed—a reassuring notion, but also one of great vulnerability at Theodora losing the unquestioned loyalty of the Imperial spymaster.

"I prayed for your recovery," Theodora said once we were alone.

"You know I loathe Cassiodorus. Show me your injuries."

"Highness?"

She insisted. "Where the scourge lashed your back. I would see Cassiodorus' judgment. I am as much to blame for not defending you, and I would bear witness to the pain of my oath sworn servant."

"Highness, I am not sure it would be… proper." In fact, I knew it would not be—undressing to the waist before Theodora, especially inside the Imperial Palace.

Theodora pursed her lips, sharp dimples forming in her cheeks. "I am rarely in the habit of asking for something twice, Varus. Please do me the courtesy of acquiescing."

Beneath her heavy gold and pearl regalia, Theodora wore those rare shades of violet reserved for the embodiment of Caesar. As only Theodora could, she struck a figure both of traditional modesty—her hair was wound in a tight bun and veiled with black silk—and the far bolder ensemble of a fashionable Roman woman—her dresses were cut to fit snug against her body, unlike the shapeless mass of linen and wool of more common women. From worry and overwork, Imperial office had aged Theodora, but the strands of gray hair only added to her allure. That, and the raw confidence.

I bowed, surrendering to her will. "I will need the assistance of a servant to unstrap the lamellar," I admitted. "I could normally manage alone with some difficulty, but the scabs tear with too much motion. Shall I summon—"

Theodora shook her head vigorously, beckoning again with an outstretched hand. "I will help you. Come—tell me where to address the knots."

With a hand, I gestured to a few sections along my shoulders and lower neck. "It may be coarse against your fingers, Highness."

"What little you must think of me!" Theodora laughed. "Leather ties won't kill me, Varus."

With a surprisingly firm grip, I felt her fingers tugging at the knots, freeing the armor to slide easily over my head. After lifting the metal covering free, I then untied my sweat-strewn shirt, tugging it free of my body and placing it in a neat pile atop my armor. With no further words, I turned my back to the Empress, feeling a chill despite the tepid air of the hall.

"Mother of God," she muttered.

I heard her step forward, quite close, so that her breath was light across my skin. An icy finger traced near one of the scabbed cuts, bringing me to shudder against a light stab of pain. At that, she withdrew for a heartbeat, but soon continued onward, albeit keeping her fingertip hovering just above the still-healing wound.

"What did it feel like?" she whispered.

"Not terrible, at first," I admitted. "But later... like my skin was burning. Or a hundred bees lancing me with their sting."

Theodora murmured incomprehensibly to herself before continuing. "It hurts still?"

"Only when moving suddenly. Sleep is still difficult."

"They shall pay for doing this, in time." Her voice was so soft that I hardly heard her, even just paces away, yet I shivered all the same.

Indeed, Theodora's simmering anger, spoken in husky tones, would have made any sane man tremble. The one truth I could depend upon in Justinian's court was Theodora's will, for when the weak would run from deadly conflict, Theodora embraced the challenge, refusing to abandon her claim as empress.

"Doing this to me?" I asked. "Or to Rosamund?"

"Both," she said. "That savagery has no place in my empire. You may dress, Varus."

I obeyed, eager to return to a more proper state of modesty. Though I doubt any slave could discern our conversation, someone must have spied our exchange, and any unwise word would easily find its way to the ear of Narses and the Emperor. From my recent bout of ill luck, I could not afford the wrath of a jealous husband, especially one who was lord of us all.

"I know you are very busy, Varus, so I will not keep you long," Theodora continued. "You still provide board and succor to Antonina, for which I am grateful."

I nodded. "It is my pleasure, Highness."

Theodora rolled her eyes. "One day, you will give me the pleasure of using my name in private conversation. And I doubt you enjoy Antonina's company, from what I have gathered of your past interactions with her as children. But I appreciate your kindness to her all the same." She paused, folding her hands above her stomach. "What do you know of Belisarius' intentions for his wife?"

I stifled a groan. "Nothing directly from him, for it is not a polite conversation to raise. But from Antonina, I know that divorce papers have been dispensed."

"But why now?" Theodora demanded. "Belisarius could have done so in Carthage, or far sooner."

Confiding Belisarius' actions to Theodora felt strange, somehow wrong—even though I did not know the answer, and little of Antonina's infidelity had been kept secret. "Only he knows. But I can guess."

Theodora's eyes fluttered, suggesting a deep fatigue stemming from far too many hours of heeding court affairs. "Your speculation is as valued as anyone's."

"He still loves her," I replied, pushing through the reluctance I felt about Belisarius' privacy. "She could have cuckolded him with half the army, and he would still love her."

"And you would not, if you were in his situation?"

Exhaling a thin stream of air, I surrendered to the truth. "I doubt it. From my experience, marriage is more than love, it's trust. With adultery, trust is broken. No amount of poetry or courtship could render the pieces whole again."

Theodora laughed. "Honest, of course. But why does Belisarius not share your sense of reason?"

Another shrug. "He's the most loyal man I have ever met, enemy or friend. Finding Antonina with Sergius... it changed something within him."

Theodora frowned. "Bitterness?"

"Betrayal," I suggested. "Belisarius never complains. He never speaks ill of friends or superiors. But from all the hardships thrust upon him, Antonina was the only person to strike a wound. I thought he would never speak as friends with me again, given that Antonina's indiscretions were discovered in my Carthaginian house."

"And you believe that friendship is repaired?" Theodora asked.

"Looking back, it was never in any jeopardy, but Belisarius needed time to heal," I replied. "But wouldn't Narses' spies tell you of my more recent interactions with Belisarius?"

Theodora's lids fluttered again, leading the Empress to rub at tired eyes with her thumb and forefinger. It was a delicate action, carefully practiced to avoid smearing layers of kohl and powder carefully refreshed by palace slaves each hour. "You are no fool, Varus. If Narses is not here with us, what does that tell you?"

At that, my suspicions were confirmed, and the worries of Petrus and Liberius validated. The Imperial spymaster, risen high in Theodora's service, had gained a far more powerful patron in Justinian.

"That my fellow ringbearer is not to be trusted," I whispered.

"Correct. Which means that, in all the world, I only have you to confide my secrets and fears. Does that concern you?"

While I often struggled and worried under the weight of Theodora's burdens, I never truly wished to be free of her trust—not the way I often desired release from the army. "No, Highness. But it does mean we must tread carefully."

"Carefully, indeed," Theodora agreed. "After Nika, my stature swelled throughout the provinces. I am not so much a fool to believe such love and respect is lasting or impermeable."

With two gold-ringed fingers, Theodora teased at a sore spot along her forehead. Wincing, she brought her second hand to join, massaging from arched brows to the corners of her closed eyelids. It was a careful exercise, likely conducted many times daily in her more intimate moments. Likewise, it was a gesture that hinted at a weakness, one that I never observed from my time in the presence of petitioners or ministers.

"Highness, shall I call a servant?" I offered. "When I was a slave, my dominus suffered from a throbbing head as well."

"I have a mind to request Rosamund instead, from what I observed of her healing prowess during the riots," Theodora mumbled.

"I am certain she would be delighted."

"No," Theodora countered, ceasing her ministrations. "As Justin likely knew all too well, there is only one cure for the stresses of the purple. And I have no intention of dying just yet."

Death. Theodora was not young, but neither was she slowed by a crooked back or gout-riddled joints. And in death, she had hit upon an equally uncomfortable subject as Belisarius' shame.

Breathing deeply, Theodora used a silk cloth to dab at sweat along her forehead before re-affixing her diadem. Satisfied, she turned her attentions back to me.

"I hold authority as long as I am seen to be authoritative," she mused. "As a woman, competence is not enough to hold loyalty in the Empire. Patricians must fear my wrath, and plebeians understand that I shall protect the weak."

At this, I gathered courage to guess at her intended subject. "Antonina is no plebeian, and far from weak."

"But you are incorrect!" Theodora cried. "Antonina may be the daughter of a consul and the child-bearing wife of a beloved general, but it makes little difference. In the eyes of our society, Antonina is a woman. Aside from the few coins she possesses from Basilius' will, Antonina is one ill-fated month from penury and beggary. Our history shows this to be true."

"I do not understand, Highness," I said. "I have sworn to provide Antonina comfort, regardless of cost in coin or in favor with my friends."

"And you have my gratitude," Theodora replied. "But Antonina is also one of my attendants. I will not allow Belisarius to divorce her."

"Highness!" I gasped.

Though all who knew of Antonina's plight understood that its conclusion would be difficult, I doubt any other than Theodora would have guessed that that conclusion would be a painful reunion with her spurned husband. Having witnessed Belisarius' pain, I certainly had not. To remain married after such infidelity defied a thousand years of Roman custom and deprived Belisarius of his most basic legal recourse.

"Do not worry, Varus," Theodora added. "I will not ask you to deliver the message to Belisarius, for that would be exceedingly cruel."

I struggled for words, finding little justice, let alone sense, in Theodora's ruling. "Highness, Belisarius will be ridiculed for this. This is no misunderstanding—both Belisarius and I discovered Antonina in the embrace of her lover."

"I appreciate your opinion, and I understand the facts of Antonina's charge," Theodora said. "But my judgment is unmoved. I cannot allow a daughter of Basilius, one of my closest allies, to be condemned to disgrace and penury. There will be discomfort, but Antonina may yet find redemption should Belisarius forgive her."

Antonina regretted her actions—if not at first, then certainly by now. But that did not absolve her of such dishonesty, such wanton betrayal of the noblest man the Empire had produced in generations. Theodora might have been Antonina's patron, but Roman law was clear: As an aggrieved husband, Belisarius could do with Antonina as he wished. Banishment. Penury. Enslavement. Worse, even, though I doubted that either Belisarius or Theodora had the stomach to see Antonina physically punished. No, not like me or Rosamund. The lashes upon my back itched as frustration against Antonina bubbled in my throat.

"Highness, this is wrong!" I cried, momentarily losing my check on my emotions before my oath keeper. "Belisarius has legal rights— by the old customs and the new laws!"

"And if he, or you, or any other man betrayed his wife for the bed of another woman, what would the law say then?" Theodora scowled. "Nothing. Nothing at all. I do not absolve Antonina of her sins, but I would give her a chance to live in peace and raise her daughter."

It was true—significantly less recourse would be available to an aggrieved wife. A Roman woman could petition for divorce only if her husband had been a proven adulterer within the same town where his wife lived, or if the husband had committed the unforgiveable crimes of sacrilege or treason. Abuse, even wrathful abuse, was tolerated, and few women achieved divorce even with proof of their husband's infidelity. Liberius had gleefully lectured on how divorce had been commonplace in the pagan Republic, requiring only seven witnesses to separate man and wife. Caesar himself had been thrice married and once divorced, while many aspiring to membership in the Imperial family would cast aside their spouse for some niece or nephew of the sitting emperor. Alas, for better or worse, much had changed with the spread of Christianity and Justinian's law.

"The law is still the law," I countered cautiously. "And Belisarius was publicly aggrieved. He has standing."

Theodora's scowl turned a light shade of crimson. "Belisarius has nothing that I do not grant him. Law or no, this is my will."

"Augusta," I protested, with even less vim than before. "Belisarius and the men won't like this…"

Theodora stood, her body seeming to expand like a great bird of prey unfurling its wings. I knew instantly that I had pushed her too far.

"If I cared for the opinions of the men, I would have fled like a rat during the riots!" she yelled. "You call me Augusta, though I have warned you repeatedly to speak to me as a friend in private. But have it your way, for now. As Augusta of this Empire, will you execute my will?"

Blazing eyes burned through me, cutting across the tangled mass of conflicting oaths within my heart. Theodora's anger was not unknown to me. However, I had only ever seen it delivered to another, and now I squirmed from its sting. Even though I knew the law agreed with my response, I wanted to apologize, to kneel at Theodora's feet. She was half my size, but in her presence, I always felt tiny. Even more so than as a child with Justin. And though I felt for Belisarius and believed Theodora's position utterly wrong against Roman law, which all sworn warriors fought to uphold, I acceded. Even though that same basket of laws had seen me flogged and Rosamund nearly scorched to death.

"You have my oath, Highness," I responded. "Tell me what you wish, and I will see it done."

At that, Theodora deflated. She resumed her seat, exhaling deeply and retaining her stern gaze.

"I know." Again, she teased at a sore temple. "But you are not a woman, and do not easily understand why I have influenced my husband's laws. If I abandon Antonina, I am a hypocrite and a weakling. With enemies like Cassiodorus inflicting harm upon you and Jakob's followers, I cannot sit passively any further."

I bowed. "May I ask a favor of you?"

"Speak your desire, and see it fulfilled."

Reluctant as I was to entangle myself further, I continued. "Let me be the one to speak with Belisarius. This ruling should not be delivered by a slave, but by a friend."

Theodora bobbed her head ever so slightly, making the pearls atop her diadem dance and clink. She closed her eyes. "Your honesty and loyalty do you credit. You have my blessing to speak with Belisarius, but please do so today. I would give him and Antonina both ample time to decide what should happen before the voyage to Italy."

I saluted, then crouched to collect my armor. As I slipped the polished metal over my head, I inadvertently yelped as the brass rim to the iron chest piece scraped across my scabbed back. Theodora jolted forward, as though ready to inspect my body for any sign of distress.

"Nothing to be worried about, Highness," I insisted. "Just another month of stretched and uncomfortable skin."

She ignored me. "Turn around. The least I can do is help you dress."

Again, Theodora surprised me with her dexterous handling of the straps. Each knot was secured within moments, with her watchful eye searching for any loose or uncomfortable fit. There was none, for she could have outshone any camp servant or even Agathias in such a duty. With my armor reassembled, I turned to leave and execute my duty. Halfway to the closed door, however, Theodora stopped me.

"Do you think he will forgive Antonina?"

I considered my answer. "I am not certain," I began. "It would make him look a fool before the men. But forgiveness is Belisarius' instinct."

"Bugger the men." Theodora smiled. "With a little more forgiveness, we would all live more prosperous lives."

With another salute, I departed the hall. I did not wish to tarry in my responsibility, nor would I need to make any delay. For Belisarius spent much of his days in the palace, and I had no difficulty in seeking out his offices. Outside his closed door, I discovered Marcellus sitting next to one of Belisarius' bucellarii, with both men appearing bored, almost ready to doze.

Marcellus groaned as he stretched his back. "Anything new, Varus? It's heartening to see you rushing about again," he said. With thinning hair and a body scarred by multiple wounds, he was not yet elderly but lacked the vigor of youth. From what I heard from other excubitores, Marcellus was well aware of his limitations, though I doubt such self-knowledge yielded much comfort. Excubitores rarely died peacefully, and infirmity left the komes excubitorum a bit slower in his reaction to nearby threats. Marcellus was once one of the fastest blades in the Empire, yet now I worried whether he could set aside his pride and allow one of the younger men to hoist the burden of fighting off possible attackers. From what I knew of him, I doubted it.

"Too much is new," I replied. "And what is new is rarely a welcome omen for spearmen. Is Belisarius in?"

Marcellus nodded and rattled a gloved fist against Belisarius' door. Not waiting for a response, he then turned the iron knob, muttering to the room's occupant. With Belisarius thus forewarned of my arrival, Marcellus allowed me to slip inside before locking the door once more.

Belisarius greeted me. "Apologies, Varus. Justinian insists upon securing my presence against assassins when I am alone."

"As long as he allows you to move freely about." Of that, I was skeptical, my thoughts briefly turning to the Emperor's questioning of Belisarius' loyalty.

Settling on an empty bench along Belisarius' table, I again took stock of the man. His beard remained uncharacteristically full and laced with gray, though he was little older than thirty. He seemed thin, with ill-fitting clothing and dark-rimmed eyes. Nevertheless, his demeanor was far warmer than I had known in the months following Carthage, and I could only hope his wellness would soon follow.

"Any update on Indulf?" he asked.

"Not yet," I replied. "But that's not why I have come."

Belisarius' eyes narrowed, but he nodded nonetheless. "Nothing terrible, I pray?"

I clenched my fist to still a jittery leg and plunged ahead. "Lord, there is no painless option to present to you this new decree, so I will inform you plainly. The Empress is blocking your request for divorce."

Little reaction from Belisarius. A hand scratching at a slowly curling beard, a small shuffle in his seat. Eventually, however, he shattered the silence. "How long have you known?"

"I was told just now, Lord." I found myself suddenly desperate that he should believe me. "Theodora was planning to send a servant, but I volunteered to deliver this knowledge to you."

"Why would you do that?" he muttered, and fixed me with unblinking eyes. Once, I thought, the hint of suspicion in his gaze would have been utterly foreign to the magnanimous general.

I struggled to meet his eyes. "Because, Lord, I would not want such uncomfortable news given to you by one who does not cherish your friendship. Better to hear it from an ally, who wishes to blunt the pain where possible."

Another pause, and a further gaze of frustration. However, he nodded, as if understanding, at least, my motive for telling him myself. "I thank you for your candor. Do you know why Theodora would inflict this shame upon me?"

I did my best to explain Theodora's motives, without betraying her trust. She had not forbidden me from such measures, although an even more compelling twang of guilt shot through my gut as I noted Theodora's need to support those women who had been her companions and attendants, regardless of their sins. Belisarius soaked all of it in, breathing growing heavy, making no sound beyond popping his knuckles.

"If only Justinian would do the same for me," he muttered when I finished.

I frowned. "You wish me to seek the Emperor's favor in this matter?"

"No," Belisarius grunted. "That is not what I meant at all."

He tore his eyes away from me and stared blankly at the table, jaw clenched, chest rising and falling as if winded from exertion. Though little had been said, the aura of tension emanating from Belisarius was palpable, and left me at a total loss for how to comfort my friend. All I could do was wait.

"Did she make other demands of me, our Empress?" he asked at last.

"Only that your household remain intact, with Antonina in it," I replied. "Theodora made it plain that the degree of your interactions with Antonina are your affairs alone."

"For now," Belisarius muttered.

I nodded, again unable to offer reassurance. Belisarius fell silent for several minutes, making the room feel uncomfortably warm. My scabs itched along my back, but I resisted squirming against the bench. Thankfully, Belisarius soon released me from my burdens.

"You have my thanks for speaking with me directly on this," Belisarius said, his features as broken and frustrated as I remembered in Carthage. "Truly, Varus, I know of your desire to help me, and it means a great deal. I also know you struggle to please two oath masters—the Empress, and myself. Let alone the Emperor, who I must satisfy. If it eases your burdens, I would release you from your oath to me."

"Never, Lord!" The words came without thinking, without even a heartbeat considering what it would mean to undo my tangled web of obligations. "Before Callinicum, you spoke to me of our shared dreams, of struggling to build peace and plenty from suffering and darkness. Despite everything, I believe that still. I will follow you into whatever hell the Emperor seeks for us to conquer."

At that, Belisarius slackened, his jaw unclenching and shoulders falling. "Thank you, Varus. I still believe in what I shared with you. In many ways, it is one of the few things that stirs my blood onward, despite it all."

"You still have friends, Lord," I added. "Many of them—more than just me—would do anything for you."

"That too." He smiled. "But I would ask a final burden of you and you alone."

I nodded, suspecting I knew what Belisarius would ask.

"I wish for Antonina to remain in Constantinople, in your household," he said. "While the city is less safe than I would prefer, it is best this way. I will provide a full twenty spearmen to guard her, and will cover their cost as well as her own from my own purse."

"Of course, Lord," I said. "Although I should note my own family will be taking the journey to Italy. There will only be a few servants lingering behind to maintain my property and affairs until we return to the capital once more."

"No matter."

A thought pricked my conscience, and I hesitated even to raise it—but, as a father, I knew I could not stay silent. "And of what of Joannina?" I asked. "Would you like her to join my children on the voyage ahead? Mariya would love to care for her," I added, praying this was true.

Belisarius sighed, closing his eyes. For a moment, I thought I spied tears welling, but it disappeared as Belisarius concentrated upon his response. "I wish more than anything for her to accompany me. God knows, my greatest regret is spending such little time with my only child."

"Of course." That, I understood all too well.

"But I could not deprive a young girl of her mother," Belisarius concluded. "That would be selfish—cruel, even. So, no, I will allow her to remain in Constantinople. I can only hope that our war will conclude quickly, and I can retire in peace."

"Retire, Lord?"

Belisarius smiled. "You and I would be terrible farmers, Varus, but what a blessed life it would be. Yes, retire—one day, God willing. But until then, I thank you for giving me this information, even if its contents bring little joy. Go, and do what you can to keep our war a brief and decisive one."

The notion of retirement stirred something within me. What a dream, a miraculous dream, where pain and duty were washed clean with the honesty of simple work. As I departed the palace, I prayed that God might honor Belisarius' wishes, and that as with Persia and the Vandals, our conflict would end soon, and with a positive outcome.

Privately, however, I knew neither Belisarius nor I believed that fate was likely. In this, at least, I would not be wrong.

THE GHOST OF ISAACIUS

After I departed from my unhappy meetings with Theodora and Belisarius, life turned to our final preparations for war. So many familiar motions and orders, repeated from past expeditions, ones with now-dead friends and healthier, younger bodies. Yet at the same time, the looming invasion of Italy seemed altogether different—though that recurring sensation of dread and exhaustion was ever present, a new sliver of excitement at touching Italian soil could not be denied. Unlike past campaigns, we truly would strike for Rome's ancestral heartland. Whether we lived or died, the Empire would return to Italy, after so many years of being severed from the Imperial homeland.

There was time to prepare for our voyage, though not enough for leisure. Instead, each day was crammed with movement, rushing from the palace to the markets, from churches to the docks, all to carry out the impossible task of keeping to Procopius' timetable. At times, I wanted to seize the secretary's writing instruments and snap them over my knee, freeing thousands from their merciless demands for thoroughness. Alas, I never did.

Instead, between sessions of prayer with Petrus and preparing my family for their journey ahead, I fulfilled Belisarius' requests in altering the voyage's intended route. Antonina was informed of Theodora's decree and Belisarius' subsequent acquiescence—something she appeared to already know and which offered her some measure of relief. She was grateful to remain with her daughter but voiced concern at being abandoned in Constantinople.

"Belisarius does not want me in Italy?" she said, half pouting and half questioning.

"No, Lady," I responded. "He will provide for your welfare and security, but his wishes are clear in this regard."

She nodded, her face haggard from a lack of sleep. "It is better than most outcomes, I assume. But will he ever call me back to his side?"

I shrugged. "God grants an infinite array of possibilities in life. As for Belisarius, I would not press the matter with him for some time."

Antonina rolled her eyes before abruptly adjusting her posture. "I should not complain. Thank you, Varus, for all that you have done."

Her gratitude left me relieved but not totally unburdened from the requirements thrust upon me as Belisarius' second. This included conferring with Indulf, who was still incensed by the death of Amalasuntha. He gnashed his teeth at the opportunity to seize Syracuse from Theodahad as we shared a cup of wine in a nearby barracks.

"Syracuse's chieftain is my cousin." Indulf grinned. "Probably hates Theodahad more than I do. If you promise to leave his daughters and herds intact, I'll convince Syracuse to open to us like a pliant whore."

"Just grant us unopposed access to the docks, and I will do the rest," I said. "Are you certain he will keep our secret?"

Indulf snorted. "As I said, he hates Theodahad. From what I have heard, the Sicilian Goths and Latins have been taxed to the point of exsanguination. If he does anything but welcome you with an embrace, I'll hang myself from the nearest dromon mast."

"Very well," I concluded. "How will you inform him of our arrival?"

Indulf looked about the room, considering his strategy. "Get me twenty gold pieces," he said at last. "I'll send a man on the fastest vessel to Corinth. From there, he will gain passage on a trading cog to Syracuse. Even with a war, trade between the two cities is considerable."

Though I had no great love for Indulf, neither had I any reason to doubt his conviction. Up to that moment, the Ostrogoth warlord had led the largest segment of foederati against the Vandals, Mauri, and Visigoths, never shirking from a battle. I loathed his cruelty and tendency to buck against command, but he had not been cowed nor bribed into treachery, even after suffering terrible burns to his face in a duel with Agila. For that, Indulf had gained a measure of trust from me, and from Belisarius.

I was no fool, however. Along with an ample purse of golden coins from the Imperial Treasury, I also secured from Narses a half-Gothic translator to accompany Indulf's designated courier. Indulf did not begrudge me this, and even showed gratitude for the further support, but he was not naïve enough to believe my gesture to be one of goodwill. By nightfall, both men were granted berths upon the swiftest vessel in Constantinople's harbor. With luck, they would reach Syracuse a full fortnight ahead of Belisarius' armada.

Even amidst the anxious hustle of those days, there were moments of temporary bliss. Perenus' wedding was one such affair, even as it was a simple gathering with little grandeur. Though Petrus chastised Perenus for his ungallant tryst with Hereka—and reprimanded him for his deficient Christianity—the old priest still agreed to marry the expectant parents, reasoning it was better for their child to be born in the sanctity of wedlock.

Perenus' wedding was an inexpensive affair, for although he was an exiled Lazic prince, Perenus never cared for pomp, and the Vandals always held a distaste for the garish, stuffy rituals common across the Empire's churches and government buildings. Instead, what coin was mustered was used upon the feast to gather great hunks of mutton and fat hen, accompanied by ponderously large amphorae of wine.

Many attended, and I was joined by many of my household as well as Sindual and Fulcaris from the Herulian foederati. The excubitores Marcellus and Chanaranges, too, sat in witness of the rushed nuptials, although they swiftly departed after Petrus concluded the ceremony, allowing the old priest to safely accompany them rather than join in upon the wanton behavior to come. Even Rosamund attended, although she was still weak and could move only with the assistance of Agathias.

As the bride, Hereka was supported by Gunderic and other Vandal kinsmen, although most of the Vandal warriors skipped the religious vows in favor of arriving for a celebratory ceremony of wine and roasted chicken in a tavern near the Valens aqueduct.

"I don't think there's been a religious ceremony I haven't fallen asleep in." Wisimar chuckled, midway through gorging himself on the succulent and spiced juices of a meaty leg. "More respectful to show up later, right?"

"Lazy bastard!" Gunderic roared, before turning to me with a whisper: "I wish I would have thought of that excuse."

Perenus relaxed, his bride's honor contented thanks to his elevated status as an excubitor. It was a happy distraction for one of my oldest, dearest friends—even if he drank himself into so violent a stupor that he urinated along a tavern wall and collapsed upon a table dressed in fragrant chicken meat. Hereka rushed to her husband's side, smacking him firmly on the back with a thud.

"Wake up!" she screamed. "Are you hurt?"

"Not hurt, just snoring like an ox!" Cephalas chortled, wine dribbling down his chin.

And so he was. Great ponderous snores, rattling the table with every rush of air into and out of his body. It was a careless display for any wedding, let alone one's own, and I saw Mariya wrinkling her nose, though it was predictable for Perenus. Were I still a simple dekarchos, perhaps I would have joined him in drunken revelry, but now, my elevated status as Belisarius' second, Theodora's ringbearer, and Mariya's husband had thrice raised me above such wanton debauchery. Nevertheless, while I outwardly shook my head at Perenus' behavior, I inwardly giggled mightily.

Gunderic placed a heavy palm upon Hereka's shoulder. "My

dear, I hate to be the one to inform you, but it looks like you will not be able to consummate your marriage tonight."

Mariya gasped. "Gunderic!"

Hereka slapped him across the face, causing the giant Vandal to weep with laughter. Where most Roman women would have cringed with embarrassment, however, Hereka joined in his mirth, leveling a closed fist into Perenus' gut. Coughing, Perenus rolled over, smashing scraps of chicken and smearing all manner of detritus along his back. Then, recoiling like a serpent, a great fountain of violet streamed from his mouth, ejecting what must have been two full skins of wine.

"Wake up, you great bag of pig shit!" Hereka said, slapping him across the face. Nearby, a dozen Vandals bellowed with humor, with many choking from laughing so hard.

Perenus shuddered, raising both arms as if prepared to exchange blows with an unseen enemy. Yet, his defenses were too slowed by drink to deflect Hereka's assault, and her fingers audibly smacked his wine-soaked beard. Mariya jumped at the sound, though even she was forced to suppress a chuckle as Hereka scolded her useless husband. Raising his head, Perenus sniffed like a rat, adjusting his eyes to the light. "What day is it?"

Kneeling to put my face level with his, I grinned. "Your wedding!"

"Oh!" He grinned back. "I didn't miss it!"

I had mere seconds to scurry away as Perenus' face contorted once more for another bout of vomiting.

Rosamund howled with laughter. Mariya, however, was less amused, frowning at Rosamund and Perenus alike. "Disgusting!"

"Quite," I replied, kicking my boot free from the few flecks of undigested wine that splattered my foot. As Perenus wiped his mouth upon his sleeve, I handed him a cup of water, which he drank greedily.

"You hold your wine like a gelded priest!" Hereka scolded, grasping her husband's shoulder. Before Perenus could mount a response, she dabbed a kiss atop his forehead and lifted the drunken warrior from his filthy perch. "But you're my responsibility now!"

Perenus stumbled, unable to hold himself upright even with Hereka's support. Fulcaris rushed over, grabbing Perenus' other arm to aid the bride with her duties.

"I'm your responsibility," Perenus slurred, "and I might be a terrible drunk, but I swear I'm not gelded!"

"I know," Hereka shot back. "I didn't marry you for your intelligence, after all."

God, but I was happy that night. With only a few cups of wine, the cares of the Empire faded into the corner of my awareness, allowing me to enjoy the company of Mariya and my friends. Regardless of the callousness or the indignity of Perenus and the Vandals, it felt good to be surrounded by friends in celebration instead of mourning.

The celebration ended all too soon, however, and our gathering dispersed into a frigid late-winter night. Many Vandals continued to another tavern, joined by Fulcaris and Sindual, who urged that I join them in their merriment.

"Act like a man for one evening!" Wisimar beamed, swaying on his feet.

"Aye, Varus," Fulcaris added. "You can abandon your worries until the morning."

I shook my head. "I'm not nearly as young, or as entertaining, as I used to be. Go, and enjoy yourselves."

Groaning with animated disappointment, the foederati bounded away with a noisy song, uncaring whether Cassiodorus' agents or an opportunistic cutpurse should hear their drunken march. My own small party—Mariya, Cephalas, Xerxes, Sembrouthes, Agathias, and Rosamund—departed together, with all but Agathias, Xerxes, and Sembrouthes numbed by the wine.

Immediately after separating from the larger cohort of celebrants, however, something made me shiver—the sensation of being watched. Though it was by now very late, there were still several men rummaging about the city streets, although far fewer than might have done so in prior years. Most staggered from inebriation and posed little threat, but as I scanned the adjoining alleyways, I choked from fear, crashing to a sudden halt.

Isaacius. Even in the gloom of an overcast night, even with my senses blunted from drink, even forty paces distant, the bearded face was as I remembered it from our doomed stand against the mist-strewn Avars.

Just as quickly as he appeared, however, he slipped back into the maze of city streets.

"Wait!" I screamed, and I sprinted off in search of him.

Hardly missing a beat, Sembrouthes sprinted alongside me, finding little difficulty in keeping pace in full armor due to his sobriety. "What did you see?"

"Lazarus," I muttered.

"What?" Sembrouthes shouted, but my focus was solely upon the alley entrance, and I had no time to explain the Bible's tale of a simple man resurrected from death.

Soon, we reached the intersection of street and alley. But nothing remained to greet us, save a stray dog rummaging through refuse and the ever-present horde of rats that colonized every corner of the Empire's capital. Cautious, Sembrouthes drew his blade, gazing into the darkness to seek any threat. I am not certain what I wished to find—the spirit of my slain friend? A flustered plebeian whose only crime was a resemblance to Isaacius? Or nothing at all?

Regardless, nothing was all we discovered. "You are sure you saw something?" Sembrouthes asked.

"I think so," I muttered, not daring to blink as I affixed my eyes upon the alley's exit.

"Well, if you did, they aren't here now." Sembrouthes sheathed his sword. "Let's leave this place before something truly does come to seek us out."

When I returned to the group, Mariya questioned my sudden departure. Though I insisted it was nothing more than anxiety and a mistaken flicker of torchlight, Rosamund eyed me with suspicion. I dared not speak my suspicions to her or Cephalas, for I had no proof, and to mention our fallen comrade would only cause them pain.

Along with Perenus, we had all befriended Isaacius in our brief time together, and all mourned his unjust death on a broken battlefield. I could feel my heart pounding against the bones beneath my chest as I strove for calm, but found little in the gloom of night.

Instead, we proceeded downhill, toward a more well-lit thoroughfare that led eastward to the safety of our rooms. As we reached the broader road, however, Rosamund insisted upon an alternate course.

"Lead us west, just for a few minutes," Rosamund instructed Agathias. "We can return home shortly."

"That's in the opposite direction, and not safe for the two of you at night," I called, eager to steal Rosamund to the safety of my home. "Can this wait until the morrow?"

Rosamund shook her head, directing a hapless Agathias as if goading a reluctant ox to till a field. He obeyed, however, either from an utter devotion to Rosamund as his teacher or a fear of her abilities and beliefs as some kind of witch.

"Sembrouthes, Cephalas, can you return Mariya to our building?" I asked.

Sembrouthes nodded, though Mariya complained, her face lined with a bemused smile from her own drunkenness. "Why can't I join? I want to go too."

"I would rather you did not, Princess," Sembrouthes said. "Same with Rosamund, but I have no authority there. Varus and Xerxes will provide sufficient protection against brigands for a smaller group."

"Fine," Mariya groaned. Rushing toward me, Mariya surprised me with a wet kiss, her hands tugging forcefully against the collar of my shirt. Separating before I could react, she smiled at me. "Come back soon," she whispered.

Wine may reduce men to beasts, but I needed little intoxication to yearn for her. I nearly called Mariya back to me, but after a sideways glance at Rosamund's melancholy visage, I placed passion aside for an hour. Instead, watching Mariya depart, I joined my remaining three companions as we followed Rosamund's direction.

"West," Rosamund said. "Just for a short while."

Our pace was little more than a trudge. Only Xerxes remained sober, while I glanced down every street and avenue for a trace of an otherworldly stalker. Rosamund still required assistance walking, reducing our progress to half of a casual jaunt. It was pleasant, however, with a breeze prickling our skin as it flooded the streets from the Sea of Marmara. Eventually, though, Rosamund suggested a deviation from our present course, and I recognized her intended destination.

Keeping my voice hushed for fear of thieves or cutthroats, I begged her to turn back. "We have no reason to go back to Bovis, Rosamund!"

Xerxes' muscles tensed, while Agathias slowed his pace, but Rosamund was determined to progress onward. "Then go back. I can care for myself."

"Rosamund!" I hissed—still to no avail.

Rosamund quickened her hobbling, although never rose to more than a mild walk. No quantity of pleading could convince her of the futility of returning to such a barbarous place; she was deaf to all but her own intentions. Slowly, but all too soon, the road widened into an opening of the Bovis Forum, illuminated only by a dozen torches and an occasional light from a nearby building.

"We've made it," I said. "Can we go back now?"

Rosamund shook her head angrily. "Not yet. If I am inconveniencing you, *you* can depart at any time, however."

Her words struck deep in my fogged mind. "Of course not, Rosamund," I said softly. "I just believe this to be dangerous."

"Perhaps." But she did not slow her progress.

There was little movement in the Bovis Forum at that hour. More rats, more dogs, and an occasional drunken sailor ambling back to the cheaper bunks by the Imperial docks. Where once thousands of braying citizens screamed for blood, all that remained was a vacant wooden dais. That, and the bronze bull.

Finally, Rosamund broke away from Agathias. He faltered, catching his balance before jolting forward to intercept Rosamund.

Made alert by Rosamund's display and seeking potential danger on the street, Xerxes rested a palm along the pommel of his curved dagger.

"We're being watched," he whispered to me in Persian. "Being here is asking for a confrontation with one of Cassiodorus' cronies, or worse."

"Keep watch," I replied, separating from Xerxes in a manic sprint. Though riddled with healed wounds, I had no trouble surpassing the younger and less athletic Agathias, his face awash with worry as he struggled forward. Rosamund was but a mere ten paces farther, seeming to ignore the pain in her limbs as she lurched closer to the bull.

Still out of my reach, Rosamund screamed. She slowed her pace to a trot, then bent down to pluck one of an uncountable number of stones that had been pried free from plodding hooves and thousands of boots from a day at the market. Once a week, teams of Imperial slaves would address any cracks and holes in the paved roadway, yet their work favored the wealthier fora closer to the palace. The Bovis Forum was a wicked place, and I doubt whether any slave master conducted repairs more often than once every couple of months. Given the choice, I certainly would not, for even at night the place stank of death.

Rosamund hurled the stone. The thing was no larger than a malnourished mouse, yet it cracked against the bull with a surprising clangor that would easily call the attention of any within a few hundred paces. As I caught up with her, Rosamund screamed again, an indecipherable torrent in the Gepid tongue spilling from her lips like venom. None of the words were comprehensible, yet I understood their meaning, and I wrapped my arms around her as she screamed and wept beneath the instrument of her torture.

Unsatisfied, she threw two more stones at the bull's head. After the second connected with the bull's snout, I wrapped Rosamund tighter in my embrace, bringing her to struggle in rage.

"Let me go, Varus!!" she shouted.

"Rosamund," I said, murmuring her name as though soothing a horse before battle. "It cannot hurt you any further."

"Let me go!!" She thrashed, and the back of a bony hand smacked me in the jaw.

Involuntarily, I stumbled, releasing Rosamund to her desired freedom. At first unsteady, she soon regained her balance and knelt to pluck another stone from the muck-riddled road. At that distance, she could not miss her target, spewing a litany of Gepid curses as she raged to the point of hyperventilation. Rosamund struggled for breath as she cried, and I dared to walk alongside her once more. This time, however, she turned to embrace me, her arms too stunted to fully wrap about my torso as she slowed her breathing. I returned the gesture, placing my palms upon her back and urging her to calm herself.

"It's over," I promised. "I won't let anything like that happen again."

Xerxes interrupted Rosamund's catharsis with an urgent growl in Persian. "Arrivals."

Three men had joined the forum. Two walked together, their coarse wool hoods discernible even in that darkness as those favored by the priests of the Empire's hinterlands. A third man, also hooded, stood along the forum's periphery, although he made no motion to join the other two. I cursed inwardly—it was foolish to assume Cassiodorus' men would not have my movements watched, regardless of the lateness of the hour. As they approached, all I could think was how much treasure this fresh encounter might sap from me, even as I raised a hand for Xerxes to still his blade.

As the closer two men approached, one threw back his hood, revealing Philip, Andronicus' disciple. He appeared pleased with himself, as if rejoining a long-departed friend.

"Lord Varus, come to pay homage to justice?" He beamed. "I did not think you had any further coins to pay anything, but I am happy to be wrong in this case."

I opened my mouth to retort, but it was sober Xerxes who

countered first. "Priest, we have no quarrel with you, but nor are you a friend. I suggest you leave now, for our affairs do not concern you."

Xerxes' cadence was slow, deliberate, with a songlike quality. His accent, which any speaker of Latin or Greek would recognize as a native Persian, seemed a touch ominous, which suited Xerxes' purposes all too well: Philip paused, eying the Zhayedan's hand resting atop an ornate scabbard.

After a moment, however, the priest resumed his taunting. "Destroying Imperial property, or attempting to destroy it, is a grave offense," Philip continued. "And half of the Empire understands that you and your witch have a grudge with the Brazen Bull."

Rosamund, wiping her face from tears, glared at her enemy. Before I could think to hold her still, she lurched forward, jerking forth like something malevolent and inhuman in the darkness. She stopped a handbreadth from Philip's face and looked up at the man who stood half a head taller than her.

"You think you have power," she said, glowering. "And with your little boys following you in the daylight, perhaps you do. But the night is my domain, and from what Varus tells me, your God does not protect the cowardly and the wicked. So, tell me again what you intend to inflict upon me."

Philip's smile disappeared. Taking slow steps forward, I tried to pry Rosamund away from the man, yet she would not have moved even if Gunderic had been there to haul her away with all of his strength. At last, Philip cocked his head and responded.

"You belong to the flames, witch. You were spared only because your master has something that we need more than your early descent to Hell. One day, you will be placed back inside of this great harbinger of justice, and I will light the pyres myself." He whistled, flashing his teeth in a grin that was soon extinguished.

Rosamund had reached into her belt and pried a needle loose from its moorings, one she typically used to knit torn flesh together. Now, though, she held it steady in one hand, raising a finger from the other to eye level. As Philip watched, eyes wide, she pressed the needlepoint to the pad of her finger's flesh, tiny red droplets escaping the open wound as she returned the needle to its holster.

"You seem to desire my blood," Rosamund began, her uninjured hand grazing her body. "Or maybe something else? I have seen you hunger for my body. I cannot abide you having my body, but I shall make you a gift to sate your lust."

She slashed her bloody finger at Philip's cheek, leaving a thin streak above the man's beard. Yelping, he leaped backward, touching his face with a slackened jaw. "You would curse me?!"

Rosamund laughed. "You are a fool." She turned her back on both priests, beckoning me to follow. "And none of us desecrated your infernal monument. We merely attempted to use a few stones to discourage cats from making their homes atop its body. Right, Varus?"

She elbowed me in the ribs when I was slow to agree.

"R-Right!" I stammered, looking over my shoulder at a stunned Philip and his confused companion. "Damned cats are everywhere. Pissing on everything."

But Philip was unconvinced—furious, in fact, for the first time in my memory. "One word from me, and Cassiodorus will have both of you hanged!" he screeched. "Even if you fuck the Empress, Lord Varus!"

Xerxes tensed again, but I merely chuckled—half confused, half amused. Philip raged further, lashing out with whatever condemnation he could grasp, but I did not rise to the accusation, and Rosamund only cackled at his sorry attempts at insults… until his shouting ceased with a sudden thud.

At first, I thought Xerxes or Agathias had finally struck the interloper. Philip's friend appeared to think as much and raised his arms to defend against further attack. Philip, meanwhile, moaned in pain, twirling on his feet as he clasped at the back of his head.

"Cease!" I yelled to Xerxes.

"It was not me," Xerxes said, alarmed and turning to Agathias. "Neither of us."

Within moments, a second stone flew, striking Philip in the back of his leg—and clearly sent from the far end of the forum. As Philip's comrade turned to meet their attacker, I finally realized: The third man was not one of Cassiodorus' followers, but instead the same hooded figure I had spied before. Because, with his hood now fallen back, a nearby torch illuminated one side of his face, and I once again saw him.

Isaacius. Not spirit, but flesh.

"Stop dawdling!" Philip castigated his companion. "Seek a town guard and seize that man! He will be whipped until his ribs shine in the sun."

Rosamund laughed again. "As I said, you have a strange hunger. I thank you for humoring me."

She turned back to us, her friends, and patted me on the shoulder. "We can leave now."

"An excellent idea," Xerxes said in Persian, his eyes wide with worry. "Let's leave before their guards come, or Cassiodorus' men decide to act upon their threats."

With that, we all departed—Philip nursing a wounded head and bounding after his comrade, their attacker far swifter, and disappearing into the city, sprinting northward and away from our intended road. As for our party, our progress was faster than before, and though still sodden with drink, the mood overall seemed far more contented. Rosamund in particular smiled to herself, ignoring the obvious pain of each step as we wove homeward toward our haven. For a while, no one spoke, but I soon found I could no longer keep private what I had witnessed three times in the past few days.

"Rosamund," I whispered, supporting her weight as she hobbled forward. "I saw Isaacius."

Confusion registered, then she shook her head. "Too much wine, Varus. Isaacius died in Tauris."

"I know—that's the thing!" I hissed. "I did not believe it myself, but he has now appeared three times. He was the one who cast the stone at Philip!"

Rosamund was silent a moment. "I wish it were so, but that is not what you saw, Varus. It cannot be. Isaacius died a terrible, unnecessary death. I can only pray to my gods that he knows peace in whatever afterlife his people strive for."

"But it *could* be," I insisted. "I never saw the killing stroke."

Rosamund, however, would not brook further discussion, instead demanding that I gain sleep and a fresh mind to wash away impossible thoughts. Seeing as we were nearly home, I ceased my argument, now much less certain of what I had seen—what I could not *have* seen, according to all logic.

As we arrived safely at my residence, two Aksumites and a half dozen of Belisarius' bucellarii acknowledged our passage, the latter assuming duties intended to safeguard Belisarius' dishonored wife. Leaving Xerxes to seek his own rest, Agathias and I helped Rosamund upstairs and to her quarters, pushing aside an overeager Haeva as she barked happily at our return. Despite her lingering injuries, Rosamund lay upon her bed with a measure of contentment I had not seen in many months.

"Thank you, Varus," she whispered. Smiling to herself, she stared at her lofted ceiling as Agathias departed and I shut her door.

With my children long asleep but morning light still hours distant, I crept to my own quarters, unlatched the door, and slipped quietly inside. There was no need for such discretion, for a household of my stature seemed to rumble with activity at any hour of day or night due to the ceaseless tasks of cooking, cleaning, and the delivery of messages or goods. Still, I was reluctant to wake Mariya, who never could withstand strong drink, and I presumed had fallen asleep immediately upon returning home.

As I secured the door upon its latch, hands thrust me against the wall, bringing the door to rattle against its mooring. My chest took most of the blow, forcing me to wheeze for breath as those same hands reached for my waist, unfastening the iron rivet that held my sword belt in place. It, along with my dagger and sword, clattered onto the floor. Disoriented and winded, I reached down for my dagger, seeking to mount some defense in my assault, but an arm knocked my grasping fingers away, pressing me further into the wall.

"Tribune Varus," came the murmur in my ear. "Disarmed and defeated by a woman?"

The floral scent of her perfume was unmistakable. Relaxing, I grinned, although my pulse still pounded as Mariya pressed me harder into the wall. "I never claimed to be competent at my job."

"To my benefit," she whispered. Her hands drifted again to my hips as, in a whiplash, she turned me about. She leapt, wrapping her legs about my hips as her fingers ran through my hair, leaning her forehead against mine. She giggled, her usual perfume mingling with the rich taste of red wine as she grasped my chin to command another kiss. "Let's see if you have competence in other things."

PROMISES UNKEPT

Sleep was fleeting, and waking brought a pounding headache. My pains were remedied by a ponderous jug of cool water, although Mariya's headache seemed forged from a particularly mischievous imp.

"Never again," she moaned, burying her head in a feather pillow. "I'm never drinking wine again."

"That's a lie!" I teased her, poking her side. "I didn't think you consumed that much to begin with."

"More than enough." With a groan, she shot out of bed and vomited noisily into a nearby iron pot.

After so much sadness brought on by Cassiodorus, Mariya's casual happiness left me giddy and somehow lighter in my boots. Dressing, I rushed into the hallway to summon a passing servant, seeking honeyed water to ease Mariya's roiling innards. I caught sight of Jamila, who winked at her shirtless master as she went to fetch a breakfast of fruit and cheese for the children.

Others waited in the hallway, and I discovered Wazeba standing patiently at the far end of the hallway. "Lord, good, you are awake. Please dress and come downstairs when you are able."

Suddenly feeling ridiculous from my appearance and recovery from inebriation, my eyes widened. "Any problem? More of the priests have returned?"

"No," Wazeba replied, seemingly unconcerned. "Just a boy that insists upon speaking with you. Sembrouthes tried to send him away, but the lad refuses to leave before speaking with you alone."

"Did he offer his name?"

"No, though we asked," Wazeba added. "Do you wish me to toss him into the street? Might he be some assassin or a common thief?"

I shook my head. "Give me but a few moments, and I will address this myself."

Waiting until the honeyed water returned to me, I ferried the clay jug in to Mariya and poured a glass. She was in no condition to speak coherently, but moaned and complained of nausea. The only words other than curses that I could decipher were "children" and "clothes," leaving me to deduce their meaning.

"Jamila is with our children, and a servant will arrive with fresh clothing soon," I explained. "Wazeba says that I must attend to a visitor now, if you feel well enough to be left alone."

Mariya waved a hand in feeble dismissal, spitting into the iron basin. I donned a clean shirt and boots and headed to the lower level of my building, finding an interloper standing at the open threshold but not fully inside. A half dozen bucellarii stood guard while Sembrouthes blocked the lad's progress into our rooms, only moving aside to grant me view of my stubborn petitioner.

And I froze. For there again was the ghost of Isaacius, with baleful eyes and a thin beard masking an otherwise friendly face.

"Isaacius," I gasped.

The youth shook his head slowly, never breaking my gaze, as though studying my reaction as I came fully downstairs.

Sembrouthes glowered. "You know this urchin?"

"I will speak with him outside," I said.

Sembrouthes nodded. "I will follow. Not negotiable."

The false Isaacius, whoever he was, wordlessly stepped into the alley. I acquired a cloak from a servant and soon followed, trailed by Sembrouthes and two of his spearmen. They kept a respectful distance behind me, but never more than the length of a single fatal spear thrust if our visitor attempted violence. The biting morning air sobered my senses, still tainted with nausea, and I directed our party toward an adjoining street.

"You say you are not Isaacius," I began, "but you wear his face. Who are you, if not him?"

"My name is Shimon." His Greek was raspy, carrying a faint lilt that I recalled from my days in Mesopotamia. "Isaacius was my brother."

I frowned in suspicion but also at the realization that I knew so little of the friend who had saved my life in Moesia and Tauris. "How old are you? Isaacius would be nearly thirty, or even older than that?"

"Sixteen," Shimon murmured. "My mother had twelve children. Seven survived past their second year. My memories of Isaacius are vague, but he cared for us. He sent a few silver coins to our family after receiving his army pay."

We paced toward the Forum of Constantine. More black-cloaked followers of Cassiodorus glommed onto various stalls and platforms like crows, but few seemed interested in my presence. Above, ominous clouds portended rain to come, yet in the moment I enjoyed the open air and dry streets.

"Why have you come to Constantinople?" I asked. "Why now?"

Shimon tossed his head about, scratching his bearded chin as he replied. "Until recently, I supported my parents and siblings. Two years ago, my father's skull was broken by the kick of a frightened horse. It killed him before he even hit the ground. After that, my mother sold her body to help feed her family, but she acquired some pox and withered into nothingness. By then, my younger siblings had perished from starvation and flux, while my surviving older brothers and sisters departed to strike their own fortunes. None took me, and I sold what remained of my father's tools and earned a pittance as an oarsman on a trading vessel to Constantinople."

"That explains how you arrived here," I countered. "But little of why."

"I have nothing in this world," he said simply. "And my brother wrote a letter to our family that if ever we required aid, to seek out Varus the Herulian. My mother was too proud to seek the help of a stranger, but I have little choice otherwise. And so, I paid a few spearmen to help me identify you. Once I discovered your whereabouts, I followed you for the past month, watching your behaviors and actions."

I grunted. "A tedious task. I did see you—last night, and earlier when I visited the palace."

Shimon nodded. "And in the Bovis Forum. I handed you a bucket of water to free your servant. That is what convinced me that Isaacius spoke the truth of you, although I lacked the courage to introduce myself then."

He reached into his threadbare cloak, procuring a worn courier's tube. Sembrouthes lurched forward, as though the lad had drawn a weapon, but swiftly relaxed. As he untwisted the tube's stopper, Shimon suddenly stopped his pacing and gently slid a brittle parchment spotted with stains and watermarks. Curious, I said nothing, waiting for an explanation.

"To convince you of my identity, these are the last words that Isaacius sent to us, before he departed for Cherson," Shimon said.

I frowned. "Isaacius could not read letters, let alone write them."

Shimon nodded. "The letters are in the hand of an Imperial clerk. They'll transcribe and transfer messages for a few coppers. The words, however, are Isaacius'. He even left his mark at the bottom."

More closely inspecting the parchment, I unfurled the document to reveal three crude Latin letters, their lines ragged as if from an unsure hand. With a finger, I outlined Isaacius' name, and though a lingering doubt mixed in my heart, I knew the missive to be genuine. That, plus Shimon's uncanny resemblance, were enough ammunition to pierce through any misgivings. Accepting Shimon's tale of the letter's provenance, I read the clerk's transcription. It was a lengthy account, but a specific passage warranted rereading multiple times.

I have been promoted to the rank of dekarchos, or commander of ten of Rome's Thracian spearmen. My pay is higher now, and I have enclosed a bonus received from exploits in Moesia. My first command will be in Cherson, against one tribe or another. I was worried that my comrades would betray my trust and reveal me as a Jew, but instead I have discovered fast friends. To be honest, I am excited to venture beyond the sea with them and explore this distant land, and I have little doubt that such a vast Roman Army will have difficulty restoring order. Cephalas the Greek and Perenus of the Laz people are among my closest friends, serving with me against the Gepids. Both are honorable men.

But if I should fall in battle, seek out Varus the Herulian. Though a new centurion, Varus joined the army about the same moment as me. He is as honest a man as I have met throughout the Empire, and he will provide aid if called upon.

Not that I intend to die! There are far too many adventures ahead. Just know that I think of you, my family, on whatever land or sea I find myself.

Grief, anger, guilt, fatigue. I felt it all, that maelstrom of emotions that had ravaged my mind after Isaacius' needless death. And now, for a heartbeat, it hit me as if still fresh, and not separated by the veil of time. I returned the document to Shimon, and he slowly rolled the scroll into a tight spiral before sliding it into the tube to secure it from further exposure to sunlight or the impending rain.

In my melancholy, I finally discerned a clearer look at Shimon's face up close and without the shroud of darkness. The bushy beard and rounded jaw seemed identical to my faded memories from a decade prior, yet the lad clearly still possessed an unstained youth that had only just begun to harden from months at an oar. I did not know how to handle him, but I refused to allow him to suffer his brother's fate.

And so, I pressed Shimon further of what knowledge he knew of his brother's demise. "Do you know how your brother died?"

"In Tauris, from what I could gather," he replied calmly. "I also heard that you challenged the man responsible for Isaacius' death in single combat. They say he was a beast of a man."

I grunted. "Archelaus was his name. And he was a beast. But not uncommon, in the new Empire. Few have any love for Jews in the army. Your brother died because of it."

Shimon laughed. "Few have any love for Jews anywhere! Why would Italy be any different?"

At that, I wanted to shake him by his woolen collar so that he might understand. "Because you might be sent to a senseless, needless, hopeless death!" I cried. "And I won't be responsible for that. Not again." Thinking of the measure of his youth, I added, "And not for a boy. The last boy who followed me into battle died weeping and afraid at Tricamarum. I would spare you that fate, and me as well."

Shimon sighed, nodding. "I would not ask you to burden yourself. Cooking your food, scraping your parchment for writing, following you into battle, I will do whatever you ask. But I do not accept your refusal."

"Why?" I asked.

"Because." Shimon sighed again. "Isaacius' letter said I could trust you, if anything happened to him. If you send me back to Judea, I'll be beaten and starved to death by the local Romans either way. All I'm asking for is an opportunity to be something more than desperate and afraid, before the last coins in my possession are exhausted."

Noticing a swelling crowd of zealots in the Forum of Constantine, I beckoned Shimon and our entourage to meander back to the safety of our quarters. As we retraced our steps, I considered Shimon's pleas, searching for an opportunity to gracefully decline his burden. After Cassiodorus' so-called measure of justice, I could not afford another household dependent. Truthfully, I could not afford those who already called me lord. And allowing a Jew to serve in the Imperial Army carried grave consequences for those who tolerated such happenings—while such measures were rarely enforced under Justin, under Justinian, Jewish soldiers and those who abetted them could be stripped of their possessions and exiled to the desert wastes. Topping all of these worries was my firm reluctance to not contribute to another avoidable death, especially of a youth.

But as we closed the distance to my household, Isaacius' words burned into my heart. He had saved my life in Moesia, my first engagement with Rosamund's village, and I promised to return such blessings in kind, just as Xerxes swore a blood oath to do the same for me. To my torment, I had not been able to balance the ledger with Isaacius, but I could do so for his kin.

"If you enter my service, you will follow every command that I give," I began. "Even if that means that you should leave me to die on the side of a flooded road or depart my service in the middle of a frost-cursed night. This is an oath you cannot break."

Shimon nodded, the corners of his eyes creasing as he smiled. "I understand, Lord."

"While I do not begrudge you your faith," I continued, "there are others that do, and would happily punish both you and I for it. I would ask for your discretion."

Another vigorous nod. "Nothing I don't already do for survival, Lord. I understand, and as long as you are not forcing me to convert, I will be as silent as a corpse."

I grimaced at his choice of words, clumsy from eagerness and inexperience. "Then face me, so I may gain the measure of you."

Again, Sembrouthes tensed, but found no reason to intervene. As I had done with Rosamund so long ago, and many servants who followed in the years after, I administered the servant's oath to Shimon. He bobbed happily through it all, stumbling on the words as he enunciated each phrase with feverish force. As we concluded the oath, I embraced Shimon as my servant, obligation, and oath sworn follower, inviting him into my home.

"So we aren't going to skewer this little rat?" Sembrouthes said dryly.

"No, but you will put him to work," I said. "He will care for our weapons and armor as a start. Cephalas remains in command, but he would benefit from the assistance."

Turning to Shimon, I prodded one last inquiry. "Have you any possessions to haul? I can send men to ferry them here, for you will stay in the servants' quarters."

"Only what I am wearing, Lord," Shimon said, beaming. "I slept in a tanner's straw pile, and already paid the drunken fool."

"Good," I said. "You will bathe and eat heartily, and rest for the remainder of the day. But tomorrow, your duties will begin. Sembrouthes will provide you a basic education with weapons, but your task will be to maintain our armor and blades. Later, we can assess your fitness for further tasks."

"Absolutely, Lord!" Shimon replied. "You won't regret it. Anything you need."

"I may not regret it, but you might," I grumbled. "Go, fill your belly in the kitchens, and gain sleep while you can. The expedition to Italy is going to have few carefree nights for a long time."

With a bow, Shimon departed. Sembrouthes, still skeptical, whispered his doubts. "Is it wise to trust this stranger so quickly? What if he accepts a bribe? Plenty of greedy servants have poisoned their master's soup for a fistful of bronze coins."

I shook my head. "Not likely. His brother was a dear friend, who I owe my life to. If we treat Shimon well, he will return to us double in effort. Let Shimon be your first test pupil before instructing my children in war."

Sembrouthes nodded. "What of Agathias? Shall I instruct him too?"

I declined. "Agathias' talent is with his mind, not with arms. He may resent my decision, but it is a far safer path, and one more beneficial to Belisarius and the army. In time, he may become as adept as Rosamund."

"Perhaps." Sembrouthes grunted. "I would settle for serviceable. It'd be difficult to gain the wisdom of our Gepid friend, even in a decade."

The addition of a servant to our household was a common affair, and few took much notice of Shimon in the few days we remained in Constantinople. Mariya initially balked at my decision, although grudgingly accepted the added expense of the lad after I explained his bloodline and the unrequited promise I held to Shimon's long-dead brother.

"The expense..." Mariya whispered.

"Will be minor," I said in a hushed tone, though privately I worried at my mounting deficits. "And you asked for additional help with the household."

Mariya smirked, striking with a playful slap. "Don't you use my words against me, Varus."

Cephalas, on the other hand, embraced Shimon so aggressively that the lad looked to me in bewilderment, but still did not complain. That was perhaps Shimon's most persistent trait in the days that followed—whether facing tedium or suffering, unfairness or excessive burden, he did not complain. If anything, he would thank me for the privilege, asking if there were further opportunities to absorb more duties and advance himself in my standing.

And then there was Rosamund. She understood my weakness for the lad and recalled Isaacius fondly, but held a greater apprehension for my foundling.

"He may promise to keep silent, but Romans have a tendency to root out those who look different and speak in an accent offensive to their ears," she warned. "The kinder thing to do would be to give Shimon a bag of silver and send him east to Persia."

"Persia!" I chuckled. "In what age does that notion become sensible?"

Rosamund shrugged. "Xerxes and I speak of how the Persians tolerate other religions and peoples, and have done so for a thousand years. The Persian elite save their murder for one another, and tend to spare their people."

"That was not my experience." My bemusement turned to a growl, recalling my brief time alongside Fulcaris in Nisibis.

Rosamund raised a hand in apology. "Nevertheless, Shimon will never be safe with us. And I am not certain we will ever leave for something better."

"I need a young lad to help with my armor, especially with Cephalas less capable." I shook my head, unwilling to further engage on Rosamund's desire to escape the Empire. "Shimon understands the risk, otherwise he would not have abandoned his home to seek me out. All we can do is to take measures to safeguard him, and provide him with an opportunity to forge a future for himself."

"He isn't Isaacius," Rosamund murmured. "Just be sure to remember that."

I promised that I would, although in many ways, Rosamund had diagnosed the affliction that clouded my judgment. My guilt stemmed not only from the fact that my oath to Isaacius remained unfulfilled, but equally from realizing my companion in arms had faded from my own memories. At all of the many funeral orations I have participated in, promises are made that the fallen shall be remembered for their unique contributions to the Empire. It is all a lie. Not only because the living are quick to progress toward new opportunities, but because those who loved the dead rarely possess the fortitude to keep alive the memories of the lost. I have failed much in my life, and though Rosamund was correct in her assessment of Shimon, bringing that lad into my service is not company to my regrets.

Moreover, at the time, the luxury of an additional body to prepare our voyage did ease the strain of an already overburdened household. Ponderous chests of clothing, unwieldy barrels of wine, wooden toys for the children, and all the necessary instruments for our cooks, laundresses, candle keepers, stewards, and maids. Even without all the trappings of war, transporting my extended household in as much comfort as could be expected aboard an Imperial transport required two dozen cartloads pulled by twin mares. Slowly, my building emptied of its contents, leaving behind only the barest team of servants to clear away cobwebs and vermin—and meet the needs of a lonely Antonina.

Work was ceaseless, for if Mariya's needs were satisfied, those of Belisarius and Theodora surely were not. My only respite came in the training yard, trading blows with Xerxes or Samur with wooden swords. To my surprise, however, my greatest joy was when Bessas delivered my new Nisean mount upon my visit to the Imperial stables, his dark hide glistening with sweat despite the warming air of the earliest days of spring.

"I've had my cataphracts break him in to the saddle," Bessas explained. "Indefatigable, as Niseans are, but even as a foal he had a rare calm demeanor. I thought he was deaf at first, but we discovered that he is simply unbothered by any manner of noise."

Intrigued, I nodded. "Has he a name?"

Bessas shook his head. "That task is yours. Mine was only to prepare him for you."

Stroking my mount's mane, I noticed the unflappable nature that Bessas described. Ignis, as powerful as he was, would balk and snap at unfamiliar arrivals, while my new gift treated me with a curious indifference.

"Boreas, then." I smiled.

"Father of horses?" Bessas asked, surprising me with his knowledge of Roman pagan lore.

"The same," I agreed. "Although he is also the god of the northern winds, blowing from lands of impenetrable ice and night. Calm, unflustered, but determined."

And Boreas rode just as his namesake. At first, I worried that his calm demeanor would make for an unenthusiastic warhorse, but Boreas' Nisean bloodlines were readily apparent upon my first jaunt from the Melantias Gate and into the rolling hills just beyond Constantinople's walls. Though tasks mounted and requests for meetings piled one after another in my absence, I rode for half a day with Samur, laughing as my legs tightened into knots while Boreas hardly panted.

"Out of practice!" Samur teased, navigating his own mount as deftly as if he were a centaur himself.

"Out of shape, more like it." I groaned. "Too much time in the palace and not enough in the training yard. At least I'll have time to rectify that on the ship."

Our last days passed far too quickly. Upon the morning of our departure, Cephalas organized our final evacuation from our home, leading an overexcited Haeva tugging upon her leash. Mariya and the children followed soon thereafter, fetching fresh delicacies from the market before boarding our intended transport. Rosamund, Agathias, and Shimon boarded late in the morning, just as the tide began to flow favorably into port, carrying Rosamund's growing mass of healing materials and instruments that she had refused to store on-ship in the days prior.

If anything, the pending voyage was bittersweet. Of course, I was all too pleased to put Constantinople hundreds of miles behind me, well away from Cassiodorus' grasping fingers. The Imperial Palace had always felt a touch sinister, masking all manner of sin in a façade of frescoes and marble. There was little to hold my heart to Constantine's city, for with my family in attendance aboard Belisarius' fleet, I was not hostage to fears that they might be mistreated.

But, alas, there was plenty to spoil my prospects. My family would attend me, but in squalid conditions aboard a ship, and later in the dangers of enemy soil and the muddy, stinking deprivations of an army camp. I had enough coin to see them in private quarters, and even to afford luxuries of perfume, soft cheese, and well-knit cloth, but these would only temporarily blunt the hardships that Mariya would face. Would she complain? Might her resentment fester? I feared so, though she displayed little overt concern in our final days in Constantinople, her mind fixed upon the task of packing for an extended journey.

"Rosewater," Antonina offered helpfully to Mariya. "You can't have too much of the stuff. Coats the stink that clings to the walls of a ship like fleas on dogs."

Glancing apologetically at Haeva, I cautiously monitored Mariya's reply. "I've taken long sea voyages before, but I shall take your advice," she said graciously.

"Not nearly as long, nor with armed men and horses." Antonina wrinkled her nose. "Bring fortified wine too, for the days that rosewater wilts against the heat. If you can't mask the smell, at least be drunk."

Mariya laughed, though from her steely gaze, I could tell it was forced.

"You'll have better quarters, and as much privacy as I can muster," I put in, eager to seem helpful.

Yet Antonina insisted upon adding miserable commentary, forcing me to stifle a groan. "Double the normal clothing as well, because you never know what might happen if they make you ride twenty miles on a horse."

Mariya flinched. "Twenty miles?"

In truth, that was nothing. "Oh, yes!" Antonina tutted. "It can be miserable when your moon cycle arrives. One of Theodora's slaves can help you find little sea sponges that help, although a small rag will do for a short time."

"Moon cycle?" I gaped stupidly, only to shudder as both women turned toward me, incredulous grins spreading across their faces. "Oh..."

Mariya patted me on the shoulder. "Nothing you need to worry about, dear."

Bashful, I nodded in abeyance, retreating with Haeva to private quarters to brood. Was taking my family on expedition wise? What else might I not have considered? It was safer than Constantinople, I had convinced myself, and cheaper besides. Though a noxious worry tugged in my stomach as if I had forgotten something, or had made a terrible mistake.

Ultimately, I had no stomach for this war. The thought of Italy did garner a twinge of boyish curiosity within me, though nothing of the longing that burned in my teenage years like a fever. Back before I had seen slaughter, and starvation, and the product of a conquering army. I was tired, so very tired.

But by oath and friendship, I was committed to go, and took pains to ensure Belisarius saw none of my reluctance in my daily toils to aid his planning. To ensure continuity of our expedition, Belisarius and I were assigned to separate vessels. Liberius and the clerk Procopius joined Belisarius and his bucellarii, although Uliaris remained excluded from their number. Even after Uliaris' heroics in Septem, he had yet to heal the gulf with his master, leaving him as another broken spirit under my care. I dared broach the subject only once with Belisarius two days prior to our voyage, wondering whether Uliaris' exploits had scabbed the wound where John's absence lay.

"He can remain with you," Belisarius replied dismissively. "I'll even pay his wages and kit. But I don't want him in the same building as me, if it can be helped."

"Lord," I prodded gently. "Uliaris only wishes to please you, to make up for —"

"Then he can leave me alone," Belisarius shot back, clenching a fist so tightly his knuckles popped.

I did not press further, though I did later remark upon the exchange with Samur.

"I've heard that Belisarius and John were more than friends," my brother said. "Makes you wonder, no?"

"Gossip and slander." I spat derisively. "They were like brothers, nothing more."

Samur chuckled, a wicked grin spreading across his face. "I don't care if the two of them kept each other's bed warm. Justinian might, but I don't."

Would I have cared? Would it have changed my opinion of Belisarius? Possibly. Petrus cautioned against the temptations of Sodom, and Cassiodorus' ilk condemned such creatures to death, often without trial. But a part of me cared little, reasoning that heroes like the Great Alexander had known the company of men while conquering half the world. Still, I disbelieved the callous rumors about my lord, having witnessed little to suggest their claims held truth. If Samur had perished at the hands of a comrade, or Perenus, or others I had known for less of a time in my household, I would likely react similarly to Belisarius' mistrustful spite. John had an incredible mind for battle, but he also shared rare secrets of Belisarius' youth that none could fulfill. And for that, I abided Belisarius' anger against my baleful Frankish friend.

The woe that it would cause me. On the day of our departure, Xerxes dragged Uliaris sopping wet from stale wine onto our transport, although not before receiving orders that Uliaris alone was responsible for whatever wine-induced sickness he might project on the voyage into sea. Xerxes rolled his eyes at the komes bucellarii's helpless state, but nevertheless was deaf to his moaning.

"I thought Uliaris might have abstained from drink, based upon his improved mood after Septem," I said.

"So did I," Xerxes replied. "And so did he, likely. A grueling expedition will be good for him, and the training that follows."

Unlike our past departures for Cherson, Trapezous, or Caput Vada, there was no formal ceremony to see Belisarius' forces out of the harbor. This made my burdens considerably easier, for it allowed me to embark the various transports under my command from the early violet of predawn. It was never comfortable, but far less rushed.

I saw to the boarding of my family, my servants, Father Petrus, and the ever-vigilant cohort of Aksumites. My vessel, and the hundred others like it, rumbled with ceaseless activity as Belisarius' army of some eight thousand warriors placed their faith in God and the Emperor that they would neither be cast into the sea's depths, nor be condemned to a hopeless conflict on a foreign shore.

My vessel was no flagship, for that privilege was retained by Belisarius as our strategos. However, though lacking the martial decking and catapults of a dromon, my transport was freshly hewn and bereft of the clinging stench of urine and vomit from countless prior sea crossings. Fat-bellied and overladen with supplies, our transport would win no races for speed, but its hold was larger than normal, and equipped with more comfortable furnishings. The ship's hold, separated from its crew of rowers and sailors, would be cramped but far more preferable than my prior experiences.

Samur's Huns as well as Fulcaris' Heruli were each divided into multiple separate ships, while Perenus and fifty Heruli joined one segment of Indulf's Ostrogoths. Perenus was little pleased at his assignment but did not balk when I gave him the reason for keeping him in close quarters with the Gothic foederati.

"If Indulf even sniffs at betraying the voyage as we reach Syracuse, toss him overboard," I whispered.

Perenus nodded. "I might just do that anyway. Hereka would find it amusing, at least. But do you have a reason to suspect treachery?"

"None," I admitted. "And neither does Belisarius, for Indulf has been loyal despite everything. And while I understand he has a blood feud with Theodahad and his tribe of Goths, I do not want to place our fates squarely in Indulf's palms."

As if routine, I offered my farewells to friends, and with Samur shared a skin of pilfered wine that my brother had snuck away from Procopius' stores within the hold of one of our supply ships. Though the patriarch did not come to offer blessings upon the massed men, Narses conducted a final inspection of Belisarius' forces, and I offered him a nod. Likewise, I even discovered Antonina beside two guardsmen, standing carefully distant from Belisarius' flagship.

"Keep my husband safe, will you?" she asked, her Latin as polite and deferential as I could remember.

"Of course, Lady," I answered. "And if there is anything you need, just send a messenger through Narses."

"I shall, thank you. For now, if you would be willing to relay to Belisarius my updates of our daughter, I would be grateful."

Accepting her charge, I awkwardly separated from Antonina and returned to find most of the first wave of soldiers already boarding their ships. Given the great size of the army and relative small size of the docks, the army would depart Constantinople's harbor in two clusters, with the initial wave departing for Syracuse as soon as possible. Mistakes were inevitable, and progress seemed to proceed both arduously slow and perilously quickly, but soon, the initial cluster of ships neared their time to depart.

Before boarding my vessel, I had one tardy group to contend with—the Vandals. Considerable cares had been taken to preload all their weapons, clothing, and personal items days in advance, yet still, Gunderic's unruly mass arrived after most others had securely boarded, whooping and screaming drunken cries of excitement and bloodlust. Their numbers were too great for a single vessel, and instead were divided into thirds. Gunderic insisted upon accompanying my transport, and absolutely refused any excuse I could muster to dissuade him.

"Don't worry, Varus. I'll be as quiet as a mouse around your family." Gunderic smiled broadly, his closed fist bashing me playfully upon the chest. "And Wisimar is taking the unrulier Vandals to a separate ship. He claims to have smuggled whores onto his boat, and if that's true, his sailors won't get any sleep for the next month."

I snorted, skeptical. "If your men aren't the misbehaved ones, I pity the ship that houses Wisimar."

"Me too!" Gunderic winked, rushing by me. "Hurry up, lads! Varus is going to kick all of us in the arse unless you get on this floating hell immediately!"

As the last of the Vandals filtered past, I slowly followed, praying that this patch of land would not be the last I would set foot upon. Before I had ascended the boarding area, however, a voice shouted my name from afar, just breaking through the diminishing noise of a depopulated port. Behind me, perhaps a hundred paces distant, I found none other than the Empress, surrounded by dozens of retainers. She stepped away from her sycophants, raising an arm to beckon me closer. Naturally, but quizzically, I obeyed.

"I thought I'd miss your departure!" Theodora beamed. "All is well?"

I nodded. "As well as could be hoped, for a ludicrously unwise and undersupplied expedition."

She smiled. "I'll pray for you every day," she whispered, and rose to her toes to plant a light kiss upon my cheek. "I await your reports in earnest. You know of my difficulties in Constantinople, but if it is within my authority to assist you, I absolutely shall."

"You have my gratitude, Empress," I responded, dropping to a deep bow.

She stepped away with a nod, casting a glance upon the row of ships whose sailors had already begun to unknot ropes and raise anchors that secured the ship into port. As I resumed my boarding, Theodora turned back, yelling one last note of encouragement.

"And rain hell upon the Goths, Tribune!"

Again, despite my doubts and worry, a spark of hope had ignited in my guts. I was going to see the Roman homeland, even if it ultimately killed me, and make one great thrust to fulfill Justin's dream. Snapping straight, I saluted Theodora and boarded the transport. Not long thereafter, and before I even descended to the deck containing my cabin, my vessel freed itself from its moorings and embraced the rising tide out to sea.

With an escort of dromons, we sailed through the Hellespont, leaving behind Constantinople for the greatest gamble Justinian could muster. One throw of the dice for all the hopes and dreams of three generations of Romans. Against an army undefeated in as much time, possessing more than ten times our numbers, and with none of the miserly restrictions on supplies that Narses' quartermasters had inflicted upon Belisarius. It was a journey of fools, but God forgive me, I wanted to see how it would end.

THE FORLORN HOPE

Though traveling similar routes as to Caput Vada, the entire sea journey was anticipated to last only three weeks. Barring an outbreak of flux or spoiling of our rations, the lead ships—at Belisarius's direction—would veer directly around the Greek provinces and sail directly for Syracuse. These precautions would limit the effectiveness of the Gothic spies to detect our movements and also reduce the time that our soldiers would spend in the tedium and ill air of the ships' holds. Without having to worry about Vandal pirates, we could sail unmolested through the sea, cutting our travel time in half. It was a lone mercy in a wake of gambles, for at least my queasiness would be only somewhat unbearable.

The venture was also timed to correspond with a rapid strike by the Thracian Army into broader Dalmatia. Within days of our departure, Mundus and Constantinianus would travel upon the Via Militaris toward Sirmium. Once a city cherished by many of Rome's emperors, Pannonian Sirmium had been brutally sacked by Atilla and subsequently dominated by the Ostrogoths. From the accounts of Narses' spies, Sirmium had little economic value, but its proximity to Singidunum made for a potential Gothic launching point to raid the Roman hinterlands. As such, Mundus' first goal was to secure Sirmium before the Goths could muster reinforcements, and then rush southwest through the Via Argentaria to pacify the Pannonian and Illyrian coastline. It was a ruthless pace, but we hoped the dense network of stone-lined roads would ease Mundus' task.

Yet, as uncertain and risk-prone as both our land and sea voyages were, there was little to do while sailing across the Aegean. All we could do was wait and pass the time in whatever reasonable manner was possible aboard such confined quarters. For some, like me, the time was a mixture of nausea and prayer, flavored with muted curses that my life had yet again been consumed by the Empire's infernal wooden ships.

My cabin was far larger than any I had experienced, furnished with a larger bed, a desk with benches, two weighty chests to store belongings, and even a rare silver mirror whose polished surface was like peering into a pool of still water. While Zenobia, Tiberius, and Alexander shared an adjoining berth with Jamila and Aya, and others shared rooms or slept upon makeshift beds of twisted rope suspended by iron rings driven into the walls of the ship, Mariya and I were granted the luxury of privacy. Besides us, only Rosamund slept alone, tucked away in a tiny room that seemed more suitable for storage of cloaks than for sleep. Nevertheless, she did not complain, and continued to gather her strength with extensive sleep throughout the journey.

For all her complaints and worry about the expedition before our departure, Mariya bubbled with happiness in such an intimate space. Having journeyed from Constantinople to Antioch and back during our war with Persia, Mariya was no stranger to voyages at sea, although until now had not enjoyed the company of closer friends and family. Other than Rosamund, she alone slept soundly each evening, nestling her head atop my shoulder as she dozed into light snores. Though still early spring, the lower decks of the transport sweltered with sticky heat, and I have no shame in admitting that we often slept naked in the darkness of the cabin's nights.

In those moments of privacy, Mariya was as playful as our first days together. Whenever I moaned and threatened to vomit from the light rolling of the waves, Mariya would answer with a tickle or a kiss, teasing me at each turn.

"Don't be such a child," she chastised me upon one particularly sea-churning night. "Even Alexander sleeps soundly, and Zenobia even enjoys the motion of the waves. I thought I would be the one to complain of the conditions, not you!"

With my head swimming, I could not muster anything beyond a pathetic counter. "Alexander is too young to know the difference of sea and land," I muttered as Mariya stroked my face. "And Zenobia is far too fearless for her own good."

Mariya laughed. "You do not need to tell me. A week before we left Constantinople, I caught Zenobia slipping one of your blades from its sheath. She insisted that she did not know what the weapon was, but the next day, I found her attempting the same gambit."

"I probably need to explain to her how dangerous it is." I sighed. "She's getting old enough to know what my duties are to the Empire."

"She already understands," Mariya replied, dipping a cloth into a small bottle of rosewater that she applied gently to her neck and wrists. "Jamila tells me that she and Tiberius take turns playing soldier, bashing each other with goose-feather pillows as shields and wooden spoons for spears. Whether or not you see it, Zenobia adores you." Mariya paused before adding, "And your brother as well."

I nodded. "Sembrouthes will train Tiberius with weapons soon. Eventually, Alexander as well. What shall we do with Zenobia after she loses her playmates?"

Mariya pecked my nose with a kiss, seeming to consider the predicament. Her answer, however, was the last option I would have predicted. "Train her as well."

"What?!" I gasped. "You do understand what weapons training means, even for children? Even if the weapons are blunted, the injuries can be quite severe." My mind fluttered back to my final duel with Solomon in the twilight of my days as a palace slave. "No Roman instructor would ever consider including a girl, even at the earliest stages of training."

Mariya's fingers raked lightly against my chest. "Of course I know what it entails! The Ghassanids have never known a year of peace, and my father was not one to be lenient with his sons and nephews. I am not asking you to make Zenobia a spearman, or even continue it for long. But she is too much her father's daughter, and will become restless if you condemn her to a life of silks and spinning without a taste of something different."

I groaned, resisting yet another bout of nausea from a rising wave. "Even if I permitted it, Romans do not train women for war. She could become maimed, or worse."

"Only if the teacher is careless or drunk!" Mariya insisted. "Besides, women in the east have served as guards or even soldiers now and again. Her namesake conquered half the Roman Empire at one point! Besides, Sembrouthes is no Roman and will not place her in jeopardy."

Still, I did not embrace the idea. "Why do you want this? Zenobia is not even four. And this would make her unmarriageable to most men of the Empire."

"Again," Mariya replied, "Zenobia will not be a soldier, but she will know how to defend herself. My experience in the riots makes me believe those skills may be necessary if fortunes should turn against us. And as for marriage, that just means we will need to identify a more honorable and stronger partner for her—which is a good thing, no?"

I wanted to answer no. Only with horror could I imagine little Zenobia, as undaunted as she was, with a broken nose or gnarled limbs, nursing a battered body as Samur and I had done in our childhood years under Godilas' tutelage. Mariya, however, did possess one unblockable weapon that slipped past any defense I could muster—my own weakness. When she insisted, I could never deny Mariya her desires, no matter how financially draining or socially challenging they might be.

"As you wish," I said, surrendering. "But only so long as Zenobia wishes to continue, and only if Sembrouthes approves of it. And he will treat her no differently than any pupil. If the training is to continue, you will not be able to soothe her hurts, for it is the only way to mold soldiers."

Though I could not discern Mariya in the darkness, I could feel her chin rub against my shoulder in the form of a nod. "I will explain it to her, and you can begin after we land safely in Italy. But she will impress you, Varus. I know it."

Until we did make landfall in Italy, however, I wavered between simple discomfort to cursed misery aboard the ship. For others, like Gunderic, the boredom of seaborne transport was easily slaked through all manner of games — to the extent that, upon embarkation, I worried that the coarse manner of the men would annoy Mariya, with bawdy tales of port prostitutes, bloody battles, and an overindulgence of drink.

But true to his promise, the Vandal lord behaved himself in almost a civilized manner. Of course, the Vandals gambled, and drank, and told bawdy tales. But their games lacked the threat of violence, their drunkenness did not translate into filth or discourteousness, and their tales were generally spoken in the Vandal tongue. From my past recollections of Vandal gatherings, this was a minor miracle. But what truly baffled me was how playful Gunderic and his band were with the young children.

From the first day of the voyage, Gunderic lavished in the attention of Zenobia and Tiberius. Sweltering in the trapped heat of the hold, Gunderic separated himself from his Vandal followers, plopped upon the ship's floor, and beckoned both children over to him. From his belt he withdrew a worn leather sack, its contents clinking as he unknotted the bag's fastenings and dumped it onto the ship's floor, which immediately drew the children's attention. Even little Alexander, jostling in Jamila's arms, turned to watch the fray.

"The knucklebones of a sheep," Gunderic explained, plucking one of the three dozen pieces from the floor. "My favorite game when I was but a tiny scrap of a lad. Have you seen these before?"

Both children shook their heads, befuddled looks upon their faces. "How did you get them from the sheep?" Zenobia asked.

Gunderic pursed his lips together, appearing surprised and uncomfortable at the question of explaining death to the descendant of a princess. "They were a gift from my father, so I do not know. But gather, and I will explain."

Though not a game that children of wealthier families were likely to play, the concept was familiar to many a spearman. After splaying the knucklebones in a rough pile, a selected participant would seize one knucklebone and cast it high into the air. Upon that signal, all players would rush toward the remaining bones, grabbing as many as they could before the airborne knucklebone came to a full stop along the floor. Though usually innocuous, the scramble to capture the most bones could easily devolve into animosity, although Zenobia and Tiberius were too slow and too small to exact any real harm.

Gunderic roared with false indignity as, moving slower than a tired ox, he allowed the two children to gather the greater portion of the bones in most games. On later days, he summoned other Vandals to join the fray, including those who had no qualms with thumping a would-be child warrior about the ears. One particular spearman made a point to stalk Zenobia's movements and block her grasping hand, only for my daughter to bite his arm after losing multiple times. The Vandal howled in pain, sending Gunderic collapsing with laughter as Zenobia was crowned the winner. With each of her victories, Zenobia flashed me a broad grin, occasionally rushing to show me her amassed knucklebones with unabated glee.

"I would not have picked you for a mother hen," I said to Gunderic after one lengthy game.

"I told you back in Carthage—I have a weakness for children." He chuckled. "Girls, boys, doesn't matter. There's something about not worrying about anything but winning a game and fooling your mother into letting you stay awake a bit longer."

Tiberius especially basked in Gunderic's attention. He demonstrated no reluctance to interact with the Vandals—something that many of my household, and indeed much of Belisarius' army, held concerns over. Yet, though only half civilized and just as blood crazed as before their conquest, each of Gunderic's followers encouraged the boy's willingness to fight and tussle against the stronger warriors for a stray knucklebone—Gunderic most of all. In the final days of the voyage, Gunderic handed the sack of knucklebones to Tiberius with a wink. "So you can practice."

Tiberius gaped at him, the happiest I had yet seen the boy. "Truly?"

"Truly." Gunderic nodded. "Keep them safe for me. We will play when I return."

Others on our transport kept themselves occupied in the favorable weather and calm seas. In the mornings, Sembrouthes and the Aksumites trained with sword and spear, and labored until panting and lathered with sweat. On most days, I was hale enough to join; indeed, I was concerned about my diminished stamina from long weeks of incense-smothered rooms in the Imperial Palace.

"You've nothing to worry about," Sembrouthes insisted. "Your instincts will never die. Endurance will return to you with training, if you are patient."

At least my strength had not diminished, for I found it easy enough to overpower most foes training the transport's upper deck. For those weeks, I abided by Sembrouthes' optimism and found improvement with each passing day. Occasionally, a nearby transport or dromon would hail our practice bouts, including one exchange with Belisarius' flagship. On that occasion, as the flagship pulled alongside and within fifty paces of our transport, I found the strategos waving for attention, a broad grin visible even from that distance. Beside him stood Liberius, appearing as dour as Belisarius was contented.

"Varus!" Belisarius yelled. "Liberius says you've gotten fat!"

The Aksumites hooted with laughter, while I shook my head and paced to the transport's railing, where I cupped my hands about my mouth.

"I won't be fat forever! But Liberius will always be old!"

Chortling, Belisarius clapped his hands in appreciation. Liberius shook his head, although I thought I detected a faint smile. Soon, our ships parted ways, unable to keep abreast of one another without sacrificing the all-important speed we needed to reach Syracuse. Through the duration of our travels, other transports or dromons came into view, from Valerian's ballistae-laden warship to Samur's Huns. Like me, Samur appeared to be training feverishly atop his transport's deck, clashing with a detachment of fur-clad and bowlegged Huns. More attuned to a life in the saddle, the Huns stumbled from the slightest swell, and many appeared as seasick as I was as they traded practice blows with Samur or their comrades.

When not given to exercise or moping belowdecks, I spent considerable segments of my time with Father Petrus. Prayer was expected in our interactions, although he often merely sought companionship and conversation. Petrus, normally so reserved, seemed to enjoy the idyll of the sea. When only light rolls disrupted the calm surf, I would often find him sitting on the transport's deck during my exercises with the Vandals, absorbing sun despite the faded priests' robes he was loath to part from.

"Warms my bones for a colder night below," he explained one morning.

"If you have any discomfort, I can have that remedied for you," I offered, but Petrus laughed.

"Unless you have a remedy for an aging body, I doubt that. But I would appreciate your prayers nonetheless."

Like Gunderic, Petrus enjoyed the children's games, frequently bribing Zenobia or Tiberius with hidden sweets crafted from congealed honey. He had been so stern with me that I found myself perplexed at this carefree old man and his temporarily thawed temperament. Yet I reserved other questions still—more desperate questions—about the oiled leather bag that the priest kept safely locked in his rooms, the same bag he had carried upon introducing himself to me for the first time. That bag had ferried my bronze cross and Godilas' gift of my dagger, but its weight suggested more might be tucked away. Petrus, for his part, would brook no untimely inquiries, and swatted me away when I dared to ask.

Nevertheless, his prayers for serenity must have worked, for we encountered no storms—an unseasonable bout of luck for the spring months. What few waves were encountered entertained the children, and I did what I could to keep a confident face as I chaperoned them about the upper deck. Even with the assistance of Jamila or another maid, I was ill-prepared to mind my daughter; Zenobia would skip away as soon as my attention turned elsewhere, chattering with a nearby sailor about life at sea or how the ship remained afloat. Tiberius, meanwhile, shadowed me diligently, only parting from my company when beckoned by Mariya or Gunderic.

Alexander, the youngest and predisposed to a fussy nature, gaped at the open sea. As we rounded the Peloponnese, he giggled at the hundreds of coastal birds that crashed headlong into the waters and often emerged with a wriggling fish. For the first time, he neither fought nor cried in my arms, fixated upon the teeming life all about him. With a chubby hand, he reached out, unraveling a finger toward the flying hunters.

"Bird," he babbled, his Greek sloppy but nonetheless impressive for one so young.

Jostling him about, I beamed. "Very good!"

We walked about for a full hour, quenching every bit of his curiosity, to the point where I realized my son was shivering from frigid sea spray and the occasional breeze, and I finally surrendered him to Jamila and the warmth of his cabin. It was a brief moment, but it left me pacing along the deck, awash in pleasure and relief at my son's happy attentions. It was not until later that I realized our interaction had temporarily quelled my nausea, like some powerful medicine that Rosamund had yet to identify.

But the days rolled on. After separating from the Greek coastline and making for the open sea, our final week before disembarkation seemed to slow time itself. Though there was little we could do but pray that Indulf's messenger would grant us safe passage into Syracuse's ancient port, I searched my memory for any unfulfilled task. I was not alone in my worries, for in those final days before reaching Sicily, even the Vandals heightened their training in anticipation of the campaign to come.

"I never thought I'd fight a war in Sicily or Italy," Gunderic confessed. "Our grandfathers boasted of their spoils, but I always imagined my fighting would be in Hispania or Egypt."

"Sicily," Petrus cautioned, catching the Vandal warrior's attention, "is but a foothold. The real prize is farther north. I always believed I would return, but to live it firsthand…"

He trailed off, unable to bring to words the hope that many in his generation carried through decades of fear and loss.

"You will step foot in Italy again, Father," I promised. "I swear it."

"Aye!" Gunderic shouted. "With Belisarius' mind and Vandal arms, we cannot be beaten."

I prayed it would be so as, on the final morning of our voyage, the coastline of Sicily came into view. For many on the voyage who had landed in Syracuse during our prior war, stepping foot on the ancient island lacked the luster of the Italian peninsula itself.

However, the less worldly Vandals all clamored for a view of Ostrogothic territory, excited whispers and boasts of strength rising with each passing stroke of the transport's oars. Between Petrus and the Vandals, I, too, surrendered to the hunger, and as Syracuse's port drew nigh, I assembled all the warriors of my transport to the upper deck. Encased in freshly forged armor from Constantinople's smiths, they obeyed. Gunderic touched each man on the shoulder, then nodded as he deemed attendance complete.

"Men!" I roared. "For sixty years, our forebears have dreamed of reclaiming the heart of the world. Today, their wait ends!"

Shouts rang across the deck, Vandal voices whooping their cries of war. *"Varus! Varus! Varus!"*

I echoed the words of Justin, spoken so long ago yet still echoing in the hearts of many. "We must reclaim Rome. We have no other choice." A clangor of spears upon shields answered me. "Do no violence to those who would offer peace, but if any should wish us ill, send them to the afterlife!"

Gunderic roared, calling out in the Vandal tongue. Whether from my words or Gunderic's foreign call, the Vandals cheered once more, watching the harbor draw closer. Our ship was not first in the collection of vessels—that responsibility belonged to Perenus and Indulf—but our captain piloted our ship just behind. Instead, we awaited a signal from the city's walled port, eyeing teams of arches arrayed along the battlements. I did not doubt that we could take Syracuse by storm if need be, for in this rare moment we had the benefit of superior numbers and ballistae-laden dromons, but such an assault would be bloody and treacherous. We could not afford such losses so early, and with far more perilous targets ahead.

Thankfully, any threat of violence quickly evaporated. The sigil of the Gothic king, a cross atop a yellow sun, descended from the ramparts, though a half dozen banners of local lords continued to flap against the coastal breeze. In place of Theodahad's banner, an Imperial Chi-Rho rose above the highest tower, followed soon behind by Belisarius' wolf. Indulf had kept his promise, and without even stubbing a toe, we had liberated Syracuse in the name of Justinian.

Formally, the Gothic War had begun. Unknown to all of us at the time, its ending would not come quickly.

THE SCRAMBLE FOR SICILY

Unloading the fleet required double the time I required to embark within Constantinople's harbor. Over two full days, the army transferred nearly all of our supplies and arms into Syracuse's wharf. We drew a crowd of local Goths and Greek descendants of Syracusan heritage, although none dared to venture too close and risk the wrath of some Hun or Heruli. The Vandals in particular drew muted hisses from Syracuse's locals, and rather than ignite a riot from a drunken brawl between Gunderic and the local residents, I ordered the Vandal foederati to camp outside of Syracuse's walls.

"A bunch of mewing sheep!" Gunderic spat.

I shrugged. "We aren't staying in Syracuse long, anyway. Be prepared to invade the interior within two days."

"Gladly," he replied. "Although I doubt that any man here has the testicles to challenge me. I'll never find someone worthy to take my life in this dung heap."

Belisarius, too, seemed possessed by urgency. He observed the hospitality of Indulf's kin, promising vengeance for the murders of Amalasuntha and her son, and only accepted the invitations of a single feast of friendship on the first night of his landing in Sicily. It was risky, rushing out of Syracuse so quickly, for the Goths could be easily offended by perceptions that Belisarius cared little for their loyalty or prowess as warrior men.

"Justinian shall reward all of you for your loyalty to the Empire, on my honor," Belisarius exclaimed before a gathering of local chieftains. "Indulf can attest to this."

Indulf, a bemused grin on his face, nodded. "It is true. Justinian will allow me to cut the heart out of that pig fucker Theodahad. Goths do not kill children or women without cause. Amalasuntha was one of the last of Theoderic's blood, and I intend to exact vengeance."

Though the local lords swore fealty with words, Belisarius made sure to seal their allegiance with gifts of gold and weapons. Indulf identified those who'd need the greatest bribes, ensuring that only a couple dozen Romans would need to be stationed in Syracuse to dispatch messages to Corinth and Constantinople. "For centuries, Goths do not desert oaths lightly," Indulf explained. "Especially when it's profitable to stay loyal."

Though outwardly respectful, given Indulf's achievement, I did voice concern to him privately. "Didn't these men just abandon their oath to Theodahad?"

Indulf snorted. "He never came to Sicily, let alone Syracuse. Theodahad is a treacherous bastard, and a slothful one."

"Slothful?" A child killer and oathbreaker, of that there was little doubt. But a layabout?

"Oh, yes," Indulf explained. "Theodahad might thirst for the blood of others, but he's no warrior. Never lifted a spear in his life if the rumors are true. Instead, he gorges on wine and books and sends gutless thugs to seize and murder my queen."

It was a strange denouncement, decrying a man for preferring learning and luxury to bloodshed, but I preferred not to argue. "Why do you think Theodahad would kill them, then, and break the Gothic custom?"

Indulf shrugged. "Who knows? Every report tells the same tale, and I intend to write the final verse of Theodahad's worm-riddled life. Until that day, however, my kin in Syracuse will not betray Justinian... as long as he does not provide them with a reason to do so."

My recollection of Syracuse is a blur. We ate a great many fish, drawing exasperated groans from Perenus and frequent bouts of stomach pain amongst those Greeks less acquainted with the sea. The day after disembarkation, I ordered the bulk of Belisarius' army to follow the Vandals toward an outdoor encampment, of which few complained due to the meager fare served from the city's granaries. Selected dekarchoi were granted permission to barter with Syracusan merchants, while a retinue of army servants followed Procopius to restock provisions of salted meat, twice-baked bread, and hardened cheese.

Though I accompanied Belisarius in many formal gatherings with the Syracusan leadership, I rarely spoke, and never revealed a headcount of our men or their strategic intentions. Granted, neither would be difficult for even a raw recruit to discern—even just by counting Roman ships, one could accurately guess Belisarius' strength, and our only true direction was an eventual foray into Italy proper—but nevertheless, Belisarius whispered concerns to me about the fidelity of our new allies.

"Perhaps later they will be useful additions to the army," he said in hushed tones when walking on a noisy street, "but I would sleep better without worrying of Theodahad's hired knives."

If Belisarius felt any worry, it did not show. Indeed, he appeared happier than at any time since before John's death, his beard neatly cropped and his face warming when even a more junior spearman crossed his path. Belisarius seemed to have supped on some unknown well of limitless vitality, for he rose well before dawn, and I had never seen him fall into sleep firsthand, but only watched as he sketched new maps from Syracuse's libraries and learned all he could of the still-fragmented situation of Theodahad's control over the various Gothic tribes and clans late into the night.

On the night before departing Syracuse, Belisarius called me into his chambers. I yearned for sleep, yet Belisarius appeared fresh and hale, pacing about his desk.

"The campaign begins tomorrow, Varus," Belisarius began. "In some ways, John and I planned for this all our lives. In my bones, I understand what must be done, but how our progression shall unfold is less certain."

Yawning, I flexed my legs and arms, forcing my mind alert. "How can I assist, Lord?"

"Sicily is not our goal, but a necessary milepost," Belisarius said. "I do not wish to become engrossed in a drawn-out conflict. How can we seize the island quickly, without taking many losses, and still leave time in the fighting season to carry on toward Campania?"

He paused, and I initially believed that a proposed answer would spill from his lips with renewed fervor. Yet he looked to me, patient and inviting. "Liberius taught you Pyrrhus' wars, as well as the great battles of Carthage and Rome," he went on. "How would you claim Sicily for the Emperor in haste, but without loss?"

In my mind, I searched for the hundreds of stratagems prepared for this moment, centering upon the only one that had a chance at achieving such aims. "Split the army, Lord. Two mounted detachments to sweep along the coastline, and the bulk of the infantry and bowmen to rush diagonally to Panormus."

As I spoke, Belisarius snatched up several figures from a pile and slid them across a map of Sicily, sketched by his own hand from a reproduction of local navigators. "The northern detachment captures Messana," he narrated, "and the western portion seizes Lilybaeum." He paused, considering. "A long journey, and hard riding."

"But no worse than Armenia, Lord," I reasoned. "And of all the nights spent on planning this attack, this is the only approach that makes sense now that we have Syracuse. Sprint across the island, take the major cities before the Goths can react, and fortify ourselves against whatever pathetic navy Theodahad might mount as a counterattack."

Belisarius nodded. "Bold, and as you said, reasonable. How would you divide our forces?"

"The northern route is the most challenging ride, so send the Huns there," I said. "The Heruli can move west. But split light Roman cavalry to accompany each branch of foederati, for we do not wish the natives to believe that the Emperor champions barbarian tribes who will turn Sicily to ash."

Belisarius chuckled. "Indeed. Valerian desires to lead our fleet, but I will give that duty to Ascum for now. I will have Valerian's horse join with Samur, Sinnion, and Aigan. Bessas and half of my cataphracts will join Perenus, Fulcaris, and Sindual. As for the center, the remaining thousands will rush diagonally for Panormus."

I nodded. "Syracuse was the prize of Sicily, but after that, Panormus is the best-defended city and the most critical harbor. If we cannot capture it quickly, anything we gain here will be in jeopardy."

"Then it is done," Belisarius said. "I will command Ascum to use our dromons to blockade Panormus from the north. With luck, we'll take every city before they even know we're here."

"And if any resist?"

"Then we pray that God sends fine weather and easterly winds, because we will require twice the men from Constantinople. By Narses' accounts, all but Syracuse and Panormus were lightly defended, and we still have Indulf to secure the local loyalties. Sicily held Amalasuntha's staunchest supporters, and we will use that to our liking."

The deadline to evacuate the city was swift in coming, and by the end of the second day, Belisarius ordered all but the few stationed within Syracuse to join the assembled army outside of the city walls. Just after dawn on our third day, we all gathered in three massive squares, with each senior officer instructed on the course they would follow. Belisarius granted me the right to select which column I would join, ensuring that my household would be safely included in the baggage train of our unmounted forces. Liberius and Petrus, too, would take the more leisurely march, although Liberius balked at the idea.

"If I want to burn and pillage with a herd of Huns, that is my business!" Liberius scoffed.

"Lord, the Huns fully intend to eat and even sleep in the saddle." I could only hope that this business of joining Samur, Sinnion, and

Aigan was meant in jest. "And there will be far more opportunities for violence than the other divisions of the army."

"No respect for your elders." Liberius groaned. "But if you insist... I will join the clerks and priests in the rear, with the other useless things."

I deduced that, yes, Liberius only meant to joke, but his lack of clear approval brewed a sour sensation in my gut. Assigning him to a task might sway his favor, I reasoned. "Lord, perhaps I could ask a boon of you?" I asked him.

"A boon? Of a decrepit old fool, apparently unworthy of riding in the countryside?"

"Would you look over Mariya and the others?" I asked, bowing my head in a deliberate show of deference. "Though they will all be well guarded, I would find greater ease if their guardian were you."

Liberius' pretense dropped, his face turned to a solemn blank stare. "Of course, Varus. You need not even ask. Go and perform what you must."

Saluting, I mounted Boreas and galloped hard to Syracuse's landward gates for a final meeting with my family and household. Cephalas handed over my assortment of weapons and shield, the blades polished and honed to wicked points by Shimon. Rosamund secured the white wolf pelt about my shoulders, its added warmth welcome against the morning chill.

"Liberius promises protection over you and the others," I said. "If you encounter any difficulties, no matter how insignificant, seek him out."

Rosamund nodded. "I don't fear the Goths nearly as much as the Greeks of Constantinople. But I appreciate the gesture."

She did not offer an embrace, but touched the hilt of my sword and muttered a prayer in the Gepid tongue. Moments later, she nodded again, leaving me to trot Boreas toward Mariya and the children. Sliding from the saddle, I first gave Haeva a hearty scratch, triggering contented panting and an equally disappointed nudge from her muzzle once I stopped. Spotting Tiberius, I gestured for him, and he all but jerked forward with an urge to obey.

"I want you to help Cephalas care for Haeva," I explained, handing Tiberius the leash. "She is a war dog but far too young for work. Can you do this for me?"

He nodded excitedly. "Yes, Lord."

Patting his tangled mop of hair, I turned next to Mariya, her arms barely restraining a wriggling Alexander desperate to be placed on the ground. "It won't be long," I promised. "A couple of weeks, and Sicily will be at peace. Sembrouthes will attend me, but Wazeba will lead the other Aksumites to protect you."

"Do what you must, but come back to us whole," she whispered, and offered a lengthy kiss that enflamed my limbs and body, then reluctantly pulled away. As I ruffled Alexander's hair, he cowered from the motion but giggled nonetheless, reaching out with his plump fingers. For a moment, I set his small hand within my gloved one and placed my lips upon it for a heartbeat.

And then there was Zenobia. "Pater, do you have a horse?"

"A new gift!" I beamed. "Want to see?"

She nodded, and I swept her into my arms. Positioning a foot in a Hun-style stirrup, I swung my body back into the saddle, placing Zenobia carefully before me as she allowed both feet to dangle just beyond the saddle's rim.

"Varus, the men are waiting," Sembrouthes called.

"I know," I called back. "Give me a moment."

Grabbing the reins, I placed the leather strap in Zenobia's hands, careful to retain control in case she yanked at them. She did not, however, and remained stationary even as her whitening knuckles gripped the leather. I kicked Boreas forward into a slow trot, bringing my daughter to bob with glee.

"Faster!" she shouted.

Chuckling, I obeyed, rising to a slow gallop that I knew would draw Mariya's ire—something I'd willingly bear, just this once, for the prize of Zenobia's laughter.

Our time together was altogether brief, and hardly more than a hundred paces. "Pater, can't I come with you?" Zenobia begged as I slowed our course. "Please?"

"Not this time, anaticula," I said, wishing nothing more than anything to accede to her wish. "But soon, you will learn to ride, just as me. Far more than that."

"Like you?" Zenobia asked. "I would like that."

After plucking her from the saddle, I lowered her gently to Shimon, who saw her safely to the ground. With a final farewell, I kicked Boreas back into a canter and made my way back to the massed soldiers awaiting Belisarius' orders. Sembrouthes followed, galloping to catch up.

"You truly want me to train Zenobia in combat?" he asked, once at my side. "And Mariya approves of it?"

"It is Mariya's notion," I answered. "And perhaps she is right. With so much risk from riots or Cassiodorus' men or outright invasion, the ability to defend oneself might prove useful to Zenobia. At any rate, she can quit whenever she chooses, but I doubt that she will."

"Agreed," Sembrouthes muttered. "Even young, you can tell a person's spirit. Zenobia is a stubborn one, but fearless. I will not show favoritism."

"I'd expect nothing less."

Galloping past the Vandal foederati, I saluted Xerxes and Gunderic, nodding in recognition of the Vandal cheers. "I'm bored, Varus!" Gunderic yelled. "I need something to kill!"

"Patience!" I called back.

Xerxes rolled his eyes as the Vandals again howled for blood, reverberating with the same war cry that had once stripped Rome of its wealth and pride. Soon, I reached Belisarius, and the general saluted my arrival.

"Did you offer parting words with your family?" he asked, calm before the eager eyes of thousands of men and servants.

I nodded. "Yes, Lord. Thank you."

"And have you decided which wing of the army you will join? Not the infantry, I am assuming."

Grinning, I nodded. "Yes, Lord. If you shall lead the infantry and archers, Perenus and Bessas will need no help with the western horsemen. I think I'll join my brother, make sure he behaves himself."

"Sensible, for though the Huns are our best fighters, they're the least controllable with Sunicas gone." Belisarius rose in the saddle. "Let us begin, then."

He trotted toward the center of the frontmost ranks. As he did so, I signaled for the army's horns to beckon all to attention, the soaring brass notes cutting through all voices, the clinking of armor, and the braying of horses and oxen alike. All conversation ceased as thousands of eyes followed Belisarius' plumed helmet, dancing atop his head as he guided Xanthos farther away and slightly uphill. It was an ideal spot to speak to thousands, if there ever was one. As the horns faded, Belisarius raised his arm to salute the army.

"Soldiers!" Belisarius yelled, his resounding voice fuller than in private discussion. "We come here, to this hallowed island, not as conquerors, but as liberators!"

His veterans pounded their shields against the turf in response, the iron rims thudding against hard-packed ground. Despite the chill, I could not have asked for better weather in that moment for Ascum's dromons, as well as the horses, carts, and boots that would slog throughout every corner of Sicily.

"Our cause is just!" Belisarius continued. "Our enemy would send assassins to murder women and children. This is unacceptable!"

He trotted Xanthos around the army's front ranks. "The Emperor offered Theodahad an opportunity to explain himself. For we are merciful! But"—he shook his head—"Theodahad spat upon the Emperor's offer and slew the Imperial messengers. Theodahad started this war, but by the bones of Christ, we will end it!"

The pounding of shields quickened, sounding at once louder and more chaotic. I wondered whether such a display might frighten Mariya or the children—I doubted it, but the massing of the army must have appeared an incredible sight to those not used to seeing so many soldiers prepare for anything beyond parades or triumphs. Casting any worries aside, I fixated on Belisarius, who allowed his horse to plod slowly before the ranks as he barked his declamation.

"I will not lie to you. Theodahad has far more warriors under his thrall. That truth is important for you to know." He paused, trotting farther down the line to face the Herulian foederati. "But what my veterans already know, as if embedded in their very souls, is that their numbers mean nothing when we stand united. For not by numbers of men, nor by measure of body, but by valor of soul is war to be decided!"

By now, the percussion of shields had been joined by cheers. Even I felt an elation that had been absent for years, and a desire to destroy Belisarius' foes. In that moment, I was desperate to prove myself worthy of my role, and added my voice to so many others.

"Belisarius! Belisarius! Belisarius!"

"As you go forth to reclaim the lands of legions' past, I make this vow to you." Belisarius was now sitting high atop Xanthos. Unbuckling his helmet, he tucked the plumed headpiece under his arm, sucking air to provide force to his shouts. "No matter how massive the walls we must scale, or how dark our nights may seem, we will prevail if we stand together!"

Amidst further cheers, Belisarius reached for his sword, ripping it from its sheath. The polished metal glinted against the sunlight, its tip thrust toward the heavens as if challenging the great celestial universe to battle. "Any man who stands with me is my brother, and I will fight against all enemies for you until my final breath. By God and the Emperor, I swear it!"

The army's crescendo was deafening. My voice fused with thousands of others, yet its words were muffled to the point of silence amidst the crowd. I have little doubt that, as dire as our situation truly was, Belisarius could have asked his men to charge against every Goth in Italy without hesitation. He was the victor of Dara and of Ad Decimum, the savior of Constantinople, and the most hailed military commander in over a century. Despite any obstacles we faced, he was ours, and we loved him for it. *I* loved him for it, and believed every word he spoke.

Belisarius nodded to me, ceding the final order for the sweep across Sicily to my control. John had wielded such authority with a confidence that stemmed from raw intelligence, and now, as I stepped into John's role in a far more expanded capacity from Septem, I wondered whether he ever felt the anxiety that now rooted in my guts, making me question our plans and the risks that we faced. Whether he did or did not, I was determined to follow his example and show a face confident in both the Imperial cause and our strength in arms. If nothing else, I'd prepared well for this moment.

"Men, forward!"

"Forward! Forward!"

The effect was immediate. To Syracuse's south, the combined horsemen of Bessas and Perenus surged to the southwest, tracking toward the favorable roadways that would speed their journey toward Lilybaeum along Syracuse's western corner before turning back for Panormus. More heavily armored and laden than the Huns, Bessas' contingent moved at a steadier pace, careful not to lame their burlier stallions with overwork. Likewise, the vast bulk of Belisarius' infantry initiated their march, taking the shortest path to Panormus, but slower, due to the snaking trail of servants and baggage that followed the army. Touching my fingers to my lips, I saluted to that great mass of men and women, praying that all would reach their destination without hardship or issue.

That left Valerian's light cavalry, and the combined Huns under Sinnion and Aigan. Though I was undeniably the most senior officer of the group, none would have confused Samur's right to lead the swifter band of horsemen along their more treacherous path. Before giving the signal to commence, a beaming Samur weaved his horse to me, his arms stretched wide.

"Here we are!" he called in Heruli. "Just you and I, and the path ahead. Are you sure you can keep pace?"

"I'll keep pace," I muttered, though I inwardly groaned at the arduous trek ahead, already regretting my decision to forgo the more leisurely pace of Belisarius and our unmounted forces. "Give the order when you're ready."

Still grinning, Samur whistled, his keening note signaling the Hunnic horns. Their shriek brought the Hunnic riders to howl in unison, raising their fists as they fell into a column of five riders abreast. Valerian, though a skilled rider, lacked the effortless agility of even the rawest Hun recruit, and struggled to follow their example.

Careful to not question Samur's authority before his men, I whispered to my brother in Heruli. "I thought only a Hun could command other Huns. Sunicas often said as much."

Samur shrugged. "The Huns follow strength. They just don't recognize Romans as equals in that capacity."

"And they don't consider you Roman?"

"Do you?" Samur laughed. "Do you even consider *yourself* Roman, truly? Even if they grant you laurels, men like Solomon will only ever see you as a mud-eating savage. Why try to impress them?"

Before I could reply, Samur cocked his head toward the front of the column. "Come, let's show Belisarius the Huns have no reason to fear the difficult path."

Kicking the haunches of his mount, Samur galloped to his position of leadership alongside the two Hunnic warlords. I followed, with Sembrouthes urging his borrowed mount onward close behind. In my haste to reach Samur and prove my ability to match the Huns' stride, I did not see the man who stalked Sembrouthes' progress.

Uliaris—a sober, if pale and haggard, Uliaris at that—galloped hard, overshooting not only me but Samur as well. Samur croaked with laughter.

"Do you wish to race me to Mount Aetna, Uliaris?" he called to the struggling Frank. "Perhaps we should let you set the gait."

Uliaris merely cursed, allowing we officers to catch up before yanking again on the reins. It was a canter half again as rapid as the progress of Bessas or Perenus, although neither the Hun riders nor their ponies appeared concerned at such a blistering rush.

"We have what, two hundred miles to Panormus?" Uliaris said gruffly.

"Three hundred," I corrected. "If you want to go elsewhere, decide now. Samur is ruthless when placed in command."

Ignoring Samur's hooting affirmation, Uliaris only grimaced. "Xerxes told me to watch you closely. If I can't guard Belisarius, I should follow his second."

Sembrouthes shot me a private glance of skepticism, wordlessly begging me to send Uliaris away. It would have been simple to redirect him, but the thought of abandoning Uliaris now seemed unpalatable, especially given that, after Septem, I owed him my life.

"Very well, bucellarius," I confirmed. "But none will be able to help you on this ride, for I am not entirely certain that I shall make our intended timetable. All you can rely upon is your training and stamina."

"It will be enough." Though adorned in a rich coat of lamellar armor, Uliaris' mount appeared healthy and swift of foot, and at least would not likely be the cause of Uliaris' capitulation.

"Stop jabbering!" Samur yelled. "We must reach Messana in three days. Save your wind for the ride." Turning back, he took stock of the Romans that trailed the Hunnic foederati. "And lower the banners! They will only slow us by flapping in the breeze. I'd rather not give away our identity until necessary, anyway."

Finally reaching the front of the column, Valerian nodded in welcome. "Your brother is a cheerful sod, then?"

"Oh, I'm an absolute *joy* after winning a fight," Samur bit out. "Three days to Messana, one day to pacify the city, and another four days to Panormus. You can thank my idiot brother for such a comfortable schedule!"

We rode hard. That first day was easy enough, with flat grasslands and firm ground making easy footing for Boreas and the other horses. We made progress even beyond Samur's intention, ending in the southernmost foothills of the fabled Mount Aetna: Its vast, snow-capped peak pierced distant rolling clouds, this volcano that had captured Virgil's wonderment at once serene and altogether insurmountable. Its size made the sprawling villages along its southern slopes seem pathetic, like ticks nestled in the folds of a great giant. For Samur, however, Aetna offered precious cover from prying Gothic eyes, and few sizeable settlements capable of supporting a garrison that could bar our path.

"I haven't seen any outposts or banners for miles," Valerian panted, rubbing at a sore thigh.

"Nor have I," Sinnion agreed. "Surely there must be some ahead?"

Samur shrugged. "Eventually. There's the city of Catana, which must have at least a hundred men."

Sinnion scoffed. "Easy enough. A few volleys from horseback, and they'll turn their shields and run. The Goths were always cowards, and that's why they will only fight when massed in huge numbers."

"We cannot get bogged down in a standoff with a smaller city," Samur said. "Stay well away from the roads around Catana. We will make camp on the northern slopes of Aetna tonight. Our orders are to seize Messana, and that is what I intend to do without distraction."

Though his order showed the wisdom of discretion, it also extended our journey for that day well into the darkness. Our ride-path melted from firm grasslands to swooping hills, the twilight hours chilling the layers of sweat that matted along our clothing and hair. None of the Huns complained, for lengthy excursions were common amongst the famously nomadic people, but Valerian's Roman riders groaned in the saddle with every twist and canter.

Navigating by the stars, Samur kept well away from the best-lit paths and signs around Catana, instead guiding our column around the graded slope of Aetna. Eventually, our horses began trotting downhill, a sign that we had reached his desired stopping point. Camp was quickly struck, with most men—save a detachment of six Huns—asleep within an hour of the end of the march. Many did not even bother to eat, with the Huns having gnawed at dried beef while mounted and the Romans simply too exhausted. I, too, felt the press of fatigue, but still convinced myself that we would be provided for upon the morrow.

At dawn, we made to leave: bread distributed, tents folded, and leaves and branches tossed about the campsite. That last measure struck me as unnecessary, for we were well in the wilderness and far from coastal Sicilian society, but Aigan insisted.

"I would not fall victim to a shepherd boy stumbling across the camp of a war band only to alert the local chief," he said, ordering a dozen Huns to disguise our presence.

Whether they were eventually alerted to the Roman invasion or remained blissfully ignorant, the garrison of Catana never saw Samur's progress around their outer defenses. By the sun's zenith on the following day, that coastal stronghold was well to our south, with Messana ahead. Along with Rhegium on the Italian mainland, Messana controlled the narrow straits that separated Sicily from the Calabrian isthmus and Campania beyond, and had once, in the days of Severus and his successors, been among the wealthiest cities in all the Empire.

Though Messana was still vital as a point of control over sea lanes, our spies had told of a city fallen into disrepair, deemed only mildly important by the Ostrogothic kings who had their sights set on the northernmost cities. Those poor defenses made for an appetizing prospect, but still left me, at least, with an air of unease about the place.

Uliaris was among the first to give voice to such doubts. "What if Messana resists? We have no siege weapons, nor even an adequate force of spearmen to scale the city walls, even if Valerian's men all dismounted."

"No siege," Samur insisted. "If Messana does not capitulate, we burn its fields and outlying manors. It must be taken quickly or rendered too cowed to mount an offensive while Belisarius is occupied around Panormus."

I grunted to catch Samur's eye. "Belisarius would not approve of wanton destruction of property of civilians—in the east or against the

Vandals. We must find an alternative path."

"This was your strategy, brother," he retorted. "And it is a wise one, but not without its own measure of brutality. Even Belisarius, the noble Belisarius, must have understood that."

I disagreed, but speaking my discontent would have turned the men's faith in Samur moot at best, and hostile at worst. And though I would like to claim impartiality in my judgments of Samur's actions, I also wished to spare him any public denunciation—scruples that few Roman officers would have shared.

"Very well," I said, "but refrain from violence unless they strike at our men with deadly force. Keep to properties and outposts of the military alone."

Samur smirked but did not contradict me. "Ever the diplomat, Varus."

We had intended to camp another evening in the hinterlands and take Messana in the predawn hours, but all our plans unraveled as we gained sight of the open sea. Rather than a vacant expanse of churning sapphire waters, our horsemen crested a coastal hill to see a herd of dromons surging toward the port of Messana. Though nestled against the coastline and charged with the protection of a few narrow landward walls, Messana had little of the defensive strength of Septem, with its own walls visibly crumbling and its port lacking any chain to guard against seaborne assault.

"Luck is on your side today, Varus," Samur mumbled, taking in the sight. "Can Messana hold against Ascum's ballistae?"

Valerian shook his head. "Not a chance. When I led my dromons against the Balearics, I pounded towns far stronger than Messana into submission. Ascum is less gentle than I am."

We did not have long to wait for Messana's capitulation. A lead dromon, its identity undiscernible at a distance, fired twin ballistae bolts, which splashed into an unoccupied section of water within a hundred meters of the city's dock.

From atop a nearby hill, I could see the few defenders dividing themselves, scrambling to a water-facing tower and the primary landward gate, with perhaps a half dozen bowmen staring upon our massed horsemen meanwhile. The detachment of dromons drew around Messana in a half circle, halting their progress only after a horn blared from the city's interior. Afterward, the iron-reinforced doorway to the city rose, and the sole Gothic banner—professing loyalty to Theodahad—sailed from the rafters and fell to the dusty soil below.

"Simple." Samur grinned. "But we should not stay more than a day. Keep our men camped well beyond the walls, so I don't have to pry them from their whores and drink the following morning."

Messana's surrender was little to remember. Against what followed, it is the merest speck of history, made important only by its position along the sea. It would be hardly worth recounting, except for a sole conversation held with the city chief—a crook-backed man of some fifty years. Entering Messana with Uliaris, Sembrouthes, and Valerian, Samur guided the remainder of our forces toward a western camp, deaf to any complaints of relief, comfort, or the prospect of pillage by the Hunnic warriors. Samur brooked their nagging, but nothing further, and no Hun or Roman dared cross his will.

Messana's chieftain had aged poorly, missing more than half of his rotted teeth, and possessing a bald, spotted pate. His name, Adalfuns, had once struck fear against foes in the shield wall, yet a half dozen wounds and arthritic fingers made him a vision of pity. And perhaps pity is what warranted him lordship over such a place as Messana, for he had gained such a prize twenty years prior as spoils from Theodoric, whom Adalfuns once served as a personal bodyguard. Yet the man, broken of body but resolute in spirit, had little option under his authority than to surrender without a single arrow shot in anger.

"A damned pitiable state," Adalfuns grumbled, his Latin limited but conversant. "If Theodoric were still alive, the skins of every Gothic councilor would be peeled into coats for allowing Sicily to fall."

"Theodahad is no Theodoric," I said. "A child killer sits upon the throne of Romulus. Belisarius and the Imperial family intend to reclaim it, after all these years."

Adalfuns spat. "You youngsters, so full of notions of fancy. Theodahad may be a prattling woman, and as soft-bodied as a eunuch, but he is no child killer."

I frowned. "Amalasuntha and her son, your former king, were slain by Theodahad's henchmen. This is not debatable. Whether Theodahad is warlike or not makes little difference to me, for he is guilty of treason and effrontery to God, in his own way."

"You Romans... you know nothing of guest right." Adalfuns snorted. "Theodahad invited Amalasuntha into his household, guaranteeing her protection. Within my people, he who violates the sacred responsibility of a guest is worse than a worm, a soulless beast unworthy of trust or friendship."

"But—"

"You shall have Messana, Roman," Adalfuns cut me off. "But understand this: Aside from guest right, Amalasuntha was Theodahad's cousin by blood. I have heard the rumors your singers tell, and they are all lies. Lies spun by your insipid emperor, no doubt. If only I was younger, I would carry my blade to Constantinople and carve out the gossip-mongers root and stem."

I stiffened, resisting the instinct to seize my sword. "Careful, Adalfuns."

He shrugged. "You have won, and now I have nothing. Theodahad does not even deign to send me a messenger of what to do, let alone men. What few guards I have are all kin of my followers, all bound by oath. It may mean little to you, but if you spare Messana and our livelihoods, you have my oath that we shall do no harm to your campaign."

Relaxing, I agreed. "I shall recommend to Belisarius that your authority here be unchallenged. Despite what you may believe, the Empire has come here to restore order and reclaim our lost lands. To do that, we need to build harmony, whether or not you believe in Theodahad's guilt."

Adalfuns grunted. "You have my gratitude. But heed my words: Amalasuntha's killer did not come from Theodahad's care. I would wager the souls of my grandchildren on it—and I never wager."

I nodded, offering a slight smile. "Never trust the wager of a man who never gambles. They either know too much or not enough of what is at stake."

Adalfuns snorted. "The former. Do as you like, Roman. You know my beliefs on the matter."

Normally, I would have left a detachment of men to hold Messana, but Valerian's Romans were sorely needed against Panormus, for even that dilapidated city would have risen in fury at the prospect of being governed by Huns. Even then, so many years after Attila's demise, the memory of Hunnic ferocity haunted the Gothic people. Instead, I trusted Adalfuns at his word and privately assured myself that the city, so swiftly taken by such a small force, could easily be recaptured if necessary. Instead, as our dromons signaled their advance along Sicily's northern coast, we left Messana in the control of their longstanding Gothic elite.

As I rejoined Samur's forces, my brother belched in welcome. "Anything interesting? Anyone put up a fight?"

"No fight," I answered in Heruli to avoid eavesdroppers. "But their chieftain insists that Theodahad did not order Amalasuntha's death. Something about guest rights."

Samur shrugged. "Justinian seems sure of it, although he's a treacherous slug."

"And Narses' spies found ample information to back the accusation," I added, careful even then to offer no insult to the Emperor. "The chief must have spoken bluster, making excuses for their sorry state."

Another shrug. "At this point, it matters little. The Romans want Theodahad dead, and dead he shall be, unless he can kill all of us first."

I was less at ease than Samur. Of course, I doubted Adalfuns' accusations. A lifetime in Constantinople's palace made me skeptical of all salacious claims—especially those rendered by enemies and on the subject of blood or children. Yet, in the pit of my stomach, a wriggling worry nested, along with the dozen other concerns that only grew from the passing years.

We departed Messana and left behind our limited view of the Calabrian coastline that led to Rhegium beyond. Rhegium was so tantalizingly close, yet our encirclement of Sicily remained incomplete. And so, with raw thighs and a sore back, I mounted Boreas and desperately sought to keep pace with the Huns, wishing to God that I had marched with Belisarius instead.

Not all were so fortunate as to keep pace, however. No Huns took injury, but a half dozen Romans complained of bleeding thighs and twitching muscles that could no longer secure their bodies atop the saddle. One Roman, not careful enough to anticipate the ground around him, led his horse into a hidden gully. The horse's body collapsed, bearing its full weight on a leg that snapped cleanly in two, and the beast screamed in pain. Sinnion, wary that the noise would prove a beacon to ravaging enemies, muttered a prayer to some Hunnic god before driving his blade into the horse's brain, killing it instantly. The Roman, along with others incapable of continuing, were left behind in a small camp.

"We will send for you as soon as we get to Messana," I promised. "Just keep out of sight, and no pillaging."

They grumbled assent, and I pretended not to see their widened eyes darting about, fearing exposure on enemy territory. Some may deem me cruel, but I had a duty to fulfill, and those men were plenty capable of staying alive on such hospitable terrain in the middle of spring. I rejoined Samur, and we rushed headlong to the west, finding no interlopers as we closed the distance day after day toward Sicily's great fortress.

I nearly wept in relief as we arrived within five miles of Panormus' walls, the moss-covered stone markers set hundreds of years ago in a far more peaceful time. Billowing masts of dromons again appeared at sea, their captains angling for a seaward blockade of Panormus' port. Among them was Ascum, whose far larger and more heavily armed dromon was easily spotted even from a distance.

"At least we didn't arrive early," Valerian quipped. "Any faster and I'd be dead."

As we closed the distance to the city, evidence of Roman arrivals around Panormus grew. Though the bulk of Belisarius' forces had not yet arrived, the mounted vanguard formed a tight camp outside the city, while Herulian scouts patrolled the perimeter. The discipline on display would have been a welcome sight to any expedition commander, yet the presence of guards outside the walls meant one thing.

"Panormus is preparing for a siege." I groaned. "Theodahad's banners still fly."

"What does that mean?" Aigan asked. "We can take the city, surely."

"Idiot," Samur snarled. "It means that we will be in Sicily for a long while. Theodahad will have time to organize against us, and we won't cross the sea to Italy until fall at best. It means that, unless something miraculous happens, you and I will find our skulls serving as goblets for some pox-addled Gothic whore by the new year."

LIGHT WITHOUT BRIGHTNESS,
A MOST DREAD PORTENT

Panormus was soon surrounded, but that maneuver gave Belisarius' army little joy. Ascum's dromons launched their ballistae against the city's manned towers, yet the destruction did nothing to stymie the Gothic resolve. As Belisarius arrived with the remainder of the army, I begged an audience, pleading forgiveness for this failure.

"I'm sorry, Lord," I said. "I should have sent men to seize Panormus immediately. I failed you."

"Hardly, Varus." Belisarius seemed oddly unbothered. "You've seized all of Sicily, save this rock, with no deaths and few casualties beyond stubbed toes. If we can coax Panormus' defenders to surrender, we may yet take the entire prize to our liking."

Belisarius' calm demeanor made little sense to me, especially for a man who appeared happier when navigating the hazards of life than sitting peacefully in an office. Still, there is no doubt that Belisarius, despite Theodora's blocking of his divorce from Antonina, felt a measure of liberation in this voyage. Time away from brooding and strides into the flames of activity had melted the bloated flesh around his middle and ignited a life in his eyes that made even the worriers like myself more composed in his presence.

Despite the reassurance, however, the impediment of Panormus felt too daunting to swipe aside with confident words alone. "Lord, what can we reasonably do? We do not even know who commands the enemy."

"We can learn," Belisarius replied. "Call the senior officers, plus the commanders of the foederati. They are to provide all scouting reports of Panormus' defenses and any estimates of the forces arrayed before us."

Inside Belisarius' vast tent that signaled his position as strategos, men responded to my courier's messages within the hour. Joining them was Liberius, whom I summoned via a hasty message carried by Shimon. "If you want something from an old man, Varus, have the manners to come offer greetings yourself."

"Apologies, Lord." I grinned at his petulance. "But I could use your aid once again."

"Panormus." Liberius nodded. "We really found ourselves neck deep in a dung heap here."

I sighed. "Any advice?"

"You'll never take it by land," Liberius began. "Even if poorly defended. The Phoenicians of Carthage understood this well, although they were unsuccessful in their war. Do you remember why?"

"Because they lacked resources?" I shrugged. "Little different than with Belisarius, although the Goths do not seem to have prepared for our arrival."

"Precisely." Liberius offered a curt nod. "So stop dallying, or you'll meet the same fate as those hundreds of years ago. As for Panormus, you do not attack a turtle by striking its shell, but by seeking its more vulnerable flesh."

"And the flesh of our current turtle is… the port?"

Liberius rolled his eyes. "Perhaps metaphors are not for you, Varus. Or perhaps I am merely an old and soft fool. Yes, I am instructing you to storm their port immediately, before the Gothic garrison gets a notion that they might truly be capable of victory. As for *how* you take the port, well, that is why we pay you fine soldiers such considerable coin."

After Belisarius' officers gathered, I relayed Liberius' words to an audience at once intoxicated by the swift conquest of Sicily and equally anxious from the unclear path forward. "Liberius insists that the port is our only way inside," I explained. "At least, the only way with minimal casualties."

Belisarius concurred. "Our scouts indicate well-maintained stone walls encircling the city, with watch towers at every fifty paces. A landward assault would cost hundreds of Roman lives. If the harbor is our only option, how might this be achieved?"

Ascum, freshly landed from his ship to attend our gathering, chuckled. "We can set the gates aflame with naphtha! Varus knows well how that may gain us success."

"No naphtha," I muttered, silently recalling the towering pyre of flame as the *Serapis* burst asunder, ripping Septem's sea walls apart. "Can we stage landing parties?"

Ascum's mirth switched to irritation. "I can position our ships next to the walls with no difficulty. And even our smallest ladders will reach well above Panormus' walls. But as soon as our men try to climb ladders to seize the parapet, they're little better than any spearmen attacking from the front."

"And that's assuming the boats can anchor to still their rolling," Xerxes added. "I would wager half of our ladders would tip into the sea and send our climbers below the waves."

"Miserable death, drowning," Valerian put in.

It all seemed pointless. "Well, if we cannot take the walls be land or by sea, how shall we gain control of Panormus, then? I doubt we can ask the Goths nicely to open their gates."

Others chimed in with some thought or another, but each notion offered either required resources we did not possess or could too easily descend into the slaughter of our men. Through it all, Belisarius said nothing, until finally he nodded to Xerxes in a gesture for him to speak. It seemed curious, my oath lord seeking the guidance of a man who had savaged Belisarius' forces at Thannuris, yet as I turned to share Belisarius' gaze, I found Xerxes brimming with enthusiasm.

"Xerxes?" I offered, quieting the room.

"Forcing our way onto the battlements is too costly," Xerxes began. "But it may not be necessary. All we need to do is convince the Ostrogoths that their position is impossible, and their deaths imminent."

"Unlikely chance of that," Indulf blurted out. "You won't scare a Gothic garrison into surrender. Not after they've sworn to resist. If it were me, I'd climb to the top of the walls and piss down upon any Roman who charged at me, and prepare myself for a lengthy siege."

Gunderic opened his mouth for a retort, but Sembrouthes elbowed the Vandal warlord hard in the gut, preventing what almost certainly would have been an insult against Gothic courage. I pretended not to notice, although I caught a glare from Indulf to the Vandal officers. Xerxes, however, thankfully continued before any true anger could manifest.

"I agree, Lord Indulf. That's why we must show them something different."

Belisarius grinned. "Different how?"

At that, Xerxes turned to Ascum. "You say the sea walls are short?"

"Aye," Ascum rasped. "No taller than a man and a half. Our masts reach well above Panormus' highest sea tower."

"Then that's your way forward." Xerxes beamed. "Place teams of archers along the masts, and fire down upon the defenseless city guardsmen. They'll have no choice but to sue for peace, or risk their entire garrison falling before we attempt a rally with our ladders."

Ascum seemed to consider Xerxes' plan but scowled in frustration. "I can position no more than two archers on each mast while still allowing them to draw their bow. Perhaps I can fit four or five dromons into Panormus' unguarded outer harbor outside the walls. Even if they have a clear shot, though, that's not nearly enough to clear the walls of defenders."

"Nor prevent the Goths from returning with their own arrows," Bessas added. "You'd need three times as many bowmen to keep the Goths cowering behind shields."

"Five times more." Belisarius was staring into the middle distance, eyes unfocused and mouth agape with a grin. "And I know how to do it. Brilliant plan, Xerxes."

"I do not doubt you, Lord," I replied. "But how can we fit so many men in such a small space, where even experienced sailors would falter?"

At that, Belisarius nodded to Liberius. "By using intellect over brute strength. We will raise landing rafts to the masts of our stoutest dromons, and fit ten bowmen apiece with three full quivers per man."

"Lift rafts?" Ascum frowned again. "With pulleys, yes, but how?"

Liberius straightened. "Leave that to me. When youth falters, the wise blaze a trail. I only request Belisarius' aid, and three dozen burly spearmen not afraid of heavy lifting."

"As you wish." Ascum shrugged. "But I will believe in our miraculous flying boats when I see them."

"Agreed," Belisarius concluded. "Let us be finished with Panormus in one week. If we are successful, there will be ample time to attempt a landing at Rhegium before the winter ends."

Though Belisarius expressed resounding confidence in his plan, I myself felt less sure of how he would engineer boats to soar into the air. Dromon masts might be able to handle the weight of men, lumber, and weapons, but at that height, they would have little stability, and that wasn't even considering the slightest wind blowing along the Sicilian coastline.

Nevertheless, Liberius and Belisarius huddled with Ascum, procuring additional labor from Belisarius' bucellarii. In Belisarius' absence, I commandeered the command tent, writing missives to Theodora in Constantinople and Mariya in Syracuse. In a way, I could even describe that evening as peaceful, although howling squalls blustered through our camp, rendering the braziers useless at staving off chill within our tents. All could be explained by a typical spring storm looming on the horizon, with more temperate climes to warm our bones on the morrow.

The following morning, however, did not lend itself to warmth. Indeed, it dawned cold; the sun shone weakly, allowing frost to form from morning dew upon the freshly grown grasses. It was Procopius who first noticed the peculiar heavens, hustling into the command tent and brushing aside Uliaris and Sembrouthes. Both guards followed, with Uliaris huffing with irritation as he snatched at Procopius' robes.

"Unhand me, barbarian!" Procopius screeched.

Uliaris shrugged. "Want me to beat some respect into him, Varus?"

"Leave Procopius be," I ordered. Though the Imperial scribe had violated decorum in seeking me out, Procopius rarely sought my attention, and his visible worry stimulated my interest.

"If you're certain." Uliaris shrugged and released him. "If you change your mind, we can tie him upside down and watch him shit on himself for a day. Men can take beatings and humiliation, but if you force a man to stain his body with his own dung, I've found he will be far more receptive to orders from then on."

Procopius glared, his lip quivering as he mustered a response, but I raised a hand. "I shall keep your observations on discipline in my thoughts. For now, leave us."

As both men departed, Procopius rearranged his sleeves, brushing at dirty fingerprints that stained the bone-white robe. "Lord, with Belisarius absent, you are in command of the army. Have you ventured outside today?"

"Not yet." I yawned. "Writing reports as soon as I awoke and broke fast, although I regret the lack of exercise. Why?"

"The sky, Lord," he mumbled. "God has blackened the sky."

"Blackened the sky?" I repeated.

Procopius repeated his claims, speaking the words as if they were pagan curses. I rose from my seat and, after donning my cloak, ventured outside the command tent. In truth, other than the morning frost and continued chill, it would have been easy to miss the change in the day's temperament, and at first I did not understand Procopius' blathering. As he followed me out and skipped carefully around Uliaris, Procopius rushed to my side, pointing at the sun.

"Do you see it?!" Procopius hissed, shielding his eyes from the morning rays.

"Truthfully, no."

"Focus on the horizon, and then scale to the sun. I tell you, it is different than any other morning I have ever lived to see."

Sighing, I humored Procopius, my eyes tracing the distant sea upon the horizon. However, as I turned my head toward the sun, I saw it for myself. I could not help but gasp, even clutching at my cross.

"Merciful Christ," I whispered.

"Problem?" Sembrouthes had appeared at my side.

"Look!" I yelled, instructing both of my guards to follow Procopius' instructions.

Sembrouthes frowned, while a lagging Uliaris staggered as he gained a careful look at the sun. "It's… like a veil."

And so it was. Our sun, the provider of life, worshipped by millions of pagans as a preeminent deity, seemed to have slipped behind a translucent web. It was unlike any cloud I had ever seen, both fully formed but so thin it might have been missed by a careless eye, and formed of grays and blacks as if billowed from a great pyre of the dead. Though the sun was still visible, its orb was hazed and dull. It was an evil omen, perhaps the worst of all, and there was naught that all the armies in the world could do to resolve it.

"Light without brightness," I muttered to no one, although Procopius nodded energetically.

"A dread portent, Lord," he said, his voice a hush of awe and fear. "We must find Belisarius and write to the Emperor. God shows his disfavor upon us for some reason. Even in the scriptures, Revelation tells of such signs as a harbinger of the end."

For a heartbeat, I trembled. My urge was to vault atop Boreas and gallop headlong to Syracuse, rush to comfort my family who had undoubtedly seen the great orb of our sky dulled as if it were dying above us. For Procopius was correct: Such signs had been well discussed in the scriptures, burned into my memory from years of study under men such as Petrus. From memory, I recited a verse, speaking louder than I intended as I gazed at the diminished light from the heavens.

"But immediately after the tribulation of those days the sun will be darkened, and the moon will not give its light, and the stars will fall from the sky, and the powers of the heavens will be shaken."

Uliaris spat, squinting further at the sky. "It's odd, and cold, but terrible? And what tribulation?"

"You think our past few years would not qualify as tribulation?" I countered. "Invasion, riots, famine, and the destruction of empires?"

Uliaris, still fixed upon the skies, shook his head. "Could be worse. It could be us behind Panormus' walls. I doubt the Goths like the look of a cold sun more than us."

Procopius was less inclined to dour humor. "Lord Varus, we should send messages to the Emperor *without delay*. Belisarius should be consulted as well, wherever he has ventured to."

I knew I must act, yet my chest knotted with apprehension at the skies, which seemed to grow darker with each passing moment. The sun was now obviously filtered through a shroud, as if God wrapped the fiery orb with some unburnable linen stola. Though still early in the morning, the dimmed orange light seemed as if in the final hour of daytime. More, the blowing winds and muted warmth from the sky made it seem as if winter had returned to the world. A nagging panic once again sparked the desire to flee, yet I still had far too many duties to perform. Instead, forcing my mind to order, I turned to Procopius.

"Write your letters to our Emperor," I commanded, "but show good cheer. Soon, more will recognize what we have seen and will look to leadership for comfort. If you show them fear, this army will collapse into a mob inside of an hour." Sharing a glance with Uliaris and Sembrouthes, I added, "That goes for both of you, too. Seek out the other officers and inform them of my command."

As the three men rushed away to fulfill my orders, others sought my attention, begging explanation for the darkening skies. It was no eclipse, one man reasoned, so how could there be darkness during the day? Christians muttered fears of the End Times, while pagans hissed about the displeasure of gods of some land or another. To all, I merely nodded and listened, insisting that all was well and repeating Uliaris' observation that the shrouded skies applied equally to the Goths as they did to us. Valerian, an ardent Christian, was unconvinced.

"All this did not happen until after we landed here," he whispered. "What if God is angry at our conquest? Surely it is a sign of disfavor."

"If you think you can know God's mind, then you should be Belisarius' second instead of me." The words were laced with an arrogant defiance I did not truly feel. "There will be an explanation, and all will be well, so long as you don't allow our men to piss their pants at unusual weather."

After that, I gathered my horse and galloped for the coastline, seeking out Liberius and Belisarius after yielding to Bessas a temporary overlordship of the combined army. They were easy enough to find, camped but a mile from Panormus' walls and near several anchored dromons in a deep-water inlet. The clangor of wooden mallets and shouting men filled the air, with little of the apprehensive awe that consumed the broader army. Belisarius soon caught sight of my approach and waved his arm, grinning.

"Come and see!"

Curiously, even Liberius seemed pleased, although he glanced toward the sun when others turned their attention toward the boats.

Dismounting, I hailed both closer. "Lord Belisarius, the darkening sun is frightening the men. Is there any explanation?"

Liberius chuckled. "Either the world is going to end in seven days or we're all going to cackle at one another for being superstitious jackals. If it is the former, there will not be much reason to worry for long, so I suggest you growl and stomp your feet until the army decides to come to its senses."

"Liberius is correct, as always," Belisarius replied, his joy briefly halted as he turned his attention to the sky. "I've never seen anything like this. As if God is changing the seasons. I am sure Procopius wants to write his missives, but we still have a duty here. If you'd like, you can see our progress."

I agreed, if for no other reason than as a pleasant distraction from the creeping chill. And to my incredulity, it appeared as if Belisarius and Liberius had already fulfilled Xerxes' strategy, for two boats soared along the masts of a nearby dromon.

"How..." I mumbled.

"Archimedes!" Belisarius grinned again, his smile as broad as I could ever remember. "You know of his pulleys, Varus?"

"He should," Liberius grumbled. "But this younger generation, their brains are like soft cheese."

I chuckled. "Yes, Lord, Liberius instructed me on Archimedes' inventions. But none of the tales told of something like this."

Belisarius paced toward the shoreline, where he boarded a landing craft and invited me to follow. We only had a hundred paces or so to row until we were hoisted aboard the dromon, and from that closer vantage point, I saw a complex web of ropes and wheels, with a massive weight that counterbalanced a small rowboat that housed ten galley archers.

"We used an extra transport anchor, and the weight helps raise and lower the archers' boat," Belisarius explained. "Beyond that, all that was required was balancing the ropes without placing too much strain on the mast. We should be prepared to attack tomorrow, unless the skies truly do open up and angels pour from the heavens."

"Lord, this is incredible." I gaped. "I had little idea you were such a craftsman."

"Archimedes, Agrippa, and many other Greek or Roman engineers," Belisarius replied. "I loved their tales the most as a child. There is something wonderful about building something entirely new for a purpose that seems impossible. Perhaps, too, this will spare many lives."

"God willing," I answered, stealing a final look at the darkening skies.

I spent the evening with Samur. He would not abandon his Hunnic followers, so I surrendered the glowing warmth of my tent for the frigid camp of the Huns, who huddled under their furs as they stoked a massive bonfire. Samur did not wish to speak of the omens of the skies, but Aigan did share the Hunnic interpretation.

"My father used to say that the world would end in ice," Aigan said. "That the sun would blot out, and giants would reemerge to dominate the land. All those animals who eat grass would starve, and men would follow them to the afterlife. In the end, there will only be cold, and wind, and silence."

"I wish Rosamund was here," Samur complained, wrapping himself in a second fur. "If there's anyone who understands how to stoke a decent fire, it's her."

"Or Ascum," I offered.

"Ascum is a crazy bastard." Samur grinned, his teeth chattering. "He would douse our kindling in naphtha. We would either sweat to death or die from burns."

"Agreed. I will see if I can get more blankets and furs distributed tomorrow. In the dark, we'd just stumble about hopelessly."

Samur only groaned. "What a mess. I never thought I'd miss the palace. It's not just the cold, but the wind from the sea. You'd think the gods were playing games with one another, seeing what new discomforts we might be able to survive through the night."

"Gods?" I asked. "Have you turned pagan?"

"You've known for a long time," Samur said. "I don't begrudge you Christians, but the faith is not for me. Give me freedom, and friendship, and a lack of guilt in pursuing both. I'd much rather throw my lot in with the Heruli or the Huns than men like Cassiodorus."

"I wish you would speak with Petrus," I said stiffly.

Samur shrugged. "Why? He's no different than any other priest. He just speaks in a softer voice. As I said, I don't begrudge any Christian their love for their God, but I cannot scrape and bow like the slave I used to be. Not for so-called holy men who tie women to pyres for inane offenses and cut the throats of anyone who won't convert. All I want is to be free, and if the pagans allow me that fate, then so be it."

Samur would not pursue the subject further. We shared what poor fare that was immediately available, which was just dried fruit and salted mutton that was carefully heated before the fire. Still, I could not help but think back to what Rosamund had warned me of: that something was broken in Samur. Though she offered no explanation, in that moment, I feared that she may have been right. This man was my brother, no doubt, but he seemed far changed from the mischievous lanky boy who scuttled about the servants' quarters, frequently about to flout the wishes of his masters but never truly crossing an unforgiveable threshold.

We only half slept. Though the blaring fire licked us with delicious heat, the warmth was fleeting, wiped away by the coastal wind. Even with a wool blanket placed between my body and the hard soil, I could all but feel the vitality sinking out of my bones and into the turf. As sunlight peered above the horizon, I flexed stiff limbs and forced tired eyes open, hoping our sudden curse would wash away before the day's assault on Panormus.

God did not hear my prayers. On that second day, the skies were even darker than before, with the sun's orb flaring into a furious reddish hue that yielded little comfort beyond piercing the darkness of night. Frost again covered Sicily's grasses, and men struggled with inflexible leather and near-frozen iron armor.

"Perhaps Aigan is correct, and this is the end," I muttered.

"I doubt it." Samur shrugged. "But if it is, at least we won't have to push through Italy. It's going to be a terrible war, regardless of what Justinian's hopes are."

Belisarius, however, was unflappable. "There's nothing we can do but pray and perform our duty as best as we can. And if we can take Panormus with Xerxes' idea, that is as beneficial an omen as I could hope for."

He handed me a roster of archers from the Cappadocian Army, all hand-picked by Ascum for their accuracy and instinct. In all, fifty men had been selected for temporary assignment aboard Belisarius' hoisted rafts, with three dromons to be positioned just outside Panormus' walls. Though I did not participate in the exercise, I stood aside an eager Belisarius as he gave the order to commence Ascum's attack at the sun's zenith, when its feeble rays would be least likely to blind our flying bowmen. Many were wide-eyed as they glimpsed their intended battlement, yet none defied the order as the dromons closed in upon the walls.

If any plan can be remembered as unfolding perfectly, it would be Belisarius' attack on Panormus' harbor. Truly, the whole maneuver approached the finest art. Ascum was correct—Panormus' sea-facing walls may have been stout, but they were diminutive against our masts. Perhaps a hundred Gothic bowmen formed atop the towers and walls, but an unfavorable wind sapped their arrows of deadly force. As our dromons positioned themselves to face Panormus on their port side, the Gothic bowmen halted their attack, with many shouting in confusion: Why would the Romans not push their assault with ladders and armored spearmen?

The answer came as Belisarius' boats, laden with Ascum's favorite archers, were hoisted to the heights of the mast's crossbeams. I doubt I moved or even breathed as the boats wavered from a sudden gust, yet their counterweights held, and no beams snapped. From that distance, I could hear little, but there was no mistaking Ascum's horn signaling the Roman archers to attack.

The effect was devastating. Perhaps half the Goths fled, while a dozen more were filleted with barbed arrows. Only a violent gale could have disrupted our attackers' accuracy, and there was little that Panormus' defenders could do to resist. They abandoned the harbor, allowing Ascum's dromons to creep ever closer until they were little more than twenty paces from the walls, still safely within the deep water of Panormus' harbor.

A horn from Bessas informed us of what we already knew— Panormus had been defeated. The Cappadocian signal sealed their defeat, announcing the opening of the enemy's gates. A sluggish call of triumph came soon thereafter from the disparate Roman forces, lacking the vigor of victory chants I had witnessed after Dara or the Vandal War. Nevertheless, Panormus fell without a single Roman casualty, and Sicily was now wholly within Justinian's grasp.

"The mind can defeat a tremendous enemy." Belisarius grinned, then called for his horse to gallop back to the main army.

"If only more of you would learn that lesson," Liberius complained. "You'll need quite a bit of intelligence on the road ahead."

Following Belisarius, I witnessed Panormus' formal transfer to his control. Flanked by five richly armored warriors, Panormus' chieftain rode out to meet Belisarius, Liberius, and me fifty paces before the open gates. Our gathering occurred just as Theodahad's banners were lowered, to be replaced by the Imperial Chi-Rho once our army could enter the city. For now, Belisarius gave the Ostrogoth leader a salute, which was crisply returned.

"To you, stranger, I surrender Panormus," the Gothic lord began, his Latin perfect, though formal. "I am Badwila. Whom of the Romans do I address?"

"Flavius Belisarius, strategos," Belisarius replied before gesturing to us, his companions. "With Tribune Varus and Minister Liberius. We are sworn to Emperor Justinian and Empress Theodora of the Roman Empire."

Badwila nodded in recognition. "And the maneuver with the boats—that was you?"

Belisarius smiled, nodding. "I can claim only partial ownership. My officers collectively identified this opportunity."

"That was, indeed, the strangest attack I have ever witnessed," Badwila said, stroking a bushy beard that curled into an unkempt fork beneath a massive helm. "I could have held you for months, had you not taken the harbor. But tell me—why do the Romans attack us now? I hear only rumors and see dark skies."

At that, Belisarius cocked his head, a look of surprise on his face. He briefly explained the events that led to Justinian's declaration, from Indulf's testimony, to even the Emperor's personal friendship and patronage over Amalasuntha. Badwila sat silently through it all, awaiting his turn, until Belisarius concluded.

"I have heard these rumors," Badwila said, "but I thought them little more than the talk of tavern wenches. All I know for certain is that Theodahad's warlords have stripped my lands of spearmen to fortify Mediolanum. For what, I cannot know, although the Franks are treacherous bastards."

"Warlords?" Liberius interjected. "Which ones?"

"All the men of renown," Badwila said. "Vacis of Rome, Uraias of Pavia, Uligisalus of Illyria, Widin of Rhaetia, and Witiges of Pannonia." All were names that meant little to me, mere passing details amongst hundreds of notes passed by Narses' spies to the Imperial court.

Still, Liberius shot a glance to me, his eyes piercing into my thoughts. Had Liberius and I fostered war between the Franks and the Ostrogoths? It was not the worst outcome for our expedition, and while Justinian had hinted at this very tension, I did not place significant faith in the Frankish and Alemanni chieftains to aid our men. Why should they? Butilinus still waged war against the Visigoths, and by allowing our Empire and the Ostrogoths to deplete one another's resources, the Franks might still benefit by seizing authority over southeastern Gaul and even the Alps without pitching a single battle against Theodahad's men. Regardless, while it was a welcome rumor that Theodahad's attentions were not solely dedicated to Belisarius or Mundus, I could not help but wonder what carnage Liberius and I may have invoked across Italy's northern provinces. Justinian, at least, would be pleased.

"You may stay here, or leave as you wish," Belisarius said to Badwila. "With all of your weapons, possessions, and wealth. I ask only one boon."

Badwila frowned, his arms still tense despite Belisarius' unusual leniency. "And that boon would be?"

"Send your messengers to the minor cities of Sicily, telling that they shall be similarly treated if they surrender peacefully to the Empire," Belisarius explained. "Theodahad has abandoned you, for whatever reason. I would make the Goths my friends, just as with the foederati who serve as equals amongst my men."

"Your foederati, under Indulf?" Badwila snorted. "I shall do as you command, for it is the only wise choice before me. But whatever Indulf whispers in your ear are lies. I have known Theodahad for twenty years, and though he is a weak man, he would not kill Amalasuntha or her son. I doubt he even wants to be king, for he prefers books to blades."

Other Goths had levied similar descriptions of Theodahad before, usually with derision. Yet Badwila intrigued me most of all due to his extensive interactions with the Gothic king. "Books to blades?"

"Aye," Badwila replied. "Not exactly an honored trait amongst the Ostrogoth warlords. It is little wonder you swept through Sicily so quickly. And while I thank you for your generosity, you will not find such meek and undefended opponents on the mainland. Theodahad's lords will not allow for easy conquest."

Belisarius waved an arm, gesturing indifference. "My duty brings me north. Theodahad can resist all he wants, but I will not quit until he is defeated or I am dead."

Badwila's brows raised. "It will come to that, in one form or another. I will not pretend I am your friend, Flavius Belisarius, but I do appreciate your mercy to my people. Sicily is yours, until someone stronger comes to claim it."

Both men saluted, ending our conversation. "That was surprisingly cordial," I remarked as we departed. In fact, I could hardly recall a similar gathering of enemies transpiring without an exchange of blows, or at least insults.

"As I said, Panormus' harbor is its weakness," Liberius said. "Between a terrifying sky and equally frightful flying boats, the Goths likely dunged their trousers in fear the moment they saw Imperial archers soaring overhead. Make sure our men know of their victory. This will keep their minds from whatever hell is spreading above us."

"Hell?" I asked. "I did not take you for a religious scholar."

Liberius chuckled. "Nor would I ever wish to be. What a dull life. No, my years have been spent chasing the dreams of one emperor after another. As for this, I have never seen anything like it, which is why we must appear supremely confident at all times."

Belisarius nodded agreement, as did I. "That's what I instructed our officers yesterday," I said. "They will obey, although the skies are worse now."

"At least you learned something from me," Liberius said, ignoring the worry in my voice.

"We must inform the men of our need for a short rest only," Belisarius said. "With Messana taken, we can sail from Panormus' port all the way to Rhegium without any true threat. By autumn, we may even reach the gates of Neapolis and take all Campania before the year's end."

It was a hopeful dream. Not entirely unreasonable, either. At that point, our campaign had unfolded far better than we could have hoped for, or even planned for.

Valerian was first to enter Panormus, raising the Imperial banners at each of the city's towers. Any Goth who desired to leave found no resistance—though few did, with most preferring to remain with Badwila, in a familiar house with whatever family they had raised. As the faded sun fell into the west, all Panormus fell into Belisarius' command, with missives sent from the city's harbor telling of our success. Belisarius' mood only brightened, for his men were safe, order was affirmed, the local populace guaranteed their safety and prosperity, and our dream of liberating Rome all the closer.

But, as with all wonderful dreams, ours would take a terrifying lurch. For, not three days after seizing Panormus, just as a half dozen boats departed Panormus for Syracuse, Greece, and Septem, one arrival cut through the surging waves, bearing unwelcome news.

It was Bessas who first gained access to the hastily written scroll, its contents sealed in a leather tube to protect against the spray of salt water. As I met with Belisarius to plot our journey to the Italian mainland in Panormus' local palace, I jumped as Bessas burst in, cracking an iron-rimmed door into an adjoining wall.

"Lord, a message from Africa," he panted, wheezing from his sprint from the harbor. "The population has risen against Solomon. Carthage will fall in a fortnight."

MEMBRESA

B elisarius dismissed all but me as he pored over the message. Its text again bore Troglita's signature, its contents not even filtered through a cipher.

The populace has revolted against Solomon's taxes for the Emperor's tribute. Stotzas leads them. I suspect he has been fomenting rebellion for months. Their ranks are primarily Romans and those Mauri of the Aurès Tribe. A clan of Vandals has joined them, although most other Vandal clans remain loyal to Justinian.

We are besieged. Our port is free, and our walls are freshly repaired, but we have fewer than a thousand men to defend our expanse when perhaps eight thousand men stand against us. Our winter stores of grain are also low, besides. If we do not receive relief in the next month, I have little doubt that Solomon will flee and those who remain will surrender.

Stotzas is no military mind, but he is cunning and possesses respect amongst the Mauri. I shall do what I can to resist, but I can no longer guarantee victory. I am sending copies of this message to Syracuse, as well as other known locations of Belisarius' army that my sailors can discover. Please care for Auria and Evanthes, for although I am committed to fight, I have no stomach to risk their safety.

I shall look for relief by sea. Do not delay.

"Well, Varus." Belisarius sighed. "It appears you were correct about your friend Solomon."

"He was never my friend, Lord," I said quickly. "All the same, I did not wish for him to fail in his duties."

Belisarius closed his eyes. For a heartbeat, again I witnessed the cumulative pain of the loss that he felt, his features weathered from worry and a lack of sleep. The greatest cruelty was that these ill tidings, though not entirely unforeseen, would come at the conclusion of perhaps Belisarius' greatest triumph. He had successfully seized a rich province with hardly a fight, and I had survived my first true test as second-in-command.

With both hands, Belisarius rubbed his face, wiping away melancholy as he returned to consider his path ahead. "I cannot surrender Carthage after losing so much," he said, pain lingering in his voice. "But any delay to rescue it will magnify our difficulties in the coming months. If you were me, what would you do?"

It was a weighty question, but the solution was obvious. Belisarius was correct; if we engaged in a protracted war against these rebels, the Ostrogoths would gain far more readiness in our further landings in Campania or Apulia. More, the cost of a battle against Stotzas' forces, so shockingly large in number, could be disastrous—in lives as well as gold. I grated my teeth in fury at Solomon, who'd dared to parade himself as some living hero as prefect of all Africa and now had come within a single city of losing all we had won. Of all Belisarius, John, and so many others had sacrificed. Of Vitalius, of Irilar, and even Baduarius farther to the west. It was unthinkable.

"We must continue both fronts, Lord," I declared. "Take two thousand men to Carthage and strike like a viper against Stotzas' rabble. Leave the greater mass of our forces to pacify Sicily and prepare a landing for Calabria."

"Bold," Belisarius said, "but risky. What if Stotzas proves to be capable enough of holding our lesser numbers?"

"Then we require Constantinople's aid," I replied. "In Italy or in Africa. For now, Carthage is aflame, and the singular maxim of warfare is to quell your greatest threat without ruining the peace. Take two thousand of your most ruthless fighters, and make Stotzas' officers regret turning their shields."

Belisarius considered my words. Truly, we had little choice, yet no Imperial officer present yearned to venture once more along the African coastline. "I shall go," Belisarius began, "and you're coming with me."

It was all I could do to suppress my reluctance. "Of course, Lord."

"Liberius will keep order, and Bessas will serve as interim commander. Enlist five hundred cataphracts from my bucellarii, Gunderic's Vandals, and all the Huns."

"It shall be done, as well as the requisite horses and equipment," I said. "When shall we depart?"

"In seven days." Belisarius' voice darkened as he stole a glance at the sky. "Give the men time to rest while we wrangle enough transports. I expect to be in Carthage's forum within two weeks."

It was decided. With Ascum's aid, Belisarius acquired ships for his band, while I carried the burden of assembling and preparing them for the unplanned assault. Horses, arrows, blades, and spear shafts were stacked across several of the ships; by the third day, men from each of Belisarius' requested detachments joined them aboard. Before I embarked myself, I dispatched a message to Mariya, informing her of my change in location.

God willing, it shall not require much time, I concluded. *But if you should require anything, seek Liberius or Petrus. I shall be rejoined with you all soon.*

My ship, to my surprise, included Rosamund and Shimon. "I thought you would fare better with your servant," Belisarius explained. "So I sent for her to join a transport from Syracuse. Apparently the lad wished to follow, and I saw no reason to deny him a chance to see Carthage."

Though still not characteristically spry, Rosamund nevertheless appeared far better rested and considerably more mobile. "Mariya wouldn't let me do much, although Cephalas and Agathias are making a bollocks out of everything," she informed me. "But I will not complain."

Her presence was like a soothing balm upon my riven mind. Outwardly, I echoed Liberius when questioned about the skies—which mercifully dimmed with each passing day—yet silently, privately, I sought God's reprieve from whatever terror had been unsealed upon the world. No people, regardless of creed, could ever consider that omen a hopeful one.

Where God was silent, however, Rosamund was lively and protective. I confess that I have always been a poor Christian, and as our days grew darker, I relied less upon prayer and more upon Rosamund to ease my troubles.

"What do you make of the sun?" I asked, intending to sound more curious than fearful. "Did Petrus discuss anything of it?"

Rosamund smiled slyly. "Your priest has no further answers than any man living. All I can tell you is that the gods do not make such statements without purpose. A change is coming, and I fear it is something evil—just as I felt before we departed Constantinople."

I pressed further, more than I would normally. "Your religion has no explanation for the end times? An end of the world?"

Rosamund's smile broke into a laugh. "Why should we? The world continues, in one form or another. Only the Christians fret about a beginning or an end."

As before, Rosamund and I were joined by Gunderic and a hundred Vandals on our brief journey south; Uliaris and Sembrouthes, too, followed, serving as my small personal guard. Thankfully, our voyage required only three nights, yet through it all, our days grew colder despite the advancing spring month, while the seas churned with unseasonable fury. Against my better judgment, I joined Gunderic in his wine drinking, wishing to blot out far too many undesirable memories from the Vandal War. Rosamund joined in our attempts at revelry, although Shimon would not allow a single drop of wine past his lips.

"Isaacius would have drained every wineskin on this boat within a day," I joked, hoping to loosen his troubles.

Shimon shook his head stiffly. "Not for me, Lord. Besides, a man such as yourself should always have a someone clear-eyed to watch over things."

I did not press further, and neither did I encourage a surprisingly restrained Uliaris. Instead, we spent our brief passage sharing tales and toasting to health, although the Vandals always added an additional pledge of glorious butchery in the battles to come.

By God, though, the weather was horrid. The ancient Greeks believed in sea gods capable of summoning gales amidst clear days, and great monsters to torment travelers intrepid enough to sail the seas. I saw no monsters, but the ferocity of the wind was second only to the rocking swell of sea, unusual for that time of year. The ship's crew assured me that our boats could handle all manner of hazard, though cautioned my footing all the same. I needed no warning—the treacherous deck tossed about beneath every step, made worse by the strange darkness that pervaded open water even during the sun's zenith.

"Still not worried?" I asked Rosamund, pointing to the thickly veiled orb.

"I never said I wasn't," she shot back. "We've angered something terrible. Something thirsting for vengeance."

At that, a sudden swell caused both of us to tumble against the ship's wall, a tangled mass of limbs. Normally surefooted on any waterborne vessel, Rosamund yelped as her elbow collided into the wall, cursing in Gepid. The ship lurched again, and I wrapped my arms about Rosamund's head as we were thrust to the floor, our combined weight pressing my body painfully against the filthy wooden planks. We remained there, cradled together like some great tortoise, until that brief tempest eased. Rosamund shivered in my grip, though soon eased as well.

I coughed, lifting her from my chest. "Hurt?"

"No," Rosamund returned with her own rasp. "Sorry. It's just, for a moment…"

She trailed off, sitting upright. The sea rolled beneath, with shockingly chill spurts of wind fluttering through gaps in the upper deck, though Rosamund pretended not to notice.

"...my mind went back to the Bull," she confessed. "Gods, why am I still here?"

It was not fear that consumed her—not in that moment, at least. Balling her fists, Rosamund pounded against the floor, shrieking in frustration as her entire body jostled about.

"You're here because I need you," I replied, my clumsy attempt at soothing words. "I'd be dead without you."

Rosamund snorted but appeared to soften. "That's true. But that doesn't make me hate those damned priests any less."

Though there is no denying the journey was terrible, I cannot ignore that brief spurts were almost acceptable, either. One evening, after a particularly lengthy bout of drunkenness, Gunderic followed Rosamund and me to the ship's topmost deck, which jostled about terrifically from the rolling waves. What we normally would have seen as dimming twilight was more like staring into a vast cauldron of fresh ashes, the ink-black skies impermeable, starless. The crew lit torches to guide their footing, careful to secure the open flames to brass posts nailed to one of the two ship's masts.

"Be careful," I called to Gunderic. "I doubt any sailor on this ship could support your weight if you fell overboard."

"Worth the risk," he grumbled. "Need the air, even if the sea wants to kill me. Why are you here, though?"

Rosamund spoke for me. "Varus? He's a weakling on the waves. And as for me, I just want a break from the drunken boasts of bored and unwashed men."

Gunderic hooted with laughter, which faded swiftly to queasiness as he fought to steady his steps. Toward the center of the deck, he plopped to the floor, ignoring the inquisitive looks of the dromon's crew. With nothing better to occupy my attentions, I copied his example, as did Rosamund.

"I never thought Belisarius would allow me to return to Carthage," Gunderic mumbled, placing both hands upon the deck to reduce his swaying. "Seems risky for him."

"Nor did I," I admitted, earning another chuckle from Gunderic. "But your men proved their loyalty at Septem, and Belisarius is one for trust."

Gunderic nodded, sipping at the gusting air. "It will kill him in the end, that measure of trust. The world does not exist for such men."

"Nor women," Rosamund added. "Cruelty is a far easier and more rewarding path. I doubt it was always thus."

"For the Vandals, I doubt it was ever different," Gunderic remarked. "My father said that the Phoenicians, those who inhabited Carthage before the Romans, fed babies to the fiery stomach of great bronze monsters like what I saw in the Bovis Forum. In the southern wastelands, where even the Vandals are reluctant to trod, he said they practiced such rites still."

Rosamund grimaced, her yellow eyes narrowing with a distant look of pure hatred. "I have found that those who claim to be civilized are the most detestable bastards to walk the earth. Cheap words and worthless sentiment."

"Oh, aye," Gunderic agreed. "That's why I don't pretend to be anything but a soldier. Strength or nothing. Keeps life simple, and makes times with friends all the more important."

By morning of the fourth day, Carthage's vast circular harbor had emerged into view, anchored along the African coast. It was as cold as any day I could remember in this distant land, including the bitter nights in siege camps outside Mount Papua. Gunderic, too, acknowledged the unfamiliar chill, although it brooked no griping or fear amongst his men. Not that the Vandals required any coddling, for all donned their armor and weapons as if lusting for a fight.

And there was every indication that a fight was imminent. For along Carthage's walls was a massive host, a giant swirling mass with few banners and little sign that they were a hardened and professional army. But their forces were vast, consuming, like a great mouth whose jaws closed just beyond Carthage's walls, eager to savor the few men loyal to Solomon. Our few ships found easy entry into the

Carthaginian harbor, and with our Imperial masts acknowledged along the city's seaward gates, saw the city's docks largely vacant for our use.

Belisarius' craft docked before my own, although he awaited the arrival of his senior staff before venturing toward the Carthaginian Palace. Aside from me, we gathered Xerxes, Gunderic, Samur, and a senior cataphract officer named Martinus. The latter had served as a member of Belisarius' bucellarii since Callinicum, replacing Barzanes as a senior officer of the cataphracts after Barzanes fell to the Persians in our infiltration of Nisibis. He was a rare Greek officer amongst Belisarius' armored horsemen, maintaining a swishing beard that fell to a point along his chest. I had come to know Martinus as a man with little education, a bit shy with respect to forming strategy, yet as loyal as any, and quite capable with lance and sword atop a horse.

"How did Carthage go to shit so quickly?" Martinus rumbled.

"From a lack of attention," Belisarius replied. "And take care of your thoughts here. Remember, even if the city remains in friendly control, spies abound."

Belisarius permitted a guard of some thirty men to accompany his officers to the palace, with the remaining two thousand to take formation in Carthage's square. No release was permitted—we had precious little time for our soldiers to seek comfort amongst Carthage's whores and winesinks, regardless of how many groaned at the rush to formation. Belisarius was deaf to such complaints, promising only that their labors would be repaid twice over from his own purse.

We did not send warning of our arrival to the palace. Doubtless, our ships would have been spotted and reported by now, although Solomon would have expected some delay in our arrival. More, Solomon likely did not know who had rushed to Carthage's rescue, for Belisarius could easily have sent a deputy to quell the situation— likely, that's what Solomon or even Troglita suspected. Belisarius, however, was insistent upon not only attending to it himself, but taking the remnant Roman leadership by surprise, and yielded no time for those officers to compose themselves: All of the palace's guardsmen could identify Belisarius by his face, and many others could do the same with me, and none blocked our passage into the palace's outer gates. From its hill, I glanced over the city walls, rage boiling in my veins.

"Fucking incompetent," I spat.

"Who?" Uliaris asked.

Belisarius turned his head, his eyes narrowing upon Uliaris. "We knew that thousands stood against Carthage's walls. Don't be alarmed at their clangor."

Uliaris bowed. "Of course, Lord."

Belisarius' glare turned to me, although he offered no further comment. Instead, he gestured that we should continue, and our gathering stomped through the palace's courtyard and climbed farther up its marble steps. Soon, we passed through the inner gate, where Belisarius asked all but the most senior guardsmen to wait in the palace's primary atrium. He led the remainder of us to the locked doorway that had once been King Gelimer's throne room—the first instance where the strategos was refused unhindered access to Carthage's seat of power. A gaudily dressed guardsman bearing the trappings of a komes stood before the closed throne doorway with a dozen armed followers.

"Lord, you must wait until the Prefect summons you," he said.

Though his voice was familiar, I could not place the officer due to the helmet wrapped about his head and cheeks. He was younger and clean-shaven, bearing a Latin lilt that suggested a childhood of wealth and privilege. Belisarius, normally patient, plucked his helmet from his head, and glowered at the younger man.

"And who might you be, komes?"

The man puffed his chest, but Samur pressed forward before he could answer. "This molting chicken is Silius, one of Solomon's cronies. Not many of you left, eh?"

"Hold your tongue, Samur," Silius snarled. "Or perhaps we'll acquire another spear butt to silence you."

Despite Belisarius' presence, I abandoned all restraint. Without thinking, I drew my sword, leveling it against Silius' throat. "Say something else, I beg you."

His face, blurred by the fog of time, had snapped back into my memory. Alongside the deceased Marcian and Gratian, Silius was among Solomon's closest friends, and his longtime second even from the Imperial schoolyard—trained under Godilas and Liberius before a swift rise through the ranks.

A half dozen of Solomon's guards lowered their spears at me. "Murderer," Silius mumbled. "You think I fear you?"

Both Samur and Xerxes drew their blades, yet only I stepped forward. "I could gut both you and all the men behind you without trying. Come now, draw your sword, whelp."

Samur grinned alongside me, licking his lips. "There were five of you that night, including that cockless guard, and three are dead. Too many funerals in your world, Silius?"

"Enough!" Belisarius roared. "All of you, sheathe your weapons."

Samur paused, gritting his teeth as he glared at Silius, but I obeyed, my oath lord's voice enough to stop me despite the spearmen still intent upon my death. Nostrils flaring, Samur followed my example, although Silius' men did not.

"That is a command from an Imperial strategos!" Belisarius bellowed. "You have one moment further before I order all of you hanged."

Silius did not hesitate, raising a hand so that the guardsmen should comply. They did, allowing some of the room's tension to deflate, yet Silius stubbornly refused to move from our path.

"Move, coward," Samur seethed. "I smell the piss dribbling down your leg. You aren't man enough to fight a bunch of starving plebes, so I know you won't raise your blade against me."

Silius hissed, unimpressed. "Barbarian bastard!"

It was Belisarius that ended the confrontation. "Komes, while Solomon is a prefect, I am the senior commander of all Roman forces at war. And Carthage, if you were unaware, is at war. Stand aside, or I will remove you from your position through my authority."

At that, Silius' reserves depleted. He saluted, stomped his foot, and then retreated to one side, allowing Belisarius to push one of the throne room's ponderous doors abruptly open. As he passed Silius, Samur made a kissing noise to the komes, who returned only a reddening furious expression.

"One day, you will be mine," Samur hissed in Heruli.

"He is nothing, a worm," I whispered back. "Leave him to rot."

The throne room was gilded with gold and jewels, resembling nothing of the spare interiors preferred by Gelimer and Belisarius in turn. Gold cups rested atop carefully smithed gold plates, while all manner of ornament dangled from the walls. Atop a stone dais, the throne itself remained unoccupied—a gesture of obeisance to Justinian—but the expensive silks that rested to the throne's right were enough to make it clear where local power resided.

Solomon's skin was darker than I remembered, no doubt from countless hours beneath the burning Numidian sun. Sweat caked about Solomon's brow as three slaves rustled about him, carrying messages from Carthage's walls. He wore the metal breastplate and cloak of a prefect, immaculate compared to the stained, burned, and torn garb of the warriors that surrounded the hall. The scene made it clear: Solomon had leveraged Carthage to mold himself into an important man, but punishing taxes and personal avarice had brought him to the precipice of losing it—the city that Belisarius and I had bled over.

Solomon initially leered at the door, then exhaled with relief as he hailed Belisarius' arrival. "Strategos, what took you so long? Does the army follow you in the port?"

Belisarius, however, showed no such warmth. "Explain yourself, Prefect." He levied a stare at Solomon, ignoring the half dozen courtiers, and even Troglita, who stood at attention behind the prefect.

Solomon tensed. Still haughty, still wrapped in privilege of birth and military rank, Solomon had never dealt well with criticism, assuming that his whims would be obeyed without complaint. And legally, Solomon retained rights of control over Carthage's military prefecture, regardless of the presence of Belisarius' army at port. For a moment, I saw the same spoiled boy who had tormented Samur in the Imperial halls, and I loathed him for bringing me back to this accursed place.

At last, Solomon cocked his head. "Explain? There's an army of rebels and thieves at our walls. We must go kill them now, in the name of the Emperor!"

Belisarius sighed. "I have two duties here. First, I am to congratulate you on your betrothal to Praejecta. May you know much joy in your marriage."

Solomon straightened, smirking. "Praejecta enjoys Carthage a great deal. I am sure the Emperor will take pleasure in our future children serving him here."

A grin widened across Solomon's face at Belisarius' recognition of his still-rising status, or so I thought at first. Yet, curiously, it seemed he was smiling just as much at the mere mention of Praejecta's name as at the acknowledgment of Imperial favor. It was odd to imagine Solomon caring for another person, yet it appeared that my rival may indeed have had an honest affection for his intended wife.

"Indeed," Belisarius replied. "But as for the second line of business, yes—I insist you explain. How did Carthage come to this unhappy situation?"

Now Solomon puffed his chest. "Lord Belisarius, the population spits upon the Emperor's name just as the mongrels in the Nika Riots." As he spoke, he finally glanced toward me, sneering, before continuing. "Stotzas, that treacherous serpent, turned them all against me. I did what I could, but the revolt could not be helped."

At that, Belisarius finally glanced about the room, finding several courtiers bearing heavy gold chains that all bowed one after another. Ignoring them all, Belisarius instead walked to Gelimer's empty throne, placed his helmet at its foot, and sat ponderously upon the hardened stool. There was no cushion—Gunderic claimed that no Vandal would ever take solace in something so venal as a feather pillow—yet it was unmistakably the mark of overlordship of Africa.

Thank you for coming, Troglita mouthed to me silently, moving a few paces distant.

"Don't thank me yet," I countered, keeping one eye upon Belisarius.

Solomon's hands clenched as his gaze moved between Belisarius, to his ministers, to even Samur and myself. Yet he did not speak further, and jumped as Belisarius interrupted the pause.

"You have led a conquered and peaceful province to the precipice of ruin. So again, I ask you—please, explain to me why this is."

At that, more guards filtered into the room, led by Silius. Solomon looked to his friend for aid, which only irritated Belisarius further. "Don't look at your friends," he snapped. "Answer me, Solomon."

Solomon, sipping air, stuttered his response. "Lord, I am a prefect, and you will address me with resp—"

"I will treat you as I find you!" Belisarius boomed. Though lacking raw anger, his stern voice carried easily through the hall, likely echoing well beyond. "Now, as I ask you for a third time, explain your situation that causes me and my men to return to a place where we have bled and lost much."

Solomon crossed his arms, hunching slightly as he turned his eyes from Belisarius to the marble tile just below the throne. "Lord, my men deserted for Stotzas," he mumbled. "He bribed them, and most accepted. After a few soldiers left, other younger men in the city followed. There was nothing I could do."

"And why were your soldiers amenable to bribery?" Belisarius questioned. "Bribery is a fact of Roman life, yet my officers do not desert me."

Solomon shook his head, his crossed hands gripping hard at his linen-covered elbows. "Lord, I only did what the Emperor required of me. He was pleased with my tribute, yes?"

Belisarius rolled his eyes. "The Emperor Justinian would not be pleased that two shipments of gold cost him one of the wealthiest cities in the whole world! Again, Solomon, how did this revolt come to be?"

"I could not pay the army!" Solomon shrieked, his face draining of color as he stood from his gaudy chair.

"Could not?" Belisarius pried after a moment. "Or would not?"

"I don't know, Lord!" Solomon replied. "I did my best, but the Mauri and the Vandals are all treacherous bastards, and Stotzas lured away enough Romans to lead them all in battle!"

Belisarius rose from the throne, pacing forward. "Stotzas is a provincial administrator, nothing more. If you have allowed him to make a fool of an Imperial prefect, that is your fault."

Solomon jerked back as if bashed with a fist. His fear of Belisarius turned into rage, granting him the courage to summon a retort. "Lord, it is not my fault when the officers *you* left me with would desert from the slightest prodding. And it was not only Stotzas who encouraged this. Many of our defecting soldiers follow a capable military leader, which is why I dare not attack."

"Not only Stotzas?" Belisarius asked, standing within three paces of Solomon. "Who, then, would give you such pause?"

Amidst his apparent discomfort, humiliation, and anger, Solomon struggled against a sly grin, placing a hand over his mouth. Yet Solomon's eyes creased as if in laughter—something that I found uncomfortable.

"Sergius, Lord," Solomon stuttered, stifling a laugh. "Many of our soldiers now follow Sergius, who knows our tactics too well for me to risk striking out."

Nearly all present flinched at the mention of the unforgiveable name. Belisarius alone did not move or even change expression. Instinctively, I raised a hand to my mouth, forgetting to breathe for several heartbeats. Solomon did not speak further, only stared at his accuser for a few silent moments, the only noises the creaking of armor and shifting of boots from men like me who were no longer capable of standing still.

And then Belisarius slapped Solomon. With an open palm, Belisarius' gloved hand smacked into Solomon's exposed cheek, sending a trail of spittle flying onto the tiled floor. Gasping, Solomon turned his face back to Belisarius, his mouth agape and eyes wide, only to be smacked again—this time hard enough to send him toppling to the ground, where he raised an arm in feeble defense against Belisarius' attacks. After the second blow, however, Belisarius ceased.

"You hit me!" Solomon cried. "The Emperor will hear of this! You think he won't send you back to a dungeon? You are nothing! Just an upjumped plebe with a sword."

Towering over Solomon, Belisarius straightened, his voice deep. "Solomon, you are relieved of your position. You will take a berth aboard the first ship back to Constantinople."

"No!" Solomon shrieked. "You can't... wouldn't!"

Samur's mouth shot open as his eyes met mine. My fists were clenched, for I had no ability to predict what would occur next, now that something incredible had just transpired.

"I just did," Belisarius replied. "And I will have messages delivered to the Emperor explaining my decision. You have no command here, nor in my army. Is that understood?"

"You can't!"

Belisarius' eyes narrowed. "Is that understood, Solomon?!"

Solomon whimpered but nodded. Belisarius ignored the incoherent mumbles and turned to face his officers. "Varus, raise our personal standards along the walls and assemble the men. We're going to break this siege."

Gunderic hooted, pounding his spear onto the floor. Samur, however, yielded one question as Belisarius moved to depart.

"Strategos, Solomon will not need his guards any further, and this mess is their doing."

Silius snarled at the insult, though Belisarius was unmoved. "Komes Silius, you will assemble any Roman soldiers not currently patrolling Carthage's walls and form along the square."

"Yes, Lord," Silius mumbled, offering Belisarius a salute as a sign of supplication.

"The rest of you, show our flags and prepare for battle," Belisarius commanded. "We will catch Stotzas unawares, before they can truly organize for a sustained fight. We advance in two hours."

I led our salute. "Your will, Strategos!"

Belisarius saluted in dismissal, and we departed for our tasks. Within an hour, Belisarius' wolf and my ouroboros soared atop Carthage's ramparts. Within two, Belisarius' lean yet hardened force of two thousand was fully armored and arrayed for battle, awaiting their leader's signal to flood out of Carthage's gates.

Instead, Belisarius offered one final opportunity for leniency. Ascending Carthage's primary land gate, I followed him as he overlooked the thousands of Vandals, Mauri, and Romans under Stotzas. Some semblance of organization was evident in the rebel army's encampment, yet most soldiers appeared outfitted in stolen or antiquated Roman gear, or cheap boiled leather once favored by the poorer Vandal horsemen. In fact, gaining view over their ranks, it seemed their camp was turning to chaos, with the rearmost detachments filtering southwest and out of sight of Carthage.

Thus observed, Belisarius nodded to a detachment of wall guards, signaling for their various horns to blo for the rebels' attention. Against a backdrop of the shrouded sun, it truly must have seemed like Armageddon had come to Carthage, with an army of angels reinforcing Carthage's under-strength battlements.

It worked, somewhat. The frontmost ranks drew silent, halting their activity as they turned their heads to the looming general. Waving his arms to attract the attackers' attention, Belisarius shouted so that as many as possible might hear, speaking in simple Latin so that most of Stotzas' followers could understand.

"Rebels! You have abandoned the Emperor," Belisarius began, speaking each syllable slowly and clearly. "But we are merciful. We understand you did not wish to turn your shields. I understand your plight. You were hungry and poor and mistreated. So if you surrender now, full amnesty shall be granted to all but those former Roman officers and ministers!"

Many in the mob turned heads, muttering unheard conversations doubtless questioning whether Belisarius' offer was genuine, whether it was worthwhile, and how to decide the best path ahead. Belisarius, however, added one final note.

"I am Belisarius, liberator of Carthage," he shouted. "And if you do not surrender now, you will be dubbed outlaws, and no quarter shall be shown to you. I beg you, heed your last opportunity for peace! You have but five minutes to abandon your weapons and kneel before Carthage's walls. After that, my army will seek out those who remain defiant."

The mob exploded with great noise and greater disarray. I discovered later that Stotzas had already struggled to retain order as soon as Belisarius' banners were raised; the standards struck panic into untested recruits and Mauri who could easily melt into the safety of the southern desert. Now, after Belisarius' speech, it seemed none desired a confrontation against the famous general where he controlled a superior defensive position. Even the most resolute traitors hopped atop a horse and fled with Stotzas' army. A few hundred remained to accept Belisarius' offer, mostly women and older men, and they were welcomed into Carthage with no reduction in wealth or status, as promised. All that Belisarius required were their weapons, and such individuals had little enough iron amongst them.

Five minutes was enough time to separate those seeking mercy from others desperate to flee. At that moment, Belisarius' horns blared a more martial tone, unleashing Samur's Huns onto Carthage's firm terrain. The Hun foederati ignored those too infirm or slow to peacefully surrender, rushing westwards towards the fleeing enemy spearmen.

The Hunnic mounts had little difficulty navigating on such favorable ground and split between two separate detachments under Sinnion and Aigan. Samur joined the former, and the two wings of Hunnic horse archers swirled along the farthest edges of Stotzas' army. Blowing across the landscape like a violent gust of air, the Huns unleashed volleys of arrows upon those few formations that resisted, stinging their targets with a hail of missiles yet staying too distant for the rebel soldiers to reply with their own strike. By the time Belisarius summoned the cataphracts or his Vandal spearmen, there was little enough to do other than cut the throats of the wounded and dying.

"I'm bored, Varus!" Gunderic yelled in my direction, where I was still atop the walls with Belisarius as the Vandals filed onto the battlefield. "Samur is too greedy!"

"You shall have your chance, Gunderic!" Belisarius replied for me. "Gather your men, for we follow the rebels to where they feel safe."

Gunderic grinned wolfishly and thrust a spear in the air. After conferring with Xerxes, Gunderic then spat orders in the Vandal tongue, which gained him a roar of approval. As the Vandals cheered, I turned to Belisarius, unsure of what to do now.

"Lord, while I am pleased Carthage's danger passed so easily, I do not know what you wish to happen next."

Belisarius smiled, the first happy expression since being confronted by the baleful memory of Sergius. "You learned all the tales of Alexander, yes?"

"Of course, Lord. We all did, under Godilas."

"Alexander always fought armies far larger than his own. Do you remember why?"

I nodded. "Alexander favored Darius summoning all his men together in a single place. Rather than fight a hundred battles for a lifetime, he conquered all of Persia in but a few engagements."

"Precisely." Belisarius grinned again. "That is what we will do here. Even if Stotzas outnumbers us three to one after today, we can crush him once they halt their retreat."

"Then we pursue, but slowly?" I asked.

"Send scouts and commence a slow march, but keep the men from becoming overeager," Belisarius explained. "Let Stotzas re-form his forces into a single mass. Then we will annihilate them all."

And so it was done. With Carthage secured under the leadership of Troglita, Belisarius' army ventured gradually to the southwest. We allowed Stotzas a half day's retreat, but no more, kindling a fear in his men of a sudden attack by a hardier, better-rested force of veterans—a fear that was further stoked by Hunnic outriders, who handily shot death upon stragglers.

We allowed the chase to continue for four days. Belisarius did not wish to tarry in Carthage any longer than necessary, yet our men were amply provisioned and well disciplined for an expedition into the African interior, unlike the trailing rabble under Stotzas. A full thousand people, mostly older men and wispy-bearded boys, threw down their weapons and surrendered to Roman cavalry, to whom Belisarius demonstrated mercy with waterskins and enough rations to reach the nearest town. Given enough time, I have little doubt that Stotzas' forces would have melted down to an inconsequential nub, yet that was not Belisarius' intent.

"Make Stotzas' men hungry," Belisarius reasoned. "Hunger begets poor morale, and poor morale slackens discipline. At that point, that is when we attack."

Through our route, we passed Tricamarum. Even then, nearly two years later, the nearby hills were littered with skeletons of those Vandals and Mauri who had been allowed to decay in the open air. We did not stop—there were no Roman dead, and Gunderic showed little interest in availing the bones of his fallen kinsmen—yet I did note the hush that befell Belisarius' officers. Upon the back slope of a hill that had once been the Roman camp, John had rasped his final and pained breath, and it was obvious to all that the memory dominated Belisarius' thoughts.

Though Rosamund would spend the majority of her days riding with Gunderic's Vandals, she and I shared a meal each night, sharing conversation about some squabble amongst two Vandal spearmen that day, or the misfortunes of a camp follower, or some other inane event. Yet as we approached Tricamarum, the evening was met with melancholy. Rosamund's words, laced with unhappy memories, are still distinct in my mind so many years later.

"Do you think we will venture near Mount Papua?" she asked, near whispering.

"No," I replied. "There's no reason for Stotzas to go there. He knows it will trap his forces, and the area cannot support so many."

"Good." Rosamund nodded, gnawing at a hardened loaf of bread. "I wish we never went up that mountain," she added.

"Me too," I admitted.

"Their souls will never leave such a cursed place," she said, shuddering. "Just like mine would have been trapped in the forum."

That surprised me, though I wished the subject of the Bovis Forum would depart me and fix itself in the past. "Like yours?"

"We burn the dead after chanting prayers for their soul and give gifts to the gods to ease their passage," she explained. "But those mutilated or uncleansed or burned cannot be known to the gods. They wander the earth as spirits, desperate to re-knit their bodies but never capable of doing so."

It was a fate I did not believe in. Both from my abeyance to Christ Jesus, but also from the simple fact that violent deaths were commonplace. "It sounds like a fate worse than death. One that many warriors would suffer after battle."

Rosamund's jaw clenched. "Why do I think I try to convince you that these Roman wars are not worth it? You sweat and bleed for Justinian, and for what? To starve children? Or butcher pagans?"

"Rosamund..." I cautioned, feeling my anger rising.

"Not you," Rosamund insisted, albeit while rolling her eyes. "But most of the men in this army wouldn't have to think about destroying others for no reason than gold or the command of some silken patrician."

There was no point in deflecting the blow. "True, unfortunately."

Rosamund nodded contentedly. "Mount Papua is a cursed place because the Emperor of the Greeks insisted that some province in Africa should be his. If that is not the mark of evil, I do not know what is."

It was an unsettling thought, though not one I entirely agreed with. Carthage had long been Roman, and the Vandals abusive to the vast numbers of Roman and Mauri who lived as Vandal subjects. The war had been devastating, true. Had taxed my wits to the point of overexertion, certainly. But it could not be all wrong. All so immoral.

It simply could not, I reasoned then. Not when we had the likes of Liberius backing the voyage. Or Petrus. Or Theodora. Or Belisarius himself, who had earned the love of the natives as he freed them from the Vandal yoke. Rosamund spoke sense, but a sense poisoned with resentment and mistrust. For that reason, I could not completely take her wisdom into my heart. Not then, at least.

By the third day of our pursuit, with Tricamarum firmly behind us, Belisarius finally broke from his melancholy.

"Stotzas' deserters are thickening in number, and our opportunity for attack is ripened," he remarked. "Where are we?"

"We're just to the southeast of the Bagradas River, Lord," I said. "If Stotzas is a half day's march ahead, then he'll soon find his progress blocked by the river."

He nodded. "And the nearest town?"

Searching my memory of the maps that Xerxes and I had used to plot our daily route, I recalled the name of some town—inconsequential, not even a mile from our current position. "Membresa, Lord. A trading post for hunters, nothing more."

"Water to the northwest, desert to the south, and mountains of pig shit not far distant," Samur put in, smirking. "I would say Stotzas is ready to be cooked and stuffed."

Belisarius smiled. "I would agree, Samur. Let's quicken the pace. The Huns will encircle the rebels from both sides, while our cataphracts and Vandals will pierce through to the heart of their army. If we can claim the rebels' leadership, mass surrender will follow."

The men did not grumble at the doubling of our pace. On the contrary, many reveled in the prospect of spoils to come. For unlike the civilian towns or our Gothic enemies in Italy, a rebel camp would be open to plunder, with no objection from Belisarius. Though the lives of captives might be shown mercy—spared and reserved for judgment or enslavement—the goods and coins of those who willfully raised arms against the Emperor's agents were forfeit. That law was as ancient as any, and could easily mean wealth for one who slew a handsomely outfitted traitorous officer, let alone Stotzas himself.

None, however, asked of Sergius. We did not need to. For his sake, I hoped the man would be killed by a stray arrow, for if he was taken alive, even I would have no stomach to temper Belisarius' vengeance. Perhaps that was what drove Belisarius, leaning forward on his mount, squinting toward the horizon and the distant glint of iron sparkling against the afternoon sunlight.

By the fourth morning, Stotzas' army lost its momentum. Our scouts reported a general halt; the more experienced soldiers were carving ditches and forming as much of a defensive perimeter as could be fostered in a treeless, flat expanse along a riverside. Belisarius' moment had come, and the order was one of the easiest I had yet received.

Overlooking Stotzas' army, Belisarius leaned over to me. "You will ride with Martinus and my cataphracts."

"If you desire, Lord—although I have little experience with their tactics." I could feel my old wariness of fighting on horseback returning.

"Boreas is armored for the task," Belisarius replied. "Trade your spear for a lance and cradle it tight underneath your arm. Beyond that, there is little you have not experienced before."

I capitulated. "Yes, Lord. And you will remain here?"

Belisarius shook his head. "No, I will take a portion of Martinus' cataphracts as my own. When you are prepared, order the attack. Our enemy is already beaten. We must simply inform him of that fact."

Saluting, I joined Martinus, who hailed my arrival. "Come to join the real men, Varus?"

"Don't let Gunderic hear you say that." I laughed. "And don't let me humiliate myself today."

"Certainly not, with a wife as pretty as yours." He winked. "Stay close to me, and whatever you do, keep close to the wedge. As long as there's a cataphract to your right and left, all is well."

Before I signaled for the attack, I discovered Uliaris and Sembrouthes galloping hard from a distance. Martinus would not allow either man into the front ranks, for they lacked the heavy lamellar armor for such a violent charge, yet they nestled firmly into the third rank. Sembrouthes glowered at me sitting atop Boreas just off the tip of our wedge, yet did not insist that I alter my position.

"Very well, men!" I yelled. "Let's sweep this field! Mercy to women, children, and slaves, but don't let any traitors escape!"

Martinus handed me a spare lance as the other men roared their approval. Though the iron-tipped wood was easily twice the weight of a typical spear, its handle was sublimely balanced, resting comfortably beneath my armpit. Though I would not be able to heft it for long, that was no impediment: Our lances were design to pierce an enemy and shatter upon contact. Reassured, I signaled a nearby horn to order our advance and seize this otherwise unknown battlefield outside the dying village of Membresa.

"For the Empire!"

Our Huns reacted first, lurching forward and separating to the far edges of Stotzas' crude square. Like the claws of a great beast, the Huns snapped at the outer edges of the enemy, loosing volley after volley without hindering their gallop. Our cataphracts came next, and Belisarius donned his white-plumed helmet, saluting me as our twin columns of armored horsemen parted into separate wedges.

"Lances ready!" Martinus boomed, leading the tip of our wedge and to my right. "We're lunging through the enemy's center right. Straight through! Do not stop your advance no matter what!"

Behind me, I heard men muttering prayers and smelled fresh piss mixing with the ever-present aroma of horse dung. Though never pleasant, it was somehow reassuring—a sign that our soldiers took this fight seriously, despite Stotzas' marked disadvantage. Following Martinus' lead, I kicked Boreas to a trot and kept our pace slow until the wedge could form and we were just fifty paces from enemy lines.

"Steady!" Martinus yelled, increasing his pace to a canter.

Just ahead, Hun arrows filleted Stotzas' men, although the rebel officers began to discern our strategy. Lacking archers and possessing few horsemen, Stotzas was nevertheless able to form a protective shield wall—one that I prayed was made of men of weak resolve and unsteady legs. As we drew closer, I first recognized Stotzas, bedecked in a red-plumed helmet as if he were an Imperial governor or a general in his own right. I barely had time to laugh at the display before spotting the man next to him, dressed in a common centurion's garb, barking instructions for discipline amongst the enemy lines.

Sergius.

"Steady!" Martinus called again, his voice trailing as his commands were echoed by the lesser officers of our wedge.

At one hundred paces, Martinus increased the pace again, swift but not quite a full gallop. Our lances still rested in a cup along our saddles, pointed toward the sky, yet the quaking earth alone must have rattled the guts of our enemies. Their shield wall seemed determined enough, yet I spotted several in their second rank cowering from a continuing hail of Hunnic arrows. At fifty paces, Martinus unleashed the full might of the cataphracts, intending to demolish the most stalwart positions of an enemy line.

"Lower, you bastards!" Martin screamed. "Charge! Always forward!"

Two lances lowered to my left and right, yet neither posed any danger to Boreas. I followed their example, at first lowering my lance too low, yet soon steadying it parallel with the ground. Controlling my breathing, all sense of fatigue, of weight, or even of fear evaporated, leaving behind only a familiar giddiness.

Battle lust was no stranger to me. I had felt its noxious pull less of late, but still I recognized it befuddling my senses amidst Belisarius' fabled cataphracts. Rosamund claimed that such madness was an offering from the gods themselves—and perhaps it is so, for I have known little else, save the love of a woman, that offers such unquestionable conviction of strength.

Ten paces out, I found my target: a younger man, perhaps five years my junior. Covered in grime and stained with sweat, his mail armor was handsome, yet fit poorly upon his thin frame. When he looked upon me, he beheld one of the wealthiest warlords in all the world, yet when I looked on him, all I saw was a dead man.

Our wedge pierced through Stotzas' lines like a hot blade through soft cheese. My lance drove clean through the young man's shield, through his mail, and finally through flesh and bone underneath. When the tip protruded from his back, it snapped in half, and I dropped the fragments to draw my sword. Roaring nonsensically, I followed Martinus' instructions, surging ever forward into the collapsing ranks of Stotzas' army, but always ensuring my flanks were guarded by friends.

Resistance heightened as we delved further into the massed square, yet Martinus' charge was never in serious danger of becoming lodged against a determined line of spearmen. After plunging into their fifth line, however, Martinus instinctively altered our path, cautious to preserve his cataphracts against excess casualties. What Martinus and I could not have known at the time was that, suffering losses against Hunnic arrows and the companion wedge under Belisarius, the rebel army at Membresa had already neared collapse. As we veered right and toward open ground, Xerxes and Gunderic directed the Vandal spearmen into the ravaged rebel formation, eviscerating any lingering resistance.

The battle was nearly over within heartbeats of Martinus' charge, yet a determined core under Stotzas and Sergius remained. And while Martinus prudently sought safety, Belisarius dove headlong toward Sergius, undoubtedly recognizing the centurion's plume and kit. My own battle lust spoiled in my gut, replaced with fear as Belisarius pushed farther toward the rebel center, finding more well-trained foes in his path.

"Martinus!" I yelled. "Belisarius strikes at Stotzas! We must charge for the center!"

Our situation was mayhem. Vandals blocked our path back to the rebel lines, while the Hunnic horsemen reduced the maneuverability of our cataphracts along the battle's periphery. We could not easily charge farther inward, nor seek escape outside the battle lines.

"The wedge will get bogged down!" Martinus yelled.

"Give me twenty men!" I called in return. "More than enough space for them."

Martinus seemed reluctant, yet he too saw Belisarius' plume at the center of the vicious fighting with the rebel center. "Twenty!" he agreed. "But don't trade blows if you can help it. There are still far more of them than of you around Stotzas."

Along with Sembrouthes and Uliaris, Martinus ordered two dekarchoi to attend my thrust toward Belisarius' stalled wedge. Forming them into our own diminutive section, I directed my followers toward the rebel's center.

"Stotzas is there, as is Belisarius!" I yelled. "Kill that bastard, and the battle is over!"

Kicking Boreas to a canter, I rushed us into the melee once more, calling for the Vandals before us to scatter. Wisimar, witnessing my fresh assault, ordered his section of Vandals to part and allow me entry into the rebel lines and far easier access to the core of Membresa's remaining fighting. Rising to a gallop, I clenched my sword, pointing it toward an unsuspecting Mauri rebel and slicing deep into his shoulder. Boreas's momentum bumped the wounded Mauri aside while knocking a rebel Roman onto the ground, allowing the horseman behind me to trample upon the man's body. I heard screams for aid, yet there was nothing anyone could do. There is nothing worse in this life than war, and Membresa was no different.

Even with only twenty armored horsemen, we blew apart the disorganized and scattered rebel ranks like a poorly constructed chariot wheel. We suffered no detriment to our progress until, thirty paces from Belisarius' dancing plume, a stouter line of fifty spearmen locked their shields together, their spears level to the height of our chests. Forcing our party to a swift halt, I began to voice an order but was interrupted.

"Move, Varus!" It was Uliaris, yelling from my left.

Still mounted, Uliaris plucked at one of the three francisca axe blades at his belt. These weapons were disfavored by most warriors I have fought with, save Uliaris' own Frankish kinsmen, for they demanded greater skill than a spear or bow. Though shaped like a diminutive axe, the francisca was designed for throwing instead of hand-to-hand fighting, its bearded edge honed to a wicked sharpness and the bulk of its iron tapered narrowed into its wooden handle. Fundamentally unbalanced, an expertly thrown francisca would twirl in tight circles until striking its target, and thus served as a favored secondary weapon for those who mastered it.

And despite his flaws, Uliaris counted himself in that number. His francisca flew so swiftly from his hand that his target had little time to react, only just raising his shield as the axe head carved itself into his exposed jaw. The soldier shuddered, dropping his spear and plucking helplessly at the wooden handle, yet finding no relief. Instead, his flailing only widened the gap in the rebel lines, revealing an opportunity.

"Cataphracts!" I bellowed. "Bows!"

Though they lacked the range of the Huns or the speed of the Heruli, the arrows from Belisarius' cataphracts had little trouble dispatching our wavering enemy from thirty paces. The bow was a secondary weapon for Belisarius' armored horsemen, yet after three steady volleys, perhaps a dozen of our enemy lay dead and another dozen twitching in the dirt, quilled with missiles. On some of their shields, I recognized the faded Chi-Rho that betrayed a onetime pledge to Justinian's service.

Yet there was no time to further explore who they were, nor even to kill or capture those who truly had once sworn allegiance to the Empire. For as we drew closer to the last remaining quarter of earnest fighting, I saw Belisarius had thrust farther into Stotzas' ranks. And though he drew within ten paces of the rebel commander, I instantly understood that Belisarius' target was a closer enemy, and one more likely to rob him of his wits.

"Push for Belisarius!" I yelled. "He's going for Sergius!"

"Mother of Christ," Uliaris growled.

Remounted, I kicked Boreas into a canter, instinctively riding toward an embattled Belisarius. Remnants of our recently butchered enemy scattered, allowing me passage to Belisarius' stymied wedge. Twenty paces out, however, I realized that while Belisarius himself was surging forward, his guardsmen struggled to keep pace. Still too far off, I saw Belisarius surrounded, trading blows with Sergius' shield even as rebels struck at our strategos' body—failing, mostly, save one spear that slipped the iron web of scales armoring Xanthos and pierced the horse's neck.

My breath caught. "No!!" I yelled. "Hurry!"

Xanthos reared, legs flailing. One rebel, kicked by a wild hoof to the chest, choked and fell to the ground, while others rushed away from the dying beast. Belisarius half jumped, half fell from his mount, falling somewhere I could not see.

"Hit them!" I yelled, at last closing the distance. "Defend the strategos!"

Amidst the chaos in battling Belisarius' guards, we caught a line of rebel soldiers unawares. Here, too, many carried shields with Imperial regalia, including all remaining soldiers about Stotzas. From the saddle, I gripped hard upon Boreas' reins with one hand, then took my sword in the other and sliced down upon an enemy. The sword's edge cut deep into the man's exposed neck, which fountained blood as I tugged the blade free. Behind me, Uliaris and Sembrouthes followed my example, carving a path to Belisarius. Not ten paces distant, cataphracts of Belisarius' wedge pushed closer, yet were still too far to save their commander.

At that moment, I saw Belisarius' plume rise, only for three Mauri soldiers surge forward to meet him. "Dismount!" I yelled.

Before waiting for my men, I unstrapped a shorter shield from my back and vaulted from the saddle. With my sword slick with blood, I sheathed it in favor of my axe, chopping down upon the nearest enemy I could find. Anticipating my strike, my foe raised his shield, catching my axe plum in the shield's center, yet his face contorted with pain—Uliaris had jammed a sword beneath his armpit, where mail is typically weakest. Sembrouthes struck down another in my way, allowing me to free my axe and rush forward.

Until I caught sight of Belisarius once more. Pressing his shield tight against his left side, he slashed viciously toward Sergius, yelling something I could not hear. His strikes mostly landed, yet with each blow, he earned twice as many attacks from Sergius' men. Even an adept warrior like Xerxes could not withstand such unequal fortune for long, and Belisarius panted between his shouting, visibly winded, as Sergius calmly struck forward.

Sergius' blows mostly clattered harmlessly against Belisarius' shield or thrust into air where Belisarius' body once stood—until one sudden jab slipped past, and the blade's edge grazed against Belisarius' hip. Belisarius growled, slashing, as he limped two paces backward, now unsteady atop a weakened leg.

At that, I abandoned any hesitancy. Around us, Stotzas' army fled into a rout—Stotzas himself included, though many of the rebel spearmen were unable to free themselves from the tangle of Roman attackers. As such, I did not engage any man who did not impede my progress toward Belisarius, happy to allow them to escape and further sap the rebels' lingering strength on the field. Dust plumes billowed all around in the confusion, yet I could still see Belisarius pacing forward once more, attempting to strike at a hale and fresh Sergius. To Sergius' right, a rebel lowered his spear, ready to thrust against that injured right hip and disembowel him.

I lunged forward with my own attack. It was a foolish maneuver, and one that would have seen Godilas whip me bloody. Yet I leapt forward, brandishing my axe as far as it could reach. The blade bit into the lunging spearman's wrist, cutting flesh and breaking bones, and he cried out. His spear fell from senseless fingers as he pressed the bleeding limb into his chest, granting me just enough time to gather my balance and shield myself from a slash by Sergius.

"On me!" Sergius yelled. "Orderly retreat to Stotzas, but smartly now!"

A dozen spearmen filed around their centurion just as my own followers rushed to defend my position. Keeping my shield angled toward Sergius, I shuffled closer to Belisarius.

"Lord, how bad are you hurt?"

"It's nothing," he rasped. "Let's end him here, Varus!"

Locking my shield against Belisarius', I paced forward. Somehow, Sergius called more men, who swelled his ranks even as they backed slowly away, step by step. To our left, a second detachment of rebels crashed into our position, threatening to cut Belisarius away from the protection of the wedge once more. I glanced behind me: Xerxes and Gunderic were still too far to intervene. Yet Belisarius still pressed forward.

"Lord, we are about to be exposed!" I yelled over the din.

Belisarius ignored me, stepping forward again to slash at Sergius' shield. Sergius responded in kind with a swift thrust at Belisarius' hip that I was only barely able to parry with my own shield. Though several dismounted cataphracts attempted to block the rebel attack on Belisarius' left, our position was hopeless. Belisarius must have known that too, for his attacks against a steadily retreating Sergius grew far less disciplined and far more frantic.

Then, as the pressure on our left flank heightened, someone managed to push his way between me and Belisarius. "Lord, we are leaving now," Uliaris panted to the strategos, "and you are coming with me."

Belisarius' face pinched in confusion, then scowled. "Bucellarius, we are not leaving this battlefield!"

A heartbeat later, a rebel charge pressed hard into the left flank of our lands, sending Belisarius stumbling into my shield with a yelp of pain at his injured hip. He struggled to remain upright, leaning a portion of his weight upon my shoulder.

"Lord, the battle is already won," I barked into his ear. "But we might still fall if we advance further without support."

Still, Belisarius screamed wordlessly, slashing forward at Sergius' shield and receiving twice as many blows in return. Both Uliaris and I absorbed many of the enemy strikes, maintaining our perilous march forward in pace with those of Sergius. One spear, however, sailed far too high for either of us to block, searching for Belisarius' skull. To his credit, Belisarius managed to jerk aside, but the spear's wooden shaft still hammered against his helmet. Hearing a crack as loud as a mallet upon an anvil, I reached for Belisarius, holstering my axe and maneuvering to support his sagging weight.

"Sergius, you coward!" Belisarius yelled. "Fight me, man on man!"

Sergius laughed, raising his chin in mock triumph. "That would be difficult, as only one of us qualifies!"

Belisarius snarled in fury, even as he struggled to remain aloft. He pushed ever forward, now plucking a dagger from his belt and hurling it clumsily toward Sergius. The blade only rattled against Sergius' shield boss, earning nothing more than laughter, and the rebel centurion ordered a continued retreat.

It was then that Uliaris fully intervened. Grasping Belisarius by his belt, Uliaris hauled the general backward and away from the fighting.

"Willingly or unconscious, you are leaving with me!" Uliaris shouted.

"No!" Belisarius screamed. "He's mine!"

"Lord, if I don't remove you from this battle, you will be slain by some no-name goat herder," Uliaris said. "Hell, I'll butcher that bastard Sergius myself, but not today."

Weary and uncoordinated, Belisarius spat feeble defiance. "I order you to send me back, Uliaris! I will charge alone if you will not go with me."

"I swore an oath to protect you, Lord," Uliaris replied, his strength overpowering Belisarius' flagging body. "Even if it is from yourself."

"We will guard you, Lord," I yelled in support of Uliaris. "You have won the field, and the day."

"But Stotzas lives," Belisarius mumbled, resigned but still fuming. "As does that godless bastard."

As they separated from Sergius, the remaining rebel forces were able to retreat more swiftly. Several fell to the occasional Hun arrow, yet neither Sinnion's nor Aigan's detachments were willing to venture close enough to aim for either rebel commander. Our Vandal infantry swept across the surrounding valley, dispatching the desperately wounded and taking prisoner those still hale enough to bear chains. Even Silius' Thracian detachment was caked with dirt and gore, although the shared suffering had not made Silius any friendlier in his demeanor to me. With the battle concluded, both Xerxes and Samur sought me out.

"Is Belisarius injured?" Samur asked.

"Yes," I replied, "but not badly. And the enemy is swept aside."

Samur nodded. "They won't make a good pace, but those who remain will be the more disciplined ones—the better soldiers. Men that Stotzas trusts in battle."

"Should we pursue?" Xerxes asked. "What does Belisarius want?"

"Revenge," I murmured. Xerxes narrowed his eyes before I added, "The day is done, and we should not risk any of our soldiers to some ambush. Take Stotzas' baggage train, and let the men take plunder."

"Plunder?" This from Gunderic, running to join our gathering. "So we aren't chasing Stotzas?"

"The battle is done," I said. "Tally your casualties and spread wealth amongst the men. They've earned it, for such a resounding victory."

"A victory against Vandal turncoats, listless Mauri, and Roman oath-breakers," Xerxes muttered. "But yes, it could have been worse."

And so, what gold, food, and other treasures had been amassed by the rebel armies were greedily hoarded by Belisarius' veterans. We made camp, dressed our wounded, and gained rest for an abrupt return to Carthage on the morrow. The skies, veiled in a cold light throughout the day, faded into true night. Membresa's battlefield surrendered to a summer frost, watered by the icy blood of hundreds of bodies.

Today, if men even remember Membresa, they discount it as some minor skirmish. Something that began and ended within an hour. Something that solved little, other than preventing Carthage's capture by Stotzas. Yet while Membresa lacked the awe of Dara or the finality of Tricamarum, it changed the lives of many, from a dozen nations, for decades to come. I could not know at the time, but it affected our army as well.

EXILIUM

B y any account, Membresa was an unmitigated success. Through desertion, death, or capture, Stotzas had been deprived of half of his forces. Admittedly, as Xerxes mentioned, these casualties were the sickest, oldest, and least fit, yet the loss still left Stotzas far less capable of maneuvering in the African hinterlands. More, the battle was a blow to his reputation; a battle lost to a force one-third as large as his own made him appear ineffectual, even if his enemy was Belisarius.

For our leadership, however, the greatest victory was our own lack of casualties, with only four men slain and a further dozen wounded enough that they would not be capable of departing Carthage for some time. For that, I offered a great many prayers of thanks: thanks that Stotzas' rebellion had been tamed with minimal loss of life or supplies, and thanks that it had not substantially complicated our mission to Italy, aside from wasting time.

That is not to say there were no costs to the expedition. Notably, Belisarius took minor wounds. Rosamund tended to him directly, stitching together a cut along his hip and applying a poultice to a nasty bruise along his left temple.

"Any permanent harm?" I asked Rosamund in the privacy of my tent.

"None of the body," Rosamund answered. "Although he veers from anger to melancholy. I understand his hatred of Sergius, but I never knew Belisarius to be impulsive."

And nor was he. Yet, where Antonina was concerned, Belisarius was but a servant to love. Even then, hundreds of miles distant and separated by resentment and betrayal, I have little doubt that he loved her. Perhaps killing Sergius would have help stitch closed an open wound, or at least offered some element of finality. For although Theodora denied Belisarius his divorce, a defeat of Sergius was one thing that none could prevent or forbid. Unfortunately, that was not our fate, or Sergius', as Stotzas fled beyond the Bagradas River.

Before leaving Membresa, we said honors over the corpses of our few dead, their bodies sticky with dried blood. They were each given their own pyres, still adorned in their armor and grasping at spears and swords, and burned to smoke as Belisarius and I looked onward. This task was more difficult than expected, for the soft earth had stiffened from days of the waning sun and was worsened by flakes of frost that lined patches of grass. The veil before the sun had become so thick that it had taken on a reddish glow, like a bleeding eye against a gray field. I felt wrong, somehow exposed, as I labored with the men, desiring even the thin veneer of protection of our tents against that circle of crimson judgment.

With that duty concluded, Belisarius dismissed the rest of his men to enjoy their newfound plunder, yet asked that Rosamund and I attend him directly. Whatever the cause, I was simply relieved to gain protection from our baleful observer.

Belisarius desired to offer Xanthos a private rite, and I found my friend red-eyed and sallow as he led us to his longtime mount. Xanthos' corpse had been stacked atop hewn logs and kindling, more than enough to consume his vast and muscular body.

"Justin gifted me Xanthos, did you know?" Belisarius said, his voice hoarse, wincing and rubbing his sore hip. "After I rescued Petrus Sabbatius, our Justinian, against a Hun war band."

"I did not know of the gift, Lord," I replied. "Godilas did tell me of that raid, and that you saved Justinian's life, but little else."

He smiled sadly. "Justinian granted me patronage that day,

promising to raise my fortunes along with his. But in some ways, I doubt he ever forgave me."

"For saving your life?"

"For making it appear that he lacked the competence to save himself. Justinian has the vision for leadership and a rare dedication to his dreams but little tolerance for hearing the names of others chanted by the masses."

Sighing, Belisarius plucked a leather glove from his hand before running his bare fingers across Xanthos' hide. "I'm going to miss him. Is that odd?"

"No, Lord," I answered. "Ignis was like my family. I have no notion of how I would handle the death of one close to me—Ignis' death after Tricamarum was like a stab to my own heart."

"Perhaps that is a good thing, then." Belisarius gave Xanthos' body a final pat. "We should grieve our losses, however they come. Without that, all life would be little more than the urge to eat and to kill our enemies. Perhaps this means we are more than just killers."

"It is a wonderful thing," Rosamund said, finally joining our conversation. "Feeling grief at loss means that we have loved. And there is nothing more important in this life."

We stood together as Belisarius lit Xanthos' pyre. He offered the traditional words of honor for a fallen soldier—words that I have heard far too often in my life. Will others offer such respect to me when God finally does pry my soul from this coil? I doubt it, given the present circumstances. Some may try, but if they read this tale first, do not bother. My soul is gone, departed to a distant place where many have preceded me, to bliss or torment. Wherever I am sent, I hope I find some of my beloved there, for after writing so much of this tale, I miss them dearly.

We returned to Carthage. Belisarius rode a borrowed mount, while captured pack animals hauled away a trove of silver, jewelry, candles, spare weapons, and food that had been intended for Stotzas' host. Nursing his sore hip and swollen head, Belisarius still did not begrudge the rampant celebrations of Gunderic's Vandals, although he did insist that the natives were not to be molested under any circumstances. And though we returned to Carthage as saviors, we lacked the time to celebrate our achievement. Belisarius ordered me to prepare for our departure within a week—a near-impossible feat given the logistical constraints of our forces.

Rosamund assisted where she could, overseeing the correct allocation of plunder to each ship as our transports were readied and goods hauled aboard. I wrote letters to Conon, Thurimuth, and Theodora, using coin from the Carthaginian vault to send swift dispatches to Septem and Constantinople. Samur urged me to break from my tasks and enjoy a brisk ride beneath the darkened sun, and though I obliged one afternoon, my thoughts rarely strayed from my duty. For with luck, my duty would guide me back to Mariya and the children and some measure of comfort.

One of my final duties would be to witness Solomon's departure. Requiring whatever rest he could get, Belisarius declined to observe the former prefect's disgrace, and instead delegated the responsibility to me.

"In the days of the Republic, a Roman citizen could trade many grades of punishment for exile," he said. "Most chose punishment. Now, however, I am not certain that exile is nearly as grave a punishment as it once was."

I shrugged. "Want me to drag Solomon to the forum? Samur would love to flog him bloody."

Belisarius grunted. "No. I fear that Solomon may speak true, and that my authority in removing him is overstretched. His father will be less than pleased."

"You had no choice, Lord," I insisted. "Solomon has always been a prat. This time, however, his actions nearly endangered the Empire. Surely that must count for something."

"One would think," was Belisarius' only reply.

Though I did not mean to derive too much pleasure in Solomon's humiliation, I still could not help but indulge myself. With Shimon's aid, I donned my full war regalia, freshly polished and cleaned of the blood and detritus from Membresa, for the ignominious sendoff. Then, with an escort of Xerxes and a half dozen Vandals, I marched to Solomon's quarters in the Carthaginian Palace.

Though his goods — an inhumanly vast assortment of barrels and crates — had been stowed aboard his transport the evening before, Solomon's slaves still scurried about, loading odd trinkets and garments that Solomon had been loath to part from until the morning of his release. Their labors were further burdened by Praejecta, who had boarded Solomon's vessel with considerable baggage an hour earlier. I felt sorry for Praejecta, a dour girl who appeared happiest when left in solace and away from the trappings of court, now condemned to another lengthy voyage to join her betrothed. Alas, life is unfair, and even as Solomon chided his servants, I knew Praejecta at least would be cared for in comfort.

I found Solomon chastising a slave, presumably for dropping a mirror whose glass lay shattered across the marble floor. "Shit-eating whelp! Do you know how much that cost? I'll sell you to some whoremaster as a catamite for this, but even then, I would be short on the silver."

"Dominus! A thousand apologies!" the man begged. "Please forgive me!"

A resounding smack indicated forgiveness was not forthcoming. Frowning, I signaled for Xerxes to stamp his spear on the ground, and burst into the room. "Enough, Solomon!" I cried. "If you had shown such fire before, perhaps you would not be running like a coward."

"Eat shit, Varus," Solomon spat, palm still raised. He struck his slave's face once again, and a yelp echoed through the room.

Xerxes, however, was in no mood to accommodate Solomon's insolence. Stepping forward, he raised his spear and slammed its wooden shaft downward upon Solomon's outstretched forearm.

"You hit me!" Solomon hissed, cradling his injured limb as he fell in a clump upon the ground. "First Belisarius, and now you! You both will be flogged raw!"

Xerxes shrugged. "Keep talking, and I will hit you again. In Persia, we do not abide the weakness of the entitled."

"Stay away from me," Solomon snarled, tears brimming along his lids. "I think it is broken."

Xerxes crouched, examining the limb as Solomon tried to scurry away. "Looks fine to me. But perhaps you should cease beating your slaves while it heals." With a wink, Xerxes added, "Just for now."

"I'm surrounded by foreign savages," Solomon grumbled.

I grinned. "That you are. Now, are you ready to get on your boat, or must I have another mirror delivered to your cabin first?"

Muttering curses, Solomon rose. After a quick flex of his fingers, he abandoned any pretense of serious injury and hobbled well ahead of my escort as he bounded toward the Carthaginian docks. His vessel was prepared for launch within the hour and included one of Belisarius' bucellarii to deliver the strategos' condemnation of Solomon for his negligence. As we herded Solomon aboard, I found Samur staring silently not twenty paces away, his unblinking eyes fixed upon Solomon's every footstep. As Solomon reached the gangway, Samur jogged forward, his hands behind his back.

"Solomon!" Samur yelled. "Something urgent for you!"

Solomon turned. "What now?"

He was too slow to react. A wet, well-packed, and particularly pungent pile of cow dung struck Solomon's tunic, splattering inside his shirt collar, where it oozed from his chest to his stomach. Solomon gasped, too stunned to dodge the second. An equally viscous glob of dung slapped against Solomon's shocked face, with droplets staining his hair and filtering into his open mouth.

He gasped, vomited, and swiped helplessly at the mess, which only rubbed the foulness into a thicker, deeper smear along his skin. Outraged, Solomon roared, only to once again gag from the stench and taste.

Samur cackled at Solomon's suffering. "A hearty meal for the journey ahead!"

"You bastard!" Solomon screeched. "You think this is funny? My father will send assassins to gut you all like fish!"

"Oh, Solomon, this is nothing against what I still owe you."

Solomon began a further retort but only managed to vomit once more. "Water," he panted, his eyes frantically searching for relief. "New clothing. Immediately!"

I shook my head. "Not possible, my friend! Your boat leaves now. I wish you well upon the seas, rough as they are."

Solomon moaned, turning a bitter gaze to Samur. "You'll always be a slave, Samur," he spat. "No matter what you do or where you go. That's what separates you from me."

"Probably true." Samur grinned. "But you'll always be a shit eater. Enjoy your feast."

As Solomon gagged and retreated to the far side of his temporary home, Samur strode to the edge of the pier to scrub his hands in the waves. "Solomon must be more moronic than I thought," he said, returning. "Calling for water like that. There's water all around him!"

I chuckled. "I wonder how long he'll smell of dung. His trip will be at least six weeks."

"Hopefully every day," Samur said. "At least then he will smell as rotten as his soul."

Later, after Solomon's transport departed for Constantinople, Samur volunteered to remain in Carthage. It was sensible — Carthage would require reinforcing, given that Stotzas remained alive and scheming in the distance — yet struck me as curious why Samur would request the assignment. He insisted there was no reason, that Carthage was not so much more preferable to toiling against the Goths in Italy, yet in my heart I sensed dishonesty. Still, I did not pry, but instead conveyed Belisarius' denial of Samur's request.

"Belisarius needs the Huns in Italy," I explained. "They're his most effective fighting force."

Samur shrugged. "If he insists. But Africa will fall apart sooner or later."

Belisarius, weakened and exhausted from Membresa, was wary of Carthage's predicament. After Solomon's departure, Belisarius designated Troglita the temporary military governor and empowered him with martial law in a separate meeting of local leadership.

"All of Solomon's men who did not join Stotzas may remain here under your command," he decreed to Troglita. "I will spare twenty cataphracts and fifty of my Vandal foederati under Wisimar. God knows it will not be enough to pacify the region, but it is all I can spare at this time."

Troglita bowed. "It is enough, Lord. And Germanus will bend Justinian's ear. As soon as reinforcements arrive, I will return your men to you."

Belisarius grunted. "I pray you are correct. But in the interim, rely upon local levies to hold the major coastal cities. Stotzas may be defeated, but he is not yet beaten. Is that your estimation, Varus?"

"Yes, Lord," I agreed. "From what our Hun scouts observe, Stotzas still has some two thousand men under arms, and perhaps another thousand stragglers who could wield a club or mattock."

Troglita sighed. "Enough to cause trouble. He will seek out more of the Mauri tribes to flock to his banners. I can sway most to remain neutral, but farther west is still lawless."

"Which tribes?" I asked. "Can Auria bind their loyalty?"

Troglita shook his head. "The Mauri rarely cooperate outside of their clans. The Dorsale and the Nemencha are with us, but the Aurès were already supplying Stotzas with warriors for the siege of Carthage. I would not worry about any of these tribes on their own, however."

"Which concern you, then?" Belisarius asked. "You know the local customs better than any other Roman officer."

Scanning a nearby map, Troglita traced the African coastline westward. "The Frexenses are led by a man named Antalas, who agitates for independence from the Empire. But the most concerning are the Mauri of Altava, under a certain Mastigas. The Altavans are too distant for me to safely strike with so few men, yet they are the wealthiest and most numerous tribe. It is said that Stotzas was betrothed to Mastigas' daughter."

"If they are so distant and lack ships, how can they harass Carthage?" I asked.

"They don't need to. They have inspired other tribes like the Aurès to destabilize our trade routes for them. That way, Mastigas loses no men and incurs no direct retribution."

Pale but alert, Belisarius considered Troglita's map, detailing the dozens of scattered Mauri tribes. "What makes Stotzas so appealing to the Altavans? When I ruled Carthage, Stotzas was capable but hardly a man to burn nations over."

"Stotzas grew hideously rich under Solomon's leadership," Troglita explained. "And he promised the Altavans independence in return for following him. Stotzas makes the same promise to all the Mauri. The Empire ruined Stotzas' streams of wealth and influence, and so he offers the Mauri an opportunity to expel us. It does not hurt that Stotzas understands the terrain better than most, and knew of all our logistics in the province."

"Clever," Belisarius concluded. "But little we can do for now. Send an emissary to this Mastigas, and let us pray that Germanus arrives with an army. I have a premonition that you will need it for the fighting to come."

Though it is embarrassing to admit, I found talk of Mauri tribal squabbles dull. After all, my path lay in Italy, and while I cared deeply for Troglita, there was little I could do to shift the outcome of that conflict in Rome's favor. Besides, the Mauri were undisciplined warriors, fighting as individuals rather than in an organized formation, and lacked both the iron and the wood to fashion plentiful weapons. Their greatest defense was the endless southern desert. With three to four thousand men, I believed Troglita could sweep all the Mauri off the map.

In truth, I yearned to leave. Carthage and its surroundings were locations of sadness and regret, and I would not linger a day longer than necessary. Yet before we could leave, Belisarius insisted upon one further meeting—a meeting between me, himself, and Uliaris. It would be the first formal conversation between the two men since John's death, and there was little joy in Belisarius' face as he summoned his senior bucellarius.

Belisarius did not explain his purpose beforehand, nor offered any kind of warning. Still, I could surmise his intent, yet felt powerless as Uliaris walked into the Carthaginian throne room.

"Strategos." Uliaris bowed. Turning to me, he added, "Tribune. How may I serve?"

His eyes were bloodshot, and his hands shook as if freezing in an icy gale. That was not entirely unfounded, for the evening coastal breeze smacked of winter, with each day less hospitable than the last. Indeed, earlier that day, a beggar had been found dead in a gutter, his flesh chilled underneath thin garments that normally were well-suited to the African heat. Uliaris, however, likely suffered from being separated from his wine, sweating as he shook, yet no alcohol stained his breath.

Belisarius, however, wrinkled his nose.

"Uliaris," Belisarius said, the word shot from his lips as if poisonous.

Uliaris stood straight, offering a salute as he struggled to remove the quivering frown from his face. "Yes, Lord?"

"You are formally released from my bucellarii," Belisarius declared. "You may remain in this army with your usual wages or depart without hindrance."

"Lord?" Uliaris moaned, swaying lightly atop unsteady feet.

Belisarius, breathing deeply, did not render a response quickly. When it came, it was laced with pent-up fury, spilling forth like a lanced boil. "You are unfit to serve as my chief bucellarius. At John's dying request, I gave you more opportunities at redemption than would be owed to any man. As your oath lord, you have failed me in this regard. And so, you are removed from my service."

Uliaris bit his lip, his voice little more than a squeak. "Lord, may I speak?"

"No," Belisarius growled. "You are dismissed for today. Find another position in this army or take your spoils elsewhere."

As cruel as they were, Belisarius' remarks were more a reflection of what already had come to pass rather than a sudden change in circumstance. Yet, though Uliaris could remain with me, the disdain stung all the more—formally, Uliaris was condemned in the eyes of his oath keeper.

Uliaris bowed, yet paused as he faced the floor, shaking. He panted as he stood, yet would not allow his face to be seen. What he waited for I do not know—perhaps nothing. It was one of the few moments I had ever witnessed Belisarius' bitterness, which he neglected to show even Antonina after her affair was revealed. In a small way, I loathed Belisarius' actions, but I said nothing to contradict them. I regret that to this day.

One mote of clemency was that Uliaris could remain a soldier. Like Xerxes, I doubt that there was any other profession, or indeed any other life that the Frankish soldier could survive within. As atonement for my silence to Belisarius' condemnation, I invited Uliaris to my household guard, knowing full well that his cost was one I could not afford.

"I don't want your pity, Varus," Uliaris murmured.

"Not pity," I insisted. "I need men to keep me alive in the battles to come. If Theodahad has his way, we'll all be hanging from the Via Flaminia by next autumn."

"Theodahad's wish or Justinian's?" Uliaris grumbled. "Do you know how many men I have killed, Varus?"

The hairs on my arms rose, chilled by the sudden breeze from the friendless sky. "No."

"Neither do I." He chuckled. "I lost count after fifty. I lost count, but I see their faces every night all the same."

In an instant, I found myself falling backward in time, after my first raid as a slip of a man, into Rosamund's village. Mundus spoke of the permanence of the nightmares after a battle, when a man's soul escapes his lips and all that he might do is extinguished in a single act of violence. As my time in the army stretched longer, I came to know full well the meaning of Mundus' warning.

"Do you regret any of it?" I asked.

Uliaris shrugged. "Most of them probably deserved dying. Some did not. John chief among them." Wiping his face, he clutched his hands together, not fully stifling the shaking. "I don't regret the killing. I regret what we did the killing for."

"The Empire?" I asked. "What else is there?"

"The world. Something better. I would take a thousand lives for my friends. But to raise a blade in anger for that cunt Justinian?"

Uliaris rose to his feet, staring out at the sea. With the veiled sun, the twilight hour was somehow more breathtaking than before. The dying gasps of the day drew more vivid, with pinks and reds dancing on the horizon. It was like blood against the western skies, spilling from that crimson eye that taunted us from the heavens.

"Why are we here?!" Uliaris yelled into the distance. "What is it all for?!"

I could not answer. Instead, I allowed Uliaris to pant, and to grieve, and to seethe. As he calmed, I patted him upon the shoulder.

"Fine," Uliaris muttered. "I will join you. I owe Belisarius a life for John's. Franks believe in blood debts, and I will settle my ledger one day."

And so we parted. I tasked both Xerxes and my Aksumites to keep watch over Uliaris, yet after that moment, he never touched another drop of wine. Not before our departure for Syracuse, nor on the voyage across the sea, nor after our arrival. The abandonment saw something die in Uliaris, but by the same coin, it also stoked in him a hardness and determination to do right. He would be sorely needed in the battles to come, in one of the most desperate clashes any of us would struggle through.

And it would not be long in coming.

A YEAR WITHOUT SUMMER: THE SCALES OF THE BLACK HORSEMAN

Our sailing back to Syracuse, though brief, was memorably violent. Even Rosamund's labors did little to stymie my misery. As I secluded myself in a cabin with her, Sembrouthes drilled Shimon in the basics of combat. Each time he attended me, I spotted fresh welts and lacerations, yet Shimon embraced it all with a rare smile.

"This life may not be for you," I cautioned. "Most quality warriors begin training at half your age, or even younger."

"More reason that I should train harder and make up for lost time." Shimon grinned. "With your permission, of course."

Others suffered from the unfeeling bloodred sun and the churning waters, yet most were in good spirits. Plunder will do that to a man—the spoils of war are better than a richly seasoned dinner or a surprising gift, or even sex. There is something to seizing one's just rewards from the battlefield that is dissimilar from all other actions in this life, generated by the knowledge that one gambled their life at a chance for such wealth.

As Belisarius' second, I was granted a portion of Stotzas' looted treasure, which would secure my finances for another year. Similarly, I was granted a portion of the proceeds of the enslavement of captured enemies who had previously sworn an oath of loyalty to the Emperor—to this, I did not object, not at the time. The threat of civil war was a heinous sin, and such men would have happily butchered my own to pry their independence from Justinian in the African provinces.

It was not nearly enough to compensate from my winnings seized by Cassiodorus, unfortunately, but my chest lightened at the knowledge that unwelcome visits from debt collectors could be pushed further into the future—although that assumed I ever returned to Constantinople in the first place. Fortunately, the Emperor's law made it plain that no soldier could be struck with a creditor's judgment while serving the Empire in war. Many, including Caesar himself, legally fled from debts while they journeyed on campaign—a fate that I'd considered if fortune did not replenish my coffers. In the meantime, I rejoiced despite my misery, watching others drink and make merry as Rosamund sang soothing Gepid songs.

Syracuse could not have arrived sooner. I was among the first to depart our ship, followed by Rosamund and Shimon, as the others unloaded our goods and newfound wealth. Though Syracuse is an ancient city, it is not particularly large, and I found my household's quarters with little delay. Greeted by Cephalas at the door, I rushed inside and up two levels of wooden stairs, finding Mariya conversing with one of her servants. I swept her in my arms, not even allowing time for a shriek of joy as I kissed her.

In the privacy of Mariya's rooms, we coupled together with an urgency unmatched by any other time in memory—save for, perhaps, during the Nika Riots. Servants assisted with the unloading of my goods, and attendants cared for the children, allowing me to lie naked with my wife despite the early hour. Through all our time together, I never lost the enchantment of her scent, of the floral perfume that clung to her skin despite not applying it for days. It was that allure that first enchanted me to her, bewitched to senselessness. A gentle madness, but one that I would risk everything to preserve. Wrapped in the arms of one another, I told her of my sojourn to Carthage and Membresa.

"Poor Solomon." Mariya grimaced.

"He's lucky Belisarius did not have him hanged," I countered.

"Samur would happily prepare the noose."

Mariya frowned. "I do not forgive him his transgressions, but nor do I believe him a willful idiot. I promise you, Solomon will never be the same after this loss of respect, even if Praejecta bears him many sons."

"Nepotian," I grumbled. "I cannot believe he convinced Justinian to allow Solomon into the Imperial household."

"I can." Mariya grinned. "Nepotian is rich, and one of the few elder senators who survived the riots. I am sure Justinian was given a handsome gift in return for Praejecta."

I grunted. "No matter what he does, Solomon always floats above the mire."

"Which is why we must be careful with our remaining gold, Varus." Mariya lowered her voice to a whisper, face darkening. "One day, it might be you that needs wealth to dissolve a problem."

"Remaining gold?" I whispered back. "What is your meaning?"

Mariya sighed. "I know the troubles of our household fortune, especially after Cassiodorus. What I do *not* understand is why you could not trust me with this information. I am not stupid, Varus."

"I..." I stammered, a tightening sensation creeping across my skin. "I did not wish to worry you."

Mariya slapped my cheek—playfully, at least. "All the way to poverty? At least give me a chance to help you. Had I known, I would have been more proactive about limiting expenses."

I could summon nothing perfect to say. No words of explanation, nor assurances that the situation would be securely resolved. All I could muster was a clumsy reply. "I'm sorry, Mariya."

She responded by rolling on top of me, her legs straddled about my stomach. Her eyes, so dark despite the light peering through nearby curtains, seared into my own. "Varus, if I wanted a husband with boundless silver, I would have remained with Solomon. I chose you because you honor me, not my father or brother."

"Mariya, I know—"

Her fingers squeezed my shoulders. "I don't wish to live a poor life. I know the terrible ends such a life leads to. But if that is what God intends for my family, I will embrace it with a soul of love and my chin high. However, you make it difficult when you keep secrets from me. And that I cannot allow."

"I'm sorry," I said again, burning under her gaze. "You have my promise to be more forthright."

Mariya nodded and leaned down to peck at my cheek. "I know some things you feel most comfortable discussing with a woman. I just wish that person could always be me."

That exchange left me in a Janus-faced combination of humiliation and relief. Relief, in that I did not need to withhold information from Mariya our struggles with coin. Humiliation, however, in that both my inadequacy and my secrecy had been discovered. Together, it left me feeling unclean and desperate to correct my error. Before we dressed and parted, Mariya slid back to the feather mattress, reflecting on a different revelation from my time in Membresa.

"Belisarius will never quite be himself until either he dies, or Sergius does," she said. "I would expect rashness from Samur or Gunderic, or even of you, but not Belisarius."

"Agreed," I said. "But there's nothing we can do about it now."

Belisarius granted our armies a full three days of rest after reaching Syracuse. Other elements of the army were informed of our return, as well as Belisarius' intentions to cross the narrow strait, seize Rhegium, and advance along the Campanian coastline to seize Neapolis. I fielded missives from across Sicily, preparing a plan for the next phase of our attack on the Ostrogoth kingdom.

Alas, as with most plans in life, it all collapsed as summer unfolded. Or the lack of summer, as I remember it.

Whether from darkened skies or some additional calamity, the violent seas and occasional snow delayed our voyage to the Italian mainland. No amount of cursing, of bribing, or of pleading with the ship's captains could sway a different result—the danger posed by transporting thousands of men and beasts even a short distance was far too great. Belisarius demonstrated no irritation in meeting with his officers, yet in our private conversations, his worry was palpable.

"Theodahad will now know of our conquest of Sicily, and will have ample time to prepare Campania," he muttered. "I fear we will have little choice than to fight a much greater army head on, rather than rush the provinces while the Goths lack coordination."

And so we waited. Many occupied their time preparing for the campaign ahead—salting fish and other meats, storing grain, and otherwise provisioning an army for what could be an extensive march defined by deprivation. Our soldiers trained, and our officers updated their maps, updating the locations of Gothic leaders and armies based upon what little Narses' network of spies was able to slip into Sicily. Curiously, Theodahad and his warlords showed no initiative to march southward, yet Belisarius never abandoned his wariness of a sudden assault by a massive host.

Though not an immediate concern, the extended frost caused the local wheat to wither and crack. Within two weeks of our return from Carthage, a quarter of the island's planted fields had died. Two months after that, half the fields again were consigned to flames, and what immature stalks remained yielded so little that even the native birds began to fall from their nests, emaciated.

Through prudent planning, Belisarius' army had rationed stores through the coming winter, and shipments from Greece amplified the stores from Sicily, yet when that produce was expended, there was little hope for future relief. Before vast congregations, Petrus prayed that the sun would return its warmth and that God would again show signs of favor upon the Empire. Privately, however, Petrus hinted that such a symbol might be more than a test, but one of the horsemen that carried portents of a coming apocalypse.

"None living have seen such times," Petrus said, his voice a wispy hush. "But those who hear God's words have described such events in detail."

Though normally I would be skeptical of such claims, Petrus' hints rattled my confidence. "If it truly is God's displeasure, what would be the next sign?"

"Whatever He elects to do," Petrus replied. "But since Atilla, we have seen war, and now we see famine—indeed, what might become the worst famine of my lifetime. That leaves two others."

"Pestilence," I whispered, shivering, "and death."

"Which are often bedfellows," Petrus concurred. "Be sure that your family and loved ones commit themselves to God, Varus. For in this instance, I am fearful of what might come next."

I do not consider myself prone to superstition, but neither do I consider myself a fool. If neither Rosamund nor Petrus had answers for the slow death of our world, that was all the evidence I needed to be fearful of the months to come. As letters from more distant locales told of similar destruction amidst the creeping chill, I understood that no aid would come from more hospitable climes. All I could do was uphold my duty, stretch what rations our army had stored, and distract myself as best as I could with the hope that God did not intend for our world to end in the coming months.

Amidst the flurry of action, Sembrouthes commenced his training of the youth and children. For Shimon, it was a welcome continuation from the voyage from Carthage, his spirits unshakeable despite whatever cruelty Sembrouthes thought to inflict that day. On one dawn, Sembrouthes barked for Shimon to wake and marched him beyond Syracuse's walls and a hundred paces from the coastline. He was ordered to dig a pit ten paces wide and two paces deep, with only a common spearman's shovel to till the ice-hardened earth. It took Shimon all morning and the greater portion of the afternoon, but, caked in frothing sweat, he completed the task.

"Excellent," Sembrouthes said. "Now, run to the sea and fill the pit with water. You can return home when the water reaches the top."

Shimon was handed a wooden bucket and pointed the hundred paces toward the coastline. Again he continued, shivering from cold spray and the feckless sun, splashing one pail after another into the hole. I was certain that he would fail, either from injury, exhaustion, or simple surrender, yet he halted only to sip at a waterskin and gnaw at a tough strip of dried beef. As I awoke the following morning, I found Shimon still battling the pit, his labors ending as the sun fully rose to above the horizon.

"The lad never complains," Sembrouthes remarked. "Was his brother the same way?"

"Oh no!" I laughed. "Isaacius moaned constantly. But he was dedicated and loyal."

Less punishing but equally focused were his initial instructions to Tiberius and Zenobia. Both struggled to keep attention to Sembrouthes' commands, leading him to growl and threaten violence. Indeed, eavesdropping upon one of Sembrouthes' sessions, I heard him crack a leather belt against a nearby rock. Both children jumped in fear.

"You think you are safe because you live in a wealthy household?!" Sembrouthes shouted. "In a fight, cutthroats and thieves drool over the opportunity to grapple against rich brats. You will listen to every word I have to say, or one day you will find yourselves stuck with a rusted dagger, bleeding in some shit-stained gutter. Is that what you want?"

"N-No," Tiberius stuttered.

"No, Sembrouthes," Zenobia replied calmly.

Another crack. "You have not earned the right to speak my name in the training yard!" Sembrouthes yelled. "You will refer to me as master, and I will speak to you in a manner that pleases me. Do you understand?!"

"Yes, Master," Zenobia replied, her voice as steady as before.

"Y-Yes, Master," Tiberius blurted. He sounded as if prepared to weep, yet I heard no sobs as Sembrouthes continued the lesson— ordering both children to run the length of Syracuse's walls while he trotted behind atop a horse.

The brutality of his words against such young children—my children—pulled at me to intervene. Yet Mariya, far more patient than me, prevented that. Not even after thunderclaps sounded in the distance and further darkened the skies with the threat of an impending gale.

"Sembrouthes will not allow either of them to come to harm,"

Mariya promised. "He loves these children. Were you treated any differently by Godilas, who loved you as well?"

"No," I admitted. "And probably worse, because Samur and I had neither wealth nor status."

"Precisely," Mariya said. "So do not deprive either of them an opportunity to learn strength from one as Sembrouthes, under the care of Rosamund, who soothes their aches. Better Sembrouthes teach them than they learn at the hands of one who would truly mean evil."

Mariya's logic was sound. It nearly always was, balancing out my own tangled web of oaths and instincts to react aggressively. So I yielded to Sembrouthes the authority he required to train his pupils, whose numbers swelled with each passing week until he had acquired a veritable class of some two dozen foundlings. In a way, this expansion pleased Mariya the most, and when I raised the concern of cost—for it seemed these urchins needed provisions, too—she secretly bartered portions of her jewelry. No quantity of begging would change her mind.

"They are baubles that I have far too many of," Mariya explained. "And the coin is enough to feed and clothe these children for several years. If you wish to honor me, allow me to perform this act."

There was no resisting. I knew the closure of Pella had been a terrible blow to my wife, and when Mariya was happy, my heart felt lighter. She doted in the foundlings, yet was careful not to interfere with Sembrouthes' lessons, for the purpose of such work was to train warriors.

Tired and pocked with bruises, Zenobia nevertheless rose with a lurch each morning, eager to return to Sembrouthes' latest lesson. Nevertheless, it was Tiberius who truly flourished under the regimen. Not from the ceaseless physical demands that Sembrouthes inflicted upon their small bodies—Tiberius never became comfortable with Sembrouthes' instruction—but rather from the presence of newfound friends. Though many young boys, largely orphans and foundlings, would enter and exit Sembrouthes' teachings, there were two in particular who stand out in the earliest cohorts.

I first met those two—one with the unmistakable straight black hair, smaller eyes, and flat nose of a Hun, and the other a bushy-headed Roman, and both perhaps a year older than Tiberius—while sitting in the shadows of a nearby portico with Xerxes. I witnessed the Hunnic youth creep behind a gathering of older children, almost sliding across the sands. Then, as Sembrouthes departed the training yard to seek instruments for the next drill, the Hun pounced.

There was no malice in the maneuver. Instead, the Hun's fingers slipped beneath the collar of an older boy far burlier than he and lifted a necklace from his neck. It was an action of dexterity but little guile, for the burly Greek child's companions immediately noticed the theft.

"Cours! You pig fucker!" one boy shouted, his voice cracking with looming manhood.

The Hun sprinted away, yet tumbled not five paces into his retreat as his legs collided with a discarded wooden staff. Older boys launched themselves atop the Hun called Cours, their clumsy attacks little more than open-handed pawing than true and hurtful blows. Cours did not strike back, and instead covered his head with his arms, shielding against their attacks while protecting the necklace in his interlocked fingers.

I rose, but Xerxes, who observed along with me that day, shot an arm out to stop me. "Let us see the ending of this escapade," he whispered in Persian. "If you interrupt now, the other children will never treat this Hun boy with respect. He must learn to defend himself, even as young as he is."

"For now," I agreed, yet remained standing as I watched the yard descend into chaos.

Cours was not without his own companions. All younger, from four to seven years, including the young Sicilian Greek, Tiberius, and my own Zenobia. The Greek lad dove headfirst into the pile, throwing ineffectual fists at Cours' attackers that only earned the boy beatings alongside his friend. Tiberius was more measured, grabbing a boy from the outer edge of their circle and yanking him away from the assault.

However, it was Zenobia who caused the most substantial disruption, leaping upon the back of the boy who'd worn the necklace and snaking her arms about his neck and chest. He jerked backward, attempting to throw Zenobia free, but she held on, her legs dangling as she tugged and forced the youth away from Cours' prone form. Again I motioned to intervene, yet Xerxes grabbed my cloak.

"It is nearly finished," he whispered urgently. "We know not the reason for the fight. Whether from honor or selfishness, let the children complete their exercise."

And so I did. As the older boys pummeled Cours and his Greek companion, Tiberius finally skipped into the fray. With a wild, scything fist, he swung at the boy who wore Zenobia as a cape. Though clumsy, the blow drove into the softness of the boy's stomach and forced the lad to his knees, gasping for air, until he eventually fell backward onto Zenobia. Tiberius was slapped in the face in kind, yet still he pushed his way toward Zenobia to free her from the fallen boy's weight.

"Enough!" Sembrouthes roared. "All of you, in lines! Now!"

Those who could scrambled to their feet. Many limped, others gasped, and Cours and his friend struggled to stand at all. Sembrouthes barked and snarled and spat upon the sands, chastising the children as undisciplined cretins.

"Explain yourselves!" he roared. "The first one to tell me why the fight started is excused from drill for the day."

Some of the older children grumbled, but none stepped forward. "As you wish," Sembrouthes said. "All of you will run along the perimeter of the training yard until I decide you have had enough."

Still, the children did not break, though they did not quite have the endurance to continue much farther, either. Within a half hour, the younger children had fallen to the ground, and even more lurid threats could not spark further movement. By the end of the hour, the remaining children had collapsed, panting and asking to water. Many moaned, although none surrendered to Sembrouthes' questions.

"Dismissed!" he spat. "Do not squabble in my yard, or you will pay."

As the older children staggered away and Sembrouthes departed to train with his Aksumite spearmen, I finally descended to the training sand. I understood the exhaustion of the children well, for Godilas had subjected me and Samur to similar kinds of toil—and was indeed often a great deal unfriendlier than Sembrouthes. Leaving Xerxes at the edge of the sands, I paced close to the foursome, taking note of their sniffles and moans.

"Hello, Pater," Zenobia acknowledged me, a light scowl lining her soft face.

"Are you harmed?" I asked. "Anything bad?"

Zenobia shook her head, a droplet of blood slipping from a tear in her lip. Tiberius, too, stood alongside Zenobia. "I feel fine, Lord."

I nodded, turning to the two boys who remained seated. "And you?"

"My chest," the Greek boy garbled. "They kept hitting me."

"Be quiet, John," the Hun named Cours mumbled, coughing with a wince.

Grunting, I knelt down. "I heard the others call you Cours," I said, nodding to the Hun, then turned to the Greek. "So your name is John? Where are your parents?"

John was a common name, with mothers christening a great many children of the Empire and in the Christian dominions beyond with the name of the great apostle. Nevertheless, it was a name that I could not speak without muffling my voice, fearful that I might somehow slander the man who served at Belisarius' side, or that Belisarius himself might take some unintended offense.

The Greek boy nodded. "Yes, my name is John. And my parents were hanged by a Gothic chieftain when I was little. Cours and I only have one another."

"The others call him Johannes exiguus," Zenobia added helpfully. "But why? What does it mean?"

John the paltry. An epithet intended to hurt or demean, and one a boy who did appear scrawny was unlikely to be easily absolved of. He was the only member of their group to weep from the fight, although I credit him with the bravery to lend aid to his comrade.

"Nothing kind, and I will not allow it in my hearing." My eyes turned to Cours, and I switched my words to the Hunnic tongue— one that only he and I understood fluently, although Zenobia likely grasped a word or two. "The army does not abide thieves. If your friends had not intervened, the other boys might have seriously hurt you. I have known men to be slain for nicking a leg of roasted goat, and I warn you that you will not find leniency forever."

Cours replied in Greek, eyes narrowed. "It was not stealing, Lord."

Raising his hand, he unfurled his grimy fingers, revealing a bear claw underneath. It was a fine specimen, possessing an unnaturally large hook that seemed more likely originating from a mythical beast than any animal who stalks the land or swims the sea. "Speak your truth, then," I said.

"This was my father's." Cours cradled the claw as if it were the most finely forged pendant fit for an Emperor. "It is all I have, and the older boys would take it from me."

I surveyed him slowly, unsure whether the lad told lies. Yet he yielded a passionless gaze in return, his unblinking eyes locked upon my own.

"Cours speaks the truth, Lord," John blurted out. "Right, Tiberius?"

"Yes," Tiberius said, his voice wavering. "The older boy wanted to take it for himself."

Zenobia shuffled forward. "It is true, Pater. My friends do not steal."

Her friends. A word so simple, yet with such an effect. Zenobia was no longer a mere babe; she was capable, and of more than I had credited her for. At that, I felt a note of pride—and oddly, at the fact that they defended one another without the aid of their teacher. They were so young, yet perhaps both Mariya and Xerxes were correct in pushing for such training.

"Take John to see Rosamund," I commanded. "And take care of

one another. This is only one day of hundreds that you have before you."

Zenobia stepped forward, not yet willing to let the conversation drop. "Pater, we will not be punished?"

I shook my head. "Cours did nothing wrong. Sometimes, even if the law forbids it, we must use force to preserve ourselves and others." Smiling, I added, "Just don't let Sembrouthes catch you fighting, or anything else disruptive. When Samur and I were not much older than all of you, we learned to exact retribution without our weapons master becoming wise to our plans."

Cours beamed. "Yes, Lord."

After ruffling Zenobia's hair, I beckoned at Xerxes and paced away from the training yard. If all such encounters in Syracuse had been so uplifting, I might recall those early months of our conquest with fondness. Alas, much of the information we received from abroad was either puzzling or downright disheartening.

Occasionally, an intrepid sailing vessel would limp into Syracuse's harbor, its sails battered by overwhelming gusts. Though fishing along the coastline remained safe, travel atop the open sea had become unusually perilous. Yearly, and absent a war at sea, perhaps one or two larger transports would capsize from such a vast port as Syracuse. Now, a full third of the cogs and hulks that roamed any farther than a half day's sail from shore would find themselves gripped as if by some angry sea god, slipping to the deep as churning waves tossed our tiny vessels about. Though safely landside, little Alexander wept bitterly during one such storm, shaking as gusts of wind smacked against Syracuse's harbor and its stone buildings beyond.

"Just the wind, my love," Mariya cooed in his ear.

But Alexander was not so easily consoled. "Want it to stop! Stop!"

"I am here with you, darling." She snatched Alexander into her arms. "And so is Pater, and Zenobia, and Jamila, and so many others. We won't let anything happen to you, my love."

She planted a kiss on Alexander's forehead, though he squirmed all the same. Eventually, he calmed, but the near-constant darkness of the storm seemed to further ignite his fears, which were then brought to climax by the occasional bolt of lightning. In this, I did not blame the poor boy—there were plenty of grown men in the city who cowered against the tempest, broken solely by the bleeding eye in the heavens. I confess, at times, I was one of them.

Any reprieve from such sea storms was unpredictable and brief, making the more superstitious of our sailors seek out pagans for answers of how to ward off such evil. Rosamund did not encourage these attentions, but neither did she dissuade them, and would merely repeat her premonitions from Constantinople. Something terrible was coming. Whether in a month, a year, or a decade, a great harvest of souls would commence, and it would make the darkness we currently suffered through seem comfortable by comparison. To my mind, her words prompted unpleasant flashes of Hakhamanish, whose curse never seemed far. Both had warned of the great darkness to come, and now Rosamund argued its first breath had already been taken as winter ruled the land and the sea alike.

Thanks to one fortunate vessel, we learned of Mundus' thrust into Moesia, where he had seized the Gothic border city of Sirmium before turning southeast toward the wealthier Dalmatian coastline. Opposing him were the twin brothers Uligisalus and Asinar, both seasoned chieftains who had previously earned renown warring with the Franks near Narbo. Beyond from the liberation of Sirmium, we heard accounts of minor skirmishes between scouting parties, nothing more, though both armies seemed to stalk one another as Mundus trudged his path toward Salona. Mundus offered praise for our speedy conquest of Sicily and promised to sap Theodahad's reserves and tie down Gothic soldiers in Dalmatia as much as possible.

A second missive, however, told of a far more dire situation in Constantinople. Scratched in Theodora's unmistakable script, the wax-sealed letter was delivered only to me, although I shared its contents with Belisarius in the privacy of his offices in Syracuse.

An earthquake struck Aleppo, leveling its walls and nine in ten of its buildings. That, along with the veiled sun and biting frost, have only emboldened Cassiodorus' men. Our guardsmen still keep order, but even many of them have taken oaths to Cassiodorus. Justinian claims all is well, but Cassiodorus' zealots have only grown bolder in harassing Constantinople's residents and any who do not practice their faith. Some have been hanged and others burned, to lift God's wrath in the black skies and red sun. The remainder of Jakob's followers have departed for safer cities, though I would fear for my own well-being if I were to depart the palace.

Cassiodorus' men claim that God's pact for Revelation is at hand. Rubbish, I say, although some days I wonder... I fear that, if any further calamity were to pass, Cassiodorus would gain full control over Constantinople's life—and with it, the Empire itself.

Speak carefully in your future letters to me, even if in a cipher. I cannot vouchsafe their privacy any further.

"If Cassiodorus' followers are so bent toward violence, perhaps they could reinforce us," Belisarius grumbled.

"They are only good when bullying the unarmed," I said, equally discontent. "And anyways, Lord, does this curse not bother you?"

"The sun?" Belisarius asked, his brow furrowing. "We aren't dead, Varus. And the cold affects our enemies and allies alike, regardless of what the priests say. God will claim my soul one day, but until then, I do not intend to walk about fearfully."

Amidst the unwelcome tidings, there remained little I could offer Theodora other than prayers and a promise to serve. I possessed no desire to return to Constantinople and face Cassiodorus' swelling ranks—my beloved were nearly all present in Sicily, and I had no desire to again live under the constant threat of assault by an Armageddon-obsessed mob.

In spite of the grinding fear of such ominous skies and seas, life was, at times, quite pleasant for Belisarius' soldiers during our stay in Sicily. There was always training and frequent evening gatherings with Belisarius to scour what reports could be mustered from Italy, but also there were considerable swathes of time allocated to our idyll. As summer waned and tempestuous seas prevented our travel, I was able to spend most every evening meal with my family, and watched the children grow and explore Syracuse's wares and hinterland.

Occasionally, Samur and I even took the children riding, placing them safely on our saddles and trotting toward the nearby hills. Zenobia, giggling, would urge Samur to a gallop, her black hair whipping out behind her. Sitting with me, Tiberius was far more reserved, squeezing the reins even with the slowest walk, while Alexander bobbed and burbled as he patted Boreas' mane.

And so we rested, and waited, and prayed that what food remained from the ruined harvest would tide the region over. Ever the planner, Belisarius vouchsafed his prayers by commissioning additional fishing vessels along Sicily's coast, and by summer's end, nearly every meal included one form of fish, even as bread crept upward in price.

By early autumn, Belisarius declared our stasis at an end: Preparations would be made to strike toward Rhegium regardless of the hardships we faced. It was that or await destruction by the far larger Gothic armies, which posed a greater peril to our survival than a few hours aboard frothing waves. Reluctantly, I agreed, for he was correct—we had already delayed our attack for far too long, while Mundus proceeded ever onward toward his objective.

The last information of note was passed to us not by ship but instead by a Herulian scout. And its tidings were worst of all, for they told of loss far closer than distant Constantinople. Though the note was sent to Belisarius, he quickly handed it to me, his face lined with sympathy.

"If you would wish to attend him in Panormus, please do so," he said softly. "But please seek him out soon, for we cannot remain in Sicily forever. I plan to leave after harvest."

Curious, I unfurled the letter. It was brief, yet its few lines demanded to be reread. Hereka, Perenus' wife, had perished in childbirth. Bakuris, the infant son, yet lived, and while a nursemaid had taken over the child's care, Perenus had locked himself away, taking neither friendship nor nourishment. The only signs that he lived were the occasional creaking of the floors and a low moaning that emanated from the room's interior.

Instantly, I grieved for my friend. With only Uliaris as my companion, I galloped for Panormus that day. Days of hard riding revealed ongoing pacification of Sicily, with smaller towns of the interior displaying Imperial banners where once the Ostrogoth king's sigil had hung. However, we also witnessed the extent of the harvest's desolation, with enormous tracts of wheat bent and decaying. One village burned the useless husks, while others ground what little edible material could be yielded into a fibrous meal and boiled it in a bitter soup. Full-fledged famine had not taken hold, yet I had little doubt that the poorer plebeians would struggle by winter's end—more than they usually did. Many sick, elderly, and infants would be consigned to graves before next summer, when the prospects of a fresh harvest could replenish depleted stocks.

For all my title and duty, there was nothing I could do to aid these poor souls. Seeing us camped, some were hospitable enough to share what little they possessed, although Uliaris and I politely declined. Others attempted to thrust young children into our care, burdened with one mouth too many.

Of course, I was unable to take further wards, least of all on my urgent journey to Perenus. "Have your local leader write to Syracuse," I told them. "Those old enough to carry weight and aid our soldiers may be granted entry into Belisarius' army."

"And the younger ones?" a woman pressed further, her features haggard from age, strife, or both. "Will the Emperor let them die?"

"Send to Syracuse for aid," I repeated, reaching for my cross as a hundred hollow eyes focused upon my richly attired mount and body. "We will do all that we can to send fish and supplies to you."

Our promises gained us little love. Those farmers knew too well that an army quartermaster would never relinquish precious food amidst a famine. Neither would Justinian. No, they would be left to God's mercy. Some would ask for aid, of course, and a more courageous few would travel to Syracuse to seek greater fortunes in the city. Most, however, would weaken in their ancestral homes; a few would even snuff out the lives of their youngest children, from mercy or simply harsh practicality.

After the misery of the few days' journey, Panormus granted us easy access through its walls. Upon our arrival, a city slave informed Liberius, who ventured out to meet me in the forum.

"So, Belisarius finally would continue?" he asked.

"After harvest," I confirmed, eager to slip away and seek Perenus. "Only small garrisons will retain Sicily's larger cities."

"And Carthage?" Liberius pried. "I hear that Belisarius severed Solomon's manhood."

I chuckled. "Nothing so serious as that, but he did remove him as prefect. He should be in Constantinople now, with Praejecta."

"Assuming they made it, in these seas."

I shrugged. "The devil loves Solomon far too much to let him die so anonymously."

Liberius nodded. "I wish I could have seen the look on his smug face. I doubt Belisarius will keep Solomon down for long, but at least Carthage will be under more capable leadership for a few months."

Before we parted, Liberius guided me toward a nearby storage building that had been repurposed as a temporary barracks. "He won't speak to anyone."

"He will speak with me," I said, hoping the words were true.

Uliaris excused himself, allowing me to entreat with Perenus alone. Due to his rank, Perenus enjoyed private quarters adjacent to Fulcaris, and it was Fulcaris who both hailed my arrival and warned me of Perenus' wild mind.

"I was the one who told him," Fulcaris whispered, eyeing Perenus' locked door. "He did not believe me. Not until he saw Hereka's body. Even then, he initially insisted that she lived and beat an attendant bloody when another attempted to speak logic to him."

"He believes this still?" I asked, puzzled.

"No," Fulcaris answered. "But he did for three days. The chill kept the flies away for a time, but eventually…"

I nodded, thanking Fulcaris. "See that I am not disturbed, regardless of what you hear within."

"Are you… certain, Lord?" he asked. "It might be a good idea to have a guard or two. I took away his sword, but who knows the other weapons he hides in his bunk."

"He will not harm me." Nevertheless, I did unbuckle my sword belt and hand Fulcaris all my weapons. "Don't leave. I don't plan on staying long."

I knocked on the door. No reply. I knocked again, and now a voice moaned through the doorway, unmistakably Perenus.

"Whatever it is, leave it at the door," he yelled.

"It's Varus," I replied, keeping my voice as mellow as I could while loud enough to pierce through to him. "Unbar the door."

"Go away, Varus." His voice sounded weaker.

The feeble protest, compounded by rumors of Perenus' debauchery, convinced me that calm words alone would not gain my friend's attention. Instead, recalling my earliest days in drilling the Herulian foederati, I assumed the booming shout of a military instructor. "Open the door immediately, Perenus!"

No reply.

"Perhaps we should leave him be, Lord?" Fulcaris asked.

"No," I replied. "Give me my axe."

Fulcaris complied and tugged the half axe, half hammer free from my belt. Rather than the bladed edge, I levied the blunted iron of the handle against the door's latch, holding fast with both hands.

"If you're near the door, Perenus, I suggest you move away!" I yelled.

After a waiting few seconds' warning, I swung. A deafening crack rang out as metal crushed into metal, yet still the door did not yield.

"You crazy bastard!" Perenus yelled from within.

With the latch holding fast, I turned my attentions to the center of the doorway. I chopped the hammer into its mass, rattling the wood and shivering sections into splinters. After a third blow, whatever barred the door from the interior made a cracking noise, and after a fifth, the door burst asunder, blowing inward with a shower of wood and iron.

Before entering, I turned to Fulcaris, his eyes wide and mouth ajar. "Make sure we are not disturbed," I reminded him, and handed off my weapon.

The scent of filth in Perenus' quarters was palpable, and I gagged, unprepared for such an unpleasant welcome. I found Perenus sprawled on a straw cot, not three paces from a basin overflowing with piss and dung. Lank hair streamed over his face, while his darkened eyes signaled a lack of sleep.

Poets describe the Empire's warriors as unfeeling creatures, bent toward executing the Emperor's will through death to our enemies, insensible to any manner of suffering. At times, there was some truth to that, but mostly, they are utterly wrong. Perenus, the first friend I had made after freedom from bondage, had been gravely hurt, and with a far keener weapon than any spear or arrow. My heart ached for him, especially knowing I could do little to ease the sadness that tore across his face: gaunt cheeks, swollen eyes... a breathing, weeping skeleton. Perenus, who had been a living legend in the chariot races and survived all manner of calamity with an incomparable love of life all the while, had been visibly broken.

I knelt beside him. "My friend, words cannot convey how much I hurt for you."

Perenus snorted. "She's dead, Varus. Save your pity for someone else." His voice wavered with each snarled word, absent any of his usual vigor.

Bitterness. Resentment. A joyless void had replaced the soul of my friend, the sadness clasped about his body like a poor-fitting carapace. I wanted to help. No, I desperately needed to help. But this was not the Hippodrome—I knew not how to pluck Perenus from the captivity of death and depression.

"You speak from anger, and I forgive you," I said. "But your quarters are filthy, and Fulcaris tells me you will not take food."

Perenus scoffed again. "So?"

"When I was imprisoned at Barbalissus, and later in Antioch, you came to my aid. I am here to return the favor."

"Now?!" Perenus roared, rising to a seated position. "Have I disappointed the mighty Varus so much that he must come and baby me?"

I was genuinely taken aback. "Perenus, what is this? No—you are my dearest friend. Since we marched bloody footed to the Euxine Sea."

Perenus snorted. "Since Tricamarum, it's like I am a worn-out pair of boots, happily discarded for a fresh pair. You disappeared on me, and now you come and offer your sympathies for my dead wife, who you hardly knew? Eat shit, Varus."

I leaned closer, grasping at the stained collar of his shirt. "You're in pain, and you want to lash at others. I understand—I understand better than you realize. But this moping does no good. Not for you, not for your infant son, not for the hundreds of others who would help you if you only ask."

"You have everything!!" Perenus screamed. "Wealth, family, authority, trust..." His eyes closed as he shook his head. "We survived three wars together. Yet as soon as you rise to Belisarius' trust, you abandoned me. Still, I thought perhaps that I might carve my own happiness... but now, I have none of that."

I slapped him. Not forcefully, but enough to awaken his senses and shake loose any self-pity. "You *do*, you blind idiot!"

I hated myself for lashing out, though in hindsight, it felt like the correct action to take. I wanted to sit with Perenus and laugh as we had in our earliest days together. Tipping over, dizzy with drink, cocksure that life would provide many more happy times to come. Feverishly, my thoughts fluttered through all manner of ways to aid my friend and came up short through it all. I was simply not trained in the art of condolences—my skills were inducing fear and pain, not relieving it.

"Oh?" Perenus asked mockingly. "I'm so pleased to hear it."

"I love you, you stubborn ass," I roared. "I waded through a river of death to free you from the Hippodrome, when all others insisted it was suicide. I would do it again without question. And yes, perhaps I have neglected our friendship this past year. But if you think, for one heartbeat, that you are not my closest comrade, then you're a bigger lunatic than you appear."

With that, tears streamed from Perenus' eyes. His weight sagged against my grip. "Hereka was so scared, Varus," he wept. "The attendants made me leave the room. I did not even get to comfort her when she... when..."

Perenus sobbed. There were no casual jokes, nor the black sense of humor that I had come to depend upon in our years together. Perenus seemed hollow, as if the flame of his spirit had been snuffed out by the gales of the ongoing storm. He leaned against my body, as though unable to sit unassisted, and I allowed him his moment of grief.

Privately, his accusation struck a sour reaction in me, though I had been unaware of his unhappiness toward me, and though his words were honed by anger, their meaning was laced with truth. Perenus and I were no longer the carefree recruits marching to a centurion's cadence—we had grown into far grander, yet far more lonesome, more separate lives. It was a rift I intended to mend, though how, I did not know.

"You have a duty now, whether or not you are prepared for it," I told him. "Hereka's son, *your* son, needs you. And I will stand with you in that duty, every single day."

"Fucking black skies and bloody sun." Perenus laughed, even as he sobbed. "Maybe the world truly will end, eh? At least the babe won't need to worry then."

"Don't tempt fate with such talk," I snapped. "Gather your belongings. You're coming back with me."

Frowning, Perenus stopped his weeping and wiped his face with a grime-covered palm. "With you?"

"The foederati will function under their individual warlords until we disembark in Italy," I told him. "You, your son, and whatever servants or followers will come back to Syracuse. You are correct in that I have failed you as a friend, and I intend to rectify it now."

Perenus bit his lip. "Belisarius won't be—"

"Belisarius is concerned for you as well," I interrupted. "He will understand." Sniffing the air, I made one final request. "Before you leave, take a bath. You smell like cow shit."

Perenus' shoulders dropped. "What will the others say? I will be a laughingstock. A man who fell apart because of his wife."

"They can go to hell," I countered. "Belisarius was no different. Nor would I be."

Shivering, Perenus moaned. A long silence stretched between us. "I don't know what I'm going to do, Varus," he said at last.

Standing, I loomed down upon my friend. "As you said, you have lived through three wars and the riots, none of which we were intended to survive. If youthful tongues wag, then perhaps it is their turn to shoulder the front ranks of the shield wall."

"Harsh." Perenus chuckled. "I will go... but I could use a meal," he added as his gut roared.

I nodded. "And you shall have it. Lastly..." I paused, reluctant to dig a finger into Perenus' open wound, yet unable to delay our stay in Panormus. "Are there any funeral rites Hereka requires?"

"I burned her body myself," Perenus mumbled. "Although I could use your aid in writing to her father. He can't read, but I feel like I should send a message all the same."

"Done," I replied. "Tell me what you wish to say, and I will craft the letter in my own hand."

We required two full days and nights before departing for Syracuse. There would be no swift gallop across the Sicilian farmland—along with a sluggish Perenus, the infant Bakuris, his wet nurse, and a further three attendants whom Perenus had sworn into his personal service joined us on the return. All were younger women, and each had been procured to serve Hereka, yet Perenus was loath to dismiss them now that their intended mistress was no longer of this life.

"Save yourself the silver," Uliaris suggested. "There's plenty of work for servants, now that the Empire is here. Before long, Justinian will appoint governors and all manner of useless administrators, who each will need a small army of slaves to satisfy their urges."

"I know, but they'll be useful to my… to Bakuris," Perenus replied. "And it's not like I don't have an endless list of tasks to perform either way. They will make my life easier."

Before departing, I also informed Liberius of my decision to temporarily relieve Perenus of his duties.

"Fulcaris and Sindual can rule the Herulian foederati, and Gunderic the Vandals," I reasoned. "And Indulf rarely listens to counsel that does not originate from his own mind."

"It is not me you will need to convince, although I concur with you," Liberius said. "There will be little disruption for now, but someone will need to lead the combined foederati once we establish a fort in Italy."

"I could do it," I said. "Until Perenus returns."

Liberius disagreed vehemently. "You have enough to worry about. If Perenus requires leave, someone must assume his position. The problem is, there are few enough we can trust with such authority."

"Perenus will recover," I insisted. "He just needs time." This earned me only a raised brow from Liberius.

We departed Panormus as the already-gloomy skies grew heavy with clouds. Only a light rain fell upon our traveling party of three mounted warriors and a horse-drawn carriage bearing Perenus' household and possessions.

Perenus did not speak much on our journey. Nor did he cradle his child, preferring to entrust all care to servants. Aside from a drizzling rain, it was not an unpleasant journey, although the unkempt roads sent the carriage jolting about. Nevertheless, we kept warm with furs and blankets, subsided on rations donated by the Roman garrison of Panormus, and journeyed southeast to Syracuse.

When we arrived back in Syracuse, the city bustled with afternoon noise. Perenus and his household joined with ours; he submitted to an embrace from Mariya, yet merely nodded as she discussed how she would aid Bakuris and swiftly left her to dote on the babe. In the days that followed, as the ships were prepared, Perenus appeared only for meals, the stench of sour wine about his breath.

I ignored it. Grief is a fickle thing, and all are entitled to absorb the finality of death in their own manner. That is not to say I cared nothing for Perenus' suffering—indeed, his accusations of my abandonment still stung three weeks after I recovered him from Panormus. Indeed, I made my fears known to Mariya and Rosamund, vowing to do better.

Belisarius was as understanding as I had anticipated. "Inform me of Perenus' progress, but let me know if he will be unable to perform his duties in Italy."

I promised that I would, although knew I would exhaust all options available to me before removing Perenus from his hard-won rank as lord of the foederati. For the time being, we supped together, he occasionally shared cups of wine with Cephalas and Rosamund, and I made myself willfully ignorant of other activities. I ignored gossip that he frequented the prostitutes of Syracuse's wharf—a common activity amongst many of the Empire's soldiers, yet uncommon for Perenus. Nor did I take note that his visits to the wharf grew in frequency, including the very morning we were set to depart for Italy.

Led by Father Petrus, we prayed for calmer seas and safe passage. Belisarius had selected multiple landing points for each segment of the army. Our primary target was Rhegium, an older city that opposed Messana along the Calabrian coast and possessed a port capable of sheltering the larger transports from Constantinople until a grander city, such as Neapolis, could be seized. It was a blessedly brief trip, requiring only half a day with fair wind, yet the surging waters of the channel posed an outsized threat to even storm-tested vessels. I found Belisarius directly monitoring the progress of the embarkation, something that he normally entrusted to others.

"Anxious, Lord?" I asked.

"More than I would have assumed," Belisarius admitted. "I've dreamed of Italy since I was a boy but have never set foot on its soil."

"Nor have I," I replied. "I could name you all the cities and all the rivers and provinces, yet all I know of its people are the tales I hear from Petrus and Liberius."

Belisarius laughed. "John and I used to whisper dreams of liberating Rome. Part of me always wondered if I would get the chance."

"Well, fate has led you here," I said. "And me as well. One way or another, the Eternal City will see Imperial soldiers once more."

"Indeed," Belisarius concurred. "For better or for worse."

With favorable tides, our boats cut into the surf. I begged God that Narses' spies were correct, and that Theodahad had prioritized the looming Frankish hordes over Belisarius' tiny expedition. For the day of our attack upon Italy, presaged so many years ago by Justin, was underway. With that, the Gothic War had now truly begun.

NEAPOLIS, CAMPANIA FELIX

The initial stages of our attack were anticlimactic—not so much from happenstance, but instead from diligent planning, for Ascum and Valerian had veered their dromon fleet to capture the soft and thinly defended towns of Locri, Croton, and Medma without a hint of resistance. Rhegium followed as soon as Belisarius' transports neared the adjacent beaches, and the sun-draped cross of the Gothic king was cast to the ground. God blessed us all with a beachhead that required not a single drop of Roman blood. Compared to Neapolis, such prizes afforded little defensive value, yet yielded a gateway to the wealthier cities of the Italian heartland.

I should have been pleased, but stepping foot upon Italian soil offered no special swell in my spirit. Not even when Mariya and the others joined me, landing in Rhegium's harbor to a clangor of drums and horns. Shortly after we docked, an Imperial flag rose above the battlements, declaring their allegiance for Justinian just as the scattered cities of Sicily had. It was a welcome development, though Rhegium's air bit hard, alternating blowing winds and unholy cold. Amidst the darkness, I began to wonder whether the poor bastards who remained to guard Rhegium from our advance believed the bloody eye of the sun an ill omen against Theodahad's reign, just as many in our army worried it was a sign of Justinian's disfavor amongst the heavens. Regardless, Belisarius trudged forward, undeterred.

Though I could not know at the time, messengers told of identically peaceful occupations of the surrounding towns—Fulcaris and Indulf in Medma, Samur and Martinus in Locri, Bessas in Croton, and a force of Cappadocian and Vandal spears in more distant Metapontum. Despite the risk, Belisarius lost only one vessel—a supply ship bearing spare grain, rope, and shovels. Prudent logistical planning ensured it was not our only one, yet the gratitude that few lives were claimed by the sea would soon be replaced with pangs in our bellies from its now-drowned stores of food.

Upon arrival, Father Petrus seemed close to weeping. "My God," he murmured. "But we are here."

"Just the beginning, Father," I promised.

"If only Liberius were here with me, Varus," Petrus said, his voice hushed with awe. "We have planned and hoped for so many years. Decades, even."

Though still taken by cautious apprehension, Petrus' passion intrigued me. "Have you visited this part of Italy before?"

"Oh, yes," Father Petrus replied longingly. "Long, long ago. Weather so lovely that one would not know of the terrors lurking in the hills." Looking toward the still-shrouded skies, Father Petrus whistled. "And certainly, we never saw a year without summer, and especially not in the sweltering heat of the local sun."

After sailing from Panormus, Liberius had joined the Herulian and Gothic foederati at Medma. He also expressed his gratitude at living long enough to see such a day, yet the missive he wrote also bore a warning.

The locals tell of few Goth armies in the region, but an excessive disruption to their harvest. Frost claims the stalks, leading to rot in the fields. Tread carefully as you proceed into Campania. Hunger will afflict the people here before long.

Belisarius took Liberius' words to heart. All excess food from every dromon was to be unloaded in Rhegium's port, with its soldiers instructed to rejoin a land-based formation. Valerian was permitted to remain in command of a reduced cohort of a dozen dromons, yet Ascum disembarked, watching carefully over dozens of laborers as they lifted ballistae from their moorings atop each warship.

"Damned grateful to be on dry land," Ascum grumbled. "I was beginning to sprout fins and gills."

"I need you here," Belisarius explained. "We won't win Italy at sea. Your bowmen and ballistae will have plenty of work ahead of them."

Ascum hummed agreement. "So it's Neapolis, then? So soon?"

"No time like now," I said.

"Indeed," Belisarius agreed. "I cannot explain Theodahad's inaction. He either does not wish to fight or is foolish enough to believe us not a threat. Either way, I plan to sup on as much of this hospitality as Theodahad's chieftains allow."

The bulk of our attendants and families would remain around Rhegium. Though the mixed Roman and Gothic residents seemed relieved that Belisarius' army would swiftly depart, they did offer up stores of arrows, spears, and even a bundle of ballista bolts that had been stored in a local church in the time of Theodoric.

"Why a church?" I asked Father Petrus.

"My boy, few are willing to steal from a church." Petrus winked. "You would be amazed at the amount of weaponry that is stored in the vaults and storage of a hallowed place. If God minds, I doubt it is little compared to the greater goings-on."

Rosamund, Shimon, Petrus, and Cephalas were to join me, with Mariya and the rest of my household remaining behind in Rhegium. What surprised me most is the general contentment that the populace seemed to show to their Gothic overlords. True, few civilians were cloaked in lavish silks, and most of the local chief's men were armored in crude iron that had been mended from a half dozen rents that likely killed their previous owner. Despite this, there was no evidence of famine on the bodies of the masses—not yet, anyway—and relative harmony throughout. Though they were pleased to watch Belisarius depart, they were happier still that our civilians, with all their food and silver, would remain behind for at least a month.

With kisses and farewells, I separated from my family for a

long ride atop Boreas. Before departing, I dispatched messages to Theodora, updated Belisarius' maps, and sent requests for an update from Mundus, though I was unsure when a reply might be garnered or how a courier might find me. Still, such worries were the challenge of others, for at that moment, all I could do was follow Belisarius north and into a land once sworn to Roman heritage.

Belisarius had been rejuvenated by the journey. Beaming, he trotted across our marching lines, hailing novice spearmen and grizzled veterans alike with his characteristic dedication to learning the lives, hopes, and worries of his men.

"He read that Alexander did the same," Ascum explained to me one evening, resting from the day's march. "Alexander could identify the name and family of each of his warriors. Whether this is *true*, of course, I cannot say; I only know Belisarius tries to emulate that ridiculous feat."

"It's not ridiculous," I insisted. "Belisarius took the time to learn of me in Tauris. Made me want to fight for him all the more."

"Aye, worthless bag of Herulian shit that you are." Ascum cackled. "Perhaps Belisarius' mind is better than my own, but I can hardly remember the names of my slaves, let alone a thousand farting men with no greater desire than to hump the first woman they find."

With much of Calabria surrendering absent any contest, Belisarius ordered the disaggregated portions of his army to re-knit outside Metapontum. Despite the lingering rain that nightly turned to frost, the men's happy morale was evidenced by singing in the ranks as we plodded north, mile by mile—until Belisarius reduced their rations by a quarter. To compromise for the loss, Belisarius instructed me to distribute a second ration of wine for each soldier, and sure enough, that announcement converted dissenting grumblers into pliable cherubs.

"Lord, is it… wise that the men should drink more?" I asked.

"No," Belisarius replied, "but neither is allowing them to rise to the point of mutiny over lost meals."

I scoffed. "Mutiny? The men would not do that to you, and

especially not over such a small reduction."

Belisarius dropped his voice to the lightest whisper. "It may not be the last reduction if we are not able to replenish our stores—and believe me, the army is little more than three days from descending into anarchy. Allow men to get hungry enough, and they'll butcher their friends for something to eat. Wine dulls that anger, for a time."

At the end of the second day, Liberius and the foederati joined their strength to ours, with Bessas and Martinus doing the same by the end of the seventh. Our pace was neither leisurely nor strenuous as we wound through the Calabrian valleys, guarded on each side by a tossing sea and snow-capped mountains respectively. There were few settlements here besides a few fishing villages, their tiny populations largely unperturbed by Gothic kings of the preceding decades.

"This is Italy?" Perenus snorted. "What a shithole. If I wanted to scratch at rocks and beg fish to jump from the sea, I could have stayed in Lazica."

Petrus smacked Perenus across his scalp. "Show respect. If the seas were calm and the sun cooperative, Calabria is an idyll equal to any in the world."

"If," Perenus retorted, grinning.

When atop his mount, Perenus often parted from Belisarius' column, although never beyond eyeshot of our outriders. His spirits seemed to improve when surrounded by his friends, and I took heart at his banter with Petrus, although it was plain that his attentions were divided between past and future. And though his child, now a hearty babe, remained in Rhegium, he never once asked to send a message back.

At last, after nearly two weeks of weaving through the Calabrian mountains, we reached the more accessible and temperate province of Campania. Ancient stone markers, leftovers of more prosperous times, noted our distance to Neapolis at a mere hundred miles. It was there, less than a day's march from Metapontum, that the last remnants of Belisarius' distributed army were reunited with our greater whole. Galloping far ahead of the Hunnic foederati to reach me, Samur saluted Belisarius and waved to me. Samur voiced his sympathies to Perenus, who only shrugged and insisted that our war be attended to.

"Any conflict?" I asked, shifting Samur's attentions.

"Very little," he replied. "Valerian's dromons were already docked in Metapontum by the time I arrived. The Huns dispatched a small Gothic war band as we scouted to the west." He snatched at his waterskin, gulping the liquid as he nodded to the joint Hun-Vandal forces behind him. "This is too easy, Varus. And it does not make sense."

"No chieftains?" Belisarius prodded. "No armies?"

"Hardly any scouting parties, Lord! Only one or two mounted riders, and another fifty men traveling from the road to Brundisium that are now all slain, but otherwise nothing."

We awaited the Hunnic and Vandal leaders before continuing our makeshift command gathering. There was no camp—despite the gloom, there was enough light to continue for a while yet, although Belisarius yearned for collective guidance about where to tread. Standing a hundred paces away from the main column, Perenus initiated our proceedings.

"What is Theodahad playing at?" he asked, frowning.

"I do not know," Belisarius said. "But he has granted us two choices. One, we proceed carefully, fortify our existing position, and send wider-ranging scouts to explore the Gothic position."

Liberius grunted. "That does not sound entertaining at all."

"And the second?" I asked.

"We plunge headfirst and take a gamble for Neapolis," Belisarius said. "Theodahad must defend such a critical city, and will do so with armies that we have limited understanding of."

Turning to our Gothic foederati, I nodded at Indulf. "What do you make of this?"

Indulf shrugged, scratching at the scattered skin that bore evidence of his duel in Septem with Agila. "Whether you believe me or not, I have no contact with the Ostrogoths. I am here with you, after all."

"None question your loyalty after serving the Emperor for years," I replied hastily, hoping to mask the nagging concerns that I had felt since meeting Indulf during the Vandal War. "All I ask is for your interpretation. As Perenus said, what is Theodahad doing?"

Another shrug, with a deep sigh. "I have told all of you many times. Theodahad is a schemer, not a fighter. The only reason the Goths treat him with respect is that he was Theodoric's nephew. My guess is that he does not trust his chieftains to take full control of the army, but dare not fight to lose men." Indulf spat. "Cowardly. Fit for mice and women."

It seemed too farfetched: a Gothic king capable of murdering his kin but too fearful to fight with a vast array of trained spearmen. "If what you say is true, then we should march north until we face resistance," I said.

"It will bring you closer to avenging Amalasuntha if you do," Indulf replied. He licked his lips as if relishing a meal to come, unbothered by the confused situation or the numbers arrayed against us.

Gunderic heartily agreed. "Let's go kill the bastards!"

"You might be correct, Indulf," Belisarius put in, "but before we proceed, I would ask for each of your opinions. The road north will not be so simple, with far greater spoils to be won."

"What is the risk you see, Lord?" I asked.

"Eventually, we must face an army in the field. The Ostrogoths show favor to their kin, far more even than the Visigoths," Belisarius remarked. "It makes their armies fight harder, for nearly all Ostrogoth spearmen have a brother or a cousin fighting alongside them. Their ferocity and strong kinship is what made the Ostrogoths king of all Italy, after all."

"And what makes them reckless," Gunderic added. "Cut the belly of one, and within moments a hundred men are pulled into a fight, unthinking. I've done it myself, years ago."

Now Bessas spoke up. "Lord, we have little choice. We have

momentum on our side, and according to Indulf, a superior command than what Theodahad can bring to bear. This is a war, and a fight was inevitable."

Belisarius concurred, yet nevertheless proceeded to hear the opinion of each of his officers. All nodded varying degrees of assent, from Gunderic's vehement hunger for battle to Ascum's desire to rid ourselves of Justinian's ploy for dominance. None, however, questioned Belisarius, including when he arrived at a conclusion.

Mine was the last opinion he sought.

"And you, Varus?"

"We fight," I said, which drew hooting cheers from Gunderic and the Hunnic warlords. "Press the Goths into a single battle and seize Theodahad."

Indulf grinned at my final inclusion, while others growled their approval. Liberius—whose opinion was not sought amongst the council of warriors—even allowed a smirk to crease his wrinkled face. "No one tells tales of men who stayed home."

Belisarius, too, could not help but smile. "Very well. To Neapolis, and whatever lies beyond."

In a broad arc, we swept through the Campanian foothills, seizing both the coastal and inland roads that linked Italy's southernmost provinces with Rome and Ravenna to the north. This included the fabled Via Appia—that critical roadway that once had borne Spartacus to Italy's south, and later was decorated by the crucified bodies of thousands of Spartacus' slave army that had been defeated by Crassus and Pompey.

Scouts ranged far beyond the twin Roman columns, yet three days' march north of Metapontum, Samur's assessment proved valid—there was little, if anything, of our enemy to see. Rain stung our faces, yet did not fall so hard as to muddy the roadways, allowing for fair progress toward Campania's capital. Occasionally, our outriders encountered Gothic scouts, yet few of those escaped Hunnic arrows and none drew close enough to gain an estimate of our numbers. More the better—even after leaving only a few hundred men to garrison all of Sicily and Rhegium, our invasion was pitifully small in number. All we could do was proceed and hope that fortune would hold out.

It did not. Though no Gothic army blocked either road, evidence of evacuation was undeniable as we reached the final three days of our march to Neapolis. Few villages were still inhabited; many were charred to cinders. Some still blew pillars of smoke, evidence of a conflagration not a day prior to our arrival. There was no livestock, and only chaff-heavy wheat and half-frozen grapes that the residents did not bother to collect in their rush to depart. In one village, a group under Sinnion discovered a buried hoard of silver candlesticks, spoons, and other trinkets, yet for the most part, the plunder in Campania was stripped to little more than the bodies of the dead and the barren harvest of the fields.

And then there was Neapolis. Centuries ago, the city had been overshadowed by its wealthier neighbor, Capua. Now, however, centuries of ravishment had left Capua little more than a walled husk of its once-great self. Instead, in the shadow of Mount Vesuvius, Neapolis sprawled well into the Campanian countryside. By the density of construction and the stench of dung, all knew that a great city was imminent, and its well-maintained roads sped our path onward. Even in the darkness, I gaped at Neapolis' sparkling walls, rising on a low hill that jutted into the sea as if a rival to Vesuvius.

It was a glimmer of majesty that not even the mournful, ashen skies could extinguish. Despite the sullen crimson orb or the flurries that fell from diabolically unseasonable clouds, Neapolis stood as if guarding Rome's ancient honor. Clean, well-maintained, and vaulted toward the shrouded blight, our target was proof that Italy had once been something beyond the reckoning of simple minds.

"I know what you mean now," I muttered to Petrus.

"Beautiful," he murmured. "Better still in peace. But this region has seen little enough of that in my lifetime."

Liberius scoffed. "I don't understand what is so wonderful. It is pretty enough, but its port stinks of refuse, and its aqueducts leak. A waste of good land."

As Shimon readied me for combat, Cephalas aided Perenus and Uliaris in a similar fashion. There was little delay, and after donning my armor and gripping at the cross and pendant tucked beneath my collar, I gathered Boreas' reins from Shimon.

"When does it end?" Rosamund asked in Heruli, approaching from behind me.

"If we don't die today? When Rome is also taken, or perhaps Ravenna."

"So *never*, then." She slumped her shoulders. "I would tell you to take care of yourself, but you never listen to me. All I get in return is torn flesh and bones in need of mending."

I laughed. "Have faith, Rosamund!"

"Oh, I do," she replied. Rising atop her toes, she planted a kiss upon my cheek. "I am the most faithful servant you have."

I blushed, not knowing how to reply. Instead, I nodded and mounted Boreas, followed closely behind by Uliaris, Sembrouthes, and the Aksumites. Perenus, however, separated from our contingent.

"I'm joining the foederati," Perenus explained.

I frowned. "So soon? You're sure?"

"Certain," Perenus replied. "Although I will see you in the evening for whatever passes for dinner, if some Gothic bastard doesn't rip my stomach out first."

Belisarius ordered the army to sweep in a great crescent, severing Neapolis from Capua and any traveling caravans beyond. As Belisarius was reluctant to press an attack against an unknown enemy and an unfamiliar city, most of our army was ordered to rest, while those few tasked with night duty carved moving palisades from trees hewn along the roadway. Again, there were no war bands to contest even the few hundred horsemen that encircled the northern terminus of Neapolis' adjoining farmland. Nor, indeed, were there any people, just as with the prior villages. I almost would have thought Neapolis abandoned had the glow of fires atop the city's vast walls not given evidence that something living remained inside.

Then came the following morning. In the clearer light of day, we saw Gothic sentries illuminated against the clouded skies, while teams of archers strung their bows and gazed upon the massed Roman Army. I even spied at least two ballistae housed atop each of Neapolis' gates, although whether the Goths knew how to operate such engines, I could not know. Based upon my experience at Dara, I did not wish to learn.

"They intend to resist, then," Belisarius rumbled. "Form the men into ranks."

Fulfilling Belisarius' orders took an hour, allowing a still-rising sun to yield what little warmth it could against our backs. Though it was still only autumn, a light snow began to fall, and the breath of thousands of men hung about their bodies like mist. Belisarius' men moved closer, hauling forth the wooden barricades that would shield detachments of ten men at a time—solid against arrows, although less so against a direct strike from a working ballista. Likewise, Ascum spat and barked at his teams of engineers as Belisarius' own ballistae wheeled forward to within range of the Neapolitan walls. There was no exchange of arrows, but a great many Goths formed on the walls.

"How many do you think?" Sembrouthes asked my group. "A thousand? Maybe two?"

"No more than two," Xerxes said. "Otherwise, they would have already launched a sally at us."

"Get the men ready for an assault on the walls," I commanded. "And if any ask, it is one thousand Goths, maximum."

With the army in battle array, Belisarius beckoned for me, and we trotted closer to Neapolis' walls. Each step made me lurch in the saddle, wary of a rogue bowman seeking a fortune for slaying the Roman commander. None came, yet I kept my shield prepared for anything, ready to cover Belisarius' body at the first hint of flying metal. We halted fifty paces before Neapolis' gate, and Belisarius withdrew his helmet.

"Neapolis!" Belisarius yelled. "I am Flavius Belisarius, strategos of the Roman armies. Our quarrel is not with you, but of the illegitimate king, Theodahad!"

A heavyset man, draped in pitch-blackened furs, emerged atop the gate. He, too, removed his helmet, revealing a head of prematurely thinning hair and sweat streaming from his jowls. "I am Optaris, Lord of Campania. You are trespassing, Roman. My people do not embrace uninvited guests."

Belisarius sighed, visibly annoyed at the fruitless exchange of bravado. "Lord Optaris, the Emperor Justinian has dispatched his innumerable armies to take vengeance for Queen Amalasuntha, who was notoriously slain by your current king. We would have justice for her, and her son!"

Indulf roared approval, and, without Belisarius' permission, vaulted atop his horse and galloped alongside me. Unable to react, lest he acknowledge insubordination in his ranks before an enemy leader, Belisarius merely reddened, his breathing slowing as he squeezed his reins.

"Optaris, you goat's arse!" Indulf yelled. "Why do you follow that gelded incompetent? Theodahad would sell you and your entire family into slavery if it would gain him a fistful of silver."

"Indulf?" Optaris sounded confused at our Gothic foederati. "You traitorous whelp. You always were a little cunt."

Indulf growled, then turned to Belisarius. "Let me fight him, Lord!"

"Indulf, leave," Belisarius said shortly. "That is an order."

Indulf's nostrils flared, yet he nodded. His shoulders arched as Optaris hooted with laughter at the retreat.

"Let's compromise, Roman," Optaris called once again to Belisarius. "Give me Indulf, and I will let you return to Sicily peacefully."

Belisarius trotted a few paces forward, forcing me to match his position as I gripped hard at the straps of my shield. "Last chance, Optaris. Your kinsmen have opened their gates to me with honor. Will you do the same?"

"There are no real Goths in Sicily," Optaris spat. "As evidenced by Indulf in your ranks. Close your holes and leave. I've heard enough of your talking."

Belisarius nodded, signaled at me to retreat, and slowly backed away. We returned to the safety of our forces, absent the hoped-for outcome of yet another bloodless victory.

"This is a siege, so no cavalry," Belisarius explained to me. "Have Martinus lead our Cappadocian ladder teams to the walls. There is no trench or moat, so we should swarm the walls in at least a dozen places. Ascum will position archers with each ladder team, and ballistae will strike at Neapolis' towers."

"Yes, Lord," I replied. "All we can do for now."

"No," Belisarius murmured. "But it's all I can think of for now."

With a half dozen armored couriers following Belisarius' movements, I ordered two of their number to dispatch our final orders to different sections of the army. The approach was a cautious one, but sensible—our Cappadocian veterans would probe for weaknesses along the Neapolitan wall, while Ascum would soften their defenses where possible. It was also, however, an obvious strategy, one that Optaris could anticipate, if not counter, and that worry lingered on my mind as Roman horns blared, Cappadocian banners dipped forward, and Martinus led the first Roman lines toward Neapolis.

It was not a shield wall but rather a grouping of some forty or fifty men in crude squares, heading a centurion's orders to encase the unit in a protective shell of shields. At one hundred paces distant, Optaris loosed his first volley at the rolling squares, followed shortly thereafter by a second and third.

"Not many bowmen," Xerxes muttered. "The volleys are thin."

He was correct, although such welcome information did not eliminate all hazard from Martinus' advance. Most of the Gothic arrows merely slid off of Roman shields slicked with a layer of light rain. Others thudded against a wooden bulwark, and some, perhaps two or three, slipped past the roving Roman tortoise, even striking one Cappadocian in the neck, who stumbled away from the square, jerking as the steel arrowhead did its work. Leaving him as he lay, the squares continued onward, for that was the only hope they had to eliminate the threat of the wall archers.

"Send in the Ostrogoths," Belisarius said, his eyes fixed upon Martinus' advance. "Tight squares in support of the ladder teams. And have Ascum commence firing."

Couriers sprinted through the Roman ranks, sending shouts of glee amongst the Gothic foederati. "Amalasuntha!" Indulf yelled. "Amalasuntha!"

"You would think she was his mother, the way he worships her," Uliaris whispered to me.

"Don't let him hear you slander her," I bit back. "I'll be peeling your skin from the walls next if he does."

As Martinus drew within thirty paces of the walls, with Indulf not far behind him, sonorous horns blared near the anchored palisade walls. Though I could not see Ascum, all present could hear the winching of the ballistae and the pulsing thrum of massive bolts. Most sailed wide of their mark, yet two hurtled directly for a tower beside the south-facing gate. Angled upward, one bolt carried clean through the lumber and stone roof, while the second smacked against a stone wall that shielded several Gothic soldiers. Two Goths were launched from the walls as sections of stone exploded outward, their screams cut short as, encased in iron mail, they clattered against the dirt-packed ground.

Our onlooking ranks cheered, but in that din, few of us saw the Gothic response.

"Cover!" I yelled instinctively. "Cover Belisarius!"

The two Gothic ballistae facing our forces had launched their missiles, which whistled downward at the approaching Romans before exploding into one of Indulf's squares in a mist of blood, dirt, and splinters. Of forty-some Goths in that square, no fewer than four were killed upon impact, and an equal number screeched in pain as enemy arrows rained down from the walls.

"Damn." Belisarius groaned. "Signal Martinus to rush."

There was little need, however. By then, half of our ladders were anchored against Neapolis' walls, with others close behind. The Cappadocians, including many who had experienced the siege of

Septem, demonstrated no reluctance as they snaked up the ladder's rungs. Those waiting on the ground hurled spears at opportunistic archers, finding an occasional victim who leaned too far forward from their stone defenses.

The climbers, however, made terrible progress despite their eagerness. I can only imagine the difficulties added by the persistent sprinkle of rain, making leather boots and wooden rungs slick and prone to tripping. I witnessed at least one man tumble from the rungs, while others hauled their shields above their heads as they carefully navigated upward. Such delays only allowed the Gothic defenders further time to coordinate their response—a reprieve which more than made up for their deficient numbers.

Two burly Goths hauled a stone near a Roman ladder, struggling against its onerous weight. As a wall defender exchanged blows with the closest Roman climber, they heaved the stone downward, crushing a second Roman climber and shattering no fewer than four rungs. Those who could jumped free of the breaking structure as it cracked from its injury, bent in half, and eventually sent an unlucky man tumbling to the ground.

Roman and Gothic ballistae traded bolts, but none of Martinus' men could carve a path atop Neapolis' walls. Be it due to poor footing or ingenious methods of defense, our injuries began to mount despite the reinforcements of Indulf's foederati. Defenders hurled stones atop the Romans who swelled against Neapolis' walls, and soon it was clear our attack was nothing more than toothless and chaotic.

"That's enough for today," Belisarius said. "Sound the retreat."

"Nothing else for today?" I asked.

"No," Belisarius replied. "While we may find success in better weather, we find ourselves in the same predicament as Panormus. Brute strength will cost too many losses, and far too many cities remain ahead. Let the men rest and dry themselves, and we shall consider another path into Neapolis."

I acquiesced in commanding the army to retreat, and our attacking forces re-formed their squares to comply. Protected by the consistent thrum of Roman archers and ballistae, Martinus and Indulf retreated far quicker than they advanced, although many carried or dragged wounded and dead companions to the safety of our lines. As the exchange of missiles ceased, we tallied nine dead and fifteen gravely wounded, and none of us any closer to gaining control of Neapolis.

There was no further fighting that day. Nor the second day, when the rain further softened the grasses and turned dirt into sucking mud. Occasionally, fleet-footed teams of Roman archers would send a volley toward either of Neapolis' gates, yet it did little more than keep Optaris wary that an attack could occur along any point of the walls. By the third day, a violent gale had pulsed from the west, making both accuracy and force impossible.

Of all the battles I have fought, only in Neapolis was boredom such a terrible enemy. Rain and wind gave Ascum little to do, and our men stood mostly idle, with even our horses cropped against the grass as they were herded from one section of outer fields to another. Though Optaris lacked the force to attack us, Belisarius could not bring his full strength forth either, given the conditions. Instead, we could do little more than scout every pace of Neapolis' walls and triple-count the dwindling rations remaining to our army, our bellies never quite full.

One week after arriving at Neapolis, we did attempt a further assault, but it was barely an improvement upon the first. Again, there were few casualties, but poor light and bitter cold sapped the men of their strength. Our only success was in Ascum's ballistae destroying one of the enemy siege engines, striking it directly with a resounding snap of taut wood.

"As ugly as you are, I could kiss you." Bessas laughed to Ascum. "What luck!"

"The only luck I ever need is with women." Ascum chortled. "That blow was guided by a decade of experience and nothing less."

A further stroke of fortune came in the form of a half dozen dromons that surrounded Neapolis' harbor. Joining the percussion of Ascum's assault, Valerian's seaborne catapults tossed stones into

Neapolis' wharf, but what little damage they did was of only small aid to our attack on the land-facing walls.

Two weeks after arriving, we launched a more dedicated assault at a ballista-weakened section of Neapolis' southern gate, yet this, too, was only marginally more successful than its predecessors.

As Belisarius' men retreated once more, a roar erupted from Neapolis, contrasting from the general silence that Optaris' men had usually opted for. The weakened southern gate opened, revealing a single warrior strutting into the hardening mud, bedecked in a thick web of mail and fur that would have cost a small fortune in Constantinople's markets.

"Romans!" the warrior called in harshly accented Latin. "You fight like sheep! Leave, before Arareiks castrates you!"

"Arareiks?" I questioned, stumbling over the foreign word.

"His name," Indulf explained. "'Ruler of eagles.' I do not know him well, but I've heard tell he's a skilled fighter with many weapons. Deadly."

Belisarius shrugged. "How should we respond?"

"I can fight him, Lord," I replied.

"No," Belisarius said quickly. "And neither you, Indulf. Select someone else."

I never enjoyed sending another to fight in my stead. It seemed cowardly in some way. Yet Belisarius refused me, and I could not refuse him as my strategos. Another must bear the burden of single combat, and in that situation, I knew there was only one man I could call upon, one bored to tears of the eventless siege and begging to be used.

Summoning Cephalas, I requested the massive two-handed blade that had been among my spoils from Gelimer's downfall. Cephalas returned, struggling to balance the fur-bundled blade.

"Gunderic!" I roared. "Gunderic!!"

The Vandal foederati, fallow until this moment, erupted. Clattering shields and guttural howls soared above Belisarius' army, infecting even Indulf's men, who added to the clangor. Gunderic was easy to spot as he approached, weapons in hand, his body encased in armor that even I would have struggled to move within, yet that still could not to hide his glee.

"Yes, Varus?" He grinned. "You called for me?"

I nodded toward Arareiks, some thirty paces distant. "Our army needs a victory. Can you defeat him?"

"Dead?" Gunderic asked. "Or just defeated?"

"Whichever is best," I answered. "Do you wish to hear of his strengths? Indulf knows the man."

Gunderic chuckled. "Does it matter? A man is a man. Rest easy, Varus. Now is my time."

"The men want to see what you can do." I grinned, raising the bundle toward my elected champion. "But with this, if you like."

Stone-faced, Gunderic snatched at the fur, withdrawing the ponderous steel inside. "Gaiseric's blade," he murmured, clutching fast to the hilt.

I nodded. "You gave it to me, but it will be in better service in your hands."

Kissing the naked iron, Gunderic laughed throatily. "It was too big for you, then?"

I chuckled. "Just not my preference. Now, go cut down that stinking goat."

The full swell of our army, including Belisarius, roared as Gunderic stepped forward. Arareiks lowered his spear in acceptance of the challenge, showing no outward intimidation at the raw strength of his opponent. I later discovered that Arareiks had been a victor of a great many duels against the Franks, and thus likely supposed Gunderic just another large but clumsy foe to dispatch. Stepping forward, Arareiks turned to the walls of Neapolis and shot his arms to the sky, earning a counter-cheer led by Optaris—yet whether from distance or a lack of voices, it seemed muted against our own din.

At twenty paces apart, Arareiks squared his body in anticipation of the first blows, but Gunderic halted. Seeing this, men around me muttered in confusion, the booming cheers gradually ceasing. Arareiks screamed some provocation at Gunderic, yet the Vandal warlord remained still. Confused, Arareiks turned around, shrugging to his lord before levying a taunt at Gunderic.

"Big men are always the fleetest cowards!" he yelled. "I can smell your piss from here!"

At that, Gunderic chuckled, a rivulet of laughter that burst into a veritable river as Gunderic hooted in delight, almost unable to catch his breath. As his merriment rose in a deep crescendo, he unstrapped first his helmet, then his shield, letting them tumble to the ground.

"What is he doing?" Xerxes muttered, his face lined with concern and irritation.

"Being Gunderic." I winked. "All is well."

With his helmet gone, I could see involuntary tears wetting Gunderic's eyes as he struggled to breathe from laughter. Arareiks, still dazed, offered no further taunts but began to shift weight from one foot to the other. Gasping, Gunderic finally unbuckled his sword belt and lay his weapons gently atop his shield, rendering him unarmed and defenseless. Even Gaiseric's blade remained far from his reach.

At that, Arareiks could not resist a final jibe. "You surrender, coward?"

With a single hoot, Gunderic sipped air, wiping his eyes from tears of amusement. "You call this a man?! I've eaten chickens bigger than this!"

I could not hear Arareiks' reply. Gunderic's Vandals all cackled in unison, resurrecting their cheers. Rattling shields drowned out Arareiks' rage as Gunderic took his first ponderous step forward.

"No discipline whatsoever," Xerxes grumbled.

"None," I agreed. "But I could not imagine Gunderic behaving any other way."

Arareiks rushed forward, outpacing Gunderic as he closed the remaining distance, and showing showed no reluctance in striking an unarmed opponent. With a whipping thrust, he plunged his spear toward Gunderic's chest, and only then did Gunderic display his agility as he sidestepped the jab, allowing the iron spearhead to strike only air, and just as swiftly grabbed the shaft and yanked. Unable to resist, Arareiks released the spear and hopped backward, allowing Gunderic to inspect the weapon.

"You are not worthy of my death." Gunderic grinned. "You are hardly worthy of your life. Run back to your mother, and I won't chase you."

Roaring, Arareiks instead drew a sword from his belt. Gunderic laughed again, snapped the spear atop his knee, and tossed its remnants to the ground. As Arareiks closed in again for an assault, lowering his sword for a more disciplined jab, Gunderic kneeled, as if in waiting. Seeking an easy strike against the undefended Vandal, Arareiks finally hopped forward and jammed the tip of his blade toward Gunderic's hip.

Only to watch the weapon sail unhelpfully past Gunderic's body. This time, Gunderic launched himself toward Arareiks, bashing into the Goth's shield as though his body were a ballista bolt all its own. Hopelessly off balance, Arareiks flew backward and landed a full three paces distant. Both sword and shield clattered against the turf, leaving a breathless Arareiks only enough time to reach for the pommel of his weapon. Smirking, Gunderic stepped forward, driving a boot into Arareiks' stomach and leaving the Goth gasping for air.

The Gothic defenders were silent as their champion struggled to stand. Gunderic, meanwhile, only turned to face me, shrugging.

"Live or die?" he yelled.

Before I could respond, Arareiks rushed forward in a final frenzy, slashing with his sword in an attempt to send Gunderic backpedaling for safety. Gunderic did not oblige, and simply dodged each slash with a tilt of his head or a twist of his hips. From my view, Gunderic had only grown swifter since our own single combat atop Mount Papua, and I offered silent thanks that I would not have to face this deadlier warrior who now toyed with Arareiks as an enemy.

Screeching fury, Arareiks raised his sword for a further attack. As he lowered the blade, however, Gunderic captured his wrist with a single hand, squeezing hard into the tendons. Arareiks screamed in pain and smashed his free hand into Gunderic's neck, which barely even curried Gunderic's attentions. Upon a second attempted blow, Gunderic seized Arareiks' other wrist, squeezing as he gritted his teeth in a broad smile.

"Pathetic." Gunderic laughed.

Within heartbeats, the blade dropped from Arareiks' useless hand. I doubt he even noticed, for the man screamed and jerked about with a wild desperation of a frightened animal moments from butchery. Despite the tossing about, Gunderic's grip only tightened, and I could hear the gruesome popping and grinding from the trapped wrists even with a cheering Roman Army at my back.

Desperate, Arareiks attempted to strike Gunderic with a boot. When that failed, he swung his head back, only for Gunderic to smash a knee into his gut and send him crumpling to his knees. At that, Gunderic released Arareiks' shield arm, and with a yell, snapped his sword arm clean in half.

"Any others?!" Gunderic yelled to the walls of Neapolis, stomping on Arareiks' face as a measure to keep his opponent docile. "No? Fine."

He plucked Arareiks' discarded blade with one hand and snatched up the man himself with the other, lifting him into the air by the throat. The Goth hardly had time to beg before Gunderic thrust the blade into his chest, twisting the iron to pulp the heart underneath. Arareiks shuddered, blood spilling from the wound and from his lips, and went limp. Gunderic tossed him aside like a cornhusk doll and wiped his hands upon the corpse's trousers.

"Looks like I didn't need Gaiseric's sword," Gunderic said with a bloody grin, offering me back the blade.

"Keep it," I told him. "You've earned it."

It was a gruesome death, fulfilled by a brutality known only to the Vandals or the Huns. Yet our army loved the display of strength, evidenced by chants of Gunderic's name as he shot a salute to Belisarius and me before retreating to his foederati. Belisarius' face was impassive—I doubt he approved of the excessive violence—but I imagined he was content to win at least a small victory against the stubborn Goths of Neapolis.

Unfortunately, it was the last victory we would enjoy for a month. Belisarius permitted an Ostrogoth detachment to reclaim Arareiks' body, yet Optaris was no more inclined to surrender after that duel than before. Instead, Ascum's ballistae thundered against Neapolis' gate and towers, and we mounted an occasional assault on the walls. Other than temporary boosts to morale, however, our efforts accomplished little.

"They have so few defenders," Xerxes complained to me. "With a few siege towers, we could swarm their walls."

"No point in wishing for what we cannot produce," I countered.

Our situation worsened still. Though the rain halted, the days grew colder, bringing the soil to freeze each night. Likewise, our limited rations made many listless, and flaring tempers sent small disputes spinning into full-blown fights. Worst of all was the appearance of the flux, forcing many to carve new latrines from the frozen and rock-strewn earth each week. Neapolis could hardly have grander food stores than ours, even with its populace stripped bare and sent northward prior to our attack, yet its warriors at least slept in better conditions than frost-laced tents, and its sentries sat warmed by blazing fires at each tower.

Petrus particularly hated the cold. "My father told me that hell is a burning waste, and that we should embrace the cold," he complained as a small party of my companions shared what little was available for an evening supper. "Foolishness. Hell is pain, however it comes. I would go without food for a week if it meant that God would return the sun to us, even if only in winter."

"It could be worse," Perenus muttered. "You could also be ugly."

"True, true!" Petrus agreed. "I was a handsome lad, I will admit."

I chuckled. "It's impossible to imagine you were ever young, Father."

He tossed a piece of unlit kindling toward me. "You'll see, if God graces you with my years. One day, you will understand what is important in life."

Today, I must be nearly the same age Petrus was during our stay outside Neapolis. I cannot claim to be wiser—Petrus was far more a paragon of patience and virtue than I could ever hope to become. But through this tale, in all its joys and sorrows, I did learn. There is no escaping suffering, for that is what life is. We all suffer and die. What is important, for however long we remain amongst the living, is that we share our burdens with the loving shoulders to bear them. That is what makes life worthwhile—for a time, anyway.

As Belisarius galloped daily along Neapolis' walls, we did our best to survive God's wrath. After sharing in the depleted nourishment of my men, the only comfort I knew was Rosamund's company. Wrapped in furs, she alone seem unperturbed by the cold, never complaining of stiff hands and sore joints. "The trick is to embrace fire," she explained. "Fire is the most sacred element we have, and the only one capable of changing everything around us. Stoke a fire, and all your shivers will depart."

"But you sleep without a fire," I said.

"Not all fires are of wood and kindling," Rosamund replied. "Mine is in my heart, and it is never extinguished."

Tireless, she treated all manner of injuries and half-frozen limbs. Absent Agathias, Rosamund deployed Shimon as her assistant. Shimon was capable and willing, yet never seemed comfortable with Rosamund and happily departed her presence upon some minor assignment or another. Though he never admitted to this avoidance, he rarely sat with her at meals, preferring the company of Cephalas and Perenus. Rosamund showed no offense, yet did admit to fatigue after a month of constant labors. She resisted my entreaties to rectify her plight, but eventually I insisted that she trade her private tent for my larger command posting. She acquiesced, but only after I agreed to share a cup of heated wine with her before departing for sleep. Samur occasionally joined us, yet often we gathered separately, sitting near a stone-lined fire as we watched sentries pace the perimeter of Belisarius' camp.

One frigid evening, we even enjoyed tiny cuts of deer slain and butchered by Hunnic scouts that morning. Our portions were a mere mouthful, yet the scent of meat roasting over an open flame made me groan, my stomach lurching in fury at its diet of hardened bread and frozen fruit. Dressing it with an herb plucked from her medicine chest, Rosamund used an iron poker to spear a piece of meat and handed it to me. In my eagerness, I thrust the meat right into my mouth, searing my tongue in the process. Rosamund giggled as I sought relief from my waterskin, yet I cared little. After months of reduced rations, the venison was nothing less than ecstasy. Soon thereafter, a wind billowed from the nearby coast, the biting gale leading me to shiver uncontrollably.

"Damned cold," I grumbled, prying off my frigid leather gloves and blowing onto stiff fingers. "And damned useless sun."

Rosamund placed wine in a fire-hardened jar and nestled it in an iron holder over our fire. As we waited, she covered my callused hands in her own smaller ones, an undeniable warmth to her grip. "How are you not freezing?" I asked.

Rosamund sighed. "You never listen to me. So stop questioning what benefits you and enjoy the moment."

And so I did. The wine further aided my recovery, thawing out a body made stiff by the icy darkness. Our evenings never fully slaked the pain, but as we parted to our respective sleeping quarters, the mixture of fatigue and partial relief were enough to bring on sleep. Indeed, I should count myself fortunate, for as autumn dragged on and our desolation continued unabated, a few unlikely members of our army did freeze to death. They had no one to blame but themselves, for both men had overindulged on wine and stumbled beyond the camp latrine and into a nearby forest, where they eventually fell asleep. On different occasions, our sentries found each respective man curled up and frozen. After that, Belisarius forbade sojourns beyond his established pickets.

Amidst flux, weakness, and the nagging cold, our officers debated options to end the stalemate. We could not depart, for a Goth-held Neapolis would harry our supply lines should we proceed northward. Nor could we rush the walls, which stood higher than most and atop a hill that left little protection for those climbing its ladders. Even our dromons were useless, for Neapolis' sea walls were as stout as those facing land, and we lacked the transports to affect a beach landing. Ascum even suggested naphtha, yet Belisarius denied that request.

"Our goal is to gain loyalty of Italian cities, not bully and destroy," he insisted. "We must be more than bloodthirsty conquerors."

Belisarius never expressed concern about our conditions, yet I began to wonder whether retreat would become a necessity. Without Neapolis, it would be near impossible to hold Calabria, forcing Belisarius' army to return to Sicily and pray that Theodahad would not mount his own invasion with five times our number. And I would have privately suggested that option to Belisarius, too, if it had not been for Liberius.

Through a light snow, Liberius sprinted like a lunatic as he called out my name, grinning widely. I had not seen Liberius so pleased since his success at Nisibis, procuring whatever scroll he had sought. "Varus! I have been looking everywhere for you!"

"Lord?"

"Get Belisarius, and call a meeting of the officers," he insisted.

"Lord, the men are busy—"

Liberius groaned. "Damn it, Varus, this is more important. Summon everyone now. This cannot wait."

I obeyed. Though Liberius had no formal rank in Belisarius' army, I doubt that any would have willingly ignored his counsel—even if the purpose of such counsel was unclear, the timing of its delivery was urgent. All of Belisarius' officers gathered in his command tent, with some shivering and many clutching growling and underfed stomachs.

"We must take Neapolis within three days," Liberius said. "Otherwise, this army will fall to anarchy. No amount of wine will sway the difference."

Veins throbbed about Belisarius' forehead. "It isn't like we haven't tried, Minister. Neapolis' walls weaken, but we lack the men and the ladders to force our path over the top."

"Ladders are not the only path past Neapolis' walls," Liberius said, his eyes widening. "I'm a fool to not have seen it before."

"How, then?" I asked. "Through tunnels?"

"Apparently, I am not the only fool," Liberius said. "If you want to be a mole and dig through ice and rock, you are welcome to your strange proclivity. No, not digging."

There were no further ideas. Not even a suggestion or a guess. Liberius chided us all for our lack of ingenuity, we officers granted authority over thousands. "Use what little minds you have! If Neapolis is sealed tighter than a tortoise shell, how does it get water?"

"Wells?" Gunderic offered, drawing an exasperated sigh from Liberius.

But Samur identified Liberius' intention immediately. Just as he had in Liberius' classroom, Samur bobbed to the tips of his toes, his face bright with enthusiasm. "The aqueducts, Lord."

"The aqueducts!" Liberius cheered, pumping his fists in the air. "And, poor samples of Roman architecture that they are, how are the aqueducts near the city fashioned?"

"Like closed tunnels, Lord," Samur replied again, his speech fast and confident.

"Tunnels indeed!" Liberius cried out. "The Aqua Augusta, or the system of aqueducts that services Neapolis and its surrounding cities, is enclosed at multiple points. It was beautiful when Agrippa first built it, true, but I doubt that decades of Gothic rule have made for promising upkeep."

Belisarius' frown disappeared, his head cocked as he considered. "We could carve an entryway into the tunnel, but the channeled water would make for perilously slow passage."

"If it retains running water," Liberius countered. "Ice, more like — which is the only reason this foolhardy attempt would even work. Otherwise you would all drown. Ancient cartographers suggest that men of the northern icy wastes would attach spikes to their boots. If we find the aqueduct filled with ice, we can supply a hundred men with the footwear necessary to trudge through. From there, all they must do is open the gates and allow our army to spill in."

"Just like Troy," I murmured.

Liberius nodded. "Far better, for we are not gambling on the enemy's stupidity. All we need are a hundred willing volunteers who aren't fearful of tight spaces and can blend into Neapolis without detection."

There was little choice in the manner. All turned to Indulf, who threw a glance at his subordinate Gothic officers and sighed with indignation. "Christ, but what a mess."

"You are the only person who can deliver this," Belisarius said. "It's risky, but it's our only hope of ending this quickly."

Indulf tossed his head, appearing to weigh out the strategy. "It makes sense," he agreed, "and I'll do it. But I want Varus to join us, with whomever he would care to invite."

I shuddered, unable to understand why Indulf would insist on such a demand. Others grumbled, while Xerxes outright refused on my behalf. "Varus doesn't speak Gothic. It's asinine."

"That's my price for slugging our way through a half-frozen tunnel," Indulf said. "If he comes with us, then I know all of you will do anything required to rescue us if things go poorly."

Gunderic spat. "Typical Goth."

Indulf laughed. "My last condition: Varus cannot bring that brute along." He nodded at Gunderic. "His fat arse will get stuck, and we'll never make it."

"Enough!" Belisarius roared. "Indulf, if you have my oath that we would not abandon you, would that suffice?"

Again, Indulf considered. "Respectfully, Lord Belisarius, no. My men take on all the risk of this plan. Besides, Varus knows us well and will be useful in a fight. I doubt he crows complaints like the others, no?"

Belisarius turned to me, his unwillingness to speak or make an order plain in his fatigued eyes.

I acquiesced and freed him from that unhappy task.

"It would be my pleasure," I lied. "When do we depart?"

"Tonight," Liberius said smartly. "The moon is near empty, and the rains have temporarily ceased. It must be now, before fate makes our predicament worse."

With Belisarius' assent, we departed, although both Belisarius and Liberius offered to free me from my obligation. I refused—shaming Indulf before the other officers would be foolish at this point, and I reasoned that I would remain relatively safe toward the rearguard of our infiltration. Privately, I requested aid from Xerxes, Uliaris, and Sembrouthes, assuring each man that I would not feel slighted at their refusal. All insisted upon joining, and we spent the remainder of the afternoon preparing our weapons and armor.

Not all portions of the Neapolitan aqueducts were easily accessible from the ground, and Liberius insisted that we move beyond eyeshot of the city's defenders. Before we left for the predetermined location, Rosamund procured woolen blankets for each of Indulf's men, and mine as well.

"To quiet the clinking of your armor," she explained. "Line your scabbards with fleece as well."

Wool and fleece were among the few materials abundant to us, and their effect was not only immediate, but provided an additional layer to insulate heat as well. Given the enclosure we would worm through, we left behind all shields and spears, taking only those swords or daggers that could be quieted with Rosamund's wrappings. In total, Indulf selected a hundred men for the task, all of whom were familiar in their service in our prior conflicts, and all of whom were given fresh boots laced with iron stubs to better grip the ice.

Accompanying us to our intended entryway, Belisarius was accompanied by a dozen Cappadocians bearing mallets and iron spikes. Liberius directed them to a portion of aqueduct closest to the ground, requiring only a simple wooden riser for a man to climb inside. Careful to avoid carving holes in the underside of the aqueduct and rendering it useless to ferry water, the hammerers smashed their mallets into its upward-facing sides, turning smooth stones into shards and prying mortar that had been lain perhaps five centuries prior. It was exhausting on their bodies, but after the first hammer succeeded in crushing a hole into the aqueduct, prying apart nearby rock went far quicker.

Soon, it was wide enough for a man to slip through, and Indulf designated a fellow Goth to investigate. A few moments after climbing atop the riser and pulling himself into the hole, he landed with a thud.

"All's well, lords!" he called. "It's mostly ice, with some pockets of slush. Just as Lord Liberius said."

"But will we fit?" Indulf asked. "At least, those of us the size of actual men?"

"Yes, Lord Indulf," the man replied unhappily. "All will need to crouch, and the bigger of us will have sore backs, but it will work."

"God in heaven." Indulf snorted. "Crawling a mile in freezing darkness. How will we know we have reached the other side?"

At that, Liberius straightened. "Agrippa engineered this system to have many outlets. Avoid the open fountains and the toilets, or you'll be wading in frozen shit. But any enclosed thermae will be ideal, for there you can gather your men in a building absent prying eyes."

Before allowing Indulf to depart, Belisarius added further instructions. "When you reach safety, any gold and silver you find are the just rewards of your valor, but spare the inhabitants."

"Spare them?" Indulf mocked. "They would happily kill us, Belisarius."

Belisarius nodded patiently. "Yes, but after we gain Neapolis, they will all be our fellow citizens. Restore the children to their parents, the wives to their husbands. Wherever you can, show them your generosity, of what friends they have obstinately deprived themselves by remaining in Theodahad's service."

"No sack." Indulf sighed. "Fine. But my men deserve to be paid the value that they would get from the spoils of this city."

"It will be done," Belisarius said. "And God be with you in the darkness."

One by one, we ascended to the opening, with Indulf's foederati scurrying toward Neapolis as more men filled in the spaces behind them. Toward the end, my turn to ascend came, and I was the first of my group to enter the aqueduct.

"Remember Troy, Varus!" Liberius called to me. "Discretion is a more powerful ally than any blade. For now, you are all Goths under Optaris' control, and your lives depend upon the ruse."

My three companions followed, forcing me to bend forward and half crawl toward the darkness. One hundred Ostrogoths shuffled before me, and the acrid stink of unwashed bodies permeated the enclosed space. Our passageway was perhaps a bit more than the height of a child—plenty of space to fit a moving body, but far from enough to do so comfortably. As I was larger than most before me, I in particular struggled, continually knocking my back against the stone enclosure as I placed one awkward foot before the other.

"Quiet, Varus!" Sembrouthes hissed. "You knock about like a drunken lecher."

"It's not my fault!" I shot back, wishing that I had allowed Belisarius to pluck me from this unhappy assignment. "You're smaller than I."

Indulf and two Gothic companions were the last to enter the aqueduct. I found the gesture odd, yet it was Uliaris who spoke against the Gothic leader.

"Afraid to go first, Indulf?" Uliaris said.

Indulf chuckled, his throaty laughter echoing from the walls. "From here, I get to make sure you won't run, even if I find myself downwind."

"Insolent bastard," Xerxes muttered in Persian.

We crept forward, each laborious step taking us farther away from the narrow band of light at our backs. Within fifty paces, it was as dark as pitch, as if naphtha had caked into our eyes and blotted out what little moonlight snuck through the veil of the heavens. Many stumbled and cursed, only to be chastised for excessive noise, and many a time I found myself reaching blindly for the Goth before me as steady reassurance that I was not completely lost. God help me, but if our journey had been anything other than a straight line, I might still be in that aqueduct today.

I will not pretend that the darkness, as complete and impenetrable as I have ever known, had no effect upon me. At times, I wanted to scream, to rush backward and toward fresh air. The atmosphere was fetid, and even the scratching of the men's boots seemed sinister in such a void. I clung to Petrus' teachings, that God, too, inhabited such forlorn places, where even a sliver of light can penetrate the most pervasive darkness imaginable. We trudged for an hour, our pace agonizingly slow and seeming never to end.

Worse, though my limbs and body were being slowly sapped of its heat, the ice at our feet warmed from our breath. The ice slowly melted, and by the time the rear of our column passed through a given point, it was a veritable stream of stinking liquid and acrid air. My boots became soaked through, and my feet stung with each sucking step. It was then that we heard the scratching.

The noise was ominous, as if something terrible had discovered our plot and was digging to reach us. Too soon, the scratching grew louder. Claws against chunks of ice and plodding against pockets of running water. My chest pounded as I focused my ears upon the intruder, the grinding approaching at an ambling pace. Others before me murmured in Gothic, yet their meaning needed no translation, for it was laced with fear. It drew closer, seemingly just a pace from my ears. And hungry. I could not know why, but I knew it was hungry. At last, it brushed against my boot, ricocheting between my feet, even tugging at my leg.

And then it squeaked. Behind me, Xerxes jumped, slamming his back against the ceiling with a painful "Oof."

"What is that?!" he yelped.

This was the first note of true fear I had ever heard from the vaunted Zhayedan. "Rats," I replied. "Probably half starved. We must be close to the city."

"Disgusting." He shuddered.

"There were plenty of rats in Barbalissus, and you didn't complain then," I teased.

"We were not friends then," Xerxes hissed. "And at least I could see them scurrying about. There could be hundreds of them here, and I wouldn't know."

"Oh, thousands, surely," Sembrouthes added. "About your head, even."

Xerxes seethed. "*Bokhoresh,*" he muttered in Persian, suggesting that Sembrouthes should eat something untoward.

"Quiet!" Indulf hissed. "If Optaris finds us because you're jabbering like washerwomen, I won't stay behind to save your skins."

After that point, the passage of time becomes indecipherable. Most of the rats scurried by, although occasionally one bumped into my leg. No words were exchanged about me aside from Xerxes, who flailed about from another encounter with a rat.

"It bit me!" he whispered. "That motherless bastard bit me!"

"Bite back," Uliaris grumbled.

Suddenly, our stone enclosure began to vibrate. It felt like the tremors I had come to expect during my youth in Constantinople, yet this was far less dangerous. Placing my ear against the frigid stones along the side of the tunnel, I heard the unmistakable sound of voices.

"We are in Neapolis," I whispered as lightly as I could. "Keep everyone quiet."

They obeyed. There was no more complaining, although each step felt somehow more exhausting and more infuriating. Ahead, I detected a small light, yet the man in front of me whispered not to follow it.

"Too many voices coming from that end. Keep going straight, and pass the message along," he said.

We passed two further exits, all of which rumbled with the voices of men upon the other side. However, the fourth such entry was promising, and our column halted as the leaders of our pack inspected its providence. Eventually, after an eternity, I was given the word that our escape was nigh. It came, although when two men helped me stumble into the gloomy room, I wondered whether we had actually improved our situation.

It took several moments for my eyes to adjust, yet I could tell that Liberius' conjecture of thermae had been proven valid. The room was vacant and waterless, yet plenty large enough to gather our men, and insulated to dull their noise. As I popped my back, I groaned instinctively, relieved to be freed from that minor hell, only for Uliaris to throw a hand over my mouth.

"Silence," he warned. "We are here."

Indulf designated a scout, bedecked in Ostrogothic mail that would have been indistinguishable from any of Theodahad's adherents, to inspect our location. Until then, we waited: flexing stiff limbs, rubbing frozen toes, and praying that frostbite would not claim anything. The pain in my foot was promising, for Rosamund had once warned that frostbite comes not as a painful injury, but as a blissful escape from hurt—until the dead flesh thaws and the digits require amputation, that is. Our scout returned, dragging behind him the stunned body of a Gothic warrior. Though he still breathed, the Goth grasped listlessly for his head.

Without hesitation, Indulf withdrew his dagger and cut the throat of the guard. "Idiot! His sentry friends will know he is missing."

"No, Lord," the scout replied. "He was pissing against the wall of the thermae, clearly drunk. I thought we might use his shield to blend with the others on guard."

"We can use the shield," Indulf snarled. "But you're still an idiot. Where in Neapolis are we?"

Per the scout's description, the thermae were perhaps a hundred paces through Neapolis' walls, not far from the southern gate. "We can take hidden alleys, all vacant, all the way to the gate," the scout muttered. "I couldn't get too close, but the gate only has a standard guard. Perhaps a dozen men?"

"Excellent," I replied. "We must find a way to signal Belisarius, though. Overpowering the gate guards will be easy, but their reinforcements will overwhelm us if the Roman cavalry doesn't storm through the gates to support us."

"Also easy." Indulf shrugged. "Seventy men will open and hold Neapolis' gate, while the remaining thirty will ascend to the battlements and light a guard's spear butt against a brazier. Between the flames and the noise, Belisarius will understand."

"Sensible," I agreed. "But that means we abandon the northern gate. All success rests upon one entryway."

The scout interjected. "Separating us from the northern gate is another two or three hundred paces, and the forum. We would definitely be seen, and possibly discovered as imposters."

"Unwise," Xerxes said. "We wager on Belisarius forcing his way through. Might as well use those cataphracts for something useful."

After checking our weapons and readjusting the fleece lining against our scabbards and armor, we formed into five groups of twenty. Though we still made far too much noise, I doubted a gate guard would think much about such small detachments. In my days as a centurion, Archelaus would frequently test his sentries for their alertness, shifting timetables for replacement to prevent any from growing too comfortable in the evening shifts. The Ostrogoths were likely little different, albeit less disciplined, and so we placed the safety of our lives in a single thrust toward the southern gate.

Our pace was something of a fast walk—light footsteps, but as fast as we could go without plodding in our boots. It helped that Neapolis was encased in darkness, with few stars and only a shrouded sliver of moon illuminating the streets with their glow. Curiously, there were few torches to light the alleys, which masked our presence within twenty paces of the walls. Reaching our target, Indulf's hundred gathered together once more, readying themselves for the attack.

"No mercy to the soldiers," he whispered. "Slit their throats before they make noise. Any man of mine who gets wounded keeps his mouth shut. Otherwise, he joins Optaris' men."

There was no debate. Instead, Indulf nodded for his first team of twenty to venture forth, walking casually toward the gate. After they passed into the light of the gate's torches, a duty guard saluted them in Latin. "Orders from Optaris?"

"Aye," one of Indulf's men replied. "He wants to double the guard, and here we are. Wants us up top, he does."

The gate watchman frowned but shrugged. "Not enough of us to double the night watch, but if it's what Optaris wants, we comply."

Indulf nodded, and his men filtered between the two towers of the southern gate. Beneath, an iron-reinforced wooden doorway was barred shut by twin logs, a weight that doubtlessly required at least five men to budge. A few of Indulf's Goths remained at the ground level, again catching the attention of the gate watchman. They chatted in the Gothic tongue before switching back to the bastardized Latin that many Goths had begun to favor in recent years, the guttural, clipped words corrupted by all manner of Germanic phrasing.

"Is Optaris shuffling the gates again?" he asked.

Indulf's companion shrugged. "I assume so. He doesn't ask me anything other than to obey."

The guard laughed. "Fair. Although he's kept us alive this far."

At last, the guard turned round, pacing back to the gate. Indulf raised a fist, suspending it above his head for a few heartbeats before splaying his fingers in each direction. That was when the killing started.

"Go," I whispered. "It starts now!"

Indulf's soldiers did their work well. One gate guardsman fell from the wall all the way to the ground, air bubbling from an open gash in his neck. Others were gored and fell where they stood, slain by a pierced heart or a severed neck. In a way, it was the cruelest art anyone living could experience, with the canvas the souls of the enemy and its paint their flowing blood. It all went so well that by the time our second group of twenty arrived in support, there was no more violence to be conducted.

Save one man. His collarbone snapped but windpipe intact, he sprinted away from Indulf's men and toward the main street of the forum. He screamed in Gothic, and with that I knew that our fortune had turned to dung.

"Uliaris!" I yelled. "Stop him!"

A swift flick of a francisca ended the guardsman's chanting. Uliaris stepped forward, tugging his axe from the man's back and cutting down into his spine. Quiet returned to the gate, yet none of us took comfort in our circumstances.

"Do you think anyone took notice?" Sembrouthes asked. "We were fairly loud, even without the screaming."

A blaring horn offered an immediate answer.

"Hurry!" I yelled. "Light a torch for Belisarius! Open the gate!"

"Move your arses!" Indulf roared, signaling to the remainder of his men. "Steal their shields and form what wall we can. Get the bars off of the gates!"

Indulf's men formed a wall, though only twenty of their number possessed shields. Others drew swords, while some plucked fallen spears from the slain guardsmen, searching the darkened streets for attackers. Some five Goths struggled to lift the ponderous wooden bars from the gate, cursing as it budged only a hand's length.

"Out of the way!" I ordered. "Sembrouthes, add your shoulder to the effort."

I thought my shins might shatter from the exertion as we strained ourselves to lift the bar. Faring little better than before, I stole a glance to the heavens, praying for the gate to open. God answered: I glimpsed a hanging pulley that jutted from the stone walls along the sides of the gate, carefully concealed in the darkness.

Liberius was correct. I was a fool.

"Release!" I yelled. "Strap the pulley onto each end of the bar. Two men to crank the pulley's wheel and another five to lift the bar!"

From the streets near the gate, the horn sounded again. Gothic voices, urgent and furious, spilled toward us. Optaris' reinforcements had arrived. It was all I could do to train myself on the pulley, looping its straps around each end of the bar, disciplining my mind to not turn around to glimpse at the oncoming hundreds of Optaris' Goths.

"Varus, why is the gate not open?!" Indulf screamed. "They're coming!"

"Wheel, pull!!" I yelled.

With the pulley channeling the force of our backs, the bar rose and lifted free from its iron holster. Xerxes guided the bar to the side of the gate, lest it trip Belisarius' relief force. Quickly, they unstrapped the bar and allowed it to slam noisily to the stone street, turning the pulley back to the second and final bar that blocked Neapolis' gate.

Behind me, iron cracked against wood and flesh, and I knew the battle had been joined. My discipline temporarily broke as I looked back, finding Indulf's hundred slipping backward as they resisted Optaris' men. Indulf had shoved his warriors into five lines, yet all most could do was press their bodies against those few who held shields and hurl what few spears we possessed against Optaris' attackers. Slowly, Indulf's men were pressed closer to Neapolis' walls and gate, severing any paths of escape.

Uliaris' eyes widened. "We're going to be crushed!"

"Shut your mouth, weakling!" Indulf roared. "Varus, get that fucking gate open!"

Xerxes nodded to me. "Pulley's ready!"

"Wheel, pull!!" I cried again.

Sembrouthes yelled, I screamed, and a chorus of shouts erupted from our throats as we hauled the beam loose. Lacking space to maneuver, Xerxes guided the pulley to the side of the gate's interior, depositing the enormous wooden beam where it would be the least impediment.

"Free!" I yelled.

Indulf turned around, livid. "Don't tell me!" he bellowed. "Just open the fucking gate!"

I gathered a half dozen Goths, and together we unfastened three iron bolts, allowing their chains to hang limp. At last, the gate's hinge moved freely, and nothing further inhibited our path. Behind me, the rearward ranks of the Goths threatened to bump into my assistants, the clash of weapons rising in ferocity as Indulf's men began to fall from their wounds.

"Last time, light another torch up top!" I yelled. "Push!!"

At that, Neapolis burst open. Roman horns blared not a hundred paces distant, and the thunder of thousands of hooves rattled against the frozen Campanian soil. Such a sweet melody, signaling freedom and the news that we would not be squashed like trapped mice. In the darkness, I still spotted Belisarius' white plume, his armor reflecting flickering braziers and torchlight that emanated from Neapolis' walls.

"Belisarius comes!" I shouted, my voice cracked and straining. "Move out of the way!"

Outside Neapolis' walls, Belisarius' charge slowed as his cataphracts formed into a wedge. Though other horsemen pushed their way to the front of the attack, I could still see Belisarius in the third or fourth line, bouncing in the saddle as the cataphracts compressed into a compact stream of armored death. With Optaris' men pushing at our backs, the only path open to us was outside Neapolis' walls.

"Quickly! Leave the city!" I yelled. "Make room for Belisarius!"

Most did not need to be told, although Indulf acknowledged the order with visible relief. His over-matched foederati backed away and out of the Neapolitan border, cleaving in two on either side of the gate just as our cataphracts pushed their way into the city. If Optaris' men saw the looming attack, they did nothing to turn it away. Martinus told me later that the Ostrogoth shield wall broke and ran, allowing our cavalry to burst through the patchwork defenses and force their way into the city's streets. A veritable wave of men, concentrated through a tiny gap in Neapolis' walls, that seemed to never end. As the Cappadocians and later the Vandals followed Belisarius' progress, relief washed over me, for the siege of Neapolis would come to a victorious end.

Except fate never allows for such tidy circumstances. As more Imperial warriors pushed through Neapolis' gates, a horrified groan spread across many a Greek voice. At first, I assumed it was the press of battle, of men pushing and dying as they have done for thousands of years. After a few moments, however, I understood what they cried out with such urgency.

"Belisarius is dead! Belisarius is dead!"

ATONEMENT ON THE APPIAN WAY

I am not sure how long I went without breathing. Even with the fury of the Roman Army swirling about me, I could hear the pounding in my head and in my heart. My body stiffened as if momentarily separated from my soul. All I could hear was a swelling rage, fueled by the shouts of the army.

"They killed Belisarius!"

"Fuck Neapolis! Revenge!"

Whether for a heartbeat or for an hour, I stood outside Neapolis' gates, my body propped against the frost-lined stones as I watched the stragglers of the Roman assault rush toward the sack of a city. I had witnessed such atrocities before in Scythian Neapolis, yet even the death of Godilas had not left me like this, a breathing corpse. There was no hatred, nor even grief. I was numb, unsure of whether what I heard was real. It was not until Uliaris slapped me that my senses returned.

"Varus! We need to go find Belisarius!"

"He's dead," I mumbled, my cheek stinging from the noxious mix of a gloved hand and the night's chill.

Uliaris slapped me again. "Come to, man! We know nothing. Grab your weapons and let's go find him."

Shivering, I checked my blades. "The others?"

"Here, Varus," Xerxes called, nodding to Sembrouthes. "We are ready."

By then, Neapolis' southern gate was bereft of the living. All that remained were lines of corpses, their blood and entrails slathering the paved road. By then, I recognized the soreness in my feet, for the spikes that preserved my footing in the ice-crusted aqueduct now abraded firmer ground. There was no time for a replacement, however, and we stepped over a few dozen bodies as we reentered Neapolis. There, at least, we found no slain body bearing Belisarius' face.

Inside, Neapolis had descended into havoc. Where once there was darkness, fires blazed from one building to the next, igniting all manner of screams as gangs of soldiers stole their way into each enclosure. Some fighting continued, evidenced by the clang of steel from the direction of the forum, yet Optaris lacked the men to turn away thousands of vengeful Roman soldiers. Near the gate's opening, we found one group of Cappadocians standing about, pointing toward a nearby building not yet consigned to fire.

It was difficult to hear, and my throat burned raw as I yelled for the attention of others around me. "Have you seen Belisarius?"

One man straightened. "Lord Varus, I heard men say that Belisarius had been killed after passing through the gate."

"How?" I asked. "Did you see the body?"

"I saw nothing," he admitted. "But others tell me that a beam that barred the gate tripped a horse near him and sent Belisarius crumpling to the ground. One of Optaris' men slew him." Seething, the man turned his gaze back to the building. "Now we repay his death a thousandfold."

My chest tightened, yet I fought to retain my wits. "Belisarius despised sacking a city."

"I loved him," the Cappadocian replied. "But some things deserve to be butchered. Fuck these Goths, and fuck this city."

I did not prevent their assault. There was little point in even trying; I could not afford to fight my own men in a still-hostile land. It all seemed pointless now, and I had no notion of how to proceed. All I wished for was counsel, advice, someone who could tell me what to do next.

"Xerxes, go find Liberius," I said. "He should still be outside the city with the reserves of our men. Inform him of what you heard."

"We haven't heard anything yet!" Uliaris snapped. "Varus, please!"

I nodded. "As Xerxes leaves, we will search for Belisarius. He deserves peace, however we find him."

Together, we filtered through Neapolis' streets. If that city had been a living thing, it would have been in the throes of death that night, for its remaining residents wailed their last as they sprinted away from Roman attackers. The farther we walked into Neapolis, the greater the signs of rampage, painted in gore and carved in smoldering flame. Entire city streets were engulfed in fire, including at least one enclosed pen for the city's hogs. Squeals of terror pierced the crackling timbers before Belisarius' food-deprived forces realized their lost bounty. Several disappeared into the burning pen, but only a few emerged before its roof collapsed in a heap of smoke and dust. The survivors grinned, guiding their terrified chattel away from the attentions of others.

For years, I had thought Belisarius' army too honorable for such savagery, or at least disciplined enough to resist its call. Petrus warned at the warrior's lust for plunder, the pursuit of theft, of rape, and all the fruits of violent conquest that could turn the sons of threadbare plebeians into veritable lords. Hearing this, I had often clung to Petrus' teachings of our shared God, yet only partially due to a desire to please our Lord. Though years had passed, I remembered the senseless destruction of Rosamund's village and the screams of mothers and children who knew not why desolation had visited their hovel. When remembering such screams, my earliest memories of another emerge, a voice of anguish begging for mercy.

"I should stop this," I muttered. "This is madness. It goes against Belisarius' direct order."

Sembrouthes grunted. "It's too late, and they would not listen to you. Your position matters nothing now. I'm only surprised we didn't witness something similar in Carthage."

"All you'll do is earn a knife in your ribs," Uliaris agreed. "Our duty is to find Belisarius. Nothing else."

Yet when we paced all the way to the forum, we found only bodies writhing in blood, wine, or both. "They wouldn't have carried Belisarius this far," I reasoned. "Let's turn back to the gate."

"If they bothered to guard his body," Sembrouthes muttered.

"He's not dead!" Uliaris yelled. "It makes no sense!"

Uliaris suggested that we separate to cover ground, yet Sembrouthes adamantly refused. Instead, we quickened our pace, the throbbing in my feet pounding all the worse. By my reckoning, I had only another hour before my boots were awash in my own blood and I was rendered at least temporarily crippled. In our urgency, I swallowed the pain and trudged on.

Returning to the gate, we found ten men bedecked in the armored scales of the cataphracts. "They weren't there before," I said. "Do we recognize them?"

"Can't tell with the helmets," Sembrouthes replied.

As we approached, it became apparent that the dismounted cataphracts guarded the wide-open southern gate. One man, ostensibly their leader, jerked his head as he detected our noise.

"That's far enough!" he yelled, stomping forward. "Identify yourself, soldier!"

Hearing his voice, I now recognized the armor. "Martinus?"

"Varus? Where have you been?" Martinus said, relaxing his shoulders and removing his hand from the scabbard at his waist.

"Martinus, I…"

"Where is Belisarius?!" Uliaris roared.

I raised a hand for quiet. "We heard he was slain at the gate," I explained to Martinus. "Do you know what happened with his body?"

Martinus' friendly recognition receded into a glower. "It happened so quickly. We yelled for calm, but once one man yelled that Belisarius was slain, the cry spread like the most insidious plague. I've never seen so many sensible men lose their wits all at once, but here we are."

Gesturing toward the forum, he shook his head. "Disgraceful. Disorderly. Illegal!"

Uliaris sagged. "So he is dead?"

"God, no!" Martinus shot back. "I admit, he looked terrible. But God has designs upon our strategos, and it seems like Belisarius will emerge from this with little more than a few bruises."

I shuddered, relief flooding every pore of my body all at once. "Why didn't you begin with that?" I shouted. "Lead me to him!"

"Very well, but quickly," Martinus said. "He ordered me to hold this gate, given that no one else could be bothered."

Martinus struck a brisk pace, even wearing cumbersome armor better suited to horseback. The building was not far, but nestled in a nook along the wall, one of thousands still separated from the blazing ruins near the forum. A full dozen guards stood outside, their spears lowering as our small party approached.

"It's just Martinus, with Tribune Varus," my guide said.

Uliaris stepped forward, recognizing one of the armored men as an oath sworn member of Belisarius' bucellarii. "Gouboulgoudou, is Belisarius awake?"

The Hun, one of many granted patronage in Belisarius' bucellarii, nodded. "He will not be pleased to see you, Uliaris."

"Just let me see that he's alive, and I'll leave," Uliaris said, his tone almost desperate.

Gouboulgoudou frowned. "Why do you care? You were dismissed from service."

"Christ's bones," Uliaris blasphemed. "I swore an oath. Until Tricamarum, my service to Belisarius gave my life purpose. Now, will you allow an old friend the affirmation that his master lives, or will you cast me into the gutter?"

Gouboulgoudou nodded. "Briefly. And if he protests, you all leave."

"You have my word, and thank you," I replied.

As we moved to the door, a thundering roar spilled through Neapolis' southern gate. All of us, from my companions to Belisarius' bucellarii, drew our blades, expecting the long-awaited ambush from Theodahad or another of the Gothic warlords. Instead, we found only Romans, marching in neat array as they streamed across the road. Led by another of Belisarius' appointed gate guards was Liberius, trotting atop a horse as he approached our location.

"Belisarius lives, Lord!" I yelled.

"Thank Christ." Liberius sighed. He had never been one for protestations of faith; to hear him say as much only proved the near-disaster we had courted if Belisarius truly had died. "He's here?"

"We're going inside," I replied. "He's injured, so speak quietly and tread carefully."

Liberius concurred. "Bessas and Ascum, lead the reserves. We will reinstall order and discover whether Optaris has saved any surprises for us."

Ducking through the wooden doorway, I led Liberius and the others through a maze of rooms built half a head too short for me. Toward the building's rear, sprawled atop a worn sort of carpenter's workbench, Belisarius lay in relative stillness. Around him were another half dozen bucellarii, who nodded to me as they departed the tiny quarters to allow our entry.

Uliaris' eyes widened. "Lord..."

"Lord, you're alive!" I whispered, a curious tear forming in one eye.

Bereft of his helmet and his chest armor, Belisarius was unrecognizable, a far cry from the shining plumed figure atop an iron-ringed mount. His forehead was wrapped in a cloth torn from a nearby curtain, and small splotches of blood stained the cloth and his clothes alike. His hand reached upward, grasping at air yet reaching for nothing.

"Varus," he croaked, the single word spoken painfully slowly. "Neapolis is ours?"

"More or less, Lord," I replied. "The final resistance is being swept aside. The siege is over."

Belisarius coughed, wincing, and rubbed his forehead. "Martinus will not tell me what has happened and insists all is well. But you will not lie to me, Varus. Why do I hear chaos outside the walls?"

He seemed so frail. With unfocused eyes, he at last seemed to reach for my hand, which I slipped into his. "Please, Varus. Tell me."

"Lord…" I sighed, wishing I could be relieved of my burden. "Neapolis is put to the sack."

He nodded. "My men say that I was pushed from my mount and fell to the ground. I cannot remember, but at least nothing appears broken."

For emphasis, he craned his neck, wiggling his feet. "My head swims, Varus. We must stop them from destroying Neapolis, but I am not strong enough to walk."

Liberius strode forward. "It is already done, Strategos. A great many of your men stayed loyal to your command, and the sack only flared because your soldiers believed the Goths had slain you. I will see to the peace."

"I'll summon Rosamund, Lord," I offered. "Just rest. All will be well."

"Sleep," Belisarius muttered, his eyelids fluttering. "Pray for our sins. For they are many, and they are growing."

It was a painful night. After my encounter with the strategos, I dispatched one of Liberius' attendants to fetch Rosamund and Shimon, and to seek fresh boots for myself and my companions. Rosamund hissed when she gazed upon my swollen and blistered feet, yelling that I should refrain from walking. However, she soon switched her attentions to Belisarius and ministered to his hurts throughout the evening.

"No serious damage, but his skull will be fragile for a few days," she declared. "No riding for at least three days."

Liberius, meanwhile, marched five hundred men into the forum. Any plunder was ordered ceased, and any evidence of rape, murder, or arson of the local populace warranted summary hangings. Incredibly, Belisarius' army grew docile as the weak morning light peeked over the horizon, their rage slaked from pilfered meat, overabundant wine, and the knowledge that their strategos yet lived. Though none of the senior command were found to have committed serious offenses, both Perenus and Gunderic were discovered to have requisitioned an abandoned tavern, where they gulped at a half-full wooden cask and searched for forgotten morsels of bread or cheese. As an offense, it was benign enough, yet Liberius chastised both men for their lack of discipline. When Perenus appealed to me, I refused to absolve him.

"We didn't do anything terrible, Varus," Perenus insisted.

"No, but it was against Belisarius' orders. None wish to speak of it again, but I am depending upon you to help me keep order for any other cities we take."

Perenus rolled his eyes. "And Gunderic?"

"Gunderic too," I said. "Although it will be hell convincing him of anything. Belisarius will speak with him directly, for that's probably all that will work."

It took three days to put Neapolis to order. Smoldering embers were doused with water from the shoreline, and those buildings whose wooden supports had been fatally weakened were torn down. Belisarius ordered those who committed minor sins, including those who engaged in looting, gluttony, and a general disorderliness that was contrary to his orders, to bear the brunt of such labors, unceasing by day or by night. A hint of fear lingered amongst our men—a fear that was only heightened when Belisarius did not emerge to oversee the clearing of the city's destruction, although I, at least, knew the reason for this was Rosamund's insistence upon rest.

Roughly half of the city had been torched, with nearly every building containing food or goods ransacked by lusting hands. After the ash and debris were hauled out, Liberius organized an Imperial court, organizing a few borrowed tables and benches in one corner of the forum. Couriers spread notice that all new citizens of the Empire could seek justice for their losses in that tribunal, encouraging a deluge of frightened Neapolitans to form lines as they awaited their turn to be heard. By the fifth day, Rosamund approved Belisarius for light work, and he joined Liberius in hearing the petitions of many hundreds of recently impoverished Goths and Romans. Even with two dueling courts processing the masses, it took another week before all cases were seen, judged, and repaid in kind.

Though I resided in the city for only a few weeks, Neapolis stands in my memory as the first city whose business was conducted solely in Latin. Nearly all in Constantinople and its adjacent provinces conversed in Greek, with Latin saved only for formal Imperial activities that many in the capital would have struggled to translate. Though Belisarius and Liberius were both native speakers of Latin, many others in the army found themselves unable to fluently communicate with Neapolis' residents. Often, I found myself translating words of Greek, Hunnic, or Heruli into the Roman mother tongue, though I knew the obligation to do so only fostered greater distrust amongst the locals against their new Imperial overlords.

Though Belisarius could distribute gold to compensate for ruined property or stolen possessions, some infractions could not be made just through dispensations of Imperial coin. Liberius had already overseen the hanging of a half dozen rapists and three murderers, yet claims emerged that warranted consideration of severe punishment. A further dozen men were flogged in the forum for attacks against unarmed civilians. Others were required to compensate their thefts from their own purse, including Gunderic and Perenus.

"You will each return five times the cost of the goods you unjustly absconded with, payable in silver to the aggrieved," Belisarius ruled, scowling at both men.

Perenus nodded in silent capitulation, but Gunderic furrowed his brow. "Lord, we committed no violence. The tavern had been abandoned before I arrived."

Belisarius glowered. "You were given plain commands to leave the city intact, Lord Gunderic. You do not know the reason why the tavern was abandoned, despite all its goods remaining inside. Your actions jeopardize our entire army, and for that, you will yield enough coin to demonstrate penitence."

From his expression, Gunderic did not understand. He showed

no anger, nor resistance; I suspect it was the simple fact that few Vandals had ever been scolded for sacking a conquered city. To his credit, Gunderic saluted, loyal to the man who had soundly defeated his former king in twin battles. "It will be done, Lord Belisarius."

We spent another week in Neapolis, with the full capacity of Belisarius' army spent repairing those buildings that had not been demolished and rebuilding those that were struck down. Even with thousands of men, the work was slow, and by the week's end only one in five plots had been resurrected to Belisarius' liking. Cold sapped at sore muscles, and several of my joints popped against the strain of swinging a mallet or lifting debris. Likewise, darkness was so pervasive that all work had to temporarily cease, leaving precious few hours for productive labor.

Simultaneously, though the seas remained inhospitable and the skies a tainted blight, Belisarius and I wrote our obligatory missives to Constantinople, begging Justinian and Theodora alike for support after informing them that the jewel of Campania had been reclaimed. There was no question that our campaign had been successful, yet our many injuries, along with the men required to garrison so large a city as Neapolis, had drained Belisarius' army to a dangerous level.

"I'm appointing Martinus as the military governor until Justinian offers a permanent official," Belisarius explained to me. "I'll leave three hundred men behind to continue rebuilding. Those who stayed in Rhegium will relocate to Neapolis as soon as they are able."

"So we're leaving?" I asked, surprised that we would not winter in Campania. "So soon?"

"We must," he said. "It seems like madness, but Theodahad still has not summoned his armies to oppose us. We will not have this advantage for long, and so we must take what is offered."

I nodded. "Then where do we go? Barium? Brundisium?"

"No, Varus. We go north," Belisarius said, his voice trailing as he seemed to fall into a trance. "We travel to Rome, through the Appian Way."

Rome. The Eternal City. The mother of all Romans, whether they hailed from Italy or far beyond. A city that seemed more fable than reality. "Truly, Lord?"

"Truly," Belisarius confirmed. "We will take one further week and gather what excess harvest we can. But I intend to see the walls of Rome by the onset of winter, regardless of what Theodahad must be planning. I only ask one thing before we leave."

"Something I can procure for you, Lord?"

"No," he replied. "On the dawn of our departure, assemble as much of the army as you can in the forum. I will address all, and we shall leave to go north."

Though the aftermath of the siege had left a shroud of fear and embarrassment draped over Belisarius' army, whispers that Belisarius would challenge Rome itself kicked our hive of officers into a frenzy. With coin and excess goods such as nails and lumber, we purchased all the dried grain that Neapolis could spare before the winter ahead. City blacksmiths mended armor and honed iron-bladed weapons just as feverishly as the army continued its reconstruction, forcing Belisarius to spend even more.

From what I could gather amongst the men, there was a desire to leave the awkwardness of Neapolis behind and exchange it for the promise of witnessing firsthand Rome's ancient heart. Some, such as Indulf, had seen the city before and scoffed at the childish curiosity of those sharing third hand tales of Rome's enormity.

"Ten times the size of Constantinople?" Indulf scoffed. "It's a big city, but nothing special. Smells like cow shit, besides, and is populated by pale old men who squabble in the forum as if they are still important to the world. Give me fresh air and freedom from that hell, and I would thank you a thousandfold."

In a separate conversation, Liberius concurred with Indulf's assessment. "I haven't visited Rome in decades, but after the thrashing it took from Alaric and Gaiseric, I've seen mud hovels more pleasant."

"Then why bother fighting for it?" I asked.

"Because it is our home," he said simply. "Rome means everything, even when stripped of its wealth and robbed of its virtue.

It is the promise that our civilization will live forever, regardless of the setbacks we face from time to time."

Personally, no blathering from Indulf could quell my excitement, although I longed to be reunited with my family. Instead, we readied our army for its final, if brief, journey along the Via Appia, which hugged Italy's western coastline. Two days before our departure, however, Belisarius insisted that Optaris be brought before him.

Few of Neapolis' Gothic defenders survived the sack. Through both the chaos and its aftermath, we could not acquire a clear assessment of Optaris' numbers, but we guessed based upon the corpses we stacked in massive pyres outside of the city's walls that he now commanded no more than a thousand men. Optaris and a few dozen men had defended Neapolis' northern gate for a time, yet were swarmed by a cohort of Vandal foederati. Optaris himself only survived when Wisimar recognized his rich set of mail and captured him rather than mow him down.

In the days that followed, Optaris spat defiance to any who would question him, and only grudgingly accepted the rations provided to him at each meal. He resided in the relative comfort of a governor's manse and saw few visitors after his initial capture.

Until Belisarius decided to free him. There were no demands for payment, and only one small condition: that Optaris would carry a warning to the Ostrogoth king.

In a meeting of leadership, however, Bessas voiced hesitation. "If we release Optaris, he'll tell all of the Gothic warlords of our disposition and intentions."

"I'm depending on it," Belisarius replied. "His words will spread rumors amongst the Goths that our army will annihilate anything that resists its aims, and that Theodahad lacks the courage to stop them. The sack of Neapolis is shameful, but I intend to use it to our advantage nonetheless."

Internally, I agreed with Bessas. My greatest concern was that Optaris might inform a Gothic warlord that Belisarius' army was a mere shadow of available Gothic forces, emboldening a foe who had yet to confront our advance. Nevertheless, Belisarius had led us from one triumph to another for so long that it was easy to trust in his instinct, even if it conflicted with my own. And so, Optaris was summoned to a meeting of Belisarius' senior officers, allowed to move without chains but escorted by Belisarius' new leader of the bucellarii, the Hun Gouboulgoudou. Optaris was not even invited to sit, for Belisarius explained that the confrontation would be brief.

"God has weighed heavily the crimes of your king," Belisarius began. "But those sins are not your own, and you defended the honor of your people well. For that, we grant you freedom from Neapolis, barring one request."

"You are all fools!" Optaris screamed. "Your entire cause for war is a lie! A nothing! But here you are, puffing chests like conquering heroes. You will all burn for this evil."

"The evidence presented to our Emperor says otherwise," I shot back.

Optaris turned to me, his teeth clenched as he strained his neck forward. "Amalasuntha held guest rights with Theodahad, and no honorable Goth would kill a child. Think!"

"You may depart in peace, Optaris," Belisarius continued, ignoring the accusation. "Let Theodahad know that we are coming but will offer clemency to any who does not resist our justice."

"Theodahad is a weakling," Optaris spat, "but not a monster who violates guest right."

I stepped forward. "We will grant you a horse and a week's rations. Travel in amity. If we see you take arms against the Empire again, we will not treat you mercifully twice."

"I shall speak with Theodahad," Optaris grumbled.

Within an hour, he departed. Two Huns stalked Optaris' progress as he galloped free from Neapolis and toward the Via Appia. They would follow him within eyeshot of Rome, yet depart to scout the region while Belisarius' army snaked northward. At the time, we were uncertain of whether Theodahad had taken residence in Ravenna, Rome, or elsewhere, yet Belisarius' message to the Gothic king was secondary to the frustration and fear that we hoped news of Neapolis' destruction would spread.

Upon the morning of our departure, all spearmen and much of our cavalry assembled in Neapolis' forum. Every nook was filled, and the light dawn snows seemed inconsequential against the heat of so many bodies clustered together. Our ballistae and the cataphracts remained outside the walls, although their officers joined Belisarius near a raised dais. After the final detachment of Vandal spearmen took their position, Gouboulgoudou fetched Belisarius from a nearby building, and we awaited the strategos' address.

Though recently dented, morale was undeniably high—boisterous, even. Whether decade-long veterans or recent recruits, all present understood the opportunity before us to fulfill a dream that millions had fought and died for—a dream that millions more desperately yearned for. That we could do something deemed impossible not long ago and revive the decayed Roman Empire, in truth as much as name, was nothing short of a chance at glory, endless glory. The men sang chants once bellowed from the throats of legions, taught to them by Liberius and the dozens of other educated men who could reach into the past and connect our soldiers with their brothers from centuries prior. I doubt the hope and zeal would have been quite so fevered had we not been led by Belisarius, who might be the only man to achieve such an impossible dream. I know that I, had least, would have felt differently without him.

And so, as Belisarius rose atop the dais, a reverberating cheer echoed from the throats of thousands, but what followed was confused chatter. For Belisarius had eschewed his armor for the tattered robes of a simple country priest, joined by an identically clad Petrus.

I was standing behind Liberius and bent to whisper in my teacher's ear. "What is Belisarius doing?"

"Being an altruistic fool," Liberius said, and hushed me.

Gouboulgoudou stepped to the front of the dais, raising his hands for calm. It was an impossible ask, for the whisperings of thousands of men in so tight a space could foster a deafening roar, yet most hung eagerly on to any sign of Belisarius' plans.

"Silence!" Gouboulgoudou yelled. "Belisarius, strategos, addresses you."

With that, the bucellarius retreated to the rear of the dais, allowing Belisarius and Petrus to pace to the dais' center. Removing his hood, Belisarius revealed a darkened bruise along his forehead, though his features were otherwise haler than they had been the week prior.

"Men of the army!" he yelled, enunciating each word. "We have come to this place to bring justice. In doing so, however, we ourselves have committed a grievous sin. The citizens of Neapolis did not deserve to suffer, regardless of what their Gothic overlords have done."

More mumbling and confusion rolled throughout the crowd. Many frowned or averted their eyes, while a defiant few openly scowled. However, Belisarius raised his arm once more, ordering silence, and continued.

"One day, when I truly am gone from this life, I ask that you not forget your oaths," he said. "Obey the Emperor. Love your God. And as always, protect the people, who without their love and labors, nothing in this life would be possible."

Liberius leaned back to me. "As I said, flights of foolish altruism."

I had become accustomed to Liberius' goading, although it was not always easy to stomach. "Are our desires any different?"

Liberius chuckled. "No. But I don't make speeches about it either."

After a pause, Belisarius paced about the dais, nodding to so many that he doubtlessly recognized. "Our mission is sacred, and it is I who must atone for the sins of our army. That is why I am adorned in the frock of a penitent and will spend our journey ahead in prayer and fasting. To pray for our forgiveness, and for the souls of those living and dead of Neapolis. For today, I ask my friend Father Petrus to pray over our army, as he has over me."

Petrus stepped forward, stretching his arms over the amassed army. Belisarius beckoned all to kneel, and most obeyed as Petrus began his incantation. Standing behind the dais, I watched as many of our soldiers muttered their own prayers, while others shared befuddled glances at one another in respectful silence. Either unaware or unfazed, Petrus asked that God forgive our many sins and protect the Empire's army on its hallowed task to rejoin Italy to the light of our civilization. There were the obligatory praises for God's magnanimity and further pleas to return the warmth of the sun as well as bountiful harvests, and a concluding prayer that our Emperor may be rightfully guided by divine will.

As Petrus concluded, Belisarius stepped forward, gesturing for all to rise once more, and took in hand an Imperial banner atop a long wooden pole that caught the coastal winds winnowing over Neapolis' walls.

"Men! Everything we have done has led to this!" Belisarius yelled. "Today, our boots will land upon the dressed stones of the Appian Way, a path that so many legends have trod upon a thousand years before us."

As he paused, Belisarius' chest rose and fell, allowing time that others might translate his Latin into one of a dozen languages. Grins spread across hundreds of faces nearest me, while many fidgeted as they hungered for the strategos' final command.

Belisarius did not disappoint. "We go to Rome! And all who come after will remember that it was we who fulfilled the dreams of millions! No matter the strength of our enemy, in my heart I know that we shall prevail!"

At last, cheering erupted. A rolling thunder of shields slamming against the forum's stones made the ground rattle against my boots. Leaning forward to Liberius, I chuckled into his ear. "Looks like a bit of altruism is what we needed."

Liberius raised his hands. "I admit, I am routed. But we shall see where fate takes us. If I could see the Aurelian Walls once more, I would die a happy man."

"Men!" Belisarius bellowed, his voice all but drowned out against the ceaseless din. "We go north!"

A chorus of horns sounded, signaling the centurions to guide their respective units from the forum and through Neapolis' northern gate. It was a slow process, taking perhaps an hour, yet eventually the vast bulk of our warriors had slipped into the surrounding fields and formed into columns as they proceeded toward the Via Appia. Martinus stood atop the gate as our stragglers departed, which included both Belisarius and myself.

"Give Theodahad a swift kick and end this war, yes?" Martinus yelled down to us. "And send messengers if something is needed."

Hugging Italy's western coastline, the Via Appia connected Neapolis and Rome with about a hundred and fifty miles of well-maintained stone roads. Bypassing the hills and mountains of the interior, it made for an easy march, one that our mounted vanguard might have comfortably accomplished within a week. Belisarius, however, insisted that the men's vitality should be preserved for the fight ahead, and he set a pace that would place us at Rome's southern gates nearly three weeks later. Unlike in Sicily or much of Campania and Calabria, mounted Gothic scouts seemed to haunt our progress along distant northern hills. Samur offered to subdue those inferior horsemen, yet after two forays of Hunnic horse archers failed to reach their prey, further sorties were denied.

While our army trudged along the Via Appia, Valerian's dromons split into two factions. One sailed south, its goal to round the Italian peninsula and harry Gothic settlements on the eastern coast in hopes that an ample port might fall under Roman control and ease the transfer of reinforcements from Epirus or Greece. The other trailed the army north, its intention to blockade Rome's all-important port of Ostia, enclosing it from resupply by sea while Belisarius' army besieged it by land.

It was a ridiculously optimistic plan, for Belisarius possessed only a fifth of the men necessary to guard Rome's many gates, and our dromons would have to battle treacherous winds as much as any Gothic wall guards. Nevertheless, Belisarius pressed forward, intent upon leveraging the one advantage he possessed: Theodahad's baffling unwillingness to render combat.

By then, an early winter entrenched itself along the coastline and grew fiercer as we entered the region of Latium. What furs and fleeces we possessed were distributed amongst the men, yet there were too few fur-lined gloves, and many a frustrated traveler lost a patch of skin from pressing too firmly against one frigid iron implement or another. The greatest danger was at night, when the frozen soil was drained of all its preserved warmth and a man could freeze in his sleep with little forewarning. Anticipating such danger, our spearmen and riders over-packed their tents, using the heat from their bodies to ease the challenge of sleep. Though officers were exempt of this order, most still obliged out of comfort, and Shimon and Rosamund both shared my tent each night. There was plenty of grumbling amongst the men, but morale remained at a giddy high as we clambered closer to our destination.

On the second week of our march, I fell ill. Some ague, leaving me prone to shivering all day and night, my body feverish and pale. Frigid drafts worsened those fits, their tendrils like knives upon my skin even with heavy furs draped over my body each night and riding on the back of a grain wagon during the day. My head throbbed as if to the cadence of an Avar drum, while breathing became labored.

"A cold, nothing more," I insisted to Rosamund, shortly before sneezing with the force of an army horn.

"Probably," Rosamund said dryly, her eyes narrowing as she pressed fingers to my forehead. "You've always been a babe when it comes to illness."

Great globs of phlegm took residence in my nose and chest—first clear, then the yellow of acrid piss in the tanner's pits. My body's movements grew labored as I struggled for air. At that, Rosamund took greater notice. She slathered my chest with some unguent, muttering Gepid prayers all the while. Shivering, I forced myself to stay as silent as possible, eager to avoid seeming weak before the men. Lord Varus, excubitor, victor of battles, reduced to a sputtering mess in the back of a grain cart. The display brought me to recall my first weeks with the Herulian foederati, when such frailty would have meant the loss of my men's respect evermore. As fever gripped my body, evil thoughts danced about in a great procession, never ceasing, as if in an endless tale.

A man who is thrown from his horse is not a man.

Scion of sin!

You do not belong here.

I remember little of that time, save Rosamund's hands about my body. Later, I was told that I sweat through multiple changes of clothing, leaving me in a near-constant state of undress that would have brought me to blush had I not been delirious. Gradually, as the deep blues of one predawn morning stretched along the skies, my thoughts became fixed and my eyes aware of their surroundings. My joints quaked, and I struggled for breath, but Rosamund forced me still.

"Am I..." I choked, "...going to die?"

"No," she cooed. "Not yet. Today is not the day you die."

Spitting a yellow gob, I groaned. "You don't know that."

"I do," Rosamund answered, cleaning my face. "The gods love you, and I simply won't allow some evil spirit to claim you today."

My condition worsened to the point that Belisarius prematurely halted our day's march so that I might rest, and met with Petrus and Liberius in hopes of learning of any changes to my disposition. Rosamund allowed no visitors, though I could hear her speaking with the three men.

"Varus will be fine in a couple of days," Rosamund explained calmly. "Too much activity. It would not surprise me if many of you similarly fall ill."

Yet Belisarius sounded unconvinced. "You're certain? Should I send him back to Neapolis or fetch a physician to attend him?"

"Keep those quacks away from both of us. And you as well, if you wish to live," she added.

Belisarius' answer was deferent. "I do not doubt your skill, Rosamund. I just have never known Varus to grow so ill."

"Nor I," Liberius countered. "Not in the palace, at least."

Rosamund groaned. "It has been a decade of constant war. Varus is still young, but not immortal. As I warned you, constant deprivation is no nourishment for the soul. Your men would never refuse your orders, but what you and your emperor ask is slowly killing them all." Petrus mumbled an intervention, but Rosamund shouted a reply. "Even without the displeasure of the gods. And believe me, a little cold and a few dead crops is far from the worst we will suffer. I will heal Varus, but I hold further worries for others I care about."

Our march did not halt again until twilight, for to stop for any man would give the Goths more time to scout our numbers and prepare for our arrival. Instead, I jostled about in my grain cart, shivering as friends paced by with a playful jibe, yet each man whispered fearful tones to Rosamund about my condition. She shrugged each man off, refusing to entertain anything other than my improved health. Rosamund even refused entry to Perenus or Samur, with my brother spitting in anger as his demands to see me were denied. Likewise, Shimon was instructed to stay in the Aksumite tent for several days, allowed to assist only by fetching water and distributing our meager rations. After receiving them, however, Rosamund prepared everything by herself.

Those days are a blur in my memory, and I have difficulty separating fevered dreams from the unbridled discomfort of being tossed about in the cart. One evening, however, stands out as one that I believe was more than an imagination fired by illness and hunger.

"If you gain Rome for Justinian, will the war end?" Rosamund asked, offering a bowl of thin gruel.

"*When*," I corrected, teeth chattering. "Probably not. Ravenna and Mediolanum are farther north, and Ravenna was the final capital of the Western Empire."

Rosamund sighed. "And then? If those cities, too, become Justinian's, the fighting will be over?"

I earnestly hoped for that conclusion, but superstition prevented me from thinking beyond the looming battle. "If all Italy is returned to Justinian? That would be a miraculous day, and I cannot imagine even the Emperor's appetites would demand more than that."

Rosamund grimaced. I admit, in the gloom of that tent, lit only by a single candle to pierce the winter darkness, she appeared lovely. Hard living had not deprived her of vitality, while dancing shadows traced a lithe body, triggering lustful memories of long ago. I could blame fever, and perhaps sickness addled my thoughts, though I would be dishonest to ignore the fact that I wanted her. In that moment, were I hale, I might have been fool enough to act upon it.

It was difficult to discern, but I thought I spied a tear in her eye, her hands tying her still-shortened hair into a compact knot. She replied only with a simple phrase, stuffed with meaning from our long years of suffering alongside one another.

"I doubt it."

Little more was said. I lacked the vitality to converse, and Rosamund was one who thrived in quiet. Indeed, it was as if Rosamund could speak directly to your mind, with no words spoken, still communicating all the passion and confidence that she possessed. On that evening, I could sense her revulsion for this war, perhaps even more so than those that came before it. Unique from those engagements, however, was a note of fear. For since I escorted her from her burning village in Moesia, I had not seen Rosamund truly afraid in all the years between us.

Rest was not easy in coming any of those nights, but especially that one. Coastal gales brushed against the sides of our tent, and at times I worried whether the wooden pegs that secured each corner to the ground would be lifted from their moors. Normally, I took pleasure in resting in a tent far larger than others, as befitting a tribune, yet now I regretted its loftier ceiling and expansive floors making it so difficult to heat. Chattering, I moaned as a draft slid beneath my furs, making my flesh prickle and limbs convulse with an unquenchable urge for warmth.

It was then, in a total absence of light, that I felt Rosamund's touch about my forehead. She must have been rummaging about, for she held a cup full of some unknown liquid on my chest, wiping away sweat that laced my brow. "You must drink this."

I gave a ragged cough. "What is it?"

"Something I'd rather not give you, but it will ease your pain," Rosamund whispered. "You must heal, but healing only comes with sleep."

Her words had a sobering effect. Sucking air through clattering teeth, I voiced further concern. "What do you mean, you'd rather not give it to me?"

"You've taken this before, at Dara," she explained. "And you became irate with me. It is a toxic herb, besides, although I am confident that I prepared it safely."

"You're sure?"

Rosamund brushed my hair with her fingers. "Do you trust me?"

"Yes," I answered instinctively.

With that, Rosamund raised the cup to my lips. Its fragrance was sickly sweet, and it flowed with the same unpleasant viscousness that I remembered from my time in Mesopotamia. I gagged, so Rosamund slowed the progression of the cup's contents, granting me a brief respite before draining the remainder.

The effect was not immediate, but neither was it long in coming. At first, I felt a tingling in my limbs, distinct against their ceaseless shivering from the blowing cold. My body grew heavy and my breathing slowed, while my racing thoughts dulled to a stupor. Yet still I shivered, the cold seeming to penetrate my bones as I moaned in pain.

"Patience," Rosamund whispered.

She rolled my body onto one side, facing away from her. Then, slipping underneath the furs, she wrapped her arms about my chest, cradling my head with one arm underneath my neck. Even through her shift, her skin burned against my own, heating the insulating furs as my mind dimmed to the world. Aside from raging gusts against our tent, the last I remember was, embarrassingly, that I yearned for her.

Rarely had dreams been so vivid. Every skirmish and battle

I had fought blended together in a titanic conflagration of men, struggling and dying underneath a thousand banners of a dozen kings. Simultaneously, the world was awash in rolling plains and impenetrable forest, searing sands and frigid mountaintops. All were capped by the same veiled sky, the sun and moon swirling about as they fought, hopelessly, to bring light to the world.

My dream turned far more intimate. Swept from endless war, I instead flew as if upon the back of a vast eagle to some nameless collection of huts, engulfed by a sea of billowing grasses. I saw only two men amongst those huts, yet as I drew closer, all the signs of destruction burned about them. Crumpled on the ground, one fur-clad man pressed a hand onto a bleeding wound in his gut and raised the other in a plea to his onlooker.

"Please!" the man croaked, his voice a half dozen languages spoken simultaneously.

The other, dressed in the polished mail and plumed helm of a Roman tribune, did not reply. Instead, he plucked a sword from the ground, leveling it against the dying man's chest.

"Stop!" I yelled, yet neither man reacted.

Behind me, a weightless voice whispered in my ear. "They cannot hear you. They do this every afternoon and are doomed to repeat so forever."

Turning round, I found Rosamund staring off at the murder. She was as I first remember her in Moesia, her long hair flailing against the breeze and her face absent all the cares and worries of the present. Even her garb was cut in the manner of the Gepids—verdant and close-fitting, stained by all manners of herbs and powders of her trade. She appeared carefree, or at least happier, yet her face streamed with tears as she watched the Roman approach his dying victim.

"Why do they do this?" I asked.

It was then that behind Rosamund, hazy and nearly amorphous, appeared a man. Encased in black, atop an onyx steed, glaring angrily with glowing crimson eyes, he seemed a ghost, yet I recognized him from memory: the dark rider of Rosamund's prophecy.

"It is their nature. They know no other path," she whispered. "But it does not have to be this way."

"How, then?" I yelled, begging for the answer.

The rider trotted forth, seeming twice the height of a man as his shadow fell upon the two others. Just as with me, neither of them seemed to notice to the rider, and the Roman lunged forward upon his victim with the sword. Yet before I could scream, the images blurred once more. By then, it was I who held my own sword, adorned with runes that had once brought Justin such melancholy, and stared down at the dying barbarian.

"Please..." he garbled, blood seeping from the edges of his salt-lathered mouth.

It was as if I possessed no will in the matter, for I drove the blade into the man's chest. Above me, amidst the huts, the sound of a woman's wailing pierced the man's dying rattle, followed by the cries of another. Behind me, the rider laughed, galloping toward the huts with his own blade held aloft.

"It doesn't have to be this way," Rosamund whispered.

And, just as suddenly as the dream had formed, it vanished. I awoke. Prying crusted eyes apart, I discovered the white wolf pelt, taken so long ago from my spoils in Tauris, draped atop layers of blankets and furs. Tensing my arms, I battled into a seated position, my heart pounding as I looked about for anything I had seen.

"Lie back!" Rosamund hushed. "It's still early, and it snowed last night. Sip on this broth and see if you can sleep."

Nodding, I relaxed. "I—I saw him again," I stammered. "But... more."

"What you saw is a gift from the gods, nothing more and nothing less," Rosamund replied. "As for your body, your fever broke not long ago, but your body is still too weak to rise yet. So sleep while you can, for in a few hours the army will move once more."

After that, I did not resist Rosamund's efforts to bolster my health. I ate what she asked, rested when she told me, and subjected myself to whatever infusions she demanded. And, despite the falling snows,

I began to feel better. Through the next week, I even grew well enough to ride Boreas, although never far from Rosamund's unblinking watch. Our path through Latium even became pleasant, and we shared scanty biscuits passed about the evening's campfires and told wine-soaked tales of better times, when our slain friends remained with us. I joined in their swirling merriment and melancholy and basked in the relief of Belisarius, Liberius, and Petrus, who each offered Rosamund thanks for my recovery. And though I once again felt the stir of purpose as we stomped closer to Rome, a whisper echoed in my mind, stalking my thoughts each hour.

It doesn't have to be this way.

At the end of our travels, with one day's march separating our camp from Rome, Belisarius ordered the men to silence. Such an order was impossible—the movements of thousands of men and beasts hauling goods along the stone-lined road generated deafening noise. Nevertheless, the centurions distributed the command, and all singing and idle chatter ceased. However, the order could not extinguish the urge that so many felt, including me, to look upon the city. Especially after Samur's scouts returned with an assessment of Rome's defenses.

"The gates are locked," Sinnion said. "And they definitely saw our riders, but there weren't many Goths defending the towers."

I gasped. "You're joking."

Sinnion shook his head. "Not about this. Whoever leads Rome is going to allow us to approach uncontested."

In the final hills separating us from the city, evidence of nearby villas, their fields of grapes and olives just as devastated as those in Sicily, signaled that we had entered Rome's orbit. As if without thinking, many lines accelerated their pace, making officers hiss orders to follow Belisarius' intended timing. With each hilltop, we expected to gaze upon our destination, that desire only rising after passing one mound after another.

Until, at last, Rome's Appian Gate came into view.

Streams of midday sun illuminated the towering Aurelian Walls, the sheer expanse of which nearly filled my vision. Only the Tiber River broke the wall's integrity, flowing south and through the western expanse of the old Republican city, though looming ivy-wrapped towers stood half again as high as the crenellated walls to dissuade any foolish attempt to infiltrate Romulus' city through its sacred waterway.

It was a city of stone and marble. Of buildings that soared to impossible heights, visible even behind the city's forbidding carapace. And when I first saw it, it was a city of life. Of hundreds of thousands gathered at the home of any who call the Empire their mistress. Constantinople might be known to the Greeks as the Great City, but it paled against Rome. The Eternal City, mortared by the lives of millions who worked and fought to carve an impossible dream onto seven hills. When men speak of Rome today, they whisper or weep, or wonder whether the ancient tales of splendor were ever true. As I hope that God will forgive my countless sins and grant me entry into Heaven, I swear just as fervently that Rome, that day, was everything the singers' tales promised. The Eternal City lifted my burdens. It was as if we approached the abode of Christ himself and were now empowered with the duty to bring order and justice into a world draped in shadow.

"Rome!" I gaped, riding alongside Belisarius' senior command. "My God!"

I wanted to gallop ahead, to be the first to reach its gates. Regardless of the risk, I lusted to touch the city's walls, to verify that Rome was a place not merely spun from Liberius' wild tales. I could have wept if I had not giggled maniacally, my arms shaking uncontrollably as the reins nearly slipped from my trembling fingers.

Liberius laughed. "It's still here after all."

"Thank God," Petrus said, and mumbled a prayer.

"Careful," Belisarius murmured. "Watch for the enemy. This must be an ambush."

But against all logic, no attack emerged. Nor did any catapults strike as Belisarius unfolded his column into a half circle. Nor even did any Goths seek to parley with our leadership as Ascum's ballistae was hauled into place, or when our men began carving trenches facing the Appian Gate, connecting our current roadway with the Circus Maximus. Aside from a few onlookers, no Goths came to challenge us, and no Gothic horns sounded resistance. Instead, the few present atop the city's walls scurried away from our view.

Searching my memory of the city's geography, I failed to see the advantage in such a careless defense of Rome's southern gates. "Lord, if this is an ambush, it's the least-effective ambush I have ever witnessed."

"Agreed. It makes no sense."

"Send an envoy," I suggested. "We cannot attack, or even lay siege lines, until we know who we face."

Trailed by a dozen Cappadocians, Liberius took that mantle. He galloped forth, leaving his escort midway between our army and the walls as he trotted next to the sealed gate, stopping just below a looming battlement. He was so close to the nearest Gothic defender that the man could have stuck Liberius with a spear, yet my teacher only glared at his opponent. Neither man spoke for a while, until Liberius lost his patience.

"When I was a boy, Romans would acknowledge their guests," he yelled in Latin. When this gained no response, he repeated himself in Latin, in Frankish, and even Hunnic, yet each effort was unimproved. Shrugging, he retreated back to our lines.

"My Gothic is incomplete enough that I don't dare entreat directly," Liberius said. "I wouldn't want him to think I'm insulting his cock or his mother. All Gothic words sound like one or the other to me."

"We wait, then," Belisarius said. "Send a scout toward Ostia and determine Valerian's progress. For now, our only other movement is to position Cappadocians about the Caelian Hill and block the city's southern roads all the way to the Tiber."

"Nothing more?" Ascum prompted, sounding disappointed.

"No ladders on the walls yet," Belisarius answered. "Although you may form teams of archers to fire on the towers. Let's make sure these Goths are alive."

"Theodahad is a pig-fucking coward," Indulf grumbled. "Theodoric would have ridden out and challenged us in the field."

A bemused look stole across Liberius' face. "Theodoric would not have allowed us to land in Sicily, let alone get this far. If Theodahad is disinclined to fight, we must assume there is a reason. And if it is because he is busy pleasuring pigs, as you say, who am I to complain?"

From my assessment of the state of morale, if Belisarius ordered an assault upon the walls, every man present would have climbed the ladders, regardless of the foes we faced, including our servants. Atop the walls, soaring buildings formed a towering line of civilization along the sky, a tease of hundreds of years of Roman achievement just a brief ride from where we stood.

Belisarius' army cordoned off Rome's southern roads, and only Ascum was granted the limited capacity to engage in violence with the Gothic enemy. After an initial volley, however, even those men hid behind stone merlons.

"Lord, if you give me command of two hundred men, I will seize the gate," I whispered to Belisarius, unwilling to publicly contradict him.

"Just wait," he replied. "Something is happening, I can sense it."

And we waited. Noise rose behind the Roman walls as we ate, watching the sun trail lower into another uninviting afternoon. I considered ordering the men's tents formed into camps when our Hunnic scouts returned, marking their progress from Ostia.

"Lord Belisarius," the Hun Chelchal panted, tugging against the reins to allow his mount to rest. "Roman ships have surrounded the harbor. One gained entry. Ostia belongs to Valerian."

Belisarius' eyes grew wide. "You witnessed this?"

"Less than an hour ago, Lord," Chelchal confirmed. "Do you wish us to send further scouting parties?"

Before Belisarius could reply, a series of horns blared from deep within the city. Drums followed, their percussion urgent and out of sync. Those few Goths who spied our position atop the Appian Gate scrambled away once more, replaced by little more than a light dusting of snow. At first glance, it seemed Rome's southernmost gate was undefended.

"Prepare the column!" Belisarius yelled. "Ladder teams from the Tiber to the Asinarian Gate! Send scouts along the walls to scout Rome's north!"

"We attack?" I cried, surprised.

"No." Belisarius beamed, his fists vibrating with a longing I had not seen since Antonina's disgrace and John's death. "We have won. To positions!"

Gothic horns sounded again, yet no reinforcements came. Instead, the Appian Gate creaked, its solid oak doorway budging only slightly.

"Ascum! Mass your archers in range of the Appian Gate!"

"Done!" Ascum replied.

Turning to face his forces, Belisarius next summoned Xerxes. "Bring Gunderic and two hundred Vandals. They will protect our archers if any Goths come storming out of the gate."

"Happily, Lord Belisarius."

We waited. The gate creaked and groaned and occasionally seemed to open, yet nothing happened. All we heard was an increasingly distant blaring of horns, mixed with the deep tenor of thousands of voices calling in unison. Until, the iron hinges of the gate creaking open, the Appian Gate finally unsealed, pausing to reveal a narrow sliver of light.

"Ready, men!" Belisarius yelled.

Nothing could have torn our attention away from whatever was behind the gate. I fully expected ten thousand screaming Gothic spearmen, furious at their loss of Neapolis and the humiliation of their kinsmen. Gunderic organized his spears while rows of archers nocked their arrows, focused upon the first sign of resistance. Slowly, the Appian Gate rose further, revealing a hint of light beyond.

But no warriors. Only a group of young Roman men, their bodies draped in white linen and wool, lifting their arms out as if in an embrace of every man in Belisarius' forces. Immediately thereafter, on the army's right flank, the Asinarian Gate opened as well, revealing a gathering of priests who waved for our attention.

"Roma! Roma Victrix! Roma Victrix!"

Belisarius hooted with laughter. His eyes swelled with tears of happiness as he thrust a fist skyward, rising high atop the saddle as he faced up toward the heavens. "Men! Form a column! Rome is ours!"

And euphoria set in. For all our sacrifices, at least for a time, had been made worthwhile. And the Empire, for too many years a shadow of its hallowed memory, had truly become Roman once more.

THE ETERNAL CITY

If Justin still lived, he would have kissed every man and woman present on that day. While many in Rome's soaring buildings viewed our procession to the forum through windows and behind columns, a fair number sprinted forth, cheering, to wrap one of our men in an embrace. One man, crook-backed and gray-bearded, hobbled to our banners and brushed their cloth with his hand.

"The Emperor truly came," he said, touching his forehead to the Chi-Rho banner. "I was a boy when Odoacer came. I never thought this day would arrive."

Dismounting, Belisarius placed his hands about the man's shoulders. "We never forgot you. And now, we will make things right again."

Rome was overwhelming. In the size of its buildings, the maze of its winding roads, its statues and monuments, and all the markers telling of the glory of Romans long dead. Constantine. Trajan. Vespasian. Agrippa. Augustus, of course, yet many others not commonly held in the hearts of Imperial citizens outside of the Eternal City. Yet as stunning as the city was, the love of the people, bedecked in whatever faded or hand-sewn Imperial regalia they could muster, was what consumed me. For years, I always assumed that Constantinople, with its Hippodrome and palace, housing hundreds of thousands of denizens, had been the center of the world. After an hour in Rome, I knew that all of that was a lie.

If I was overpowered amidst all the emotion and majesty, most of Belisarius' men were like children within that city of soaring stone. Many residents tossed flowers toward Belisarius as he rode past, while others offered gifts to one spearman or another. One young Roman woman sprinted forth to peck a kiss upon my cheek, darting away before I could react. Liberius hooted with laughter as Petrus wept with joy, surrounded by walls of noise that longed for us. And Belisarius most of all.

Even the muted warmth from the veiled sun could not diminish Rome's splendor. If Neapolis was a triumph of Imperial architecture, Rome was a dream carved into marble and stone. It was a victory that defied all convention, for none would have predicted that Theodahad would surrender such a prize without even so much as a message to negotiate. Optaris, the exiled lord of Neapolis, had been discovered in Trajan's forum, insisting that he had elected to remain behind as the bulk of the Gothic garrison fled north. Optaris' presence only kindled our hope for negotiated victory, although doubt never lingered far behind.

The suspicious ease of it all was the only disconcerting note in an otherwise glorious afternoon, but one that could not wait. Thus, with Liberius assigning sections of Belisarius' army different quarters throughout the city, Belisarius summoned those senior leaders that could be identified in the chaos of celebration. Many were discovered, from Roman senators to even Pope Silverius, who had been confirmed to his position less than a half year prior at the personal recommendation of Theodahad. Yet it was a different figure altogether who captured our attentions, for he was one we did not expect to see so soon. We gathered all about the Temple of Neptune, a once-pagan building honoring the sea, benefitting from the fact that the temple had been sealed for decades, ensuring that eavesdropping would prove difficult.

"Theodahad abandoned us," Optaris murmured. "He just gathered his men and left."

Along with me and a dozen other officers, Belisarius paced about the temple, gazing upon a nearby altar portraying the sea god and his trident. "Why did you not go with him?"

Optaris groaned. "He left before I arrived, perhaps a week ago. His remaining men ran out of the northern Flaminian Gate just as yours entered to the city's south. I remained behind to demand fair treatment of those Gothic civilians that remain in Rome."

"Demand?" Ascum snarled. "You only live because we pity you."

Belisarius turned from the altar, raising a hand for Ascum's silence. "Any who would reside in peace are welcome in Rome. You have my oath that their goods and homes will not be harmed."

"Gratitude," Optaris said, sneering at Ascum. "What would you do with me now?"

"What I originally planned," Belisarius said casually. "You may depart, with a fresh horse and full rations, to seek Theodahad wherever he has scurried. Tell him that Belisarius comes for justice."

Optaris nodded. "As you wish, Lord Belisarius. I shall find a way to make my king listen this time."

Optaris went to depart but was halted by an interjection from Indulf. "Lord Belisarius, if you would grant me leave with a hundred of my foederati, I would escort Optaris on his journey."

"I would rather sleep with rats," Optaris grumbled.

Optaris' revulsion aside, the suggestion was reasonable. As wintry bluster worsened across Italy, there was danger in traveling alone, especially in the confusion of war. Belisarius turned to Indulf, seeming to consider the offer, but it was me he approached.

"Varus, can we spare the men?" he whispered to me.

"Not easily," I replied. "But if the loss must be suffered, I will manage."

Indulf repeated his request. "Just a hundred men, Lord. The rest I leave to Perenus. I will guard Optaris all the way to Ravenna, if required, and deliver Theodahad's reply to you."

With that, Belisarius was convinced. "A hundred men. But travel swiftly, for I will likely have need of you before long."

Optaris was dismissed immediately, instructed that he would

depart through the Flaminian Gate by the coming dawn. Indulf, too, separated from our gathering to prepare his chosen men, selecting mounts and packing rations and tents for the cold nights ahead. I did not envy Indulf, yet neither would I miss his presence amongst Belisarius' forces.

Others were permitted an audience in Neptune's Temple. From various individual accounts, we managed to knit together a story of all that had transpired in Rome and in the surrounding region over the preceding months, including Theodahad's flight northward. Absent their king, Rome's remaining forces had little stomach to resist the Empire's famous general, nor to quell rising discontent amongst a Roman populace longing to reunite with the provinces. Theodahad even met with Pope Silverius, who encouraged the Ostrogoth armies to depart in peace.

"Why would you discourage a king who was so instrumental to your ascension to the papacy?" Belisarius asked. "I am told that few Gothic kings have ever exercised such influence in the affairs of prior popes."

"No indeed," Silverius replied. "But I serve God, and hoped to prevent unnecessary bloodshed."

In many ways, Silverius struck a similar image to Father Petrus. White-haired but speaking in tones of an educated elite, his words were that of a need to protect the innocent—something that resonated with any who adopted the Imperial oath of service. Yet I, too, had heard rumors similar to Belisarius' accusations, telling that this pope held more loyalties than only to God. And while Petrus kept his appearance humble, Silverius adorned himself in all manner of gold and silver. Rumors—collected by Narses and distributed to me by Procopius—even suggested that Silverius had purchased his position from Theodahad outright, although such a sin is too grave to consider.

Nevertheless, I could not resist acting upon my suspicions of Silverius' simony and affinity for Theodahad, unqualified though they were. "Father, how have you kept peace with so many

Arians?" I asked. "In Constantinople, any hint of disagreement fuels demonstrations in the fora."

Silverius laughed. "Cassiodorus? Yes, he was always one for theatrics. Even when he was a member of the Roman Senate decades ago, he never tired of howling for the blood of others. I heard that he had recently grown fat and slothful, and was surprised to hear tales of his activities with your mob."

It was not unreasonable that Pope Silverius would know of Constantinople's doings, yet the revelation nevertheless left me feeling off balance. "Cassiodorus was changed by the Hippodrome riots."

"As were we all," Belisarius added. "Hopefully, however, toward paths more gracious than sinful."

"Hmm." Silverius frowned. "I also heard that it was you, Lord Belisarius, who ended the riots. Have you atoned for those deaths? How many comprised the final tally?"

Only a lifetime of instruction by Justin restrained me before the Pope. Not that I wished to harm the old man, but rather to lash out with my own accusations, questioning why the Ostrogoths were so willing to abandon Rome and leave the Bishop of Rome in his seat. Surely, if Silverius were not a reliable supporter of the Goths, he would have been carried northward to Ravenna and kept as a valuable hostage. Belisarius, however, merely bowed his head in supplication.

"Too many, Father, and I think of them every evening," he replied. "I beg God for forgiveness in pursuing my duties to the Emperor, and I would appreciate your prayers as well."

Silverius nodded, grazing Belisarius' scalp with a ring-lined finger as a feeble gesture of blessing. "Of course, we all have duties to fulfill. Your atonement is to consider whether you might be a better servant to the Church, just as you are to the throne of Caesar."

Belisarius nodded. "I shall pray upon this, Pope Silverius," he responded, before any of his officers could inject anger into the conversation. "It appears that we shall require faith as we wander through our own desert, just as Christ did."

The other meetings were far less antagonistic, yet revealed diminishing insight into Theodahad's intentions. Most helpful was speaking with a young soldier of the city watch named Tarmutus, who, after the Gothic abandonment of Rome, had become the city's most senior military leader. Half Roman and half Burgundian, Tarmutus had been brought to Rome as a slave in one of Theodoric's campaigns. Like me, Tarmutus had demonstrated an early skill in battle due to his great size and was freed at age fifteen when his elderly Gothic master died of a seasonal chill. Illiterate and not of the Gothic warrior class, Tarmutus would neither be trusted in the Gothic shield wall nor capable of organizing its war bands, but he had proved incorruptible enough to gain position as a member of the city watch.

"A year ago, Rome teemed with Gothic soldiers," Tarmutus recounted. "But most were sent north against the Franks, for whatever reason. More recently, others traveled to Dalmatia, although they did not explain to the guardsmen why or for how long. I was not aware that Justinian's men were attacking the Goths until survivors of Neapolis flooded our gates."

"And the Goths left you behind?" I asked.

He shrugged. "The Goths were happy to let the Romans organize the city's life but were never willing to inconvenience themselves for us. While I cannot vouchsafe for any within the Roman senate, my guardsmen will not disappoint the Emperor."

"Excellent," Belisarius said. "I am raising you to the rank of komes. Any of your guard who requires weapons or armor will receive them from my stores, and all will be required to train with my bucellarii. Their pay will increase, but so will their responsibilities, and it is important that they prepare themselves for any battles ahead."

"Battles, Lord?" Tarmutus replied, unfazed at his promotion. "I have no fear of violence, but isn't the war over, with Theodahad running away?"

"No." Belisarius was firm. "It has hardly begun. The only question is where it will be joined, and with how many Goths."

We continued our interviews until well after the sun had set.

Eventually, however, the rumble of cheerful shouts that vibrated through the temple's stone walls convinced Belisarius to cease the day's labors. Fatigue had also begun to set in for most of us, although Belisarius showed little weariness despite the lengthy day.

"Time to go see the fruits of Liberius' effort!" Belisarius exclaimed. "And take in the celebrations."

"Finally." Ascum yawned. "I've been sober all day. Time to correct that."

Belisarius chuckled. "Just show kindness to the Romans. Beyond that, I merely insist that all of you walk the streets and absorb the city. It's Rome, after all!"

Others cheered, hopping off their benches and hurtling toward the doorway. Before I joined them, I pressed Belisarius further. "You are certain you do not require aid, Lord?"

"I always do." He smiled. "But I will have tremendous need of you soon. Go and enjoy an evening of few responsibilities, and in the morning we shall dispatch letters to send for your family."

I surrendered to Belisarius' demand, following the others, the last of the senior officers to depart the temple. Before slipping through its doors, I glanced back toward Belisarius, who sat alone, his table layered with maps and drafts of written orders. He seemed to ignore all of it, however, and instead clasped his hands together, staring off upon a far wall. I doubt he knew that I remained, believing himself in solace.

"Rome," he whispered, a broad smile on his face. "We made it, John. After so many years, we are here."

Relief swept through my veins. Oddly, I felt a greater sense of joy at Belisarius' triumph than my own. This is not to say, in those first weeks in Rome, that I did not feel a sense of awe, a measure of pride that I had fulfilled Justin's dream. That meant a great deal to me—and still does, to this day. Yet it was Belisarius' private moment of happiness that provided the greatest reassurance, both in that we had accomplished something wonderful, but also that our achievement had torn through my friend's suffering for one glorious evening, if a fleeting one. Today, men recall Belisarius at Dara or as Justinian's savior amidst the riots, or even the liberator of Carthage. Having stood beside him for each of these trials, I knew it was Rome that granted him the greatest joy, although the cost would be a crushing one.

And so, wrapping my cloak about my armor-encased body, I ventured into the streets of Rome. No amount of snow could dampen my spirits; if anything, it lifted them, giving the city a mystical veneer, as if its walls and buildings were being polished clean of sixty years of bondage to foreign kings.

Guided by Tarmutus' thousand-strong city guard, many of Belisarius' men already occupied various posts on the city's walls and gathering places, yet the greater mass of our army rummaged about in the streets. I saw one Herulian dig his gloved hands into a coating of snow along a nearby statue and pelt a mud-covered ball at a passing Vandal, launching a mock war of filthy snow flying in all directions. Beyond these streets, the roars of joy filled Rome's expanse, with fires raging at all corners of the city as men and women ambled about, sharing wine and precious food with Belisarius' soldiers as they shouted commendations to their strategos.

The celebrations were raucous and quick in coming. Though Rome was a massive city and a significant chunk of our army was required to guard its gates and streets, every alley that I passed swelled with celebration and drink. Even absent anything other than crusts of bread, the city's popinae never seemed to run short of wine, nor even the beer favored by Rome's various Germanic peoples such as the Franks and Langobards. It was as if the whole world had erupted into competing and inebriated songs, defying the snow-laced darkness with flaming torches and an inextinguishable joy of reunion.

I discovered Perenus amongst the first crowd of revelers. His cloak was soaked in wine, and a fresh dribble of vomit trailed down his shirt. His beard and hair were greasy, while his eyes were unfixed, at once dancing wildly about but fixed upon nothing. He was the most boisterous amongst his group, which consisted entirely of strangers, with none of the foederati in his company.

"Decided to move quickly, no?" I asked, eyeing Perenus' soiled clothing.

Perenus grinned, his jaw slack. "It's a celebration! Rome, Varus!"

"Indeed," I replied, accepting a wineskin thrust forcefully into my grip. "Just slow down."

Perenus' face pinched, and he minced his words in mockery. *"Slow down, slow down!* Varus the truth-teller, Varus the lucky! Come to tell us scullions how *poor* our behavior is!"

There was no reasoning with the man, yet I did not wish him to set an example for the others. Leaning close, I whispered a few parting words, careful not to foster anger that could quickly turn to drunken blows. "I only worry about you, friend. Nothing more. Remember that."

But Perenus' mind had already fluttered elsewhere. Seizing a nearby woman who wore the slight shift dress preferred by many a city prostitute, Perenus planted a wet kiss upon her mouth before shouting to the forbidding skies. "Rome, lads! We did it!"

Other than Perenus, I begrudged none their celebrations, but I pitied the fifteen hundred or so sober men who kept order along the streets and walls. Absent Mariya, the only person I desired to rejoice with was Rosamund, who had been out seeking an optimal location for when my household arrived from Neapolis. Unbeknownst to either of us at the time, Belisarius had gifted me temporary residence of much of the Domus Augustana, shared only by Liberius and Belisarius himself. In the interim, however, I discovered Rosamund with Uliaris and Shimon, strolling aimlessly through the center of the Great Forum.

"Uliaris, Shimon," I called. "Go and enjoy yourselves. Keep watch over Perenus if you cross his path."

Uliaris frowned. "Too many people here that I don't know. Any of them could be a cutpurse or worse. You might need me."

"I can handle myself for one evening," I replied. "You too, Shimon. Go find Sembrouthes, and see if you can make him smile without breaking his face. Perhaps you'll learn something of our new home."

Uliaris shrugged. "If you're certain."

"Do not hesitate to summon me, Lord Varus," Shimon said.

I retrieved two silver coins from my belt and placed them in Shimon's hand. "Enjoy yourself for a night. It isn't every day that you liberate a historic city. Most every other war I've fought has been terrible, so a peaceful victory is something to celebrate."

Both slipped away, leaving Rosamund looking upon me with frustration. "And me? What am I to do?"

"I thought we could explore the city together," I suggested. "Unless you're going to be cross the entire time."

Rosamund rolled her eyes. "Very well. Show me what you will."

Of course, I had never visited Rome before. But its history, as well as its many monuments and temples, had been etched into my memory. Ambling about the major roads and gathering places, we journeyed to the riverfront along the Campus Martius before turning back to Palatine Hill. When we lost our moorings, there was always a guardsman or reveler just a few paces away to offer directions. Near the Campus Martius, Rosamund balked at the Circus Maximus and voiced disinterest in the theaters and noble houses that lined the streets. She had particular disdain for Augustus' tomb, as well as the tomb of the Emperor Hadrian residing across the River Tiber, just beyond Rome's walls.

"It's a stone monster," she murmured. "An atrocity against the natural world."

Nevertheless, she gawked at the vast dome of the Pantheon, the onetime abode of countless pagan gods. Shrouded in darkness and snow, its dome and decorated interior seemed not of this world, as if the ceiling floated effortlessly above the ground. We shared cups of wine with a passerby as we gaped at the vast dome from the street.

"Theodora tells me the Hagia Sophia is copying a similar style, but larger," I said.

"Impossible," she whispered, stepping into the Pantheon's center. A hollow oculus formed at the Pantheon's center, like a great eye of light that poured from the hollow center of the arched dome. Rosamund stood directly beneath that opening, peering up toward the clouded heavens. "It snows outside, but none reaches the open eye. If the gods were to visit this city, they would not be displeased to reside here for a time."

As for me, I had no ears for Rosamund's criticism of the Eternal City. All I saw were visions of dreams, of the greatness that is possible when a people dedicated to civilization and betterment gather to build something impossible. Rome was full of the impossible—perhaps even comprised of nothing *but* the impossible. In every sense, it was overwhelming even for one such as I, who spent all of his childhood years weaving through Constantinople's fora and alleys. Every corner of Rome held stories, and those stories were shrouded in secrets, and it all could seduce any person desiring ambition. As we walked southeast and discovered the Colosseum, I nearly wept with joy, realizing then the full extent of Belisarius' own private triumph.

"I wish Justin was here," I murmured. "I wish he could see this."

Rosamund wrapped an arm about my back, tucked beneath my cloak. "He is here. In this place, he sees you. You have fulfilled your promises to his dream, many times over."

When I close my eyes, I can still see the Colosseum amidst the snow. Its uniform arches and soaring columns, framed by three rising tiers, were lined with blazing torches and reflecting what little moonlight could pierce the clouds and haze. Like a vast open bowl, the polished white stone seemed as if it had been carved yesterday, revealing little of the wear of hundreds of years and two sackings of the Eternal City. How it still stood, I cannot say—in this, I believe Rosamund's explanation of magic might be correct. It was the city's fabled house of gladiatorial combat, surpassing even Constantinople's Hippodrome as a center of Roman culture and heritage. And aside from a handful of guardsmen, it stood empty in the night.

"Do you wish to see inside?" Rosamund asked.

"It's probably barred for visitors," I said. "No reason to hassle the guards."

She slapped my arm. "You don't get to drag me around half the world and then deny us both an innocent pleasure! Follow me."

"Rosamund!"

But she did not heed my reluctance. Instead, she approached a nearby guard, who rose from a word wooden bench and yawned lazily at the approaching Gepid.

"Where is the entrance?" Rosamund asked.

"Closed at night," the guard replied. "Come back tomorrow with a permit if you wish to see."

Rosamund scowled, pointing to me. "Do you see this man? This is Tribune Varus Veridicus, the second to Belisarius. He requires access to this building for reasons I am not free to explain to you."

"Lady—"

Rosamund groaned. "Shall I retrieve some of the foederati? Varus trained the Herulians himself, and they, too, would love a private audience of this building."

The guard turned back to face his colleagues, shrugged, then saluted me. "No offense intended, Tribune. Just performing my duties."

Blushing, I nodded. "Good lad. Keep watch. I do not intend to be long."

"Unless we decide to stay awhile," Rosamund added. "Tribune Varus may consider hosting an event in this monument, after all."

After fumbling out a ring of bronze keys, the guard unfastened the lock on a nearby gate. As we stepped inside, he handed us a torch and warned us to keep away from the underground hallways, where gladiators and beasts alike had once been readied for their duels to the death. Then, with no escort, Rosamund and I entered the Colosseum alone, enveloped only by snowfall and the spirits of thousands who had lived, fought, and died in this place.

The Colosseum's interior was more jarring than its outer façade. It was like a giant stone bowl for some massive god, its oval ringed with stone benches only interrupted by the enclosed Emperor's box. Above, the Colosseum's velarium, a looming awning decorated with all manner of fantastical animals and Imperial sigils, further darkened the interior, yet afforded the stands even to the lowest levels of seating an unobstructed view of the skies. Brushed white with flakes, the Colosseum was unlit, with only our single torch to guide our footsteps.

"So gloomy," I mused.

"Only if you do not have eyes to see," Rosamund shot back. "It is not possible for men to build such things. In my village, we heard tales of structures fit only for giants, but I assumed it was all a jest."

"You've lived in Constantinople. There are plenty of monuments there."

Rosamund tossed her head, her mouth slightly open as she turned about to absorb the Colosseum's interior. "Not like this. Nothing like this."

We descended stone steps, eventually striking snow-covered sand. Our feet left prints as we ventured into the Colosseum's center, and I turned about as I peered into the shadow-kissed stone of the stadium's empty benches. Shivering, I lowered the torch closer to my face, its feeble comfort thawing skin exposed to blustering wind.

Unslinging a leather bag from her back, Rosamund freed a half-full wineskin. "For the cold." She winked.

"You think of everything." I gladly traded her the torch for the skin.

As I gulped down the lukewarm liquid, my skin flushed, the ache of the winter cold dulled. Soon, I traded back with Rosamund, who drank her fill before replacing the wine in her pack. "Is it true that many died here, in this arena?"

"Yes," I said. "Some voluntarily as gladiators, others through force as slaves or condemned criminals. Animals too. Long ago, it was even flooded to reenact battles at sea, although that was well before even Liberius' time."

"The Gepids have a long tradition of contests of strength and skill," Rosamund said. "But never to the death."

Frowning, I reached out for another swallow of wine. "Your

people train for war like any other. How is that different?"

Rosamund considered, eventually turning to meet my gaze with unbroken conviction in her own. In that darkness, her one yellow and one clouded eye blazed, seeming to absorb the light emitted from our torch. "We never took lives for sport. And those who committed offenses against the village were punished, but rarely in public, and never for humiliation or pleasure."

We paced about the Colosseum's sands, drawing closer to the Emperor's box and sharing in further drink with little caution, even when Rosamund mentioned the strength of the vintage.

"What will Belisarius do now?" she asked at last.

"Winter in Rome, probably," I guessed. "Our supply lines are already stretched to hell, and most of the eastern coastline remains loyal to Theodahad. If we could gain support in men and supplies from the Emperor, we could pressure the Goths to retreat farther north come spring."

"Justinian won't help you," Rosamund said. "And you know that just as well as I."

"Even for Rome? He would be remembered as the greatest emperor since Augustus if we can hold what we've earned."

Rosamund sighed. "You're wrong—although I will never understand Roman fascination with legacy. Anyone with a modicum of sense would give praise to Belisarius. All Justinian has done is thrown his men to war like fodder, and pouted about cost the whole time."

"But it was Justinian's vision!" I cried, just as I'd heard from Belisarius countless times.

"It was *Justin's*!" Rosamund shouted. "And some decrepit emperor before him, and another insipid braggart before him. All Justinian has ever done is wager with lives and succeed."

I could not restrain myself from an unwise reply. "But he did succeed."

Rosamund turned, stepping so close to me that she all but drove me toward the center of the Colosseum's sands once more. Up close, her pale skin had reddened, and her speech was beginning to slur. "Justinian's success will kill us all, in one form or another. All he reaps is sadness, and all he sows is death." Closing her eyes, she brushed snow from the knot of her hair. "I won't let myself be Justinian's currency, nor will I let you. The gods have smiled on you thus far, but their patience has limits."

Though I was much taller, I still felt inadequate and chastened as she spoke. Around us, the Colosseum's spirits observed our standoff, with the only noise a wind that whipped along the stone benches and between soaring columns. Despite the dulling effect of the wine, Rosamund seemed ablaze, as though scorching the air around her, removing the lingering bite of the cold. It was then that she grasped me by the collar, rose atop her toes, and kissed me.

A weaker man would blame the wine, but in the clarity of old age, I can say that inebriation alone was not behind this dalliance. Parts of me had always wanted Rosamund, this woman who repaired that piece of my soul that shattered upon my enslavement to the Empire, and had not quite re-knit to wholeness as I came to manhood. Even in our first months together, when she was barely more than an enemy captive, my every instinct had urged me to trust her, to *entrust* her with all the secrets and worries that I might bear. Others in my life had given me priceless friendship, and I possessed an endless, ceaseless love for Mariya, but it was Rosamund alone I trusted without reservation. In that moment, as our mouths met, I felt as if we had been transported back in time, to her first visit to Constantinople, when I still possessed all the blind hope of youth and had not yet been deprived of friends from death on the battlefield.

So, as this tale is true, I must be honest—I returned her kiss. I hungered for it, her body pressing against mine as she drove me first to my knees, and then vaulted atop my body as I lay in the snow.

But wrongness tainted our every move. And it was not something that I could ignore.

"Rosamund," I whispered, prying myself from her kiss.

"Stop talking," she whispered back.

I wanted to, but could not. "Rosamund, stop."

Breathing heavily, she rose to a seated position, still pinning me against the ground. "There is nothing wrong with passion," she murmured. "You want what I want."

My chest heaving, I gripped her arm. "I made an oath to my wife, Rosamund."

"Oaths!" Rosamund hissed, slapping a hand against the snow. "Love is not possessive. Only Romans are so jealous and backward."

"I made an oath, and I won't violate my promise," I said. "The same as I would uphold my oath to you."

With that, she shifted her weight to slide off my waist. She simply curled against the snow, her cloak and hood tossed aside as her bare head dug into the sand. We said nothing as our torch, discarded along the ground, expended the last of its embers, leaving us with the faintest sliver of light from the masked moon. I lacked any idea of how to address the situation, conflicted by guilt and longing yet unable to address either. Instead, I remained silent, waiting for Rosamund to lead.

Her shoulder nestled beneath mine, her face fixed upon the skies. After a time, she broke our silence. "Varus, sometimes I wish you had left me in my village."

I bit back a gasp. "What do you mean?"

"I told you years ago that my grandfather scried my future, and said that I would forgo children and family to lead a great conqueror to liberate the world. That doesn't mean I never wanted those things, though."

Turning my face to glance upon hers, all I could discern was the faint outline of her eyes and nose and the glistening of melted snow atop her hair. "You never told me."

"No," she replied casually. "There was no benefit to wishing to alter the past. But sometimes I wonder, if you had left me behind, and I managed to escape and survive, what would my life be like?"

"You have people who love you," I told her. "Many friends. And you've saved the lives of dozens of people. Hundreds, even."

She nodded. "I know. And I don't regret any of that. But all your Empire rewarded me with was attempting to burn me alive. If I hadn't promised to serve you in all things, I would have left for the north years ago."

My chest felt knotted, as if some ponderous flaxen rope were squeezing out its vitality. "If you desire freedom, I could release you of your oath. You may leave with however much coin, whatever goods you desire."

She shook her head. "No, my place is with you." At that, I felt quick heartbeat of relief. "But it does not mean I cannot wonder at what might have been," she went on. "Just as how you must wonder if the Romans had not enslaved you and your brother, what life you might have enjoyed, freed from the burdens and oaths of these Romans."

There was nothing further I could say on the matter. Instead, we lay on the Colosseum's ground, staring up at the shivering heavens. Though I desperately desired to offer her comfort, I lacked the courage, worrying what I might signal in doing so. After a time, Rosamund took that responsibility on herself, pressing more of her body against my own. Her head rested upon my shoulder as she gazed at the falling flakes.

We lay there for a good while. Absent a torch and befuddled by wine, how long is impossible to say. Eventually, however, Rosamund lessened the blow of her prior revelation.

"The gods sent you to me for a purpose," she said, still cuddled against my body. "Most times, I am grateful for that."

"Most times?"

"When you actually heed my advice," she teased. "And when war doesn't threaten to take away someone that I love."

Our brief conflict, it seemed, was swept aside. Relaxing, I felt my wits slowly reemerging as I considered our current plight. "The torch is out. How will we find our way out of here?"

Rosamund giggled. "Leave that to me. Sometimes I agree with Liberius—you are a poor listener."

We rose, departed the sands, and navigated the Colosseum's innards. Rosamund grasped my hand, leading me through bends and corners until we at last found the gate by which we had arrived. Rosamund stubbornly refused to explain her ability to find her way even in pitch blackness, possibly goading me with silence, allowing me to wonder if she possessed some mystical power. In fact, after years of living alongside her, I rather assumed that she possessed a near-perfect memory—something I had only witnessed in Liberius, and perhaps Theodora. Whether by pagan magic or memorization from our initial entry into the stadium, however, Rosamund eventually found her way to Rome's streets, still mobbed with revelers even more raucous as the night, and the wine, had worn on.

But it would not be so for me. Instead, Rosamund led me to a nearby house that she'd commissioned for our stay. After unstrapping my armor and lifting free its interlocking lamellar, she bade me peaceful sleep and retreated to a different room. Again, guilt spiked my thoughts, my skin burning and hands twitching as I wished that my sojourn with Rosamund could be undone. I slept poorly, my head pounding from the undiluted wine and mind conjuring dozens of scenarios, all ending in hurt and anger from my family.

That sense of guilt did not evaporate come morning, although it was dimmed just enough to be bearable in public. Men may scoff at such concerns as insignificant, or even praiseworthy. If anything, most of the army would have dubbed me a eunuch or worse for ending our tryst before it reached a more desirable conclusion. For me, however, a lifetime centered upon oaths and honor, as well as the love for my wife that all but consumed me, left me unwilling to abide the amorous pursuits of others and layered my conscience with regret such that I was reluctant to reveal the truth to others.

Had Antonina felt thus? From our time together traveling from Carthage to Constantinople, she had insisted so. The weighty burden of a secret, the feeling of one's soul split in two. The nobler part wishes to cleanse itself, to confess and sin no more. Yet the part of great yearning, of original sin, and indeed of raw humanness, compels all but the saintly toward the pursuit of earthly delights. Antonina had been tempted, albeit by a man of strength and stature, where refusal would have met with its own mesh of gossip and problems. Antonina had sinned, and gravely, though in that moment I wished that I had not judged her so harshly to others. Perhaps Theodora saw the virtue in forgiveness where I could not.

Alas, I said nothing to anyone. I was even able to keep my scruples unknown to Father Petrus, whom I sought out for our typical morning prayers.

"You look terrible." Petrus grinned. "I'd chide you on a reckless evening, but I think you might be excused, given the circumstances."

I could not meet his gaze. Part of me, the warrior, hardened by years of deprivation, saw nothing untoward in Rosamund's advances. Little enough had happened, and I had eventually resisted. So it was nothing, the warrior reasoned. Yet an honest mind, honed by years of education in the Imperial Palace, believed the warrior dishonest. Yes, I had prevented my evening with Rosamund from becoming a true dalliance, though the encounter would have been enough to doom others to a life of marriage-destroying gossip. But, in full account of the truth, I knew what Rosamund had intended that evening. And I wanted it. The excitement and desire, fueled by drink and the rush of joy at Rome's liberation. Even such a desire, unconsummated, was a sin.

"Apologies, Father."

Petrus frowned at my dour reply. Whether he suspected anything, however, I was doubtful.

"You have no idea how much this means to those few who remain from the old days," he marveled. "Your achievement is remarkable. It changes everything."

"Remarkable," I agreed, my thoughts still of Rosamund and Mariya.

Mariya. God, but hearing rumors of infidelity would destroy her. Especially after losing her livelihood to the Brazen Bull and my own intransigence. Had there been eavesdroppers in the Colosseum?

How silent would the building's guards be? Fear wriggled through my veins, even as I reasoned that enveloping darkness would have prevented any observation. Besides, why would the guard care, when most men in the army spent themselves to penury on whores? My secret was safe, I reasoned, and calmed my thoughts as Petrus droned on about the day's lesson. That calm was fleeting, though, and seemed to swell once more as a new fear took root in my thoughts.

Our prayers continued with no unusual disruption on that morning, and for the next two weeks. Likewise, each day, regardless of the snow or wind, each segment of Belisarius' army and its Roman volunteers trained in the Campus Martius or along the hills to the city's north astride the Via Flaminia. I joined as often as I could, with Samur as my most frequent companion, though I dragged Perenus with me for several mornings. Perenus' mood had darkened since his drunken revelries upon our first night in the Eternal City, and though he swung his training blade with vim, he remained aloof and sour. No words of mine could raise his spirits, though I heard that nightly he turned to the city popinae for drink and women.

The Campus Martius was vast, capable of training and sheltering most of Belisarius' army in a single flat plain. Most of our daily exercises were conventional—exchanges of swords, spears, and bowshot, with additional time spent clashing in mock shield walls or in formation on horseback. One novel inclusion was the additional preparations taken to shore up the walls of Rome for a possible siege, to which I sought Belisarius' guidance.

"Theodahad must attack at some point," Belisarius declared. "And we risk losing everything if I proceed northward. Rome's walls are stout and its towers capable of sheltering our ballistae, so it's as good as any a position that we could defend."

"But a siege, Lord?" I pressed. "With grain as limited as it already is…"

Belisarius nodded. "We must do what we can to bolster our depots. If food is difficult for us, it will be thrice as concerning for the Goths, for their numbers are greater and their lands less likely to yield crops in this frost. Pray that next year is better, or we'll be reduced to eating our boots."

"That or rats." I chuckled. "Plenty of vermin in this city."

"It may come to that sooner than I would like." Belisarius' tone turned serious. "Of everyone here, only you have successfully defended against a siege. I will have need of your guidance from Septem in the days ahead."

It felt odd, having a measure of experience in battle that Belisarius did not. Nevertheless, I plunged into my task, not least because it kept my mind from Rosamund and the uncomfortable knowledge that I held an undesirable secret. Not that I ignored her completely— after receiving word of our commandeered home in the Domus Augustana, Rosamund set about preparing for the arrival of Mariya, the children, and many other attendants who trailed my progress in Belisarius' army. She served my meals, and along with Shimon, executed my will.

Yet I grew anxious in her presence and asked that Shimon attend to my person whenever possible. I had to be away from Rosamund. Distance, I reasoned, would be defense against any hint of scandal. God, but I was an insecure fool, at a time when the Imperial world had been turned on its head.

Aside from Rosamund, my worries multiplied once I understood what Rome truly was. With twelve smaller gates and six grander ones, the Eternal City made Septem seem little more than a backwater village, especially given the hundreds of thousands residing within or in the fields just beyond. Though the city had clearly fallen from its pinnacle from prior desolation by the Vandals and sixty years of indifference by the Goths, Rome remained one of the most thickly settled points in this world, and maintaining a modicum of order demanded that every person and beast had water and nourishment.

More, our commitment did not cease at the traditional limits of Rome. Other than Ostia, Rome's all-important port city fifteen miles to the southwest, most critical amongst these was the Mausoleum of Hadrian. Once a vast tower that had housed the dead emperor's ashes, it was recently transformed into a military fortress along the Tiber's opposite bank. The Tiber, that sacred river that defined the earliest days of the Roman Kingdom, bisected the walls, while the western walls of Janiculum lay on the opposite side of the river and were connected to the rest of the city by a few key bridges. In total, Belisarius tasked me with rebuilding and defending twelve miles of stone wall, roughly three times the height of a man and marked by nearly four hundred towers and fighting platforms at regular intervals.

"You're overthinking it," Liberius chided me when I voiced my exasperation. "It's simple mathematics. Divide Belisarius' army to cover first the essential defensive points, and then the secondary ones, and then everything else that looks pretty but has no strategic value."

"We have five thousand men!" I exclaimed. "Even if all of them never stopped to eat or sleep, we would be twenty thousand soldiers short of a reasonable garrison."

Liberius shrugged. "Do what you can with what you have. In the meantime, I shall labor with Tarmutus and our gaggle of squawking hens that is the Roman Senate to find you citizen militia."

And then there was Ostia itself. We were obligated to defend it, not only to guarantee the provision of what little grain might be received from Carthage or Alexandria, but also to provide Valerian's dromons with a port to refit and reorganize after sweeping attacks at sea. There was little I could do besides station a hundred Herulians under Sindual and pray that Belisarius was wrong. Even a naïve child could see that we were woefully thin, liable to break from even a mild raid upon certain points of the northern and western walls.

Belisarius attempted to address my concerns by stationing his military quarters along the city's entry to the Via Flaminia and the Pincian Hill, yet even the presence of his bucellarii did little to plug our gaps. Instead, I was reduced to dispatching couriers by sea to all Roman garrisons in the former Western Empire, begging Conon and Thurimuth, and even Troglita to offer what reserves they could spare.

We have Rome, I wrote to my comrades stationed in Carthage and

Septem, *but we face twenty times our numbers. If the enemy were to awaken from their fear, they would not hesitate to attack as soon as possible.*

After dispatching those missives, I commissioned a thousand carpenters and stonemasons to strengthen decaying portions of the Aurelian Walls, while common laborers stacked stones, arrows, and bolts atop each tower. Others carved and lengthened trenches outside the walls, while the most gifted masons devised outerworks for the more critical gates, fashioning a small stone postern that would hinder any who would hope to rush an open Roman gate. Atop the walls, Ascum personally oversaw the installation of each of his siege engines, dancing in glee as he requisitioned two hundred ballistae and twenty catapults from the city's storage yards.

"With force such as this, I will never understand how the Western emperors fell." Ascum grinned lustily as he inspected a nearby ballista bow for any signs of wear or defect.

"Keep Belisarius in command of the city, and we will prove your thesis," I told him.

We drilled, we planned, and with Samur's Huns and Fulcaris' Herulians, we scouted every road and field within three days' ride of the Roman walls. Through it all, I plunged into my work, eager to occupy my mind with labor rather than thoughts of the Colosseum. No rumors had spread in the weeks that followed Rosamund's kiss, sparing me the worst outcome of the news reaching Mariya's ear. Still, the virtuous corner of my soul insisted that I speak with Mariya, to confess the event and insist upon my innocence in refusing Rosamund's advances. After all, honor in love comes not from a lack of temptation, but from a refusal to act upon temptation, no? Mariya would understand—or so I desperately wanted to believe.

But such a confession would doom Rosamund. Though she might absolve me, Mariya would never consent for Rosamund to remain after learning of such advances—especially given her proximity to me on expedition. Plenty of wealthy Imperial men kept mistresses, with some supporting dozens, but Mariya could never accept such a fate or anything approaching its resemblance. No, cleansing my mind of its secrets would cost Rosamund dearly, and that was equally something I could not allow.

I did not know what to do and had no one that I trusted wholeheartedly to listen, keep secrets, and yield impartial advice. As such, I alone weighed both paths for myself, leaning toward secrecy, yet stung with far too much shame to commit to a choice so sinful and self-serving.

At least my work for the army was well-received. Belisarius approved nearly all of my recommendations, save two. One, he insisted that the men have additional days of rest, arguing their bodies would soon be pushed to overexertion and uselessness. Second, he delayed the transfer of families from Sicily and Neapolis to Rome, insisting first that the Via Appia be guarded by trusted riders as we sought the capitulation of Italy's southeastern towns.

"I would not endanger your kin, nor any others, unnecessarily," he explained.

Meanwhile, all of Belisarius' senior officers took interest in learning more of our Gothic adversary, benefitting from hundreds of Roman guardsmen, clerks, and senators who had lived with Gothic overlords all their lives. For me, the guardsmen's guidance was most useful, signifying the tactics that Theodahad might use.

"The Goths loathe archers," Tarmutus said. "They will have small numbers of bowmen, but they will likely be Suevi or Langobard mercenaries. The wealthier Goths will ride into battle on horseback, but most prefer the shield wall."

"Any chance we could ride them down?" Bessas asked. "Break one flank and send the rest running?"

"Unlikely," Tarmutus answered. "The Goths aren't crafty, but they won't flee lightly. Each man will fight bravely to impress those of his tribe, and so your task is to find opportunities to exact casualties without becoming entangled with a more powerful force. That is how the Goths took Italy by storm, and how they've kept it from the clutches of the Franks."

It all felt impossible. There was too much information to digest and enough work to occupy a million men for two lifetimes. Yet we pressed onward, constrained by poor weather and a lingering lack of understanding of Theodahad's intentions, and the uncertainty of whether he would assault Rome at all. But as exhausting as it all was, the labors of so many interlocking parts fell into a routine. It was then, as he approved our semblance of order, that Belisarius requested a final boon of me. Unfortunately, it was far from simple.

"I need you to lead a party back to Mundus, and then to Constantinople."

I did not understand, though whether that was from lack of knowledge or distraction as my inner thoughts turned to memories of Rosamund's lips, I cannot truthfully say. "Lord, we still know little of Gothic dispositions, and my place is here."

Belisarius shook his head. "You were correct from our first morning here, Varus. We need more men, and we aren't likely to gain sufficient numbers from the old men and young boys of the Roman populace. Mundus needs to know of our success and need for aid, and the Empress must intervene on our behalf. If neither moves in our favor and Theodahad regains his courage, we will all die in Rome within a year."

"Theodora?" I asked. "We could send any courier to carry my words, and your own."

Again, Belisarius denied me. "You are the only person who might affect the Empress' understanding of our war," he said. "If Theodahad decides to unleash his warlords, even Hannibal couldn't hold Rome with six thousand men. If the Emperor will not be moved by my begging, perhaps Theodora will with yours."

God knows, I did not wish to leave. Not with my family approaching, nor with my men destined to stare down a Gothic enemy, nor especially when I still squirmed when thinking of what Mariya might say if she heard of my entry into Rome with Rosamund without me there to explain. I conjured a dozen excuses, first insisting, and later begging to remain. Belisarius was unmoved, however, reiterating the vital importance of reconnecting with our companions in Dalmatia and later with the Imperial leadership in Constantinople. "You are the only man I can trust with this assignment, Varus. You know Mundus and Theodora well, and I would ask, as a favor to me, that you find a way to save my army."

I could not refuse. Not due to violent seas, nor a longing to await the arrival of my family—because, doubtless, Belisarius was correct. He almost always was, despite all the pressures of the Imperial court. There was no other but me. And so I agreed, sending a glimpse of relief washing across Belisarius' face. What he did not see was the surprising relief that I felt bloom in my own chest: Away on a mission, I would no longer be immediately pressed to choose what to do after Mariya's arrival in Rome. Secrecy or honesty, both options would be temporarily deprived of me.

"Tell me whatever you need for your journey, and I will guarantee that you possess it," Belisarius concluded. "Mariya and the others will be safe and warm in Rome upon your return."

And so I prepared—though not without complaint. At the time, my groans were for little more than the prospect of yet another cursed boat, tossing about the waves and lurching up what little food I could force down my gullet. Perhaps, even, for my reluctance to go begging the Empress for aid, when I lacked clear vision of what she realistically could do. I had no notion of what truly awaited me on the voyage ahead, which would make any misgivings I felt utterly insignificant. Nor did I hold any premonition of what awaited me at Salona—a name that is reviled in my memory forever after.

THE FEAST OF SALONA

I departed two days later. Rather than recruit a larger following, I requested only Uliaris, Sembrouthes, and Xerxes accompany me. Rosamund was furious and insisted that I reconsider.

"I need you here to get the domus in order," I explained, which only stoked Rosamund's irritation. "And Belisarius may need your aid as well, for he will occupy a portion of the Domus alongside me."

"You need me with you at sea," she insisted. "Everyone knows that evil is rising."

I shook my head. "I'll be well cared for by my soldiers. A small party will not attract attention, and our route is well clear of Gothic garrisons."

"Fools with sticks. You think violence solves everything, but it is nothing more than a blunt instrument in your hand." Still, she surrendered. "But go, if you must. Just know that I warned you."

Others wished me well, although none expected that I would be absent longer than two months—three at most. Procopius saddled me with a copper tube stuffed with accounts of local grain and tax capacity, as well as invaluable up-to-date maps of Italy's provinces, which would replace antiquated diagrams last charted during the reign of Romulus Augustus. With Shimon's aid, I gathered any simple requests from sections of the army for weapons or goods from the Imperial capital, as well as a more complex ask from Samur.

"Keep safe in Dalmatia. And when you reach Constantinople, see if Narses can send recruiters to the Huns," he asked. "I could always employ more horse archers, given how sorely they will be needed in the months ahead."

"Narses can probably find more Herulians," I said. "But even the friendlier Hunnic clans will be hard to reach in winter."

Samur shrugged. "Can't hurt to ask. The Huns are the best warriors the Empire has, and even the morons in government understand that."

Our journey to Mundus, perhaps only a few hundred miles flown straight by an eagle, was fraught with greater hardship than Belisarius may have wanted to admit. From Rome, there were two routes to Dalmatia—one by sea through Ostia, weaving through the narrow passage between Sicily and Calabria before turning north toward the Ionian and Adriatic Seas. It was a far safer journey, for we could avoid any enemy engagement and travel through waters seeded with Roman warships. Yet it was slow, with the indirect circle to reach Mundus' moving army adding several extra weeks.

The second and far quicker option was partially by land: We would transect the Italian interior, galloping hard for the eastern coast, where we would board a ship bound directly for the outskirts of Salona. Given the still-unknown disposition of Theodahad's armies farther north, the only practical embarkation point would be somewhere along the coast of Samnium, likely along the natural harbors just south of Ortonoa. When I chose this latter route, however, Uliaris chastised my foolhardiness.

"A few weeks of extra sailing is an easy trade over getting ambushed and skinned alive by a Gothic cutthroat."

"Likely," I replied. "But in this surf, I'm not sure I would survive those additional weeks at sea."

Belisarius had anticipated my choice and ordered Valerian to make available a dromon to carry us across the Adriatic and into the coves of Dalmatia. It was a simple enough journey, for the Roman fleet had harried the coastal harbors of Barium and Brundisium in the preceding weeks and were unlikely to encounter serious Goth resistance at sea when sailing into Samnite waters. As such, before we galloped through the Via Latina, Belisarius delivered the intended location of our expectant dromon.

"They will wait for you for two weeks from today," Belisarius explained. "Once you reach Salona, write to me about the condition of Mundus' army and their skirmishes against the local Goths. Travel safely, and let us pray you find the same easy success I have enjoyed thus far."

Our rush to the eastern coastline commenced well before dawn, the darkness allowing us to avoid the Gothic scouts that continually stalked the region's outer limits. Eschewing Boreas, I borrowed a mount, fearing we'd need to abandon our steeds before boarding the dromon. We carried shields absent an emblem and removed the plumes from our helms, masking our identity as Romans for curious onlookers. Fortunately, my three companions already bore armor foreign to any Roman soldier, further discouraging gossip that Romans skulked through Gothic lands. To be sure, sightings of a Persian, an Aksumite, and a Frank would prompt any serious warlord to investigate, yet at least their suspicions, and their response, would be relatively small.

When men and women speak of Italy, their tones grow hushed as they recall the sprawling veins of its roads or impossible grandeur of its monuments. Few, however, regale others with tales of its land, which I find a considerable oversight. Even Procopius, to whom most turn for knowledge of Belisarius' campaigns, is no better in this regard. For me, the Italian landscape, from Latium to Calabria, Samnium and Apulia, and also those battle-scarred provinces to the north, were nothing short of lands carved by the hand of God.

As we entered Samnium, we wound through snow-tipped mountains and valleys sprinkled with villages. Some settlements showed the heritage of centuries of Italian wealth, their roofs fashioned from brick and clay and walls built in the style of old villas. Others, doubtlessly newer, favored the simple yet sturdy Gothic thatched huts, capable of housing a dozen or more individuals comfortably within a single hearth. Interestingly, some of the wealthier settlements flew the Imperial banners from a nearby outpost or small forum—though none sought contact with our party, incognito as we were.

The Via Latina, one of so many stone roads in Italy, cut through mountain and meadow with relative ease, although often winding about to avoid more taxing ascents. Our mounts trod over dressed stone for all of their sojourn through Latium and northern Campania, and a fair distance into Sirmium proper, rarely seeing more than a thatched Gothic village or a smaller Roman town in our four-day ride. Given invasion and the threat of a ravenous plunder of precious food and valuables, it is unsurprising that these smaller settlements did not send messengers to greet our passing, and one went so far as to douse their fires and shutter their doors as we passed within a hundred paces. More the better—all I wanted to do was to bring this expedition to an end, absent conflict or begging for aid that I could not provide.

Nor could we deal with distraction against a backdrop of black gloom. Soon, lightning clawed at the sky, illuminating the sullen canopy of clouds in stark, terrifying flashes, as if a great celestial beast breathed flame across the dead sky. The blinding brilliance of the lightning was a stark contrast to the frozen grays and dull red-orange hue of daylight, and it made our mounts jittery. In such a small party, though the countryside was hauntingly beautiful, the forever dusk of Italy's lifeless sun imparted a sense of unflagging danger.

And through it all, the cold continued unabated, leaving my gloved fingers numb and my limbs stiff with no chance to warm them; even the meagerest of campfires was too great a risk. It was a journey that could not end soon enough, when we could sleep in warm beds, gnaw at cooked food, and otherwise heat our bodies before a roaring hearth without fear of signaling enemy scouts.

Our final twenty miles split from the road. The riding was not arduous, but a slick sheet of wet snow made for treacherous footing for our mounts, and progress slowed. We clung to denser woods, avoiding detection whenever we encountered any Samnite village.

There was no serious threat of discovery until our final stretch to the sea. It was Sembrouthes who saw it first, urging our party to a halt.

"Quiet!"

At first, it was easy to miss amidst the cover of trees, which dampened sound from the open plains and disguised our progress. Yet what troubled him soon became evident as the rattle of boots clapped against the nearby road.

Xerxes bobbed his head, seeking my attention with a whisper. "What's our nearest settlement?"

"We can't be far from Ortona," I chattered back, unable to stop my teeth from clicking against the frost. "Perhaps less than a half day's ride to the coast?"

Soon, we saw them. Spears aloft, perhaps two hundred Ostrogoths marched northwest. Judging by their noise, including a fair amount of idle talk, they seemed to care little to hide their presence.

"Undisciplined fools," Xerxes muttered.

"Should we continue?" Uliaris asked. "They aren't likely to spot us."

Inexperienced with scouting, I shrugged. "What is the risk?"

"We stay," Sembrouthes insisted. "Wait for them to pass. All it would take is a single zealous picket, and we'd be discovered immediately."

Uliaris groaned. "They don't have horses…"

"We still wait." Sembrouthes would broker no compromise. "The coast is far enough to be worrisome, and we can't risk laming the mounts."

I acceded to Sembrouthes, and we dismounted for a rest. From our place in the trees, the Ostrogoths were hard to see, yet in what I could make out of them, they seemed little different from the now-deceased defenders of Neapolis: a few draped in iron lamellar, yet most bearing shirts of mail and leather. On many, that simpler armor showed evidence of repairs, chain re-stitched where it had been pierced by an arrow or torn by a sword. Compared to Belisarius' forces, the Gothic band was poorly equipped, yet all appeared thickly muscled and above average in size. In many ways, these men reminded me of Baduarius and Dagisthaeus, and that raised the private worry that we might be forced to battle against a thousand copies of those dead heroes. I prayed it would not be so—there were simply not enough men living to withstand that kind of prowess.

The Gothic progress was painfully slow; their soldiers seemed in no hurry to reach their destination. Blessedly, as the sun stretched toward its afternoon hours, the last of them disappeared over the nearby hill, their cacophony dampened to a dull, distant thunder. At last, Sembrouthes nodded, and we remounted for the final stretch of our race to the sea.

Only then did I realize what else struck me so about this band. "Those are the first Goths I've seen patrolling in force," I observed aloud. "Should one of us trail back and warn Belisarius?"

"No," Sembrouthes insisted again. "We know nothing if where those men may go. Likely, back to Theodahad in Ravenna. If they venture close to Rome, your brother's scouting parties will tear those Goths apart. Trust that Belisarius can defend himself, for all we can do to help is to find more men to wield a sword."

We trotted onward, taking greater care to venture away from paved roads. As the final rays of daylight disappeared to the west, the sounds of waves echoed just ahead. In that dark, however, there was no safe approach to seek out our dromon, and so we made camp where the Samnite tree line met the Adriatic Sea, using the near-leafless trunks to break the chill of the sea breeze. At dawn, we rose and scouted for evidence of Belisarius' designated ferry toward Dalmatia. Trailing southward and away from Ortona, we trotted for half a day, with none of us willing to voice the fear that our ship had either not yet arrived or had been waylaid by weather or enemy attack.

Around the sun's zenith, however, our fears were quelled. What we found was no small vessel, but the Imperial flagship, rocking lightly where it had anchored in an inland channel, perhaps a hundred paces from the shoreline. Even absent the Imperial sigils, the build of the warship was unmistakably an Imperial design, with platforms for archers or ballistae to hail missiles upon a nearby foe and a particularly deep hold. It was a vessel I had gazed upon countless times in so many godforsaken sea voyages, and that I could recognize anywhere even today. Galloping forward, I unfurled a smaller Imperial banner that I had tucked safely in a saddlebag, and short bursts of the ship's horn met my request.

It took three trips within a shallower-keeled craft to transport us four, and our four horses, to the flagship. After that craft was hauled aboard using the ship's pulley for the last time, the flagship raised its anchor and rowed toward the Adriatic's open waters, embracing the churning swell.

"Have trouble finding us?" Valerian asked, hailing my arrival.

"Not as bad as it could have been," I replied, coughing violently into my hand, as my stomach already roiled from the rolling waves. "I expected a smaller dromon, so thank you for seeking us out."

Valerian nodded. "I was turning to this direction anyway, and I was concerned that a lighter vessel might lack the ballistae to ward off the Goths in the northern ports. Ascum left me with only a half dozen engines across the entire fleet."

"You should see what Belisarius is doing to Rome's walls," I said. "So we've taken all the towns of Apulia?"

Valerian nodded. "Those that matter, anyway. Barium, Tarentum, Brundisium. With any luck, Belisarius will receive resupply from Corinth next year."

"And our ships will have safe harbor to raid deeper into the Adriatic," I added. "Ravenna, even."

Valerian grinned. "I'd say that the Goths not having a large navy takes the fun out of this. But I'll be damned if I don't enjoy winning every engagement."

Before I could reply, the deck lurched from a nearby wave and sent me kneeling to the wooden planks, spray clapping about my shoulders. I again rose to my feet, grumbling as Valerian chortled. "You're still confident despite the weather?"

"It's not so bad, once you get used to it," Valerian said. "And if you keep close to shore. After we take you to Dalmatia, I plan on harrying Ortona. I'll leave you my smaller transport, but hopefully you'll find Mundus quickly."

"No word from Mundus' forces?" I asked.

"Little enough. The Goths crawl along that coastline like mites. Huge armies. If Mundus wants Salona, he'll be in for a scuffle. The frost cut Illyria hard, and there isn't enough grain to go around. Mundus will need to fight before the winter comes."

Our voyage should have taken little more than half a day, but thwartwise winds delayed our approach to Dalmatia. More, with no light to safeguard our passage, Valerian grew wary of hidden shoals and shifting sandbars that lined the jagged Dalmatian coast. Instead, Valerian's sailors fought to anchor the ship not far from an inlet, using dim moonlight to identify the presence of solid ground.

By morning, Valerian's captain had maneuvered the flagship farther northeast, until larger swaths of land could be detected. "Salona isn't far."

Squinting, I gained view of a coastal Roman road, but no settlements. "You're sure?"

"Less than half a day." The captain grinned. "I used to stalk these waters before the Emperor begged my service. Salona is a den of cheats and liars, and I would recognize its surroundings even if I were stone drunk."

Xerxes glowered. "You were a pirate?"

"I was a merchant of the sea." The captain winked. "Just not of cloth or grain. Be thankful you have men like me guiding your boats against the Goths."

One after the other, we boarded Valerian's boat. Our mounts, however, remained aboard the flagship, with Valerian's officers insisting that a boat would make for a safer approach. "The Goths have few ships, and the roads here are poorly kept. Row north until the zenith, and peek your heads inland to see if Imperial banners are flapping about."

I obeyed, although I had no firm inclination of how we might find Mundus' army, even if the local weather held back its sleet and snow. By then, however, our only option was to press onward, clinging to the railings of our boat as we tossed about while the pulley lowered our keel into the sea. Icy spray splashed into my face as we thumped free of the pulley's straps and snatched the oars as Valerian shouted for us to separate from the flagship.

"Tell the Emperor we need more boats!" Valerian yelled as we parted. "And men to pull the oars!"

Initially, we four were painfully uncoordinated. My experience with oarsmanship was limited to training with the Herulian foederati along the outskirts of Philippi, while neither Xerxes nor Sembrouthes had ample education in seamanship. Uliaris, however, barked a cadence that soon brought our strokes into rhythm, and we lurched northward.

The Roman road along the Dalmatian coast wandered between hills and crags, and just as Valerian's captain warned, even from a distance, it was visibly eroded, with frost-widened gaps that would inevitably weaken any remaining mortar that united the road's stones. Occasionally it disappeared from view as it turned inland, only to reappear a few hundred paces northwest. One minor miracle was a calming of the waters that, while tossing our craft about, were weakened from the protection that Dalmatia's outer islands could afford.

There was no talking. Only cursing and grunting and an occasional spout of vomit—mostly from my own soured gut, but not always. Our initial views were terrible, blocked by rock-strewn knolls that told little of any living person in the Dalmatian interior. Yet as the sun ascended, the coastline flattened, and the occasional fishing village denoted some settlement in the region. Unfortunately, all were deserted, and we paused at one such hamlet to take rest.

"No scorch marks," Xerxes said, after ducking carefully into each hut. "But all the rooms are ransacked. I doubt we'd find any insects, let alone food."

"Raiders," Uliaris observed. "No villager would do this to their own property. The only question is whether the pillage was conducted by Goths or Romans."

We gnawed on our rations, rubbed our chafing hands, and hauled our boat back into the water for its next jaunt up the coastline. Thankfully, after more cursing, growling, and a yet worse episode of regurgitation, the walls and port of a great city rose in the distance.

"Salona?" Sembrouthes asked.

"It's the only sizeable port city in the area," I reasoned. "Keep silent, and hide any metal that might catch what little sun is available to us."

Yet our fears did not materialize. Instead, all that greeted our arrival were dozens of Imperial banners, all emblazoned with a golden Chi-Rho that told of allegiance to Emperor Justinian. Salona's walls swarmed with glinting helmets, the faint outline of red plumes blowing in the sea breeze.

"Mundus took Salona?" Uliaris gaped. "Should we steer for the port or pull aside and disguise the boat?"

"Pull aside here," I replied. "Better to proceed warily."

Still several hundred paces distant, we steered for a stretch of beach where the surf was broken by boulders half the height of a man. We hauled the boat ashore, its keel driving a wedge in the wet sand as it rose from the water and well beyond the grasping edge of the high tide line. After safely disguising the boat behind a nearby boulder and with a cover of fallen branches, we gathered our packs and snuck toward Salona.

"Nothing worse than a wet arse," Uliaris grumbled.

Xerxes hushed him. "Better than being dead. Look for officers you recognize."

Our progress was slow, dogged by a need to keep low to the ground and avoid more vigilant sentries upon Salona's walls. Yet as we trudged closer, we heard nothing but sounds of merriment, with Greek voices roaring victory chants and pealing out in laughter. More, once we crested a low hill along the beachfront, we caught sight of a massive tent city that lay in orderly rows outside of Salona's walls, capped in its center by the Imperial Chi-Rho and the banners of the Thracian Army. A great pen had been erected along the tent city's land-facing edge, but rather than sheep or cattle, it was an assortment of bloodied and stunned warriors, their clothing and beards cut in the Gothic style.

"Mundus must have struck a victory," I whispered.

"Likely," Xerxes replied. "All the same, let's wait to find someone we know well."

Perhaps another hour passed before Xerxes' caution was sated. Amidst the outlying tents, we witnessed a helmetless Constantinianus jogging toward the pen that held many Gothic captives, trailed by an entourage of clerks, spearmen, and even a mounted courier and stumbling scribe, awaiting a message to be dictated and delivered. At my signal, Sembrouthes raised a horn to his lips and blasted the rolling notes that signaled the arrival of friendly Roman forces. Oblivious to our position, Constantinianus snapped to attention, ordering his spearmen to form a defensive ring as they scanned the tree-and-rock-screened edges of Salona's tent camp.

Gesturing my followers to rise, I paced away from my hiding perch, my arms stretched wide. "Friends!" I yelled in Greek, before switching to Latin and tugging my head free of my helmet. "Friends!"

I doubt Constantinianus understood me across the distance. Yet as his men approached, one recognized me and barked at the others to rest their spears. "It's Tribune Varus, Lord Constantinianus."

"Varus?" Constantinianus said, his brow furrowed. "Him too?"

My hands still outstretched, I paced closer. "Yes, it is Varus of the Herulians! And I bring tidings from Italy!"

Trotting closer, Constantinianus hailed me, yet did not shed his confused gaze. "That Rome is taken?"

"Yes," I replied, now sharing his sentiment. "How did you know?"

"The Goth foederati," Constantinianus said. "Indulf arrived last night."

The idea held no logic. Indulf? Why had he not returned to Rome after protecting Optaris on his trail to Ravenna? And, I wondered, gaining a clearer view of the prisoner pens, who were these hundreds of Goths gathered about, shivering in the cold?

Constantinianus beamed, seeming to understand at least one of my questions as I gawked at his prisoners. "We beat those Goth bastards bloody, Varus. Not a week ago now. I took one of the Gothic commanders, some shit-mouthed brute named Uligisalus, prisoner, although his brother Asinar escaped with a few hundred men."

Though his braggart tone irked me, the words themselves brought nothing less than elation. "Mundus defeated the Gothic army here?"

Constantinianus smirked. "Not just the army, Varus. We've taken the entire goat-fucking province. Dalmatia is ours, and with it we have a direct path to Aquilea."

God protect me, but I could have kissed that young runt. Though Belisarius had taken both Rome and the southern half of Italy, no sizeable Gothic army had fallen to our blades, leaving Theodahad's strength intact. Mundus' victory signaled not only a reclamation of these ancient lands back into the Emperor's bosom, but indeed a potential end of the war altogether. All my worries were shed, if only temporarily, and replaced with a reckless hope that the Gothic War would be brief, triumphant, and sparing of both lives and coin. With such developments, anything was possible, for Ravenna was surrounded by two veteran armies under the overlordship of the finest Roman military leader in hundreds of years.

"Your men can rest in the city while I take you to Mundus," Constantinianus offered. "You will stay for our feast, no doubt?"

"Feast?"

Constantinianus' brow arched. "You truly arrived here without coordinating with Indulf? Yes, there will be a feast in two days. You will wish to stay before returning to Belisarius?"

"I'm headed for Constantinople next," I explained. "Although with Salona under Roman control..."

"The war might be over by the time you depart Constantinople for Rome." Constantinianus laughed. "It seems like the Goths are too divided and don't have the belly for a fight. Not that I blame them, given how our men acquitted themselves in battle."

He led me through Salona's gates, weaving through a series of narrow streets before escaping through the city's northern gates. Perhaps a further thousand paces along the coastline, Constantinianus escorted me to a structure abutting the sea, its walls painted a glinting white while the shingles on its towers were a faded crimson. It would have appeared a permanent fort for several bandae, except that its interior resembled three interconnected villas constructed in the style of the Republic.

"Diocletian built this," Constantinianus remarked, gesturing with a toss of his arm. "Housed him in retirement. Pretty enough, but such a dismal land!"

Inside, the villas were latticed with dying vines, their leaves withered and falling from brittle branches. Many Thracian officers were discovered bustling about—most of whom carried stacks of parchment toward a central villa, yet others appeared at rest over a midday meal. Many greeted me, with a rare few remaining from my days as a lowly dekarchos, shouting plaudits for Belisarius' capture of Rome. Constantinianus stopped for nothing, insistent upon depositing me with Mundus.

"Very busy today, between the feast and dealing with the prisoners," Constantinianus half complained, half boasted. Leading me to the largest villa, he ordered the guards to open its doorway. "You won't mind if I leave here?" he asked. "Mundus is just through the atrium in the feasting hall."

He turned away before I could respond, and I felt relief at his departure. Constantinianus appeared capable enough as a leader, yet his haughty tone was, I felt, as yet unmerited, one victory in battle be damned.

Mundus brightened as he greeted me. "I didn't expect Belisarius to send you, Varus, but you're welcome all the same."

The new general of the Thracian Army carried a number of small cuts upon his face and arms; his temples were bruised where his helmet had pressed against his skin. Nevertheless, he was in as happy a mood as I could ever recall, flashing an uncommon grin as he gestured for me to commandeer an empty bench. Beside him were several other centurions, all decked in mail and red cloaks common amongst Roman spearmen. Only Indulf stood out, his mail covered in a heavy bear pelt.

"Nor did I expect to find Indulf here with you, General," I replied. "It seems you have already received what information I was tasked to offer."

Indulf shrugged. "A happy circumstance I am here. After depositing Optaris in Ravenna, I rode north with my men to find old kinsmen in Pannonia. They, too, have declared a blood feud with Theodahad, and do not trail me by much distance. Perhaps we will see them tonight."

"A great omen!" Mundus exclaimed. "With Pannonia and Dalmatia under our control, Theodahad will have no choice but to surrender. Indulf tells me that the Pannonian warlord, Witiges, commands a vast host as well."

"Twenty thousand hardened killers." Indulf grinned. "And another thirty thousand young men itching to wet their blades for the first time."

Though I was elated at Mundus' independent acknowledgment that our war might draw to a rapid and bountiful conclusion, I could not ignore some traces of irritation and skepticism that tainted the moment. Irritation in that the purpose of my meeting with Mundus had been rendered moot upon Indulf's arrival. Skepticism in that the prospect of a massive Gothic horde, nearly thrice the number the warriors under Belisarius' command throughout all of southern Italy and Sicily combined, would rampage toward Ravenna and demand Theodahad's capitulation. This scenario was not only unpredictable but also invited selfishness; surely both Witiges and Indulf would seize a significant portion of spoils from the war's end. Personally, I stood to receive a significant bounty from our success, while the Emperor likely expected sustained dominance over much of the Gothic kingdom.

"You were able to convince Witiges so quickly to turn his shield?" I asked. "At what cost?"

"Nothing you should be concerned about over the longer term," Indulf answered. "Theodahad's demise was the most important bargaining piece. I can vouch for the Pannonian chieftains in this regard."

"See, Varus!" Mundus beamed. "Who would have thought a battered centurion and a freed slave would rise to conquer the West, eh? Not me, that's for certain."

It was impossible to deny my friend his happiness, given Mundus' long history of seizing no personal glories despite sharing in every hardship of his men. Throughout the evening, I discovered that Mundus' victory had been near flawless—the encirclement of two-thirds of the Gothic forces of Dalmatia. Cataphracts borrowed from Belisarius alongside swifter spearmen rushed forward, engulfing the forces of the warlord Uligisalus within an hour of the battle's commencement. Asinar, Uligisalus' brother, attempted to carve a gap in the Roman stranglehold, yet relentless arrowshot blunted Asinar's wedge. By early afternoon, Uligisalus had tossed his blades to the grass, surrendering thousands of Theodahad's famed mountain warriors while many hundreds lay dead or bleeding.

"It was as if Uligisalus didn't know whether to fight or flee, and instead did neither," Mundus replied, brushing off his daring strategy as mere good fortune. "Nothing like our fight with the Avars. None of the viciousness or desperation."

A tray of olives and bread was passed about, and I snapped at it I greedily. "And you're able to feed them all?"

"We've been fortunate with local forage," Mundus replied. "The region has suffered from a terrible harvest, although not nearly as troubling as Sicily or Italy from what Indulf tells me. The Emperor promised me a grain shipment from Egypt as soon as Salona's port was conquered, so it appears our long-term issues will not matter. For now, I have food to feed all through winter, although by spring, we will have to make difficult choices."

Hence the feast. Mundus assured me it was not his idea, for the extravagance seemed wasteful against the broader needs of the Empire. It was Constantinianus who had goaded him into proceeding, arguing that such displays were necessary to demonstrate pleasure to the victorious Thracian Army. Upon Indulf's arrival, the feast took on a second meaning—to greet the liaisons of Witiges, welcoming him into Justinian's embrace, and to toast the end of the war. Witiges himself would not join the delegation, Indulf explained, although thousands of his men would arrive to bolster Mundus' command in preparation for a thrust toward Aquilea.

"Witiges will strike toward Noricum before turning south," he explained. "He will meet our forces near Pavia."

It all seemed so simple. So inevitable. Only Xerxes expressed private skepticism later that evening, although his worries were affixed upon our decision-making. "Even the greatest kings fall victim to hubris. If taking Ravenna were as simple as Indulf insists, the Gothic kingdom would not have survived for as long as it has."

Nevertheless, I enjoyed the raised morale, as well as the considerably improved food offerings available to Mundus' men. Even the Gothic prisoners ate heartier meals than my men in Rome—and for that, I stomached a measure of guilt along with my soft cheese, saliva leaking from the corners of my mouth as I popped a berry in my mouth for added flavor. Mundus' forces kept good order, maintained their watches, and kept clean—all the while keeping all but a hundred spearmen outside Salona and in the army's tent city.

"To discourage any dalliances with local women," Constantinianus explained. "Or livestock. Couldn't tell you which one is more in demand these days. You'll all want to be fed, I presume?"

To Constantinianus' dismay, we imposed upon Mundus' stores and took ample respite from open beds and roaring fires. I groaned in delight as a slave aided me in scrubbing all manner of dirt from my face and body with heated water. After that, my muscles yearned for sleep, until camp slaves ferried in a bowl of thick stew, simmering with hewn vegetables and even chunks of overcooked rabbit meat. The taste was sparing, lacking in salt and tough to chew, but I swallowed it all and belched my appreciation, my torso flushing with warmth.

Outside, Illyria's coastal winds howled, somehow even less inviting than Italy's frigid interior hills. It was only then that I saw two of the slaves near my tent shiver, their lips blue and fingers stiff, though silent all the same.

"Warm yourself by my fire," I said, and insisted again after the slaves' initial refusal. "Frost is no friend to the body."

"No, Lord," a diminutive slave replied, his words slurred as if from too much wine. He lacked his front teeth, though he put a hand before his mouth to shroud his disfigurement. In that, he reminded me of Cephalas—good natured but cursed to a homely appearance.

I remember little else, other than the crackle of hewn logs against the fire and the rising beat of wind from the Adriatic Sea. By the time I woke, the slaves had departed. In their place were clean clothing and oiled weapons, the iron so cold that it could easily snatch layers of skin from one's fingers if taken outside for too long.

My party rested for two days, taking no part in the drills, ditch-digging, or wood-cutting that livened an army's winter camp. Absent Petrus to insist upon morning prayers, I even slept late for those two blessed mornings, waking after the army's morning meal. Instead of laboring, I spend my days conversing with the men, listening to their exploits, and sympathizing with their injuries or deaths of friends. It was a skill I had learned from Belisarius, one that required considerable patience but was a universal requirement for anyone seeking to lead men into war. I had even gained a view of Uligisalus, although the Gothic warlord spoke no tongue I was fluent in.

Pannonian Goths filtered into Salona just as Indulf foretold. As with Mundus' forces, all were amply provisioned and eschewed Salona for the open air of camp, yet kept well apart from the Thracian spearmen. Few Pannonian Goths even ventured to consort with their new allies, leaving Indulf's few Gothic foederati to serve as translators and go-betweens to facilitate interaction and trade. However, the

Pannonians had prepared for Mundus' feast by slaying two dozen full-bodied deer, then carefully skinning their hides and rubbing salt over the exposed meat. The scent of roasting venison blew about the camp for an entire night and morning—teasing my senses as I recklessly considered stealing a morsel while none were looking. On my oath, I did no such thing.

When men today speak of the Feast of Salona, they often show their ignorance by speaking of a meal in the city's forum. In fact, the city's only contribution was the use of its bakers to fashion soft bread; even then, the grain came from Mundus' wagons, and the pay for their service was rendered double. The feast was held at the center of Mundus' camp, with hundreds of tables and benches hewn from local trees and wooden cups provided from the baggage train. As always, wine was overabundant, and many of Mundus' men were roiling drunk before the sun's zenith.

Festivities began as scheduled—midafternoon, as the winter sun slowly sank from its heights, dimming even further given the constant shroud of haze. I recall it to be an overcast day, yielding a light snow but always threatening a deluge that loomed but never struck. After gathering the entire Thracian Army around their benches, Mundus ordered his men to stand as Constantinianus and Indulf led the Pannonian Goths into the fleet of tables, instructing the Goths to separate into groups of five. Indulf separated each group of five to join with Roman counterparts of the same quantity, making every table half Goth and half Roman. For both parties, swords were only permitted amongst the senior officers. Only a handful of guards were posted with the Gothic prisoners—with Indulf recommending that such men still be deprived of their freedom.

"We don't know who amongst them are true loyalists of Theodahad and who merely follow the crown," Indulf explained. "The Pannonian tribes will take no offense at feasting before their captive kinsmen. If anything, any Goth who surrenders willingly deserves little respect. Let them gawk at our merriment."

From my party, Sembrouthes and I joined a table near Mundus, while Uliaris and Xerxes moved to the far end of the Thracian gathering. Several slaves stacked logs in stone-lined circles every hundred paces, igniting a blaze to ward off the creeping cold of the late afternoon. We sat just a mere two hundred paces from the beachfront, where occasional gusts whipped against the bonfires, casting warmth about the hundreds of bodies seated nearby. In all, it was as pleasant a day as any that year, with most giddy from victory, wine, and the allure of camaraderie that is as rare as it is cherished in this life. Though I no longer claimed affinity to the Thracian Army, I, too, shared in the cautious hope that all would be set right in the world, and all of us who dared to fulfill the dreams of so many before us would be rewarded in gold and tales that other Romans might tell of us in the centuries to come.

Though the fare was pitifully limited, the cooks from Salona applied what magic they could to the grains, cheeses, dried fruit, and scraps of meat. The initial offering was freshly baked bread and skins of olive oil, which the slaves insisted was recently pressed. It was a meal that I had supped upon hundreds of times as a palace slave, yet given our recent deprivations, I savored the tangy sweetness of the oil as it soaked into the nooks of the crust.

"Jesus Christ, it's still warm," Sembrouthes garbled lustily, shoving the bread into his mouth. He struggled to chew the overlarge hunk, sucking air between bites.

I nearly choked from laughter. "I've never heard you speak of anything so lovingly, Sembrouthes."

"You have no idea how hungry I've been," he said. "I thought I was going to weep when Mundus first fed us upon our arrival."

Though I imbibed wine with our Thracian and Gothic hosts, Sembrouthes did not. I was certain that Xerxes would abstain, too, for he was never comfortable with anything that would befuddle his senses, especially in the presence of any whom a false word or a sudden contest of drunken bravado might render a foe. "In Persia, the drunkards rarely survive the Ctesiphon court for long. Too easy to manipulate," he'd once told me.

It was Uliaris I worried over, for though the man professed extended bouts of sobriety, he still drank to the point of gluttony from long-held sadness. All I could do was hope that Xerxes would rein in the man's baser instincts and exercise caution.

The second and third courses were served shortly thereafter, including heaping baskets of overripe figs and later hunks of pungent cheese from local goats. Again, Sembrouthes groaned with happiness as he tossed an ample portion into his mouth, hardly bothering to taste the fare as it slid down his gullet. Admittedly, I was little better, grasping at the plate of figs and palming extras in my fists. Wine flowed freely at all times, loosening tongues between the Thracians and Goths. Though some angrier growls could be heard throughout the feasting tables, most conversation seemed borne of mutual curiosity, with the Pannonian Goths having significantly less interactions with Romans or Greeks than their southern brethren.

"You fought the Vandals?" one Goth asked me. His Latin was halting, yet fluent enough to follow, and his boiled leather chest guard set him apart from his more haggard brethren.

"Yes, I even captured the Vandal king." I grinned, not bothering to stop the boast before swilling another drink.

"Terrible people, the Vandals," the Goth replied. "If we were not at war, we would be friends for what you have done."

I nodded. "Perhaps the war will end soon, and we may yet be friends."

He considered the statement for a few heartbeats, then nodded. There was no animosity in his speech or gestures, yet he appeared skeptical of me somehow. At the time, I believed him suspicious of my rich armor, custom forged in Constantinople; as battlefield plunder, it would be enough to fetch a lifetime of silver for the spearman who claimed it. Indeed, between gulps, I caught one Goth or another starting at my armor, with one even rising from his seat to regard the dragon-hilted sword that hung from my belt. I tossed such moments aside as playful curiosity and embraced conversation with Goths and Thracians alike as inebriation relaxed cultural sensitivities and language barriers.

In a lull, I spied Mundus sitting at an adjoining table, finally separated from a herd of Gothic chieftains and nibbling upon our fourth course—strips of salted mutton heated in olive oil. Leaning heavily upon an elbow, Mundus took no part in the merriment of army drunkenness, nor did he seek out those who descended into ludicrous games of overindulgence. After excusing myself from my tablemates, I shuffled to sit beside the victorious general.

"I couldn't be happier for you, Mundus," I said, clapping him on the back. "But you seem displeased!"

"Oh, I'm pleased with the outcome," he replied. "I'm just wary of wine in such a gathering."

Frowning, I shrugged. "Why? Even our priests drink wine, albeit not to the point of losing control of their bowels."

"Last time I was drunk was Barbalissus," Mundus confessed, hunching awkwardly. "Haven't forgiven myself for being useless that night."

Shaking my head, I filled two cups of wine for both of us. "That was not your fault, and there's nothing to forgive. For God's sake, man, you've just won a battle!"

"Aye." He grinned shyly. "It's off-putting to think about, in a way. I was always the man enforcing the orders of others, not outfoxing the enemy with my ideas."

"And look how it turned out!" I exclaimed, raising my cup. "If it weren't for you, I would never have succeeded in Archelaus' banda. I was too naïve and cocksure of my abilities."

Mundus punched my shoulder playfully. "You still are. Some moments, I miss our smaller group, sitting about a campfire and leaving the cares of the world to wealthier men. Even with all of Archelaus' troubles, I enjoyed it all the same."

His worries sated, Mundus took the second cup from my hand and clinked it against my own. "To our fallen friends."

"Indeed," I replied. In one motion, I drained the cup's contents, and Mundus did the same. Soon after, others begged his attention, pulling him toward other conversations with some Gothic chieftain or another.

Returning to my table, I chuckled as I saw Mundus sharing cups with one Goth, and then another, and then another. Constantinianus joined in several toasts, boasting grand speeches to the gathered leaders and regaling all present of the Thracian Army's achievement. At that, I was grateful to be away from such conversation, and instead enjoyed the fifth course, this one of fish, and sixth of another cheese with dried fruit. Sembrouthes and I gobbled up all that came to our plates, reaching a point of painful gluttony. Nevertheless, I would not have stopped unless I fell from my bench, for the long-term deprivation of rich foods will reduce a man's temperance to little more than a forgotten suggestion. Clutching my gut, I belched to make room for another slice of cheese, though I would wish soon thereafter that I had paced myself more prudently.

By then, the sun was setting along the western sea. I would wager that nine in ten men present, both Goth and Roman, had become ruinously inebriated; many stuffed hoarded scraps of prior courses into their mouths. Sembrouthes, though abstaining from drink, followed their example, although soon complained of a squeezing in his gut.

"Ate too much," he moaned. "I'm going to the latrine."

Chuckling, I directed him to Salona. "Go to Diocletian's palace. Far less competition for an ideal spot to relieve yourself. Mundus won't mind."

Waddling uncomfortably, Sembrouthes left not long before a horn blared from Mundus' table—the long, sustained blast needed to render thousands of drunken voices silent. Constantinianus leapt atop his table, wavering as he stole one final swallow from his cup and gestured for all to listen.

"Friends! We have one final course to enjoy in celebration of our victory!" he bellowed, his speech uneven. "Our friends from Pannonia have reserved the finest meal for last and will serve it to their new Roman allies!"

At that, Indulf raised his banner, signaling both the Gothic foederati and Witiges' Pannonians to rush toward Salona. Not every Goth ventured forth, but at least two men from each table excused themselves to fetch the delicacy—the platters of roasted and dressed venison. Though my own stomach was in little better condition than Sembrouthes', the prospect of such rich fare made me salivate all the same. I had no ears for Constantinianus' blathering, which continued for a good while, though I did take notice when he invoked his general. By then, the sun had nearly disappeared into the west, leaving crimson streaks across the dying skies above.

"Mundus won't willingly speak to you, so we'll need to summon him!" Constantinianus shouted. "Mundus! Mundus!"

All who could hear took up the cry, and it swept across Salona's valley in a boom of adulation. "*Mundus! Mundus! Mundus!*" Through it all, I beamed, shouting the man's name as two Thracians hauled him to his feet and atop Constantinianus' table. From there, Mundus was left to stand alone, absorbing love of his men amidst the falling snow.

"*Mundus! Mundus! Roma Victrix!*"

A sweeping smile across his face, Mundus ran both hands through his thinning hair, sending beads of sweat and melting flakes of ice trailing from his forehead. Laughing, he waved in acknowledgment, yet the chanting only continued. And I joined them, thrusting my fist into the air with the thrum of each repetition.

"*Mundus! Mundus! Mundus!*"

"Thank you!" he shouted, his voice inaudible but the words clear upon his lips. "Thank you!"

Another bout of cheering commenced, now somehow more intense, until Mundus ordered his horns to blare for attention. As the Thracians obeyed, Mundus nodded in approval, sucking in air with a tear in his eye.

"Thracians!" he began, eliciting another roar. "Through your courage, Dalmatia is ours!"

"*Roma Victrix! Roma Victrix!*"

Mundus joined the victory chant before continuing. "When I joined the Thracian Army, just a slip of a boy, I begged to whatever gods would hear me to give me the chance to see this day. And now, more than twenty years later, I stand before the Romans who delivered that dream!"

"Mundus! Mundus! Mundus!"

"With Belisarius in Rome and our allies guiding us to Aquilea, the Emperor's grand vision is all but accomplished. And it is because of you!"

Mundus strode to the edge of his table, hopping the narrow gap to another as he gazed into the massed audience. Though snow fell, the heat was incredible, although whether from sour red wine or the press of unwashed spearmen, I cannot be certain. None complained, however, for the fires beat away the still-insistent winds of the Adriatic, seemingly furious that we all had escaped its frozen clutches. It was impossible to turn my eyes away, not even to gaze upon the setting sun, that bleeding, angry eye fading what little light it was capable of to a naphtha-black darkness. As I followed Mundus' every footstep, he momentarily found my gaze, offering a nod that I returned in kind.

"I have no father but the Emperor," Mundus began. "No brothers but those who rose through the ranks with me. And most of all, I have no sons but the men of Thrace. And I would not trade that privilege for all the gold of Croesus!"

"Mundus! Mundus! Mundus!"

By then, a stream of Goths had emerged from Salona; pairs of men hoisted vast silver platters, steaming with strips of venison. Others carried forth clay cups on their trays of silver, the sloshing contents bearing even greater quantities of wine. I eyed the venison as it reached the table, yet temporarily eschewed the special silver cup offered to me.

"In a moment," I replied. "Need to make room for the meat."

The savory scent seemed to have reached Mundus' nostrils, for he beckoned the Gothic leaders forward. "Our allies honor us. This food and drink are a symbol of their friendship and ours. I would call

Indulf, lord of the Gothic foederati, to stand with me!"

There were fewer cheers now, but many of the Goths stomped their boots as Indulf hustled toward Mundus' table. Arm outstretched, Mundus hauled Indulf to the table's heights, then embraced him before the combined armies.

"The Emperor has personally bestowed Roman citizenship, as well as the status of patrician, to Lord Indulf," Mundus explained. "He has served nobly with us in Africa, in Hispania, in Sicily, and Neapolis. Rome depends on friends such as Lord Indulf, for together we shall rebuild our world!"

Gesturing toward the tables, Mundus beckoned for Indulf to speak.

"You all know me." Indulf grinned. "I am not a man for pretty words. I asked Emperor Justinian for justice, and he kept his bargain."

He signaled a nearby Goth, who carried food and drink to Mundus' table. Snatching an empty tray, Indulf stacked hunks of steaming venison upon it, grabbed a silver goblet, and handed both to Mundus. With a light bob of his head, Mundus accepted, popping a strip of meat into his mouth with a smile. Meanwhile, Indulf grabbed a clay cup for himself, taking a single strip of venison for his own meal.

"My people place honor in granting our guests the very best we have to offer, whether the harvest be plentiful or meager," Indulf continued. "Silver cups for those we—I—have bled alongside against countless foes. You have my gratitude for bringing justice to Amalasuntha!"

Though Indulf spoke in Greek, many Goths echoed their fallen queen's name. After acknowledging their mourning call, Indulf gave those men some order in the Gothic tongue, and many snatched iron knives to carve chunks of venison and splay them about the platter. Likewise, others distributed wine, serving their Roman guests first. With the bounty thus distributed, Indulf raised his clay cup to the heavens, then lowered it to his mouth for a deep gulp. Mundus copied his example, as did many in the procession. Others, such as myself, were too preoccupied with the venison to take notice of the wine, ready to compete with the Goths for strips of meat as it cooled in the winter air.

No matter that by then my stomach was roiling from the excessive labor of overfill, I could not resist the meat. "Sembrouthes is going to be so angry when it's all gone," I said to myself, spittle running from my mouth and matting my beard.

Scattered cheers rang throughout the crowd, while others conversed in drunken song. It was a beautiful end to a day of celebration, a foretaste of the glory and plenty to come upon the cessation of war.

Finally, I relaxed, abandoning all worries—of Rosamund, of the darkened skies, of famine, and of even the prospect of travel back to Constantinople by tempestuous seas or snow-blocked roads. All was pleasure, as if some starving piece of my soul had finally been satiated after a lifetime of yearning.

Until the men began to fall around me.

Some slumped over, so drunk that even their laughter slurred to nonsense. One nearby Thracian hunched over the table, dropping scraps of venison and his half-empty cup. I heard no complaints— only the chuckles from livelier men as they attempted to shake their comrades back to consciousness to enjoy the feast. Then, the Thracian to my left sagged as well, dropping his cup onto the dirt.

"All right, friend?" I asked.

He grunted, struggling to keep his head up. "Just tired. Head hurts. Think this will end soon?"

"I doubt it," I answered. "Even if only a few of us remain awake."

After perhaps another ten minutes, more men succumbed. My neighbor began to snore, replying with only a moan as I pulled on his shoulders. "Too much food?" I spoke aloud, directed at nobody. "Perhaps meat from a tainted deer?"

"Must be," my Gothic conversationalist suggested. "My stomach feels heavy too."

At the table next to mine, laughter turned to murmurs, and then, swiftly, shouting. Though my own vision was blurred from drink, I trained my sights upon what had recently been Mundus' dining location, where the Thracian general struggled to prop his body atop the table. Closer to me, Constantinianus fell back from his chair, sending a puff of dirt sailing about his body as he connected with the ground.

It was then that the hilarity of drunken antics smoldered into horror, the realization of our true predicament now manifest. For it was then, as a handful of sober men sought to raise Mundus from his perch, that Indulf surged forward. Indulf's sword, one of the few present due to his status as a patrician, thrust toward Mundus' ribs, spearing the general just as a half dozen Gothic followers jammed their carving knives into the throats of Mundus' guardsmen.

"No!"

I cannot be certain who yelled. Perhaps many. Likely me. What I am certain is that I did see blood spurt from Mundus' chest, his body jerking instinctually away from his attacker. Yet Indulf struck again, jabbing his sword before Mundus could parry. Screaming, I reached for the hilt of my blade, but it was no use: The Goths before me had pushed their feasting table toward us Romans, tipping our bench and many of our men backward. By the time I could rise to my feet, I still tripped against a leg of the falling wooden table and only barely staggered away from the Goths.

Near Indulf, I heard the blare of a foreign horn, a call briskly echoed throughout Salona's campground. I stumbled, a silver goblet brushing against my foot, droplets of red liquid still clinging to its interior, but my wits sharpened as a Goth hopped over the upended table, jamming a serving knife into the eye of a Thracian trapped beneath the bench and table. I drew my sword, yet found my hand wavering as I leveled its point toward three oncoming attackers. One sparred playfully, intending to do nothing more than drive me backward, yet all I could muster was a sloppy parry that nearly sent me toppling to the ground. My conversation partner smiled at my pathetic display, stepping carefully closer as he weaved through my clumsy thrusts.

A moment later, his face seemed to lurch forward, elongating his nose to a bloody point. It took a heartbeat for me to realize the Goth was dead, a sword passing through his brains with little difficulty. It was Sembrouthes, now slashing at the two other Goths too swiftly for them to react: one slashed across the face, the other's neck half severed, and both hit the ground alongside their comrade.

"Sembrouthes—*Jesus!*" I cried.

"I saw the Goths cutting the throats of Salona's guardsmen," Sembrouthes said, securing the tube of Procopius' messages and lashing it against his back. "I will explain later. We must find the other two and leave before Indulf gains control of the area."

It was only then that I viewed what had become of the Feast of Salona. Thousands of men brawling like wrestlers, with every Goth in eyesight wielding a carving knife or wooden clubs. The Thracians were poorly matched and outnumbered, since the Goths had slain the guards, freeing their once-imprisoned kinsmen. It was a foretaste of hell, I thought, the carnage and chaos mixing into an elixir of utter hopelessness.

My respite from assault was brief. Two other Goths descended upon me—only for Sembrouthes to dispatch with them in two thrusts to their bellies. Then, before engaging a further enemy, Sembrouthes snapped me from my shock.

"Varus, we need to go now!"

It was then, searching for other foes and wishing my senses to clear, that my thoughts returned to that traitorous whelp Indulf.

"I'm not leaving without Mundus!" I yelled.

Sembrouthes shot a glance to a nearby table, easily the most hotly contested scrum of the feast: there, a dozen armed officers slashed wildly at the Goths who encircled Mundus' table. "No time!"

"There's nowhere we can go!" I yelled.

Sembrouthes grasped my collar and shook me with uncharacteristic frustration. "We left our boat on the beach. Get control of your senses. This battle was lost before it began."

Screams of rage and pain flew as sluggish Thracians fell to swarms of Gothic attackers. Pockets of resistance emerged, yet even those Thracians who managed to wield blades were far from fit to fight. Like hounds sniffing the blood of wounded prey, Goths swarmed about the shrinking Thracian circles, allowing no escape.

"We grab Uliaris and Xerxes," I said, "and then come back for Mundus." I could not bear to accept the general's likely fate.

Sembrouthes groaned. "Very well! Keep close!"

Perhaps the only reason I survived that ordeal was the shelter of our fallen table; it had little behind it besides frost-covered grass, beach, and sea, and Sembrouthes utilized this advantage to its utmost, at times snatching my shirt and dragging me behind. He kept his sword low, only revealing its edge when a Goth directly impeded our progress. By that point, most Goths had grown lazy hunting befuddled Romans, and the three that Sembrouthes slew had no time to retreat or even scream. Nevertheless, Sembrouthes refused to rescue any other party of nearby Thracians, even when I felt our sword might thwart nearby Goths and spare our allies.

"Shut your mouth!" Sembrouthes hissed back at me. "If I had any sense, I would smack you in the face and carry you back to the boat. I'm already taking a risk by searching for the others."

After another twenty paces, Sembrouthes pointed toward his destination. Xerxes, with his copper-lined iron mail, was easy to spot in the scrum, where he handily turned the momentum of his attackers against them as they thrust forward with their knives. One managed to get close enough to slash uselessly at his armor, only for Xerxes to grab his knife arm and slam it into his knee, easily shattering the elbow and leaving his grip on the weapon slack.

As Sembrouthes jabbed the point of his sword in the belly of an unsuspecting Goth, I drew behind Xerxes, yelling for his attention. "Where is Uliaris?!"

With his free hand, Xerxes pointed along the bench. There, lightly rolling upon the wine-soaked wood, was my Frankish bodyguard, clearly unable to move despite no visible wounds. As Sembrouthes warded off nearby Goths, Xerxes lifted Uliaris to his feet, eliciting a painful moan.

"At attention, you sack of shit!" Xerxes bellowed, throwing Uliaris' arm about his shoulders and propping the Frank's ponderous weight upright.

One Goth rushed from our flank, rushing toward Xerxes' defenseless arm as the Persian attempted to maneuver free from Uliaris. As the Goth closed in, however, I rushed for him, just in time to slam my shoulder against his and send him spinning to the ground.

"Use your sword, you drunken lunatic!" Xerxes yelled.

I obliged, and had no sooner driven its tip between the man's shoulders than something tugged me by the shirt—Sembrouthes, dragging me along the edge of the gathering, as the Thracians quickly collapsed under the rabid surge of triumphant Goths. He hustled as quickly as he could, as did Xerxes with his own charge, distancing us four from the fray, until, with a sigh of relief, my bodyguard pointed to the beach.

"To the boat!" he yelled. "Go!"

Xerxes obeyed, hefting Uliaris' body toward the beach. I, however, refused.

"Not without Mundus!" I insisted again.

"God damn you, Varus!" Sembrouthes snarled. "In a few minutes, this entire camp will pounce on us. We need to leave while there are still others to deflect the Goths!"

"Then leave," I replied, my courage buoyed by wine. "I can do this alone."

Sembrouthes let slip a torrent of words in the Aksumite tongue, likely cursing me in ways that cannot be sufficiently explained in any of the languages I know. Regardless, when I left, he followed me, and we trailed back toward the feast. The commander's table still held a fair thirty Romans that, while not yet encircled, almost surely would be in mere minutes. Ignoring Sembrouthes, I ran toward the Thracians, who allowed me entry as they recognized my armor. "Tribune!"

I swiveled about, frantic. "Where is Mundus?!" I yelled to any who would listen.

Most could not, however, for they faced twice their number. Goths battered our limited numbers, shoving the paltry Thracian shield ring backward. The centurion pointed to a nearby table, where several bodies lay slumped atop one another. "Not with us, Lord."

Heedless of the carnage about me, I found Mundus' body prostrate on the feasting table. To this day, no man can convince me that Mundus had yet died, for I swear upon Christ and all the apostles that I saw him rasp a bloody breath, one tired eye gazing upon my form. I am convinced that he saw me, too, though others later denied it was so—that I had been too late. But I cannot deny that his wound, a savage puncture between the ribs and directly above a lung, was fatal. Mundus said nothing to me, nor did he move, but upon every oath I've ever taken, he saw me.

"Sons of bitches!" I screamed, gripping hard at my sword. "I'll kill them all!"

"No, you won't." Sembrouthes was right behind me. "We need to leave and take this useless turd with us."

He nodded to where Constantinianus shuddered helplessly upon the ground. Although nothing now could separate Mundus from his creator, his second-in-command moaned and wept nonsensically. Sheathing my sword, I reached for him, finding his eyes glossy and movements as sluggish as the rest. As pathetic as Constantinianus seemed, sparing his life was the most I could do in the circumstances. However, I could not run to safety easily or without a sacrifice. For that, guiltily, I turned to the Thracian centurion, finding him five paces distant.

"Centurion, I need to take Constantinianus to safety," I replied, enunciating each word in hopes of masking my own drunkenness. "Cover my retreat, but break for a run as soon as I am clear. Salona has fallen, and no help is coming."

It was a foolish thing to say, given the desperation of our camp, and the certainty that any Romans who did not flee would be surely killed. Within a heartbeat, three Romans sprinted away from our formation, racing toward the coastline. However, the centurion and a loyal cadre of his men remained. "Go, Tribune. Quickly."

At last, I obeyed Sembrouthes' orders—I left. Heaving Constantinianus over my shoulder, I stole one final glance upon Mundus, his pallor white as a corpse's. I muttered a prayer as I hobbled to safety, asking God to accept Mundus, my longtime friend and former protector, into his comfort and mercy. Whether Mundus was a devout Christian I cannot say; looking back on our experiences together, I doubt it. But never a more just man lived, nor one more humble. I still miss him terribly.

The Thracian band allowed us enough space to escape. A handful of Goths surged forward to attempt encirclement, though Sembrouthes cut the hand from one while two Thracians tackled another. We had perhaps a minute before the Thracian circle was fully surrounded, granting just enough time for our escape. Yet the Thracian stalwarts could not last long, and within a short time I could hear Goths howling behind me, rushing toward the beach. Laden with Constantinianus' helpless weight, I lagged behind Sembrouthes, fighting against an urge to retch.

"Move, Varus!" Sembrouthes yelled. "Nearly there!"

Away from the heat of bonfires and amassed bodies, the sea wind had a sobering effect as it stung my cheeks. With each lumbering step, I struggled to keep Constantinianus aloft, hampered even further by his occasional squirm. A tugging pain knotted in my gut, yet I forced each ponderous step forward as we shifted from firm soil to sucking sands. Sembrouthes never faltered, screaming demands for those ahead and to me behind.

"Xerxes!" he barked. "Push the boat out! They're following us!"

Constantinianus moaned. "I left Mundus behind."

"Nothing we can do," I muttered, gagging as bile flooded up my throat with speech.

"It was a feast," Constantinianus continued pointlessly. "How could they do this?"

Something sailed overhead—a dagger, barely missing my shoulder, that buried itself in the sands immediately before me. Only then did I sneak a glance backward, finding Indulf and at least a dozen Goths in pursuit. Indulf cackled with glee, while all I could do was force my body onward until waves lapped at my boots.

Heeding Sembrouthes' words, Xerxes had uncovered our boat and hauled it into deeper waters, although it must have exhausted him to push such weight. Waist deep in seawater, Xerxes hailed our approach, while Uliaris thrust his head over the railing and vomited noisily.

"In the boat!" Sembrouthes yelled.

Crashing into the waves, he steadied the boat with Xerxes just long enough for me to toss Constantinianus in alongside Uliaris, then grabbed my shirt and pushed me in as well. Xerxes followed immediately thereafter, prying an oar from its holster and using it to pole ourselves into deeper water.

"Varus!" Indulf howled, reaching the beach in a full sprint. "I always knew you were a coward!"

"Rot in hell," Sembrouthes grumbled, hauling himself aboard. "Get us out of here."

Grasping an oar, I joined a shivering Xerxes in poling our boat away from the shoreline—surprisingly effortless, with the tide tugging our boat outward along with our pushes and grunts. By the time Indulf reached the waterline, our oars no longer struck ground, and we were rowing freely away from Salona.

One of Indulf's followers flung a knife toward our boat, but it splashed harmlessly several paces short. Indulf did not bother to follow us—we were too far, and his heavy kit would pull him down besides. Instead, he laughed as waves lapped his boots, raising a fist into the air. All around us, the Adriatic winds howled with renewed vigor, ravenous at the opportunity to claim the warm bodies of more men.

"You can scurry away, Varus!" Indulf boomed. "But we're coming for you! And give Belisarius my thanks for his aid against Theodahad!"

I did not respond; there was nothing I could do except grieve. For in the span of less than an hour, Indulf had butchered five thousand Roman soldiers, annihilating the Thracian Army in an orgy of blood and food. Half of Rome's western armies now entered the afterlife, led foremost by Mundus. As we further separated from shore and Indulf's figure grew faint, I screamed into the darkness of the sea, tossing about in the waves as the wine slowly released my wits from its clutches. It was only then that I realized that the Gothic War had turned, and all would be ash and sorrow.

God damn Indulf. God damn him.

THE GATHERING HORDE

Perhaps the greatest frustration that first night after Salona was the darkness. Absent torches, and with the light from the moon and stars still dimmed, it was reckless to navigate with land out of eyesight. Thus I ordered the boat turned southward, so we might trail the jagged coast for several miles, and then, with enough distance between us and the ordeal, ordered us to the shore.

Wet, cold, and three of us soaked in wine besides, sleep was an uncomfortable challenge on the lightless, forlorn outline of Dalmatia. Though Uliaris and Constantinianus moaned and snored, we remaining sentinels three each took shifts watching the tree line for any sign of movement, though nothing disturbed our tiny party. By then, I think I would have welcomed disturbance; whether it brought a chance to exercise my craving for vengeance or to painlessly snuff out my life, I would have happily accepted.

"It was the wine," Xerxes hissed, unknown hours into our vigil. "Those treacherous bastards poisoned the wine."

"How can you be certain?" I replied.

Xerxes sighed. "I can't prove it now. But the Thracians, including us, were served silver goblets, and the Goths clay. Indulf must have dosed the Thracians with something to weaken our bodies."

"Aye, my head still pounds," Uliaris confirmed, now fully awake. "I've woken many a morning from a prior night's drunkenness, and I've never felt so awful."

"You should not have been drinking at all," I bit out, and took a deep breath before continuing. "But Xerxes' theory seems possible. I doubt the meat was poisoned, for I saw the Goths eat from the same cuts as I. If my belly had not already been sour, I would have tasted Indulf's wine with the others."

"Some god must love you, Varus," Xerxes said.

His words were tinged with the memory of Rosamund, her own insistence at the same, and brought me to shudder. Xerxes' lifted a brow, but I briskly shook my head as if there were no cause for concern, even as her heresy hissed in my ear, as reassuring as it was damning.

The gods love you, Varus. And they will use you as an instrument of their will, even if you don't believe in them.

"At any rate," Xerxes continued. "The venison was not so much for poison as a way for the Goths to sneak in their blades. The serving knives were a brilliant maneuver around the weapons ban. I left my sword in Salona, by the way."

"And I mine, along with my franciscas," Uliaris added.

"They will all be replaced," I promised. "With the same or better quality. Just get us safely back to civilization."

Despite the gluttonous feast, my stomach growled by dawn. We gathered back into our boat, discovering two stale crusts of bread from a previously forgotten pack, and split one between the five of us.

"We'll need more than that before long," Xerxes warned.

"One now, one later," I said. "We can venture inland to forage, but we risk discovery. The quicker we reach safety, the quicker we'll eat and find dry clothes."

Constantinianus vomited, then rubbed his eyes. "Where are we headed?"

"Dyrrachium." I guessed the distance at three days' sail. "Unless Valerian discovers us rowing about."

Constantinianus grumbled. "Christ. Might as well steer for Corinth. Why not one of the villages a day away?"

"Anything closer and Indulf's Goths will ride us down like pigs."

Waves pounded against shoreline rocks as if in agreement with Constantinianus. Even by boat, it would be a long, arduous journey. Worse, tossing seas could easily work against us, sapping our strength rather than guiding our bow toward the ancient provincial capital. The icy spray only added to my misery, taxing my resolve and strengthening an internal voice that insisted we would be safe completing a much briefer sail.

It took a painful level of resolve to refuse that temptation. Repeatedly, I envisioned capture by Indulf and the inevitable torture that the bastard Goth warlord would inflict upon us. He would deliver me to Mariya one piece at a time, just to gnaw at the morale of my men safely inside the Eternal City, while torturing my wife and children. More than merely seeking comfort away from the sea, I wanted my wife and my children.

"We must assume the Goths are charging into the border provinces," I explained. "And from Dyrrachium, we can acquire berths on a transport to Apulia, and perhaps all the way to Ostia."

Sembrouthes nodded. "Not returning to Constantinople?"

"No." I gestured to the tube that Sembrouthes had rescued from Salona's interior. "We will send Procopius' missives onward. But Belisarius must know of Indulf's treachery. We know nothing of Goth dispositions, but they must be preparing for an assault on Rome."

Constantinianus winced as he licked chapped lips, made swollen by too much drink and overexposure to sea spray. "Why not sail west, direct for Italy?"

"The water is already rough near shore," I replied. "It'll be worse farther out. We'll never make it."

"Some confidence," Constantinianus muttered, his face still an unhealthy shade of green.

And so, we trailed southeast, never allowing our boat to venture too far out to sea; I doubted it would survive in such treacherous waters. Sturdy but full from carrying five grown men and their armor, our craft sailed each day until just before total darkness, when we carved a small camp to extract what rest was possible. For the first two days, I forbid any fires to be lit, even though it was unlikely that Gothic war bands could have followed so swiftly in our escape. Uliaris complained mightily of the cold, yet we persisted through dead skies and the loveless, bloody eye of the sun.

Food was a greater concern. From poor planning and the gnawing hunger brought on by hours of rowing, our loaves were consumed by the first day, and our stomachs roiled by morning of the second. Though I did my best to ignore the demands of my body, it was not so easy for others. Tensions rose amongst our party, and tempers flared. Constantinianus in particular mumbled incessantly to himself, prompting what would be our bitterest exchange.

"Shut your hole!" Xerxes yelled. "I can't listen to you whine any further about how you let Mundus die."

Constantinianus shifted angrily on his bench, wound back his arm, and smashed Xerxes with a fist—or aimed to, anyway; the Persian was too agile and ducked the blow.

"I've taken shits more capable of violence than you," Xerxes spat. "If you weren't Theodora's kin, the recruiters would have died of exhaustion from laughing at your enrollment."

"Xerxes, enough!" I yelled.

"Bastards," Constantinianus muttered. Yet moments later, he continued his inane blathering, drawing an exasperated sigh from Xerxes but no further blows.

Late in the afternoon of our second day at sea, we took shelter in a hollowed-out fishing village. A mere five squat huts total, the settlement had only one thatched hovel intact enough to shelter us five (along with its usual tenants, a family of mice). Again, no fires were permitted, but Uliaris did unearth some measure of relief: a small trove of stored food in clay amphorae, hidden in a covered hole.

"Desiccated," he complained. "Too tart."

"It's still food," I retorted, my thoughts drifting to the memory of gluttony in Salona, before life slipped into hell.

We each took a mouthful of grapes so dry they felt like chewing leather, and chewed pieces of their sour skin caked our mouths long after swallowing. It was just enough to stave off my body's cravings and allow sleep, but not enough for the gnawing to disappear entirely; my sore arms and salt-blasted face still yearned for deeper nourishment. Still, I slept, for at least in sleep, hunger could be kept at bay.

That night, I had drawn final watch—that dreadful sequence of predawn hours that bled right into an overlong day. I had not sat a final watch since my days as a centurion, and it was a duty that brought no nostalgia. Surprisingly, Constantinianus awoke to join my vigil and sat with me upon an abandoned bench in the center of the village. Though I was hardly eager for his presence, Constantinianus seemed to yearn for companionship; still, I waited for him to broker whatever conversation he desired.

"Varus," Constantinianus began, his voice not even an echo of the cocksure officer from Salona. "Why would Indulf kill our brothers?"

I sighed. "Indulf has always been a pain-loving jackal. The only reason the Emperor tolerated him is because he was loyal and offered a conduit to Amalasuntha and the Ostrogoth chieftains. If Indulf is willing to butcher an entire Roman army, it's because he plans on giving loyalty to someone else."

"Theodahad?"

"Who knows. But I do know this: Indulf hated Theodahad. That, I never doubted for a heartbeat. Some of the Goths I encountered in Messana and Neapolis insisted that Theodahad neither desired a crown nor could have violated guest rights to kill his kin. However, Indulf makes me question whether that custom is truly held dear."

Constantinianus frowned. "About Theodahad, Uligisalus said something similar. That Theodahad preferred his poets and his books to swords, and never would have consented to be king on his own. Do you think that has anything to do with Indulf's treachery?"

I shrugged. "The Goth chieftains would deny Theodahad's guilt. But the fact remains that Amalasuntha is dead, and someone took a knife to her throat. In such circumstances, all we can do is ask who stood to gain from her death."

"Who stood to gain," Constantinianus murmured, thoughtful. "Well, Justinian did."

Justinian. In a heartbeat, with a single accusation, Constantinianus had spoken more truth than anything I had ever beheld. I nearly toppled over, flooded with foreboding from Hakhamanish and Theudis, of Adalfuns and Optaris, all who warned of the evil in the West. To think that this was it—that Justinian was that evil—and more, that I was an instrument of that darkness, or even had a hand in its creation... it nearly tore my soul to pieces. Perhaps that is why I denied it so heartily.

"Justinian treasured Amalasuntha's friendship and deference," I shot back. "If he was discovered to be the author of her death, even Marcellus and the excubitores would find it difficult to defend such a man."

"Just a thought, nothing more," Constantinianus said, quick to surrender. "Although, if he isn't caught... killing Amalasuntha might be the most daring action Justinian has ever taken."

I did not reply. As an excubitor, I was bound by oath to rebuke Constantinianus, to insist that he cast aside his words as filth, nonsense, spoken in sadness. But I did not, because a piece of me wondered whether it was true. In many ways, Justinian as the distant assassin of a Gothic queen held no logic at all. In others, however, it made all the sense in the world. A long stretch of silence passed before Constantinianus spoke again.

"Did I cause Mundus' death?"

"No," I said, still considering Justinian in the privacy of my mind. "Mundus was a grown man and an experienced officer. We all placed faith in Indulf."

Constantinianus shook his head, his eyes brimming with tears. "Then why didn't you leave me with the rest of them? Why didn't you let me die with my men?"

"Because we need you," I growled. "The Empire, Theodora, me, even the memory of Mundus. The Thracian Army is dead. But you have the authority in the Imperial court to stitch together something to replace it."

"I do?"

"You must. Someone needs to flay that son of a bitch Indulf and do honor to Mundus and our fallen brothers. But if you're going to sit here and mope about how guilty you feel, then I'll let Xerxes toss you overboard in the morning."

Constantinianus chuckled, cuffing his eyes. "Xerxes really doesn't like me, does he?"

"No." I actually laughed. "But he doesn't like many people. Prove yourself in battle, and he'll be the first one to embrace you."

After that, Constantinianus said little, but neither did he retreat into the drier comforts of the hut. Instead, as morning dawned, he helped me ready the boat for our departure, gathering all our packs and storing them safely in the boat's small hold. He even took his share of the rowing once we set off, offering others the opportunity to rest as he labored behind the oar. It was not a pleasant day—our stomachs groaned, the five of us bickered, and the sea tossed our craft in ways I cannot adequately describe—yet we made progress.

The following day, a forceful wind blew us toward our desired direction, relieving us of the need to row entirely. By midday, the outline of a walled city emerged in the distance, with Imperial banners flying overhead. We five must have seemed like sea-cursed vagabonds, stinking of sweat and waste, our shirts and trousers worn to rags. Dyrrachium's port guards greeted us with lowered spears and were only somewhat pacified as I identified myself. They allowed us to disembark, taking our armor as we separated from our boat for the final time.

On firm ground, Uliaris retched, but nothing emerged. "I'm never getting on a small boat again."

"Don't say that," I warned. "I've sworn that oath a dozen times. Fate thinks it hilarious to offer additional helpings of this sour meal."

The guards desired to bring us to the Epirote governor, but our weakened limbs and ravenous stomachs demanded a meal first. At first, all that was offered were hunks of salt mutton, yet we each scrambled for our portion, gnawing at the tough flesh with grunts of pleasure. Another guard then procured twice-baked biscuits, which also disappeared with nary a word of gratitude. Immediately after finishing that poor meal, my body convulsed, threatening to upend its long-awaited nourishment. Xerxes, however, was not so lucky, and as he vomited, I finally agreed to greet the governor.

It was a formality, and rather dull. Dyrrachium's palace was a forlorn place—worn from a century of neglect, its hallways whistling with blasts of sea air surging through cracked walls. Cold and damp, it was one of the least luxurious Imperial residences I had yet seen, although it was far preferable to the confines of a tiny boat in winter. The governor was named Elegius, rotund but with the telling loose flaps of skin that indicate a sudden loss of fat, and he greeted me with little suspicion, acknowledging my status as a tribune and an agent of the Empress. Upon informing him of the destruction of Mundus' army, Elegius banished all but a single slave from his presence, ordering the rest to prepare food for Dyrrachium's latest guests.

"Of course, we will provide what fare can be mustered, although the harvest was poor," Elegius explained. "Fish are plentiful, as Jesus intended, although one can never seem to catch enough of them."

The prospect of fish, that detestable creature I dined upon too frequently in Carthage and Septem, made my mouth water. "You have my gratitude, Governor. Our last feast was bountiful, but had a conclusion to be little desired."

With that, I conferred my tale, halting only when a meal was presented before the two of us. With dirt-crusted fingers, I tore into the fish as soon as it left the slave's clutches, consuming a third of its meat before realizing the governor had paused first to pray. Against protests from my gut, I joined him, wondering whether additional portions might be made available if the meeting continued much longer.

My audience was a brief one, however, concluding shortly after I'd recounted the army's poisoning and subsequent slaughter. "You mean there are no other survivors?"

"Some," I guessed, "but less than a hundred. We had no reason to doubt Indulf, and paid dearly for our trust."

"Such is life these days." Elegius sighed. "It was not always thus. Two hundred years ago, prosperity reigned. Now all that remains are dilapidated stones and the teasing notion that life need not be so difficult."

I had not anticipated that the governor might have information of his own to reveal to me. "A lovely achievement, taking the Eternal City," Elegius commented, after I informed him that Belisarius had dispatched me to Constantinople to seek reinforcements for Rome. "But you won't find any ready reinforcements in Constantinople."

"No?" I asked. "Why not?"

"The Emperor wrote to me to request many of my transports, which I obliged." He smiled. "Please do tell the Empress of my hospitality, if you would. At any rate, in the Emperor's letter, he also informed me that Germanus would lead a small army to Carthage to quell the rebellion there."

"Stotzas," I confirmed. "I fought him at Membresa. They have no notion of leadership, but Stotzas commands a sizeable force with the Mauri at his back."

Elegius groaned, digging his knuckles into his protruding belly. "Germanus won't have many men, but plenty of gold to bribe locals. It seems Nepotian is taking Carthage's governorship into his own hands, paying to secure his grandson's inheritance."

I needed a moment to understand his full meaning. "You mean Solomon is returning to Carthage?!" I gasped. *Grandson*—Praejecta must have given birth to a son. "He's the one that almost lost it to Stotzas!"

"Possible as that is, Nepotian seems too formidable to resist," Elegius replied. "Even for one such as me, or as you. All we can do is pray that Germanus can foster peace in Africa. If not, we'll all be bled white by taxes by next winter."

He did not keep me longer, affording me a comfortable room secured on an opposite corner from the sea. More biscuits were delivered, as well as pails of water for washing, yet I forsook my habitual need for cleanliness in favor of rest. With biscuit crumbs on my lips, I fell asleep as soon as my head lay upon a wonderful layer of fresh straw.

I slept badly that first night. Not from the ache in my muscles or a roiling gullet. Instead, a suffocating grief made every breath I took fetid and lifeless, as the reality of Mundus' death became manifest. In our desperate sail away from Salona, I had little time to consider the enormity of what had transpired there. Yet, safe in Dyrrachium, the knowledge that I would never again share time with an old friend became too much. In the darkness, I wept, visions of listless Thracians cut apart like chaff racing through my thoughts. I wanted nothing more than to leave that place, and my initial urge was to seek Rosamund's protection. She had been correct, of course, and perhaps if I had allowed her to attend me at Salona, a different fate may have awaited my party. Instead, Mundus had been butchered. In my fury, I swore an oath to God that I would see Indulf scream for his sins.

Initially, I hoped to leave Dyrrachium for Italy within a day or two at most, but Elegius demanded that we rest for a full week. Though I insisted that Belisarius needed to hear of Mundus' demise immediately, Elegius was unmoved.

"You are a free man, and able to leave if you wish," he said. "But if you wish me to commission you a transport across the sea, you will grant your body the gift of sleep and food. You will do no good to your strategos if you perish before reaching your destination—which is likely, with the Adriatic as evil as it's been these past weeks."

And so I accepted Dyrrachium's safety and gathered my strength. The others did as well, going a full three days without so much as training, although by the fourth both Uliaris and Xerxes had taken up wooden swords to substitute their stolen property in Salona. Our first day was brief—only an hour before fatigue set in, and our overworked bodies could be pushed no further. By the seventh day, although none of us had fully regained his pre-Salona vigor, I felt my vitality had returned enough.

On the day before our departure, Constantinianus informed me that he would not be joining us.

"You would be welcome in Rome," I said. "Our army is already short of officers."

Still, he declined. "You swayed me to stay. If it kills me, I will raise an army in Greece and strike back at those Gothic shit-eaters."

I was not sorry to see the back of him. If he had not been Theodora's relative, Constantinianus would never have risen so high in Justinian's army—not for many years, at least. Beyond his incessant complaining, he lacked the grit of a hardened warrior, the kind born from countless hours of sweat and suffering in the training yard and on the march. He'd likely only survived because of me and the others, and while it would be beneficial to have a favorable voice in Constantinople, I doubted that the headstrong young man could sway the Emperor to do much more than balk at Mundus' misfortune.

"Good lad," I replied, masking my doubts. "You won't find men in Constantinople, but Theodora should be able to find gold for your efforts. See if you can gain recruits in Macedonia and Corinth."

And so, Constantinianus' plans were set. Borrowing a horse from the city's stable master, Constantinianus set off early, laden only with food, skins, and a sword gleaned from Dyrrachium's barracks. Before he departed, I transferred Procopius' messages to him, indicating they should be delivered to the attention of the Emperor and his ministers. I last saw him at Dyrrachium's gate, where he hailed me from horseback.

"Thank you for saving me, and tell the others," he said, "I won't squander the gift."

The following morning, a full week after arriving as starving and threadbare survivors of a slaughter, the remaining four of us boarded a transport and left Dyrrachium for Italy. Unlike our departure from Rome, there was no feeling of boundless optimism, nor a willingness to blind ourselves to the frigid and inert world that was the cursed winter around us. All I could be grateful for was that my duty to return to Constantinople was alleviated, and we would instead travel toward friends and family.

"Do you think Indulf will try something similar in Rome?" Sembrouthes asked. "Betraying Belisarius and our household?"

I shook my head. "Wouldn't work. Belisarius is too well guarded, and word of the massacre will reach Rome through some tradesman or another. Salona was small, and Indulf was able to manipulate Mundus in the confusion of its conquest—not that we weren't also foolish for trusting the arrival of the Pannonian Goths, mind you. The capture had been so easy that I assumed the war was over."

"So did I," Xerxes replied. "It's easy to see fault when standing on the shoulders of the present, but at the time, I was of a similar mind as Mundus. Don't forget—I led Indulf in our attacks on Septem. He was stubborn, yes, but he never demonstrated any sign of treachery."

Except that was not entirely true. No overt treachery, of course, though Indulf did seem to loathe taking orders from Roman officers— especially when mercy was required, which Indulf viewed only as weakness. After his duel with Agila, Indulf's injuries only made him more difficult to control, but still, I had assumed the drive to revenge Amalasuntha's murder would steer his passions in support of Belisarius' campaign. So much had come from the death of that woman—someone I had never met, nor came within a hundred miles of—and all the world would be different.

To my relief, our transport was a deep-hulled vessel, and while it still tossed about atop the seas, it was a far less violent voyage than aboard our raft the prior week. At an ideal tide, we departed with neither celebration nor well-wishing, and instead took residence in the ship's lower decks for the next several days. The journey was little to be desired, but it did afford an opportunity for further rest, albeit one tainted by nausea.

Our voyage required a further week: to traverse the Adriatic, split the channel between Messana and Rhegium, and turn northward past Neapolis and toward Rome. Near Brundisium, we spotted a lone Imperial dromon, yet the warship was far swifter than our cog and cut the seas in a similar direction as ours. Our ship's captain disembarked briefly in Syracuse to deposit goods from Dyrrachium, yet elsewise we battled the waves along the Italian coastline. As we neared Ostia, however, the ship's captain summoned me abovedeck.

"Can't land here," he grumbled. "Need to turn back."

"Why?!" I demanded. "Rome is just a few miles distant. Is there no open berth in port?"

The captain shook his head and beckoned me to follow him to the ship's bow. As he edged to the ship's closest point to shore, he pointed into the distance, where the glint of iron reflected in the dull sun.

"Weapons," he explained. "Nothing throws light like iron weapons. And if you look closely enough, those are Ostrogoth banners. If my eyes don't deceive me, Ostia will be crawling with Goth agents. Our ship could be seized, and you'd be captured."

Squinting, I discerned the colors of the Gothic king. My hand quivering, I scanned the horizon, finding a distant trail of men and weapons around the hillside, perilously close to Rome. At last, the Goths deigned to attack, and at the worst possible moment that Belisarius could have asked for.

"But I—we—need to disembark!" I insisted. "If not at Ostia, then where?"

The captain did not disguise his exasperation. "If you insist upon killing yourself, we can retreat south a few miles toward Antium. You can find a horse there, but you'll have to ride thirty miles to Rome. And pray your fortunes don't land you at the end of a Gothic spearhead."

"Done," I said. "Make it happen, and you will have my thanks and a draft for a handsome payment from Constantinople."

Though close by sea lanes, Antium and Ostia were more distant on land, separated by hilly terrain that made Antium's more distant port less favored for those seeking entry to Rome. As such, the port was small, nothing compared to the hive of piers at Ostia, yet there was little competition for a berth. Neither was there any competition for the few horses available for trade, allowing me to procure four mounts of old yet sturdy stock with silver gifted from Dyrrachium's treasury. The owner, a balding man with mottled skin that hung loose about his frame, seemed pleased to be relieved of the burden.

"There's no fodder nearby," he said, counting the silver coins as he shuddered against a sudden gale. "And if I take the horses inland, they'll get stolen by some Greek or Goth. Better sell them now while they still have value."

"The Emperor's men would not steal from you," I assured him. "The Goths, though…"

The tradesman shook his head vigorously. "I've seen war. Morality falls away like mites off your head in a steaming bath. And the hills are teeming with Gothic spearmen anyway. Best hope to be mistaken for their kinsmen if you're planning a journey, then. Your mounts will not fail you, but they won't move quickly."

With only two days' rations each, we did not tarry. Somehow, Latium had grown colder than what I remembered. Darker. Devoid of life and all signs of it, save the remnants of the dead Western Empire in its roads and decaying buildings. Shivering, we rode through a frigid sludge that molded even along the dressed stones toward Rome, silently praying that the frost would not steal a toe or a foot as grimy spray coated boots that hung on either side of our mounts. Numbness pervaded both night and the cruelly insufficient day, and my mind began to wander after a full day's march from Antium. That bloody eye blurred in my vision, appearing more the baleful gaze of a man than a dying sun.

"The Dark Rider," I whispered.

"Who?" Xerxes chattered.

My mind worked slowly. "Nothing," I replied after a few moments. "Just wild thoughts."

"Silence, then," Xerxes grunted. "I've considered cutting you open and using your blood to warm me up. It's disgusting, but I swear it'll work."

The Via Appia led from Antium toward Rome's southern gates, and while we again followed that fabled road in the first few miles from Antium's diminutive gates, Sembrouthes insisted that we keep to the hills after only an hour. It was not a terrible burden, for the snow in that area were no serious hindrance to our mounts, yet it did add additional time to our march. Nor did we dare continue in darkness, and instead made camp with less than ten miles remaining to Rome's southern gates.

Our slumber was interrupted not by the rising sun but due to a great rumbling from the east. One unfamiliar with the noise might assume it came from storm clouds and distant lightning. For me, however, it was too familiar: the sounds of an army on the march.

"At least a thousand, by that much noise," I reckoned, packing our tent.

"More," Xerxes said, "for that much sound to travel through the hills. I would guess three or four times as much."

We dared not scout the enemy, for Antium's horse monger was no liar—our mounts could not carry a canter for more than a few minutes, and stubbornly ignored any crop to their haunches. I ordered the others silent as we proceeded, careful to avoid eyeshot of the Via Appia.

The noise, creaking and rumbling, grew ever more sonorous as we trotted our final miles to Roman gates. Xerxes' initial assessment, if anything, was likely an underestimate—only Kazrig's horde, or perhaps the Persians at Dara, had sounded so fearsome for so long. Every step I took was riddled with fear, my fists clutching tight around the reins, intimately aware that there was nothing I could do if we were confronted by Gothic outriders. All we could do was press north and pray.

Until Rome's walls came within notice. My first reaction was a rush of relief, signaling the end of a journey that I would soon trade for comforts, allowing me to place the slaughter of thousands of Thracians far from my thoughts. As I quickened my pace, however, I again witnessed the glint of iron and traces of embroidered cloth that were the Gothic royal banners, streaming in the distance along Rome's eastern gates.

"We need to hurry," I whispered, gesturing toward the Gothic force. "The city is being surrounded."

"Another siege," Uliaris griped. "This time, a city that's impossible to defend with thirty thousand men, let alone a sixth of those numbers."

"Complain later," I hissed, rubbing stiff fingers against my chest.

As we reached the final mile of the Via Appia, a Gothic horn blared to the northeast. I paid it little heed; it seemed little more than a summons to those forces already assembled. By then, there was nothing we could do but push forward and hope that God would favor our steps. As we drew within five hundred paces from the Appian Gate, it appeared that Rome would open us to a safe, if taxing, arrival.

Except the Goths were not prepared to allow me to flee so easily. The Gothic horn blared again—and this time, it was not muffled from the protection of a nearby hill. I looked to the east, where a Gothic banner rose against the skyline, followed by no fewer than fifty Gothic horsemen.

"Rush!" I yelled. "They're coming!"

They were only a few hundred paces behind. Though few Goths were any kind of horsemen, and those who did ride paled against the centaur-like instincts of the Huns or the Heruli, these Gothic hunters galloped atop sturdy beasts that far outstripped our own. Their armor, a carapace of mail and leather, signified a wealthy detachment of the Ostrogoths' veteran warriors, and complemented the crisp line that they maintained even while charging at speed.

Next to me, Uliaris glanced backward, his breath seizing. "Faster! We're not going to make it!"

"Open the gates!" I barked in Latin, praying that a Roman might hear me, then repeated the order in Greek. "Open the gates! It's Tribune Varus! Open the gates!"

I dug my boots into the haunches of my mount, and he turned his head backward, nipping at my thigh. His pace quickened, but to little more than a lazy canter. I fared better than Xerxes, however, whose horse appeared lamed from the two days of exertion.

"Leave me!" Xerxes called to us.

I looked ahead once again. "Open the gates!!" I yelled. "Now!!"

We had just over a hundred paces to go, with our pursuers a bit more than two hundred behind us. If we abandoned Xerxes, and the defenders obeyed my command, three of us would likely reach safety. By then, Xerxes had stopped urging his horse forward and instead drew his borrowed sword, yelling aimlessly at the approaching Goths.

At that moment, the Appian Gate creaked open, the clanking of chains pulling the immense barrier of wood and iron up from its moorings. Freedom was at hand.

But I could not abandon Xerxes. "Dismount!" I yelled.

"Fool!" Sembrouthes shouted back at me. "What are you playing at?"

"We go together!" I replied. "Dismount and run for the gates!"

"Barking madness!!" But Sembrouthes obeyed, as did Uliaris.

"Run!" I cried. "*Hard!*"

Xerxes soon followed, and we abandoned our horses to the mercy of the Goths. Slowly, we closed the distance to the gate, moving my legs as quickly as they would go. Only once did I steal another glance at the enemy, finding them a mere hundred paces behind. We would not make Rome in time—just a stone's throw from safety.

"Form a line!" I yelled.

"God damn it!" Sembrouthes roared.

We turned, and with no shields, no protective barrier of any sort, drew our swords in the most pathetic wall of men that had ever defended the Eternal City.

"Fuck!" Uliaris groaned. "Oh fucking hell."

"You should have left me," Xerxes barked.

"Hold firm!" I yelled, ignoring the others.

The Goths were less than fifty paces distant when a yell rang out behind me. Distracted as I was, I did not recognize its provenance, but instinctively obeyed all the same.

"Down!" it yelled. "Get down!"

"Down!!" I echoed, dropping to the grass.

Above us, dozens of arrows sailed through the air where our bodies once stood. Soon after that volley came another, and another, a stream of flying death. Many arrows sailed short or fully past the Gothic riders, but several connected with horse or warrior, and eventually sent a dozen men sprawling to the ground not ten paces from where we lay. Germanic voices, heavy with fear, shouted orders that sent the rest of the Gothic line retreating to safety, leaving behind their wounded and dismounted brethren.

Still, I lay prone in the half-frozen muck, watching as thirty Hunnic riders trotted around us and toward the fallen Goths. Several Huns slipped from the saddle and onto the ground, stabbing unresponsive Goths in the neck or shooting arrows at those with shattered legs or bolt-riddled chests that dared to resist. All Goths still present were dead in heartbeats.

A pair of hands lifted me to my feet before arms wrapped me in a crushing embrace. "I've never been so happy to see you, you stubborn ox."

At last identifying Samur, I returned the gesture. "You saved my life. I thought I'd be ridden down."

"Not the first time, either," he joked, giggling with manic glee. "We heard you died with Mundus! But here you are!"

"I'll explain later," I said. "Take the others to the Domus Augustana, and me to Belisarius. I need to understand what's going on."

Samur nodded. "Nothing good. Our outlying forts were overrun, and Belisarius himself was almost captured. He arrived back in Rome just a few hours before you."

"God, what a mess," I groaned. "And Mariya, did she…"

Samur grimaced. "Shut herself away. She thinks you're dead, too. Will hardly speak with anyone, even the servants."

My heart pounded for Mariya, who had suffered far too much in the past year. "I'll make things right. As soon as I see Belisarius, I'll head for home."

Recovering our mounts, we trotted into Rome and toward the city's northern gates. After Uliaris, Xerxes, and Sembrouthes parted from us, Samur guided me to Belisarius' command quarters along the Pincian Hill. In my time approaching Rome's northern gates, as well as on the Via Flaminia, I still had only acquired a small taste of what the Goths had brought to contest Belisarius' army.

From Samur, I learned that a handful of Goths had spread tales of the Feast of Salona, reaching Rome even before the besieging Gothic force. Yet those tales, as could be expected, were tainted with rumor and ridiculousness, insisting that Mundus betrayed his allies at a feast. Brave Indulf, and the valiant Pannonians, the tales said, overcame Mundus' treachery, slaying not only Mundus, myself, and other senior officers, but every man and beast assigned to the Thracian Army.

"Ludicrous, all of it," I said. "Indulf poisoned most of the army, then overpowered the Thracians when all were disarmed."

Samur raised his hands in deference. "I know, although none of it makes sense. Why would Indulf do this?"

I had no answer. All I could do was pray that Belisarius understood more of our current predicament and had a plan to prevent battle. After all, Salona was only a Roman loss due to treachery—the Roman Army remained undefeated in the field, while the Goths ran like sheep from any serious confrontation. As I climbed the Pincian Hill, I assumed that the Gothic positions around Rome were just another feint, or some strategy to devise peace between Justinian and Theodahad.

Now, any child could tell you that I was sorely incorrect. But not, however, due to anything we could have foreseen.

Belisarius was not in a closed building, but instead atop the walls near the Pincian Gate. Each of the four larger northern gates swarmed with Romans, many bearing Belisarius' sigil as a member of his bucellarii, others the Imperial Chi-Rho or some other warlord or foederati; I even spotted several detachments of Herulians wielding my ouroboros. Not since Aetius' great stand against Atilla had Rome amassed such a motley array of warriors, melding clashing fighting styles and famed swordsmen under the banner of a single strategos.

As I ascended the stairs of the Aurelian Walls, I believed our roster of heroes would be sufficient, for even if the Goths held greater numbers, who could stand victorious against us, the men who had done so much?

One glance from atop the walls, and all bravado melted away like spent wax. Thousands, tens of thousands, swarming about in a chaotic web, carving trenches and erecting palisades opposite Rome's stone walls. As far as I could see, the Goths stretched from the distant eastern gates to the Tiber River, with smaller detachments lurking on the river's western bank. They had not brought an army to Rome. Instead, they'd arrived with a horde, and there was none other than us to resist them.

It was Belisarius, however, who truly rendered the deathblow to any hopes of a peaceful resolution. His face and arms were caked in mud and gore, while his fingers teased painfully at a shallow cut along his temple. Upon first sighting us, he trotted forward and embraced me with as much desperate strength as Samur had.

Though the gesture was unusual amongst men outside of kinship, I returned it all the same.

Belisarius pulled back. "I thought you were dead..."

"I nearly was, Lord," I said. "They betrayed Mundus—"

"I know. Indulf and Optaris led a force of Goths into Ravenna after leaving Rome. Of the Goth foederati Indulf left in Rome, all have been sent to Constantinople. Theodahad is dead by their hand, from what I've just learned. Another man, a chieftain named Witiges, sits upon the Gothic throne, and any civil strife amongst the Goths has ceased."

"Theodahad is dead," I echoed. Somehow, this made Indulf's betrayal all the more frustrating and bile inducing.

Belisarius nodded, sweat pouring from his brow. "And now we're alone, in a city that we dare not abandon, against the might of an entire tribe."

As he spoke, more Goths poured in from the north. They seemed endless, like a massive hive of ants all darting toward a would-be meal.

It was Belisarius' most desperate trial yet. No retreat, no surrender, and nowhere near home. How I prayed for deliverance as I stood atop the Aurelian Walls. If God heard me, all He did was laugh. For the worst was yet to come.

THE SIEGE OF ROME

Belisarius insisted that I take rest upon my first day returned to Rome, offering what little he could spare to nourish my tired body. Brooking no resistance, he escorted me back to the Domus Augustana, where we parted with a whisper of warning.

"Our enemies are not only those outside the walls," he said, leaning close to my ear. "Most in the city appear loyal for now, but some never left Gothic loyalties. My men tell me Pope Silverius is chief among them."

Rumors had surrounded Silverius' accession, and I held my own suspicions of the man's character, though hearing them reflected by Belisarius added grave weight to the accusation. "You're certain?"

"Keep quiet, but keep vigilant," Belisarius cautioned. "Tarmutus is our loyal man in the city watch, but I cannot trust the others for now. Whoever's loyalty you can commend without reservation—make a list of those men and submit it to me. The walls are too long, and our officers too few, to safely cover everything. All we can do is patrol ceaselessly, watching for attack or another betrayal."

The Domus, though massive and assigned to the joint households of Belisarius and myself, felt cavernous and empty. Looming columns and vast cloisters made the onetime domicile of the Western Emperor's family seem like the dwelling of giants, for it was a space that could have fit many hundreds in comfort and luxury. Dressed in marble and leafed in gold, it was as much a gaudy display of power as it was a marvel of architecture, and though I had once resided in the Imperial Palace in Constantinople, I felt unease in such surroundings.

Not that the Domus was vacant—although the first inhabitant I met approached me upon four legs, lunging at my ankles with all her weight.

"Haeva, it's just me!" I laughed, scratching behind her ears as she rose atop her hind legs, sniffing toward my face. "You've become enormous!"

"Varus!!" This from Cephalas, sprinting close behind. "My God…"

I grinned. "I can't tell you how happy I am to be here. Everyone has arrived from Neapolis?"

"Y-yes," he stumbled. "Is it true about Mundus?"

My face hardened as I turned my gaze to the mosaic floor. "Indulf stabbed him during a feast celebrating the Thracians' victory near Salona. I can still see the blade piercing his rib cage when I close my eyes."

"Bastards," he rumbled. "I will snap Indulf's neck with my good arm, even if it kills me."

Suddenly weary, I sought to be reunited with the others, with hopes I might tell my tale once to everyone rather than repeating the same story of treachery and massacre a hundred times. "Take me to the others. You will know everything of my journey, I promise."

Passing through two atria, several immense corridors, and a feasting hall that likely had once served two to three thousand with ease, Cephalas escorted me into the private rooms that had been allocated to my household. Haeva tugged hard against her leash as she heard Zenobia's voice.

"I can't believe how much Haeva's grown!" I unhooked the leather strap and handed it to Cephalas, allowing the dog to sprint off and lead me the final distance to my family.

"She'll be ready for war duties soon enough," he replied. "We've spent every day with her, me and Agathias. You won't be disappointed."

Our private residences encompassed two levels, including a

kitchen, a fuller's laundry, a solarium, two private bathhouses—one for men, one for women—a mosaic-decorated impluvium with a surrounding garden, and quarters for servants and nobles alike.

The centerpiece, however, was a hall that rose to the full height of the Domus, with an arched ceiling that flooded the expansive space with light. In centuries past, the hall had seen private gatherings and celebrations while doubling as the center of organization for daily life. It was here that I discovered many of my household, running about to fulfill tasks or idling about on the benches. I ignored them all, rushing through in search of my wife. Some gaped and others whispered, for I must have appeared a terrible sight, thin from overexertion and mottled from long days pulling an oar in a shallow boat. Running soon took its toll, and though my chest burned from want of air, I searched for her. Mariya, who had stolen my heart the instant our fates collided, so long ago.

She spotted me moments later, sitting along a bench at the edge of the hall. Wrapped in black robes, Mariya, too, seemed thinner, though no less lovely than I remembered. Gasping, she abandoned her conversation with Jamila, hitched up her gown, and sprinted toward me. She struck with such force that I fell back two paces, squeezing her arms around my neck as she jumped to reach my height. Such a display grossly violated decorum in the audience of others, but she did not care, and neither did I.

"Belisarius told me that you had been killed!" she wailed, in between covering my face with kisses.

At last, she paused, squeezed me one last time, and allowed her feet to fall back to the ground. Then she buried her face into my chest, sobbing for a few heartbeats, until she straightened to meet my gaze. And in one swift movement, she slapped me with such a stinging blow that I struggled to breathe—my senses fogged not just by the strike but also from the sudden barks from Haeva as she sensed Mariya's distress.

With my wife's face so blotched and wet with tears, and my own cheek still smarting, my thoughts turned to Rosamund and the

Colosseum. *Had someone seen?* I wondered for the thousandth time. No—unlikely, I reasoned, for the building had been shuttered and no light could have identified me should an onlooker gain entry.

Or worse, had Rosamund confessed? But that, too, was highly unlikely, as Rosamund prized confidence and loyalty above all things, as proven by her years of service to me. To be sure, I had no desire to add additional sadness to my life after all I had witnessed at Salona, preferring to keep the secret of Rosamund's kiss and the sanctity of a peaceful household. Still, as Mariya's face drained of color, doubt slithered through my mind, and I could only assume some awful confrontation was moments away.

"I thought I was a widow, and your children without a father!" Mariya wept. Behind her, I caught sight of Rosamund, who merely nodded to me. She tucked Alexander into her hip and took Zenobia by the hand, both of whom chattered at their Gepid servant. Soon thereafter, Rosamund guided the children to Jamila, and all departed to grant me privacy with my wife. Though Mariya and I had survived destruction before, she had never appeared so distraught.

"Such a foolish risk! I thought you were dead, Varus!!"

"I never expected danger, Mariya," I replied. "You have my word."

She slapped me again, and then pressed her body against mine. Her chest shuddered against my stomach, her arms shuddering as jeweled fingers dug into my arms. Wrapping my arms about her waist, I squeezed, hoping that the moment would never end.

"Don't leave me in this place alone."

"Never," I promised. "Even if the world truly is ending."

Her pitch-black garb cast a haunted pallor over Mariya's face, while her face remained absent any paints and powders. That revelation brought renewed guilt, not only for my secret with Rosamund but also that Salona's butchery had nearly left me a forgotten corpse and Mariya ruined. Doubtless, Theodora or Belisarius would have provided some aid, but equally sure was that Mariya's expenses— inherited from me—would soon surpass even the generosity of my wealthiest friends. Now, with Cassiodorus milking Justin's estate in Pella for its bounty, I could only count upon my plunder in Membresa for another year. Just as with the humblest spearman in Rome's army, I was growing desperate for wealth. Unfortunately, a siege offered little such opportunity and might yet extract my health or life and leave my household as vulnerable as if I'd died at Salona.

"Everything will be fine now that we're together," I assured her. "You're safe, behind huge walls and an entire Imperial Army."

"You're lying." Mariya sobbed. "You were always a terrible liar."

I had no response, for she was right. She had not laid eyes upon the Gothic horde, and had no need to. Worse, this present situation was a possibility that I, at some level, always knew could happen, or even likely *would* happen—eventually, Witiges would threaten our army's stronghold and every civilian that clung to our banners.

Rather than dwell upon an inevitable fate of suffering, Mariya and I held one another, enjoying what precious little time Belisarius had bade me rest and return to fitness. Mariya led me to our private quarters, where we shared a simple meal of fruit and cheese and coupled with an urgency I had not experienced since the first night of the great riots. Perhaps two hours later, she guided me through the Domus, trailed by an eager Haeva, where I answered the many questions asked of me of the Feast of Salona.

Elsewise, I was pleased to learn that the Domus' daily life mirrored what Mariya had organized in Pella, Constantinople, or Syracuse. Rosamund executed Mariya's will, Ghassanid servants attended the care of Mariya and our children, and a dozen Aksumites guarded the vast building. In my absence, Cephalas and Shimon had paid a blacksmith to repair my armor and hone my weapons, while Agathias shadowed Rosamund in her healing arts and received all missives submitted for my review. The burgeoning size of my household, beyond what I could remember, including an untold number of cooks, candle men, fullers, and servants, only added to my anxiety, although I allowed none other than Mariya to know the state of my dwindling fortune.

Many demanded my attentions before I was to return to Belisarius' side. Zenobia was most urgent, desirous that I witness all the exercises taught to her by Wazeba in Sembrouthes' absence. Along with her classmates, her tutelage had continued uninterrupted from Syracuse to Neapolis, and now here, leaving my daughter with plenty of bruises wreathing her body.

"Wazeba let me wrestle Cours, and I almost beat him!" Zenobia beamed proudly, rolling up her sleeve to show a pronounced dark mark on her shoulder. "Wazeba says that I'll be as good as you when I'm older! Tiberius too!"

Though the injuries concerned me, and I never embraced Zenobia's training like Mariya did, I could not help but grin. "Then I'll be watching for you, anaticula. Perhaps I'll study your moves before you challenge me."

Her little arms reached out to shove me, although she brightened at my interest. "Do you think Alexander will train too? And Bakuris?"

"In a year or two, he will start," I said. "Just as Samur and I did when we were little."

Rosamund interrupted my moment with Zenobia, offering a nod in greeting. "I knew you were not dead, for the gods have need of you yet," she said. "But I grieved for Mundus. He was one of the few Roman commanders who was decent to me. He did not deserve his end."

"No, he didn't," I answered, motioning for Zenobia to return to the other children.

Stepping closer, Rosamund pecked my cheek. "I am grateful you've returned, regardless of my faith."

The skin burned where her lips grazed my face. Speaking in careful Heruli, I dared to raise my fears. "Rosamund, did you tell anyone of our time in the Colosseum?"

She laughed. "I'm not a fool. And there isn't anything to tell."

Sighing, my chest lightened. "Thank you, Rosamund. I missed you in Dalmatia."

"And I you." She smiled and gripped my hand for a heartbeat.

"Although I don't believe you are much safer here. I will take you to Agathias, who can explain."

We paced to the servants' quarters, where I found the private rooms of a more honored household retainer equipped with candles, a worktable, and even a small collection of stitched books. Agathias greeted me with an enthusiastic yelp. "I knew you weren't dead, Lord!"

"Quiet, you." Rosamund chuckled. "You sobbed like a babe when word of Salona reached us."

Agathias reddened, but Rosamund graciously continued before he could express his gratitude. "Show us Theodora's message," she prompted.

As Rosamund had little skill and no patience for letters, Agathias filled that role for her. Nevertheless, he seemed to have little appetite to repeat this missive from the Empress, which had arrived not long after my departure from Rome. Reading aloud, he skipped over the usual pleasantries and began right at Theodora's assessment of the ongoing conflicts.

"My husband thanks you for pacifying Carthage and will be deploying Germanus with two thousand Isaurian spearmen to garrison local towns. However, the Emperor is displeased that his agent, Solomon, was deprived of office. With his wife and child, Solomon will return as prefect while Germanus leads the army against Stotzas, Sergius, and the Mauri. Of course, you understand the sensitivities of Sergius' participation in the local uprising."

"Nothing I didn't already know, although it's unfortunate," I remarked. "Anything beyond Carthage?"

Rosamund clicked her tongue. "Patience, Varus. Agathias, please continue."

At this, Agathias' tone become more somber. *"The initial reports from Aksum and the Himyar indicate that the plague has spread slowly up the Nile River. Narses' spies have reported the presence of disease in Persian-held lands of Arabia. While it seems little different from the plagues of past centuries, its arrival during a time of famine is most concerning. If you see signs of disease in Italy, send me news at once."*

"Hmm." I considered this. "Theodora mentioned this new plague after we returned from Septem. Nothing we can do, though, except pray that it steers away from Roman lands."

Rosamund rolled her eyes. "Finish, Agathias."

"The Emperor has heard Belisarius' request for additional forces. Narses is building a separate reserve force, yet Justinian is disinclined to send reinforcements to Italy while Carthage and our border along the Ister are under threat. If Belisarius is of civil mind, he should be happy to know that Antonina is one of his few supporters in court and has actively recruited volunteers willing to join you in Rome. Whether the captains will risk the seas and famine, I am less optimistic. Take care of yourself, Varus, for I believe the coming year will be a challenging one."

"No reinforcements," I muttered. "They must change their thoughts here, given what we face."

"You know as well as I that this will not be," Rosamund replied. "As always, we are on our own."

Rome could not be held with so few. Of that, I was certain, though I dared not show my despair outwardly. Instead, I spent the remainder of my day of rest sharing information with Petrus and Liberius, enjoying the company of my friends and family, and seeking what fleeting sleep I could. By dawn, officers arrived at the Domus to escort me to the walls, allowing time only to don my weapons and armor. Before returning to the Pincian Hill, I stole kisses from both of my children, tousled Tiberius' hair, and accepted a final kiss from Mariya. With me followed Sembrouthes and Shimon, yet others were readied in the event that orders would command the army to activity. Liberius, however, could not help but join our foray, although he seemed decidedly less carefree than usual.

"The last time the Goths attacked Rome was the beginning of the end for the Empire," Liberius mused. "A damned shame that Mundus isn't alive to provide rescue. He was a simple man, but a good one. That is as rare as emeralds these days."

Again, I found Belisarius atop the walls. Leaving Shimon and

Sembrouthes at the Pincian Gate, Liberius and I climbed to the summit, with Liberius leaping from one stone to the next far quicker than I or any other younger man. As before, the enormity of the Gothic army stunned me, as their chaos had seemed to swell and take a more organized form.

"They've been arriving all night," Belisarius said, greeting both of us. "From what we can tell, they're split into camps along the main roads, just out of range of our bows and engines."

I nodded, glancing at the complex network of trenches facing our walls. "How many do you suspect?"

"Fifty thousand?" Belisarius' guess made the number seem insignificant. "Perhaps half slaves or camp followers. But more still come from the north, including a chained procession of Roman slaves hauling ballistae from the Via Flaminia."

"Fools," Liberius grunted. "They'll never be able to do much more than lob bolts blindly over the walls. Not if they don't want to risk coming into the range of Ascum's men."

Belisarius nodded without turning his gaze from where a team of Goths lashed together logs to create a wooden wall. "They also have at least two dozen siege rams and a handful of moving towers I've only ever heard of in Alexander's campaigns," he added. "They're massive, and can allow a full banda to climb in safety to the tops of the walls within a couple of minutes."

And so they were. Great lumbering towers atop massive wheels, requiring eight oxen to drag even a short distance. In the Gothic camp opposite the Pincian Gate, three of the towers wheeled about, reaching well above the height of the Aurelian Walls. No archer, nor even a ballista, could easily pierce the hefty layers of interlocking wooden planks.

"At least winter will be over in a few weeks," I offered.

Belisarius sighed. "That won't change our predicament in the immediate term. We have food, but rations are scarce, and I cannot allot more than a half day's portion for any man or woman."

Gazing wide-eyed upon the Gothic armies, Liberius spoke at last.

"I will write letters to the Emperor. If Basilius were alive, he would solve this predicament for us. Alas, I'm fast running out of friends."

"You can try," I told him, not mentioning Theodora's discouraging letter. "But what should we do now?"

Belisarius turned back to the Goths, mouthing inaudible numbers as he counted new arrivals along the Via Flaminia. As I looked closer, the camp followers, slaves, and servants became more apparent: boys running messages between camps, bronze-collared slaves cooking meals over an open bonfire. The only advantage in our enemy's massive number was that they, like us, must have been suffering from a shortage of food—although, judging by how much meat and bread I could see shared amongst the smaller fires of spearmen, I felt less certain that it troubled them to the same degree. Belisarius, however, had seen enough.

"We go and speak to them," he concluded. "Let's see if there's something we can learn from our guests."

It was the last suggestion I expected Belisarius to offer. "Lord?"

"Why not?" Liberius beamed. "At least we can get a sense of their condition. I had thought this siege would be dull, but it seems a bit of cultural exchange is in order."

Within moments, we descended from the walls, and Belisarius ordered our gate opened. On borrowed horses, we three clopped through the narrow crack, trailed by a dozen bucellarii, who hoisted their shields high in the air to signal a desire to talk rather than to fight. We paused not far from the Pincian Gate, for none of us knew where the enemy commander might reside, and shouted a greeting to the cautious Goths.

With an interpreter at his back, Belisarius bellowed in Latin. "I am Flavius Belisarius, commander of the armies of Rome. Who among you has the right to speak with me?"

It was bold, impetuous even, quite unlike Belisarius' normal character. Yet, in that moment, he showed nothing but a grim face of resentment. It was a gaze that any Roman general, back to the time of Romulus, might have adopted against a disdainful enemy.

A hum resounded amongst the Gothic ranks. At first, none came forth to confront our force. Within a few minutes, however, as Gothic soldiers darted amongst their camp, a contingent of a half dozen Gothic warriors emerged. All were bedecked in mail and scales that would have been welcomed by any komes or tribune, with their leader covered in gold ornament about his neck, arms, and even a tiny golden hoop about his nose. However, it was the chest armor that commanded attention, decorated in silver inlay of various creatures from the distant east. It was he who hailed us, curiously offering a customary Roman salute as he halted five paces off, while eyeing Belisarius' archers with a casual indifference.

"I am Witiges, King of the Ostrogoths," he began, his Latin flawless. "And you occupy lands that are mine. I yield a week for you to collect your women and belongings and depart for Greece. After that, you will all die."

I find no dishonor in saying that Witiges was a handsome man. The wiry beard that spread from his chin had been flattened by carefully applied grease, while the unmarked face it framed gave this new Gothic king the look of a specter more than a grubby warrior. Next to most Romans, their skin marred by disease and malnourishment, Witiges' tidy appearance might have been welcomed as a clerk in Justinian's staff, for aside from the unctuous beard, his features were soft—quite like Procopius, in fact. Of lean build and above average height, Witiges likely had never struggled in the shield wall or worked the land with his hands, yet he possessed a confident ferocity in his gaze that made me consider him an equal nonetheless.

Belisarius laughed. "Bold talk from a king whose throne is stained in blood. What happened to Theodahad, exactly?"

Witiges clasped hands at his chest, as if grasping at his heart. "Alas, Theodahad shamed all the Goths. I weep for him, but I do not mourn him."

Belisarius then nodded at me, that I should speak. "Lord King," I began, "I was among the few survivors at Salona, and I witnessed how your Pannonians treated their guests under Indulf's guidance.

Why should we trust anything you say, or even that you indeed are a king?"

Witiges' head jerked, facing me, as if he had not realized I was present. "What is your name, friend?"

"Varus of the Herulians, tribune of the Roman Empire." This proud answer sparked a flicker of recognition from Witiges. "Rome belongs to Romans, regardless of however many boys you dress up in mail and cavort about our walls. If you do not leave our city in peace, your reign as king will be of a similar end as its previous occupant."

No Goths were moved by this. Instead, Witiges mimicked Belisarius' earlier laughter, shaking his head as if I had said something both tragic and utterly foolish.

"For everything, there is a beginning and an end," Witiges said, accenting each Latin syllable with a lilt of patrician education. He nodded first to Belisarius, and then to Liberius. "Birth and death, sunrise and sunset." Turning to me, he added, "The origin of an empire and its inglorious destruction."

I did not expect a Goth to speak in grandiose terms, and admittedly was puzzled with how to respond to Witiges' threats. "And you claim to be the harbinger of Rome's end? Better men than you have tried."

"Not Rome's end, my fellow traveling warrior," Witiges chided me. "Rome died six decades ago, and only the old men remember its waning days. No, I merely seek to prevent the end of us all."

The declaration, so boastful in its pronouncement, confused me. "So, you're mad, then?"

"Maybe." Witiges shrugged. "But not stupid. There are more deaths than babes with each passing year. Crops die and are not replanted. My kinsmen build thatched huts where marble circuses once stood, and house their cattle in fora once home to theater and education. You regret the passage of Rome, my friend. I weep for the passage of us all. The portents all direct us to that outcome, sadly."

"Then go north and correct those shortcomings." It had come time, it seemed, for Liberius to add his voice. "The Romans abandoned their Gothic overlords with such complete joy that they will never accept your dominion again. So leave while your army is intact, and husband what lands remain to you. As my pupil Varus explained"— he nodded to me—"the Empire has withstood the great and the terrible before, and shall do so again."

"A terrible waste!" Witiges exclaimed. "But you shall have your wish, my friends. But know this—what you see here is but a tiny portion of the strength available to me. More will come—oh yes— and they will all dance and bay for your demise. Perhaps I shall be merciful, but then again, perhaps not."

Indifferent, uninterested, Witiges turned, and he and his chieftains departed from our presence. As he walked away from us, the Gothic king threw a backward salute, his extended arm jutting backward and toward the heavens. No Goths came to contest our presence outside the city walls, nor indeed did any seem to be preparing for an imminent fight. And so we returned to the city, attempting to make sense of who our enemy was.

"A madman," I put forth. "But a well-educated one."

"As if such things are usually exclusive!" Liberius chided me. "But yes, Witiges is odd for a barbarian king. It might be a ruse, his demeanor... but somehow I doubt it."

At the open gate, Belisarius paused, stealing a final glimpse upon the Gothic army before passing back into Rome. "It seems that we are committed to fight in whatever manner the Goths decide, then," he said.

"For now," Liberius countered. "But you should still have learned something valuable, if the Gothic numbers did not cloud your eyes."

Belisarius shrugged. "Theodahad is dead, and the new king is more apt to fight?"

"You're better than that!" Liberius scolded. "Varus?"

"I was going to say the same thing as Belisarius," I admitted.

Liberius groaned. "So imperceptive, both of you. What we've learned, or at least should have, is that Witiges has no choice but to retake Rome. He's even present to oversee the fighting himself, where a king such as Theodoric would delegate the task to another.

And the longer we hold out against so desperate a foe, the weaker Witiges' position becomes. Especially with a horrendous harvest and the looming threat of a Frankish invasion to the north."

Liberius' words offered a glimmer of hope, but they came with a caveat that I could not easily dismiss. "Only if we hold out, that is," I pointed out. "All Witiges must do is seize a single gate, and Rome will fall."

"Then see that he does not," Liberius said simply. "That is what we have you warriors for."

The Goths did not attack that day. Nor the following day, nor indeed throughout that week or the one that followed. Instead, seven Gothic camps took shape amidst their army's efforts to build palisades and position rams and siege towers, all well beyond range of our missiles. I even spotted a half dozen ballistae being dragged to each of the forts east of the Tiber, their wheels rolled atop raised platforms that stood twice the height of a man.

"Idiots will get all their engineers killed." Ascum cackled at the sight. "Just wait until one of their ballistae recoils badly and rolls off that platform of theirs. Dead or screaming, everyone working there."

"Yes, but they still might kill plenty of us," I replied, "or smash our gates to splinters if we aren't careful."

Ascum pursed his lips and shrugged. "Maybe. I'm working with a few Roman architects and engineers, so perhaps I'll devise an adequate response. The Imperial libraries are stuffed with designs of weapons that would make even your dour heart sing, Varus."

Ascum was granted whatever resources he needed in his research, although I held little hope that anything he discovered would make a measurable difference against the brute force of tens of thousands of men simultaneously rushing our walls. Uneasy peace reigned for the moment, yet both defenders and besiegers worked day and night to better their own predicament.

For the Goths, this meant fortifying their separate positions and seizing lands and bridges surrounding Rome, including the port of Ostia and the Tiber's western bank. For our part, I could not help but notice the tantalizing fact that Rome's southern gates lacked an opposing Gothic settlement, and even appeared clear enough to seek aid from Neapolis, although any Roman scouting parties were quickly intercepted by roaming Gothic sentries. Meanwhile, Goth movement swelled as further reinforcements arrived from the north, including a man I could easily recognize even from a hundred paces away.

"Indulf," I muttered to Fulcaris, who now commanded the Praenestine Gate. Defined by shorter walls that nestled against the Caelian Hill, the area around the Praenestine Gate was known centuries prior as the Vivarium, housing the thousands of animals intended for display in the Colosseum.

"Bastard," Fulcaris muttered. "But who's that with him? Isn't that a Visigoth banner?"

Squinting, I spied a banner displaying a hawk with wings outstretched. This was an emblem well known to any on our expedition to Septem, and had nearly led to all our deaths. For it was the sigil of Theudis, king of the Visigoths and one of the most uncompromising men I have ever encountered.

"Yes, but Theudis is at war with the Franks," I replied, hoping that the banner was either a mistake or some trick. "And the Visigoths have no large fleet to transport an army."

Yet, trailing Indulf, multiple hawk banners flapped against the wind. Many of the Visigoths dangled leather leashes from their hands, guiding the war dogs from whom Haeva drew her bloodline. The men did not seem numerous—perhaps less than five hundred all told—but all were richly adorned and armed. Somehow, Witiges had brokered the use of veteran Visigoth soldiers, although I spied neither Theudesgel nor Agila amongst their ranks. Instead, at Indulf's side strode a younger lordling, bearing a thick black beard and limbs that stretched his cloth and mail alike, who scowled as he gestured toward our gate.

"At least there aren't too many of them," Fulcaris said. "Maybe the Visigoths and Ostrogoths will kill one another over something foolish."

"If only." With that, I excused myself to write a missive to Belisarius to inform him of the arrival of both Indulf and our new enemy.

While the Goths developed their camps and defenses, we Romans bolstered the Aurelian Walls with every technique and fortification I had gleaned from my experience at Septem. Belisarius denied me nothing that was in his power to procure, be it vast sheathes of wooden stakes, depots of boulders and arrows stacked within each Roman tower, or men to deepen and widen the ditches adjacent to the walls. Teams of archers guarded the ranks of diggers, sending warning shots to any Goth who ventured within a hundred and fifty paces. Amazingly, however, our progress went largely unhindered, a relief that nevertheless made our predicament feel all the more unsettling.

"If Witiges isn't trying to stop us from improving our defenses, it means he isn't concerned about them," Samur said to me privately. "And he isn't even the king we set out to fight, anyway! If Theodahad is dead, what cause for war do we have here?"

I, too, was frustrated that we would never confront the infamous and now-dead Gothic king that set all events in Italy into motion, but I forced a better answer. "We cannot surrender Rome after just taking it back," I replied. "Theodahad does not matter anymore."

"Foolishness," Samur muttered. "Listen, when things go badly, and they absolutely will, you and your family are coming with me. I'm not staying here to be massacred like Mundus."

I took several breaths to calm myself before responding. "If I survived a besiegement by Theudis, Belisarius could do so against an untested Gothic king. There will be no massacre."

Samur groaned. "God damn it, Varus! Look around! We can't even occupy every battlement without stretching our forces too thin. If Witiges realizes how weak we truly are, he'll rush the gates with everything he has and topple Belisarius by nightfall. Do you really want your wife and children to become Gothic slaves or worse?"

"Of course not," I snapped. "And if the city falls, we will act accordingly. But for now, the best option we have is to kill every Goth bastard that tries to scale the walls. Otherwise, we're stuck in Italy, hoping that some war party doesn't stumble onto us."

"Fucking Justinian," Samur mumbled. There was no need for a reply—this was a sentiment I had heard all too often, even as a member of the Emperor's excubitores.

Samur's views were not uncommon amongst Belisarius' army but were most sorely felt amongst the foederati. In my experience, it was those men of the foederati who were relied upon for the more desperate assignments in battle, yet they were rarely offered glory, let alone recognition, from the Imperial population. Belisarius attempted to address their disquiet by spending a portion of each day walking the walls and listening to each of the men's complaints and worries. He also paid each man an additional bonus of silver from his own holdings, and relaxed restrictions against visiting Rome's various popinae, provided that no malice be visited upon the local citizenry.

"If any man claims to not have been paid his wages, inform me at once," Belisarius instructed me. "I will pay them all myself, if there is no other option."

"That's generous, Lord," I replied, "but likely ruinous." I could not help but consider my own difficulties in still maintaining expenses for my household and much of the Herulian foederati.

"Better broke than dead." Belisarius chuckled. "Rations are already due to be limited throughout the siege. But if the men also lose their pay... well, honor alone won't keep many from shirking their orders. It is an expense I can cover, for a time."

Between maintaining morale and preparing the city, my days burgeoned with demands. Of Rome's eighteen working gates, I ordered masons to seal six, stacking bricks and mortar until the gate became useless to man or beast. It was hazardous, both in construction and as a finished structure, but while such fresh sections of wall had not yet withstood centuries of weather and abuse, they offered a modicum of defense, or at least encouraged the Goths to seek entry into the city elsewhere.

As each day brought further preparation for defending against assault, my confidence improved, only to taper somewhat from the still-increasing quantity of Goths. With Procopius' aid, we tallied all manner of weapons and shields stacked at various points around the city, as well as recruited members of the Roman citizenry to serve as fire teams. They would see no fighting, but instead be assigned in groups of twenty men and boys to a gate, ready to carry water from a nearby well should Witiges launch flaming arrows or ballistae bolts over the walls.

Most important were assignments to each gate. Belisarius' bucellarii—mostly dismounted cataphracts and Cappadocian veterans—occupied the Flaminian and Pincian Gates at the northernmost points of the city. Likewise, Bessas commanded a fledgling force of the remaining cataphracts and Cappadocians along the Via Tecta—including the Aelian and Cornelian Gates opposite the freshly fortified Tomb of Hadrian and the Campus Neronis. Tarmutus' guardsmen, less adept in combat than Belisarius' army, were granted positions along the Via Aurelia, protecting the city's less-vulnerable western flank along the Janiculum Hill.

To the northeast, Samur and the Hunnic warlords were granted control of both the Salarian and Nomentana Gates, using the steep embankments and taller stretch of walls to maximize the effect of Hunnic bowmen. Lastly, to the east, the Herulians were assigned the Vivarium, and Gunderic's Vandals were granted quarters along the Tiburtine Gate, all of which fell under the nominal control of Perenus. At the southern gates, we mingled our wounded Cappadocian veterans with a larger force of Tarmutus' volunteers, praying that this particular section would not be tried in battle. Though Gothic raiders galloped along the southern horizon, Witiges did not form further Gothic forts along the Asinarian and Appian roads, providing perhaps the only reprieve we Romans would enjoy.

"Southern gates are too isolated," Perenus offered in our second week of the bloodless siege. "We could sally out with horse archers and kill scores before Witiges could mount a response. Do that, and even with all his numbers, Witiges would need twice as many men to safely garrison the Appian Way."

I prayed he was correct. I found myself frequently at prayer in those first weeks, far more than at other periods in my life. For so many of the problems I faced, all I could do was pray and hope that somehow, we might hold out until Justinian could send reinforcements. Regardless of his jealousies, the Emperor, I was convinced, would have no choice but to send aid once he heard of our predicament and the looming threat that Belisarius' army might follow Mundus bloodily into the afterlife.

And still, the Goths did not press our activity. If anything, those first sixteen days took on a tedium that I had not expected but was nevertheless grateful for—and in this I was not alone. The youngest and most naïve of Belisarius' forces even shared in bawdy japes at the Goths' expense, believing their reluctance to commence violence a sign of cowardice. The other veterans and I, however, knew better. Of all the calamities one might encounter in the course of their lives, being the victim of a siege is unique in its suffering. No, Witiges would swarm to the Aurelian Walls—of this I was certain. My only curiosity was what the opening strike in their conquest of Rome would be.

When the Goths finally rose from their doldrums, however, it was not to storm our gates. Indeed, their attack did not even commence with any visible sign of aggression. Instead, our first tribulation in Rome came from inside the city walls, as our aqueducts ran dry.

At first, the disruption of one or two aqueducts was dismissible. By that point, Rome still possessed eleven water-bearing systems that drew its contents far from the interior of Latium, and occasional blockages or reductions in flow were commonplace. Yet two became four, and four became seven, and by the end of a single day, only two aqueducts remained in service, and at a trickle from their once-dependable flow at that.

The sudden loss of vital water prompted Belisarius to gather not only his officers, but also any trusted man who had experience in the city of Rome. Alongside Tarmutus and a collection of Romans from the city guard, he requested the presence of Liberius and Petrus.

"Rome has so many aqueducts because its population far outstrips what the Tiber can provide," Petrus explained. "Although it's not for need of fresh water to drink."

Ascum frowned. "Then what good are they?"

Petrus sighed. "The aqueducts give strength to the gristmills. While even poorer families can carry water from the river, no mill can safely reside along the Tiber's riverbank without damage from flooding."

"And no gristmills mean no bread," Liberius concluded. "Even Augustus suffered riots from a hungry mob. Give the Roman populace a month of hunger and they'll toss us all out in exchange for Witiges' embrace."

It was not an exaggeration; none present doubted the fury or the likelihood of a mob. A creeping dread consumed my thoughts as the situation, and our safety in Rome, appeared to slip beyond Belisarius' authority—even before Witiges had struck a single blow.

"There's no opportunity to restore water to the aqueducts?" I asked.

"Not unless you can dislodge Witiges," Petrus replied, sounding genuinely sad. "All the sources are beyond the walls, and the Gothic camps occupy the lines. Even if God granted you the safety to reclaim an aqueduct, the Goths have likely incurred enough damage that it would take a month to repair the lead and stones to carry water."

"We can't depend upon shipments of food, either," put in an equally grim Bessas. "Neapolis and Sicily are near starvation, and even if we received grain from Egypt, we'd have no way to grind it. The mills won't run without a powerful water source."

"I can solve that problem."

Turning, I found Belisarius grinning widely, as giddy as he had been outside the walls of Panormus. However, I did not see a path beyond the trap that Bessas and Petrus described. "You mean to attack Witiges, Lord?"

"For this, violence will not be necessary," Belisarius answered.

"Just fifty men, a few boats, and a willingness to move several of the inoperable mills to the Tiber."

Petrus coughed, shaking his head. "Strategos, the Tiber's bank is no safe place for a mill—"

"Not the bank." Belisarius beamed. "The middle of the river. You'll see."

After agreeing to send dispatches to other cities in the Empire with requests for food and men, we parted as Belisarius rushed toward the barracks that housed his bucellarii. Though I meandered to the walled riverbank, my attempt at eavesdropping bore no fruit, for Belisarius had cloistered his men in a nearby warehouse.

"Patience, Varus." It was Gouboulgoudou, saluting me as I ambled aimlessly along the Tiber.

"Another creation?" I inquired. "Something to frighten the Goths?"

Gouboulgoudou shrugged. "My people know life on horseback. Whatever Belisarius does is not of my world. But he's convinced it will work."

Belisarius did not emerge that afternoon, nor did he leave his workbench as darkness consumed the Eternal City. Instead, he left command of the Aurelian Walls to me, with our wall guardsmen staring into the surrounding hills. Gothic camps were illuminated by hundreds of cookfires and a thousand smaller hearths, with an occasional song and guttural laughter reaching the tops of the walls.

"They seem cheerful," the bucellarius spat in the direction of the Goths sheltering from the occasional blowing winds in a Pincian gatehouse.

"If they're milling about in their camps, they aren't attacking us," I said. "Let's pray it remains thus."

At second watch, I gave command of the walls to Perenus, seeking the comforts of the Domus and the restful comfort of Mariya. Before dawn, Cephalas rustled me awake. "Belisarius needs you on the Tiber."

"Which part?" I mumbled, struggling to pry myself from the feather bed.

"Not far. Opposite the Via Aurelia." With that, Cephalas excused himself.

It was a struggle, forcing my body from its slumber and out into the cold. Mariya grasped at my arm with an annoyed moan, and I nearly surrendered to the urge to remain, yet nagging duty soon overcame even that temptation. No sooner had I left the bedroom than a team of servants prepared my excubitor's armor and weapons, with still others outfitting Sembrouthes and three other Aksumites. Then, after stuffing meager rations of hard biscuits and a swallow of heavily diluted wine into our mouths, we were led by Cephalas to Belisarius' staging ground.

When we arrived, the lone figure of Bessas stood against the bluish predawn hour, and he hailed us. He sat stiffly atop his own mount, yet held the reins of another to his right. "Took you long enough."

"Getting lazy as I age." I nodded at the spare mount. "Someone is joining us?"

Bessas shook his head. "A gift for Belisarius. With Xanthos dead in Africa, he needs a new mount. I trained this Nisean myself, although it was a headache finding enough feed to build his strength."

Indeed, Bessas did not seem to have skimped in cultivating the young stallion, which stood even taller and wider than my Boreas. If anything, this horse was so broad-muscled that the common cataphract armor would have left it uncovered and vulnerable to spears and blades alike, forcing Belisarius to rely upon custom skirts of iron scales when riding into battle. "Impressive. I was with him when Xanthos was slain, and I know how difficult that was for him."

Bessas nodded. "His name is Balan, and he will not disappoint."

"Balan?" Sembrouthes said, the word unfamiliar in the Greek or Latin tongue.

"It's Gothic." Bessas grinned, pointing to a patch of white hair between the otherwise gray-coated horse's eyes. "It means *star*. A Goth I met in Sicily called him this name, and it's embedded into my memory."

Soon, Belisarius emerged, followed by teams of bucellarii that hauled three great devices. Two appeared to be boats, albeit boats that would be useless to ferry men over water; their benches had been torn out and replaced by lengths of iron chain. The third was more recognizable: a mill, although much smaller than the wooden wheels that churned against water and ground chaff in their hollowed interiors. All three were brought forth atop a succession of rolling logs, which were periodically removed from the rear of the device and placed before it as they were all pushed forward.

"Varus! Bessas!" Belisarius yelled, waving to summon us. "Come see!"

Even then I did not understand Belisarius' intention. Despite the darkness, I could see the man's eyes were marked by deep crevasses from lack of sleep, although the air about him had never seemed happier as his creation rolled to the edge of the Tiber that was unobstructed by wall. At first, men boarded smaller craft and paddled into the river, and eventually beckoned the two hollowed-out boats to be pushed into the Tiber.

"What is this, Lord?" I asked.

Belisarius laughed. "If it works, it will solve the gristmill problem. I can't make water appear throughout the city, but at least the city can fetch water from the river."

Then, and far more gingerly, the mill was lowered downhill and toward the water's edge. Only then did I see that the mill rested upon a number of coracles lashed together by flaxen rope, the knots stretched tight to prevent the boats from clanking into one another. As a result, the mill rested securely atop its perch, and Belisarius gave a sigh of relief as the contraption floated atop the water.

"It's not sinking, Lord!" one waterborne bucellarius said.

"Good, good!" Belisarius clapped. "Let's see if it works now. Connect it to the anchor boats!"

The entire scene felt ridiculous, with thousands of Goths just a few hundred paces distant and ready to murder us all, but Belisarius' enthusiasm was hard to resist. He guided the boats into position near the center of the river, where its ambling current was strongest.

"Careful now!" Belisarius yelled. "Get the boats in alignment!"

As the bucellarii hurried to fulfill an order I did not yet understand, the floating mill was secured between the two smaller boats.

A bucellarius waved his arm. "Ready, Lord!"

Belisarius clapped his hands. "Good! Now, together, lower the anchors!"

They obeyed. The boats, whose drift had moments before been corrected by struggling men paddling against the current, halted. Chains along the boats drew taut as iron anchors sank into the Tiber's depths, with each boat equidistant from the mill. At that, Belisarius gave one final order, seeming to hold his breath as he awaited the result.

"Lower the mill! Let it take on water!"

And, God help me, I then understood what Belisarius had created. Then as now, most men cared little for the technical arts, and fewer still for the construction of roadways or common buildings, with many believing such skills are too difficult to master or too dull. Perhaps both are true, yet our world would collapse overnight without the toil of men such as Belisarius, who we now know was as ingenious with construction as he was with warfare. Some today scoff at Belisarius' floating mill, yet any still living from the Siege of Rome will recall that act of magic as important a victory as any Belisarius ever authored.

What made it so wonderful was its simplicity. Connected to the two other anchored boats with links of ponderous iron chains, the floating mill rested above the flowing Tiber, allowing the river's current to push against the mill's wheel and rotating the mechanisms to grind wheat therein. Such an approach was far more labor intensive than with the larger mills on land, yet with not so much as a full evening's work, Belisarius resolved the Goths' attempts to starve the Roman populous.

I felt foolish for not having understood the design, yet at that point I marveled at the floating mill. "Lord, it's incredible!"

"Fun, too!" Belisarius beamed. "We'll need at least a dozen more,

I'd wager. And boatmen to prevent the Goths from floating debris downriver."

Belisarius' orders were obeyed, just as his predictions manifested into truth. As additional watermills were positioned in the Tiber's swiftest sections inside Roman protection, their caretakers complained of logs and even the maggot-riddled corpses of horses and dogs floating downstream. Most were little more than an unsavory nuisance, but one did jam the watermill's function, the dark viscera of a recently slain horse catching the individual blades of the mill. A half dozen men were stationed farther upstream but still inside the walls to intercept further attempts at sabotage, allowing Rome's precious supply of grain to be ground safely in the mill.

Still, through it all, the Goths did not attack. My soldiers appreciated the respite from violence, although Rome's citizens ungratefully made their many complaints known. Grumbling rose from the forum as rations of bread were reduced, despite the constant operation of Belisarius' watermills. Though complaints were rarely addressed in a formal manner to Imperial ministers such as Liberius, Belisarius preemptively alleviated the overconsumption of our dwindling supplies by seeking volunteers to sail to Neapolis, or even more fertile Carthage beyond.

"Your property in Rome remains your possession upon your return," Belisarius said, addressing a crowd in the forum one day. "The Emperor shall grant every man, woman, and child an allotment of silver upon their voyage south, and will pay full value for any property you would sell to the state. Our prefecture in Africa is underpopulated, and we will welcome all of you with plentiful food and opportunities for commerce."

Near the start of the third week of the siege, I executed Belisarius' vision to depopulate Rome of as many growling stomachs as would willingly depart. Several thousand Roman civilians, mostly those with young children, gathered along the Tiber to be ferried downstream toward the Ostian Port and the Tyrrhenian Sea. Samur's Huns were dispatched in advance of the flotilla as protection, yet Witiges did not challenge Rome's partial evacuation.

"Either Witiges is a fool or he's blind," Samur said upon return from the journey. "He just allowed Belisarius to rid himself of thousands of useless mouths."

Though I also struggled to understand Witiges' logic, having witnessed the massacre of thousands of his Thracian allies just a couple of months prior, I ventured a guess. "Perhaps Witiges believes attacking civilians would only drive the Romans toward Belisarius?"

Samur snorted. "Who cares what the Roman populace thinks? The only thing that matters to Witiges and his chieftains is that he takes this city and sends us all to the afterlife. If he's playing the role of some mythic hero, then he has no mind for battle. The winner here will be the one less hampered by social niceties."

This is not to say that there was no risk in riding out beyond the safety of the walls. Many scouts, dispatched through Rome's southern gates, never returned from their ranging in the surrounding countryside. One merchant, refusing to board a boat down the Tiber, rode a horse through Rome's southern gates in a mad attempt to reach Neapolis by road, only to be seized within eyeshot of the Appian Gate. His belt was emptied of silver and food, yet the man was allowed to continue onward, curiously unharmed.

A day after the last boats of refugees departed Rome, a party of Goths rode before the Pincian Gate, prompting Belisarius to order all his forces to prepare for imminent attack. As before, however, none came. The Gothic envoys only raised their shields high above their heads, signaling a desire to talk once more. Belisarius summoned Liberius and me, and the three of us ventured toward a midpoint between the Gothic armies and the walls of Rome, where we were greeted by five richly clad Goths led by Witiges.

"I grant you safety in this meeting of truce," Witiges began, gesturing a welcome as we gathered about a smoldering fire. "No man or woman shall harm you until you return to Rome."

Such words did nothing to allay my suspicion. "I've seen Gothic honor and guest right. Forgive me if I intend to keep my sword close."

Witiges bowed his head. "As is your wish, although I remain unarmed."

And so he was, along with the five other Goths flanking him. Though I recognized the face of a young man who I had spotted leading the Visigoth cohort, the only Goth I knew by name was Optaris, the onetime lord of Neapolis, whom Belisarius' scouts believed was responsible for Theodahad's murder.

"Allow me to introduce my companions," Witiges continued in his flawless Latin as he pointed to each warlord in turn. "Lord Vacis of Latium, Widin of Rhaetia, Uraias of Pavia, Optaris of Neapolis, and Totabadws, nephew of King Theudis."

All names I knew, save the last. Unlike Witiges, each of the Gothic warlords was a looming hulk of a man; their faces were mottled by years spent training in the burning sun and biting winds, their hands callused through exertions with the sword and the spear. Most appeared to be slightly older than me, with thin streaks of gray in their unkempt manes. One man—the one called Widin—appeared a decade older than the rest, with more hair on his chin than his pate and the edge of his nose hewn off from a long-ago injury.

Only the Visigoth Totabadws stood apart from his comrades. Though a red-tinged beard trailed down to his chest in a broad fork, his face was otherwise that of a younger, athletic man who had not yet been subjected to a life of grinding toil. He fidgeted as Witiges spoke, yet demonstrated no outward emotion, his features impassive as he scanned us three Romans.

"I stood against King Theudis at Septem," I declared. "He signed an extensive peace with the Empire. Is he as dishonorable as that worm Indulf, who skulks in your camp?"

Totabadws smiled, speaking before Witiges could interject. "My men are all volunteers. All I wish is to aid my kinsmen who suffer an unjust invasion. My uncle keeps your peace, Lord Varus, though your empire forced it upon him by goading the Franks into rampaging along our northern borders."

"Prince To-Totabadws—" I wished to deflect the accusation, yet my tongue stumbled over the strange Gothic name.

"Totila, as speakers of Latin prefer," he cut in smoothly. "And I doubt your friends have gathered here to debate the politics of Hispania, no?"

"If only," Liberius remarked, his eyes narrowed. "But understand that your volunteers will be given no quarter if captured. This war does not concern you."

Witiges arched his eyebrows. "I would disagree, Minister Liberius. Your empire is a dying thing, as evidenced by all manners of deserters and traitors in your ranks, as well as the riots in your city streets. Yet your pack of Vandals and Huns have come to Italy, threatening all the tribes who have brought peace in the wake of your chaos."

"If there is chaos, it is of your making," Liberius replied. "The world has never been perfect, but before so many tribes ravaged the Western Empire, it was not a bad place to live."

Widin spat, while Totila sneered. Witiges, however, nodded politely. "You speak as one who has lost something precious. If I could restore your losses, I would, but such a reversal is outside even the power of kings. The past belongs only to shadows, and the future to those with the might to seize it. You blame the Goths for your demise, and such is your right. But we stood firm against the Huns, throwing off the yoke of his sons at Nedao and Bassianae, and freeing your world from doom. Yet still you come to my lands, squatting in your latrines and bringing death and starvation in your wake, and I will not have it."

His Latin was songlike, a voice too light for a king of tribesmen famous for their capacity for violence. It seemed more appropriate for poets than battle, more fluid than any courtier I had ever witnessed in Justin's court, and brokered few opportunities for reply. Indeed, Liberius and Belisarius remained silent as the Gothic king continued.

"I have not come here to insult you three, or any other in your command. You are not your Emperor who causes this war. Still, your entire cause for enmity with the Goths died with Theodahad. And so, I would ask you, as one leader of warriors to another: Do not prolong the sufferings of Goths and Italians. My vaunted predecessor, Theodoric, fostered in a life not only of soft luxury but also of freedom. If you would put up your blades and return Rome to my control, I give you my oath that I shall treat Goths and Italians with equal dignity, and count you as my friends."

It was a speech that I doubt Belisarius had anticipated, given the raw violence that Witiges promised upon our previous engagement. Witiges' chieftains appeared less conciliatory, and I have little doubt that they preferred to charge against veteran archers and ballistae and scale the Aurelian Walls against Belisarius' vaunted army. Nor would I, if our fates had been changed.

Belisarius considered the eloquent offer and gave only a terse response. "And if I am unable to acquiesce to your demand?"

Witiges sighed, shaking his head with eyes downcast. "Then you, and all who follow you in this folly, will die. You know as well as I that your position is hopeless. Those Romans who have not abandoned you will soon understand the danger as well, and shall turn on you. We will burn your bodies on the Campus Martius, adorn ourselves with your possessions, and dance upon the ashes. All you must do to avoid this fate is return Rome to the Goths, gather your valuables, and depart from Italy."

Liberius offered a toothy grin, but no words. Neither did I speak up, for the truth that Witiges rendered in his songlike speech was plain: our walls could not hold for long. Witiges' chin rose as he sniffed a trailing breeze, as though savoring the gathering like a longed-for meal.

Belisarius, however, was unmoved.

"I honor my oaths, and my oath to the Emperor and the Roman people is to liberate and hold this city. The Emperor holds nothing that belongs to others. It was you who trespassed upon this city in former times, though it did not belong to you at all. Whoever of you has hopes of setting foot in Rome without a fight is mistaken in his judgment. For as long as Belisarius lives, it is impossible for him to relinquish this city."

And there it was—the oaths that bound us to a hopeless situation, committing thousands to death based upon a promise to reclaim Rome. Paramount to this were our oaths to Justinian, who had condemned us to this path. Likewise, however, we were committed to legions of long-dead Romans, having promised to reunite their bones with the rump of their Imperial heritage. And, no less, we made promises to those who had longed for our return, though their voices were often forgotten by Procopius and his scribes. Rosamund had protested at Roman reliance upon oath-taking, for it compelled us to behave in manners that were otherwise reckless, even suicidal. That may be so, but Belisarius, more than any man I have ever known, would not be moved from an oath, especially to the Emperor. And so we committed to a fight, placing Rome in a siege far more ludicrously unbalanced than any in its memory.

"So be it," Witiges spat. "I shall pray for you, though I wonder if you will live long enough for my prayers to reach God's ears."

We returned to Belisarius' command quarters along the Pincian Hill. All senior officers gathered soon thereafter and were informed of Witiges' offer and Belisarius' reply. None grumbled. Indeed, none, including myself, would have expected Belisarius to behave differently. Whether by choice or by necessity, war was our life. We planned, we ordered additional supplies, and we wrote missives to various other Imperial cities to inform them of our plight. And then we slept, with every man knowing well that what happened next would change everything, and all of us.

By morning, the Gothic battle lines drew together. And then, the Siege of Rome truly began.

THE STORM

Looking back to those trying months, I see that the only true advantage we held was a near-total foresight of Witiges' plans. Of all the monarchs I have met, Witiges was easily the strangest, keen on his own honorable reputation as much as displays of brutality. The scribes tell me that he behaved similarly to Theodoric so long ago—half Roman and half Goth. Little different than myself, in so many ways, except that Witiges had been acclaimed king over millions of Goths. Unlike Theodahad, Witiges, for all his polished manner, could not be called a weakling, nor seen as impassive before a Roman army, and so we knew he must attack us with everything he possessed.

Not that Witiges attempted to disguise his attentions, either. He could have swept south, as I feared, and ravaged both our slim hold over southern Italy and even Sicily, forcing Belisarius to depart Rome's walls and challenge a far more numerous host in the open field. Were I a Gothic warlord, that's what I would have urged. Doubtless Indulf demanded the same. Such an alternative path would have brought the Gothic War to an anticlimactic end, for I am not certain that we could have stood for long against such numbers. The Goths were more disciplined than the Avars, more numerous than the Persians, and understood Roman tactics far better than the former Vandals. Yet Witiges did not go south, and instead staked his reputation and kingship upon Rome, in a cataclysmic showdown, perhaps appealing to his Roman half yearning for a glorious conclusion.

Summoned to report before dawn, I embraced my children, shared a kiss with Mariya, and rushed toward the Pincian Hill for a final encounter with Belisarius. Aside from my usual guardsmen, I was accompanied by Cephalas, Shimon, Agathias, and Rosamund, the last of whom brooked no dissent on her attendance and arrived already dressed in the thin coat of mail she'd owned since before the Persian war.

"Did you sleep with that on?" I joked, watching Rosamund gather her box of healing unguents, needles, and wrappings.

"Whatever it takes to keep up with you," she shot back, visibly irritated. "You would not listen before, and now you have no choice. If Belisarius is intent on suicide, I'm not going to allow you to follow him alone."

After mounting prepared horses, we trotted toward Belisarius' quarters, eventually depositing Boreas and the other mounts with Belisarius' servants. He dismissed what few attendants remained to him as I entered his rooms, instructing all to rush to their gates and collect what sleep and food the Goths might permit us before attacking.

"The Gothic camps have been stirring for hours," Belisarius began. "Confident enough to not rush us in silence. Any final words of advice?"

I sighed, eager for the anxiety that brewed in my gut to ebb away. "Don't let them goad you into something foolish. That's how I almost lost Septem."

Belisarius nodded. "Godilas always warned me to avoid sieges. Nasty business. But I doubt he would have been pleased if I handed Rome back to the Goths without a fight."

"No indeed." I smiled as memories of my weapons master came to memory. "Are you worried, Lord?"

Though I expected Belisarius to shrug with his usual confidence, he nodded, and my heart fluttered. "I didn't want to tell the others," he admitted, "but I received a message from Constantinople yesterday."

I was already guessing at the letter's contents as Belisarius handed the parchment to me. Though scribbled in the neat writing of an Imperial clerk, its words were distinctively Justinian's, the tone simultaneously superior and disgruntled.

"I commend you for liberating Rome from the usurper Theodahad. However, my coffers cannot permit a further expansion of the army. Given your failure to pacify Africa, it has become my responsibility to pay and armor forces so that Germanus might counter Stotzas and the Mauri. Between that, and the usual requirements that our border along the Ister be well guarded, I cannot spare additional resources beyond the bounty I have already bestowed upon you. You have my full faith that Rome shall not fall once more. You have my blessing, and that of God, who endows me as Emperor of the Romans."

"We're alone, in other words," I muttered.

Belisarius nodded. "Don't tell the others. They already know, in their way, but the hope of reinforcement might help them hold out a few moments longer."

Horns rattled our room, their rolling notes foreign to any Roman commander. "Where do you need me, Lord?"

"Stay with me at first," he replied. "Then go to where the fighting is worst. With any luck, we can discourage the Goths enough to slow their assault, or at least focus them toward one gate rather than others."

"Of course," I replied, though I believed we'd have no such luck. Even the genteel Witiges would not hesitate to swarm each section of Roman wall if it meant ending the day in victory, regardless of the suffering.

Armored and accompanied by both of our bodyguards, Belisarius and I proceeded atop the Pincian Gate. Neither Uliaris nor Belisarius acknowledged the other, although the Frank kept his eyes upon the general as we ascended to the peak of the walls and took residence in a nearby tower. For a heartbeat, the waves of noise that crashed overhead made me believe I had returned to Septem, staring out at thousands of Goths who clamored for my death.

Each of the seven Gothic camps was now emptied of men, who

now stood in dense lines of units arrayed in groups of a few hundred. Before each section, a plumed leader strutted about, barking in Gothic and using his spear to tidy segments of the overeager Gothic lines. Dozens of ladders were strewn about along the grasses, perhaps one ladder per forty Goths. What stole my attention, however, were Witiges' siege engines. The rams were fully encased in husks of lumber, with furs lining the outermost layer to prevent the spread of fire. These weapons would have been an uncommon enough sight on their own, and would have been daunting to any warrior defending a city, but then I saw the siege towers fully readied for battle. Lumbering closer, I guessed that fifty men could stand atop each tower's fighting platform, sheltered from all manner of arrows or pitch by fur-lined wooden casings that must have stood at an arm-length in thickness. They were moving forts, and God help me, but I had no notion of how to counter them.

"Sound our horns," Belisarius ordered a bucellarius. "Prepare for battle."

The Goths were well into their rituals, with champions shouting at their massed kinsmen for bravery, and overfilled skins of wine or ale passed amongst their ranks. There was little hurry even amongst Witiges' guardsmen just opposite the Pincian Gate, and the Gothic king himself seemed to be laughing amongst his men, wine dribbling down his cropped beard as he gorged himself upon a skin.

And the banners. So many swirling flags, most bearing the sun-crowned cross, with others displaying the beasts and symbols of other Gothic warlords. There was a beauty to that sea of billowing cloth, a sign of unity amongst tens of thousands of men united in common cause. Each banner carrier raised and lowered his flag as Gothic horns blared and cheers boomed from their ranks, the percussion of thousands of voices slamming into the Aurelian Walls like a gust of wind. Just as Witiges' voice could entrance a listener, so, too, would this display of color and strength, these fearsome instruments of war, numb any observer into shock.

"Romans!" Belisarius roared, struggling to rise above the Gothic clangor from where he stood atop a parapet to look down on the ranks. "Know this: If I could wager on this battle, I would place all that I own upon you. Witiges outnumbers us by a mere five to one! Any Goth should stain his trousers at such odds!"

The bucellarii hooted laughter, while Uliaris grumbled in my ear. "More like ten to one."

Thankfully, Belisarius did not hear. "We stood firm in the sands of the east," he continued, "and along the hills of Africa. Are there any in this world stronger than us?!"

"No!!" the bucellarii called in return. "No!!"

Belisarius nodded. "I have said to all who would hear throughout my life. It is not by numbers of men, nor by measure of body, but by valor of soul that is war to be decided. And by that standard, none can stand against us!"

"Roma! Roma! Roma!"

More cheers as Belisarius drew his sword, met swiftly by a rising swell of Gothic horns. "Romans, this is our city! We shall prevail!"

Even I was caught up in the thunderous roar that followed.

"Roma! Roma! Roma!"

At the beckoning of an adjacent Gouboulgoudou, a hundred of our own Roman horns blared from the walls. The echo snaked in all directions, filling the city behind us with a call of defiance, of Belisarius' army standing against the might of Witiges. And I joined in such cheers, with my eyes fixed upon Belisarius. Despite the forces arrayed against us, I, too, could never bet against Rome's army—not if Belisarius stood at its helm.

In reply, the Goths slammed spear shafts into their shields, rattling the stones beneath my feet. Witiges galloped before the arrayed squares of men, shouting above the din to stir ever more lust for Roman blood as the Goths screamed in rage. Unsheathing his sword, he pointed it to the heavens and mouthed what must have been a prayer as his eyes raised toward God.

"Give the order, Varus," Belisarius said, gripping my shoulder. "They will be upon us soon."

"Right." I nodded, breaking from my reverie. "Archers, draw arrows! Ballistae, load your bolts!"

Belisarius' bucellarii responded immediately, with each man turning his eyes toward the nearest centurion relaying my commands. I paused, waiting for Witiges to conclude his prayer.

"Two hundred paces!" I commanded. "Stay your arrows until two hundred paces!"

Gothic horns roared again, and at last the Gothic sections milled about, lifting the ladders from the grass. Witiges guided his mount in a loop as he turned to face us, his sword still pointed toward the skies. Facing our tower, he scanned the tops of the walls, then paused, seeming not to breathe. Gothic screams fell to a hush, awaiting Witiges' command.

And in moments, he obliged. Witiges lowered his sword arm, and a chorus of horns blared as the Goths surged forward with such force that their leaders struggled to maintain order in the lines. Singing as they approached, they formed their shields into a moving wall. I was happy to test them, and gestured for Shimon to hand over my bow.

"You don't need to stay," I whispered in his ear. "The children require guards and would feel better from your company."

Shimon, however, refused. "With respect, Lord, but the only future where I leave you is if I'm killed."

In that—in both his casual confidence and his steadfast friendship—he seemed a twin of Isaacius. "Very well. But keep close to a merlon, and move only when my men require arrows or spears."

Sembrouthes nudged me. "Five hundred paces, Varus."

Slinging my shield behind my back, I plucked an arrow from one of the dozens of huge wooden holsters positioned along the walls. The Goths pressed forward, granting me a final moment to survey Belisarius' bucellarii as they awaited my order. Belisarius clutched a bow, his chest rising and falling as he stared at an approaching Gothic banner. His immediate guardsmen held their shields close, protecting their strategos against an opportunistic enemy arrow. Others, including many of the younger men, gripped hard at their bows; two of them shivered as the Goths closed in upon our walls. One Cappadocian, a man likely no older than twenty whom I did not recognize, turned away from the walls and retched violently behind us.

"Get command of yourself, man!" Uliaris snarled.

The Cappadocian bobbed his head. "Apologies, Lord."

"Nothing to be sorry for," I replied. "I don't care if you run about the lines naked, as long as you're sending a dozen Goths to hell."

Several bucellarii laughed at that, although none tore his eyes from the Gothic advance. At three hundred paces apart, Sembrouthes nudged me to attention once more.

"Romans, nock your arrows!"

The centurions echoed the order, their voices like crackling thunder. "Nock! Nock! Nock!"

Another nudge from Sembrouthes. "Two hundred fifty paces."

Time seemed to slow as I measured each Gothic step. "Romans, draw!"

Within moments, men along the line drew their bows taut, their arrowheads plucked toward the wooden center of their bows. My own bow, a massive recurve that had been treasured by the Hephthalite warlord Khingila, curled as I tugged the arrow shaft to my cheek, the bowstring demanding a strength that most men would have struggled to muster.

"Two twenty-five."

"Hold!" I yelled.

At that point, Gothic horns blared again; the leading lines, now ascending the low knoll that led to the Pincian Gate, roared a war cry in reply. Groups of ten and twenty raised their shields, quickening their pace and placing a shifting barrier above the heads of the Gothic ladder carriers. Yet the uneven lines of advancement yielded gaps between Goths—something that any Roman bowman was trained to exploit. As the Goths crossed our predetermined marker for range, I did not require Sembrouthes to goad me into my next order.

"Loose!" I screamed. "Loose! Rain hell on them!"

It was the cleanest volley that any Roman officer could pray for. No man within eyeshot fired early, with all releasing their arrows within two heartbeats of the initial command. Joining them were the creaking triggers of a half dozen ballistae and one stone-throwing onager, the former hurtling their bolts toward clumps of Goths nearest our lines, and the latter hurling stones toward the greater mass of Goth reserves that yet remained distant.

The ballistae struck first, bursting asunder at least two dozen Gothic warriors in a mist of blood and splinters that plumed thrice the height of a man. One bolt even struck a rare horseman in the Gothic advance, piercing the beast's unarmored chest and splitting its body in twain; I want to believe the poor beast died immediately upon impact. Filling those bloody scars in the Gothic lines were hundreds of Roman arrows, quilling the frontmost ranks and slowing the Gothic advance as the enemy took cover under shields. Though most of our arrows smacked against shields or were deflected overhead, several found the softer flesh of men and sent them sprawling to the ground.

Sensing an opportunity to blunt the Goth charge, I ordered another volley. "Nock and loose!"

"Loose! Loose!"

The ballistae would require more time to crank their winches and load their bolts for a second attack, but Belisarius' archers managed to spring their second flight of arrows before the first volley had fully reached the ground. Farther back, the onager's stones crashed into a more distant Gothic square, just twenty paces short of where Witiges sat atop his horse. As I watched, the projectiles crushed at least four Goths and sent men struggling to move the stones and free their dying kinsmen. Witiges himself trotted forward to inspect the onager's payload and spat animatedly into a patch of grass.

Yet still the Goths came. I ordered a third volley, and then a fourth, until the desperate need to hail arrows upon the enemy overcame any desire for orderly attack. At one hundred paces, even the least-experienced bowman could strike a target without much difficulty, and the sheer force of Roman arrows from the height of the walls now punched through Gothic shields three to four at a time. Our ballistae added to the chaos, with one bolt striking several ladder bearers and shattering wooden rungs. Indeed, ballistae and onager strikes pounded masses of flesh and iron along the line into bloody pulps, leaving only pillars of dust, and a gap in the Gothic advance—albeit a temporary one—was soon filled by the still-living thousands who bore Witiges' emblem.

Because despite all the punishment we could muster, they still came. A sea of men, the breeze billowing over their heads, ignorant or insensible of the wails of pain and the butchery of broken bones and spilled blood as they closed within fifty paces, singing and chanting. By then, their ladder bearers had repositioned themselves opposite targeted points between the Pincian and Flaminian Gates, somehow undaunted by the accelerating pace of arrows.

"They aren't advancing the towers yet," Belisarius called to me. "Are they in range of the onager?"

"No, Lord!" I answered. "All we can do is wait and discourage them from moving further."

Belisarius nodded, plucking an arrow. "If they're waiting to deploy those monsters, it's for a reason. Keep close watch on their movements."

He was right; yet in the moment it felt like nothing more than a lone stroke of good fortune not to have to counter the towers or even the wood-encased rams, which held back. Unlike Belisarius, I could hardly see beyond this temporary reprieve, too preoccupied with the dozens of ladders to care why Witiges would not deploy all his weapons at once. My attentions were further distracted as a Gothic spear sailed in a gap between two stone merlons, its tip finding the mail-covered chest of a bucellarius. The man gasped and jerked forward, falling to the earth below before his comrades could grasp at his body.

"Stones!" I roared. "Drop stones on their heads! Form rings around the ladders!"

Handing Shimon my bow, I grabbed at one of hundreds of stacked spears upon the walls, seeking a target for its honed iron point. There was precious little space to maneuver atop the Pincian Gate, yet the bucellarii managed to part somewhat as I pushed to the front of the walls. Pressing my body tight against a stone merlon, I spied a ladder bearer struggling to secure the base of his ladder against the churning soil at the base of the walls, not watching for Roman attackers.

In a single breath, I stepped into the gap between the merlons, shot my spear arm upright, and hurled the weapon toward the Goth's unguarded body. With only hardened leather encasing his chest, my spearpoint pierced through the front of his stomach and burst out the opposite end. He collapsed to the ground. I stood a moment longer, watching the ladder fall absent his steadying grip, until a pair of hands grasped forcefully against my cloak, pulling me backward just a heartbeat before a Gothic spear cut through the open air where I had stood.

"Keep your fucking head down," Sembrouthes roared to me. "Your plume and armor might as well be begging for a spear to the chest. I haven't kept you alive this long so that you can behave like a moron."

I nodded. "Gratitude, as always, Sembrouthes."

"Brace!" Belisarius shouted just paces away. "Don't give them a single step on our walls!"

Stones flew from atop the Pincian Gate's walls, striking iron helmets and wooden shields with booming thumps. Most might see these attacks as juvenile, and even desperate, but dropping a stone from a considerable height was the most effective weapon I have yet witnessed to inflict pain upon a climbing enemy. Our gathered stones, from the size of a fist to those requiring two outstretched hands to lift, could easily be tossed from behind the safety of stone battlements, or at least rolled through gaps in the walls to fall upon attackers below. Shields offer little shelter against a direct strike—the hurtling weight of rock would easily shatter a wooden bulwark, crushing the bones of the hapless man underneath. Better still, stones required no special military training to deploy; I even spotted Rosamund and Agathias plucking a few of their own and hurling them upon the Gothic masses below.

Still, for all their brute simplicity, stones would not be enough. With twice as many defenders, they would not have been enough. Under the gaze of their king, the first of the Gothic climbers were ascending the rungs, shields guarding their heads. Yet we persisted, and for every two Goths that ascended to the Pincian walls, one would fall screaming onto the swirling mass of warriors below, with the luckiest dying upon impact rather than suffering a severed spine or twisted limbs. I, and any with the strength to hurl a spear or rock or fire a bow, rained death down on our attackers, yet still far too many reached their ladders' pinnacle.

"Brace!" Belisarius yelled again. "Cut and thrust! Three Romans to every Goth! Toss them from the walls!"

Unslinging my shield and drawing Justin's runed blade, I pushed my way to Belisarius, with Sembrouthes close on my right and Uliaris at my back. A full two paces away from the frontmost portion of the battlement, all I could see was a swell of Goths in the far distance and the iron-hooked top of an empty ladder facing me. In that moment, all fear leaked away. Gone were the worries for Mariya, the children, and the many others who depended upon me for survival. Gone, too, were any anxieties about Rosamund or suspicion of Justinian, or even the threat of the still-veiled sky above and barren crops below, all of which had hollowed my days with sleeplessness and fear. There was only Belisarius to my left and Sembrouthes to my right, and the gushing hatred of an enemy that sought to end my life. It was that same battle joy that Godilas had spoken of with an equal measure of caution and awe, that feeling as if the ichor of the old gods now flowed through the veins of us mortal men on the precipice of combat. In that blessed moment, though I mouthed a prayer to God, I felt neither fear nor holiness, but only a hunger to destroy any foe. And, though Christ tells us that it is sinful, destruction was something I excelled at.

The first Goth that reached our top was a fool. Overextending himself, he did not bother to lead with his shield and instead reached with a gloved hand to grasp at the top of his ladder. Shuffling forward, I thrust the tip of my sword through his forearm, piercing sinew and muscle just above the elbow before withdrawing the thrust. Behind me, Belisarius jumped toward the flailing man, jamming his blade beneath the man's armpit and eliciting a keening howl of pain. The Goth's boots must have been stuck upon the ladder, for despite his twin injuries, he did not fall, neither able to retreat downward nor jump past us Romans who tightened our circle around the ladder's top.

"No! Please!" he gargled, his guttural Latin choked by spittle.

Screaming, I thrust my sword toward his neck. The man's body twitched backward, wriggled for a heartbeat, then slumped forward, dead before air could escape the ragged cavern I had carved along his throat. His head rolled toward the walls, making his corpse seem to embrace the ladder, while jerking motions from below came as his kinsmen attempted to pry him from his climb so that the living might try again.

Those few moments offered me the respite to scan the length of the Pincian and Flaminian walls. Down the line, several Goths had been more fortunate than mine, able to exchange blows with a Roman defender or even transfer their feet from a ladder and onto firm stone. Despite their labors, few lasted more than a few moments. For the bucellarii heeded Belisarius' instructions, surrounding each ladder so that multiple defenders could strike against a single Goth. Gore slicked the Aurelian stones, although I witnessed at least one defender use the rim of his shield to push an off-balance Goth free from the top of his ladder, careening to the masses below. It was an auspicious start, although the morning was still early.

At last, the Goth's body was plucked free from its perch, leaving a layer of viscous crimson along the rungs that sprayed up toward the battlements. The man who followed was far more cautious, covering his body with his shield. As he neared the top of the walls, he paused, shouted in Gothic, and a half dozen spears hurtled upward just a pace from my body. Five of those spears sailed well over the battlement and toward Rome's interior, the first of many such projectiles that would hail upon the city. One, however, arced higher and slower than the others, reaching its apex and falling to the top of the wall. Its iron spearhead buried itself in the collarbone of a bucellarius not five paces from me. The momentum sent him backward and nearly to the ground below, had not his comrades grabbed his cloak. The struck soldier grasped at the spear shaft and moaned, unable to pry it free.

"Bring him to me!" Rosamund screamed, pushing her way through the crowd.

"Rosamund! Stay where you are!" I yelled, watching carefully as the Goth before me clambered up his final rungs.

She ignored me, and slipped behind Belisarius to the wounded Roman. As I struck at the climbing Goth's shield, I could hear the wailing bucellarius stumble behind me, with Rosamund snarling demands for Agathias to follow and her ward to stay conscious.

"Focus on my voice!" I heard Rosamund yell. "Keep your eyes open, and don't touch the gash!"

My instinct was to chastise her for disobedience, but the fighting continued. Belisarius and I chopped at the climbing Goth, finding only an overlarge shield as the man steadied his feet. Shifting his weight, the man seemed about to hop onto the walls and use his shield to bash us apart, making room for further Goths to follow.

"Cover!" I yelled, blocking Belisarius with my body.

Lunging with my own shield, I smashed its boss against the center of his bulwark. By the grace of God, my strike occurred just as the man's feet left the safety of his rungs, and the force sent him flying backward. Yelping, he reached with a free hand at the ladder, yet found no purchase on the blood-soaked rungs. He screamed as he fell, suddenly halted only a moment later.

"Back!" Uliaris yelled, tugging at my cloak.

More spears struck our walls. While most fell as useless as in the first volley, some indeed found their target, and each wounded bucellarius felt as if five men had been removed from Belisarius' strength, while the Gothic storm seemed endless. I cut the throat of our next Gothic climber, and Sembrouthes jammed a spear in the unprotected ribs of the one following, yet still there seemed no shortage of young men willing to hazard the Pincian Gate. If anything, the Goths became more ravenous, eyeing the rich plumes of Belisarius and me as a particularly rewarding target for plunder.

After dispatching five climbers, we swapped our positions at the front of the wall with fresher reserves. Though mere minutes after the onset of violence, I already needed the break in action to clean the sticky blood from my sword and to gain a better view of our nearby defenders. As before, most Roman positions protected a concentrated perimeter about the Gothic ladders, stymying the progress of any who succeeded in reaching the top. However, several Romans bore visible cuts; others winced from wounds to their hands or arms, and altogether Belisarius' defenses had grown more porous.

With each failed wave, more ladder climbers succeeded in stepping foot atop a section of our walls, with one ladder temporarily producing two Goths who simultaneously stabbed and pushed at the nearest defenders. Both men were cut down, their bodies thrown over the walls and onto the massing Goths, yet the remaining climbers seemed to take this as a sign of our weakening resolve.

Few Romans sustained wounds serious enough to remove themselves from the fight altogether: Those who were struck by a fatal spear thrust or sword slash toppled from the walls, unable to support their weight and crashing to the ground in a broken heap. Those wounded fortunate enough to not plummet toward the Goths were carried to a nearby tower, where Rosamund had established a makeshift medic enclosure, using silver tongs to pry spearheads from wounds and washing all gashes with splashes of wine. Her hair, normally bone white, was dyed garnet from her patients, most of whom screamed as she healed what she was capable of and stitched flesh together. Some, however, were beyond saving, like one man I stumbled upon in my respite from battle.

"Please!" a bucellarius cried in Latin. "Please!"

His feet wriggled as Rosamund inspected a puncture along the man's side, where an ooze trickled from the gap. Agathias held the man's shoulders against the stone floor until Rosamund looked up, shaking her head. She leaned toward her box of medicines, procuring a flask filled with colorless liquid that she gingerly moved toward the man's mouth. Only then did she realize I stood above her, waiting to speak until I crouched to her level.

"His intestines are torn," Rosamund said in Heruli, pointing to the stinking goo that mixed with the man's pooling blood.

Leaning close, I recognized the injury as the same that struck down Alaric, my long-ago centurion who died amidst the carnage of Dara. "Anything that can be done?"

"I can ease his passing," Rosamund replied, lifting the glass jar. "Either that, or days of suffering. Death has chosen this man, regardless of what I do."

It was an injury that all warriors feared, and the bucellarius likely understood as well. Clenching and unclenching his fist, the man moaned, mumbling words I could not understand. I nodded to Rosamund, who trickled a portion of the poison into the man's throat, wiping sweat from the man's eyes and brow as he swallowed. He muttered again, at first in agony, yet soon thereafter with a growing distance.

"What is it, brother?" I asked in Latin. "What can I do for you?"

"Mater," the man gargled, blood filling his mouth as a tear streaked from his eye. "Mother..."

With a rasp, I heard the soul slip from his body. Rosamund muttered a prayer in the Gepid tongue, taking but a few moments of solemnity before rising to her feet and inspecting a broad cut along the next man's forearm. With no rest, she grabbed a needle and thread, washing the wound with wine before knitting it together as tightly as her fingers would allow.

"She's a godsend," Belisarius remarked. "Saved dozens of my men over the years."

"Hundreds, even," I muttered, my eyes fixed upon Rosamund's face, at the lingering evidence of her initial injury at the bidding of

Cassiodorus' thugs, and the faint burn marks upon her neck and fingers.

Before Belisarius and I readied to reenter the scrum, both of our names rang from the base of the Pincian Gate's walls. The figure bore an ouroboros shield and spoke in accented Greek—a Herulian.

"Lord Belisarius!" He plucked the helmet from his head, revealing the familiar face of Sindual. "Lord Varus!" He sprinted up the stone steps of the walls along the interior edge of the walls, panting laboriously as he reached the summit. "Lord," he gasped, unclear as to whether it was directed at Belisarius or me.

"Calm yourself," Belisarius replied, offering an arm to the exhausted centurion. Belisarius then requested a waterskin from one of his guards, offering a swallow to Sindual.

"My gratitude, Strategos," Sindual sputtered between gulps. "I ran here in full armor from the Vivarium. My horse lamed itself in the forum."

Blood soaked the man's neck and collar, while his sword arm quivered. Sindual was never a man to cower from danger. Likewise, though the Heruli were noted athletes, their skills were better applied atop a horse than on foot. I gave Sindual several moments to slow his breathing and turned away politely as he cocked his head to retch down from the walls.

"Lord," Sindual continued, cuffing a speck of vomit from his mouth as he nodded to both Belisarius and me. "The Gothic rams are advancing on the Vivarium. Perenus asks you for reinforcements as soon as you are able."

I was irritated hearing this, for I doubted Perenus' situation was much worse than at any other Roman gate. "How bad? Can you hold out for a time?"

"We're being struck by ballistae," Sindual explained. "We're holding the Goths at bay, but we're taking losses anytime a Herulian sticks his head out from the battlement."

Behind me, a chorus of Gothic horns blared, and for a moment I feared our gate had fallen. Besides a continual exchange of blows, however, Belisarius' bucellarii retained control of their walls, albeit with a growing number of tired and wounded men. Nevertheless, the horns echoed again and again, their urgency causing a shift in the massed Goths at the foot of the Pincian and Flaminian Gates. And movement, absent the desperate call for retreat, was rarely a good thing.

"They're letting up!" Gouboulgoudou yelled. "Still coming, but fewer now."

"They've hardly begun." Uliaris frowned. "That was just a probe against our defenses." Pacing to an open enclosure in the tower, Uliaris peered out to Witiges' men. "The rams are moving west."

"West?" Belisarius questioned. "To the Tiber?"

Sketches of the city walls flashed in my mind, and I immediately discerned the Gothic target. "No. Hadrian's Mausoleum. It's the weakest portion of the northern walls, given its disrepair."

"It must be more than a mile to the nearest bridge across the river, and then another to the Mausoleum," Belisarius said. "And we strengthened the walls. Why attack there now?"

I shrugged. "It's still exposed, and difficult to reinforce. There will be a thousand priests sheltering in the enclosure, given that they had to evacuate their Basilica. And it's a giant circle, so it's harder to defend. If I were Witiges, and I learned how few men Bessas had to guard the Mausoleum, I'd attack there too."

Sindual coughed, seeking an answer. "Lord, I must return to the Vivarium. Will you be accompanying me?"

"Tell Perenus to hold for now, and that we will ride to you as soon as we can," Belisarius ordered. "Just an hour, no longer."

Sindual saluted. "I will tell Perenus. But the situation is dire, Strategos. Fulcaris and I are used to numerous enemies, but the Vivarium is nigh indefensible."

"One hour," I echoed. "Hold until the zenith. Borrow a horse from the stable master below to carry you back to Perenus."

Sindual saluted and obeyed. A scream behind me tugged my concentration back to the siege, where a bucellarius had been speared in the hip by a climbing Goth. One comrade dispatched the climber with a spear thrust of his own, while a second carried the injured warrior to Rosamund along the inside of our walls. Rosamund jammed a wooden bit in the man's mouth before pushing the wound together and stitching it shut. The man grimaced through it all, staring at Rosamund's deft fingers and snorting when the needle pierced a scrap of dangling skin.

"Varus, go to the Mausoleum and inform me of Bessas' situation," Belisarius commanded. "God knows I have no reserves to offer, but if it's truly dire, I will find a way to assist."

I saluted. "And the Vivarium?"

Belisarius shook his head. "Other than the Huns, the Vandal and Heruli foederati are the best brawlers I possess. We must trust Perenus to hold out until we gain a greater understanding of Witiges' plan. His attack at the Mausoleum makes little logic to me, which is why I am so worried about it."

And so, with Uliaris and the Aksumites, Rosamund, Cephalas, Agathias, and Shimon, my party left the Pincian Gate. Many of the bucellarii appeared reluctant to allow Rosamund to depart, yet she refused to remain behind as we absconded to Hadrian's Tomb, and Belisarius would never have commanded her to stay.

"I can't guarantee your safety," I insisted, cuffing sweat from my brow.

"You don't need to," Rosamund insisted. "And I don't intend to allow you to leave me for this fight. Not after Salona."

There was no benefit to argument. If anything, Rosamund's presence calmed my mind, and I curiously realized that I wanted her there.

"Gratitude, Rosamund."

Snatching our horses, we rode hard for the northwest. Hadrian's Mausoleum, long ago converted into a vast fortress, was little more than a half mile's ride from the Pincian Gate. Nestled against the west bank of the Tiber opposite the Campus Martius, the Mausoleum was the only section of Rome's walled city that required crossing the river, approached by the Cornelian Gate. It was designed as a sort of massive brick cylinder decorated by dozens of looming sculptures of the Roman pantheon, carved in bronze and stone alike.

Hadrian had never intended it as a defensive building, given that it lacked the platforms to house ballistae; that the Western emperors over a century ago had decided to envelop the tower inside the city's walls seemed idiotic to me. Hadrian be damned—his grand architecture only further overstretched our lines that otherwise would have been guarded by the Tiber, and instead required a substantial garrison to protect the nearly full circle of merlon-lined stone walls. Worse, though Bessas invested each day of his stay in Rome to bolstering the Mausoleum's defenses, decades of neglect had left plenty of sections of wall crumbling, and therefore difficult for our archers to safely guard.

Still fresh due to only limited combat, I expected the fighting at that fortress to be little different than Belisarius' defense of the Pincian and Flaminian Gates. If anything, the fortress should have had far fewer Goths to contend against, with only one of the seven Gothic camps positioned on the Tiber's western bank, and with the surge of men from the Pincian Gate delayed by the extended distance traveled to the nearest sizeable bridge.

However, as we crossed the river and drew within earshot of Bessas' men, the clangor of blades and contrasting screams of Greek and Germanic voices had me rushing toward the Mausoleum to ascend its tower and gaze out to the walls.

Though the battle was not yet over, many Goths had scaled our walls. Only a thin line of Romans remained to hold back a swelling horde. Witiges' victory unfolded before us.

THE MAUSOLEUM
OF HADRIAN

They're as good as dead," Uliaris growled to me, gesturing to the Roman detachment.

"Then so are we," I argued, dismounting and handing the reins to Shimon. "Find Bessas, and seal this gap."

The tower connected to the outer walls via an extended stone bridge, every pace of which was littered with deposited weapons and the sprawling bodies of the twitching and dead. I ordered Rosamund and Agathias to establish their healing center within the tower's protective enclosure, then led the remainder of my posse onto the tower's bridge, where I scanned the battlements for signs of Gothic progress.

Upon a closer view, the Cornelian Gate showed no sign of imminent collapse. Thirty paces distant, however, a section of wall saw three Gothic ladders spilling men atop the walls, their ranks swelling with each passing minute. Though armored Cappadocians flanked either side of the gatehouse, Gothic helms popped into view one after another, signaling imminent collapse of Imperial control.

"Bows," I ordered as the last of my warriors dismounted and prepared for the fight. "Eighty paces. Aim high, because I'd rather miss altogether than have a gust of wind blow arrows into our own men."

My retinue was small by then, only a dozen Aksumites and Uliaris, plus an overeager Shimon. It was he who handed over my bow as the rest sought weapons from a nearby depot.

"Lord, can I join?" Shimon asked, near begging.

There was no time to argue. "Have you practiced from this range?"

"Every day, Lord." Shimon beamed, lifting his arm as if to impress me with his acquired strength. "I can make this shot."

"Do it," I ordered. "But make sure the others are armed and tended to first."

Each of us hurried, testing bowstrings and snatching an arrow from Shimon. "Nock!" I called, watching the Goths push the defending Romans farther away from the troublesome ladders. "Draw!"

Of the twenty or so Goths at the walls, only one was bedecked in a rich set of scales, his blackened plume dancing with each jostling step. As he roared commands, I could see his attentions were preoccupied with the Romans before him, and not upon the newcomers stationed along the fortress bridge. It would be foolish to pick such well-armored target at this distance, yet Khingila's bow possessed far greater killing force than any Greek counterpart, and an officer was an impossible target to ignore.

"Chests and heads!" Sembrouthes added. "Aim high, as Varus says!"

"Loose!" I yelled, and allowed the bowstring to slip from my fingers.

It was no great volley; many arrows sailed a full arm's length above the tallest Gothic plume, but at least five found their mark. Two struck the Gothic officer—one that dug into the man's shoulder, with most of the barb dampened by thick layers of armor. The other, however, split the officer's eye, sending him reeling backward and crashing into a Goth still climbing from the ladders. He disappeared as he fell, while his companions called in confusion for their orders.

"Again!" I yelled. "Pick your targets, and aim high!"

In the second wave, two more Goths fell from our arrows, but by our third volley, their shields were up, deflecting all. Still, my tactic succeeded, for the necessity of a shield wall slowed the progress of the ladder climbers, allowing the Roman defenders time to reinvigorate their press to close the gap in their walls.

Two other sections of the Mausoleum's outer walls were under threat of being overrun with Goths, and both earned our volleys in turn. If I were one of Witiges' oath sworn, I would have raged at the unfairness of our bow fire, hungry to butcher such archers as I struggled in the shield wall. By the standards of the German tribes, our reliance upon bows might have been dishonorable, I do not deny. But in desperation, honor is an inferior currency to survival, and all of Belisarius' men were desperate to persist for as long as we could against the combined might of the Ostrogoth nation. And so, we plucked casualties from the ascending Goths, granting Bessas' men enough time to shore up their defenses and strike at a distracted enemy.

"Varus!" Bessas yelled, limping along the bridge with a half dozen blood-soaked cataphracts. "Is Belisarius sending men to aid me?"

"Just me," I answered. "You're about to get swarmed. Witiges is sending at least five thousand men here, with one ram."

"I'm already swarmed," Bessas cried, gripping a limp shield arm with an unwounded hand. "Twice as many attackers have hit us than Belisarius planned for. It's as if Witiges knew the Mausoleum would be our weakest point. I sent for more bowmen from Ascum an hour ago but have heard nothing thus far."

"The Goths have lived here for eighty years," I answered. "They likely remembered the Mausoleum was in disrepair."

"Maybe. But it still doesn't make sense, given that Witiges' army camped upon the opposite side of the Tiber." As Bessas spoke, Gothic horns blared beyond the walls, and a hail of arrows soon followed. Yet they only struck Roman targets, their barbs crashing inside the Aurelian Walls. "And there's the volleys."

"Few Goths use a bow," I replied, unstrapping my shield to protect against any future arrow fire.

"Not Goths," Bessas replied. "Suevi. From Lusitania. The Visigoths used to use them as ranged mercenaries, and it seems that Witiges has taken up the tradition."

More horns blared, signaling another Suevi cascade and a renewed surge of Goths along the walls. The flourish was echoed by a more distant series of horns—the ram, I guessed, and the thousands that Witiges deployed from the Pincian Hill. With the sound, I wanted to scream, for our situation was hopeless.

"Can we evacuate?" I asked. "Destroy the bridge connecting the Mausoleum gates across the Tiber?"

Bessas shook his head. "A stone bridge like that could take days to dismantle. If we lose the gates, I could hold the bridge for an hour, but no longer."

Another volley. Another cataphract quilled along his chest and gut, yelping in pain as he collapsed. An urge to run brewed within me, ironically rendering my legs weak. My confidence seemed to drain onto the bridge with each passing scream of agony and roar of Gothic success.

"What can I do?" I asked.

"Ask for reinforcements. The other leaders will listen to you." Bessas sounded resigned, almost frustrated, as if mine was a foolish question. "Other than that, I'd ask you to stay and fight with me."

"Done."

Though I knew he would be loath to depart, I ordered Cephalas to seek out aid elsewhere. The Vivarium was no option—Sindual's desperation made that clear, and I could only assume that the foederati faced as overwhelming a force as what Bessas faced along the Cornelian Gate. Samur was an option, for I had no doubt that my brother would cut a bloody swathe across Rome to come to my aid, yet he was too distant, and too close to the Vivarium. Neither Belisarius nor Gunderic and Xerxes would have been in an improved position, especially with the vast bulk of Witiges' army still on the eastern bank of the Tiber. That left only one realistic option, and it was one least likely to yield hardened warriors.

"Go to the Via Aurelia," I ordered Cephalas. "A half mile distant. Determine their situation, and if it is favorable, ask Tarmutus to send five hundred men to the Mausoleum. Tell them Varus requests this with all haste."

Cephalas departed immediately, sprinting down the tower and seeking a mount. Bessas nodded approval at my order, wincing as his bloodied arm jostled about with each step atop the bridge.

"Go inside and get Rosamund's help," I told him. "Rejoin us when you're ready. I'll take command of the gate."

"Thank you, Varus," Bessas said. "I mean it. When I met you in Scythian Neapolis, I thought you were little more than some cocksure recruit who wouldn't survive life at war, but you're the most dependable comrade I have known. Regardless of how this ends, I wanted you to know that."

Bessas, ever reserved, was not a man to give voice to his emotions, and initially his words offered unease, and even offense. Yet when he held his hale hand out in a gesture of friendship, I grasped him at the wrist, understanding the honor that he conferred.

"Let's make sure we survive this, and you can buy me wine as repayment." I grinned. "Now get your arm stitched so you can rejoin me."

As Bessas departed, more horns echoed in the distance, signaling Gothic reinforcements drawing closer. "What shall we do now?" Uliaris grumbled. "I'm not sure that you will live long enough to keep any promise to Bessas, at this rate."

"Go seek Ascum, wherever he may be," I countered. "Bessas' instincts were correct. We need more range to hold the Goths back. Tell him to bring an onager immediately, even if he bloodies a hundred horses dragging it here."

Uliaris griped but obeyed, following Cephalas' movements toward nearby horses. However, uneasiness gripped at my stomach.

"You have a plan?" Sembrouthes asked.

"Clear the walls before the rams come." I shrugged, and Sembrouthes rolled his eyes. "That's all we can do until Ascum arrives. Follow me."

Amidst the chaos, I began to discern the semblance of order that Bessas had wrought along the Mausoleum's inner and outer defenses. From upper windows and the topmost platform of the tower, archers strung arrows down upon the Goths, although there was precious little space for more than a handful of men to launch a volley.

Likewise, along the ring of the outer walls, swordsmen and spearmen in scaled armor fought hand-to-hand against Gothic climbers. Though their layers of reinforced iron gave them ample protection against all but the most forceful sword jabs or spear thrusts, it also deprived them of precious agility. Indeed, slowly, some of the luckier Goths had managed to exploit Bessas' less mobile defenses, but only upon certain sections of wall and none near the gatehouse. Added to our woes was waning visibility, for the bloody orb of our lifeless sun had dimmed, and now cast deep shadows despite its position at the zenith of the storm-wrought skies.

There was little else I could do but trust the centurions charged with defenses along the stretch of wall. Instead, I grounded my efforts upon the two smaller guard posts overlooking the Pincian Gate. It was there I found the bulk of Bessas' command, and what few reserve fighters that were available to plug gaps along the Mausoleum walls.

"Tribune!" a Cappadocian centurion saluted me. "Did Bessas send you? Are more coming?"

"Soon," I promised. "You have an entire section of Witiges' army, perhaps five thousand, rushing toward this position as we speak. They have a ram. What is our disposition, and how many men can you spare me?"

"Four hundred cataphracts, and another three hundred Cappadocians," the centurion answered. "I have seventy men here at the gate in reserve. We have more bows and spears than we know what to do with, but few opportunities to deploy them outside of groups of four to six men at a time."

I nodded. "Give me command of thirty men. If the gate is under threat, sound the horn, and I will not be far."

The centurion seemed visibly hesitant to part with what few warriors remained to him, but he nodded. "Of course, Lord. But if Belisarius doesn't reinforce us soon, there's nothing you or I could do to make a difference."

From the gatehouse, the centurion guided me up two levels of stairs, ending in a covered battlement. Three archers parted so that I could peer out to the north, well beyond the walls. Though I anticipated a great host of Goths, what greeted me was a sea of banners. Most bore the sun-crowned cross, yet several were stitched with a galloping horse. That foreign sigil stood above a row of several hundred bowmen—presumably the Suevi that Bessas had warned of, mercenaries from the distant coast of northwest Hispania. Farther into the distance, I spotted the faintest outline of approaching horsemen, the color of their banners identical to Witiges' men before me.

"Suevi bowmen, a siege ram, and thousands of Goths," I counted.

"For now, the bowmen are the greatest nuisance," the centurion remarked. "There aren't many of them, but my men can't move about safely, nor garrison the tops of the towers. Get rid of those men, and the Mausoleum's defenses become far easier."

But how am I to push back hundreds of archers fifty paces or more from the walls? I wondered privately. As before, there were no simple answers, nor indeed any foolish ones that had a hope of working.

"We wait for Ascum or Tarmutus," I said aloud. "Until then, I'm going below to fight. Instruct your bowmen to focus upon Goths standing atop our walls, for they are the greatest worry I have."

Descending to the ground level, thirty Cappadocians joined my dozen Aksumites, all awaiting my orders. Several I recognized as having served in my command in Tingitana—something I hope stoked their confidence rather than doubt.

"Our task is to strike like vipers!" I explained, noting both their overall fitness and their fresh condition. "Let other Romans control the walls, but if any Goths place two feet upon dressed stone, we shall send them to hell. Understood?"

All present saluted and followed me onto the grasses that separated the Mausoleum tower from the outer walls, quickening to a trot as we gazed upward at each section of our defenses. Every fifty paces, stone steps protruded from the walls and down to our level, affording the ability to pop in and out of battlements in danger of being overrun. In this, at least, the fort's designers had planned well. After trotting a third of the Mausoleum's circle from the Cornelian gatehouse, I discovered a section of walls that again threatened to be overrun, with a half dozen Goths forming a shield ring around twin ladders.

"On me!" I yelled, unsheathing my sword. "Close-quarter weapons only! Men at the rear of the column, find spears and stones to toss upon the enemy!"

Sprinting up the ten steps that linked us to the top of the walls, I waited until half of my followers filled in space behind me before pushing forward. A dozen armored cataphracts separated us from the Goths, with each man sluggish in his movements.

"Friends!" I shouted in Greek behind Bessas' men. "Scatter so we can pass!"

In the din, I had to repeat the order before it was understood and obeyed. I lowered my shield, joined thereafter by Sembrouthes and Wazeba with interlocking shields, leading our column three men abreast.

"Get ready!" Sembrouthes roared.

As the last cataphract slipped around our formation, something struck my shield — a Gothic spear, followed immediately by a sword slash. The scrape of the blade's tip against my iron boss rattled my mind to sudden attention. Again, a lust to kill infected my heart as I snarled at the enemies before me, jabbing the tip of my sword toward the thigh of the nearest Goth.

A swipe of his shield tossed my blow aside, but Wazeba thrust his own short sword at the unbalanced Goth's hip, piercing the thin coat of mail. The blade's tip pressed against the man's hip bone and toward his groin, yielding shouts of pain and a desperate flurry of less-disciplined strikes. While two other Goths stepped forward to challenge our shield wall, I again struck at the now-wounded Goth, using my shield to batter him backward.

The maneuver had far more destabilizing effects than any sword thrust. Rather than slaying the man, it sent him bleeding and stumbling backward, pushing one taller Goth careening from atop the walls and driving a gap amidst the others. Ultimately, climbers on that section of wall had lost their surging momentum, affording the briefest moment of opportunity.

"Push!" I yelled. "Push them over!"

To push our enemies was to live. At all costs, our mission was simply to keep the enemy, their ladders, and weapons away from the parapet. If we succeeded, Belisarius' thin defenses about the vast circle of Aurelian's Walls might still hold. However, a single failure, a temporary lapse in vigilance, and hordes of slavering Goths would spill onto the battlements, puncturing our positions like a blade through a wineskin.

Though the Siege of Rome lacked the sweeping formations of Dara, our diminutive wall atop Hadrian's Mausoleum obeyed the most ancient principle that any true warrior knows—most battles are won by the side with substantially greater numbers, rather than those more adept with blades, especially when applying such numbers at the appropriate positions on the battlefield. Belisarius' past victories proved this maxim was not always true, though even if you asked him, Belisarius would not have sought battle at Dara or Callinicum, or various others unless the fight had not been thrust upon the Imperial Army. To be sure, I claim none of the genius of John or Belisarius, yet in that moment, and to this day, I took great pride in our ability to simply barge upon our enemy and toss them about.

The Goth opposite me, bedecked in mail and plume that signified a junior officer, recognized the threat too late. He could not have been older than twenty, with a wispy beard, a mouth stuffed with crooked teeth, and mottled skin that told of a childhood illness. As I grinned at the young Goth, I must have appeared some Roman demon, an unholy figure cursing him in Latin as I led my column one pace forward at a time.

"Push them over!" I yelled in Latin. "Over the wall!"

At that, the young Goth's eyes widened, and he smashed his shield against mine. He called out in Gothic, and others moved to fill the ragged gap in the line, to no avail. In this single instance of the siege, my men were far more numerous, far stronger, and infinitely angrier.

"Down you go!" I yelled to the Goth, watching him abandon all discipline in his panicked movements.

"Sweep left!" Sembrouthes roared. "Send them over!"

In hindsight, there was little the Goths could do by then. One man closest to their ladders tried to climb down to safety, yet tripped and fell headfirst toward the massed ranks below. Another jumped from the walls and crashed into a handful of men below with a clank of metal and a chorus of pained cries. Stunned and deprived of their strength, the pocket of five Goths along our section sagged as we swept about. Given their resistance, I opted to press my shield at the defending Goths against the front edge of the walls, forcing them to shuffle dangerously backward.

"Please—surrender, I surrender!" Mouth agape, my young Gothic opponent blurted in clumsy Latin. "Please!"

Given the desperate circumstances, it was ludicrous for an attacking Goth to expect that we Romans would take prisoners. With the Goth's guard dropping as he begged for mercy, I took a step back, granting the lad a temporary cessation of our advance.

Hope spread across his eyes as he reasserted his desires. "I surrender!"

Using that extra pace, I squared my legs against the Goth, pressing my shoulder against the top of my shield. With a sudden roar, I burst forward, smashing my shield high against his own. He was far smaller, and visibly exhausted, and had no reserves of strength to stop himself from stumbling backward. As he did, his boots caught the edge of a merlon, and his body plummeted backward and upside down to the Goths below. He did not have time to scream, and though the man would have happily cut me in half, I am thankful that his departure was swift.

Sembrouthes and Wazeba followed my example, taking advantage of the press of warriors behind them to overcome the now-isolated

Goths atop our walls. Those still living followed their officer over, while men behind me launched spears at the massed Goths below. Still, however, men climbed.

"Spear!" I yelled, sheathing my sword. "Poke the bastards!"

Within heartbeats, a wooden shaft slipped into my outstretched hand. "Ready, Lord!" Shimon yelled, standing behind me in the second rank of our men.

"Get out of here, Shimon!" I barked.

But I could not enforce the order, for a climbing Goth was now chopping an axe against my shield—clumsy blows from one wavering atop rungs ten paces in the air, but ones I had to answer. Using Shimon's donated spear, I thrust downward at the ladder climber, only for him to deflect my jab with his shield rim. Simultaneously, a Gothic spear shot toward my face, but Sembrouthes flicked the weapon aside with his own shield, thus granting me a second attack upon the climbing Goth. I feinted a thrust again toward the man's lower body, but shifted the angle of the spear midway, sending it sailing past his defenses and plunging through his unarmored throat. Unlike the young officer, this death was neither merciful nor quick, and he wriggled helplessly as the strength was sapped from his legs. Unable to free my spearhead, I thrust the shaft once again, pushing the climber free from the rungs and crashing him against two of his ascending comrades.

"Clear the ladders!" I yelled. "Whoever has an axe, break the rungs!"

In truth, it was a dangerous gambit. The flying spears thickened after we cleared the walls of Goths, sending many of us cowering behind shields. More, the topmost rails of the Gothic ladders were sheathed in coarse iron to prevent shattering. Yet as I peeked downward, I spotted that the second-most rung from the summit lacked that protective covering.

"Still there, Shimon?" I yelled back.

"Still here, Lord!" he chirped.

"Then hold tight to my belt, and don't let me fall!" I commanded. "Sembrouthes, cover me!"

Hefting my axe, I paused until I felt the rustling of Shimon's fingers wrap about my sword belt. I paused only a moment longer, pressing my knuckles against the reassuring lump of the bronze cross and golden dragon, long enough for an instantaneous prayer that I was not about to die. At that moment, a Gothic horn boomed, and a dozen arrows sprung from Suevi bows directly toward my face.

The underside of Sembrouthes' shield blocked my vision as he covered our bodies. Three arrowheads buried themselves well into its panels, splintering fragments near my face. At least two Greek voices nearby hissed in pain, and although I remained unharmed, my shield arm quivered as, breathlessly, I stared at the arrowheads.

"Hurry!" Sembrouthes barked.

Clutching my axe handle, I sprang upright as Sembrouthes removed his barrier. Only one Goth had begun to climb the lowest rungs of our ladder, granting me just enough time for a sudden strike against the vulnerable rung.

"Throw spears now!" I yelled. "Down below!"

A dozen men near me obliged, causing the Gothic momentum to falter as they defended behind raised shields. Less than a hundred paces away, I spotted a group of Suevi preparing their bows for another volley, leaving precious heartbeats until we would be attacked again. Jerking my axe above my head, I lunged forward, crashing the edge against the rung's center with all the momentum and strength I could muster. The rung snapped cleanly in half, but my joy was brief—the extended downward slash had carried my shoulders and chest over the walls. With terror, I realized I all but dangled above the ground.

Halted only by the strained grip of Shimon. "Help! Pull him back!" he cried.

Behind me, I sensed Shimon slip as he gripped my belt, my body tipping further toward the Gothic horde. Unable to wrest myself upright, I could only swing my shield about my body to shelter against a cascade of Gothic projectiles. One Suevi arrow punctured a lower panel of my shield, while Goths below the walls thrust up clumsily in an attempt to pierce my boots.

Still, I held all at bay—at first.

A Goth, climbing upon my previously emptied ladder, thrust his spear at my chest—a soft blow, but enough to send the iron edge of the spearhead slicing through my shield-bearing upper arm. I felt hands upon my back struggling to haul my body to safety, yet knew they were too slow. Blood slaked down my arm and hand, and I prepared myself for a killing thrust, unable to protect more than a portion of my body.

It was a foolish way to die. And I have no doubt that I would have, had a blur of yellow and metal not whooshed past me, slamming into the Goth that wounded me. Whatever—whoever—it was, its great weight drove the Goth downward and snapped the ladder in half, sending it clattering to the ground. In the seconds that followed, Shimon, Sembrouthes, and Uliaris dragged me backward, and, once stable, I saw now the cause of my survival, the mass of yellow cloth and polished iron scales that now lay sprawled in a heap atop a half dozen dazed Goths.

"Wazeba!" I cried.

Gothic spearmen swarmed around Wazeba's twisted limbs, jamming their weapons into his chest and gut. Wazeba flailed and screamed as his body was torn apart, the sound ceasing only after a dagger severed his spine. Jerking once, Wazeba fell limp, then disappeared in a forest of Gothic spearmen.

"God damn it!" I yelled. "Wazeba!"

Sembrouthes placed his hands about my shoulders, shaking me violently. "He died to save you. Stop crying and get your arm mended while there's a lull. We've saved this section of walls for the time being."

"I'm so stupid…"

"You made a decision. So did he." Sembrouthes drew closer, ducking to avoid an opportunistic Suevi arrow. "He died so you might live, and it's your task to honor that."

Swallowing a knot in my throat, I nodded, and only then spotted an arrow jutting from Sembrouthes' shoulder. "You're hit!"

"Aye, that's why I'm going with you." Sembrouthes winced. "Just a sting. It happened when we were struck by the Suevi volley. Nothing notable."

I nodded. Sembrouthes was obviously masking the extent of his injury, so there was little time to waste. "Uliaris! Take our column and clear sections of wall threatening to be overrun. Move quickly, before the ram arrives."

Uliaris nodded, pointing to a target a quarter circle away along the outer defenses. "All right, you bastards! Let's see if there's a cock amongst you!"

I ordered Shimon and the remaining Aksumites to attend Uliaris as Sembrouthes and I rose to a higher level along the Mausoleum's inner sanctum. From that vantage point, the Mausoleum's defenses appeared brittle but holding, with no section in serious danger from swarming with enemies. Every section of dressed stone was caked in blood or bodies as arrows fell sporadically across our defenses, yet still Bessas' men held.

Bessas was returning to combat just as Sembrouthes and I arrived. "Jesus, what happened? It's been maybe a half hour!"

I sighed, wincing as I grabbed my bleeding arm. "We cleared the most concerning ladders from the walls. We're holding, but it will become far more difficult when the ram arrives."

"Mend yourself and come back out," Bessas replied. "Ascum won't let me down. We just need to hold a bit longer."

Attending to the wounded inside the Mausoleum's protected center, Rosamund gasped as Sembrouthes and I stumbled into her collection of suffering Romans. Most were beyond saving, their only hope a peaceful death rather than the slow suffering of a rotting cuts, yet Rosamund and Agathias had managed to repair many cataphracts whose heavy armor had borne the worst of an arrow or a blade. Grasping my arm, Rosamund bent closer, using her one hale eye to inspect the cut.

"It needs stitching, but the muscle is intact." She exhaled. "A clean cut."

Turning to Sembrouthes, she clicked her tongue as she touched the arrow jutting from the underside of his shoulder, bringing him to hiss. "As for you, the arrow isn't deep, but it needs to come out immediately."

Sembrouthes nodded. "Seal it with flame, and then allow me to go back out."

Rosamund shook her head. "Your day is done, Sembrouthes. Extracting the arrow is going to give you great pain, and you'll need to take something to calm you. I would do the same for Varus, but he is beyond reasoning with at this point."

Sembrouthes groaned in frustration but did not argue, and I could see in his eyes that the pain was greater than he was willing to admit. "With Wazeba dead, Nzamba is next to command the Aksumites. Tell him of my injury."

"Wazeba died?!" Rosamund shrieked.

I nodded. "He saved my life. His body is with the Goths now."

Rosamund bit her lip. "He cared for me during the riots. A quiet man, but gentle."

In all the years I had known her, Rosamund rarely displayed considerable grief upon news of a comrade's passing—something that I presumed could be explained by a mixture of pagan faith and a general loathing for Roman culture. She mourned Isaacius long ago, but in the considerable violence that followed, I can recall few instances of her showing any outward grief for the dead. Indeed, seeing her just then, I wondered whether she and Wazeba shared something more than mutual respect, but quickly shrugged the suspicion away.

"We will pray for his soul later," I told her, echoing Sembrouthes. "But if I do not pacify the Mausoleum, none of us will live to offer ritual blessings."

Regardless of the extent of her sadness, Rosamund did not let it affect her skills as a medic. After unfastening the rip in my armor and peeling away the torn sleeve underneath, she washed away crusted blood with wine and stitched my arm together within minutes. When

I inquired whether the injury would be debilitating, Rosamund rolled her eyes.

"You'll feel some weakness, but nothing permanent," she informed me. "But do not tempt fate any further, Varus. Even the gods have their limits, and you've tested their patience many times now."

Her work complete, she replaced my armor, tying it securely at the wrist before slipping my fingers into my glove. Though only a few hours had elapsed since the start of battle, Rosamund's face was already creased with worry, and her mail and hair were drenched in the gore of dozens of other men. Nevertheless, her touch was delicate against my skin; she managed to just gingerly graze my wound as she properly secured my armor deftly enough to make Cephalas jealous.

"You have my gratitude, Rosamund," I said. "And that of so many others. I hope you know that."

Rosamund offered a weak smile and stole the briefest of embraces. "Just survive this, Varus. That's all I ask." With that, she whipped out of sight, seeking the next soldier requiring her care.

Departing the inner tower, I glimpsed a small cohort of Romans crossing the Tiber, entering the Mausoleum's defenses. An initial detachment from Tarmutus' city guards, I thought at first—but no, for I then discerned the burned visage of Ascum, his arms piled full of pieces of lumber. He flinched as another Suevi volley swooped nearby, while his followers hustled to reach the Mausoleum's center and place as much distance between themselves and the Goths.

Hailing Ascum, I jogged quick as I could to intercept his progress, and was greeted only with a handful of wood, iron, and rope tossed from his arms into my own. I hissed as a section of rope rubbed against my stitches, hoping that Rosamund's work had not so soon been undone.

"Where are the archers?" I demanded.

Ascum frowned. "Couldn't be moved. Perenus and Gunderic needed them in the east. I've got forty men, but something far better for you."

"Better?" I asked. "What is all of this?"

"Scorpions!" Ascum grinned. "They lack the raw punch of ballistae but are far easier to maneuver and construct. All I need is to reach the top of the Mausoleum to set them up."

Skeptical, I nodded. "And the amphorae?"

"Naphtha." Ascum's smile hardened. "It worked against Theudis' men, and I can only imagine their cousins in Italy would be equally predisposed to burning."

I shivered. "Just be careful, and don't blow holes in my walls like the sea gates of Septem."

Ascum rasped in laughter. "Give me ten men to haul these beasts to the top of the Mausoleum tower, and keep your worries to yourself. All will be well."

"Only if Tarmutus arrives," I muttered. "We're short on men, and growing shorter with each attack."

Ascum's mirth faded, a flicker of fear on his face. "Belisarius is short on men everywhere, Varus. In the east, Roman women have joined in throwing rocks at our besiegers. Perenus is reduced to using children. Though the others suffer, you still have me. Direct me to where I may best be useful."

Women. Children. A bilious fear rose in my gut that I struggled to quench, wondering whether Sindual's warning of Perenus' crumbling forces had been truer than I'd accounted for. "What do you require?"

"The top of the tower, and any platform in between. We have all the naphtha and bolts we could desire but did not dare carry torches. If we want the naphtha to do anything useful, I'll need fire."

"Easy," I said. "Agathias keeps torches in assisting Rosamund as a medic."

I guided the Alans inside the tower and up its spiral stairway. Ascum's men split into teams of three, requesting additional archers to accompany them as they fixed scorpions along the Mausoleum's open balconies. There were to be ten scorpions in total, and as Ascum and I panted and wheezed our route to the tower's apex, I questioned whether such instruments would truly aid in our defense.

"They're tiny!" I complained as Ascum reconstructed his first scorpio. "Not much larger than a recurve bow!"

Ascum raised an eyebrow at my lack of respect, but chuckled. "They're small, yes, but they strike harder than any bow I've seen. Even yours. Their bolts aren't as large as with the ballistae, but they're much easier to operate. Any simpleton can operate the crank and load the bolts, as long as he isn't drunk."

Another Gothic horn blared. This one did not signal the arrival of another volley of arrows, however, but of Witiges' ram and reinforcements nearing their destination. From atop the tower, I could only guess that the ram was a mere thousand paces distant, while teams of Goths galloped hard alongside the siege weapons to reinforce the constant influx of ladder climbers and bowmen.

"Any other gates facing rams or towers?" I asked.

"Not that I've yet seen," Ascum replied. "It's odd that Witiges would hold back such an advantage."

I shrugged. "He's softening us for an easier breakthrough. If your scorpions can keep the Cornelian Gate secure, I'll name my next child after you."

"And be a horrible father in the process!" Ascum chortled. "Stay a moment and watch a volley if you don't trust me. No naphtha for now, while we test the range, but you'll see the benefits of these beauties."

With the construction complete and bolts loaded into the five scorpions atop the Mausoleum's heights, Ascum ordered a runner to seek the status of the remaining five engines stationed on platforms on lower floors. Soon, the man returned, indicating that all were prepared for the initial volley. With that, Ascum plucked a horn from his belt and raised it to his lips, struggling to purse the flame-withered skin as he blew a rolling, flat, ominous note.

"Launch," Ascum roared. "Prepare for more."

I watched the scorpion bolts, perhaps half again the weight of a typical arrow and twice the length, whip downward toward our attackers. Many crashed into the rows of Suevi archers, puncturing armor with ease and even severing one unlucky man at the thigh. The Suevi scattered in confusion as more Goths stared up at the towering threat. The lithe missiles of the scorpions were undeniably effective, yet held little of the stunning awe that our ballistae wrought with each massive blow.

I began to voice my disappointment, selecting words to not offend Ascum. "Definitely helpful, but I'm not so certain—"

"Load and fire!" he yelled. Within half a minute, all scorpions had been cranked and loaded, and we launched another round toward the Suevi. This time, the fire butchered a plumed chieftain and sent many bowmen sprinting away, retreating far beyond the range of their inferior bows.

"You were saying?" Ascum teased.

"Mother of God, you're brilliant." And he was, for what the scorpions lacked in destructive strength, they made up for in sheer speed, able to shoot ten arrows before a ballista fired a single reload. It was like nothing I had witnessed before—and doubtless, nothing the Goths had either.

"I admit, the ancient Romans were touched by creativity." Ascum bowed. "I only wish I had discovered this before. Imagine these in Mesopotamia! Callinicum would have gone quite differently."

More, they were so simple to operate that Ascum invited me to participate in one volley. Each scorpio needed only three men to manipulate its three levers—one to alter height, another to adjust the angle of fire, and the third to crank the ropes, release the tension, and release the bolt. With the aid of Ascum's trained assistant, I aimed my scorpio toward a particularly dense array of Gothic spearmen that had gathered about three ladders, each man waiting a turn to attack Uliaris' diminishing forces.

"Loose!" I called.

With so many warriors packed together, it was impossible *not* to find a target. The three scorpions capable of angling a volley toward that portion of walls loosed one bolt, and then a second, and immediately thereafter a third. Blood misted the air, and though the Gothic assault continued, it was with far less vigor than before. Below, I glimpsed a lone figure—Uliaris—turn briefly to gape at the angels from heaven that eased his burden.

After a fifth volley, Ascum produced a waterskin and dribbled a tiny stream along the ropes that turned the cranks of each scorpio. "A lesson learned from Callinicum," he explained. "Flax heats from overuse, and frays to the point of snapping. Taking a short reprieve to correct this issue is well worth it for all involved."

A single glance at Ascum's face and withered arm attested to the truth of that sorely won lesson. At Callinicum, when Ascum's ballistae fired for a day and a night, the ropes of one machine snapped upon firing, sending a flaming bolt into a stack of naphtha-filled amphorae. The resulting pillar of flame burned throughout the night, killing many of Ascum's prized siege engine operators and covering over a third of his body in scars.

"And the naphtha?" I asked.

"That is up to you," he replied. "But with the ram coming, I would wait until it reaches a hundred paces from the walls. Then, I'll see if I can get the naphtha to reach its target, though it will be your responsibility to set it alight. Agathias' torches will work adequately... but then again, you'll want more than one to get a quick enough blaze to catch them unawares."

Aside from larger amphorae, Ascum commandeered a smaller stack of clay jars, each no larger than a table cup at a popina. "I can tie two of these to each bolt, but it's better to use only one for safety. That's ten jars per volley, for however long you need. I have three hundred ready for use."

I nodded. "Send me a few larger amphorae in case it might be useful down below. Beyond that, I will track the ram, and our horn will signal the time for attack."

I gazed northward. Many of the Gothic reinforcements had begun to trickle toward the Mausoleum's walls, while the ram trudged slowly but consistently closer. Aided by one of Ascum's Alani attendants, we carried several amphorae of naphtha down below, stacking them in a secured entrance to the Mausoleum. I assigned the attendant to stand watch as I reentered the battle, where I was embraced once more by the deafening boom of suffering, confusion, and death.

And something far stranger. At first, it appeared as if men of stone and bronze danced about the Mausoleum's bridge, their antiquated armor and flowing robes recalling Latin customs from a century ago or more. As I trotted closer, I discovered four men hauling each statue, cursing as they balanced the ponderous weight toward the outer walls. Among them was Shimon, who jumped at the sight of me, nearly dropping his burden.

Initially, it appeared as if the men were committing an unholy mixture of sacrilege and plunder, abandoning Rome's walls to Gothic control. "What in God's name are you doing?!"

"More missiles, Lord!" Shimon pointed happily.

"Missiles?"

"Uliaris' idea!" Shimon added. "We need to break the ladders, just as you ordered. These statues are heavy enough to snap any wood without risking our men."

I couldn't help but laugh. "That's insane!"

"Maybe!" Shimon replied. "But I doubt the old Romans will mind. They liked to think of themselves as warriors, and now they can do that in death."

I did not forbid their lunacy, nor even their desire to cut down more statues to use as ammunition. The Mausoleum, so richly decorated, was adorned with hundreds of such figures, the cost of which I deliberately refused to consider. The only resistance we met was from a gray-bearded priest, one of dozens who were sheltering inside the Mausoleum.

"That's Saint Dathus!" the priest said, pointing to a particularly hideous bronze statue of an elderly man in a bishop's attire. "You can't use that as a weapon!"

"Why not?" asked a Cappadocian. "What'd he ever do?"

The priest straightened, his voice lowering with reverence. "The saintly Dathus was named as a bishop of Ravenna when a dove landed squarely upon his head. A sign of his holiness in a time when pagans ruled!"

Still grunting under the weight of the bronze, the Cappadocian and his two comrades burst into laughter. "So a pigeon shits on the man's head, and now he's a saint? If that's a sign, consider me your man."

"It was a dove!" Horrified, the priest crossed himself. "The holy Dathus—"

"Would not wish to see his beloved Church subject to desecration and plunder as it suffered under Alaric," I interjected. "Father, I shall offer prayers of forgiveness to Saint Dathus, but we need his statue. Perhaps the saint might guide its weight to splinter a Gothic ladder or two."

The priest's gaze narrowed upon me as he scanned my armor and plume. "You are Belisarius' man, Tribune?"

"I am Lord Varus," I answered. "And you are?"

"Father Markus," he said. "I lack the strength to prevent your sacrilege, although I pray to God that he teaches you lot humility. The Ostrogoths might be barbarians, but they treated us clergy, and the Pope Silverius, with utmost respect."

Silverius' name made me shiver as Belisarius' warning of the man's rumored disloyalty streaked through my mind. "A thousand apologies, Father. I will see the injury corrected."

With that, the statues continued to descend from the Mausoleum's outcrop, although other priests wept and moaned at the loss of the likeness of some long-dead emperor or holy man. As Ascum's scorpions thundered above, the ponderous bulk of Roman artistry trailed from the Mausoleum's bridge and toward each fighting platform of the outer walls. I even joined the effort myself, lifting a stone likeness of Emperor Theodosius with three other Cappadocians until we reached the front of the walls.

"Clear the front!" I yelled.

As we waited for the increasingly familiar thrum of the scorpions, a half dozen defenders aided me in lifting the statue above a ladder and dropping it forcefully below, where it crushed two Goths and splintered the wooden rungs to the point of uselessness. Others followed along the line—some obliterating a ladder, others simply dumped atop the packed heads of dozens of Goths immediately below our stone walls. A gaggle of priests wept and prayed at the destruction, regardless that some stone figures portrayed notorious pagans, their crushing weight offering the slimmest advantage we could extract from the Gothic procession.

For a time, we appeared to be turning the battle, with Roman cheers soaring above Gothic roars for blood, despite the thousands of reinforcements that an arriving warlord had yielded. With few ladders still standing, our walls became simpler to defend, and hope kindled that this section of battle might conclude.

Until the ram wheeled into motion, five hundred paces from the Cornelian Gate. Lumbering forward, it appeared a floating hut, enclosing both its log and the men driving it forward in a sealed wooden carapace.

"To the gate!" I screamed. "Archers, to the gate!"

Soon thereafter, Bessas met me before the gate, followed by Uliaris and my prior entourage. "If they break through—" Bessas began.

"They won't!" I yelled. "Uliaris, take five men to the Mausoleum. I've stored amphorae of naphtha. Have two men carry torches, and the rest bring the naphtha here, but gently!"

"Sweet Christ, naphtha again?" Uliaris moaned, but he nevertheless picked five followers and sprinted toward the Mausoleum.

Bessas was skeptical. "Unless you have a river of that infernal muck, it won't be enough."

I pointed up at the Mausoleum's platforms. "Ascum has more that he'll launch from the scorpions. He just needs our signal."

"Lunatics!" Bessas grinned at last. "I guess it's the only plan we have. I'll follow your lead."

As we gathered men to defend the gate, a horn sounded from the city's interior. I jumped, initially fearing that the Goths had broken through from a different section of the city. Yet as the horn rang out again, spilling the notes of a Roman march, I rushed toward the Tiber and discovered the procession of the Roman city watch.

"What took you so long?!" I shouted, saluting Tarmutus.

He returned the gesture. "Sorry, Lord. The Goths rushed from Janiculum. Most of my men are still defending the western gates, but I was able to spare a hundred men."

"Only a hundred?" Bessas whispered, fear flickering across his face.

"More than I should have stolen away," Tarmutus answered. "Half of my men are wounded. But I came nonetheless, Lord."

I nodded. "Thank you, Tarmutus. Fall in toward the Cornelian Gate. The Goths are rushing us with a ram, and we're going to set it aflame."

"With naphtha," Bessas hissed.

Tarmutus made a sign of the cross. "God help us. What a terrible way to die."

While most of our forces lined the Mausoleum's outer circle, the bulk of our reserves clustered about the Cornelian Gate. I waited for Uliaris to return with his hazardous amphorae before muscling my way to the top center of the gate, where I overlooked the swarm of Goths. Though most ladders near the gate remained intact, there were now few climbers, with most Gothic formations sheltering beneath their shields as they awaited the progress of the ram. When the ram was three hundred paces from our gate, a great cry rang out amongst the Goths, who cleared an approach for the ram haulers. I had precious little time remaining, and asked Shimon to hand me my horn.

"Romans!" I yelled. "Do not let this gate fall! Throw everything you have. One last defense, and they will run screaming!"

We were a piteous lot, with only a few hundred men healthy enough to mount a defense. Yet we cheered as best as we could, with spears and arrows distributed to all present.

"Amphorae are ready," Uliaris whispered to me. "We have four lit torches."

My eyes were fixed upon the ram. "It will suffice. Be prepared for anything."

"Christ Almighty," Uliaris muttered, readying his shield as he stood to my right.

The ram cleared a marker for two hundred paces distant, and all the gate's defenders awaited their orders. "Romans, nock your arrows! Keep your heads down, and aim for larger gatherings!"

Most obeyed, while three separate teams hauled our few remaining statues atop the nearest merlon. Among them was Bessas, who nodded my way as he ordered the ponderous weights to hold for our order.

Pressing my horn to my lips, I blew as forcefully as I could, directing the noise toward Ascum's heightened battlements. Depleting my air, I blew the note again and was met by an equally vigorous response from Ascum's men. I spied the scorpions' operators scurrying about and knew the time to strike had arrived.

"Launch!" I yelled. "Kill the bastards!"

Bows thrummed, spears rattled, and stone statues crashed against the thousands of Goths around us. For the unfortunate targets, the consequences were terrible, with mangled limbs and pulverized bodies no Gothic shields could prevent.

"Keep going!" I yelled, wondering why the scorpions attack was delayed. "Everything you have!"

After two further volleys, each more ragged than the last, the surviving Goths responded in kind. Gothic spears and even a handful of Suevi arrows sailed toward the gate, striking several of my men. Furious, I placed the horn to my lips once more, believing that Ascum had misinterpreted my signal.

Until, with a whistling hail, the scorpion bolts smashed against the Gothic formations. Small pockets of blackened muck splattered shields and armor, and many a Goth found the viscous naphtha covering exposed flesh and eyes. For those men, the pain must have been unimaginable.

In the second volley, Ascum's scorpions struck the ram, burying its bolts into that vast shed of hewn lumber that glided slowly across the ground. I could hear the Goths inside that enclosure gasping and shouting, yet I doubted that any were in danger of serious injury. As with the Gothic spearmen, however, splotches of naphtha decorated the ram's encasing, with few Goths seeming to recognize the danger.

But the siege ram's progress continued. More scorpion bolts quilled the ram, with discernible effect upon its progress. And though the naphtha was promising, the coverage was too thin to guarantee a continuous blaze once lit.

"Ready, Uliaris!" I yelled.

He handed me an amphora, while Shimon took a second in his arms. With diminishing success, our men continued their barrage; Ascum's scorpions tore the Gothic defenses into ribbons. No fewer than ten bolts jutted from the ram's covering, yet still it trudged toward the closed gate. Fifty paces. Forty. Twenty. Until finally, it was within range.

"Toss them!" I yelled.

Both men shot upright, heaving the amphorae toward the ram. The pottery shattered, splattering naphtha onto the ram's roof and many men besides, leaving me but a heartbeat to grab two torches and drop them below. All I could do was pray.

To this prayer, God was not silent. An instant, searing heat burned the naphtha-soaked conflagration, with flames licking all corners of the ram. Other Romans followed my example, tossing torches upon the massed Goths and kindling smaller fires along the length of the northern walls. The fires soared, illuminating the Mausoleum as liquid flames spread over shields and helmets like an infernal fluid with endless kindling to sate its appetite. Inside the ram, I heard men scream, a keening howl as the ram rocked about. Some men managed to escape for a few moments, only to be greeted by a wall of burning death all around.

Compared to Septem, our defense of Hadrian's Mausoleum was little more than a cookfire. Though I cannot be certain, I would wager at least a hundred Goths were burned alive; their corpses still smoldered the following morning. I pitied them, for the fires ignited by naphtha cause a horrible death, indiscriminate as they spread across wood, metal, or living skin. For a moment, I even feared the heat might weaken the gates, and ordered buckets of water to cool the wood and stones where possible. Ultimately, Hadrian's Tomb only glowed with light as the Gothic surge burned away.

Not that the threat of battle had been extinguished, for many ladders remained, and thousands of frustrated and vengeful Goths stalked the outer walls. But that threat had finally become manageable, leaving the real possibility that, for today, this section of the wall would hold. Ascum's scorpions volleyed every minute as I scanned the horizon for a second ram or one of the accursed siege towers. Only rolling hills and a lazily flowing Tiber lined the north, and for a few beautiful minutes, Bessas and I believed we had triumphed.

Until, as fate always commands, desperation galloped into my midst. But now, rather than Belisarius or Sindual, or any warrior altogether, it was a balding man, far too old for such exertions, who hailed me, barely remaining atop his mount with the effort. When I saw him, I knew that our fortunes had turned dire.

"Varus!!" Father Petrus rasped as he slowed to a trot, jerking in the saddle as he rode around me. "The Vivarium is falling! Perenus asks that you either send all men available to you or that you commit to paying for his funeral rites."

"You've seen it?" I asked.

Petrus nodded. "Half the gate's defenders are citizens. Belisarius told me to find you. You must come at once!"

Whether out of a sworn oath or friendship or necessity, I had no choice but to comply. I handed control of the Mausoleum to Bessas, choosing a hundred men to venture to the opposite side of the city. Exhaustion reigned everywhere: in the sick bays where Rosamund and Agathias ceaselessly treated others and in the frontline's hours of resisting Gothic attacks. But still, with our weapons, Rosamund's healing equipment, and even a few jars of naphtha, we rode, galloping to the eastern gates.

To something far worse than anything the morning had inflicted upon me.

FINAL STAND
OF THE VIVARIUM

The ride to the Vivarium drained life from me. Though the path was dressed in stone, each hoofbeat of our canter amplified the pain in my arm, the weariness of my limbs, and the fog in my mind. As had happened at the Mausoleum, one of my hands began to quiver, and though I attempted to disguise that infirmity by gripping hard against my reins, Rosamund, my riding partner, was not fooled, and she frowned when she caught my gaze.

"You are well, Varus?" she asked in Heruli.

"Fine," I replied tersely. "Just tired."

We all were, Rosamund included. So much gore caked her face that her skin showed none of its usual Gepid translucence. Amongst the men, there was no banter, only worried looks from Cephalas and a resigned silence as we followed Rome's streets east through the Campus Martius.

I expected barren streets, yet discovered many curious faces peering from behind windows and doors toward the nearest wall. Some ventured forward to shout encouragement, and one older woman distributed cups of diluted wine to our procession.

"God bless you!" she called to me. "God bless you for protecting us!"

Nearing the Suarian Forum, we encountered an equally spirited column of riders led by Belisarius. Leading a gathering of some hundred or so bucellarii, Belisarius galloped forward to intercept my progress as we hugged the road along the Quirinal Hill.

"Heading toward the Praenestine Gate?" he asked.

The straps of my helmet caught against my beard, and I adjusted them for easier speech. "Perenus sent Petrus. The Vivarium is under assault."

Belisarius nodded. "Two siege towers are moving in that direction. I've requested aid elsewhere, but no confirmations yet."

Though we had little time to converse, I briefly explained my defense of the Mausoleum. Pleased, Belisarius in turn informed me of all he had learned throughout the morning.

"Witiges abandoned the northern gates not long ago, although a thousand Goths remain. Our southern gates are relatively uncontested, thanks be to God, and now you've secured the Tiber."

"Any serious losses?" I asked.

Belisarius' optimism turned grave. "The Vandals were hit hard, although Gunderic and Xerxes smashed a Gothic ram with their onager. Your brother's Huns have fared far better, probably inflicting the most casualties of all our men. But it seems that Witiges is concentrating his strength against the Vivarium for a final assault."

"Makes sense," I replied. "Other than the Mausoleum, it's difficult to defend. Attackers can approach from the south and east, and the Praenestine Gate is too distant to easily shift men."

"True," Belisarius agreed. "But I still worry that the Goths might have agents acting for them inside Rome. From atop the Pincian Gate, I thought I spied men signaling to Goths along the Viminal Hill, although I cannot be certain."

Again, an unwelcome hint of treachery spiked further doubt in the challenge ahead of us. "Bessas thought the same of the Tomb of Hadrian. Too many Goths knew to strike that position, despite the Gothic camps positioned to the east of the Tiber."

"We shall delve into these suspicions later," Belisarius concluded. "For now, lead us to the Vivarium."

Leading the combined host of soldiers from the Mausoleum and the Pincian Gate, I trailed southward. At the Salarian Gate, I spied

Samur, his Huns launching one disciplined volley after another, and my brother spared the briefest of moments to hail our progress. From there we rounded the Viminal Hill, where the rattle of clanging metal rose in a deafening crescendo. The smell of fresh corpses and burning lumber billowed around the Tiburtine Gate, and the unnerving Vandal howl pierced the clangor of battle. For a moment I spied Gunderic, his rumbling laughter seeming to make the ground quake as he lifted a Goth cleanly from the ground and tossed him helplessly outside the Aurelian Walls. Though I spotted the Vivarium in the distance, I was stopped once more as twenty men trotted from the gate directly toward me.

"The truth smiles upon you," Xerxes greeted me, grinning. "That's the only way you're still alive, my friend."

His armor, normally glittering with copper and gold-lined iron scales, was chipped and damaged, with pieces bent or missing altogether. Like Rosamund, he was painted with the dark ichor of gore, and his shield was battered from dozens of strikes. Led by Wisimar, the Vandals at Xerxes' back were in little better condition, although where the Persian prince embraced this cataclysmic siege with solemnity, Wisimar and his comrades were all smiles.

"Perenus asked for men," Xerxes explained. "Our gate is secure, but the Goths keep coming. All Gunderic can spare is twenty."

I nodded. "Will Gunderic be able to hold? Is he handling well?"

"Are you joking?" Wisimar laughed. "This is the happiest day of Gunderic's life. I'll never understand why you lot are so upset when you're called to arms."

To the south, Roman horns sounded a dozen abrupt notes, signaling an imminent attack and halting all conversation. Belisarius and I kicked our mounts forward, trailed by our swelling retinue. Evidence of extensive battle welcomed us well before entering the Vivarium's streets, including bodies that had fallen from the walls and now lay discarded as the living resisted Gothic surges. The stench of death grew more pungent, accompanied by a chorus of pain and rage as we reached the Praenestine Gate.

The Vivarium was a horror. Centuries ago, it had been an entrance dedicated to the transfer of livestock for butchers and game for the Colosseum, its gate an arch so vast as to allow such foreign creatures as elephants to enter the Eternal City. Now, it rattled against the thundering bodies of men, with only a pitifully thin line of Herulian foederati to resist.

"Lord Belisarius!" Fulcaris yelled, sprinting from the gate. "They're coming!"

A sodden bandage, occasionally leaking a trickle of blood, was wrapped around Fulcaris' head. His body was similarly wrecked, complemented by tiny fragments of wood and stone dust clinging to his armor. The ouroboros adorning his shield had been lashed by countless punctures and scrapes, while my sigil above the Praenestine Gate was checkered with tears.

"Calm yourself and explain," Belisarius said, dismounting from Balan and readying his weapons.

"Easier to show you, Lord," Fulcaris said, sucking deep breaths as he wiped salty sweat from his brow. "But keep your heads down. Their ballistae are quieter now but aren't yet ready to quit the day."

Leaving only a handful of men to escort the horses to safety, we climbed the gate's steps so we might gaze into the field from the safety of the enclosed tower. Goths surged from all directions, stretching as far back as could be discerned behind a cloud of dust. In the distance, I spotted enemy ballistae, two of which appeared operational atop their elevated platforms. Accompanying them were twin siege towers, with Gothic officers lashing the wheeled monstrosities onto oxen. Another armored battering ram wheeled into position several hundred paces distant, already grinding its axels atop earth packed by thousands of stomping feet. That alone would have been enough to terrify any Roman, for we simply lacked the remaining vitality to resist such combined might.

What made it worse was not the presence of Witiges, nor even the young Visigoth warlord Totila. Standing amidst the Gothic lords was the once-handsome face of Indulf, the traitorous bastard who had yet to atone for Mundus' murder.

As Rosamund and Agathias tended to the wounded, I stole a moment away from the other officers and crept atop the walls. The Herulian foederati resisted a slow yet continual onslaught of ladder climbers, with small groups circling each climber as others too wounded or exhausted to continue sprawled just paces away in what clearings could be found. It was there that I found Perenus, seated with his back to a merlon. Pressing a hand against his hip, he greeted me with haggard rasps.

"Not too late," Perenus joked. "You almost missed the best part."

Beneath his hand, an open gash trickled blood onto his stomach and legs. I had witnessed Perenus suffer grievous wounds before, but atop the Vivarium, he seemed all but deprived of life. "I'm getting you to Rosamund."

"No, no. The best part is when I stand up and single-handedly disembowel every Goth in Italy." Perenus grinned, his eyes unfocused. "Might have to wait for a bit, though."

Ignoring his japes, I signaled for another Herulian spearman, and together we lifted Perenus about our shoulders and hefted him back to the gate. Rosamund immediately tucked him into a corner, beside a man who had been blinded by shrapnel from a ballista strike, and leaned over his body to unfasten his armor and shirt.

"Slow down!" Perenus quipped. "How about a little wine before you take liberties with me, Rosamund?"

She slapped him. "You stupid ox! Why didn't you seek care as soon as you were hurt?"

Prone, Perenus shrugged. "The Vivarium was my job. Now that my replacements are here, I might steal a nap."

I leaned forward, my head accidentally grazing Rosamund's. "I didn't give you permission to die in Tauris, and I'm not doing so now. If you go to your Hades, I'm going to drag you back to this shithole."

"Aye, Hades would be an improvement." Perenus winked. "Varus, I don't know if we're going to win this."

There was nothing I could offer in encouragement. At that moment, I realized a dozen Heruli eavesdropped upon our conversation, each man bearing wounds and struggling to stand. "Well, Perenus, what do you recommend we do first?"

Perenus shrugged. "I was never one for the clever ideas. But there's a store of naphtha down below, just like how you won Septem. If the Goths were going to take my gate, I was going to burn as many as I could before joining them in hell."

Cephalas, delayed in climbing the walls, interrupted our gathering. "Perenus!"

Perenus nodded. "It'll be fine, old friend. At the rate I'm going, you and I will be brothers with maimed limbs."

But my mind had already wandered. Naphtha. The devil's wine, and all too often, my savior in battle. "How much naphtha do you have?"

"Twenty jars, or thereabouts," Perenus guessed. "Enough to bake a pie with."

Leaning forward, I pecked a kiss on his head. "You've saved us, you arse."

I left him speechless as I sprinted up into the tower, perhaps for the first time in his adult life. When I whispered to Belisarius of Perenus' stored naphtha, he, too, recognized the opportunity to destroy the Goth siege weapons, although he tempered his enthusiasm with more practical worries. "That's only enough to safely destroy the ram or the two towers. A boon for certain, but not enough to halt ten thousand determined men fighting for their king."

"Down!" Xerxes yelled.

And then the world went dark. It took several moments before I realized that my body lay sprawled on the ground, my shoulders and chest atop the legs of a Herulian centurion. With unfocused eyes and ringing ears, I wanted to vomit, choking on the dust-strewn air as I grasped at anything to stabilize my body. Eventually regaining enough of my senses to rise, I was joined by twenty other men that had been thrown about in the tower. My eyes were slow to adjust amidst the dust, though once they did, I noticed the ragged gash in the tower's frontmost window.

Much later, I pieced together what had occurred from those who were sheltered in a nearby tower. Soon after Belisarius and I entered one of the main gatehouses, Witiges' two ballistae had loaded their engines and connected against our battlement, their aim trained by an entire morning and afternoon of unchecked attack. Our own three ballistae and one onager returned the gesture and smashed against the massed formations of Goths, but to little observable effect. Witiges could afford thousands of casualties, while each injured man of Belisarius' army was a mild tragedy.

"Are you hurt, Varus?" Belisarius called to me a few paces distant, coughing angrily as he snatched a nearby waterskin.

"Just my pride, Lord," I croaked.

The tower had saved our lives, yet its crumbling front gave little confidence it could do so again in the future. "We need to separate, give them less of a temptation to concentrate their attack," Belisarius said. "I'm taking thirty men to the southern towers and will command the ballistae. Any chance that Ascum can reinforce our engines?"

"No, Lord," I replied. "If we pull him away from Bessas, the Mausoleum becomes a target again. And we lack the men to defend opposing corners of the city."

Belisarius cursed under his breath. "Then we're on our own. Let's see what the Goths attack us with, and God shall decide where our naphtha goes."

Another crash struck our walls—ballistae again, albeit less concentrated than the first volley. In the aftermath, Belisarius gathered his bucellarii and scurried southward, where they would seize the most vulnerable point along the Vivarium for his command. That left me with the Vivarium's gatehouse, where I gazed down upon thousands of men and more siege equipment than I could count.

Worse, with the Heruli overstretched and bleeding, a fair portion of my defenders were simple Roman citizens, flocking to Tarmutus to borrow weapons or simply tossing stones upon the heads of the enemy. These men and women were unarmored and undisciplined, although they were at least enthusiastic in their defense. As I strode from the gatehouse to a nearby tower, however, I spied familiar figures amongst the Roman populace—ones that demanded my immediate attention.

"Cours!" I yelled, storming toward the orphaned Hun boy who had become one of Mariya's foundlings and Sembrouthes' trainees. "What in the deepest hell are you doing here?"

A spear whistled overhead, and we both crouched behind merlons to guard against further stray darts. "You trained me to fight, Lord," he said. "I don't want to sit back with the children."

Clenching my fist, I would have choked from laughter if I had not been so angry. "You are a child! No more than seven?"

"Nine," Cours corrected, puffing out his chest. In his hand was a smooth stone the size of a quail's egg. Few would cower from such a tiny missile, yet from that height, Cours was able to toss the stone with enough force to crack a Goth's helmet, sending the man spinning around dazed.

"Go back to the Domus, now!" I yelled. "That is an order!"

Cours frowned. "All of us?"

"All?" I murmured stupidly, my anger quickly transforming into a chimera of terror and fury. "Show me."

As I temporarily returned command of the gate to Fulcaris, Cours fearlessly led me across the battlements a full hundred paces northward. Though the fighting slackened somewhat atop this section of wall, Gothic climbers still continued unabated, with Herulian men exchanging cuts and thrusts in a struggle to keep their section of walls clear of the enemy. In a nearby tower, Cours directed me to his companions, making my fears manifest.

"Lord!" Tiberius gaped, bowing as he stuck close to an enclosed stone wall. "We came to help!"

"If Perenus recovers, I'm going to beat his arse bloody," I seethed.

Other than Cours and Tiberius, another half dozen foundlings skulked about—including the young John. None were older than twelve, and all were filthy, their skin and clothes decorated with dust and an occasional blotch of blood. None appeared wounded, either, thank God, and while none cowered in terror, all seemed tense as death raged about them. That gathering alone would have captured my attention, yet the inclusion of one further member made me abandon all thought of the duties weighing upon my shoulders.

"Pater!" Zenobia shouted, among the youngest of the group.

"Zenobia!" I roared. "You're leaving now! All of you!"

At that, Tiberius strode before me, his darkened eyes far too sad and far too worldly for a child only a few years older than Zenobia. "It is not Zenobia's fault, Lord. Cours and I planned to sneak to the walls and heard that this gate had the greatest need. The others discovered us as we were leaving and came along."

Nearby, a Goth screamed as a spear was stuck into his guts, his body crashing against our tower as he fell from the walls. I knelt, my eyes square with Tiberius' own. The lad must have viewed me as a terror, a demon, a gore-spackled thing from hell, completely unrecognizable as the lord and master of his household. But he did not flinch, returning my gaze for several moments before bowing his head in deference.

"Please, Lord," Tiberius repeated, stifling an outburst from Zenobia with a raised hand. "You trained me for this, and I wanted to help. We all do. But if you must blame someone, it is my fault, not the others."

Growling, I shuffled closer. "Do not wish your childhood away so easily, my boy. I trained for a decade before seeing war, and I still trembled at my first taste."

Zenobia abandoned her silence as she sprinted to Tiberius' side. "Pater!"

"Enough!" I roared. "I'm sending two men to take you below. Mariya must be frightened to death at your absence. You will go now, and I shall speak with you later."

"But I want to fight with you!" Zenobia screeched.

"And you have," I glowered. "Now take your friends down to

Petrus, who should be near the gate. He will take you all back to the Domus."

"Pater, I want to stay with you!" Zenobia yelled again, grabbing at my bloodstained armor. "Don't leave again!"

It was senseless. Zenobia had no benefit to staying in such a hell—none of them did. I worried of Tiberius' mind most of all, for despite the passage of years, I feared what memories he guarded of his time in the Hippodrome, surrounded by corpses and the suffering of thousands. Did he remember Hypatius, his father, who had been raised by others to challenge Justinian, only to hang for his crime? Mariya insisted that Tiberius was too young, and that children's memories fade quickly, one year to the next. I wanted to believe her, but a bitter part of me knew she was wrong. In my dreams, I could still hear the screams of my own childhood—and in that moment, in the most desperate hour of Witiges' attack on our walls, I wondered whether those screams were from my mother.

Despite it all, Zenobia tugged at my heart. I wanted her nowhere near such danger, but neither did I wish her to leave. She yielded no aversion to my dirty, stinking body as she offered a clumsy embrace, pleading with me to stay.

"Not now, anaticula," I answered. "Your task is to defend your mother and your brother. You all are very brave, but now it is my turn watch over our walls."

Turning to Tiberius, I elected to give him a charge. "You shall lead the others, just as my officers guide my men. Take them to Petrus and see that all are safe. I shall demand a report from you in the evening."

Tiberius straightened and offered a salute—one that he doubtless had observed hundreds of times from my men and likely practiced in the privacy of his rooms. "It will be my honor, Lord."

Despite it all, I held back laughter, proud that the lad had taken his responsibilities with honor. "Two of my men will escort you. Go, now!"

A tear welled in Zenobia's eye, and I squeezed her arm one last time before I watched her descend to safety. Immediately thereafter, my mind retrained itself upon the Vivarium's swelling needs, resisting the danger of collapse despite the reinforcements Perenus had been conferred.

Upon my return to the gatehouse, I was greeted by Fulcaris, Xerxes, and other assembled officers. Having served at the Vivarium the entire day, Fulcaris spoke first. "Well, Varus, Witiges is positioning his men. What should we do?"

Our options were few, and none would enjoy favorable odds from even the most degenerate gambler that stalked the popinae of Constantinople. "We have an onager, six working ballistae..."

"Five," Sindual corrected. "The other twenty granted to us either need repairs or are well beyond range of the gatehouse."

"Five ballistae, then," I continued. "Enough bolts and arrows to butcher every boar in creation and enough naphtha to safely destroy one piece of siege equipment. Anything I forgot to include?"

Wisimar grunted. "We're better fighters than these milk drinkers. That counts for more than any of the others."

"Skill, perhaps," I allowed. "But we're tired and outnumbered, and facing towers and a ram."

Xerxes was more helpful. "Witiges is powerful but not a military mind. I can understand testing the mettle of an enemy with feints and smaller attacks, but Witiges should have stormed our walls with every man at his disposal by now. Something holds him back, and it might be either fear or incompetence."

I nodded. "Or honor. Witiges argued to Belisarius and me that he wanted an honorable end to war, something similar to how Theodoric was said to behave."

"Incompetence it is, then." Wisimar grinned. "So, we defend long enough for Witiges to make a mistake, and then ram it up his arse?"

"Precisely," Xerxes replied. "He's already making mistakes now by attacking in gradual waves. While we're taking casualties, his incrementalism is easy to predict."

His thinking was sound, although wagering our fates on poor decision-making by the enemy left me uneasy. "We still need to contend with his siege weapons. The few ballistae he has are too far for us to counter. Where should we prioritize our naphtha?"

"The ram," Xerxes blurted out. "The towers are dangerous but only allow a few men at a time to rush the walls. If the ram breaches our gates, Gothic cavalry could storm inside, outflanking our men."

Fulcaris concurred. "It's easier to kill a ladder climber than those sheltered in the wooden towers, but those men would still need to challenge our fighters atop our walls. I agree with Xerxes."

"As do I," I said, concluding the debate. "However, that means all we can do is wait for the ram to draw close and cover it with naphtha. The timing must be perfect, but the effect will be terrible for the Goths nearby."

In our final preparations, I ordered that any man—foederatus, reinforcement, or civilian—who could wield a bow do so. Our ballistae were ordered to save their bolts for the towers as soon as they came within range, while the onager hurled rocks at the massed Goths outside our walls. It was a simple plan, and obvious to any attacker, yet no intricate alternative emerged. Moreover, for exhausted warriors, simple is divine, and I prayed that our strategy would be rewarded by a further mistake from the onlooking Gothic king.

Then suddenly, the bulk of the Gothic reserves lurched forward. The towers, the rams, the combined elements of richly armored Gothic veterans and the so-called Visigothic volunteers from Hispania all moved toward the Vivarium, their slow pace dictated by the siege engines. Though dust wafted in their wake, I noted that Witiges remained behind his attackers, barking orders to his ballistae and shouting encouragement to the thousands who pushed toward us. The only welcome tiding was the pause in men climbing atop the ladders, as if they awaited an easier assault upon the arrival of Witiges' most dangerous forces. I paced into the open walls where the greatest bulk of the Herulian foederati lingered, all of whom panted and leaned upon merlons or spears to support their weight.

"Herulians, I am returned to you this day!" I yelled, drawing my easily recognized blade. "This is it, the last attack that Witiges can muster. I promise you, neither Belisarius nor I shall leave this place until every Goth is swept from our walls! What say you?"

There was no cheer, nor did I expect one. Minding what reserves of vitality remained to them, the men simply smashed their spear butts against the stone floor, concurring with an unyielding will to defend their post. I did not doubt their honor for a moment, for I had trained these men, and they had plunged through all manner of hell in service of duty. They would not run, even now, when Witiges had worn them all down to nothingness.

Ballistae bolts smashed just ten paces from my position, forcing me to duck below a merlon. One Roman citizen toppled forward, screaming before he smacked against the earth below and his cries were ended by a merciful Gothic spear thrust. Through it all, Witiges' killing blow rolled forward, closing within two hundred paces of our gate.

"Ballistae, concentrate your attentions upon the nearest siege tower," I yelled. "The rest of you, ready your bows and defend against the ladders. We will make them weep over every step they take toward the Vivarium!"

At a hundred and fifty paces, Witiges' force came into range, and the commanders of the assault plain. One warlord I recognized from my prior gathering, but I could not recall his name. The two others beside him were more easily discerned: Totila and the hated Indulf, each marching before segments of the Gothic army and adjacent to one of the siege elements.

"Loose!" I roared. "Make them suffer!"

Again, the punishment of even that diminutive volley was terrifying to behold. At least two dozen Goths collapsed from arrow wounds, while a handful of others disappeared altogether in a strike by our onager. Our ballistae, however, were less promising: Most bolts sailed wide of their targets, and the three that did connect yielded little more than the echoing crunch of wood. Two bolts jutted from one siege engine, yet its protective outer layers remained intact, its progress unhindered.

"Reload the ballistae!" I yelled, fighting against a bilious panic. "Faster!"

But there was no time. Goths cheered as they closed in on our walls, jeering at Belisarius. In my soul I knew we could not resist a successful attack by both the towers and the ram, yet no answers emerged in my mind to prevent that outcome. The Herulians looked to me for guidance, firing arrows every ten heartbeats, yet all I could do was stammer.

Until Belisarius, in all his splendor, came sprinting toward my battlement.

"Shoot the oxen!" Belisarius yelled, gasping as his chest heaved. "Varus, shoot the oxen and the tower will halt!"

"What?" I asked stupidly.

"Oxen pull the towers!" Belisarius roared, pointing to the base of one tower. "Look through the dust. Stop the oxen, and you stop the towers!"

"Oh," I muttered, my skin burning hot with embarrassment.

Who remembers an ox? They are dull creatures; though vital to the economic life of the Empire, few would write poems about them, and other than those clerks tasked with maintaining an army's progress, even fewer within military command would pay those beasts any heed. It was as if my eyes could not see their shaggy hides amidst the swirling dust and Gothic howling until Belisarius altered my perception. Perhaps Liberius had been correct so many years before, and I truly was daft, for it was a simple yet elegant resolution.

"You heard Belisarius!" I boomed, though my voice was cracked and sore. "All arrows on the oxen, now!"

Shimon handed me my bow, and I joined in our desperate volley. "Loose!" I yelled.

Many along the battlements had a poor angle at the oxen, and many likely could not discern them within a swirling mass of men, metal, and churning earth. But enough, perhaps three dozen, did find their target. I doubt most did little more than annoy the oxen, buried within their matted and greasy fur, yet at least a few dug into the animals' flesh. Still, though I could not discern an injury upon the beasts, one of the towers began to tilt—one side had ceased hauling forward.

"Again!" I roared, joined by Belisarius. "Find an ox! Nock and loose!"

After that strike, the off-center tower halted altogether. Yet the second tower continued, getting close enough that I could hear its wheels whining under the ponderous weight of lumber and men.

We had only one volley remaining before the tower closed upon the walls. "The second tower! Loose at the ready!"

Across a short distance, Herulian and Roman arrows poured downward. Indulf roared as he ordered a shield wall to cover the oxen, yet his Goths appeared either confused or hesitant to defend beasts at the expense of their own bodies. The result was a perplexed milling of men, some with shields guarding the oxen, some guarding themselves, with neither effort sufficient to protect against our attack. Nocking and releasing arrows as quickly as my muscles would allow, I aimed directly for one ox's head, joining fifty other bowmen in that steady barrage.

At last, the second tower halted too, albeit less than fifty paces from our walls. "Keep firing!" I yelled. "Fillet the bastards!"

At last, the Herulians cheered as many Goths scrambled away from the derelict device, that looming column of wood that soared higher than our towers by the height of at least three men. Unmoving, and at such close range, ballistae operators from the two closest fighting platforms reoriented their aim and launched against the sides of the tower. The first bolt cracked into the tower's sides, while the second pierced cleanly through a portion of wooden wall that had been weakened by prior strikes, revealing a network of stairs that Goths would have safely climbed to reach our walls.

"Eat shit!" Fulcaris yelled wildly to the Goths. Other Herulians roared approval, spilling their own insults upon the failed attack and subsequent disarray of swathes of the Gothic army.

"Stay alert!" Belisarius yelled at me. "We still have the ram!"

And it was a mere fifty paces distant. I ordered our bowmen to strike against the covered wagon that housed the battering log even though I knew the effect would be minimal. Only naphtha could easily disable that device, and we had just enough of the noxious muck to engulf the ram in flames.

"Uliaris, ready the naphtha," I ordered. "Shimon, light torches and bring them to the top of the gate!"

But it would not be so simple. Wisimar sprinted up to seize my attention. "More ladders, Varus. They're climbing again."

Grunting, I spat. "Tell the men to drop their bows and deflect the climbers. The naphtha will destroy the ram."

Wisimar saluted, then keened a howl as he unsheathed his sword and stabbed at a would-be Gothic climber. Other Vandals followed their officer, brushing aside tired Herulians as they gutted any enemy who drew close. Unlike other defenders, who preferred to thrust spears at climbers as soon as they drew into range, Wisimar allowed the Goths to reach chest high above the walls before grabbing their shields with a free hand. Once his enemy was unbalanced, Wisimar jammed a dagger beneath their unarmored chins, leaving their bodies a lifeless weight that plummeted downward and knocked others from the rungs. Catching my gaze after a successful kill, Wisimar grinned at me.

"I'm merciful!" He laughed. "They die quickly this way!"

Soon, the ram lumbered into range of our amphorae, leaving only moments to strike. Uliaris, myself, and Nzamba, the temporary Aksumite commander, all took two amphorae into our arms, steadying our aim. "Torches ready, Shimon?"

"Yes, Lord!" he yelled. "But I could only find two."

"It's enough," I answered. "Throw them as soon as the naphtha settles. Don't let the ram reach the gate."

Shimon nodded, handing a torch to Gouboulgoudou, who stood next to Belisarius. The Hun bucellarius accepted the charge, wary as he took his place beside Uliaris, yet uncomplaining.

"Ready?" I asked.

"Ready to drop," Uliaris confirmed, echoed by Nzamba and the other Aksumites.

Exhaling, I paused for only a moment, just long enough to peer out from a tower window down to the ram. I aligned my amphorae, offered an unspoken prayer, and dropped my first jar, and then the second. "Release!"

The others followed, allowing the clay to shatter and release the black liquid just as had been done outside the Mausoleum. It seemed perfectly aligned, that end to the Vivarium's danger.

Then ballista bolts struck our tower. Again, Xerxes saw them before any other. "Brace!"

Though not as debilitating as the first strike, both Shimon and Gouboulgoudou dropped their torches, with Gouboulgoudou's smothered out by dust and rubble. The need to attack was urgent, and I choked as I urged Shimon forward.

"Shimon, throw!" I rasped. "Throw now!"

And he did. It was well aimed, despite the delay, falling downward toward the rear half of the ram. Yet I knew it would not meet its target. For in that brief interruption of our attack, the Gothic leader amongst the ram's warriors had discerned our intentions, staring up, watching for our torch. As I peered from my window, I saw Totila and four others block the torch with their shields, sending it falling a useless twenty paces from the nearest splatter of naphtha.

"Fuck!" Fulcaris moaned. "The ram..."

A rattling boom from the gate eliminated the need for explanation. We had failed. The Goths were at the gates, with the ram's naphtha-lined exterior blocked by an overcrop of the Vivarium's stone walls.

"Down below!" I yelled. "Brace the walls!"

"I'm coming with you!" Belisarius called. "Do not let them through!"

So much screaming. And new amongst my warriors, so much fear. Most were ordered to hold their posts along the walls, watched over by Sindual and Tarmutus, the latter particularly wide-eyed as he accepted his charge.

"Lord, I will fight to the last, but I'm not certain I can keep the Goths off the walls," he said.

"All you need to do is hold," I explained. "Bend, but keep hold of the walls intact. As soon as I address the ram, I'm coming back with all our men to reinforce you once more."

Clenching his fists, he nodded. "I will not run, Lord. I will wait for you."

Most of our men obeyed wordlessly, forming their smaller parties to defend against the Gothic ladders. Some, however, insisted on accompanying me. Leading them was Perenus, lifting his weakened body from the inner courtyard of the Vivarium's gate, too stubborn to surrender to rest.

"I'm coming too," Perenus croaked. "I'm not staying here to die in a puddle."

Cephalas hustled behind Perenus, half propping up his friend's body. "Me too, Varus."

I groaned, lacking time to argue. "Very well," I conceded. "But Cephalas, you stay in the rear. Aid the men in the fight, and—" A third figure trotted to join the other two: Rosamund. I shook my head. "No. You must stay in the gatehouse, Rosamund. Too many need you here, and I will return shortly."

Rosamund scoffed but did not push back. "I'll be praying for you, even if you don't want me."

Her bitterness struck my heart with the force of a dagger, the same way Zenobia's had. But she departed to care for her wounded wards, leaving me to rush down the walls and toward the Praenestine Gate.

"Hurry!" Belisarius yelled. "Brace!"

The gates rattled, lurching backward for the briefest moment. Hinges creaked and dust scattered over our heads, with the muffled noise of Gothic voices testament to the swarm of enemies hungering to gain entry to Rome.

"Brace!" Belisarius repeated.

Leading a party to the gate, I slammed my shield against the gate's wooden doorway, pressing my weight at its center. Uliaris and the Aksumites followed me, while Wisimar muscled his way to my left. "I say let them in! I'll geld all of them!"

"Concentrate!" Belisarius called, filling the space behind me. "No talking!"

In that confined space, the hundred or so men we had gathered to block the ram felt far more numerous. The pressure of Belisarius' shield and the bodies of so many men behind me was suffocating, pressing my body against the wooden panels and allowing only stale air to reach those of us in front. I forced myself calm as I steadied for the next blow, entirely unready for the magnitude of force it would yield. It came sudden and hard, knocking me four paces backward and forcing me to rush forward and slam against the walls once more.

"When the wall breaks, form a wedge!" Xerxes called over the din. "Let their ranks crash against us. Do not let them pierce our lines."

"As Xerxes says!" I repeated. "Be as unyielding as a stone against the waves."

But Wisimar was still unimpressed. "Just kill them all and use their bodies as bricks in a wall. Blood is wonderful mortar once it dries."

Another boom. This time, however, it was followed by a sickening crack, and slivers of wood splintered away from the hinges. The gate's bars had begun to warp, too, bending with each hammer of the ram against the outer doors.

"Out of the way," Gunderic yelled, tossing men aside as he stepped toward Wisimar's left. "What in Hades' stinking arsehole are you doing letting the Goths take our gates?"

"What are you doing here?!" I yelled, bracing for another strike.

"I killed all of mine, and the rest ran away." Gunderic snorted. "I figured you weaklings might have some left for me, and I was correct. What a battle!"

More Vandals filled in behind him—yet still too few to counter the Gothic hordes facing us. The gate rattled again, and more splinters showered our heads. One of the two bars on the gate cracked apart entirely, while the other seemed not far off. I felt hopeless, although there was little else I knew to do. Near me, a Herulian began to pray, joined by others as they asked for God's protection and deliverance from the swarming enemy.

"Beg *my* protection instead!" Gunderic snarled. "Shut your holes and ready your blades."

Belisarius offered a calmer perspective. "When the gates open, hold the wedge," he yelled. "Hold the gate and do not let the Goths get into the city. Make them bleed for every step forward."

Another boom, and the gates loosened to the point of futility. All noise dulled about me as I focused upon my shield, offering my own prayers regardless of any sneering from Gunderic. Despite everything, the prayer eased my worries, washing away distractions as I thought only on the enemies that would soon crash into us like a great wave. I was not foolish enough to believe that Belisarius' strategy could work, but neither was I willing to turn and run. Not with my family in the city's interior, nor so many friends at my flanks and back. And so I held, joining in a guttural yell as the Gothic ram surged forward for a final time.

The gate burst apart. Its doors blew backward, pushing aside our massed men and sending many stumbling to the ground. Had not Belisarius held firm to my armor, I would have joined them. Instead, I merely shuffled backward as sections of wooden gate fell from their moorings and a rush of naphtha-scented air rustled through the Praenestine Gate.

"Wedge!" I coughed. "Form up!"

I attempted to assume the position of the frontmost man, yet Gunderic refused me, unwilling to stand behind anyone. "Watch how it's done, Varus!"

Only then did I glance at his body. He was riddled with puncture wounds, his ponderous layers of lamellar and mail torn from spears or blades. He limped but showed nothing less than vigorous contempt for the Goths, taunting their hesitancy after the gate's destruction.

"Come on!" Gunderic roared.

I stood in the second rank adjacent to Uliaris, while Belisarius stood nestled between Xerxes and Gouboulgoudou in the third. Had Sembrouthes been present, he would have forbidden me to be separated from the Aksumites, but I would not allow Gunderic to stand up front without my sword defending his sword arm.

"Come on, you cunts!" Wisimar yelled from several ranks back. "Come hit me!"

After a rustling of Gothic taunts, the gate drew quiet. An impenetrable forest of helmet plumes blocked our view, and the screams and blows atop the walls drowned away any noise upon the ground. I should have been grateful for the reprieve, but by then, all I desired was an end to the uncertainty, and to finish this endless battle.

And then, a shout. The first Goths rushed through their breach, pushing the gates farther apart as a stream of Goths swelled into a torrent of Witiges' veteran spearmen.

"Yes!!" Gunderic cheered. "Who among you can take my life?!"

"Hold this line!" Belisarius barked from over my shoulder. "Whatever you do, do not become separated from the men to your sides!"

The initial Gothic charge was no wall, but a disorderly mob leveling spears with hopes of an easy victory. They were wrong. And not only were they wrong, but they were also facing the greatest assembly of killers that existed in Justinian's empire, drawn from a dozen tribes and far-flung provinces to serve and to die in defense of Rome. Gunderic was testament to the power of our motley array, swinging the hallowed blade of Vandal kings in a sweeping arc that felled the first two Goths with ease: one with a severed limb and the other with bowels spilling from a split stomach. Gunderic only laughed, echoed by the Vandals scattered in our wedge.

"More men!" he yelled. "Send more men!"

The Goths obliged. Gunderic hacked and stabbed as four Goths attempted to swarm him. I seized the chance to strike, and the tip of my sword dug into one Goth's armpit, sticking in layers of metal and muscle so deep I struggled to tug the sword free. Behind me, Xerxes gored a second Goth with his spear, driving its point clean through the man's chest and puncturing his heart. After freeing my blade, I aided Xerxes in retrieving his spear, allowing the dead and dying bodies to form a macabre wall just as Wisimar recommended.

Their first assault was a bloody waste. Undisciplined, the Goths clattered against our wedge, falling one after the other. For a time, it seemed as though our wall could not be breached, with the Vandals jeering and the Heruli singing as we stabbed and chopped, protecting the men in front with each attack.

"Shields tight!" I yelled. "Rotate with those in the interior if needed!"

Suddenly, the mad rush stalled. From behind the dust, a wall of Visigoths marched before the ram, with Totila stepping a pace before his men. With his spear, he rapidly organized his Goths into two separate pincers, filling their ranks with an endless supply of Ostrogoth reinforcements.

"They're coming for our flanks!" I called back.

"Brace and hold!" Belisarius yelled. "Don't let them in!"

Satisfied, Totila leveled his spear toward the city, and the orderly attacking formation trotted forward. The approach lacked the vicious intensity of a sprint, yet the men avoided stumbling or tripping on scattered bodies and maintained ranks until the last five paces from our men. Totila positioned himself opposite me.

Where we previously held back Gothic advances, Totila rendered us helpless against a pummeling charge. At three paces, the frontmost Visigoths halted, plucking short spears from their belts, weapons I only now recalled from my time in Septem.

"Cover!" I screamed.

And we did: Belisarius' shield sliding over my head as my own layered between on either side. Multiple Visigoth spears struck my bulwark, with one piercing the wooden panel, its iron point halting but a handsbreadth from my chest. Gunderic chopped at the protrusion, easing the weight upon my shield as I readied for Totila's next maneuver.

"Attack!" Belisarius yelled, lifting his shield from my head just as Totila's men rushed forward.

Unimaginable pressure—that is the only way to describe our shield wall. Squeezed from both sides, our wedge was like a great walnut, trapped in a metal vise that lusted to crack our shell. Uliaris and I were forced to fight back to back, relying upon men of the interior to strike at the heads of our enemies as we struggled to maintain the wall's integrity.

Totila slid down our lines, leaving a younger Visigoth to push and spit opposite my shield. Unable to lift my arm, I sheathed my sword and instead drew Aetius' dagger, gripping it against my palm. With his longer sword, my Visigoth enemy attempted to duck below our shields, aiming jabs to cripple my ankles. Normally, such a maneuver would have been effective, yet I had survived too many battles to be fooled. Instead, I slammed the iron rim of my shield downward, blocking the attack, and thrust my dagger into his unguarded neck. He snapped upright, struggling to back away from further strikes, yet found himself pinned by the hundreds of Goths swarming behind him. Blood bubbled from his severed throat as he choked on an attempt at speech until, shivering, his head slumped forward, his body still upright.

The corpse and I drifted for several moments, locked in one another's embrace. In that reprieve I stabbed at another Goth that pressed against Gunderic's side, sticking the tip of my dagger into the man's ear no fewer than a half dozen times. He, too, slumped forward, falling at Gunderic's feet and sending the Goth behind him stumbling. Gunderic seized his chance and dispatched that man with a single downward thrust, sending a second body to pile at his feet.

Unlike in past battles, this raw press of men gave little opportunity for true combat. Instead, we struggled through a deadly pushing match, seeking the briefest moment to leverage open space and cut at exposed hands, joints, or faces. I struggled to breathe in that mass, my chest crushed on three sides by my fellow Romans and before me by the murderous Goths under Totila. Had I been a smaller man, I might have suffocated, and I spotted many Goths before me whose mouths gasped for air amidst the press of stinking bodies and piss-riddled corpses. There was no glory in that struggle beneath the Praenestine Gate, only an understanding that if Belisarius' men broke, we would all die within the hour.

Even Gunderic lacked the strength to carve through the massed Goths entirely, though many fell prey to his blade. One Visigoth slipped past my guard and stabbed Gunderic in the shoulder, eliciting a hiss of anger before Gunderic lifted his sword and slammed it upon the man's helmet with a scraping crack. Clubbed by the sword's hilt, the Visigoth's eyes crossed, and he dropped his weapon and his guard, allowing me to jam the length of Aetius' dagger into his neck.

"Pay attention, Varus!" Gunderic roared. "I'm tired of these bastards tickling me."

No matter how many we slew, more stepped forward, caring little whether their boots trod upon stone or bodies. One Goth attempted to leap over the corpses before me, yet his boot slipped upon the severed throat of my prior victim, sending his face tumbling into my shield boss. Alive, he crumpled to the ground, and I seized the opportunity to trample him, smashing an iron cheek guard into the man's face again and again, until he stopped wriggling beneath me. From over my shoulder, I saw Belisarius thrust toward another attacking Goth, cutting into the man's eye and forcing him backward.

Yet these successes were not enough to stop Totila altogether. Through sheer strength, the twin talons of the Gothic surge pierced into our wedge, threatening to sever those of us at the front from the bulk of Belisarius' men to the rear.

"Strike back!" Belisarius yelled. "Keep our ranks together!"

Later, I am told that Perenus attempted to counter Totila's rightmost pincer. Weak and exhausted, he and Sindual surprised Totila with a sudden surge, slaying many of the warlord's followers before the Herulian counter was deflected. We simply lacked the men, and it appeared our fate was to be surrounded and cut off, slain or captured by Witiges' forces.

A rolling wave of screams rang out from the direction of the ram. At first, I believed it a baleful sign of Goth reinforcements, ordered to complete Totila's assault. Yet when I peered at the oncoming Goths, I witnessed instead a torrent of stones from the gate and heard someone—Tarmutus—ordering his guardsmen to loose more projectiles.

"Push!" I screamed. "They're breaking up!"

Totila likely saw the danger, realized that he might yet fall victim to encirclement despite his near-successful assault. Shouting in Gothic, he backed his spearmen out of the gap he had riven in Belisarius' lines, abandoning those too slow or too injured to retreat. The other Gothic claw copied his example, backing several paces toward the siege ram.

"Cowards!" Gunderic laughed.

"That's all?!" Wisimar added. "I didn't even get to kill one!"

"Look!" Xerxes hissed.

Totila sheathed his sword and put a horn to his lips. He blew five rolling notes, once, twice, then cried an order, and a gap carved down the center of his ranks. The maneuver appeared innocuous, and although I could not discern the logic of even the slightest retreat, I still believed that a senior Gothic chieftain or even Witiges himself might come to negotiate with our men.

I was wrong. The stones at the Praenestine Gate rumbled as a stream of Gothic horsemen galloped forward, tossing spears and spilling over our wedge.

"Keep the wall tight!" I ordered.

No horse would willingly plunge headlong into a disciplined porcupine of shields and spears. It was a lesson that every Roman recruit learned in his earliest days as a bronze-capped neophyte, with the centurions demanding thoughtless obedience as each man held their position along the shield wall. All of us in Belisarius' wedge understood that lesson by instinct, and the charge initially broke into two competing halves as the horsemen sought easy prey. With most of us lacking spears, there was little else I could do but secure my aegis and allow the men of the interior ranks to poke and thrust at horse and rider alike.

Totila's horsemen, however, had come prepared. Each rider bore the short throwing spear favored by the Visigoths, which they tossed into our line as they flowed past our frontward ranks. As before, my shield rattled from the Gothic spears, with the painted ouroboros cut into splinters by their blades. Though it had not yet shattered, I doubted my shield would persist much longer against Totila's shifting attack.

Our only aid was the occasional volley from wall archers spitting arrows down upon the undefended heads of the Gothic horsemen. Perhaps only twenty had an angle to strike such Goths beneath the Praenestine Gate, and the casualties from arrow fire were few, but the disruption was enough to blunt the worst of the cavalry's charge. And, lacking the packed cohesion of Totila's shield wall, the gaps in the Gothic horsemen gave us our only opportunity to strike a mortal blow.

"Push forward!" Belisarius yelled, the first to identify the opportunity. "Drive the horses out! Fill the gaps!"

Gunderic roared with approval, while Goths from the rearward ranks broke free of the wedge to slaughter man and beast alike. Seizing the discarded spear of a Visigoth, Wisimar rammed its point into one mount's eye, causing it to buck its rider to the ground. Wisimar's followers stabbed downward before seeking additional victims, isolating groups of two or three mounted Goths at a time.

"Keep order!" I yelled. "Watch for a counter!"

Though I lacked the Vandals' lust for carnage, a reeling enemy could not be ignored. I led a party of Uliaris, Xerxes, and Belisarius' guardsmen forward, where we joined the Vandals in isolating enemy riders. Sheathing my dagger, I grasped one Goth by the belt and tore him from the saddle, sending his head cracking against the ground. Xerxes rammed his sword into the back of the fallen Goth's neck as I reached for another victim whose eyes centered upon a nearby group of Vandals. With one hand on the horseman's cloak and a second upon his hip, I tipped him backward and down, his body jostled by horse hooves and pounded into a pulp.

Totila's spearmen reentered the fight just as the Goth horsemen began to rout—although, in that confused fray, no amount of shouting or threats could have kept Totila's warriors in clean lines. Instead, they rushed upon us in ragged clumps of four or five, a chaotic melee. Totila himself soon joined the scrum, roaring a challenge as he smashed his shield into my own.

"You're going to die!" Totila grinned behind his shield.

He moved as lithe and fluid as a coiled snake. Yet he was not the fastest swordsman I have ever encountered, nor was he the strongest—of so many thousands, only Baduarius or Gunderic could claim that title. Nor was he even the most skilled, with only Xerxes possessing a rare ability to make any weapon seem like an extension of his body rather than an instrument of war. Despite this, Totila was a rare talent, and relatively fresh and uninjured, too, lashing against my sluggish movements with assured control.

My shield chipped beneath a flurry of strikes, with one weakened panel tearing away entirely. Uliaris attempted to cover my body, yet struggled against two Goths of his own, while Belisarius lashed at the Visigoth warlord from over my shoulder. Totila's thrusts allowed no space for a counter—until his boot rolled atop a horse's leg. He shrieked, and I drew my sword and lunged, aiming for the man's guts.

Slam. Totila's shield bashed against my face. He had blocked just in time. I stumbled backward, gasping, choking, blood filling my nose. My eyes blurred as hands behind me tugged upon my belt, dragging me to safety in the interior lines. I am not certain how much time elapsed until my senses returned—only that by the time I did, Belisarius' desperate charge had threatened to turn into annihilation.

"Breathe through your mouth, Lord!" It was Cephalas yelling at me, snapping his fingers to test my concentration. "Your nose is broken, I think, but no serious harm."

My vision remained hazy, yet I recognized the slack-jawed face of my friend. More caring eyes never existed, especially for a man whose livelihood had been tested by God more than most. At first, I thought I saw fires consume Cephalas' body, yet as I struggled to sharpen my vision, I saw that three torches had been roped about his chest, the flames dancing over his head like some odd crown. Stranger still, Cephalas seemed to be adorned in the cloak of a Goth, with a shield bearing the hawk emblem of Theudis strapped about his body and guarding his back. Though one arm hung limp, his uninjured hand gripped another torch.

Words came only with difficulty. "Cephalas, what..."

"Is there room to move about the gates, or are the Goths packing it again?" Cephalas asked.

I shrugged. "It was chaos, lots of movement."

Cephalas nodded. "Someone needs to end this. The walls are falling, and Tarmutus cannot hold."

"Tarmutus?" I asked, wincing as my nose throbbed and head ached. Only then did I notice the swell of noise emanating from the battlements, and flickers of guardsmen stabbing and chopping at unseen Gothic enemies.

Another nod. "Varus, you are a wonderful friend. Not many have accepted me in this life, but you did. I wanted to thank you for that. Tell Rosamund and Perenus too."

Before I could reply, Cephalas lowered his head, touching his forehead to my own. Then, wordlessly, he stood upright, leaving me in the care of others. Taking two Herulians as an escort, Cephalas weaved amongst the Roman ranks, the flames tracing his progress through the ongoing press of conflict. Only then, as Cephalas ventured twenty paces away and well into the gate, did I realize his intentions.

"Cephalas, no!!" I yelled.

"Lord, you must rest," a Roman said, his plain robes contrasting with the blood-spattered armor that clogged the Praenestine Gate.

I shrugged him away, struggling to stand. "Cephalas! Come back!!"

I believe he heard me. For a moment he paused, and although it may have been from the necessity of moving cautiously amidst the chaotic battle lines, he stopped just as I called him. For a heartbeat, I believed he was returning to me, yet the flames danced onward, beneath the ruined gate.

There was a delay as Cephalas disappeared. Combat whirled on, with all seemingly unaware of Cephalas' movements. Soon, though, familiar screams echoed from behind the Aurelian Walls, and an orange glow flickered above the gate.

Cephalas had set the siege ram alight. A great blaze choked the Praenestine Gate, narrowing the Gothic path to access. While few responded immediately to the threat, Totila banded his forces together, stealing a horse from an unlucky Ostrogoth as he and his followers plunged through the flames and out of the city. Others followed in haste, yet soon all escape was severed as the fires consumed everything before the walls.

Belisarius took no prisoners. A few attempted to surrender their weapons, but most struggled until they were surrounded and slain. I saw one man beg for mercy in broken Latin, yet we faced too many enemies outside our walls and had too little food to take on an idle mouth. So many Goths died after Totila's escape that their bodies formed a carpet of flesh that rose to a man's knees, covering an expanse thirty paces wide by fifty paces long.

"Seek masons and carpenters to repair the gate!" Belisarius ordered. "Naphtha does not burn forever. The rest of you, follow me to retake the battlements!"

Though light-headed, I rejoined Uliaris and the Aksumites and trotted to the nearest staircase. My body felt numb—more from knowing Cephalas had perished in the span of a finger snap than any of my screaming muscles or throbbing nose. Of any man alive, Cephalas deserved far better than the fate he chose. I always knew him as a man who sacrificed for those he loved, from pieces of his body to deference in conversation, yet even for that, no poets will craft songs in his memory. He was a poor Greek, spawn of poor Greeks, discarded by his village due to childhood deformities. But if he had not secured the Praenestine Gate, condemning his body to the fire, every Roman would have died that day. Of this, I am certain. I wish I could tell him that. I've missed him each day since that battle.

But mourning had to wait, for herds of Goths spilled atop the walls, their ladders twice as numerous as before. Belisarius led the bulk of the bucellarii and Herulians to a southern expanse of wall, while Gunderic split his Vandals into a separate group that surged across the northern towers. I should have joined either group, but with Cephalas' death depriving me of yet another dear friend, my thoughts were consumed by only one person.

Rosamund.

As I climbed stone steps just thirty paces from the gatehouse, the extent of Gothic success became apparent. Half circles of Roman spearmen surrounding each Gothic ladder had been replaced by desperate brawls in single combat, with the Goths trickling additional men up the walls with each passing minute. Trading my sword for my axe, I charged up the stairs and crashed into the nearest Goth, launching him from the walls and onto the nearest ladder. Voices shrieked in fear as the man's weight snapped the ladder, sending many unsuspecting of danger falling to the ground.

"Where is she?" I groaned. "God, show me where..."

Other Goths turned to challenge me, yet a surge of Aksumites sent such men scurrying away, while too-slow or less-prudent Goths fell against the disciplined Aksumite blades. From that moment of security, I gazed both upon Witiges' reserves as well as the broader walls of the Vivarium, both relieved and horrified.

Before our gate, Cephalas' fire stemmed the unchecked flow of Goths into the city, granting the men below precious time to barricade the entrance until a more permanent solution could be devised. Likewise, while the Goths had placed additional ladders long our walls, no section had been entirely overrun, although several towers were a blur of violence. This offered some comfort that our situation was still salvageable, especially with a surge of Roman reinforcements. Still, I could find no white hair amongst the bloodied rabble.

Nowhere, that is, except atop the gatehouse. There, Gothic banners pressed into one of the enclosures, resisted by thin layers of Tarmutus' city watch. Leading them, his plume soaring high along Witiges' banners, was a man far more dangerous than any Gothic officer we had yet confronted. Worse, Indulf pressed forward into the gatehouse where Rosamund had settled. Even covered in bloody mail, Rosamund would be easily identifiable to Indulf, not merely as an acquaintance in his former allegiance to Justinian and Belisarius, but also as my household servant.

"Varus!" a voice cracked behind me, hoarse from weakness and overuse.

"Where..." I choked, "... where is Rosamund?"

"Rosamund is in the gatehouse." Perenus wormed forward, pausing to gaze upon the flames. "Cephalas—"

"He's gone," I answered. "He saved all our lives."

Perenus bared his teeth and let out a furious scream. It was a hoarse, pathetic shout, straining Perenus' overtaxed body. I gave him a moment to compose himself, grasping tightly to one shoulder. Eventually, Perenus saluted the flames, mumbling a prayer.

"He asked for two guardsmen and permission to search for torches. Did he really jump onto the naphtha?"

"I can't be certain, but he spoke kindly of you before he struck," I told him. "I grieve for him too, Perenus, but we must concentrate for now. How many men do you have?"

"Ten." Perenus sighed, brushing an arm across his eyes. "For Cephalas, then."

"And for Rosamund," I added. "Indulf is here. Let's gut that bastard and be done with this fight."

The Vivarium was in chaos. To the south, Roman and Gothic horns blared in their own grapple of strength, rising in intensity with each passing moment. There was little I could do but pray that Belisarius would be capable of withstanding whatever fresh assault plagued his section of wall, and I turned instead to the gatehouse. At my command, we trod atop the walls, pushing aside unsuspecting

Goths engaged in combat with overwhelmed Roman guards with each step. Abandoning my broken shield, I seized a spare from a still-bountiful depot along the wall and allowed Uliaris to secure its straps against my arm. We pressed onward, initially meeting only reluctant resistance, but only capable of moving a single ponderous shuffle at a time.

As we drew within fifteen paces of the gatehouse's closest entrance, however, Gothic opposition stiffened, spurred by the yelps of a man I had seized from behind and pushed from atop the walls. Immediately thereafter, a Gothic shield slammed against my own and sent ripples of pain up my arm. Any eagerness for battle that had stirred my heart that morning had long evaporated, replaced by a concoction of fatigue, ache, and the tantalizing knowledge that the day might soon be over.

"Cut them down!" I rasped, my voice hoarse. "To the gatehouse!"

Although witnesses would later weave a narrative about the Roman stand at the Praenestine Gatehouse, in truth it was difficult to see beyond the cluster of Indulf's Goths. Indulf himself led the assault upon the gates just prior to Cephalas' sacrifice, and, with a collection of wounded Herulians and lesser-trained city guardsmen, Tarmutus countered the blow, blocking his tower's entrance against three successive Gothic charges. After the ram was set alight, Indulf even attempted to toss flaming torches into Tarmutus' midst, yet the Roman commander refused to cede. Instead, he fought like a demon, slaying four of Indulf's men before tangling with the Gothic warlord directly.

Tarmutus' fortunes turned as I swept across the walls, pushing toward the gatehouse. Indulf never lacked talent with his blades, and he delivered a series of cuts that snuck past the shield wall and striped Tarmutus' arms and shoulders with thin cuts. At first, Tarmutus stood his ground, but sapping strength eventually caused him to stumble, and his followers only just managed to drag his bleeding body to safety. Absent their leader, the city watch held for a couple of minutes before collapsing to Indulf's fury.

What I witnessed then was Indulf's final breakthrough into the gatehouse. Some fifteen Goths locked their shields against others as dozens more flooded into the tower, doubtless fighting up and down its stairs. There was little preventing their access to our ballistae or those too wounded to lift a sword or stand in the shield wall, and the prospect of unending plunder must have tempted even Indulf's men to break free of their master's yoke and seize what treasures might be found.

It was Xerxes who carved a hole through the Goths standing in the way of our advance toward Indulf. Seizing a discarded spear from the ground, Xerxes ducked down from our second line and thrust underneath the Goth's shields. Though I did not witness the attack, I saw two Goths collapse, squealing as they clutched at severed ankles and slashed calves.

We ceased to be an organized mass. Instead, the Vivarium's battlements devolved into a thousand separate instances of single combat, the fighters more like animals than men. With my axe, I first chopped at the neck of the downed Goth before me, then smashed into the man standing behind him, burying the axe's blade into his shield—for I did not aim to draw blood, but instead to leave him unbalanced, and indeed, he stumbled when I struck. As he clattered to the ground, he inadvertently pushed another Goth over the walls, granting us Romans the necessary opportunity to destroy the remaining Gothic wall and reorganize for an assault upon Indulf. Having dispatched my victim, I retrieved my axe, trading it along my belt for my sword.

As we reached the entrance to the gatehouse, we encountered only mild resistance, but also a booming array of Roman horns. As before, grating noise cascaded senselessly from south to north. Had a senior officer died? Had our army broken into a rout? These were the only threats I could derive, compounding my anxiety as I remembered that Belisarius had launched an attack on the southeasternmost portion of the walls. Pausing, I glanced toward the noise. At first, I saw nothing other than a slow trickle of Goths reaching the tops of our walls, continuing the dance of swords with those Romans who remained to resist.

But then the horns blared again, distinctively Roman in cadence and pitch—not from any gate, this time, but from outside the Aurelian Walls, hundreds of paces into the southeastern horizon. Squinting, the cause of the horn blowers' urgency became clear.

Reinforcements were coming. Mounted, armored, and bearing the twin sigils of Justinian and Belisarius, they rushed toward the nearest Gothic camp, launching arrows without stopping. At a full gallop, they traversed considerable ground, reaching within two hundred paces of Witiges and his guardsmen.

It was a beautiful sight, worthy of a poem. "Martinus!"

Uliaris roared with approval, echoed by many ragged yet unbroken Roman voices. Martinus' band was small—four or five hundred, I guessed at first—but all bore the horses and armor of Belisarius' elite. At least fifty thickly armored cataphracts fired arrows upon the unsuspecting Goths. Witiges countered with horsemen of his own, yet those poorly armored warriors were pitifully easy targets for cataphract bows. After deflecting Witiges' counter, Martinus swept closer to the Roman walls, switching to his sword to chop down upon panicking Goths.

"Go!" I yelled, desperate to end the fight. "Go! Go!"

Where moments before I believed us all dead men, our salvation was tantalizingly close. Judging from the animated Gothic voices echoing from the gatehouse tower, Indulf must have also witnessed portions of Martinus' attack. I ducked into the tower, where I was met immediately by the hurried thrust of a Gothic sword. I rushed my attacker with my shield, deflecting the blow and driving the shield's iron edge against the man's throat. His head snapped back, and he dropped his weapon, grasping at a broken airway. Blue in the face, he toppled over, and I moved farther into the tower as I searched for Rosamund.

Despite the spring chill, the interior of the tower was sweltering, the interior stones damp and the floors sticky from blood and piss. In smaller antechambers, I saw clusters of motionless Romans, their necks slashed and bodies still warm. One lay nestled amidst others like a hewn log, blood staining hair that had once been bone white.

My entire body throbbed, my throat tightening. "Rosamund!"

Behind me, Xerxes and Uliaris fought off small groups of Goths but were struggling to maintain order. Soaked in gore and moving stiffly, Xerxes gestured to abandon the building. "Varus, we need to clear the tower!"

But I had no ears to listen. Instead, I clawed at the corpses atop the white-haired body that lay face down in a spreading pool of dark blood. Whether from the filth on my gloves or the slick mail on the body, the corpse's limbs initially slipped from my grasp, and I had to bend over and haul the body unceremoniously upright instead.

"Not Rosamund, Varus," Uliaris said.

I coughed, resisting the urge to vomit. "You're certain?"

Kneeling closer, Uliaris brushed grime from the frozen face—a Gepid man's face, with longer hair. "Must be one of Tarmutus' men," he said, "for I've seen several Gepids in the city watch. Besides, Rosamund has scars about her injured eye, and this man does not."

"Thank God," I muttered. "But where is she?"

That answer was not long in coming. Frantic, I scaled the tower's steps, stepping atop discarded bodies as I searched one room after another. Through the passing windows, I glimpsed Martinus' men loosing arrows into one Gothic detachment after another, never entangling with any sizeable groups of Gothic spearmen. It was not until I reached the top of the tower, open air whipping over our heads, that my search concluded.

"Keep still, Varus!" hissed a voice. Indulf.

It took several moments before my eyes adjusted to the tower's interior gloom. While a ballista yet remained, its former operators were strewn about, dead, leaving the only living souls present the ten Goths standing dominant opposite the staircase.

And Rosamund. Indulf had pressed Rosamund against his body, squeezing her shoulders with one arm and holding a knife to her neck in the other.

"We still outnumber you, although I'm not sure that's the most important consideration at the moment," he said. "Now send your minions away, or I'll snap her thin neck and toss her off the battlement."

I nodded, craning my neck toward the stairs. "Do not come further. Leave the stairs empty."

"Varus?" Uliaris asked, a few paces behind near the stairs. "What is it?"

"Do as I command," I replied.

Indulf nodded. "Good. Now, kneel, and slowly."

Again, I obeyed. One knee popped as I collapsed to the stones, the weight of my armor making each movement both taxing and ponderous. Rosamund's eyes fixed upon me, impossibly wide, her face drained of color.

"The battle is over, Indulf," I said, taking care not to appear disdainful. "Rosamund has never harmed you. Hurt her, and you will never leave this gate."

Indulf chuckled. "You're probably correct. That's why you will make sure I depart safely."

"How?" I frowned.

It was then that Indulf unfurled his desperate plan for escape. "You go first," he began. "And then my men, and then this flower and me. As long as no Roman harasses me, we will all simply have a pleasant walk."

"To where?" I asked.

"To wherever I say," Indulf barked. "Do you agree?"

It was reckless. Foolish, even. No forward-thinking Roman commander would surrender such authority to their enemy. Especially not to a traitor, who had more to fear than most were he to be captured. Many chide me for my decision, insisting that no woman was worth Indulf's freedom. Perhaps if I had decided differently, the world would be a vastly different place today—mayhap even a better one. But no segment of my soul could have chosen a different path. My resolve only hardened as Indulf pressed the edge of his blade into Rosamund's throat, producing a faint trickle of blood.

Rosamund's eyes shot impossibly wide. "Varus…"

It was Cassiodorus all over again. This time, however, I would not delay in sparing Rosamund her pain. "Whatever you want."

Indulf grinned, stealing a glance toward Martinus' men below as the Roman column retreated southward once more. "I did not intend to be trapped like this, you know. But I am pleased that I had the forethought to keep your whore as security. Best decision I can remember."

"Enough, Indulf," I spat. "What now?"

"Back well away, clear of the ladders and defensive positions," Indulf demanded. "Slowly, so my men can see you. And if your men think to ambush me, you know what I'll do."

Tasting a final sip of fresh air, I descended the tower. As promised, Indulf's remaining followers trailed just paces behind, listening as I ordered my men to keep back and not engage in violence. Soon, we reached the point where the gatehouse met the walls, and Indulf beckoned me into the open.

"Keep going, Tribune!" Indulf commanded. "Send your Romans away."

There was nothing any of us could do, other than obey. Uliaris and Xerxes trailed, lacking any safe approach to attack Indulf. Likewise, the other Imperial warriors were spent, looking to me for guidance. Most of all, though he was a loathsome creature, Indulf was not unskilled. The battle had ended, and while many doubtless yearned to rescue Rosamund, most present lacked the instinct or vitality to rush headlong into another fight.

Instead, I fulfilled Indulf's wishes. Tarmutus, wheezing and exhausted, looked upon me with befuddlement as I ordered him to make way. "Do as Indulf says. Keep your guardsmen back as I pass," I muttered.

We advanced atop the walls as far as the centermost point between the gatehouse and the nearest tower when Indulf ordered a halt. "This will do. Send your minions away."

Trailed by the Aksumites, Uliaris and Xerxes had stalked Indulf's progress. "Fall back to the gatehouse, and keep watch," I commanded them. "That is an order."

"Good pets." Indulf beamed. "Now, my men are going to descend your ladders. We will even do so in peace. Understand?"

I nodded. "Fine. Just leave Rosamund with me."

Indulf smirked but gestured to two of his men, who seized the nearest ladders, slung their shields about their backs, and trailed downward. Only a few Goths remained at the bottom, most of whom were limping or flailing with wounds. Otherwise, only a mound of bodies remained, congealed into a prickled mass of twisted limbs and broken armor. After the first two, Indulf sent forth another pair, this one far faster, hopping down the rungs as quickly as they could before clambering over the corpses and sprinting to the nearest Gothic detachment. Thus was Indulf down to a final foursome—himself and three compatriots.

"Give me Rosamund," I begged. "You can leave in peace as long as she is unharmed."

Trust was not in Indulf's nature. Whether against the Vandals, at Septem, or at Tingis, Indulf had proved himself a shifting, wily creature. So it was no surprise that nothing in his face revealed trust in me—yet neither was there hatred. All I saw in him was a malevolence—that rare willingness to inflict harm upon others merely to demonstrate dominance. He backed away from me, toward a farther ladder, ordering two more of his men to escape while a third stayed close at hand.

"You were always a self-righteous idiot, Varus," Indulf said, as if to goad me. "Only fools commit to waging a moral war. All that matters is your enemy lies dead, and you do not. Mundus never understood this, and neither did you, nor does Belisarius. One day, that will kill both of you."

"Indulf, I've been patient—"

He did not wait for the rest. Instead, he withdrew the blade from Rosamund's neck, gripping tight against one of her shoulders until she cried out, recoiling from his grasp.

"You're a fool, Varus!"

With that, he lifted his knife-wielding fist high in the air and smashed the pommel down on Rosamund's head. She shuddered, her knees sagging from the blow, as a laughing Indulf darted down his ladder. Roaring in hatred, I rushed forward to cradle Rosamund's head as my guardsmen flocked about us.

"Rosamund?"

Her eyes wavered, lid fluttering, yet she breathed regularly. "Dizzy…"

Xerxes was the first to reach me. "The Goths have vacated the Vivarium, Lord. Shall we take Rosamund to Agathias?"

Rosamund gripped my hand. "The fight is over, Varus."

I glanced out to where Indulf stumbled over a corpse, struggling for the freedom of the outlying hills. "Not yet. Not for me. Xerxes, take Rosamund below. Watch over her until I return."

Xerxes hesitated. "Varus—"

"Do it!" I snarled. "I'm going down."

I checked my weapons, secured my shield against my back, and gripped the nearest Gothic ladder. Even with its casing of coarse iron, the ladder felt flimsy, with each rung bending as I jostled downward. Within moments, my feet struck corpses and filth-strewn grass, and Indulf was but a few dozen paces ahead.

I wanted him dead. I wanted to jam my sword through his ribs and watch his soul leak from his eyes, one painful heartbeat at a time. For Mundus, and all the rest slaughtered that day. For Rosamund, and for all the humiliation that Indulf had inflicted. That devil was fit to keep company only with Judas Iscariot himself. I cared nothing of whether any Romans followed me, or if Witiges intended to send a fresh army to attack our walls. Instead, with the swirling naphtha flames to my left and arrow-riddled Gothic bodies along my right, I forced myself forward, screaming the name of my enemy as I narrowed the distance between us.

"Indulf, you coward!" I screamed. "Come and face me!"

To my surprise, Indulf halted. The safety of the Gothic lines was a mere two hundred paces away, and his followers sprinted toward Witiges without looking back—yet Indulf drew his sword, readied his shield, and squared his feet against an attack.

"A self-righteous fool," Indulf yelled to me. "The world outgrew you, Varus. And it doesn't want you anymore."

Quickening to a sprint, I drove forward, slashing against Indulf's shield. Fueled by rash emotion, the blow was sloppy, undisciplined, and Indulf blocked the strike, then countered with a series of thrusts intended more to force me back than to draw blood. Recalling Godilas' long-ago lessons, I pivoted and kept my balance, yet was unable to prevent Indulf from gaining momentum in our duel.

Despite an overlong day of combat, Indulf's strikes felt as crisp as I remembered. Emanating raw power, he jabbed and prodded in a frenzy of strikes, always leading with the tip of his sword rather than an edge. Most attacks smacked into my shield, yet two required a parry, sending me chopping downward to brush his blade away.

"You think you've won today?" Indulf snarled. "You've won nothing. Just death and ruin."

As he spoke, he jabbed once more. Rather than back away, I gripped my shield's straps and leaned into the blow. The Gothic blade pierced my shield just a fingernail's depth, but it was enough to prick my chest. Indulf's face brightened with victory as I recoiled in pain, yet he jerked in panic as he understood my intention behind such seemingly careless form.

I plunged my blade toward Indulf's body, with the Gothic warlord unable to free his blade or pivot to avoid the blow. Instead, he shifted his shield, redirecting my sword outward. That maneuver would nearly have worked too, had it not been an eye blink too late.

My redirected blade cut into Indulf's hip, scraping against bone. Indulf hissed, abandoning his sword as he tugged away from my attack. Still stuck in my shield, the awkward weight of his sword caused me to stumble, allowing Indulf to back five paces away. To the south, a Roman horn signaled the return of Martinus' cavalry, banners flapping as they thundered to a gallop. Farther east, a band of Goths descended their knoll, sprinting toward Indulf with spears lowered against me.

"Fight me!" I yelled. "You deserve this!"

Indulf spat. "You're a fool, Varus. And it will cost you everything."

Furious, I cut away my shield, a move which afforded Indulf another ten paces' retreat from me. Likewise, the Gothic and Roman bands closed their distance, threatening an imminent confrontation that I was unlikely to survive.

The faces of so many dead Thracians along with, the fearful look on Rosamund filled my mind, and I screamed, backing away. There was no alternative. I had no choice but to grant Indulf's escape, for foolish as I was, I was unwilling to take his life if it earned me nothing more than a skewering by a half dozen angry Goths. Instead, I backed away toward Rome as Indulf disappeared in the Gothic camp. Too many had died that day, and it seemed neither side was willing to add to the tally.

"Are you mad?!" Martinus roared as he galloped from the south, slowing his followers as they circled around me. He offered me a spare mount, which I ascended with sore joints and unfathomable fatigue.

"Good to see you," I panted, my body spent.

Martinus rolled his eyes. "I should think so. But you can kiss my arse later. Let's return to the city."

And so we did. Surprised by Martinus' arrival, the remaining Gothic bands retreated from the Aurelian Walls, returning in the thousands to their camps. In their wake, hundreds of dead and dismembered bodies festered, crows already circling the meal below. Impossibly, Witiges' great storm against Rome had failed, and the Imperial banner remained aloft. I should have been pleased—we all should have.

Except that the siege continued. And Witiges had no intention of leaving us in peace.

THE SIXTH GIFT

What was most unusual about the conclusion of that battle was not the deaths of those close to me. Nor was it the sheer insanity of our defense against so many Goths, who somehow had managed to seize defeat in a spectacular fashion. Instead, what unsettled me most was that first evening. For rather than retreat to a military camp, I instead stumbled into the domicile of my family, both looking and smelling like a creature from hell.

That did not dissuade Mariya's joy—at least, not initially. As I strode into the Domus Augustana, trailing congealed blood and all manner of muck onto the floor's mosaics, a servant gasped before recognizing me. I stilled myself until Mariya arrived, who yelped and rushed toward me, throwing her arms around my shoulders. Her kiss felt uncomfortable, even unwelcome, though I yearned to surrender to her embrace. She withdrew, wrinkling her nose, and ordered copious buckets of hot water prepared for my use, then shooed away any servants who gathered to aid my bathing.

"Your arm!" Mariya gasped, looking upon the crudely stitched flesh.

"It's nothing," I answered. "Rosamund fixed it moments after it occurred."

Mariya stiffened upon mention of Rosamund, curdling the bile in my gut. "Is Rosamund hurt, Mariya?"

"No, Rosamund is fine," she shot back. "As are your children, if you wanted to know."

Images of a defiant Zenobia hurling stones atop the Aurelian Walls flickered in my overtaxed memory. "I had no idea that they would do that, Mariya. I sent Zenobia and the others back to the Domus as soon as I saw—"

"Of course you didn't know!" Mariya shrieked, clenching her eyes shut. "You've been running about the city, looking for opportunities to get yourself killed."

I confess, I have never been more perplexed in my life. "Mariya, it was a battle. No different than any other."

"I hear you ran to three different sections of the walls," Mariya declared. "I know you must fight. I worry myself to death, but I accept it as your wife. But it's as if… as if you're yearning for death!"

She shuddered, then began to weep. "Carthage, Salona, and now Rome," she mumbled, pushing feebly against my chest. "And you leave me behind to wonder what trouble you're searching for next. Why can't you be more careful?!"

Still, I did not fully understand the cause of Mariya's anger, though I understood it to be rooted deep, and not easily deterred. Others had warned of the risks I had taken upon myself, though as both an excubitor and a leader of spearmen, I believed those risks to be nothing out of the norm. "I was careful, Mariya. I promise."

"*I promise*," Mariya mocked, her voice breaking amidst sobs. "I promise, I promise, I promise! So many promises. But the only ones you keep are for her!"

At that, Mariya buried her face into her hands. Her shoulders heaved with each ponderous sob until, after a few heartbeats, she leaned into my sore, bruised chest. In that moment, Mariya seemed so small, as if a stiff wind might topple her over no matter how furious her temperament. When she spoke, Mariya's voice was as mournful as I could ever recall, even more than upon my return from Salona. "I don't know what to do, Varus."

"What, my love?" I whispered. "What is there to do?"

"*Something*," Mariya cried on a wave of fresh sobs. "Anything. I feel useless here. I can't help you, other than sit in the Domus and wait to hear if you've been maimed or killed. I can't do what Rosamund does for you."

Gripping Mariya's shoulders, I bent my knees so that our eyes were level. "You are my wife, Mariya. You alone. I need you more than any person or possession on God's Earth."

Mariya rolled her kohl-smudged eyes. "That's not true."

"It is!" I insisted. And though a ponderous weight began to crush my chest at the thought, I gave voice to an option that I had no desire to fulfill. "Do you wish me to send Rosamund away?"

Mariya's sobs ceased, her lips slightly agape. I doubt that she had expected that offer. And by the lengthy pause in her response, it was an enticing one. Even absent knowledge of my onetime intercourse with Rosamund in our first year together, and our more recent encounter in the Colosseum, Mariya was visibly torn by the prospect of sending the other woman away. Eventually, though, she filled her lungs with a draught of frosty air and declined.

"Rosamund keeps you alive," Mariya replied, eyes serious and wide. "She will stay."

Guiltily relieved, I nodded. "I have taken you for granted, which is wrong. I promise to do better, Mariya."

Mariya flinched at the world "promise," which I quickly regretted. Then, blotting her tear-streaked face, she prodded me about something else altogether. "Others told me of Wazeba... and Cephalas..."

After the bout over Rosamund, a more unwelcome subject could not have been conjured. Hearing Mariya speak of my fallen comrades, images of their deaths flickered in my mind: Wazeba's demise by a dozen spear thrusts, Cephalas' unseen death amidst heat and flame. Worse, a faint memory of Hakhamanish, that priest of fire, entered my thoughts, as did his curse.

Mariya altered the course of our discussion, yet I had no replies or explanations for her. Instead, she spoke of a hundred things, from her worries of the children's absence to the sounds she heard of the battle. Of ballistae and screams, reminding her of the chaos of the riots. Through it all I nodded, my eyes closing as she scrubbed all hint of battle from my body. It felt good to be clean, but my mind was only fixated upon its demand for sleep.

Not that sleep was peaceful upon arrival. In my dreams, I saw the crimson eyes of the dark rider, angry slits more lizard than human as he rode beneath a dying solar disc. I saw the death of my friends, of Cephalas and Baduarius, of John and the brothers Sunicas and Simmas, and of Isaacius long ago. In death, their eyes were dark holes, boring thoughts as they beckoned me to join them. So many dead, and for whatever reason, I had been spared their fate until now.

Though I cannot remember how I arrived upon the featherbed that Mariya and I shared, I distinctly recall awaking there in a maelstrom of terror. In the darkness, gloom hid a hundred enemies, while a persistent ringing in my ears deafened me to any noise about me. Screaming, I fumbled about, searching for my sword and failing to find it secured next to my bed.

I cannot be certain how long I stood in that pitch black, muscles taut and eyes scanning the room for those who would do me harm. My confusion was muddled further as servants rushed into the room bearing tapers, while a bandaged Sembrouthes waddled in, his sword drawn.

"Calm yourself, Varus!" he yelled.

"Listen to Sembrouthes, Varus," Mariya added from the bed. "You are with your family, and you are safe."

Part of me recognized the ridiculousness of my actions, yet portions remained fearful, certain that mortal danger surrounded me. After Sembrouthes, however, a voice stilled my anxieties.

"Leave him with me," Rosamund rasped. "He will be fine."

"Fine?!" Mariya snarled. "He's terrified. Just tell me what to do."

Cowering near the bed, I watched as Rosamund drew close to Mariya. Rosamund's voice was soft, nearly inaudible. Though my memory is incomplete here, I swear that I heard Rosamund's reply.

"There's nothing you can do," she whispered. "It's too dangerous. Leave me with him."

Mariya straightened. "No! I am his wife. As a servant to this household, I command you to aid me."

The noise was too much for me. "Stop! Stop!"

Rosamund gave Mariya a quizzical glance. "If I leave you here alone, you'll be hurt. As your *servant*..." Rosamund paused, lacing her label with venomous disdain, "...my oath is to keep you safe, even against yourself."

Mariya appeared ready to scream, and only Sembrouthes prevented further discord. "It's dangerous, Mariya. I've seen Rosamund treat Varus before. Come with me, my lady, just for an hour."

Rosamund nodded in gratitude. "Evil grips his mind after a battle, and sometimes long thereafter. You don't want witness it, let alone by yourself."

"God help me!" Mariya wailed. "I don't even rule my own house!"

But still, she complied. As she and my bodyguard departed, Rosamund latched the bedroom door and drew close to me. She cooed words of peace and asked me to lie flat upon the bed.

"Indulf struck you," I blubbered.

"And it hurt, for a short time," Rosamund replied calmly. "Still sore, but Agathias aided me. After a few days, all will be well."

"How?" I asked. "How are you so certain?"

Rosamund clicked her tongue. "You are uncomfortable with talk about my gods. But there is certainty in faith, whether you understand my meaning or not."

I wanted to believe that I did. As a Christian, faith was the common precept behind all hope of forgiveness, that there is something greater than this world of suffering and hardship. But, where Rosamund's conviction was resolute, my own was riddled with questions. At times, a shrewd observer might see my misgivings as doubt. I am no fool—I believe in God—but at times I do wonder whether he cares for our world anymore. From all I have witnessed in my life, I am fearful of the answer.

With Rosamund's aid, I spent the remainder of that darkness in blessed sleep. Yet, when I awoke, it was neither Rosamund nor

Mariya who greeted me but a fur-cloaked figure sitting lazily atop the bench facing my bed.

Samur lifted his head as I sat upright, chuckling when I moaned from the ache across my body. "I admit, Varus, as children I never thought we would rise far in this life. But here we remain, lords of Carthage and Rome. Everything Justin desired, no?"

"Indeed," I grumbled, my tongue swollen and sticking to the roof of my mouth. Slipping onto the stone floor, I paced to a nearby table, where I guzzled from a pitcher of water without bothering with the nearby silver cup.

"I heard about Cephalas," Samur continued, his tone darkening. "He was a rare honorable Greek. I will miss him."

"He threw himself onto naphtha with lit torches," I said solemnly. "I don't think very many Romans were even kind to him. But he sacrificed himself for us."

Samur gritted his teeth. "Like Sunicas. Yet Justinian's perfumed sycophants still disdain the Huns."

Silence passed between us as I drained the rest of the pitcher. "I can't believe we won," I admitted. "The Mausoleum... the Vivarium... It was a disaster."

"It's not over yet," Samur warned. "But I heard that the children joined in the fighting! I would have loved to have seen that!"

I grunted. "It was foolish. Any Goth could have cut their throats without breaking stride."

"You and I would have done nothing differently." Samur smiled. "And it is obvious that Zenobia is your daughter. None of Mariya's perfumes or jewels could ever conceal such a wild heart as that."

Sighing, I surrendered. "You're probably correct, but I don't know what kind of life that will allow Zenobia. Perhaps it was a mistake to allow her to train with the boys."

"I hear she brained a Goth climber." Samur grinned. "Her and Tiberius. That lad has the makings of a warrior, if Narses' spies don't discover the identity of his father."

"*Quiet!*" I cautioned, my voice almost too light to hear. "Even here, we must be careful." I raised my voice back to conversational. "I suppose I should speak with the children. I assumed that Alexander would take my place in the army one day, but perhaps the others might rise high, too, given the opportunity."

"Perhaps." Samur sounded skeptical. "Alexander is still young, just a babe. But Zenobia showed that stone face of hers to the world before she could walk. And Tiberius will do you honor. He only needs encouragement, and to know that he's wanted."

It was unlike Samur to show softness to others. Zenobia was an exception, but as he spoke of Tiberius, I wondered whether he saw himself in the lad. "Let's go speak with them, then. You are their uncle, after all."

Given my itching arm and the interlaced bruises covering my flanks, donning a simple linen shirt and trousers required unusual concentration. Next to Samur and his leather and furs preferred amongst the Hun foederati, I appeared a Roman aristocrat. Nevertheless, my brother seemed genuinely excited as we found our way to the children's rooms, commanding those old enough to hear and understand to gather in a single space. Servants withdrew Bakuris and Alexander, while Zenobia, Tiberius, and a gaggle of Mariya's foundlings all sat in fearful silence as I addressed them.

"For those who found their way to the Vivarium yesterday, it was a foolhardy risk you accepted," I growled, pinching my face in an exaggerated display of frustration. "You could have been taken, or killed, or maimed, or simply lost. Do you understand?"

The children, some two dozen aged three to twelve, shuffled awkwardly. Tiberius yielded a baleful gaze my way, while Zenobia scowled, her dark eyes showing an intelligence far older than her years. Others, like Cours or the young John, stared at the ground, squirming at my displeasure.

"It was my plan, Lord," Tiberius piped up, just as he had the prior day. "I deserve punishment, but the others do not."

"Not true!" Zenobia cried. "I wanted to be there as much as Tiberius. You can't be angry with him, Pater!"

"Enough!" Samur roared. "Life does not kneel to your whims. When Varus and I were boys, we scraped and bowed. We owned nothing, not even our own bodies. Any insolence might mean torture or death. You have every privilege, but still, you defy your mother."

Samur's ferocity surprised me, blunting my anger. "You must understand: Every decision you make in this empire has consequences for others, especially those in this room. Your safety is the responsibility of this household, and your actions reflect upon me as its master. Understood?"

Scattered nods—some vigorous, others reluctant, but all agreeing in surrender. "Good," I concluded. "For those who wish to truly become warriors, your training will resume in earnest."

"And I will oversee it." Samur grinned. "Sembrouthes might be your weapons master, but I shall mold you into fighters."

His words took me by surprise. That was not what we had agreed, nor was I comfortable with my brother pushing the children beyond the already strenuous activities that Sembrouthes ordered upon them. Yet at his announcement, both Zenobia and Tiberius grinned, while others looked upon Samur with adoration. And why not? Though endless riding had weathered his features, Samur was the antithesis of Roman warriors—savage, unyielding, unorthodox, and unpredictable. More, he had always possessed a charm that had saved him from multiple episodes of discipline when he had misbehaved in the Imperial Palace. So I capitulated.

"That's correct," I said. "Now, Samur and I must speak with Zenobia and Tiberius. The rest of you are to leave."

The other children shuffled off, casting curious glances toward their two young compatriots. I left the room as Samur spoke to Zenobia and Tiberius of their particular responsibilities as leaders of the household children and stole myself into the Domus' armory. From that overbearing array of weapons, I plucked two simple daggers, their wooden handles chipped of paint and worn by overuse. I tested a blade and found it small yet sharp, its edge little more than the length of my hand. Tucking both into my belt, I returned to Samur.

"I wish the world was happier, and more peaceful," Samur concluded. "And I will work to improve it for you, but I know that I will fail in the end. As will my brother here. One day, Varus and I will depart from this life, and because of that, you must learn to make wise decisions on your own—to lead others, and to act with cleverness with everything that you do."

"While I am disappointed that you disobeyed Mariya," I added, "both of you demonstrated courage despite your youth. But if you disobey me again, I will not be so gentle. For now, though, I will reward you, provided you make me a promise."

Both of their heads perked up at my mention of a reward. I plucked the sheathed daggers from my belt and handed one to each child, earning a bemused smirk from Samur.

"This gift is a sign of trust. If I discover that you have harmed others or yourselves, I will reclaim these and not show further favor. Is that understood?"

Zenobia gaped at the offering. "Yes, Pater."

"Yes, Lord," Tiberius echoed.

Ruffling Tiberius' hair, I smiled. "I'm proud of both of you."

With that, I left Samur to spend time with the children and ventured into the bowels of the Domus. The place truly was decorated to the point of garishness; every room had been adorned with frescoes, gold, sculptures, and all manner of goods that Gothic nobility had restored since the Vandal sack decades ago. It felt refreshing to amble about alone, temporarily relieved of decision-making and duties, even if only for an hour. In one room, however, I stumbled upon a stinking heap: Perenus, half snoring and half moaning in a stupor.

He had neither cleaned nor changed clothes from the day before, even though his armor was soaked with stale wine. A mixed odor of sickness and filth wafted about him, somehow worse than the usual unpleasantness of a soldiers' camp. With a kick, I jostled Perenus awake.

"What in God's name are you doing?" I asked.

Perenus initially resisted, turning his body away from me—but, unbalanced, he slipped from the bench and clattered against the stone floor. With a moan, he sat upright, rubbing his eyes.

"Is there any wine?" he asked.

"Get ahold of yourself!" I replied, signaling for a passing servant to fetch water. "You should be resting under the care of a healer, not drinking yourself to oblivion."

Perenus tried to prop his head up but found the effort too great. Instead, he lurched over onto his knees and spilled the contents of his stomach across the floor. The sickly sweet aroma of half-digested wine mixed with his already overpowering stench, nearly bringing me to gag. "We won, didn't we?" he sputtered. "I wanted to see my son."

I kneeled to meet his eyes, though he repulsed me. "You are a leader of men, Perenus. But none would recognize you as such in your current state. I promised to be a better friend to you, and I intend to do so. You will stay in the Domus under Agathias' care until further notice. When you are healed and of sound mind, then and only then will little Bakuris see you—and see you for who you truly are."

Perenus' eyes fell to the floor. After heaving again, he sniffled, cradled his limbs, and began to rock, weeping. "I don't understand what's wrong with me, Varus."

It was terrible watching so great a man whimper like a child. There was no one I would rather fight alongside in a shield wall, nor whom I would trust to care for the lives and livelihoods of hundreds of others. Many a warrior had followed Perenus' path to various ends—Godilas to his fits, Archelaus to his brutality, and countless others to lechery, bloodlust, and cruelty. All of them shared something broken, riven after too much grief for one lifetime. Perhaps I truly was as poor a friend as Perenus had accused me of being, for I had witnessed his rapid descent into this decrepit state and done nothing adequate to forestall it. Now, I could only ache for my friend, whom I knew not how to help other than to listen and promise that things would be better in time.

"You've lost someone you love." I thought first of Hereka, then corrected myself. "Many someones. I struggle with that too. The pain never leaves. But it does become manageable."

The servant returned with a brass pitcher of water. Perenus initially refused the offering, though eventually surrendered to my will. Much of the liquid missed his mouth, lathering his beard and chest, though enough was consumed to satisfy me.

"I hear their voices all the time, except when I drink," Perenus confessed. "Hereka. Isaacius. Cephalas now. Too many others. Sometimes, I wish I had died instead of them."

It was a terrible sin to wish death upon oneself. But I would be a liar if I said I did not understand, for if I had been in Perenus' position, my thoughts would be similar. "Your son still needs you, Perenus. I do, too, and our other friends."

"I know, I know." Perenus shrugged. "I just wished this fucking ache in my chest wouldn't hurt so bad."

We sat together for a time. Wordless, full of meaning in a manner that only old friends can share. Whenever words reached my lips, I failed to give them voice, though Perenus did not seem to mind either way. Whatever his thoughts may have been, eventually, Perenus sighed and gave in to aid.

"I think I'll go see Agathias now."

"Do that," I said. "Anything you need, tell me. Your worries are mine as well."

Cuffing tears from his face, Perenus spat noisily onto the ground, bobbed his head, and offered me his hand. As I accepted it, Perenus gripped hard upon my forearm. "I know it, Varus. Thank you."

Additional servants were summoned to guide Perenus to Agathias' care. After he and I parted, I again retreated into the echoing side chambers of the Domus, listening to the hum of servants flitting about behind me as they cleaned Perenus' mess and rustled about on several other tasks. Though I had a far less intimate knowledge of those rooms than of the chambers of Constantinople's palace, I also presumed that at least one attendant spied upon every step that I took, both to better serve any request I should render, but also to forward knowledge to any number of spymasters under the pay of the Goths, the Franks, or even Narses. Though Belisarius had successfully taken Rome, and its residents praised the return of the Imperial banner, none of us was so naïve as to believe that loyalties were absolute. After all, Pope Silverius himself was among those suspected of curious and concerning origins.

As before, however, my solace was interrupted by another's presence. This time, rather than stumbling upon a half-dead body, I was greeted by Liberius as I walked the Domus' vast halls, finding the older man as stern and vigorous as ever as he paced atop the Domus' mosaic floors.

"You gave Witiges a thrashing," Liberius announced by way of greeting. "Perhaps a mortal one, although he may not know it for several months."

My body ached, and my mind was far too sluggish to grapple with Liberius' superior wit. "It wasn't easy, Lord."

"Nor should it be!" he exclaimed. "Nothing worthwhile ever is. But you found a way. Belisarius told me of your exploits last night."

"Last night?" I echoed. Burning embarrassment rose along my cheeks as it became plain—I had abandoned Belisarius to oversee the battle's conclusion alone.

"Indeed," Liberius confirmed. "You held Hadrian's Mausoleum, that gaudy monstrosity, with cleverness and sacrifice against a sizeable force. Similarly with the Vivarium."

"Lord…" I began, uncomfortable accepting such plaudits. "I was lucky, and Witiges was foolish," I finished.

Liberius groaned. "You say that like it is a bad thing! Good fortune is far preferable to skill. The only challenge is to be repeatedly lucky."

I could not decipher what Liberius wished me to say, but then again, he offered me little opportunity to speak. "Well, there's no need to waste time," he went on. "I've come to give your sixth gift."

My eyes widened. "Lord?"

"Ah, now I have your interest!" Liberius teased. "So impolite, to be unwilling to humor an old man in conversation unless there's some quid pro quo. Yes, Varus, the sixth gift. Penultimate of the whole set."

He paced along the edge of the hallway wall, where he reached into a satchel for a worn tome. "You remember the first five, of course?"

I nodded. "A cross, a dagger, a sword, wealth, and Basilius' seal."

Liberius nodded. "Years ago, you asked me what I so desperately sought to rescue from the library of Nisibis," he continued. "Few copies of this survive that were scratched out by the original author. This is my personal copy, although I have long missed a sizeable section. Through theft, Nisibis allowed me to complete this account. It is now yours."

Liberius slid the tome into my hands, his touch surprisingly gentle. The calfskin binding was ringed in iron and worn to roughness through extensive handling. Gingerly, I pried the cover and glanced upon its first page, finding delicate arcs and whorls denoting the book's provenance.

A History of the East by Priscus of Panion.

Beneath the name and title, in darker block numerals that contrasted with the crisp writing above, denoted: *Volume one of eight.*

"Alas, if you desire the other seven, you will spend your life searching in vain just as I have," Liberius said mournfully. "Priscus' works were destroyed along with the Western Empire. Fragments remain, and some insist they possess copies of one volume or another, but they tend to be obvious forgeries."

As I sat down and thumbed through the pages, Liberius went on, his tone ever baleful. "A true shame, because Priscus was the last historian the Empire possessed of the old style. Christianity brings many blessings, but their historians are too often tediously inaccurate."

"Priscus was pagan?" I asked, glancing at page after page of Latin text.

"Obviously." Liberius chuckled. "And because you are particularly slow this morning, I will point out sections of my interest."

He flicked through the pages deftly, as if he could navigate the text blindly—which, given the extent of handling of the tome, came as little surprise. The titles of Priscus' chapters were both familiar and overwhelming, spanning decades of intrigue, war, and survival of the Roman people. It began with the death of Theodosius I, the final emperor to rule the joint halves of east and west, and proceeded to discuss the failings of his feckless son Arcadius. Though I understood Priscus' extensive evaluation of those Eastern men as valuable to the Empire's memory, they were dry, and would have found an audience only amongst men such as Narses or Procopius. In the following section, however, my attention sharpened.

A history of the Hun brothers Attila and Bleda, the Hunnic Horde, and a firsthand account of a dinner and embassy to the court of Attila.

"Believe it or not, few Romans ever met Attila and survived," Liberius said. "If you don't understand who your adversary is, it is impossible to understand oneself. Priscus risked his head in embarking on a visit to Attila's horde, and we are richer for it."

Though Godilas and Liberius had regaled me with tales of the Huns throughout my boyhood, reading the faded letters of a man who had himself met the Hunnic warlord left me in awe. Now I understood the true pricelessness of what I held. "Lord—"

"Read on, Varus," Liberius said, chuckling. "That's what books are for."

Priscus' account began as impenetrably verbose as his descriptions of the Eastern emperors, explaining his charge by Theodosius II to venture into Hunnic lands and entreat Attila's warlords to find an alternative to their punishing raids. After riding north for two uninterrupted weeks in the dense northern forests, Priscus was granted entry not only into Attila's court, but to a banquet of honor for the Hunnic gods to seek blessings for the journey ahead.

I was seated in a vast wooden hall, filled with hundreds of men and women, with neither expressing virtues of chasteness or modesty. They drank wine from stolen silver and feasted upon cuts of rich meats from pilfered golden platters, toasting to Attila's health with each passing course. Attila joined in their reverie but preferred cups and plates of wood, his tunic threadbare next to the fine furs of his chieftains.

It was explained to me by Orestes, one of the few fluent Latin speakers present and something of a secretary to the Hunnic king, that Attila had once ruled the endless Scythian Plains with his brother, Bleda, but the latter perished from treachery. I was ordered to refuse no drink, and to join all toasts, and to follow any other instructions if I held any value to my life.

Eventually, bloated with food and near sick with drink, I was summoned to the High King's presence. I passed by dozens of conquered kings, the bearded and the clean-shaven, the tattooed and those who shape their heads into cones as babes, and those of all manner of skin and face. Behind Attila were the skulls of those kings who did not bend the knee in submission, the bones bleached clean and covered in a blackened pitch. With a stiff hand, Attila granted me permission to attend him, and Orestes followed closely behind.

Beside the king were his most treasured client-kings, as well as his chief wife and sons. A shaman, frocked in feathers and scales, his hair caked in dung and face decorated by paints and kohl, whispered into the king's ear. Tanned pelts draped the walls and floor, warming the enclosure from the sacrifice of no fewer than a thousand slain foxes, wolves, bears, and many other creatures simple and fantastical. After a bow, Orestes introduced me to the Hunnic king, and then whispered in my ear that I should render my prepared gift to Kreka, Attila's wife.

I obliged, although my hands shook as I delivered the bundle to Kreka, worrying that the king would take offense that the gift was not delivered to him. Though the Hun ladies were all rumored to be hairy and crook-backed, Kreka was both strong-bodied and handsome, if perhaps worn from years in the saddle. Her long black hair had been tied in a knot and pinned with bone, reflecting Attila's own simple tastes. Unfurling the package that had been granted by

Theodosius II, divine Emperor of Constantinople, Kreka frowned upon the array of ornaments inside, from gem-encrusted combs to a richly enameled belt, and a half dozen other trinkets that would have each purchased a slave or two in Constantinople's flesh markets. I feared her displeasure and the unblinking eye of Attila, yet Orestes assured me that the gesture was deemed sufficient to placate any ill will.

"A fascinating view into a long-ago time," I remarked. "I will read more in the days ahead."

"Surely," Liberius answered, trailing his finger to the bottom of a page. "But read a few passages more, to satisfy an old man's heart."

Reluctantly, with fatigue, I forced myself onward. Priscus elaborated upon vast heaps of Hun treasures, looted from peoples thousands of miles apart and decorated with visages of wild foreign gods and mythical creatures. Absurdly, more food and drink was served—to the Huns' delight and Priscus' terror. This example was copied throughout the Hun camp, whose inhabitants numbered in the tens of thousands, and yet was but a fragment of Attila's strength as the Scourge of God.

At last, one passage drew my interest, for it contained information I knew little of, yet somehow made the Hun king more interesting as a man rather than a myth.

Through Orestes, Kreka asked of my family, to which I responded that I had none, with my only children the people of the Empire. Kreka smiled at this, while Attila nearly choked with laughter, wiping half-chewed strips of horse flesh from his lips.

"A man without children has no future," Attila chided me. "My blood is generously granted, but only three are my heirs through Kreka."

The eldest, Ellac, was absent, dispatched by his dread father to secure the loyalty of plains-riders beyond the distant Caspian Sea. The second, Dengizich, drank and whored with the gathered Huns, adorned in the rich furs and chains of gold that his father eschewed. Lastly, the youngest was but a slip of a man named Ernakh, bridging the divide between youth and hardened warrior. Unlike Dengizich, Ernakh was showered with his father's attentions, and he rushed to his father's side as he was summoned to greet me.

"The shamans say that I will die." Attila laughed. "But all men die, so what is that to me? But they also say that my line shall live on through Ernakh, and that demands greater attention."

The stinking Hun priest stepped beside his master. "The stars and the winds, the beast in the fields and the fish on the endless seas, with every blade of bent grass, Lord Attila, they all give voice to the same fate. You shall drive the world to its knees, but it shall be your favored son who shapes its destiny."

Attila did not chide that filthy creature, nor scoff at superstition. All he did was place a palm upon his son's scalp, holding it there before rising from his throne.

"You hear that?" said the king. "The world cannot resist us! All will be cast aside, melding with the horde, and it shall be my sons who reap what I sow."

I shivered, praying that none in Attila's audience witnessed my weakness as they chanted the Death King's name. Conquest is no stranger to the Empire, nor is cruelty, or even savagery. But Attila is something else entirely, and his people would follow him to any end. I have no doubt that Attila means to do as he says, and I wonder how much of the Roman world will survive in his wake.

But Attila was not finished. "Bring him in."

One of Attila's client-kings, an Ostrogoth named Valamir, hauled forth a squirming, dung-stained man adorned in rags that were once Roman raiment. Sackcloth was removed from his head and a gag from his mouth, yet the bedraggled figure dared not speak as he stood before the Hunnic king. Orestes translated in my ear as quickly as his tongue would allow, careful not to allow his voice to rise above a whisper.

Attila bellowed a declaration to his attendants. "This man once governed the province of Pannonia for the West Romans. He took foreign children, raped them, and left them bleeding and alone in the forests to die. I can think of no better blood to shed for our soothsaying."

Men cheered as the Hun witch skipped around Attila, positioning the Roman prisoner toward the empty center of the room. The Roman, his once-soft body wasted away from lack of nourishment, shook under the clutches of the foreign holy man. The shaman cooed soft words as he lifted a wineskin to the condemned man's lips, drawing a groan of relief from the Roman. Meanwhile, Attila stepped forward, unsheathing a magnificent blade from an ox-hide sheath.

"Behold!" the shaman cried. "The Sword of Veretragna, the divine lord of war!"

"The Scythian gods, the Roman gods, the Persian gods, and even the Christian God," Attila roared, "all chose me as their vessel. This, the Sword of Mars, embodies my right to rule all the world. I ask them all to show me which direction the horde shall pledge its fate."

In a swift thrust, Attila plunged the blade into his captive's stomach. The Roman, stupefied by the shaman's drink, lurched backward as the blade was pulled free. He stumbled in wide circles, frothing blood as he first lurched left. Slipping backward, he moved to the rightmost edge of the hall, spilling crimson droplets with each step. Not long thereafter, he collapsed, his entrails slipping onto the ground, and fell still.

"The auguries are clear, God-King!" the shaman declared. "Go east, and you shall live a life of plenty and longevity, but shall be forgotten within three generations of soft-bodied descendants. Go west, and your reign shall be brief and terrible, but your spirit shall inflame the minds of all who are yet to be borne for the remainder of time."

Attila flashed his wolfish teeth at such a pronouncement. "Then Mars shall be sated. We go west!"

"Not exactly inspirational, Priscus," Liberius joked. "Read more, when you can. You'll discover plenty about what made the West fall, and hopefully identify how to set such failures to rights."

Beyond the subject of Attila, which still rendered awe and terror in any Roman who heard the name, what drew my curiosity about this book was the binding. Reinforced with golden thread, these pages had clearly been inserted recently compared to the coarse, weathered binding of the others. Yet even though I could guess at which section Liberius had taken such care to procure from Nisibis, the purpose of the gifts was still a mystery. What I was intended to do with each offering was an even greater plague upon my mind, as I had no clearer answer in that moment than I did upon my first encounter with Father Petrus.

"Lord, so many years have passed since my first gift was granted. What difference will they make at this point, to whatever design you would have of me?"

"None at all," Liberius mused. "But then again, everything shall change. That was precisely their intention."

I closed the tome, grazing a finger over its dented spine. It was humbling, holding the testament of a rare Roman eye into such a distant world so long ago. However, beyond the intrigue of its narratives, the codex itself held no special meaning for me.

"I don't understand this gift, Lord," I admitted. "Or Basilius' before this. What lesson am I to learn?"

"That our world did not begin with your birth," Liberius shot back immediately. "And if we are strong enough to stand against men like Attila, nor shall our world perish after your death. After Attila died, his empire shattered, and his sons flew to the wind. Though the Huns remain a terrible force, they are too fragmented to fulfill Attila's dream, and are even safe to collaborate with as we now do. Justinian and Theodora would see the Empire built upon a foundation of bedrock rather than the brittle bed of hay that has caused so many other great kings to disappear into the histories."

"But why *me*, Lord?" I pried. "What do you want me to do?"

Liberius joined me upon my bench, placing an arm about my shoulder as he was wont to do when I was a lad. "Complete Justin's vision, and see Rome and Ravenna freed. Defend our way of life, and do it honor. But most of all, be a good man, regardless of what terrors your service to the Empire subjects you to. I know they are many."

Later, when I sought out Father Petrus, he, too, had no further answers to yield. "Liberius warned me you would ask, and my account will not differ from his. You were promised seven gifts, not seven well-digested opinions that would be explained in copious detail."

"But I don't understand, Father!" I cried. "I don't understand *any* of it."

Petrus' smirk faded into a frown. "You will, soon enough. For a time, I had thought it would not be necessary for you to receive the seventh gift. Indeed, if it were my decision alone, perhaps that would be the end of the matter. I worry…" But he trailed off, shaking his head. "For now, honor God and your people, and be content."

It was not the first time that Petrus had framed the gifts as something to be shunned. Cursed, even, if the pagans could be believed. Before, such baleful warnings gave me little concern. But now, on the precipice of completing the course that Justin had set for me so long ago…

Alas, I would receive no further answers that day, or for many a day still to come. Yet the ache of not knowing burned just as vividly then as it had upon receiving the first gift of Petrus' cross, and I wished for time to pass so that I might be united with the full resolution of so many unresolved questions. Why me? Why had Justin and so many others afforded me such an opportunity in life? And, given Petrus' worry, what did it all mean? I was still a fool, and while still early in my life, not nearly as young as I had been when Justin freed me for a life in the Imperial Army. I still loved Justin, though I no longer burned to learn the answers to questions that had hounded my earliest days. Quite simply, I knew too well that the answers would be accompanied by more sorrow than I was prepared for. Such weighty knowledge would come in time, whether I was prepared for the burden or not.

My sojourns through the Domus left me perilously behind on the morning's reports, and as I left Petrus, I mounted Boreas to meet

Belisarius' attendants along the Pincian Hill. Once there, I found Belisarius bare-chested atop a bench, a servant teasing at overwrought muscles and slathering a salve upon the cuts along his face and arms. It was odd seeing him so vulnerable—in most settings, he was rarely seen without the regalia of a Roman general, yet now he appeared no different than a tired spearman.

"For a time, I wasn't sure we would survive," Belisarius said after greeting me. "Don't tell the men that, of course. But what a fight it was!"

"You look terrible, Lord," I replied. "Almost as bad as me."

"I doubt that!" Belisarius grinned. "I owe you thanks, Varus. You successfully led my men through the worst of the assault. Whatever Cassiodorus' quarrels with you, Justinian will have no choice but to grant you patronage."

I felt guilty accepting that praise when Cephalas' and Wazeba's bodies still lay unclaimed. But nor could I easily refuse Belisarius' offer. "After the years my family has borne, that would be most welcome, Lord."

"It would be my pleasure to commend you to him, and I shall." Belisarius smiled. "But first, there are a thousand tasks to attend to. Witiges has a bloodied nose, yes, but he's still camped outside our walls."

Though Belisarius and I had briefly met at the conclusion of the battle, it was only upon that next day's gathering that we took a full account of the battle's destruction. We tallied casualties, shored up weaknesses in our lines, and sent copious messages to Constantinople noting both our initial success and the increasingly dire state of Rome. Likewise, teams of torch-bearing riders were dispatched to set alight Witiges' siege towers, whose wheels stood unmoving as teams of dead oxen lay splayed in the dust. There was nothing that the Goths could do other than watch as their precious engines flamed into a towering inferno and tally their dead. Per Belisarius, Witiges might have lost some two or three thousand warriors in the battle, but still retained seven bustling camps outside our walls, with more bands replacing his losses with each evening.

Some five hundred soldiers and two hundred Roman civilians lay dead, their bodies collected the following day from the base of the walls or from temporary storage points within the wall towers and placed within the Roman forum. Both the Mausoleum and the Vivarium lay in ruins—the former's gate had been blackened from the flames of the siege ram, while the latter had been shattered altogether.

Rather than commit the already overstretched labor force to rebuilding the Praenestine Gate, Belisarius ordered the opening temporarily walled off, with rough-hewn stones stacked amidst a thick lather of mortar. To discourage any Gothic forays against the open gate, Belisarius placed ample jars of naphtha along the walls while Ascum erected a half dozen of his scorpions, which Totila declined to contest further after an initial probing party was butchered within twenty paces of the walls. Other sections of wall were cleaned, and their loose stones and missiles replenished from Rome's vast storage yards, while torn banners of the Imperial Chi-Rho and our various warlords were mended and replaced. Within a week of Witiges' attack, our defenses must have appeared near similar to the onset of the siege, albeit with a bustling array of scorpions.

Wazeba's body was not difficult to find, its stained yellow tunic and his darker skin striking against the tattered corpses of a hundred Goths. Sembrouthes and the other Aksumites refused to allow any Roman to wash and prepare Wazeba's body, instead taking it upon themselves to remove the ravaged and damp garments, scrub his bloodless flesh of impurities, adorn their comrade for battle, and join his corpse with others in the forum.

Cephalas, however, required far more searching, and we did not successfully identify his remains until two days after he blocked the Vivarium with naphtha flame. The difficulty lay in the all-consuming nature of that heat—the fat of at least two hundred bodies melted away, splintering bones and dissolving organs putrefying in a stinking aroma that I doubt shall ever be cleansed from that corner of Rome. As the final embers cooled, however, a Herulian discovered a gnarled body with a twisted jaw and summoned me for confirmation.

"Cephalas…" I muttered, raising the skull into my hands. "Thank you, my friend."

"What shall we do with him, Lord?" Sindual asked. "There's not much left to burn."

"Fetch a fine coat of mail, a helm, a sword, and an Imperial banner," I answered. "Cephalas was one of the final surviving members of Godilas' Thracian Army. He deserves to be honored with all the rest."

There was neither space nor resources to respectfully bury so many dead, and Belisarius feared the onset of plague from the presence of so many corpses. As we had done after each of Belisarius' battles, we gathered the army together and stood respectfully for the bodies of our brothers, knowing well that their like would never be seen again in this life. Pope Silverius had argued that the bodies of Christians should be interred in earth, insisting that a burnt body could not find its resurrection upon the return of the Christ, but Belisarius was unmoved. There was no space, little time, rampant exhaustion, and the nagging fear of pestilence that follows mounds of dead, and the Pope's grumblings muted into feeble protest.

I granted both Wazeba and Cephalas raised pyres, while a motley assortment of Huns, Herulians, Vandals, Greeks, and Latins were all refitted for war and lain at peace, almost as if they were sleeping. Belisarius said his words, and then torches were distributed to each pyre, with Sembrouthes and I both igniting that of Wazeba, and then Cephalas.

"Goodbye," I whispered to Cephalas.

While I managed to restrain my own tears, Perenus proved inconsolable. Weeping as the flames licked at Cephalas' bones, he stumbled through one of the hundreds of songs that Cephalas had sang with our men on the march. His voice cracked and wavered, lacking any semblance of tone or melody, but it did not matter. Many of the Herulians and Vandals whom Cephalas had accompanied on past campaigns joined in Perenus' song.

"What do they sing?" Rosamund had sidled up to me, deferent

but curious. "I never mastered Cephalas' songs."

"'The Lamentation of Achilles,'" I whispered, my skin prickling as more voices recognized the tune and joined their voice to hundreds of others. "It's about the death of a hero after a victory. A great honor."

Even Belisarius added his hoarse throat to the swelling mass, and I joined in as well as flames consumed the bodies of the fallen.

Loudest of all were the Vandals, who boomed the foreign Greek words clumsily but confidently, and loudest of those was Gunderic. This was despite the array of bandages and cuts that laced his body and drained his face of color, making the Vandal giant appear unsteady on his feet. When I asked later about his ardor, Gunderic frowned, almost as if offended.

"Cephalas was a warrior and a friend to the Vandals," Gunderic explained. "He was crippled but still plunged into battle. In Tingitana, he cared for many of my men too ill to continue their retreat from Tingis. He was an ugly bastard, but we Vandals respected him for his deeds."

While our dead were treated with all due ceremony, the mounds of Gothic corpses merely sat piled outside of our walls. The mess of limbs and entrails grew taller still as we ejected bodies of those Goths who had succeeded in breaching our walls only to fall to their deaths or be slain by a Roman blade. Each gate along the Aurelian Walls soon possessed its own corpse pile, and a competition ensued amongst the Huns and Vandals over whose pile was the deepest or broadest; Wisimar and the Hun chieftains argued formalities regarding whether the victor should be determined by the number of bodies or by the sheer mass of death borne from each faction of the foederati.

"Numbers are all that matter!" Sinnion grumbled. "One dead Goth is two arms that cannot be used to climb or strike."

"Nonsense!" Wisimar grinned. "Big men count for more. I cut the leg off of one Goth that was almost as huge as Gunderic and smelled twice as bad."

Not that Witiges was passive in that week following the attack. As the stream of Gothic dead from inside Rome into one of these piles stemmed, a Gothic detachment reversed their shields and halted a hundred paces from the Pincian Gate, unconcerned with our ballistae, for a parley. As Belisarius enjoyed a rare period of rest, I tended to this meeting myself, finding Witiges and three other chieftains waiting patiently.

"I would skip the portion where we trade insults, and make my ambitions plain," Witiges began. "I will take Rome. It is only a matter of when. But I cannot sit and watch thousands of my men's corpses rot as carrion for dogs and crows."

"I would offer to burn them for you," I replied, "but I'd rather save the lumber to heat Rome's houses. What do you want?"

"No barbs, for one." Witiges raised a hand in surrender. "Two, give me a half day to recover the bodies of my men. They're outside of your walls, and I would order twenty men to retrieve their remains from each gate."

I dared not show pleasure at Witiges' proposal, as eliminating the wafting stench of thousands of corpses would dramatically improve the moods of our sentries. "If I allow this, what will you offer in return?"

Witiges outstretched his arms. "What would you ask of me?"

"Your men must be unarmed, and will have from the hour after dawn until dusk," I began. "For me, allow any civilians in the city to depart from the southern gates toward Neapolis, with your blessing and promise that no Goth will harm them. Neither you nor I would like to see the residents of this city victims of a siege."

It was a bold request, I knew. Though Belisarius had successfully depopulated much of Rome's Aventine and other residential neighborhoods, enough civilians had remained behind during the siege to noticeably draw upon our food supplies. Now, after witnessing the savagery of battle along the Aurelian Walls, many of these stragglers might more willingly depart for safer climes, backed by Belisarius' guarantee that their property would be returned at the conclusion of the siege.

Fortunately, the appeal to Witiges' sense of honor seemed to resonate.

"Civilians only, but you have my word," Witiges said, repeating the instructions to his chieftains. "The day after the corpses are claimed, any civilian may depart through the southern gates from dawn until dusk, and will not encounter any Gothic army as they travel for Neapolis. Agreeable?"

"Agreeable," I replied, seizing the Gothic king's outstretched arm.

"If only all our disputes could be handled thus." Witiges groaned. "One day, after you realize that Justinian is not the man he claims to be, all of you will be welcome in my kingdom."

"That's noble of you, but I mistrust some of the company you keep."

I found, unexpectedly, that I could not help but like Witiges. He was utterly foolish, allowing so many mouths to depart Rome and implicitly strengthen our reserves of food, yet his unyielding commitment to honorable exchange was something that I recognized. Something Justin would have recognized. For that, it was difficult to wish ill upon Witiges despite his intention to subjugate the Imperial Army. My hatred for Indulf was plenty to hone my continued desire for a fight.

Drowning in competing interests, a key need for Belisarius' senior officers was to find helpful lessons from Witiges' failed assault, and apply them to our future defense. Chief among these was Martinus' mounted assault outside the Vivarium. Though Gothic impotence against mounted cavalry and especially mounted bowmen had struck me as odd at the battle's conclusion, at the time I had been too consumed by hatred for Indulf to make sense of those developments. Surprisingly, neither did Belisarius. Instead, the value of that stratagem was revealed through conversation by Samur at a gathering of twenty of Belisarius' leaders.

"If Witiges has any wits about him, he'll mount a second attack with fresh men," Samur warned. "And if he does, we will fail, because we can no longer surprise his chieftains with our engines or naphtha. Are you certain we cannot abandon the city?"

Belisarius adamantly refused. "If we cede now, no Roman will ever trust Justinian's word again. Rome is a symbol, for better or worse."

"Fine," Samur all but spat. "If we must stay, then Martinus gives us a slim answer to make Witiges' life less pleasant."

Martinus chuckled. "I didn't do anything special, Samur. Just galloped around and fired at anyone who drew too close."

"Exactly!" Samur replied. "Did any of you notice that there was nothing that any Gothic chieftain could do to contest Martinus? All the other armies we have faced possessed a sizeable number of mounted warriors. But the Goths have only a few, and those they do have are usually the cocksure and undertrained sons of local nobles. A few volleys, and they all scatter or die."

By then, I understood Samur's strategy and inwardly cursed my foolishness in not identifying the opportunity myself.

Belisarius leaned closer. "What are you saying, Samur?"

Samur grinned. "You have trained the most vicious horsemen between Britannia and India. If Witiges will not budge from his camps, then we should send groups of one or two hundred men at a time, launch arrows, and gallop away. This is how the Huns built their empire, and I have confidence that the Herulians and cataphracts can do the same."

Belisarius grunted, weighing Samur's plan. "The Gothic casualties will be low, and this will not drive Witiges from the field."

For once, I disagreed with Belisarius. Samur's plan rooted in my mind, kindling a glimmer of hope that we might placate that overwhelming nest of Goths that riddled Latium's hills.

"It does not matter," I interjected, now quite taken with Samur's proposal. "We'll be like bees lashing a bear. A thousand stings might not kill the beast, but they will put it into such agony that it cannot muster any offensive assault."

Samur nodded to me in gratitude. "If Witiges is busy protecting his camps, he'll find it difficult to coordinate another attack. We have enough arrows and horses to last a year, perhaps more. Given their food is limited, the Goths will eventually starve and demand retreat to the north."

"It beats sitting on the walls with a stiff arse." Ascum grinned. "Although I'm not one for galloping. Let's take the fight to these bastards for a change."

More grumbles of agreement ensued, although only a small portion of Belisarius' men would be granted the opportunity to slip through Rome's gates and sting Witiges' camps. What struck me was the yearning to hit back—the sight of any Gothic chieftain harassed by our riders would be a tremendous boon to morale for any watching from atop our walls. Having survived the initial battle, centurions held a refreshed conviction of Belisarius' genius, but a lengthy siege with starvation rations would gnaw away at even the most zealous of the strategos' believers. We needed to show the city that Witiges suffered every day that he maintained his siege.

"It shall wait until after the Goths retrieve their bodies and our civilians are safely retired to Neapolis or points farther south," Belisarius commanded. "But after, we shall harry the Goths with those who are capable of firing a bow from horseback. Samur will command the effort."

Samur bobbed his head, bearing the broadest smile I had witnessed in many a year. "You will not be disappointed, Strategos."

"You have my confidence," Belisarius answered. "In the meantime, while we repair the damage from the Gothic attack, we must take measures to secure our food supplies."

Martinus perked up. "Ah, that—some welcome tidings, Lord. Thurimuth and Conon can explain."

Finding both men in Martinus' ranks had been a welcome surprise. After the battle, I discovered that Thurimuth had received my messages requesting reinforcement but was forced to take a circuitous route along the African coastline and through Messana before finally landing in Neapolis. Initially departing from his outpost on Mount Calpe, he collected further volunteers from Conon in Septem, swelling Martinus' ranks with an additional two hundred veteran spearmen.

"Baetica's harvest was fair, while Tingitana's even better, and trade improved markedly after the port cities reopened trade to Gades," Thurimuth explained. "Although I was surprised to see Theudis' banner here. The Visigoth king appears to play both sides of this war."

"Or he's using Roman coin to pay Totila's men, more like," Bessas griped. "Not that there's anything we can do about it. Belisarius cannot wage another war in Mauretania or Hispania with Italy a burning ruin."

I did not wish to downplay Thurimuth's offerings, for even at full rations, his small shipments of grain would stave off hunger from Rome's streets an additional two months. "Your efforts have greatly aided the army as always, Thurimuth. When can we expect the grain to arrive at Rome?"

Thurimuth shrugged, impassive to compliments. "It rests in barrels along Neapolis' ports," he said flatly. "With a few dromons as escort, Ostia would receive it within two days."

"Antium," Ascum corrected. "The Goths seized much of Ostia a few weeks ago. And Valerian should be able to support your transport with war ships. The only advantage we have now is at sea, and we should use it."

Ascum was right, and his assertion was backed by the slowly improving weather as the bite of winter eased and the skies improved. Though the sun had not yet returned to its full vigor, it glowed brighter in the skies with each passing week, a portent that this sickly orb would soon be restored to its more hospitable rays of warmth. With calmer seas, Valerian's dromons could resume their prowl of the Italian coast, levying further nuisance upon Witiges and his chieftains as Roman ballistae struck Goth-held harbors.

"Septem can provide more support come the harvest, Lord," Conon added. "But we'll need transports. You could have another full shipment of grain and olives well before next winter."

I nodded, internally prideful that Conon had prospered after my exit from Tingitana. "Another welcome sign, and allows us to focus upon more immediate food availability."

I did not lie—Conon's assistance simplified my task of securing and sustaining the Eternal City—but that still left us with only half of a year to provide additional grain, cheese, fruit, and meat. Even with refugees escaping Rome, several hundred thousand bellies demanded nourishment each day, draining our ledgers at disheartening rates. With this new infusion from Baetica and Tingitana, we might stretch our rations into midsummer, yet eventually we would all grumble from sagging limbs and groaning stomachs. Belisarius knew this as well as I, and though we began drafting letters to governors of various provinces, we avoided informing the other commanders of just how dire our situation was. After all, this was Witiges' intent in besieging the Roman Army—not to fight continuous and bloody battles atop scaling ladders but to starve its citizens and stoke a revolt.

Aside from planning our sallies and discreetly partitioning rations for soldiers and the broader populace, the siege of Rome soon became a frustrating mixture of too many tasks to execute in a given day and a gnawing boredom as we awaited any change in our situation. The occasional Gothic nuisance was a welcome distraction, affording wall archers or operators of our scorpions a chance to test their range against a live opponent. Besides those sentries, any soldiers not healing from their wounds patrolled the streets or guarded the granaries and watermills, with an occasional rider dispatched to scout the hinterlands for Gothic movements to the north or east. As before the attack, I used those days to rest, to enjoy the company of my household, to inspect and encourage many along the walls, and to garner what peace was possible inside the Witiges' massive open-air dungeon.

Three weeks after the assault's end, a caravan bristling with Cappadocian spearmen arrived from Antium. Messengers rushed ahead to warn of their advance, granting Belisarius enough notice to send a detachment of Huns under Aigan to guard the road from that more distant port. Aside from curious Gothic scouts, Witiges presented no resistance to our arrivals. Rather than ponderous wagons and stubborn oxen, it was horses that hauled Thurimuth and Conon's grain within overlarge saddlebags, the mounts panting with the effort as they crossed through Rome's southern gates. Those riders were all granted free wine in any of Rome's countless popinae that evening, and Belisarius did not begrudge their drunkenness so long as at least one sober guardsman stood watch to discourage fighting.

We filled our losses from the siege, allocating Martinus, Thurimuth, and Conon at different sections of wall. For those less scathed from battle, the infusion of fresh officers brought greater opportunity for rest and relaxed the taxing schedule of watches so that no officer was required to stand for more than one shift. For those more seriously injured, like Bessas and Perenus, the rest alone—and the ability to mend without guilt—was a rare blessing.

On one occasion, my own stint atop the former Praenestine Gate was relieved by Thurimuth, who replaced me as the sun sank in the western skies. Initially, he was as stiff and emotionless as I had always known him, until he asked to speak with me privately. I guided him into a gatehouse tower, sequestering a room that had been previously used to store our dead during the battle. Days later, it still stank of decay.

"What bothers you, Thurimuth?" I asked.

"The Thracians... Mundus..." Thurimuth muttered. "I should have been with them."

This was unexpected—not only the Alemanni's outpouring of grief, but also his soulful regret that he, a former first spear centurion of the Thracian Army, had outlived essentially all of his men. Aside from Perenus, Constantinianus, and myself, I did not personally know more than a half dozen other surviving veterans of that army. Thurimuth was the only other living officer I knew of, having served together since the fight in Tauris.

"I was there, and I didn't stay," I replied. "There's nothing you could have done. Between poison and Indulf's knife, Mundus was dead before any of us could react."

"Still," Thurimuth whispered. "Sometimes, at night, I see their faces. And I wish I had joined them."

Nodding, I placed a hand on his shoulder. "I see them too. But we have a duty to the living. All we can do for Mundus and our brothers is to make their killer burn for his sins. That is an oath I intend to fulfill, one way or another."

"Me as well," Thurimuth grumbled. "We should have never trusted Indulf."

I chuckled. "No, we should not have. But desperation makes fools of all of us. He was useful in Africa, but usefulness does little to mask poor character in the long run."

Soon, the morning of truce with Gothic corpse bearers arrived. At my suggestion, Belisarius ordered a senior officer present at each gate, insisting upon total silence and a sheathing of weapons as the Goths conducted their grisly work. Despite the cold, the corpses had putrefied, and each body left behind a trail of humors as it was dragged to ox-harnessed wagons. There was no cheering, nor celebration, nor taunting—not even from Gunderic or any of his Vandals. The day was long, broken only by an occasional sprinkling of rain that foretold warmer weather to come. By dusk, no Gothic body remained at the base of our walls, and the final carts rumbled away.

Alone, Witiges galloped to the Pincian Gate, arching his arm in a traditional Roman salute toward Belisarius. "Though we are enemies, you have my respect, General Belisarius. Your Emperor does not deserve you."

"...the Romans don't deserve you..."

I started at his words echoing in my mind. It was as if Rosamund, though not present, were whispering into my ear. Belisarius returned Witiges' acknowledgment, allowing the Gothic king to depart in peace. Our truce concluded as the final rays of light flooded away into darkness, returning Rome into the grip of evening chill.

"Tell Samur his time has come," Belisarius muttered to me, observing the Goths milling about their camps, hundreds of cookfires forming along the horizon.

"Tonight?" I asked.

"The day after tomorrow," Belisarius corrected. "We will see

Roman refugees depart safely toward the Via Appia, and then we take the war to the Goths."

Just as the Goths recovered their fallen brethren with no incident, so, too, did the citizens of Rome depart peacefully. I had planned for four clusters of five hundred civilians to make the stone-paved journey to Neapolis, yet after hours of a continuous southward stream, Fulcaris estimated at least five thousand had accepted their opportunity to escape. A casual glance suggested that this procession was mostly women and their younger children, although by afternoon a scattering of younger men joined the gathering. Belisarius forbade horses to any but the riders escorting the refugees; a fair quantity of donkeys bore the feeblest Romans on their backs. By dusk, any stragglers had disappeared beyond the southern hills, while no Goths galloped to contest the few hundred warriors safeguarding Roman refugees. Night fell without incident, although the Huns bristled along the Caelian Hill as they prepared for their predawn ride.

Samur insisted upon no firm strategy, opting instead to adapt to any opportunities that the Gothic camps yielded. Each Hun carried three full quivers as well as three days' rations if swift return became impossible. Further, Samur only took some two hundred black-furred riders under Sinnion, leaving Aigan and the remaining Huns to maintain their position on the walls and mute Gothic suspicions of hidden activity. At the Asinarian Gate, I personally outfitted Samur with his weapons and shield, sensing the restlessness of the Huns under his command.

"Only a Hun can lead Huns." I chuckled, earning a grin from my brother. "In the darkness, you're almost frightening."

Samur laughed. "As I told you, the Huns follow strength. They respect Sunicas' decision to mentor me." Leaning from the saddle, he murmured, "I wish he were here now."

"You do him honor," I said. "The whole army is with you. Make wise decisions, avoid entanglements, and return to safety as soon as the situation deteriorates."

Samur nodded. "If I fall into trouble, don't come after me. My best bet at safety is to flee, and I can't do that if you or Belisarius send spearmen to dislodge my men."

He lowered his arm, grasping mine as I instinctively checked his saddle and harness. After releasing me, he turned his mount toward his followers and raised a fist for quiet.

"You all know what to do," he rasped in Hunnic. "Bleed the bastards, but don't let them catch you. Anyone too slow will be left behind. Is that understood?"

Two hundred fists responded. Samur lowered his fist to his chest, pounding upon the lighter yet more flexible leather that the Huns preferred over heavy Roman iron. "Keep formation. If you find yourself alone, you are dead. The war gods will look upon us with glee if we are successful."

At that, he turned, guiding his horse to the gate's edge. "Ready, Varus."

"Open!" I hissed, commanding the operator of the Asinarian Gate to allow Samur to pass.

The Hun foederati thundered through the slim opening, riding two abreast. I watched as Samur's plume danced about, eventually disappearing amidst the two hundred others behind him as they turned east toward the nearest Gothic camps. Eyeing Samur's progress, I followed the Caelian Hill east, arriving at the Vivarium and ascending the southeastern tip of Rome's walls.

Though still dark, I was able to follow Hunnic movements as they passed before the Vivarium. Yet Samur did not falter as he closed upon the southernmost Gothic camp, nor did he pause as Gothic sentries blew horns and waved torches in alarm at the incoming enemy. Instead, after firing two successive volleys of arrows, Samur's men split into two neat columns and flooded about the camp, galloping eastward and free from enemy reach.

"What is he doing?" I grumbled to myself.

Herulian sentries offered confused glances, yet I ignored all as I peered eastward for any sign of Samur's condition. All I saw was a chaotic stream of Goths, sprinting and riding from one camp to another, forming columns of spearmen and rushing east in Samur's direction. This lasted for over an hour when, my eyes strained and the eastern sun peering above the horizon, the Gothic horns blared in warning. Then—little more than a speck at first—Huns appeared in the distance, a pillar of dust churning in their wake.

"Track them!" I yelled.

The twin column of Huns came into view as they galloped back toward Rome, tossing aside more intrepid Goths as they launched arrows from the saddle. Soon, I even discerned Samur's plume at the head of one column, saw him plucking his bowstring and sending arrows hurtling into the chests and guts of many. Within five hundred paces of the Roman walls, some Goths formed shield rings, shuffling about in an attempt to constrain Hunnic movements. They failed miserably.

Samur abruptly turned north, skirting the Gothic lines and rushing toward the bulk of Witiges' forces. As he neared another camp, Samur again split the columns, launching arrows into the camp. That particular Gothic camp suffered few casualties, as it was comprised of Totila's and Indulf's men, yet although they were better able to prepare for attack, they weren't able to slow Samur's progress.

"Samur's heading north!" I yelled.

I likely seemed foolish, for there was nothing the wall-bound Romans could do to aid the Huns. Still, I sprinted northward as I trailed Hunnic progress. About me, men cheered the Huns in a half dozen different languages, baying for more blood as one Goth after another was struck with a black-feathered arrow. Breathless, I eventually reached the Tiburtine Gate, watching as Samur circled yet another Gothic camp. Here, the Vandals hooted with laughter, jeering the Goths that had no recourse but to run or cower behind crude shields. We watched as a half dozen Gothic riders attempted to charge the Huns at full gallop, only to be quilled with two or three arrow strikes each.

"Your brother has giant stones!" Gunderic laughed, slapping my shoulder. "Boulders!"

It was here that Samur's strategy shifted. Rather than round Rome's northeastern corner, Samur pushed his mount into the Gothic camp, trading his bow for a blade as he ducked between a gap in its crude palisade wall. There was no gate, for I doubt the Goths ever considered they would be at risk of being swarmed, and this allowed a hundred Huns to flood into the encampment.

"Idiot!" I muttered. "Get free of there!"

Gunderic snorted. "Give your brother more faith than that. He knows what he is doing."

All I wanted was for Samur to return to the safety of the walls. Though only a few hours had elapsed, each minute he continued the raid amplified his risk, either in that he would lame his mount or be struck by a rogue Gothic spear. Dust blew from the Gothic camp as men roared and horns blared. Within moments, black smoke mixed with dust, and flames engulfed one section of the palisade.

"Burn, you milk-drinking cocks!" Wisimar grinned. "Burn it down, Samur!"

Gripping the edge of the wall, I neither moved nor paid heed to any around me as my eyes fixed upon the camp. Gothic spearmen burst outward, forming a shield wall against a nearby entrance, but as to the camp's interior, I could see little. Only when a flaming section of palisade collapsed did the extent of Samur's raid become clear, with burning huts and stores of Gothic grain torched. Some dared to haul buckets of water to douse the fires, yet several were struck by arrows that flew from one hidden corner or another. Any attempt to surround the camp was beaten back by the second Hunnic column under Sinnion, which launched arrows at any Goth not sufficiently protected by a shield wall. A few Goths answered with thrown spears, which, predictable and easily dodged, harmed none of Sinnion's Huns.

At last, a Hunnic horn blared. From behind the section of destroyed palisade emerged Samur, guiding his horse through narrow openings, followed by a hurried trail of Hun riders closely behind. With his sword sheathed and bow tucked away, Samur instead wielded a flag adorned with a sun-crowned cross as he galloped free of the camp to rejoin Sinnion.

Gunderic hooted with approval. "He stole the camp's banner!"

Samur did not press his good fortune further, gathering his men together and galloping southward. Rather than trail his progress atop the walls, I now descended a nearby staircase and commandeered one of the gate's spare mounts myself, and set off at a gallop southward toward the Via Asinaria. Once there, I remained below, listening as the nearby sentries readied to open their gate.

"They've returned!" a centurion yelled, ordering the gate opened. "Archers, keep the Goths out!"

I did not witness the Gothic attack, although I learned what happened soon thereafter. After Samur departed the Goth camp, a disciplined detachment of some fifty Goths had trailed the Huns' progress, able to keep pace now that the Huns' mounts had tired. The Hun rearguard kept the Goths thirty paces distant with an occasional shower of arrows, yet many continued, readying their weapons as they closed the distance toward our men. It is likely that, had Samur continued but a few minutes more, his foederati would have been enveloped by this smaller detachment, but as it was, our wall archers forced the Gothic riders to peel away for safety.

Samur was the first through the Asinarian Gate. He coughed, and I could see his mouth was caked in dried spittle, while a coat of blood and ash laced his furs and armor. Other Huns filed in, some of whom were bucked by their exhausted ponies and sent tumbling to the ground. One horse simply died, shuddering as its heart burst the moment it crossed into safety.

The Huns all scrambled along the ground, exhausted and retching. Some dribbled wine into parched throats, while others simply lay along the filthy street gutters as they sucked air. Samur propped himself against a nearby building, sucking on a wineskin between gasps. I knelt down beside him, impossibly happy, resisting an urge to wrap my younger brother in an embrace.

"You crazy arse!" I grinned. "That was incredible!"

"Aye, it worked," he rasped, tossing the Gothic banner to my feet. "We ventured to the east, disrupting Goth forage, and wrecked a camp. There was nothing they could do to stop us, as long as we kept moving."

By God, but when Samur returned, a glimmer of hope ignited in my chest. Not that we could defeat Witiges outright—contesting Witiges' numbers was lunacy. Instead, even if the casualties we inflicted were few, Samur's sally had demonstrated how hapless the Goths were against Roman horse archers. We had left the Goths miserable, so that all they could muster was a defensive siege. Eventually, they might even decamp and retire to their northern provinces.

Samur made that vision possible. Despite everything, I realized, we Romans might yet prevail.

THE VICAR OF CHRIST

W ithin the span of a morning, the Huns had captured the hearts of Rome. And for the briefest moment, it was Samur that so many thousands toasted.

As Witiges' banner was paraded through the forum, Belisarius ordered every warrior capable of handling a bow on horseback readied for sallies. Most remained within their traditional hierarchies and led by their standing centurions—Herulians, Huns, and cataphracts—although a handful of others were sprinkled into the ranks to fill gaps. Following Samur's example, Belisarius instructed that each raiding party should have no more than two hundred riders, allowing each detachment to nimbly avoid traps or barriers, yet still possess the strength to send the Goths cowering behind their shields.

"I'd also keep mounted spearmen in reserve, especially if the sally ranges farther beyond the walls," Samur recommended. "The Huns are conditioned to ride under terrible conditions, yet even their ponies will exhaust themselves after a continuous gallop. A protective guard closer to the walls will prevent the Goths from trapping us, particularly as the raid concludes."

Belisarius amply met that need. Vandals were the ideal choice for this task, for they were able horsemen and already begging for another opportunity to cross blades with the Goths. Yet their numbers were too few to act alone, prompting Belisarius to appoint Tarmutus' men to a similar task.

Tarmutus appeared overwhelmed from the start. "We're more than willing to assist, Lord, but we lack the experience of your professional soldiers."

"You are more capable than you admit, Tarmutus." Belisarius smiled. "And I intend to keep your guardsmen as a reserve. They will be used, but sparingly. Make sure your men are capable of riding short distances in full gear."

Tarmutus saluted, brightening from the compliment even though his face was still lined with worry. Nevertheless, Belisarius and Samur continued to plan the general routes of attack for future sallies, with Samur insisting that impromptu changes in course would be inevitable. Likewise, our attacks could neither occur at predictable times of day nor from our southern gates alone; thus we would prevent the Goths from concentrating their defenses.

Poor weather delayed any action for two weeks after Samur's victory, however. It began as a spring frost, then, as warmer weather prevailed, a spattering of rain that consumed broader Latium. Day and night, the gradual percussion of droplets turned Rome's streets into moving troughs of sludge, while the grasses surrounding the city transformed into a perilous morass that stymied even our burliest horses. Instead, we used this time to continue to heal, to mend armor and fletch arrows, and to enjoy the company of one another in the cozy warmth of the Domus or one of the many popinae.

For that brief interlude, I pitied the Goths, who huddled in tents against the downpour, their cookfires quickly doused and their defensive camps threatening to flood entirely. Still, absent our harassment, the Goths had repaired the damage Samur had wrought upon their camp. Seeing a fresh Gothic banner flying from its rampart, Samur's Huns waved the torn flag they had looted, yet neither party sought to advance the taunting to single combat, let alone an outright raid.

Despite the donations of Thurimuth and Conon, there was precious little food to spare. I carved a portion of my meals and snuck it into the mouths of my children, including the fast-growing and knobby-kneed Tiberius. Mariya privately cautioned against such generosity, worrying that my own strength might wane, but I tossed such concerns aside.

"We won't starve," I promised, uncertain of how to keep it. "Grain shipments will arrive in summer, and this will all be an unpleasant memory."

Mariya glared at me. "How can you be certain?"

"Constantinople will send aid," I insisted. "And Egypt will have plenty. They used to supply most of Rome's food, long ago."

"You're guessing," Mariya replied bitterly. "I've witnessed those who survive a siege. Walking skeletons."

I snatched her hand, wanting to convey as much confidence as I could. "It won't come to that, Mariya. I swear to God it will not."

But she was correct, of course. There was no way to know when, or indeed if, external relief would arrive. Worse, the palaces and other grand buildings would be tempting targets for hungry bandits. The once-abundant markets lay bare, stalls hauntingly empty, their skeletal frames a testament to the prosperity that had once thrived here. The scent of fresh bread and ripening fruit, once an aromatic siren's call wafting through the air, was now replaced with the stinging smell of wood smoke and the bitter tang of desperation.

Images of what might become of my household haunted my thoughts, first as nagging irritations, and later stirring anxieties, as the weeks of siege continued. In my dreams, the echo of the children's hollow laughter amidst the Domus' marble walls spoke of deprivation and lifelessness. Each sparse meal became a vigil, the table a battleground where insignificant scraps were hoarded greedily. In the worst of those dreams, ravenous servants would dispatch Mariya and the children in their sleep, stealing what little food remained for themselves in an orgy of self-aggrandizement. Though I attempted to forestall such thoughts with prayer, believing in the honor of those who lived alongside me, an ever-present twinge of doubt left me in constant concern of where the limits of honor lay. When would hunger conquer us all?

With additional free time stuck inside the city walls, I spent each night with Mariya, sharing cups of wine while we observed the children at play. Both Petrus and Perenus were frequent guests, though the latter abstained from drinking in the presence of his son. Occasionally, even Liberius favored us with an appearance, distributing slivers of pilfered cheese to each of Mariya's wards. Though my days were filled with soaking physical toil and the nagging worry of a possible Gothic attack, those evenings offered a rare sense of fulfillment, making me wonder whether life absent war might be so blissful.

But that dream evaporated with the rains. A week after the skies parted, we tasked our scouts with evaluating the soil's firmness, testing whether it could support the weight of hundreds of men and horses flying over the hills at once. By a month after Witiges' assault, Belisarius affirmed his desire that Samur's sallies should recommence.

The rules of those attacks were simple. Only two detachments could ride out at a time, with a third allotment of mounted spearmen trailing within the shadow of Rome's walls to prevent any Goths from encircling the horse archers. Similarly, the horse archers were strictly forbidden from engaging in melee combat, nor could they trade volleys with the remnant Suevi bowmen that lingered across several of the Gothic camps. No plunder was to be taken, nor captives hauled back to the city, for such weight would jeopardize the speed and the sting of these swift attacks. Lastly, and most difficult, any laggards or wounded who fell from their horse would be left behind. As Samur made plain, to halt the column was to commit all to death, for even the slow-footed Gothic spearmen could surround and butcher a raiding party within heartbeats.

While Samur's Huns were outfitted for the first assault after the rains, I was chosen to lead the second detachment of horse bowmen. Samur opted for the more difficult assignment: Rushing from the Flaminian Gate, his Huns would hug the banks of the Tiber, riding in broad circles around a nearby Gothic camp before returning to safety in the same gate. With Fulcaris and two hundred Herulian foederati at my back, I would retrace Samur's steps through the southeastern Asinarian Gate, seeking the southernmost Gothic camp as my prey. It was deliberately simple, allowing for a detachment of Vandals to guard my escape and several hundred Cappadocians to safeguard Samur's passage along the Via Flaminia. Belisarius assumed that, as the Gothic chieftains would be better prepared for future raids, we could not act as recklessly as Samur had in his initial attack, favoring brief excursions toward singular targets.

That did not alleviate the fluttering I felt in my gut. Samur assuaged my fears by insisting that our horses were fleeter than those of any Gothic rider, but still, I understood each attack to be a gamble, predicated on the hope that our enemy would not stage an effective ambush. By then, Rome's walls had become a protective shell, and the thought of departing them left me feeling naked. Likewise, I would travel without Uliaris or any of the Aksumites, who had no skill with the mounted bow. At this, Sembrouthes grumbled, but he soon surrendered to the need for uniformity in our sally.

"Don't take stupid risks when I'm not there to stop you," he told me.

Our appointed hour was the sun's zenith, and Fulcaris' Herulians were readied well in advance. Behind us were hundreds of mounted Vandals who, God willing, would have little to do that day. I awaited the signal of the gate centurion, shifting uneasily atop Boreas' saddle, clutching my cross as I muttered prayers for a safe return.

"It is time, Lord!" the centurion eventually called down to me.

I turned back to my followers to raise a fist as Samur had. My throat was dry, yet I summoned the Heruli words as my final instructions. "Stay close, and don't stop moving. Your life is worth more than theirs, so don't risk it foolishly for an extra bowshot. Follow me, and you will live to see the evening."

Two hundred fists shot toward the heavens in response. They were ready, for this action was something that many of them had performed countless times before. I turned back toward the gate, saluted the centurion, and awaited the clanking iron chains that drew the doors open.

"Forward!" I yelled. "Follow me!"

With a crack of the reins, I sent Boreas lurching toward the opening gate. I thundered outside of Rome's shell for the first time in nearly two months, soft earth and budding grasses replacing the familiar odors of filth and unwashed bodies. At first, the freshness stung my throat, but the cooling breeze that flitted through openings in my armor soon sharpened my senses, even offering a surge of joy as I guided Boreas in a southeasterly arc.

Though a week had dried the soil of much of the recent rains, small pools remained that were both difficult to spot and made for treacherous riding. Mindful of these hazards, I slowed our pace to a spirited trot, granting time for the final section of Herulians to clear the Asinarian Gate and for the first of the Vandals to surge forth. The Vandals would not follow our procession for long, remaining within a few hundred paces of the gate at all times, yet close enough to assist should Fulcaris or I be confronted by a mounted Gothic attack. Even then, the best defense that my Herulians held was to gallop onward and pray that no hidden stone or treacherous sinkhole would lame a horse or dismount its rider.

As Belisarius and Samur predicted, the Goths had prepared for mounted Roman raids. The nearest Gothic camp blared its horn before I had made it two hundred paces out from the walls, followed by another, more distant horn signaling that Samur's attack had likewise been detected. Rather than rush onward, I ordered the foederati to form in a loose circle, and checked the readiness of each man as we executed a continuous leftward turn for two circuits. Satisfied, I tore away from the circle, guiding the Herulians on a gradual arc toward the Gothic camp.

Raising an arm, I waved my open palm in the air, signaling to Fulcaris. "Split!"

Fulcaris responded with a flick of his hand, leading a hundred Herulians away from my followers. A gulf of some thirty paces formed between us as we rumbled toward the Gothic camp, closing within several hundred paces of its outer walls. From there, I spotted several Goths standing atop makeshift battlements, while a stout mass of Gothic spearmen three lines deep emerged from the camp's entrance. No archers gathered to oppose us, nor did the Goths yield any threatening gestures that placed our mounted procession in serious danger. As we drew within fifty paces, three or four Goths hurled spears, which, being both ponderous and easy to dodge, ultimately landed harmlessly into the soft earth.

"Loose at will!" I yelled.

Snatching my bow from the saddle, I readied an arrow, then released it at a gaudily plumed Gothic chieftain. Though he deftly blocked the arrow with his shield, he howled and fell backward: the arrowhead had penetrated his bulwark and tore into the underlying forearm. Other Herulians followed my example, and although most of their arrows were deflected by the Gothic carapace, at least three struck the bodies of unluckier enemies.

Fulcaris and I split farther apart, filtering past the Gothic camp with fifty paces of open space separating us from the nearest camp defender. Our row formed four abreast, with a horse length separating each rider. A spear clattered in the turn before me, a feeble attempt by a tower-mounted Goth as we passed along the fort's palisades, focusing my attentions on the raid at hand.

"Loose!" I called again.

At such a pace, there was little time to select targets. Instead, I steadied my arrow and drew back the bowstring, the movement etched in my memory from thousands of repetitions. Then, pushing my boots against the Boreas' stirrups, I stood in the saddle and turned for a heartbeat toward the Gothic fort, releasing my bowstring. By the time I heard evidence that I had struck true—a man wailing in Gothic—I was once again facing forward.

Others behind me followed in their arrow fire, triggering a steady rain of four to eight arrows at a time. As we crested beyond the eastern edge of the fort, however, a Herulian behind me yelled a warning of incoming riders. Glancing northward, I found some hundred Goths galloping from a thousand paces distant, riding diagonally to intercept our progress.

And to their deaths. Whoever commanded such men was either inexperienced or a fool, for no knowledgeable man would charge headlong against an enemy of foreign tactics and superior numbers. I signaled our column to move northward, sounding my horn so that Fulcaris' followers might follow, and tore away from the Gothic fort.

"Go!" I urged Boreas, lashing with the reins. "Faster!"

The distance between us and the Gothic riders shrank as both groups galloped recklessly toward one another. I slowed my column's pace just enough so that Fulcaris could catch up, with the Heruli officer signaling requests for my intended maneuver.

"Circle!" I screamed. "Circle!"

Whether from my shouting or my hand signals, Fulcaris deciphered my meaning. We continued our gallop, closing to five hundred paces, then four, and then three. By two hundred fifty paces, I could see the mail on the enemy's bodies, lances aloft as they awaited an opportunity to tangle with our men. It was not an opportunity I would allow to pass.

"Left!" I yelled back, my words carried behind by further officers.

With only one hundred paces separating our riders from the enemy, Fulcaris and I peeled away, flowing about the Gothic riders like water around a stone. Their charge faltered, with some forming smaller wedges to strike at our riders, yet they were absent strength or momentum. Most Goths had not experienced horse archery since the days of Attila; few alive in the Ostrogoth army trained for such encounters. As Samur noted, it was all too easy.

"Loose!" I demanded. "Loose and ride!"

Each Gothic horseman bore a shield but lacked the ability to shelter together in the safety of a shield ring. As I directed my column's progress to turn and complete our half circle, each of my riders shot an arrow every ten heartbeats, and although by Hunnic standards it was piteously slow, the Goths wavered against our hail of iron, neither able to attack nor defend as they clumped together in the center of our ride. My arrows found several targets, either by striking an enemy mount in the chest or digging into bellies of one horseman or another. By the time I overlapped Fulcaris and turned for a second circuit of our attack, half of the Goths had fallen from their mounts, arrows protruding from man and beast alike.

We continued a full second circle as the Gothic riders were ground to nothingness. Then, with only a handful still quivering in the center of the formation, I trotted forward, picking my targets with yet greater ease. The ground was slick with blood, while the wails of dozens of dying filled the skies. I discovered that most Goths had not died from our attack, but instead bled out into the grasses of Latium, moaning and crying, with those who retained their wits shaking in fear.

Fulcaris slew the final Goth, a stout lad who looked only a few years into manhood, driving an arrow into his throat and sending him tumbling into the grass.

"Idiots," he grumbled. "It's like they wanted to die!"

I nodded. "Better them than us. We're finished for today. Loop about the fort and ride back for the Asinarian Gate.

No Goths followed us back to the gate. If I commanded that fort, I would have done nothing different. Even with a week's preparation, they still lacked any strategy to counter our archers, and had even sacrificed a hundred of their better armored soldiers for their ignorance. Gunderic, however, was visibly irritated as we returned without any Goths stalking our retreat.

"You won't leave any alive for me," Gunderic grumbled, watching from the walls as the Huns launched arrows into the undisciplined Gothic cavalry.

"For every bastard Samur kills, there will be a hundred others," I replied.

"There better," Gunderic complained. "Otherwise, why did I come to this city? It smells like sheep shit, and the people are miserable all the time."

Samur's attack was equally unchallenged, although his Huns did not have the chance to annihilate an entire century of Gothic cavalry.

"If they hide behind their palisade walls, there's little that we can do without significant danger," Samur reasoned. "But then again, if they're hiding, they aren't attacking our walls."

All Belisarius got from this additional day of raiding was jubilation. "A hundred men, and no casualties of our own—"

"A feat we're unlikely to repeat," I interrupted, embarrassed at the unbridled praise. "We weren't able to come close to the fort, and maybe inflicted five or six arrows that caused serious wounds."

Belisarius was unaffected by my pessimism. "But we took no losses! I agree with Samur: if the Goths cannot counter our horse archers, let them skulk in their defenses, hungry and demoralized."

We did not launch a third raid the next day, nor the day after that. Upon the third day, Perenus commanded his own detachment of Herulian horse archers along Rome's eastern gates, inflicting his own casualties, yet he was less enthusiastic about the results than Belisarius was.

"The Goths are digging trenches in random lines about their camps," he warned. "They're easy enough to spot now, while they're fresh, but they'll be terrors within the next month for anyone unlucky enough to ride over one."

"We've fought through trenches before," I reasoned. "All it means is that we must plan our sallies more carefully."

"There are caltrops, too," Perenus said. "Iron spikes. Most are near the trenches, but some are scattered about. One of my men had their mount lamed, but they were able to return to safety. But the Suevi are present, at least along the eastern camps, meaning that we will not be able to attack without risk of a Gothic counter."

Perenus' premonition soon bore insidious fruit. A week later, Bessas led a detachment of cataphracts to assault the camp that housed Witiges and his household, inflicting four fatalities amongst the Gothic king's most veteran forces. However, Bessas suffered two casualties of his own. One rider weaved a few paces away from Bessas' column, colliding directly with a fresh trench. His mount fell headfirst, snapping a leg, and slammed the rider into the turf nearby, snapping his spine. A second cataphract was stymied by caltrops just fifty paces from Witiges' fort, laming his mount and sending him vaulting through the air. Though he did not die on impact, a swarm of Goths soon sprinted from the fort's entrance and gored the dismounted cataphract in a frenzy of spear thrusts. There was nothing Bessas could do except ride on—to pause the sally was to condemn all of his followers to death.

Belisarius did not halt the raids, for despite the rising threat of casualty, they still inflicted a desirous effect upon the Goths. A week after Bessas' sally, Belisarius himself led an assault against the only Gothic camp west of the Tiber, sweeping across the Janiculum Hill with his own detachment of armored cataphracts. Their progress was slow, their rear guarded by five hundred Roman city watch under Tarmutus, yet the attack benefitted from the remoteness that the fort had relative to the other six to the Tiber's east.

Belisarius' attack began identically to the previous four, with the cataphracts splitting into competing columns and driving the Goths into the safety of their palisade walls. What differed, however, was that half of Belisarius' two hundred riders wielded flaming torches, circling the fort while teams of cataphract archers sent arrows sailing over the Gothic battlements.

The camp was not entirely committed to flames, for recent rains had left sections of the palisade damp and more likely to hiss with steam than burn. Nevertheless, as Belisarius' galloping circle tossed their firebrands over the walls, several huts began to smoke, while one of the camp's wooden towers blazed along its battlement. Archers targeted any Goth who dared to haul buckets of water to douse the flames. Eventually, a thousand Gothic spearmen emerged from the singed gate, their progress slowed by their lock-tight shield wall. They succeeded in pushing Belisarius east toward safety and ending the attack, but at the cost of spending the next several days repairing extensive damage to their buildings—one of which appeared to be a food depot.

Nevertheless, our attacks slowed in frequency, and never occurred more than twice in a single week. By the spring equinox, each of the seven Gothic camps had been battered by our attacks, with Samur the most frequent group leader. With the Herulians, I championed an additional three sallies, including a repeat of Belisarius' burning of the Janiculum camp. I lost one Herulian rider in that attempt and deflected a flying Gothic spear with my shield, yet otherwise enjoyed moderate success in making the Goths miserable.

As the sun's rays stretched longer through the day, the Italian summer brought delicious warmth. That celestial orb still seemed bereft of its greatest strength, though against the hardened ground and frosts that deadened Italy's orchards in the winter months, I could not complain. Daylight softened the soil, beckoning life back first for the hardier plants, and soon thereafter great flocks of birds. The simple, rapturous luxury of walking about the city streets without heavy furs and a knotted cloak felt far too good to be true—in those initial days, I felt naked with only light woolen trousers and a shirt as I engaged in morning training. The Eternal City felt brighter, soaking in longer and longer days of summer light that warmed morale and flesh alike. It was an omen that, after so much suffering, a reprieve from God's wrath might be on the horizon.

Equally, however, the more hospitable climate eased the conditions for combat, and by early summer Witiges attempted a second assault upon the Roman walls. It lacked the ferocity of the initial attack, focused primarily upon the Pincian and Flaminian Gates, and was rebuffed after an arduous day of fighting. Belisarius suffered a hundred dead or wounded in that attack, and Witiges perhaps twice those losses, with neither party pressing their advantage in the following days. Instead, Witiges was content to allow Rome to starve as his own grain shipments were hauled in from his still-loyal northern provinces, the bounty of which he displayed with a massive feast within eyeshot of each of Rome's eastern gates.

"Cowardly bastards," Gunderic snarled.

"Just make sure that your men behave around the city's citizens,"

I reminded him. "Hunger makes men irritable and reckless."

Indeed, despite the occasional fatalities that Belisarius' raids accrued, the greatest danger we faced entering the summer months was the long-delayed threat of hunger. As Belisarius' second, it fell to me to stretch the Mauretanian grain as long as possible, and I allowed all soldiers and remaining city residents only half rations. Some of my soldiers set traps along the Tiber to supplement their dinners, and while those occasionally yielded a bounty of fish, Witiges' men soon floated logs and other debris down the river to tear nets and break traps. Likewise, we dispatched guards to protect Belisarius' watermills day and night, leaving little space for fishermen to safely conduct their craft along the river.

By summer, our grain stores had dwindled to an alarming low level. Rations were cut again, affording only a one-third portion of a typical meal. To avoid agitation, Belisarius ordered an increase in allowances of wine, which never seemed to suffer shortages, even during the worst weeks of near starvation, but even that act of generosity had a waning effect. Reports of theft increased, and Belisarius and I were forced to discipline those soldiers caught stealing from an occupied Roman household. We hung two city watchmen along the forum for the crime of pilfering a small hoard of cheese from a local merchant's family. The merchant, discovering the thieves in the midst of the act, attempted to protect his hoard, only to be stabbed in the gut and tossed into the gutter. He survived, thanks in part to Rosamund's and Agathias' intervention, and demanded retribution from Belisarius.

Meanwhile, Samur amplified our grain stores by intercepting a grain wagon intended for Witiges and hauling heavy sacks back to Rome. Yet otherwise, no trade arrived from Sicily or Neapolis, for those cities reported their own dire shortages of food. In Panormus, it was said that men had descended to boiling grass and acorns, contributing to widespread flux. Through it all, the dimmed sun and near perpetual night mocked us, stunting what pathetic crops had managed to sprout amidst frost, storms, and decay.

Nor did relief arrive by sea. Tingitana did not intend to transport a second grain shipment until harvest time, while a message from Alexandria announced a poor harvest due to the veiled sun as well as the spreading plague across the Nile. Rat meat became a delicacy amongst Rome's traders, while the once-plentiful packs of stray dogs soon disappeared from the city's alleys. Shimon, who had assumed Cephalas' duties, was instructed to securely guard Haeva at all times, although the poor animal grew as thin as the rest of us. Thankfully, our mounts were able to gnaw at grasses along the Campus Martius, although Belisarius worried that a lack of ample forage would sap the strength of even the hardiest Niseans.

Aside from fish, vermin, and our shrinking portions of bread, some turned to scavenging the eels that pooled at various points in Rome's waterways. Most professed to haul their wriggling catches from the banks of the Tiber, yet I discovered many had instead ventured into the river-flooded city underground, where tunnels drained all manner of filth and waste from the city's administrative buildings and wealthier houses. Even after a thorough roasting, eel never lost its slimy, gelatinous texture, and it clung to my teeth and throat no matter how many cups of wine I swallowed. As the Roman summer drew to its hottest months, I admit to gorging upon eel flesh more times than I would like to admit, even convincing Mariya to join me as we reserved a portion of our grain for the children.

"Eel is a fine treat!" Ascum said, licking his lips as he rotated a freshly slain creature over an open fire along Hadrian's Mausoleum. "You just don't know how to dress it. In Alania, the right mixture of spice will make you crave eel every week."

I suppressed a gag. "When this is over, I'm never touching one of these slimy bastards ever again."

"Disappointing!" Ascum laughed. "Eel hide makes a fine belt, too. Watertight, supple, and hides stains well."

He patted at his sunken waistline for emphasis, a glove brushing against the dried scales of a former meal. As the siege dragged on, even the most delicate of tongues acquiesced to those less palatable meals of Rome's underbelly; some more sinister rumors suggested that the flesh of the recently dead had been consigned to roasting and consumption. I never witnessed these horrors myself, although Perenus hauled two younger Roman men to the forum's gallows, screaming obscenities with each step.

"A child!" Perenus yelled, smacking one of the men with the naked flat of his sword.

"He was already dead, Lord!" the man replied. "He complained of his stomach, caught fever, and was dead by morning. We gave him prayers!"

Perenus signaled for city guardsmen to attend him, while I observed from a distance. Nooses were wrapped about their necks, and the men were raised atop benches as the opposite end of their rope was knotted from an overhanging post. Piss dribbled down one of the man's trousers, while the other pled his case to Perenus.

But Perenus was unwilling to listen. "You have broken a law sacred to all peoples and all cultures. Consuming the flesh of another person, especially that of a child, deserves torment. What are your final words?"

A fresh stream trickled down the blubbering man's trousers, while the other screamed for mercy. "We're starving, Lord! The boy's sacrifice would keep us alive! You must understand!!"

Snarling, Perenus kicked the chair from underneath the pleading man, sending his legs dangling a few feet from the ground. Perenus turned to the second, pausing only for a heartbeat.

"No! No, please!"

With a closed fist, Perenus smashed his nose, and blood spouted from his now-crooked nostrils. Again, Perenus kicked away the chair, and the man gagged and vomited as he twitched at the end of his flaxen rope. Neither man died quickly; it took several minutes for them to rattle out their final moments in this life, froth coming from their mouths and tongues protruding from constricted throats. Perenus ordered both men cut down and burned in the forum, then turned to me.

"I need Petrus to care for the butchered remains of a child," Perenus said. "Would he be willing?"

I nodded. "He will say the necessary prayers. Let me in what you must do."

Petrus responded to Perenus' request within the hour. I did not accompany them—though I had not caught the culprits amidst their crime, I knew what their labors had wrought, and I had no desire to add images of an eviscerated child to an already overwhelming host of nightmares in my head. Petrus was especially pale that evening, refusing aid or even to speak of his ordeal. When he refused his evening meal, I ordered a servant to deliver the bread and eel gruel to his quarters, as well as my own well-wishes for the old priest. By morning, Petrus had returned to his duties, leading prayer for myself and many of my household, yet his demeanor bore hints that he had witnessed something abhorrent.

On an optimistic note, by midsummer, word arrived from Carthage that Germanus had scored a victory against Stotzas, Sergius, and a growing confederation of Marui tribesmen. Where Solomon had sacrificed Carthage's finances in order to build defensive outposts and proffer tribute to Constantinople, Germanus worked with Troglita to offer back-pay to any Roman who remained loyal throughout Stotzas' rebellion, plus an additional half year's bonus. Germanus' Carthaginian army was piteously small—some three thousand men to patrol a vast expanse of rugged territory and unrulier natives—yet all had been equipped with the best iron that Constantinople's forges could produce.

Opposite Germanus, Stotzas attracted an increased following due to the imposition of Imperial taxes upon the ports and cities of broader Africa. With Sergius as his senior commander, Stotzas promised a freedom from taxation along with ample gifts that his raiders had stolen from Roman caravans and trading posts, disappearing into the southern deserts before Germanus' patrols could strike out in revenge. It was affirmed through multiple spies that Stotzas had completed his betrothal to Mastigas' daughter, and that the son born of that union only further inspired the war-renowned Marui chieftain to battle against the Empire. With few accomplishments and a dismal record, Stotzas nevertheless had refused to quit his rebellion, earning the backing of the Altavans under Mastigas, the Frexenses under Antalas, and a half dozen minor tribes.

As before Membresa, Stotzas and his confederates pushed against Carthage, seeking to overwhelm Germanus' remaining loyalists. The thousands of Mauri, rebel Vandals, and disaffected Imperial soldiers under Sergius marched within six miles of the city of Carthage, meeting the forces under Germanus, Troglita, and an emasculated Solomon at a village known today as Scalae Veteres. Germanus' account noted fierce fighting, with battle joined for several hours, before Troglita's banda wedged a gap between the Altavan warriors and those men directly loyal to Stotzas, causing the Mauri to panic.

There were few casualties on either side, although we've taken a few Mauri chieftains prisoner. All of the rebel leaders remain alive and hale but flee westward into Altava. Until they return, we shall fortify our region and spy on Stotzas' progress.

Though a reminder of Sergius' continued defiance must have irritated Belisarius, the strategos showed only a grim frown and spoke favorably of Germanus. "If Germanus pushed the enemy all the way to Altava, Carthage will be safe for another year," he remarked. "But I worry of the destruction this uprising will cause."

"More than in Italy?" I asked.

Belisarius shrugged. "We can end this war with minimal devastation to the lives of the plebeians. But Africa has known constant war for years, with no trade route safe from bandits."

To me, there was an obvious answer, although a perilous one. "We could ask the Emperor to forgo tribute from those provinces for several years. Since we defeated Gelimer, most of the natives have known only taxation and loss, rather than any benefits that the Emperor can provide."

Belisarius sighed but nodded. "I'm not certain that Constantinople can afford to lose the revenue, but perhaps you can write to Theodora.

Though Justinian will scold me, I must petition him for food aid if he will not dispatch the soldiers to help me break Rome from its siege."

It was all too much. Carthage, Rome, constant war, and the recurring threat of starvation. The bottomless hunger of Constantinople for not only food, but of gold to pay the cost of Justinian's ambitions. Somehow, with Belisarius' patience, I ensured that each issue was raised to the attention of our expedition's leadership. Yet, frustratingly, even Liberius had few concrete answers regarding how to improve our predicament.

"The best action you can take is to strike Witiges so serious a blow that he must end the siege," Liberius offered unhelpfully. "Beyond that, we can steal from his food stores, although the risk would be tremendous."

Samur warmed to this opinion. On one particularly far-ranging sally, one of Samur's scouts had noted that the Goths received regular grain shipments along the northern Milvian Bridge. Presumably drawn from the harvest-rich provinces of the ancient Etruscans, the grain wagons crossed the Tiber from west to east, guarded by several hundred Gothic spearmen and close to three of Witiges' camps. Rather than loot the wagons outright, Samur's riders thundered astride the bridge and extracted a dozen casualties from the Goths before galloping southward to safety.

That attack was also Samur's most desperate, for Witiges amassed a counterattack that sent Samur's men scrambling back to Rome and forced the Cappadocian spearmen to retreat as well. The Gothic counter was turned away only by a punishing batter of ballista and scorpions, allowing our men to escape relatively unharmed, but ultimately, the fate that awaited us was clear—to venture more than five hundred paces from the walls would give any Gothic chieftain enough time to encircle most of our forces, as they so nearly had accomplished against Belisarius' swiftest Hunnic cavalry.

Nevertheless, Samur was adamant about the opportunity before us. "The solution to Rome's starvation is in those wagons. If we could seize them before—or even immediately after—they cross the Milvian

Bridge, we could unload their contents and strike for Rome before Witiges could amass the spearmen to respond."

"There's an easier way," Ascum put in. "Prepare ten river craft to meet us along the bridge, and empty the wagons into the ship's holds. That way, our riders would not be compelled to race against the Goths while laden with grain."

Belisarius, however, was unconvinced of the plan. "If the Goths muster any resistance at the bridge, or if Witiges responds faster than we anticipate..."

"Then we should plan well for how we would retreat," Samur interjected. "As Liberius says, this is our only option, unless you want the Romans to riot and evict us from the city."

"That is a risk, I fear," Liberius admitted. "However, the least-helpful choice is to do nothing. We must act now, while we still have the capability to maneuver and the luxury to choose when and how to fight."

Belisarius bobbed his head in gratitude, yet appeared unmoved. "I thank you all for your guidance, but we cannot proceed rashly. I will order Valerian to man and equip more fishing vessels, now that the seas and weather have calmed. Likewise, Varus and I will beseech the Emperor for aid."

Samur clenched his fists, one boot tapping insistently against the stone floor. "And for our attacks? What shall we do?"

"We continue the raids," Belisarius concluded. "But you have my blessing to scout the bridge and determine the timing of Witiges' supply wagons. Understanding when to expect them will considerably reduce our risk, as will the preparation of riverboats as Ascum suggests."

Samur grinned, ceasing his fidgeting. "I'll station scouts along the Tiber's west bank."

"And I'll determine what barges we can use for our theft," Ascum added.

While Samur and Ascum labored, Belisarius and I again scribbled desperate requests for aid to any who would listen. To Theodora,

I described the urgency of our situation, with our current survival thanks only to an incredible fortune in resisting Gothic attacks and well-timed aid from our cities in Tingitana and Baetica. Belisarius was just as direct in his own letter, begging the Emperor's forgiveness, yet noting skepticism that the Roman populace would both survive and allow an Imperial garrison to linger safely in the city walls, should the siege continue for several more months:

> Although at the present time the Romans are well disposed toward us, when their troubles are prolonged, they will probably not hesitate to choose the course which is better for their own interests. Furthermore, the Romans would be compelled by hunger to do many things they would prefer not to do.

Against my counsel, Belisarius neglected to mention instances of cannibalism, arguing that the Emperor would view such instances as more reason to not support a godless populace rather than alleviate their slow starvation. We dispatched our letters for Constantinople, knowing well that an answer would not be received before two months at the earliest, and we set about seeking aid from other Roman holdings along the African coastline.

In the heat of summer, five months since the onset of siege, our troubles expanded further still. Isolated instances of looting by Roman citizens along the Aventine swelled into outright organized assaults upon the city's granaries. At Tarmutus' suggestion, Belisarius tripled the watch at key markets and buildings, rotating guards every three days to prevent predictable bribery and corruption of wealthier citizens preying upon the needs of Tarmutus' younger and poorer city watch.

Occasionally, an angry mob would throw stones at our guardsmen, yet most violence was reserved for softer targets, including the looting of modest homes rumored to have hoarded grain, fruit, or cheese. Such behavior worsened after an occasional burglary revealed truth to such rumors, empowering Rome's gangs and increasing the frequency of nighttime attacks. Belisarius simply did not have the men to patrol every corner and street in that vast city, and the capture and punishment of notable gang leaders did little to stifle the swelling violence. By summer's end, our patrols would discover many Romans hanged or gutted outside of their homes, condemned as hoarders by the mob.

Unfortunately, lawlessness was not even the gravest problem that Belisarius faced. Nor were the Goths, who remained docile in their camps due to the occasional threat posed by our horse archers. Distracted by roving gangs, tens of thousands of stubborn Goths, and food riots, we neglected the possibility that our most urgent foe might not only be soft-spoken and mild-mannered, but also residing amongst the heights of Roman authority.

In my opinion, what transpired in the final weeks of summer placed Belisarius far closer to utter annihilation than Witiges' assault during the frosts of early spring. Yet, rather than with booming horns and the war cries of men across the Aurelian Walls, it emerged with little more than a mumble. And unlike the prior assault, the threat came in the darkest hours of night.

Shimon burst into our bedroom, rattling the door's hinges as it crashed against the wall. Even before my eyes opened, my arm reached for a dagger stationed near the bed, while Mariya bolted upright, gasping.

"Lord, you must come immediately!" Shimon hissed.

My senses were too blurred to understand his urgency. "Shimon, why are you barging upon my wife and I in our sleep?!"

"Lord, the Goths are inside the walls!"

More sobering words have never been spoken. With Shimon and Mariya's aid, I quickly donned my excubitor armor and secured my weapons, ready for combat within minutes. Sembrouthes—by then fully healed—joined me, with Uliaris struggling to follow behind. Shimon had few further details—a detachment of Cappadocians under Xerxes had discovered a Gothic attempt at infiltration in darkness, and Xerxes had requested my aid, but the extent of the assault was unknown to Shimon. Instinctively, however, I knew that Xerxes would not raise an alarm out of panic—this threat was real and present.

Shimon guided me to the Pincian Gate, where we were hailed by a Cappadocian centurion. At the centurion's request, we dismounted, leaning close as he whispered.

"We must be as silent as a ghost, Lord," the centurion said.

"Why?" I hissed. "Where is the enemy?"

"In the aqueduct," the centurion replied. "Skulking like rats."

At that moment, I wanted to scream and laugh. The Goths had mimicked our own capture of Neapolis. I stilled my scabbard and stepped carefully forward, knowing that any clattering, rumbling, or sneezing would alert the Goths of our immediate presence. The centurion guided me to Xerxes, who stood just ten paces from a section of enclosed aqueduct.

"Where does it lead?" I whispered.

"The Aqua Virgo leads to the Campus Martius and was blocked at the beginning of the siege," Xerxes mumbled in Persian. "It leads to the Baths of Agrippa."

I frowned. "Do we have guards there?"

He nodded. "Plenty, but some are worried of causing offense."

"Offense?" I murmured, both confused and frustrated. "We can't let them in!"

"The Pope resides in nearby buildings," Xerxes replied. "Even the Greeks are worried about barging in upon your Vicar of Christ."

The Pope. Pope Silverius. I wanted to believe it a coincidence, yet too many years in Imperial leadership had embedded mistrust in my heart. That, and the occasional signaling of unidentified Romans to the Goths outside the walls had convinced Belisarius that a traitor lingered inside the city's walls. It would have to be dealt with, but only after the scurrying Goths were prevented from flooding into the city as though out of another Trojan Horse.

"We don't have much time, the baths are only a thousand paces away," I said. "Grab torches, kindling, spikes, and mallets, and assemble five hundred men."

Xerxes gave me a skeptical glance but obeyed. His men were already assembled, and only a few minutes were required to gather my requested resources. They were passed throughout the ranks a careful distance away from the enclosed aqueduct, and I explained my intended attack.

I was in no mood for mercy. Worse, I wanted the Goths to suffer for their intended infiltration, not caring that I had led a similar assault in the previous winter. I ordered the men to break into teams of five—one torch bearer, one mallet bearer, one carrier of iron spikes, and two spearmen controlling kindling at their feet. The task was simple—the mallet and spike wielders would remove a single stone from the aqueduct's roof, a spearman would light kindling from the torch, and both flaming objects would be tossed into the exposure. I doubted that the Goths would burn, but once we replaced the stones on the aqueduct roof, they would suffocate, and do so slowly—a punishment that the other Goths would not forget.

Each team separated by twenty paces and climbed atop the aqueduct. Recent rain had made the stones slick, and our noise must have alerted the Goths, yet there was little that they or we could do to alter the present course. At my signal, the teams began to wrest stones free from the aqueduct, and Xerxes and I joined one near the Pincian Gate.

At first, the stones resisted even a vigorous smack of mallets and the carving of iron spikes. Below us, Gothic voices mumbled fearfully, causing the stones to vibrate. Yet I ordered our men to continue, and in less than a minute, a stone near me wriggled free from its moorings. It was little bigger than a man's head—plenty large enough to stuff a torch, but far too narrow to allow a Goth to escape or attempt to fight back.

"Burn them!" I ordered. "Light the kindling and send it below!"

A bundle of sticks, set aflame by a torch, was lowered next to the loose stone. Then, in a single motion, the mallet wielder hauled the stone free, revealing for a heartbeat the wide eyes of a Goth, whose soft face and wispy beard gave the impression of one too old to be a boy but hardly a man.

"Romans!" he yelled.

"Lower it!" I said, staring at the lad as Xerxes stabbed downward with his spear.

The spearpoint pierced his eye, likely his brain. In that same moment, the flame bearers lowered their cargo into the aqueduct, ours dropping the fire upon the lad's corpse. The last I saw was the fire catching his leather breastplate, smoke rising from the body.

"Close it!" I yelled.

Down the line, others followed our example. Stones were raised, helpless Goths butchered, and fires dropped upon those still living. As the loose stones were reseated, I could feel the Goths' screams rumbling against the aqueduct walls, their panicked voices desperate for mercy or escape. Choking noises grew louder, and a tendril of smoke billowed from a gap in the stones, yet otherwise our attackers could do nothing but suffer.

It took an hour for the last of the coughing, scraping, and crying to fade away. It took another hour for the stones to adequately cool before we were able to loosen further stones and peer inside at the Gothic bodies in their tomb. Some were adorned in charred clothing, and all the smoke-stained corpses bore scratch marks on their throats, froth dripping from distended tongues. Though some of the Goths closest to the outer entrance may have escaped, we nevertheless retrieved a hundred bodies from the defunct Aqua Virgo, lining their corpses along the sides of the nearby street.

"Inform Belisarius of what has transpired here, and ask him to come to the Campus Martius as soon as possible," I ordered a Cappadocian centurion. "And take the corpses to the forum for burning. Watch for further intrusions."

As our order was obeyed, I commanded Xerxes to gather two hundred spearmen and join me on a walk to the Campus Martius.

"An awful way to die," he said. "Although better this than risk the lives of our men. But do you truly believe the Pope encouraged the attack?"

I had doubts, but to show anything less than supreme confidence would have led to disaster. To accuse the Pope of treachery against the Emperor, the anointed of God to lead all Christendom, was not a trifling matter. "He was elevated by Theodahad and the Goth chieftains. There are too many coincidences that condemn him. It cannot be ignored any further."

Pope Silverius' guard was laughably small—many of whom were paid members of the city watch under Tarmutus. Outside Agrippa's Palace, the head guardsman could only muster a whimper as he demanded the purpose of my visit, to which I ordered the officer and his men to disarm and stand aside. Once there, we awaited Belisarius' arrival, finding the strategos followed by a hundred of his bucellarii, yet adorned in woolen shirt and trousers.

"There was an attack tonight?" Belisarius asked, his eyes sunken yet alert.

Xerxes nodded. "The Goths tried to sneak in through an aqueduct. They were planning on entering the city through Agrippa's baths."

Belisarius sighed. "Well, then, I can guess why we're here. Let's get this over with."

Absent resistance, only ten bucellarii joined Belisarius and me as we entered the Pope's temporary quarters. Xerxes, promising to meet us just moments later, led a separate detachment to the adjoining baths. Having forced to evacuate the outlying buildings of Vatican Hill, Pope Silverius nevertheless surrounded himself in splendor, mimicking the gold, silks, and rich meats that seemed to flow without ceasing at the tables of the Greek priests. We encountered several of Silverius' followers inside the Domus Agrippa, their eyes thick with fear.

"You bring swords into the presence of the saintly Pope?!" one priest demanded.

Belisarius waved him aside. "Later, Father."

Silverius' bedroom was easy to find, located upon the second level of the palace. The two remaining guardsmen surrendered to Belisarius without resistance, allowing us to pace through the closed wooden doors.

"What?" Silverius mumbled, half awake. "How dare you?!"

"Pope Silverius," Belisarius began, his voice far deeper than his usual tone. "You are deprived of your authority as Bishop of Rome."

"You can't do that!" Silverius spat, stumbling from his bed as he stood to face us. "You have no authority over God's priests!"

"The Emperor has authority in this city, and every other in his dominion," Belisarius replied. "Lord Varus shall explain your charges, although we both know you have undermined Imperial authority in this city since I first entered it."

"Lies!" Silverius cried.

"Holy Father," I began, "this evening, at least one hundred Goths attempted to sneak into Rome. Their destination was the baths and rooms of this very Domus. Thankfully, all of the attackers were repulsed."

A flicker of recognition crossed Silverius' face, yet his lips curled in hatred. "You are the Herulian who allows pagan witches to run amok in the Eternal City. If this upstart general has no authority over me, you have less. I have received messages from Constantinople about you, Varus."

Flickers of Cassiodorus' zealots, backed by the Brazen Bull, flashed through my memory. I suppressed a shiver as I continued. "It is known that you had no qualifications to the papacy prior to your election, and that Gothic gold elevated you beyond more experienced candidates. Do you deny it?"

"Emphatically," Silverius snarled. "You will hang for this insolence, whelp."

In the hallways outside of the bedroom, a familiar clattering of hobnailed boots echoed into Silverius' chambers. At that, Belisarius seized the conversation, clicking his tongue in mock disappointment.

"I doubt that," Belisarius replied. "Even if the accusations of bribery in the Holy Church are false, your guilt in undermining Imperial authority, including as a party to a Gothic ambush and night infiltration, is without doubt. No fewer than a dozen informants will attest to this."

Silverius laughed. "Sneaks, cutthroats, and whoremongers

– 681 –

all. You will hang with your underling, Belisarius. My friends in Constantinople have made it abundantly plain that you lack the Emperor's favor, and that God's servants rule this land."

"I don't deny it." Belisarius smiled calmly. "But my dear friend Xerxes may have more to add."

At the sound of his name, Xerxes paced into the room, backed by several armed Cappadocians. Astride those spearmen, two Roman guardsmen half walked and half stumbled over the embroidered carpets, tracking grime from the city streets onto the precious silk. At Xerxes' gesture, the two men were thrown unarmed at Silverius' feet.

"Tell them what you told me," Xerxes growled.

Both men were battered, their faces swollen and lips cracked and bleeding. Rising to his knees, one man turned to Belisarius, only to fall prostrate before the strategos.

"Lord Belisarius, we were commanded to ensure that no man entered the Baths of Agrippa this night," the man stammered, sniffling as a trickle of blood meandered through his moustache and onto cut lips.

Silverius' eyes widened again. "Be silent, and remember your oath to the Church!"

"Speak," Belisarius said, ignoring Silverius. "Who gave you this order?"

"One of Pope Silverius' attendants," the mustachioed man replied, nodding to a nearby priest. "Earlier this afternoon, before dusk."

The priest made sounds to quibble but fell silence with a stern glare from Xerxes. "And why would they ask you to guard the baths? For fear of looting?"

"No, Lord," the second man added, his voice unsteady as he winced from a blossoming bruise along his eye. "We were instructed to await Goth arrival. That is all, I swear to Christ."

"Liar!"

Silverius could bleat all he wanted, but I knew then that the Pope had lost any control he may have had over us. "Why would Silverius trust you with this endeavor?" Belisarius asked. "You have committed grave treason against the Emperor and might have condemned all of us to death had the Goths succeeded."

"We did not know they would crawl through the aqueducts!" the first man insisted. "We have both served as guardsmen for the Church for more than ten years. My oath is to the Pope, although his servant threatened me with hellfire if I failed my duty."

While attendants balked at the accusation, Silverius' protests ceased. He looked upon Belisarius, scowling, refusing to surrender gracefully.

"You will be damned for what you will do to me." Silverius glowered. "What is your decision, Strategos?"

Belisarius remained unmoved. "As I possess the authority of an Imperial Legate, I am stripping you of your rights and privileges as Pope of Rome. You will remain here, under guard, until you can be safely transported to Constantinople for trial."

"You shall be treated with all the respect and comfort of your station," I added, "but you will no longer govern as pope. You are the Emperor's subject, and fealty applies to you as much as me."

A sensation of wrongness pervaded my thoughts as I monitored Silverius' reaction, his resistance fading into grumbling acceptance. As a boy, Justin had weaned me on respect for the Pope, who was the Vicar of Christ. Though I felt neither pity nor remorse at recognizing the man's traitorous intentions—intentions that would have seen my family and my men enslaved or killed—my heart throbbed with reluctance. As I had felt many a day in my expedition to Septem, I wished that another might carry such a burden instead of me, allowing me to return to my days as a dekarchos, ignorant of the games of the Empire's great lords.

Nor did my conscience ease as Silverius' priests echoed his condemnation of me. A lover of pagans and protector of heretics. Some whispered the name of Jakob Baradaeus, while the unspoken influence of Cassiodorus draped atop each lofty room of Agrippa's Palace. My situation was not eased when I thoughtlessly commanded Xerxes to guard the Pope and his entourage that first night, with one familiar priest hissing curses as I departed.

"You have learned nothing of penance from your trial with Cassiodorus," he spat. "Placing a fire worshipper over Christ's representative. Your smugness will be the undoing of you, barbarian."

Though Belisarius beckoned me to follow him in departing, I turned. "Father Markus," I greeted him. "I did not recognize you with unsoiled trousers. Did I inconvenience you in our defense of Hadrian's Mausoleum?"

Markus sneered. "The holy Dathus, and so many others you destroyed, shall be rebuilt. I will not play a game of wits with you, but know this: This land is no place for pagans and apostates, and you are known as their defender. Tread carefully, or perhaps it will be you inside a bronze bull."

I wanted to smash the grin from his face. Yet as my fists clenched, Belisarius beckoned me to leave more forcefully, and I begrudgingly granted Markus a final farewell.

"Run with your master," Markus called. "Your offense to the Holy Father has been noted. You shall not win against the righteous—you or any of your heathen followers."

We left Xerxes and his Cappadocians to guard the palace and monitor other aqueducts for skulking Goths, and rejoined Belisarius' bucellarii to walk to the Domus Augustana. Though the resentment of Silverius and Markus left me unsettled, the cool summer evening refreshed my senses, washing away the cloying scents of the Pope's quarters.

"You must learn to control your frustrations, Varus," Belisarius chided me. "Silverius and his sycophants are not fools, and they speak to you in that manner to gain a specific reaction."

My head drooped, shame burning through my chest. "I apologize, Lord. You are correct. But at least Silverius cannot cause further harm."

Belisarius shook his head. "Not quite."

"You think he has agents we have not yet captured?" I asked.

"Perhaps, but those do not worry me much," Belisarius replied.

"It is more that when many faithful Romans awake and find their Holy Father humiliated and defrocked... well, I doubt many will thank me."

"We had no choice!" I insisted. "We could have all died tonight!"

Belisarius slapped my shoulder good-naturedly. "I know, Varus. I regret not acting sooner, although I had hoped that rumors of Silverius' disloyalty were nothing other than idle gossip. But that will not affect the minds of a hungry and frustrated populace."

Despite Belisarius' remonstrations, I barely suppressed a frustrated scream. "Then what can we do? We cannot afford a riot right now."

"We go with Samur's plan," Belisarius said. "It's far too risky, with too many unknowns, but at this moment I see little choice. With more food, we can stave off uprisings come harvest time."

Seeing Belisarius so helpless, so incapable of unknotting this web of misfortune, was even more peculiar to me than having to arrest the Pope moments prior. I wanted to help, to derive some solution that would cure his ails, yet nothing emerged. Both he and I knew that I was not John—I was not half as clever, and that left Belisarius with few options than to follow Samur's strategy. And it was not one that he cherished.

"I'm going to Hell for this," Belisarius mused balefully.

"Lord?"

"I'm not complaining," Belisarius added. "But Between the Nika Riots and deposing a Pope... serving Justinian has damned me."

"No, Lord," I insisted. "Silverius was a traitor. Any reasonable priest would understand."

Belisarius sighed. "He was still the Pope, anointed and blessed. And I tossed him barelegged into the street. Would Christ be pleased with me?"

The conversation left me uncomfortable and lacking proper words of comfort. "Christ knows your heart, Lord."

"Justinian will be pleased," Belisarius continued, all but ignoring my comment. "I shall have to suffice with that."

My skin chilled at those words as we crossed into the Domus. "You are the greatest man I know, Lord. That must count for something in this life."

Belisarius smiled. "I do not know what I would do without you, Varus. At least I know that someone in this army still shares my dreams."

We parted, ending that hectic evening. The violence and disquiet had been spiked by Belisarius' closing words of friendship, and for that, I felt hopeful despite it all.

Yet the siege left our predicament more desperate than ever, and we were losing control of the city's thousands. And God help me, but we were about to place all our lives in the hands of a foolish gamble, with little chance of success.

REDEMPTION

Sleep was impossible the evening after deposing Silverius. For an indeterminate time, I tossed about in bed, my mind whirling as I recollected the Pope's condemnation of my household. Surrendering to insomnia, I collected Priscus' tome and slinked away into an adjoining chamber, where I opened its pages beneath a series of burning tapers. Though the light was poor, it offered a fitting ambience as I read of the Empire's dread of Attila, the Scourge of God, who led hordes from the endless eastern wastes to destroy us all.

Before sunrise, light footsteps brushed against the stones into my room, and I found Mariya venturing to greet me.

"Can't sleep?" She yawned.

I shook my head. "An eventful evening, nothing more."

Mariya nodded, lowering herself onto the bench beside me. Against the cold stones of that room's floor and walls, Mariya's skin emitted an alluring warmth, amplified by the familiar waft of her perfume. She placed her head upon my shoulder, wrapping an arm about my waist. As she nestled close, occasionally fidgeting to a more comfortable position, I sat in silence, all thoughts of reading disappearing. In that stillness, Mariya eventually raised her eyes to meet my own, then leaned forward to steal a kiss.

"Let's go back," she whispered. "If we're both awake, we might as well enjoy ourselves."

Chuckling, I obeyed, nearly forgetting the tome in the process.

Neither of us slept, instead wrapped in one another's arms as dawn's first light filtered through the windows. Shimon attempted to rouse me soon thereafter, yet I ordered him to grant us a few more hours' peace. He obliged, and Mariya and I held one another in bed, nude except for a woolen blanket. In that moment, I dared voice a question that had bothered me since returning from Salona.

"Do you regret coming to Italy?"

Mariya tensed. Her lips molded into the weakest smile as she curled one of her hands inside of my own. Her reply, when it came, was more unsettling than if she had outright scorned her stay in this besieged, blighted Eternal City.

"What would you like me to say?"

A knot hardened in my throat. "The truth, of course."

Mariya chuckled sadly. "It has been… difficult."

"A siege is never pleasant," I admitted, squeezing her hand. "Luxuries are scarce, and the threat of violence is always near."

"That's true, but not all," Mariya confessed. "It's… difficult to describe."

"Try," I implored, though I feared the answer.

"My grandfather, and father, and uncles all fought in plenty of wars," Mariya began. "I'm no stranger to wrath. But this city…"

She gestured about us. Though only dark surrounded us, I could tell that her mind had wandered to Rome's hills and fora, with the countless households and shops that filled the labyrinthine roadways. The knot in my throat worsened, threatening to cut short my air.

"…there's no joy here, no life," Mariya concluded. "And it's not the people's fault, I know. But every day is sad, and somehow worse than before. There's no sense that life will become happier or easier. Rome is simply nothing I learned about as a girl. It's like a giant sarcophagus wrapped in gold and glory, but dead all the same."

The lamentable poetry of her words was unlike anything I knew of Mariya's thoughts. "I did not know you felt this way."

"Neither did I, until we arrived," Mariya admitted. "But after losing Pella, and the household gold, then coming here… it's hard to overlook all of Rome's crudeness, siege or no."

Guilt is not strong enough a word to describe what flooded my heart. I had been weak, desiring the proximity of my young family regardless of the dangers of our war with the Goths. Mariya had obliged, had even presented herself as a willing and eager partner. Yet while she was unrivaled at commanding a household, she was not a soldier. War was not her domain. It was not something she craved, nor sought for her own advancement. Justinian's greed and Justin's ambitions were all the same to her—her and doubtless thousands of other wives and lovers strewn about the Empire: dangerous impediments to be feared and mourned rather than celebrated.

"I'm sorry," I mumbled. "I shouldn't have brought you here."

Mariya paused. Then, with the crack of a wasp's sting, a jeweled hand smacked my shoulder. "You brought nothing, Varus. I wanted to be near my husband and have my children know their father. And if you believe that I am a flippant, pampered lady incapable of seeing my decision through, then you're sadly mistaken."

My head swam. "But you said that you regret being here?"

"I said that it has been more difficult than I anticipated," Mariya explained, her tone more measured. "That is the truth. But I will sacrifice for my family. I may not like the circumstances or fear the loss of our gold, but I won't run away like a coward."

The guilt remained. If anything, it strengthened, mixed with a curious relief that my wife did not find me wholly inadequate a provider in this terrible war. "I... I don't know what to say."

Mariya fidgeted, her eyes less than a hand length from mine. "I won't be parted from you again. This life is too short, and I intend to live it with joy and with love. So if you attempt to send me back to Constantinople, I'll jump off the ship."

"I won't," I promised, at last eased by her smile.

Two hours after dawn, I surrendered to my duty. Armed and armored, I was joined by my bodyguard and Rosamund, and together we trailed from the Domus to Belisarius' command building near the Pincian Gate. Most of the other officers, as well as Liberius and

Father Petrus, had already assembled, with Belisarius' grim visage welcoming me to the gathering.

Belisarius' fears had been realized. As a priest as well as a man who mingled in Rome's streets each morning, Father Petrus recounted the predawn chaos that greeted him in the forum from every angle. Men, including some who were known to be Silverius' household attendants, bellowed with fury at the treatment of their lord, accusing Belisarius of jailing and torturing the elderly man. Tarmutus' guards had cleared the forum, yet bands of furious looters swept through more distant alleys throughout the city, starting small fires and stealing what food might be found in various shops and houses.

"We can reclaim peace for now by granting normal rations for three days," Belisarius began, sending my guts sinking. Draining our limited stores of grain at triple the planned rate was all but unthinkable. "But we must act now. Samur will expedite his scouting of Witiges' grain wagons, and I shall beg any city within a week's sail to come to our aid."

Samur stood. "Witiges' wagons arrive regularly, and no less than three times per week. With such an extensive army, it is his only option, lest he risk theft and rot by storing huge weights of grain and fruit in temporary storehouses."

"Varus will organize everything that Samur requires," Belisarius concluded. "Do not rush unnecessarily, but do not delay in your plans. Our lives depend upon this, both to prevent starvation and to maintain order on the streets."

With Belisarius' blessing, Samur's raid upon the Milvian Bridge was expedited. Hun scouts ventured far to the north, galloping in swooping arcs around the Gothic camps to avoid discovery or tracking. As we awaited their report, I fulfilled Belisarius' desire to distribute a gift of grain to the Roman public, though I wanted to weep as the unaffordable boon was distributed to the public. While most appeared hale enough, those of the poorer neighborhoods were wasted of muscle and fat, struggling just to walk to the forum to receive their portion. I had little doubt that such creatures would be beaten, robbed of their rations, and left for dead as soon as they walked away from the forum and the careful eye of Tarmutus' city watch, but there was little I could do to protect them, or indeed any of the thousands of dying Romans that grasped at me with gnarled fingers.

By the third day after Silverius' imprisonment, Belisarius' desired peace had indeed gained a temporary hold over most of the Roman neighborhoods. Those accused of more violent crimes were shackled and hauled to the forum. Younger offenders were flogged bloody, yet most were hanged for even the crime of pilfering grain from an unrelated household. By the end of the week, two hundred corpses swung from makeshift gallows, their bodies left to rot in the summer sun as a warning that even Belisarius' recent largesse had its limits.

A few Huns returned early in the second week, yet the farther-ranging riders were not required to return for several more days. This was the period I most dreaded: when we were still readying our forces for the attack and awaiting further insight into Gothic disposition, but the city's rations had been returned to one-third their prewar allotment. Grumbling resumed, but a doubling of the city's patrols across every gate and hill dissuaded any who would toss stones or steal from their neighbors. However, Belisarius and I knew that the peace was temporary.

Not that fortune offered nothing to grant us hope. After their losses within the Aqua Virgo, the Goths attempted no further infiltration of Rome's defunct aqueducts. Once again, they hid behind the safety of their palisade camps, mounting occasional forage parties or scouting southward along the Via Appia. Nevertheless, we monitored the openings of each aqueduct, while Belisarius ordered unarmored and disguised spearmen to station themselves along each square and hill to detect any sign of communication with Witiges' chieftains.

After Silverius' deposition, a few suspicious instances were noted along the Caelian and Esquiline Hills, yet closer inspection revealed either misunderstandings or coincidence. In my soul, I remained convinced that Gothic agents persisted amongst the hundreds of thousands that remained in the city, although I could think of no approach to pluck them from their hideaways. Of all the regrets that I have, acting against my fears in this matter is among the most devastating.

At the time, however, all I mustered was a meager attempt at organizing informants amongst the Roman populace, sparing only mild attentions for gossip and rumors. Instead, I dedicated myself to preparation for Samur's raid. The city's mood improved as, ten days after Silverius' imprisonment, one of the many priests who had accompanied Belisarius and Procopius throughout our campaigns was raised to the pontificate. Vigilius, descendant of a Roman senator's family, had taken residence in Justinian's court in recent years, where he had gained the favor of Empress Theodora. With his ascension to the papacy, a relative harmony, at least, could be restored, as Pope Vigilius demanded that all Christians in Rome dedicate themselves to the Emperor Justinian.

Most important, however, was the arrival of cargo from Septem via Carthage. Dispatched before Belisarius' latest missives, the grain reached us at the close of the second week after Silverius' deposal, unloaded in Antium's port and wheeled through our southern gates flanked by Huns and Herulians. A detachment of Goths was sent to scout and harry our supply wagons yet was unable to break through our storm of arrows before the bulk of our stores eclipsed the city's gates. It was not much, but the stores would gain Belisarius another month of half rations for the city. Enough time to plan our raid, though not enough to render it either safe or wise.

I directed the wagons toward the city's granaries. As they progressed, a merchant from their caravan hailed me. "Lord Varus?"

"Yes, citizen?" I answered. "You carry our salvation, and are welcome here. What can I do for you?"

He shook his head. "Not me, Lord. We've been paid well for the effort, and the seas were lovely. I was told to hand you this message once we arrived."

I accepted a copper-lined tube. "What does it say?"

The man shrugged. "I am poorly lettered, Lord. It should be self-explanatory."

Unsealing the tube's stopper, I withdrew a small yet thick hide the size of my hand, its cover scraped clean. Though a strange clerk's handwriting greeted me, the words were from someone familiar.

Septem thrives and is happy to help you in your hour of need. Be well, Varus Veridicus.

I flashed a broad grin as I read the name of the author. *Itaxes, Harbormaster of Septem.* In this, at least, I had made a decision that improved the lives of many. I thanked the merchant, offering a silver coin as payment for the happy words, and returned to my work in determining how long we could stave starvation from the Eternal City.

The last of Samur's scouts returned to Rome at the conclusion of summer, just when the region's farmers would begin to reap the season's harvest. Though threadbare and covered in sores, the Huns were uncomplaining, and drew out a more thorough map of Witiges' northern provinces than Narses' spies had provided Belisarius.

"Witiges receives grain from multiple trade routes, but the Milvian Bridge is the one most vulnerable to our attack," Sinnion explained to a collection of Belisarius' officers. "Their movements are predictable, as is their timing. They follow a seven-day route from Pisae."

"Could we seize them by sea, if they follow the coastal roads?" Ascum asked.

Sinnion frowned. "The wagons are closely guarded until the road turns inward. You'd face a thousand Goths as you jumped from your ships, and without horses."

"They'll swarm us without our mounts," I agreed. "But of the thousand you mentioned, how many turn back to Pisae at the road's junction? How far north does this occur?"

"Fifty miles north, or thereabouts," Sinnion answered. "Roughly half return to Pisae."

Belisarius' eyebrows arched. "Five hundred Goths in open terrain…"

"Meat to be struck down," Samur insisted. "Between the Huns and the Heruli, we could down a hundred armored spearmen within a minute. Within ten, their banda would be torn to ribbons, especially funneled along the bridge."

Belisarius' worry was palpable, but others added their voice to Samur's. "Septem offers a blessing, but we need more grain before winter comes," Bessas mused. "Many say that the harvest of Sicily and Campania will be a poor one."

"There's no choice but to act," Perenus added. "While we can spare a few thousand men from the walls and not worry about open revolt in the forum."

Belisarius nodded but maintained his furrowed brow. "What say you, Liberius?"

My old teacher straightened in his bench, rubbing his eyes as if he had ignored the conversation until now. "I've found that the opinions of old men count for little in today's times. We're all too scatterbrained, I would assume."

Belisarius nodded in deference. "You are the wisest man here, and you know Rome well. What would you do if you were me?"

Liberius sighed, running a hand through his unruly beard. "There's too much we do not know. All are correct in insisting upon decisive action to bolster our food stores. Still, worries remain."

"I don't understand, Lord," I admitted. "You were in favor of this attack yesterday."

"Ah, confident Varus!" Liberius mourned. "Just because I see something as necessary, does not mean it is not prudent to worry. Perhaps those quibbles are why I never made a passable warrior?"

"You would have made a fine officer, Lord."

"You flatter me." Liberius winked. "Regardless, the matter is simple. We need food, and soon. Starvation is not a pretty thing."

Food. The constant worry. Though as a warrior my meals were not unduly limited, the portions were less than desirable. My belt cinched tighter with each passing month, and the groans of my children's bellies were maddening in their effect. Young Alexander had taken to whining out his desires, and even hardy Zenobia had become listless from insufficient nourishment. Mariya had shared much of her allotted ration with both children, and even occasionally Tiberius, though her already-thin frame had become perilously frail, her once-radiant hair dull and brittle to the touch. When I attempted to alleviate Mariya's burden by sharing my own meal, she adamantly refused me, insisting that I needed all the strength I could muster to remain alive on the battlefield. If the thoughts of food stuck ever present in my own mind, I was all but certain such was the case for the others gathered in the war council.

Samur scowled. "What do you suggest, then?"

"Alas, I surrender, Samur!" Liberius raised his hands, flashing his palms to my brother. "I do not criticize you. But like Socrates, I complain without offering a solution of my own. For I cannot see another path, short of seeking a boon from Constantinople or the other cities."

"We've tried that already!" Samur cried.

Liberius bowed his head in surrender as Belisarius turned to me. "And you, Varus? What say you?"

Though I knew I would be among the last to speak, I wished that Belisarius had relieved me of that duty. Samur's eyes locked onto mine, seeming to plead for agreement. Likewise, Liberius sat unblinking, his weathered face hiding an indomitable soul. Though Liberius may have spoken soft words to Samur, I understood his worry to be more than mere theoretical prattle from an old bureaucrat. The wise choice was to agree with Liberius and grant Belisarius enough support to seek a safer alternative.

But I was weak. And I loved my brother.

"There's little time to delay, and the Huns have substantially improved our knowledge of Gothic territory and operations," I insisted. "We need grain, there is no denying it, and there's no guarantee that others will come to our aid. My recommendation is to attack with greater numbers than we anticipated, hit the wagons hard, dump their cargos into riverboats, and ride like hell back to the walls."

Liberius shut his eyes as Samur smacked his hands together, hooting with glee. Belisarius nodded once, still uncertain, yet was never one to cast aside the guidance of his war councils. "When will the next transport pass over the Tiber?"

"There's one in three days," Samur replied. "After that, another week."

"We wait for that second shipment, then," Belisarius concluded. "Finalize our plans. I intend to join the attack."

And so we did. With the remaining delay, Samur and I crafted details for Belisarius' approval, organizing his army into interlocking bandae. Half of our remaining soldiers would remain in Rome under Bessas, while nearly four thousand men would venture out. My contribution was to suggest a further partition—rather than gamble all our hopes on a single swift strike, we instead would mount a diversion along Rome's eastern gates. Samur concurred, and we allocated fifteen hundred spearmen for the task of distracting Witiges, requiring men unlikely to quit or run prior to the return of our raid.

Naturally, that assignment was granted to Gunderic. He whooped with glee at that responsibility, unchained from Xerxes' cautious eye. "Who will join me?"

"All of the Vandals," I began, "along with many of our cataphracts. Your task is not to defeat the Goths, but make them believe your attack is serious enough to warrant their undivided attention."

Gunderic grinned. "I'll whip them bloody. You'll have your diversion, don't you worry."

Of that, I had no doubt. "If they threaten to outflank you, draw close to the walls. Ascum will support you with archers and scorpions, although wait as long as you can before doing so."

While Belisarius accepted our guidance for assault, he did veto my initial division of warriors. "If our plan goes as intended, Gunderic will absorb the greatest strain. And we must not entirely denude the walls of Huns or Heruli to maintain an illusion that those warriors are not departing for elsewhere."

The result was a significant loss for Samur's strike, and a gain of seven hundred additional men for Gunderic. Ultimately, all that remained of our attacking force comprised most of the Huns and Herulians, two hundred cataphracts, and the bulk of Tarmutus' reinforced guardsmen. From the Tiber, Ascum commissioned four river boats with ten archers and twenty oarsmen each—not enough to counter a dedicated Gothic attack, but enough to screen our efforts to transfer grain from Witiges' wagons.

Though Gunderic's assault would not commence until the late morning of the wagon's arrival at the Milvian Bridge, Samur's wing departed that very evening. Rather than gallop along the Tiber and risk discovery by the two Gothic camps facing the Via Flaminia, we instead later departed Rome through its southern gates. Father Petrus blessed all who would listen, and we began our ride, forming a sweeping arc that looped our forces clear of the Gothic camps before crashing west into the Milvian Bridge. Samur urged a day of hard riding, with only minimal rest at night before commencing the assault on the grain wagons, with advance scouts signaling the arrival of the wagons with horns.

The ride began with little complaint, although the distance in the saddle would not be trivial. Yet all of us, other than the guardsmen, had covered vast distances on horseback, and Tarmutus' men proved capable, if less agile, riders. Donning the armor that had first been personally smithed for me prior to our war against the Persians, I rode before the Herulians, joined by Perenus, Xerxes, and my usual guardsmen. Fulcaris remained along Rome's walls with a diminished force of ouroboros-bearing spearmen, and I prayed that our ruse would not be discovered or tested. Curiously, no scout or band appeared to note our presence, and so we galloped unhindered into the lands of the Umbrians.

To his credit, Samur was careful to steer away from known Gothic positions. The rising sun yielded comfortable but not overbearing warmth, and the grasses were firm for our horses' hooves. By dusk, Samur grunted approval at the column's progress and ordered a general halt. We constructed a crude camp but allowed no fires, instead simply posting sentries in hourly watches to grant most men a much-needed rest—a boon that I accepted gratefully, although Belisarius insisted upon patrolling the camp for two consecutive patrols, insisting that his mind raced too much for sleep.

Before dawn, the sentries slipped through our camp, waking each tent and preparing the column for its departure west. Night marches were known to be especially hazardous, although Samur guarded his path with extensive scouting and insisted that the extra time would allow for a more leisurely pace toward the Milvian Bridge. Yawning and cold, I mounted Boreas, ruffling his mane before resuming our trot.

The predawn air was cool, as it had been the previous day, and the breeze slight. The Umbrian hills glistened with dew, reflecting the last glimmers of moonlight as we angled toward Latium. Again, no Goths challenged our progress, not even to scout our intentions.

"There's no logic to it," Sembrouthes noted. "It's not as if Witiges is short on men."

Silently, I clung to similar worries, but there was little I could do. "Witiges has made mistakes at every stage of the siege," I offered. "Perhaps this is just another to add to that list."

"If this works, there's no chance Witiges remains as king," Uliaris replied. "I don't care how well liked he is. And I know Samur is your brother, but nothing about this plan makes me confident."

Again, I shared Uliaris' concerns but had little choice than to profess certainty. "Rome needs to eat. We've scouted the path for over a month, and the Goths have given no sign that they anticipate an attack. In war, sometimes wagers are necessary."

"Yes, but only when the dice are weighted in our favor," Sembrouthes grumbled.

As we drew a few miles of the Tiber River, our column formed into battle array. The Herulian and Hun foederati trotted to the head of the column, angled upon either flank, while Belisarius led his cataphracts and bucellarii two hundred paces behind in the column's center. In our rear was Tarmutus, who, after our forward ranks seized the wagons, would tilt toward the distant Gothic camps and await any sign of battle. With good fortune, Tarmutus' blade would remain dry throughout the day, with his only action to gallop hard for Rome's walls after our caper was concluded.

By then, our pace slowed, awaiting the harsh Hunnic horns. Two hours after dawn, they sounded across the western hills, and a trail of scouts echoed the sound all the way back to the Pincian Gate. A boom from the south denoted Gunderic's acknowledgment, and a sign that his sally against Witiges would begin.

"Time to see how stupid this really is," Uliaris spat, tightening his helmet and checking his francisca.

I could tell Samur was anxious. He kicked his mount onward, increasing his pace to the limits of Tarmutus' abilities, occasionally glaring over his shoulder at their lack of progress. Even Perenus and the Herulians struggled to keep order at a near gallop, yet I urged them onward as Samur crested one hill after another. Though the familiar battle giddiness welled in my gut, I desired nothing more than for this day to end, and end in success, assured that the sacrifice was well repaid by captured Gothic grain.

Soon, we rose atop our final hill, glancing down upon the meandering Tiber. The Milvian Bridge was impossible to miss, its stone arch famous as the site where Constantine had reclaimed the Empire as a single entity, setting into motion the eventual dominance of Christianity amongst the Imperial government. Though Jerusalem holds a hallowed place in the hearts of today's Christians, the Milvian Bridge stands a close second, spoken of in hushed tones as a fulcrum in our history. Aside from that, the only event with greater importance in shaping our world was Aetius' repulsion of Attila's hordes, affirmed a year later by the Hun warlord's mysterious meeting with Pope Leo. All these figures once called this region their battleground, and until this day, Belisarius had acquitted himself as the greatest of those heroes.

The wagons had already begun to rise along the bridge, a vast snake of some twenty carts far more massive than any grain wagon I had encountered across my many campaigns. My spirits soared—

that much uncut wheat could easily fill Roman bellies for months, perhaps even through the first portion of winter.

"Sweet Christ," Perenus blasphemed. "I'll kiss Samur when we're done with this!"

"Concentrate," I growled. "And watch the south for any Gothic patrols. We'll have to fight before the day is done."

Samur's mood outstripped Perenus', and there was no reining in his enthusiasm. "Let's go, Varus!"

"God damn it," Sembrouthes muttered.

What reserves we restrained within our mounts were unleashed. It was a mad gallop, nigh undisciplined, with only the Huns remaining in an immaculate unfolding wedge of bowmen and lancers. By then, we made no effort to disguise our arrival, for the cloud of dust that trailed our hooves and the subsequent rolling thunder was impossible to mask. However, the overlarge Gothic carts had no agility for maneuvering, unable to turn or retreat without crashing into one another. More, Ascum's river craft rowed beneath the bridge as we drew within a hundred paces, having waited until confirming our presence to surge toward our prey.

"Don't shoot yet!" Samur yelled.

Far outpacing Belisarius or Tarmutus, Samur and I arrived as the first Gothic grain wagon reached the eastern edge of the Milvian Bridge. Before them were some three hundred Gothic spearmen bearing the sigil of King Witiges—somewhat fewer than our scouts had estimated, and none of them mounted. They formed a shield ring before the wagons, watching as we Romans drew close. Samur halted our progress, forming his Huns in a half circle about the bridge's exit, granting our Heruli the ability to reinforce his position.

"I am Samur, lord of the Hun foederati of the Roman Empire. In the name of the Emperor, I am seizing these wagons!" Samur boomed. "Toss aside your weapons, and you shall leave here unharmed."

Halted in the third rank of horsemen, the Goth leader was less than twenty paces from Samur. Equally, we stood a mere thirty paces from the nearest wagon, with the procession of twenty filling the

Milvian Bridge like a hapless sacrifice to Belisarius' army.

"You have one minute to comply!" Samur continued. "Longer than that, and I will skewer each of you with arrows and crucify you along the banks of the Tiber!"

Yet the Goths were undeterred. Initially, there was only silence, and a chortle rang out amongst the assembled Goths. It gained strength as others joined in the laughter, their overlapping shields rustling against one another. Only then did I see the leader of those assembled Goths, his face hidden beneath a stolen Roman helmet.

"Samur, get back!"

If my brother heard me, he ignored my words. Instead, he sat atop his horse, watching as the Gothic leader identified himself, remaining nestled amongst the Gothic shields.

"Lord Samur, I shall give you one half minute to toss aside your bows and kiss my feet," the leader said, laughing. "I wouldn't wait that long, if I were you."

"Totila," I muttered.

Perenus reached for his bow. "It's an ambush!"

Totila raised an arm, signaling a half dozen Gothic horns to boom from the heights of the Milvian Bridge—then more horns to the south, a rolling crescendo that swallowed any noise of Gunderic's advance. The sackcloth that covered each wagon unknotted and flew aside, revealing dozens of Gothic spearmen and Suevi archers pouring out onto the Milvian Bridge. There was no grain—only death.

Samur seemed paralyzed as the Suevi launched a ragged volley of a hundred arrows toward the mounted Huns. I crouched, locking my shield overhead with Sembrouthes and Uliaris, thankfully spared any direct strike. The Huns were not so fortunate, however, with one Suevi arrow piercing Samur's leather boot. Yelping, Samur jerked in the saddle as two Huns sheltered his body with their shields. Though scattered, the Suevi arrows continued, and time appeared to slow as I desperately sought any path to rescue my brother. In the end, unable to easily maneuver or weave closer to the Huns, I ordered the Herulians to attack.

"Bows!" I yelled. "Hit the bridge!"

The Herulians answered, and our superior bows connected against the chests, arms, and even faces of Goths and Suevi alike. Clumped together between the bridge's stone walls and the vast wooden wagons, there was little our enemy could do to shelter against our attack.

"Aim for their bowmen!" Xerxes yelled.

For a moment, our barrage shifted the momentum of battle. Yet Totila must have sensed this, for it was then that he ordered his spearmen to rush forward, their disciplined wall colliding against Samur's reeling Huns. The Huns fought ferociously, but mounting injuries from Suevi missiles and Gothic spears rendered the lighter, lesser-armored cavalry over-matched.

"Fall back!" Samur yelled. "Back east!"

Even Caesar himself would not begrudge Samur his decision, for it was tactically all he could do to keep his elite foederati from succumbing to utter destruction. Yet the sudden departure of the Huns scattered our enclosure of the Milvian Bridge and forced the Herulians to separate to allow the Huns to pass. Totila seized that opportunity, ordering his spearmen to crash against my disorganized men.

There was nothing I could do. Suevi arrows prevented us from safely attacking Totila's spearmen, and our scramble for shelter from Gothic spears—while unable to fire our own arrows—allowed their barrage to continue. It was hopeless, and even Xerxes had no advice to recoup our situation.

"Back, in good order!" I yelled, mirroring Samur. "Don't let any foederati get stranded!"

Waiting for the ranks behind me to depart and grant me opportunity to maneuver, I plucked an arrow from my saddlebag, searching for Totila's plume amongst the Gothic mass. I did not aim, but rather trusted my instincts, weaned from launching thousands of arrows over the years. The shaft sprang from Khingila's bow, and I knew its aim to be true.

Totila recognized the threat but was squashed between other Goths and neither able to lift his shield nor dodge. Instead, he gripped the collar of the Goth before him, positioning the man's body to shield his own. My arrow pierced through the unfortunate Goth's noseguard and bone, jutting clean from his helmet but leaving Totila unscathed. Totila screamed in defiance as he allowed his defender's body to fall limp and ordered several Goths to throw spears in my direction.

I knew that the day's gambit had failed. All we could do was salvage the ambush with our lives. "Back!"

Though most of my followers were able to canter away, a half dozen Herulians were swarmed by the aggressive Gothic front rank. Over my shoulder, I watched those men either be dragged helplessly to the ground or gored with multiple spears to their hips or torsos. We retreated, losing cohesion as we trailed Samur's Huns, chased by ravenous Goths who thirsted for the easy kills that came from a routed enemy with flagging mounts. One Goth drew close enough that I thought I would need to turn and deal with the man, exchanging Khingila's bow for my sword.

Yet it was not so—for Belisarius' cataphracts burst through gaps in our lines, smashing aside the closest Goths with their lances. Belisarius himself skewered my stalker, driving a lance through the man's chest that broke into a hundred shards. One shard the length of my forearm clattered against the shield slung about my back, sobering my thoughts as I sat upright.

"Fall back!" Belisarius yelled, confirming my order.

Though Belisarius could not hope to defeat both Totila's massed spearmen and the throng of reinforcements along the Milvian Bridge, the shock of his assault did force the surging Goths to temporarily halt in favor of tightening their shield wall. Belisarius' cataphracts cut down at least twenty of the greedier Goths before bracing against their advance, and gradually retreated behind my mass of Herulians. Before me, a Hunnic horn blared instructions for our column to turn south, angling our mounted procession away from Totila and toward safety.

Uliaris spat. "An ambush!! We walked right into that pile of shit!"

"We're not out of it yet," Xerxes cautioned, shouting above the rumbling of horse's hooves. "Totila did not act alone, or by coincidence."

Worse, the attack was a total failure. We took casualties and received no plunder as recompense, leaving Rome's predicament unimproved. Samur was hurt, and I yearned to gallop ahead and provide what comfort I could—yet such a move would jeopardize an already rattled column. Embarrassed and frustrated, I gave little thought to Xerxes' warning. Instead, I confronted its reality head on.

For to the south, two thousand Goths formed a tight wall. At their center was a helmetless Optaris, beaming as he directed his Goths to strike a hapless Tarmutus. Witiges had not been as great a fool as I had hoped, for the Gothic king had blocked our route of escape and entangled our reinforcements in a single motion. We were trapped, the feasible paths to Rome sealed by Totila in the west and Optaris in the south.

Worse, another detachment of at least a thousand Goths swung to seal our eastern escape, preventing even a hazardous escape back into Umbria without food or shelter. As Tarmutus' guardsmen became enmeshed with the superior fighters of Optaris, the maneuverability of our horsemen rapidly diminished.

"Varus!" a Hunnic voice called to me—Sinnion. "Your brother needs you!"

My heart fluttered. "Injured?!"

"Not badly," Sinnion said quickly. "But we need to break out before these bastards surround us."

Many outlying Huns fired arrows toward the massed Goths, and Perenus soon ordered the Herulians to do the same. Transferring command to Perenus, I ventured into the Hunnic ranks with Sembrouthes, Uliaris, and Xerxes, finding the fur-clad warriors quiet and bloodied. None showed fear, yet neither did they exhibit confidence as they gulped sips of wine between firing upon a numerically superior enemy. I found Samur a hundred paces distant, leaning painfully in the saddle as he massaged his leg. He hailed me as I approached, wincing.

"Damned arrow needs a surgeon to remove," Samur grunted, pointing to the shaft that protruded from his calf. It was bleeding copiously, leaching crimson upon his black boots and dripping onto his horse's pelt. "We need to punch through one section of Goths soon, or they'll bury us alive."

Sinnion grunted. "We'll be flanked in minutes. What is your order?"

Samur turned his pained face to meet mine. "The Huns could survive if we rode northward into Gothic territory. But would the others?"

It was a terrible plan, placing a greater distance between our best surviving warriors and the safety of Rome's walls. "We could follow, but I doubt Tarmutus would be able to move quickly enough. And there's no telling how long our retreat would take."

"Then we pierce the Gothic lines," Samur replied. "The bridge would be a nightmare to cross and puts us on the wrong side of the Tiber. That leaves south or east."

"South," I answered, watching Tarmutus' men dismount to absorb the shock of Optaris' thrust. "We need to rescue Tarmutus and make for Rome. Witiges planned for this ambush, which means he intends to attack the city as well."

Samur spat. "Agreed. I will send a courier to Belisarius. Let's hope Gunderic can hold his lines until we return."

After we parted, Samur screamed. I flinched, initially believing it the pain from his wound, yet a backward glance revealed no cause for concern. He roared again, clenching his fists as he plucked an arrow from his saddlebag, his cheeks flushed ruby.

Though we retained maneuverability, and the Goths were unable to fully encircle our position, the relentless advance of the Goths' southern and eastern contingents pushed our rabble of foederati, city watch, and bucellarii into a disintegrated mass. Along the Tiber, Belisarius was holding Totila at bay, yet a steady stream of Gothic reinforcements from the Milvian Bridge made Belisarius' position untenable. Worse, a sizeable force of Suevi remained, firing arrows into a dense cluster of Romans; Uliaris' mount was struck cleanly by one such arrow, forcing him to leap from the saddle and seize another riderless horse as his original mount wailed in pain and bucked in panic.

Slowly, the Goths swallowed our forces like an unpleasant meal. I copied Samur by ordering the Herulian foederati to aim for Optaris, snatching arrow after arrow from my quiver as I sought victims amongst the Goths. We had some success, for the Goths struggled to defend against our bowmen while also clattering against Tarmutus' spears, yet our efforts were insufficient to blunt the gaping holes that Optaris had ripped in the ranks of Roman guardsmen.

Amidst the scrum, I spied Tarmutus, barking orders as he fought from his second line. With a swift thrust, his spear pierced the throat of a richly armored Goth, earning a chorus of cheers amongst the guard and a momentary forward surge. Yet his flanks sagged under the pressure of assault by Optaris' more experienced warriors. Tarmutus attempted to rally and urged his followers forward, unsheathing his sword to stab into a fresh enemy. As the Goth reeled from the ragged gash, his neighbor jammed a spear into Tarmutus' exposed armpit, throwing him backward.

"Signal Belisarius," I ordered Xerxes. "We need to attack southward now."

Xerxes' nodded, his eyes wide. "Totila will outflank us immediately after—"

"Too late!" I cried. "It's too late for that. We need to clear a path to the south. I just saw Tarmutus go down."

The guard did not break, but with Tarmutus disabled, it buckled at an alarming rate. As the Huns volleyed the eastern Goths, I continued our arrow assault against Optaris, continuously backing away and clumping against nearby Herulians. Worry gnawed at my gut as I sent a courier to summon Samur for a breakout, knowing well that if the city watch broke, we lacked the strength to pierce through

Optaris' shield wall. Before Samur could respond, however, Perenus galloped beside me.

"Belisarius comes!" he said, pointing to the east.

It was expected, albeit delayed. "Send fifty Herulians to fire upon Totila. Do not let him push into our western flank, but don't tangle with his spears."

Perenus saluted and selected a Herulian centurion to follow, riding hard in the direction of the Milvian Bridge. I awaited Belisarius' arrival, more selective of my targets as my quiver lightened from its once-ample supply. I hailed Samur as Belisarius' mounted force approached, ready to gather and decide how we would break from our current trap.

Except Belisarius did not halt. Instead, he ordered his riders to a full gallop, charging toward a section of Tarmutus' shield wall that had curled backward from constant Gothic pressure. Just as the first Goths began to puncture the Roman wall, Belisarius' wedge slammed into the fray, tossing aside a dozen Goths from the sheer weight of the leading cataphracts.

"Defend Belisarius!" I yelled, ignoring Samur's arrival. "Belisarius is creating a hole in the Gothic lines!"

As centuries of Roman commanders understood within their bones, a steadfast line of shields and spears could deflect even the most ferocious cavalry charge. If that line broke, however, whether out of fear or lack of discipline, it was trivial for armored riders to rend terrible gaps into a shield wall. And that is exactly what Belisarius did. Sensing both a dire weakness in our defense and an opportunity to overwhelm surging attackers, he collided against the Goths, piercing deep into their ranks as armored Roman horses bullied the Goths to the ground. In such a maneuver, the most grievous injuries would come more from being violently tossed aside than from any lance or blade, and the resulting fear and confusion cascaded through a vast swathe of the Gothic spearmen. Just as with horse archers, armored cavalry was an uncommon sight for the Goths, with few of their chieftains trained to turn aside a charge from one as experienced as Belisarius.

Eventually, the surge halted, yet few Goths swarmed Belisarius' men. Instead, they reassembled their shield wall, with the occasional parry against a cataphract lance their only attempt at combat. As I loosed arrows against the Goths nearest Belisarius, I spotted Optaris rushing from behind the Gothic lines, forming a counterattack of hundreds of fresh spearmen.

Alone, that would have been a dire threat to Belisarius' safety. But heartbeats later, a horn sounded from the Milvian Bridge. Though it was difficult for me to see at the time, I learned later that Totila ordered a portion of his spearmen and all of his archers to charge toward Perenus, forcing the smaller Herulian force to scamper back toward safety. Totila pressed the bulk of his spearmen toward Belisarius, seeking to trap the strategos and his bucellarii in a cocoon of Gothic killers.

It was a move of sheer genius. A masterstroke far surpassing their initial ambush along the Milvian Bridge, and one that we were thoroughly unprepared to counter. As Totila drew closer, the realization that Belisarius would either be captured or killed brought me to jerk upright, desperate for any option to shatter the Gothic trap.

"Blades!" I yelled. "Form on me! Do not let Totila flank Belisarius!"

It was madness. The eastern bank of the Tiber was awash with men and horses, tainted by the smells of piss and sweat, of death and manure. An onlooker would struggle to make sense of the battle, with its squirming Roman force wriggling inside a three-sided Gothic grasp. It took precious time to gather my Herulians into a coherent wedge, and my panic swelled as I watched the first of Totila's men encircle our cataphracts. After a minute, I lacked the patience to wait any longer.

"Charge!" I screamed. "Break Totila!"

It was hopeless, but my men did not hesitate. Indeed, many began to rush ahead of the line—Uliaris in particular. Yet order returned as we sped to a gallop and closed upon the final hundred paces to Totila's rearward ranks. He seemed to anticipate the threat and formed a rearguard wall to fend us off as he turned his attentions toward the flailing Roman cataphracts.

Eschewing a sword, I instead drew my axe. Uliaris, possessing the same instinct, flung a francisca toward a nearby Goth as we drew close, its bearded edge snapping the man's thin iron noseguard and burying itself along the bridge of his nose. The Goth fell, and that gap was all I needed. Guiding Boreas forward, I swept my axe downward, chopping at the shoulder of the nearest Goth and biting deep into muscle and bone. I could feel Totila's rearguard lurch backward against our attack, suffering horrifying casualties as Goths lost hands, arms, and even a severed head with a well-timed strike from Xerxes.

But still, it was not enough. And just as Belisarius's bucellarii became enmeshed with Optaris, my Herulians slammed to a halt against Totila's men, unable to puncture through to our trapped Roman brethren. I had failed.

"We need to fall back!" Sembrouthes yelled in my ear. "Try again if you want, but we'll get swarmed if we stay here."

Slashing downward, I chopped my axe into the wooden panels of a nearby Goth shield, leaving Uliaris to stab into the man's undefended neck. "Belisarius needs us!" he yelled back.

But Sembrouthes was right. "Fall back and reform!" I cried.

"Varus!" Uliaris roared, but I did not heed him.

We detached from the Goths, taking light wounds ourselves as we doled out gashes to Totila's lines. Though his rearguard held, I nevertheless had gained the warlord's attention, with Totila barking commands for holes to be plugged as we trotted fifty paces away. My distraction granted Belisarius a reprieve, yet he remained incapable of breaking from the tightening Gothic vise. As I commanded another assault, a Hunnic horn blared behind me, its notes haggard and urgent.

"Charge, Varus!" a Hunnic courier yelled. "Samur is making a pass!"

Though I had little knowledge of my brother's position, I did not hesitate. "Herulians, charge!"

As we kicked our mounts to a canter, a hundred Huns rumbled on either side of our wedge. Samur sped past me, yelling in Hunnic for a volley into the heart of Totila's formation. A second volley followed mere heartbeats later, with each Hunnic column wheeling ten paces before the Gothic lines as they retreated eastward. A third volley sailed over my head as the last of the Huns disappeared, colliding against the Gothic rearguard with ease.

This time, I knew that our charge would succeed—and judging by how swiftly Totila sprinted away, he did as well. Many Gothic spearmen mustered resistance, but fruitlessly, as their shields were punctured by arrows and dozens of casualties bled out. I guided Boreas toward a plumed officer, axe ready, and swerved about his spear to slash at his chest. Though I missed, Boreas battered the man aside, and Sembrouthes skewered the gray-bearded warrior with a single thrust into his spine.

"Break them!" I yelled. "Get to Belisarius!"

The Goths yielded—some by dodging and others by simply waiting helplessly to be tossed to the ground and trampled by hooves. We reached Belisarius' position just as Optaris' men pressed against Belisarius' wedge, dragging two of his bucellarii to the ground and impaling them upon their spears. For a brief moment, my arrival went unnoticed by Optaris' Goths, and I swung my axe in great swirling scythes, cutting the throat of one Goth and slashing at the limbs of two others: The one bedecked in more protective mail merely suffered slashed skin and broken bones, while the other, armored in rotting hog leather, saw his arm severed cleanly just below the elbow, a blow so severe that it took me several heartbeats to free my axe, blood pumping from the open wound. By then, other Goths stormed about my position, and I guided Boreas closer to Belisarius' protective circle before trading my axe for my sword.

Though our arrival notably amplified Belisarius' ranks, I am not certain when the strategos became aware of my presence. As Totila regrouped his spearmen and my trailing Herulians gathered in the great circle of Roman warriors, I found Belisarius engrossed in trading blows with Optaris, his rich set of scales signifying rare wealth amongst the mass of Gothic boiled leather and brittle iron. A wave of Herulians trotted in front of me, lashing against our Gothic attackers and granting me a momentary reprieve as I struggled to worm my way toward Belisarius' position.

But in that maelstrom of beast and man, nothing, not even my rank in the army, could help me carve an open pathway toward Belisarius. Still, with my guardsmen, I had to try. "Find a way to the front!"

"Give it a minute!" Sembrouthes replied. "We can't help Belisarius if we become as stuck as he is!"

I grunted in irritation, though Sembrouthes was correct. Behind us, Totila's men began to reform their lines and block our access to Samur's Huns and Perenus' Herulians, although occasional arrow fire left them skittish and content to stand a safe distance away from my men. Farther eastward, Tarmutus' guard maintained order, although they appeared bloodied and incapable of holding their ground for long. And as fighting raged in all directions, my instincts screamed in panic, knowing well that it was only a matter of minutes until Belisarius' army was outflanked, forcing the extent of our failing lines to fight back to back. My only hope was to push forward and gallop relentlessly for the Pincian Gate, praying that Witiges had not already seized sections of the Aurelian Walls.

But pressed against the bodies of so many others, all I could do was watch Belisarius and his bodyguard battle against Optaris' spearmen. Initially, it appeared as if Belisarius maintained leverage, for he stabbed from the greater height of his saddle upon a dismounted Optaris. Yet Optaris deflected each blow cleanly, using the upper half of his shield to absorb every jab and return it with blows of his own. Suddenly, a guardsman to Belisarius' left collapsed from the saddle, a spear puncturing his chest, and crashed into Belisarius' mount. Belisarius intuitively turned his head at the disruption, and though Optaris lacked positioning and could only shuffle forward, he thrust the tip of his sword into Belisarius' knee all the same.

"Fucking hell!" Uliaris yelled. "I'm going in."

I nodded. "Clear a path!"

Belisarius shuddered in pain, yet did not lose control of his mount. Instead, as Optaris pried his sword free from Belisarius' armored leg, Belisarius drove his own sword down and into Optaris' collar. The entire length of the blade disappeared into blood and ragged flesh, and Optaris' mouth hung agape as he crumpled to the ground. My brief whoop of triumph soon turned to a gasp: Belisarius, unable to steady himself with a wounded knee, toppled forward from his mount and onto Optaris, leaving his horse Balan riderless.

"Move aside!" Uliaris snarled, hopping from his mount and weaving between the massed cataphracts.

As I began to follow, a horn sounded to the south. Its silvery notes were distinctively Roman, telling of an advancing column. Atop the heads of hundreds of Goths, I spied a flying banner in the distance, with a thin contingent of armored cavalry cresting the hill that separated us from a clear view of Rome.

"Reinforcements!" I yelled aimlessly. "Rescue Belisarius, and let's get out of here!"

Sembrouthes grumbled, and Xerxes urged caution, but I ignored both. Instead, I ordered a nearby Herulian to watch over my mount as I unslung my shield, following Uliaris as I weaved beneath the press of riders. Many brushed or bumped Uliaris as he stumbled toward Belisarius' position, yet the path he forged became easier for us to follow closely behind. As we drew closer to the front, our pace slowed, and the moans of the dying rose to a deafening crescendo. Others followed in our desperate push toward Belisarius, pressing the Goths ten paces back as men of the city watch and bucellarii alike threw themselves against the hole rendered by Optaris' death.

Yet Uliaris squeezed forward, using a short sword to cut the throat of a Goth who had been thrown to the ground and trampled by dozens of Roman boots. I did my best to step over the discarded bodies, yet as I drew closer to the fighting, that task became impossible. Instead, I found myself stomping upon stomachs and legs, many of which bore Imperial emblems, and some which even wriggled upon impact.

There was nothing I could do for those poor bastards—to stop was to jeopardize Belisarius and risk that I might be tossed to the ground as well.

Suddenly, the press of bodies loosened, and the tepid air was exchanged for blowing wind. Our front rank was ragged—few officers keeping order, with city watch and bucellarii doing so through the grinding memory of training rather than from the watchful eye of our many centurions. At my feet I discovered Optaris, his motionless corpse bleeding into the mud. Crouching, I wrested Belisarius' sword free, turning to find Uliaris standing over the strategos' lamed body.

"Reinforcements are coming, Lord!" I yelled.

Belisarius nodded. "Do what you can to break out. Signal the others behind us."

I obeyed, passing the order to the men of the interior; eventually, my words found their way to a horn carrier. As Belisarius struggled to stand, however, an approach of fresh Goths rushed toward our formation, with Optaris' replacement commander sprinting forward to capture Belisarius. Their shield wall disintegrated into a mob, yet we were little better, and counted fewer, exhausted men to withstand their assault.

"Lock shields!" Xerxes yelled behind me. "Cut and thrust, and we'll be free of this fight in moments!"

Though Belisarius' injuries appeared neither mortal nor even significant, it was impossible to move him before the Goths arrived. Instead, Uliaris pressed his shield over his commander's body, locking against Gouboulgoudou to his right and me to his left. Belisarius rose to a knee, shuffling behind our protective bulwark.

When the crash arrived, however, it struck with the power of a thousand hammers. There were simply too many of them and too few of us. Though I squared my feet and stabbed viciously at my attacker's flanks, those behind him pressed forward, stepping atop a carpet of bodies as they slammed into my shield. No amount of strength, not even from Gunderic, could have prevented what happened next.

It was not his fault, but Belisarius, injured as he was, posed a grave threat to the integrity of our shield wall. I was able to down my first attacker, jabbing the tip of my sword underneath his helmet and piercing his jaw, yet the man who followed launched his body at my shield. Unbalanced and unable to lean upon Uliaris, I fell backward into our second rank. Gouboulgoudou likewise slew two attackers, yet was struck in the hip by a Gothic dagger and pushed to the ground by the rising tide of Gothic spearmen.

"Protect Belisarius," I choked, relying upon Xerxes to aid me to my feet.

Uliaris alone stood over the strategos. Again, a Roman horn called from the south, sending the Goths into an even greater frenzy as they stabbed at Belisarius. Seated, he huddled behind his shield as Uliaris lashed at would-be attackers, tossing a francisca into the chest of a thickly bearded Gothic spearman before thrusting his sword into the guts of a younger man, where it tore at the brittle leather that covered the lad's stomach. Intestines spilled to the ground, showering Belisarius in viscera, yet Uliaris merely turned his attention to the nearest attacker.

I was too slow. With Uliaris' flanks unguarded, opportunistic Goths jabbed spears and daggers toward his sides. Roaring, I slashed at the massive Goth pressing against my shield, the man nearly reaching Gunderic's height. He snarled as my blade pierced his forearm, lathering spittle upon my nose and beard. Yet I still was unable to push toward Uliaris; this towering Goth smashed his shield into my wrist, and I screamed in pain, nearly dropping my sword.

"Support!" I called.

Sembrouthes spat, cursing the muscular Goth in his native Aksumite tongue. He batted the man's shield aside with his sword before stabbing the man's elbow, leaving both arms draining blood. With numb fingers, I tested my grip about my own sword as I pierced the Goth's chest, causing the man to erupt with vomit. Steaming bile slithered down my armor and inside my collar, and I resisted the urge to retch as the scent of half-digested wine and mutton pierced through the aroma of death and exertion.

"Disgusting," Xerxes muttered, thrusting his sword at a nearby Goth.

Still, we were stuck, pushed slowly backward by the Gothic onslaught. Farther down the line, many within the city watch were less fortunate, their officers desperately calling for reinforcements that simply did not exist. At that moment, however, I had attention only for Belisarius and Uliaris, the latter absorbing multiple wounds that bled copiously. At no point did Uliaris withdraw his shield from Belisarius' body, even allowing his leg to be skewered by a Gothic dagger rather than letting Belisarius to suffer further injury.

It was then, as our lines began to falter, that the Gothic rearguard burst asunder. Men later told me that Optaris' successor had attempted to mount a defense against the diminutive number of charging Roman cavalry, yet whether from a hail of projectiles or through underestimation of their numbers, the Romans prevailed. With them rode Bessas, his body and mount encased in thick iron scales as he gored two Goths with a well-placed thrust of his lance.

"Go!" he yelled. "I can't hold them for long!"

"Sound the horn!" I shouted behind me. "We're breaking out!"

A dozen Roman and Hunnic horns echoed within the din just as the city watch began a rout. To their credit, their persistence in the absence of their leader was unexpected, and they maintained good order until Belisarius' forces could carve an open path to the south. Lacking enough mounts, Tarmutus' survivors sprinted in groups of two and three toward the Pincian Gate, sheathing swords and tossing aside spears as they sprinted to safety. Many mounted Herulians followed them, then an irregular stream of Huns, who fired an occasional arrow to dissuade the Goths from extracting further casualties. In that chaos, I carved my way toward Belisarius.

"We only have a minute!" Sembrouthes yelled, to Belisarius as much as me. "Bessas will need to retreat in a minute!"

"It's enough time!" I insisted. "Get our mounts ready!"

As I approached Belisarius, one of the remaining Goths slashed at

Uliaris, whose sluggish parry only partially blocked the sword slash against his shoulder. I stepped between corpses to launch myself at the man and knocked him backward and stumbling over the wriggling body of his wounded kinsman. Xerxes skipped forward and thrust his sword between the man's ribs, and thus we temporarily halted the danger to Belisarius.

But only for a minute, for Bessas had begun to back away from the Gothic infantry, permitting a detachment of some two hundred Goths to march in formation toward our position. At last, I reached Belisarius, urging him to move.

"Time to go, Lord!" I said, lifting Belisarius atop his uninjured leg and steadying his body against my own.

"Not without Uliaris." Belisarius winced.

But Uliaris had collapsed, sapped of strength. His body was a ruined mess of cuts and punctures that left his armor caked in a sheen of sticky gore. Though his body rested upon the discarded limbs and torsos of the dead, Uliaris seemed not to mind—instead, skin waxy and pale, he smiled to himself.

"Get up!" I roared at him.

"I don't think so, Varus," Uliaris replied contentedly. "Take my francisca, would you?"

He could not raise an arm, so Xerxes bent down to pluck the axe from his grip and place it securely along my belt. Uliaris merely nodded.

Without warning, Belisarius leaned forward, nearly causing me to drop him. "That is an order, Uliaris! We're leaving now!"

Uliaris bit his lip as his gaze went slack. "I'm sorry, Lord. Truly, I am."

The last of Bessas' men retreated, followed thereafter by a continent of Herulians under Perenus. Though half the Hun foederati had not yet vacated the field, I spied Samur leading his survivors through our protective pocket, meaning we had mere moments before Totila's men overran our rearguard. Some city watch remained, able neither to retreat nor escape to safety, instead condemned to fight as long as their limbs could trade blows and ward off the killing strike of a Gothic spearman.

"Uliaris!" Belisarius urged, his anger exchanged for a mourning pain.

The Frank reached toward his strategos. Bloodied gloves smeared against the general's lamellar, with Uliaris incapable of raising an arm once again. His eyes fluttered, and he opened his mouth to speak.

"Forgive me, Lord," Uliaris begged, his words slurred and his skin fading to gray. "Please?"

Belisarius sucked a gust of air as he nodded. "I forgive you, Uliaris. I am indebted to you for my life."

Uliaris' body relaxed, as if freed from a ponderous pack that had been strapped to his shoulders through the years. Crushing his eyes shut for a moment, he let out a great sigh. I thought him certain to die then, but his eyes peeled open once more, sparkling with joy.

"I will tell John of all we have seen together." Uliaris smiled, seemingly unaware of his surroundings. "For a moment, it was beautiful, Rome was."

His chest rose twice more before it halted. Open eyes stopped blinking, and Uliaris' broken body stilled. Of all those I have seen killed in battle, Uliaris was the only one who embraced his end with rapturous joy. Belisarius watched in reverence, his chest heaving from grief.

"We're out of time!" Sembrouthes yelled, watching Belisarius' surviving bodyguards mount their horses. "The last of the Huns are galloping forward now. Mount up, or we'll all die here."

We obeyed. I vaulted atop Boreas, while Sembrouthes and Xerxes aided Belisarius atop Balan such that he might ride closely between us for support in the saddle. There was no choice but to leave Uliaris' body—many still-living Romans remained trapped and horseless, cut off from support and collapsing against overwhelming Gothic pressure. We galloped away as a team of Gothic spearmen drew within thirty paces of our escape, their frenetic pace only disrupted when Samur's Huns unleashed a final volley of arrows. After that, there was no serious challenge to our escape, and only a thousand paces to the Pincian Gate.

As I scanned the Aurelian Walls, I noted two Roman citizens standing guard for every healthy soldier. The walls bore evidence of a recent scaling attempt, with a hundred Gothic bodies discarded at the base of the Pincian and Flaminian Gates. I even spied an exhausted Agathias, shadowed by Haeva, whose muzzle was flecked with blood.

"Lord!" Agathias yelled excitedly to me as I crossed through the gate. "Thank God!"

"Take care of my dog!" I replied, masking my true emotions.

For although I had survived, we had suffered a horrifying defeat. Whether by the machinations of Witiges or Totila, or someone else altogether, the elite of the Roman Army had stumbled into a Gothic ambush and were nearly swallowed whole. And while we escaped, hundreds of dead lay upon the northern plains, and our granaries were none the fuller.

We had failed. And the costs would be terrible.

BARGAINING

Why Witiges did not press his advantage after our defeat was illogical. Nonsensical. Lunacy. For if he had, even with a diminished force, our wall guard would have crumbled to dust.

None can know Witiges' mind, yet if any reason exists to not challenge Belisarius' crippled hold over the Roman gates, it was perhaps the casualties wrought by Gunderic, which were indeed grotesque to behold. Sindual, leader of the remnant force of Herulians along the walls, told of Vandals eviscerating captured Goths, clattering against Gothic shield walls, and pulling men helplessly backward in sudden retreats. In lulls between clashes of shields, captive Goths were butchered like cattle, severed at the joints as they screamed and cried before their kinsmen. Indulf and Witiges, who directly opposed Gunderic, had attempted a counterattack, only to be struck by Ascum's scorpions as they drew close to the walls to intercept Gunderic's retreat.

"It was disgusting but effective," Sindual explained. "The Vandals have not gotten softer under Roman orders."

Other Gothic chieftains launched halfhearted assaults upon the northern gates, yet were repulsed by Bessas just before he gathered enough cataphracts to relieve Belisarius' trapped forces. By the late afternoon, the last vestiges of combat faded, and we were left to tend our wounds. If Witiges had pushed through the gauntlet of scorpions and wall defenders, I doubt I would be alive to tell this tale.

The constancy of the stalemate was exhausting. Of course, this was exactly what Witiges intended. While his food stores must have dwindled as much as ours, he controlled the surrounding region and enjoyed the considerable luxury of time and numbers, which allowed him to forage from the land and haul harvests from fecund provinces to the north. Witiges could afford thousands of losses and suffer no loss to his grip around Rome, while Belisarius now lacked the numbers to mount an effective sally.

The day following the ambush, Belisarius sent messengers to Witiges' camp, asking for a temporary truce so that we might retrieve the bodies of our dead. To Belisarius' surprise, our request was not only rebuffed but repudiated—Witiges allowed his chieftains to defile our dead. By the following morning, two hundred Roman heads rested atop spears that had been buried deep into the ground, with one of them bearing the proud crimson plume of Tarmutus. His fate was no surprise, yet Belisarius seethed at that wretched display and once again took up the baleful gaze that had haunted his time in Carthage.

Even then, Belisarius exercised restraint... until the crucifixions. Twenty survivors of the city watch, their clothes smeared with filth and lips crusted with dried spittle, were goaded along the Via Flaminia. Postholes had been dug and hewn logs readied, awaiting the instructions of a chieftain. It was Indulf who gave the order: each Roman handled by a half dozen Goths, his body roped against the wooden cross until his arms and legs could be nailed taut. A few died while still on the ground, yet at least half survived being raised into the air and dropped into the earthen holster, the sun burning against bare flesh.

"Monsters," Belisarius hissed.

"Barbaric," I agreed. "But Indulf does this to make us think foolishly. We must wait for a time to strike back and repay him for this."

Later, more crosses were dragged toward the former Vivarium. Rather than living, squirming survivors, however, thirty bucellarii were dragged toward the roadway, well out of range of our ballistae. Most of them were hanged, and some were butchered, yet the attending Gothic chieftain saved the most memorable punishment for the corpse of Uliaris. Nailed to a cross, his body was raised upside down, his head little more than a hand length above the dirt.

"The Apostle Petrus was tortured thus," murmured Father Petrus, speaking of his hallowed namesake.

"And I shall pray that the holy Petrus guides Uliaris to peace." Belisarius grimaced, unable to tear his eyes away from the mangled body. "Varus, have Gunderic answer Witiges' offer."

Belisarius knew what Gunderic would do but could not muster the words to describe the Vandals' love of carnage. Instead, he shut himself away for a day and a night, tended by a handful of servants and suffering through Rosamund's treatments for his leg. Later, she told me that Belisarius seemed to dream while waking, rarely paying attention to the pain of his healing skin.

Furious at Witiges' debasement of Uliaris' corpse, Gunderic was more than pleased to oblige Belisarius' cryptic order. A dozen Gothic corpses were gathered from the base of the walls, cut into sections, and launched toward the Gothic camps atop a reinforced ballista bolt. One in particular, the arrowhead wrapped inside the rotting skull of a Gothic chieftain, skittered within a dozen paces of Witiges' personal camp, yielding lewd gestures and curses from our onlooking enemy. Later, the few Gothic prisoners Gunderic had captured were paraded atop the Tiburtine Gate. Each man had his torso wrapped in chains, with onager stones attached to the end of each, and was ordered to stand at the edge of the Aurelian Walls.

As his men tied the opposite end of chain to a nearby merlon, Gunderic paced behind our Gothic prisoners, occasionally pausing as his shadow engulfed them in darkness. "If any of you shit-eating cocks moves, I'm tossing your rock over the wall. Better hope that I gave you enough chain!"

He hadn't. One by one, the wounded and exhausted Goths wavered or stumbled or downright cowered from a sudden grunt from Gunderic. Without hesitation, the stone of each offender was pushed over the walls and onto the turf facing the Gothic camps. Their bodies were dragged downward until they stopped with a jerk, swinging suspended from the falling stone and the taut links of chain wrapped atop the walls. Some struggled to their deaths, choked of air. Others died immediately, their spines snapping from the force of the blow. One man, however, screamed as the twin chains tugged his body in opposite directions, stretching his torso an impossible length. I was no stranger to cruelty, but that display was too much for me and was not what Belisarius willed.

"End it," I whispered to Gunderic.

Gunderic scoffed. "His people would sever your manhood and stuff it in your mouth. All they learn from mercy is weakness."

Ignoring Gunderic, I plucked a spear from a nearby weapons' rack and stabbed downward. It was a quick death—the spearpoint plunged through the man's neck and spine, causing his screams to halt and his body to fall limp. Only hours later did the sliced skin cause his body to finally be pulled apart, splattering gore against the walls. It was not my intention, but at least that poor bastard was already dead.

News of Samur's defeat rippled through the surviving Roman populace like an inferno. Many of the city watch had families, their wives and children sprinting between gatherings of survivors in a desperate hope that their *pater familias* had survived. Most would be devastated—including Tarmutus, over half of the watch lost their lives at the Milvian Bridge, and hundreds more from Belisarius' bucellarii and foederati. Widows wailed, their curses amplified each night by pangs of hunger. Eventually, grief transformed into rage.

It did not happen suddenly, or all at once. In those first weeks, many volunteered to replenish the watch's numbers and enlist due to the promise of plentiful silver and dependable meals. By the onset of autumn, the promise of a meal had become a more effective enticement, although those men who sought it were those either too young, too infirm, or too untrustworthy to serve had Belisarius not been desperate. The lone note of good fortune was that Tarmutus' second and successor, a Latin named Principius, had proven his valor throughout the siege and possessed a reputation for incorruptibility.

"My family claims lineage from the Furii," Principius explained to me, explaining his opposition to the Roman gangs after accepting an oath of loyalty to Justinian. "It's not so admirable to refuse bribes when you come from wealth."

"It's still better than accepting anything from the gangs," I countered.

Principius laughed. "That's true. I will keep the watch in good order as Tarmutus would want, although I cannot speak confidently of the newer recruits."

Principius, as well as our exhausted and depleted army, were soon tested as the temporary boon of grain was cut back to half rations. Autumn arrived early in Latium, and while a modest harvest had been gathered from Italy's pro-Roman south, it was simply not enough to comfortably feed so many through the coming winter, let alone beyond. Every stalk was carefully stored, and strict efforts taken to discourage theft by the city's rats. By harvest, however, few rats were brazen enough to risk discovery by clawing Roman hands, with all captured furry scavengers condemned to a household cookfire. Rats and eels—fare that few desired, yet all supped upon.

As the weather cooled and the days grew shorter, the populace's rumblings boiled into revolt. Gangs championed the cause of widows of Tarmutus' fallen watch, demanding their rations be topped off to accommodate the loss of a husband, yet Belisarius could only offer condolences and promise that those families would receive the same treatment as those of his warriors. Unsated, neighborhoods again succumbed to looting and even rampant murder, both of suspected hoarders as well as sympathizers to rival gangs. Principius identified the offenders, and I dispatched a dekarchos to lend credence to our demands for order, yet I lacked the men to regularly patrol the labyrinth of Rome's streets.

Others raised the personal banners of the deposed Pope Silverius, still enclosed in the Domus Agrippa. An Oppian gang accused Belisarius of heresy—calls that, while not overtly echoed by many of the Roman priesthood, were certainly not discouraged. Silverius, they argued, was persecuted in a manner identical to the early Christians, who had been fed to lions in the Colosseum's games. These claims were ludicrous—in my memory, Silverius was both avaricious and a glutton, with his only saintly activity being his willingness to remain quiet in the confines of his palace.

Eventually, chants for Silverius' return to power and worried audiences with Vigilius convinced Belisarius to send the deposed pope into exile, separating him from his vestiges of power. The day Silverius departed was the only time I can recall him wearing black, leaning heavily upon a cane, and offering blessings to the onlooking crowd. I wanted to bash the man's face, yet contented myself with his departure for Palmaria Island beyond the Campanian coasts, guarded by ten warriors of unimpeachable honor. I had hoped that would end such quibbles, yet as with Cassiodorus, I was wrong.

Silverius reached his destination safely, unmolested by the Gothic bands that had reduced the frequency of their raids throughout the autumn. Yet protests in the streets continued, with religious zealots mixing with the hungry, the desperate, and the lonely. At night, it became an accepted fact that Belisarius could not secure the city, his surviving and unwounded forces stretched impossibly thin between the Aurelian Walls and the Capitoline and Palatine Hills. Even our sallies against the Gothic camps slowed to one every other week, yet the Goths rarely pressed their advantage by assaulting our walls.

When those sallies did occur, the Huns rarely participated— Samur was, and remained, despondent. Though I granted him time to grieve and heal from his injuries, two months after the failed attack, I confronted him over his absence.

"My idiocy got Tarmutus killed," Samur moaned, rolling atop rotting straw in his private room. "And Uliaris. And hundreds of others..."

"It's not your fault," I assured him.

"I know!" Samur shot upright.

He reeked of sour sweat and urine; a bucket in the corner overflowed with detritus, yet Samur had refused a camp servant entry to clean. My brother had always been thin, but now it was as though flesh had melted from his bones, the effects of poor diet affecting him far worse than most in the army.

"You know?" I repeated, eyeing the room. Only his weapons had been properly maintained, with all else seeming more appropriate for a cattle pen than a residence for a lord of the army.

"It's Justinian's fault!" Samur spat. "He sent us to conquer a city of nearly a million people with the scrapings of his arse. Who is surprised that we starve and struggle? Where is that bastard now?"

My eyes widened, and I silently begged for prudence. "Samur, please. I'm an excubitor!" I whispered. "You could be flogged for saying that, and me with you."

Samur shrugged. "I've suffered and killed for that man. What has he done for me, or for you?"

"Samur—"

"Justin was wrong!" Samur yelled. "He was a sad old man who thought the Empire was something it plainly is not. You follow the ravings of a madman, Varus!"

I slapped him. Not hard, but enough to leave a mark upon his cheek. Samur spat again and touched the forming bruise, his eyes fixed upon me. "I know that is hard for you to accept. But deep in your thoughts, you know it too. Justin, Liberius, even Godilas. All old men chasing dreams." He turned to face the wall, his eyes locked upon a burning taper. "What about my dreams? I never wanted to kill anyone, just to be free. The Empire made me a killer and told me to slaughter thousands, and I have. But they would toss me aside at the slightest inconvenience, or for the slightest profit. Me, you, the entire fucking army."

"You're wrong," I insisted. "And I'll give you another day to wallow, but I need you on the walls. My family, and yours, depend upon you."

Samur nodded. "Blood and friends matter. But fuck Justinian and anyone who licks his arse."

As always, I allowed Samur's venom to wash past me, for he had plenty of good reason to hold a grudge against the Imperial elite. Yet a twinge of worry nestled in my heart, resurrecting concerns that Rosamund had raised on our sea voyage from Septem to Carthage. She had warned me that something within Samur was broken—a concern I had dismissed at the time. Now, however, I wish I better understood the hatred that Samur nurtured. For above all things, and beneath all else, he was my brother, whom I loved.

Samur's eventual return to duty was marked by a spike in violence, both outside the walls and within. From the Goths' ranks, one of Witiges' warlords launched an assault along the Tiburtine Gate, yet a mixture of Hunnic arrows, pounding siege engines, and a ravenous Vandal thirst for blood repulsed their ladders. Remnants of Gothic corpses still lingered in the chains along the walls, with carrion birds tearing strips of flesh into their gullets to the point where flight became difficult. The engorged birds were occasionally hunted for their meat, although most eschewed the prey that still held human remains in their bellies. Overall, the Gothic attack had been surprisingly weaker than we expected, with many of the Goths appearing just as sunken-eyed and underfed as those throughout the city of Rome.

Inside the city, however, the arbiters of destruction had far greater success than any Gothic assault. Isolated episodes of looting and murder now consumed entire city streets, their culprits generally able to flee before Principius' watch could respond. At my order, any man engaging in nighttime disorder was punished by hanging, and within weeks, the forum's gallows were in use throughout the day and night. Yet still, the gangs grew bolder, amplified by members of the general population who gradually joined in the lawlessness in pursuit of material gain, a scrap of food, or simply the ability to unleash their frustrations after a half year of siege.

These smoldering embers broke into a veritable conflagration when our grain shipment from Mauretania missed its intended arrival date. Fearful of Gothic attacks, Belisarius ordered the wall sentries doubled, leaving fewer men to control the hills and streets of the interior. Through Principius, I did all I could to maintain order, regretting my judgment over so many who had brought harm to the city. I ignored the pleas of the family of a man who had slain his neighbor, an elderly woman, from no provocation or right within either Rome's ancient Twelve Tables or the newer codex unfurled by Justinian's ministers. Nevertheless, the man's wife pled for clemency.

"We were starving, and the old hag wouldn't share her food!" his soon-to-be widow insisted. "Belisarius punishes hoarders, and she had stockpiled a month of rations!"

"He committed murder," I answered coldly. "He snuck into her room in the night and cut her throat like a sneak-thief. Hoarders will be punished, but by the law, not by the hands of any citizen alone."

In the preceding months, judgment for those crimes would have been accepted with minimal public concern and no outward resentment—especially if the criminal's guilt was beyond doubt, such as this instance where the man confessed to his crimes absent any torture. During the autumn months of the siege, however, that unquestioned trust of Roman law had been utterly shattered as the Roman plebeians glommed onto their various neighborhoods, threatening violent resistance from any added burden or tax that Belisarius might levy. A hundred of the condemned man's friends vouched for his intentions, cursing the victim as a miserly spinster who greedily snatched up rations she neither needed nor deserved. I did not flinch in my duty, but as the man's neck snapped as he was hanged, the Roman forum erupted into chaos.

Compared to the Nika Riots, the breakdown of order in the forum was little more than a tantrum. True, there was damage: stalls adjoining the forum were burned, and scattered looting evolved into organized theft of government supply depots. Roving bands of men armed with spike-riddled clubs roamed the once-busy streets, drunk on pilfered wine and the sudden infusion of authority that my subsequent retreat had afforded them. Nevertheless, our multiple barracks remained untouched, and the zealously guarded granaries experienced little more than crude words and an occasional drunkard urinating upon the walls. Many other Romans, terrified by the breakdown of security, appealed to Belisarius for aid and temporarily gathered within the complex of residences that housed the elite of the army and Justinian's ministers.

The Domus Augustana was among them, although our location near the forum left us in a precarious position. Belisarius and I split duties—he led the barracks along the northern walls and I oversaw the residential core—and ordered all our men to avoid bloodshed unless violence was initiated by the mob.

For two days, most gangs left the Domus and other patrician residences alone, unwilling to challenge the dozens of frustrated and bored spearmen positioned at each entrance. Only once, at night three days after the forum's descent into chaos, did the mob rush our defenses, screaming hatred and tossing stones and torches amidst the chilly autumn evening. Yet we were prepared, having learned the lessons of Hypatius' failed revolt well, and cut down those who sought to push into the Domus with merciless efficiency. Between the labors of the Aksumites, Xerxes, and various Herulian volunteers and household attendants, no rioter even crossed the threshold into the Domus' enclosed roof.

It was then that I gained a firsthand view of Haeva's capacity for violence. She was goaded toward an unruly Roman who bore the physique of a retired yet still muscular warrior. Tall and burly, he toppled an Aksumite to the ground, raising a club to bash his enemy's skull. Yet before any Aksumite spear could prevent the slaying, Haeva weaved between our spearmen, snarling as she bulled the man over and latched onto his exposed throat. The Roman attempted to push Haeva away, yet this only encouraged her to snap more aggressively, wriggling at the man's neck as she would a cow bone. The sight of such an unusual and unsettling death discouraged others from charging into our formation, while Haeva happily retreated after called upon by Shimon.

"Sweet Jesus," I muttered to Shimon and Agathias. "When did she learn to do that?"

"Cephalas' work," Shimon replied. "Why Theudis would willingly give you this dog as gift is nonsensical, because I've never seen a better killer."

Agathias nodded. "You wouldn't know it from how she acts with the children. They hop on her back like she's a horse, and she merely sighs and rolls over."

"War dogs," I muttered. "If only I had a thousand of them. Keep Haeva safe—she might not be a puppy anymore, but she has little experience in a fight. This is another thing we owe Cephalas gratitude for."

Shimon straightened. "Of course, Lord."

"Yes, Lord," Agathias echoed. "I'll make sure she is cleaned afterward."

After three days of anarchy, Belisarius and I slowly regained control of the city. First was the forum—its broad expanse and marketplace populated with many hundreds of Romans who watched in horror as the mob destroyed their livelihoods. After the forum, we cleared both the Pincian and Capitoline Hills before charging through Campus Martius. We proceeded slowly, taking a full day to sweep each target and be careful to leave each position along the walls adequately guarded. We even offered clemency to any innocent of harm to another person's body. Those initial locations came under our sway easily, although the Aventine and eastern hills were far more reluctant.

The Aventine in particular housed many of the city's gang leaders, the few men remaining in the city who somehow maintained a portly physique despite the general deprivations of the city's residents, and shared their stolen bounty with loyalists. Most of the Aventine was taken without significant destruction, but two popinae and one meeting hall were put to the torch after we encountered staunch resistance. Here, no mercy was granted—any known associate of the Roman gangs who resisted was gored by our spears. Those few who surrendered were marched back to the forum, their smallest fingers and the tip of their nose severed to mark them as known deviants who should not be granted mercy if caught committing a crime in the future.

The riots ended less from our brute force and more from their own lack of vitality—though petty crime continued unabated in the months ahead, most Romans were content to return to their homes, realizing that the defeated gangs were no more capable of filling their bellies than Belisarius was.

All of us, me included, anticipated and feared a Gothic assault as the rioters expended their anger. Yet shortly after the city was put to rights, Witiges did what no one, not even Liberius, expected. They sued for peace.

At first, I believed the sudden frenzy of movement amidst Witiges' camp was the early warnings of a looming assault, yet the Gothic king merely departed for the Via Flaminia, stopping just beyond the range of our ballistae. Once there, a hundred attendants erected a tent near the gate, raising banners and ferrying benches into the tent's enclosure. With that complete, a messenger mounted, both unarmed and unarmored, a horse and galloped just beneath our walls for Belisarius' attention.

"King Witiges would entreat Belisarius and any other leaders of the Romans," the messenger shouted. "Bring whatever weapons you wish. My master awaits you without any."

Belisarius agreed, although he heeded my wariness of the Goths' intent. "Mundus trusted agents of Witiges in Salona," I reminded him. "He even ate their bread and drank their wine."

"I have little faith in Witiges, but if there's a chance to end the fighting, we must try," Belisarius answered. "Gather whoever you deem necessary, but make sure all understand that no violence will be initiated by us."

As part of Belisarius' guard, I joined ten of his bucellarii, as did Xerxes, Sembrouthes, and the Aksumites. Liberius, too, came amongst the attendants, nursing a cough that rattled his lungs with coarse phlegm.

"Damned cold," he muttered. "This winter will probably kill me."

"Nonsense, Lord." Privately, I was uncomfortable with the thought of the man's mortality. He had joked of his decrepitude since my youth, yet rarely showed any true weakness or infirmity. He, along with Petrus, were the only fathers I still possessed in this life, and the thought that one might be taken from me fostered an implacable, if silent, dread.

More unsettling was my inability to anticipate Witiges' intentions. As we entered his presence, my hand rested upon my sword belt, and I never allowed Belisarius to move more than three steps away from me. Witiges' retinue was far fewer in number than ours, including two chieftains and three scribes, and was notably absent Indulf.

"Please sit," Witiges said, gesturing to the benches across from him. Wine was poured into two dozen goblets, offered from Witiges' own bounty.

"Lord Belisarius has little appetite for poison," I snapped.

Witiges shrugged. He rose from his seat, plucked a goblet from the table, and drained it in three noisy gulps. He then selected another, repeated the action, and nodded to me. "I am not Indulf, Lord Varus. But neither am I the invader here. You are gathered to put an end to this senseless war and end the suffering of millions."

Belisarius turned to Liberius, inviting the old minister to speak.

"Wise men say that peace is preferable to the suffering of war," Liberius began, pausing to hack into his sleeve. "But usually, they only make such statements after having won their war. This is your gathering, King Witiges. What are your terms?"

With a snap of his fingers, Witiges ordered forth a servant who placed bread upon the table. My stomach growled at the offering, and though I was tempted to seize the crust, again I refused, as did every other Roman present. Unfazed, Witiges gnawed at the hardened loaf and tossed others to his attendants. All his men were curiously thin— possibly thinner than many in Rome—and they gorged on the meager offering like dogs fighting over scraps of chicken in an army camp.

"Abandon Rome within a week, and we will recognize your claim over Sicily forever," Witiges declared. "It's a rich province that you can squeeze to pay for Justinian's folly, and will help you secure Carthage. I hear of your rebellions there, and you'll need Sicily to avoid meeting the same fate as the detestable Gelimer."

Though Liberius seemed ready to counter, Belisarius laughed, silencing all and bringing Witiges to raise an eyebrow. "Yes," Belisarius said at last, "and we permit the Goths to have the whole of Britain, which is much larger than Sicily and was subject to the Romans in early times."

"Britain is not yours to give," one of Witiges' chieftains, an older man named Widin, rasped.

"Nor is Sicily yours," Belisarius replied.

Witiges nodded. "Then we shall add Neapolis and Campania, and all the southern provinces. Everything that you have safely held might be yours. Say that you agree, and we may part in peace this very day."

It was tempting. Rome was proving too vast a city for us to hold, and the temporary peace within the city would eventually flare again into unrest if food remained scarce. Latium as a whole was difficult to defend, and bordered by powerful Gothic fortress cities. More, the war would end, and we could all go home. It was something to be desired. However, though I had been a fool many times before, I was not naïve enough to believe that the offer was one we could accept.

"Rome is for Romans," Belisarius replied. "Though I grieve for all who suffer, the Emperor has commanded me to take and hold the Eternal City. Until he changes his mind, my oath remains."

"Foolish." Witiges sighed. "Pointless. But I do not blame you, General Belisarius. You and I are the same: a hopeless idealist, caught in the ambitions of a single greedy man. But I cannot willingly surrender Rome, not when I outnumber you five to one. I will give you time to reconsider, for when you are hungry and exhausted, your mind may shift to more comfortable ends."

"Perhaps," Belisarius answered. "In the meantime, I ask that you grant me possession of the bodies of my men who perished outside the Milvian Gate."

Frowning, Witiges turned to his chieftain. They exchanged words in Gothic, not bothering to hush their exchange, before Witiges nodded.

"You may have their bones as my gift," Witiges answered. "I would ask the same of you. We need not be savages, you and I."

"Agreed." Belisarius nodded. "I will retrieve my men today, and you shall take yours tomorrow. Fighting can resume after."

Even without a cessation of the siege, the mere offer for terms of a conclusion, even one we would not accept, gave Belisarius new life, an aura of confidence returning to his every step. The exchange of corpses proceeded without issue—the Goths claimed their dead, and we received those who had been taken to the Gothic camps. I commanded a banda to retrieve the bodies of our dead beside the Milvian Bridge, requiring an entire day's labor to load hundreds of bodies onto ox wagons and haul them back to Rome.

By then, so many weeks after the ambush, their remains had shriveled beneath the sun or been peeled and consumed by any number of carrion feeders. Few were identifiable—the bodies of Tarmutus and Uliaris were exceptions. Pyres were again erected in the forum; Tarmutus and Uliaris both were lain upon individual platforms as leaders within the army. Belisarius gave Tarmutus' oration first, with the leadership of the city watch bearing torches and saluting their fallen commander as he was overtaken by fire.

Belisarius personally cared for Uliaris' body, or at least the bones and scraps of flesh that remained after his crucifixion. Brittle arms and immobile legs were encased in mail, and a sword wrapped within his bony fingers, with Belisarius aided by Gouboulgoudou and ten other bucellarii. Remembering the francisca at my belt, I pried it free from its fastenings and offered it to Belisarius.

He declined. "Uliaris wanted you to have it. You were a far better master to him than I was."

The depth of his grief surprised me. Since Carthage, Belisarius had only raised Uliaris' name in anger, ordering him away from his presence and eventually separated from the bucellarii. "He loved you, Lord."

"I know," Belisarius answered. "John would be disappointed with me for how I've treated Uliaris. On my oath, I will do better."

What remained of Uliaris disappeared as the dried kindling caught flame from Belisarius' torch. Turning to his bucellarii, he offered a final remark on the memory of a warrior vaunted in skill as well as honor.

"Uliaris was the first leader of my bodyguards," Belisarius declared. "And I treated him poorly. That sin will not be washed easily, and will be a burden I carry in all that I do. Uliaris gave everything in service to the Emperor and his brothers in the army. As long as I live, he shall never be forgotten, and we shall not look upon another like him again."

Uliaris would have liked that. At the end, I think that's what gave him peace—he had fulfilled his oath to Belisarius, and now Belisarius finally acknowledged Uliaris' sacrifice. For most warriors, and perhaps myself, it was a more fulfilling death than we dared hope for. Though he was my household guardsman, Uliaris was also my friend, and like so many others, I miss him to this day.

"Goodbye, Uliaris," I muttered over the flames. "Tell John, and Cephalas, and all the others to save a place for me."

I have no doubt that he heard me.

THE FEAST OF THE NATIVITY,
THE SUN OF RIGHTEOUSNESS

The harvest months progressed with little violence. Occasionally, a Gothic scout would be feathered with Roman arrows or a Roman outrider would depart and never return. Beyond that, we Romans gazed warily upon the Gothic camps, yet Witiges and his chieftains appeared happy to rest, to await their harvest, and save their strength as Rome withered in its stone-lined desert.

Not that our own fortunes did not turn for the better. Valerian brokered the transfer of grain from a Sicily harvest that, while not bountiful, bolstered what meager stores we had mustered from Campania and Calabria. Shipments of grain continued until Rome suffered its first snow — enough to stave off the worst of starvation, although Belisarius continued the allotment of half rations so that our newfound largesse might stretch through the coming winter.

We guarded Rome's walls, we patrolled its streets, and otherwise were equally frustrated and relieved by the chunks of time not filled by duties. Belisarius and I wrote requests to Imperial cities and informed the Emperor and Empress of our plight, yet on most days, both of us joined our men at meals. Ample portions of diluted wine stymied our grumbling stomachs, and as the daylight faded toward winter night, we sang and shared tales in Rome's popinae.

Only once did Belisarius temporarily lift the rations restriction, and we were given ample notice for the occasion. Light snow blanketed the early days of December as the last of the harvest's meager bounty was collected and stored, and it was then, in the darkest days of the year, that Belisarius commanded that all would offer celebrations for the Feast of the Nativity—the birth of Jesus, the Sun of Righteousness.

To call what Belisarius mustered as a feast is laughable. Though we offered the Roman populace a three-day respite from half rations, many stored their additional fare for later days, and the kitchens of the Domus Augustana had pitifully little to mold and bake. By the day of the feast, after prayers had been offered, the meal Belisarius provided had no chance to adequately fill our bellies.

Nevertheless, it was wonderful.

In the Domus, our cooks baked small cakes for the children, while mouthwatering strips of venison from a freshly caught deer were brushed with fine salts and roasted on a spit. With Shimon's help, I delivered a heaping tray of tiny cakes and savory meat, portioned perfectly so that each of the children shared in the temporary bounty. So, too, did Mariya and the broader household, the extra morsels marked by prayers of thanks for the arrival of the Lord.

After, as dusk settled, Belisarius summoned his officers. Baked bread and other prepared foods were hauled from the Domus Augustana into the Colosseum, where Belisarius had prepared a sweeping tent and bountiful fires placed along the sands. Torches lined the empty stadium as a hundred of Belisarius' longstanding senior officers gathered in a vast square of joined wooden tables and benches, with Belisarius seated at the head.

Of all those in our midst, Rosamund was the only woman invited to the feast—a fact that doubled the awkwardness I felt as we walked together into the Colosseum. I said nothing as we were followed by Xerxes and Perenus, with several of the Herulians following behind. Clad in their heavy furs, both Sinnion and Aigan had arrived before me, although Samur was not with them.

"Your brother is still hurt?" Perenus asked.

"Perhaps his pride, but the leg is mostly healed," I replied. "He blames himself for the Milvian Bridge debacle."

"He makes it worse upon himself by shunning his friends,"

Xerxes observed. "Failure can be tolerated, but only if you show a willingness to improve for the future."

I let the subject drop, for although I was concerned for Samur, nothing good would have come from speculating upon his absence. Instead, I guided my companions into Belisarius' feasting tent and toward an empty section of table, where I withdrew my cloak and seated myself between Rosamund and Xerxes.

Though the food prepared for Belisarius' gathering might have been simple, the decoration that Belisarius' agents prepared across Rome was nothing less than extravagant. Imperial banners bedecked every roadway, while the twin portraits of Justinian and Theodora were raised atop the larger of Rome's buildings. The Colosseum's interior, like all the major monuments and columns from the Campus Martius to the Palatine Hill, was bedecked in verdant holly, its fragrance both refreshing and piercing. All about us was a celebration of light amidst the darkest days of winter, offering promise that brighter days remained ahead. As others arrived, my companions grabbed silver goblets of wine or ventured near one of the three bonfires Belisarius prepared around the Colosseum's expanse, leaving me with a happy Petrus and a dour Liberius.

"The Christians stole most of this from the pagans," Liberius muttered.

Petrus rolled his eyes as if he wished Liberius silent, yet I found my cantankerous teacher had piqued my interest. "Truly, Lord?"

"A good amount," Liberius affirmed. "Take all this wretched holly. Pagan revelers would gift wreaths to one another for Saturnalia. "

"Because the early Christians needed to protect themselves against vengeful Roman ministers in those days," Petrus added. "The Nativity is a celebration of the birth of our Lord and the promise of salvation."

"And a copy of the old Winter Solstice," Liberius countered. "Gift giving, merriment, drunkenness, all celebrations of Saturn."

Petrus chuckled. "My friend, sometimes I believe you are miserable by choice. This is a blessed day, and I intend to keep it, for I know not whether we shall live long enough to share another."

More talk of mortality, although whether it be from age or illness, or the threat of violent death amidst the siege, I could not know. Liberius tossed his head about, considering Petrus' words, before returning his gaze.

"You are correct, old friend." He nodded. "I am grateful to be here. And I'm grateful for those who made it possible."

Similar sentiment filled Belisarius' feast. Many present were not Christians, or at least had little interest in observing Christian traditions. However, all gaped at the display of fire and celebration as silver goblets were presented to each guest, with the only instruction being to abstain from consuming them until Belisarius had spoken his piece. Even Rosamund, the most notorious pagan in Belisarius' army, rose to pace about the Colosseum's sands, running her fingers through the holly.

"If only Rome was as happy as this every day," she murmured.

As the final guests arrived, Belisarius' servants called for all present to assemble along the arrayed benches. We returned to our seats along the arrayed benches. After, there was silence, with only a light snow, blowing wind, and crackling fires filling the void. Father Petrus was first to stand, offering a brief prayer in thanks to the Divine Lord, the Sun of Righteousness, who pierced the veil of death and gave all hope of salvation in the world to come. After finishing, Petrus scurried back to his seat. Visibly pleased, Belisarius stood next and leaned over his table as if to meet the eyes of each guest. After a minute, he began.

"Friends, the Feast of the Nativity is a time to celebrate the birth of Christ, but also to swear by the notion that the sun shall come again. In darkness, we all have suffered, both in holding this city for nearly a year, and equally from all the hardship and loss that came throughout our journeys together."

Of all that made this gathering remarkable, I noted that no man offered a bawdy interjection, nor spoke words of encouragement. I, too, was still, hanging on Belisarius' words with a thirst to understand what he intended to do next. Belisarius paused for a time and then obliged.

"As I believe in God, I know that the light will shine upon us again, not long from now. The sacrifices of so many of our friends will live forever, not merely in that they stood for the Empire, but that they withstood impossible odds against terrible foes and were undaunted."

His voice was almost melancholy, yet it possessed all its strength, a faint echo ringing from the Colosseum's walls and amplifying each word before he trailed off. Even Liberius sat motionless, his face as still as the marble statues of so many Roman gods and emperors that lined the city's monuments.

"But above all else, I am grateful to be here with you. No lord has been better served than I. It is I who am the most fortunate of all here, for I may count all of you as friends. As we give thanks to the birth of our Savior, I yield all that I have in gratitude to you, my legends. You shall all live forever."

His voice wavered at the end as he reached down, seizing a goblet from the table and raising it high into the air. Finally, we countered Belisarius' speech, a rattling thunder of hope and love that had been difficult to find in the deprivations of the siege.

"Belisarius Victor!" I yelled, slamming a fist upon the table.

"Belisarius! Belisarius! Belisarius!" The benches thrummed and rumbled, threatening to tip their contents onto the sands as we pounded fists and kicked our boots at the wood. None did, though if they had, we would not have cared.

"Belisarius! Belisarius! Belisarius!" Both Petrus and Liberius joined the chant, and even Rosamund grinned and shouted the name of my lord. The chanting continued for several minutes, unflagging, yet a flicker of recognition cautioned me to pause, glancing over at one of the Colosseum's entrances.

Samur. He stood in full armor, wrapped in the same furs as Sinnion and Aigan. Unlike our gathering, no chants or celebration emanated from his throat. Instead, he stared at me, his cheeks gaunt and eyes hollow from lack of sleep. I gestured for him to join me, and though he nodded in acknowledgment, he disappeared into the Colosseum's hallways, not to return that evening.

Rosamund was the only other person to see Samur, although she did not mention him. Samur's mourning was the lone blight upon the evening; otherwise, camaraderie and rich wine masked any unhappiness at the simple and insufficient fare provided for Belisarius' feast. Though I wished that my family could share in that moment, I basked in the company of those who had bled alongside me and temporarily abandoned my thoughts of hunger, of financial worries, and of the ever-present threat of annihilation by the Goths. Most of all, I shared in Belisarius' delight, remembering the man's youth at a time when he was effortlessly content and difficult to anger.

In the weeks that followed, winter raged throughout Latium. Blowing snow rose knee deep, while the lesser streets between Rome's hills were nigh impassible. I commissioned spade-bearing teams to shovel the more important thoroughfares, yet beyond this, there was no other battle to be fought. The Goths gathered in their camps, and we in our more comfortable enclosures, embraced by the promise of vigorous fires and dry beds.

As the slurry abated, Belisarius ordered the continuation of sallies, albeit with fewer men to accommodate our losses at the Milvian Bridge. Samur, who rejoined Belisarius' war councils the day after the Nativity, volunteered to strike out first. His group took no casualties but delivered little punishment toward the enemy, even though the defense was hindered by wet snow.

"Your brother is too cautious," Xerxes privately warned me that evening. "It happens to all leaders who see substantial fighting over time, but it's dangerous nonetheless. Even if he thinks he's preserving his men, his movements are predictable. Any Goth with a mind for strategy could ambush and surround him."

"Give Samur time," I replied, unsure how to rectify the concern. All I knew was that I could not undercut his authority—that would only earn his resentment and amplify the guilt that dogged his every action.

We struggled through winter the same as we had during the harvest season—inside the walls, starvation was a constant threat, while outside, we harried the Gothic camps, their foragers, and their hunters. Only then did I understand the extent of Witiges' deprivations, for like us, the Goths suffered debilitating lapses in their diet. Gothic hunting parties ranged deep into Campania in search of prey, while others hauled berries from the interior mountains and fish from the coastline to supplement their pitiful allotment of bread.

On one raid, I slew a man who lacked the vigor to raise his shield, instead simply accepting my arrow into his chest and falling serenely onto the half-frozen mud. Later, inspecting my victim, I discovered his ribs protruding through fatless flesh—a characteristic shared by others in that hunting party, and even men of the Gothic camps. Though we and the Romans suffered, the knowledge that Witiges shared in that gnawing pain, and perhaps suffered worse, was morbidly heartening.

Two months after the Nativity, the Goths finally mustered a proper assault. It began with a revival of their platform-mounted ballistae, which launched iron-tipped bolts toward our guard towers and clattered against our walls. Many thousands participated in the storm, yet they controlled only one ram and no siege towers, with most of the thousands of Goths bearing hastily crafted ladders that reached the height of the Aurelian Walls.

It would be a disservice to Witiges to contend that the assault was insignificant, for it cost Belisarius two hundred veteran spearmen, yet the attack was definitively turned back through unceasing fire from our archers and siege engines. At one point, Indulf and Totila appeared to gain traction near the now-walled-off Vivarium, yet Perenus mounted a savage counter that drove the Gothic swordsmen from the battlements and discouraged further ladder climbers from attempting to seize that portion of wall. The fighting ended well before dusk, allowing corpse bearers enough time to transport our dead as Rosamund and other healers fought to keep our wounded in the realm of the living.

We inflicted two Goth deaths for every slain Roman, yet our numbers were already strained from losses taken at the Milvian Bridge. Again, we forwent street patrols throughout Rome. Yet rather than foster complete anarchy, Belisarius equipped representatives of each hill to keep peace throughout their streets and businesses, capable of calling upon Principius and the city watch when the threat of violence rose. That and the overall neutering of Rome's gangs allowed us to maintain an uneasy quiet, although petty theft and nightly reports of looting remained a common entry in our morning reports to Belisarius.

Two weeks after the failed Gothic attack, Belisarius secretly voiced interest in accepting Witiges' onetime offer. "The men are exhausted," he explained to me. "We are too few to allow for more than a shift away from duty stations. Even if I could somehow fortify their diets, fatigue will ruin our men more than any disease or enemy spear. If we are going to negotiate with the Goths, it must be while we still have a semblance of an army."

"How long do you think the men can hold out?" I asked, exhaustion rife within my bones. "None voice frustrations with you, Lord."

"They're loyal, and I love them for that," Belisarius replied. "But another month, and we'll see rampant illness from lack of sleep. In two, many will struggle to lift a spear in defense of the city. We won't see another planting season at this rate."

Though I concurred with Belisarius' assessment, one result of his negotiations was unacceptable to bear. "You would surrender Rome?"

"If there is no choice, I would preserve our army," Belisarius countered. "If given the choice, Justinian would do the same, were he here. If he calls for my head, then I shall surrender myself. But I will not wait another month for us to crawl to Witiges, watching deserters slip through our lines as we beg for mercy."

Beyond this conversation, Belisarius gave no indication that a diplomatic surrender was imminent. As far as I am aware, he did not seek the guidance of Liberius or any other minister, nor did he display any outward sadness or regret. Instead, we proceeded each day by refortifying damaged portions of wall, fletching arrows, forging blades, repairing all manner of armor, and sending scouts and raiding parties to the surrounding camps. We shivered in the cold but did not freeze, and though we panged from want of nourishment, we did not starve. Yet implicitly, though the thought of conferring Rome back to the Goths felt abhorrent, I yearned to pluck my family free of our current hell.

Everything changed with the arrival of Februarius, and the promise that the worst of winter would soon end. Our granaries drew low, holding only another month's rations, although morale amongst Belisarius' men remained high in the aftermath of withstanding the recent Gothic assault. It was then, as Belisarius and I confidentially crafted the terms of Rome's return to Witiges, that a messenger arrived from the southwest. A younger lad, he was checked for weapons before being admitted into Belisarius' presence, bowing to the strategos and offering me a curt nod.

"What concerns you, citizen?" Belisarius asked, ordering the man to rise. From his own hand, Belisarius proffered a cup of diluted wine, granting the messenger time to recuperate from an extensive gallop.

"Roman ships took harbor in Ostia, Lord," the lad remarked breathlessly. "The Goths abandoned the harbor and town. It must have been a hundred boats, as grand as any I have seen."

"Roman?" I questioned. "You're certain?"

The lad nodded. "They bore the Emperor's sigil."

At that, hope kindled within me, but also dread. My first thoughts were of Germanus, defeated in Carthage and absconding to Rome with what broken forces remained from his wars against the Mauri. Just as swiftly, fears permeated my mind that Indulf had seized Roman ships from his massacre at Salona, for several transports and one dromon had disappeared from our records in the aftermath. The likelihood that this arrival was of grim tidings, or a Gothic attempt at deception, dampened my expectations. Belisarius, too, was skeptical.

"Send a scouting party," he ordered me. "Discern what language they speak with one another, and if any faces might be recognized. Our gates remain closed to all except those who can prove their identity."

I obeyed, conveying that responsibility to Samur and his Huns. They disappeared just as the southernmost Gothic camps mustered their men into fast squares of spears, Suevi bowmen, and small clumps of light cavalry. From the blocked Praenestine Gate, I commanded our officers to prepare for an assault, knowing well that whatever came from Ostia would only add to our confusion and likely aid in our defeat. Of this, I was convinced.

Yet my conviction waned when two of the Gothic camps emptied of their men. In a northward march, they merged with four other forts Witiges had erected on the eastern bank of the Tiber, leaving a filthy yet depopulated husk of their two camps behind.

"It has no logic to it," Xerxes whispered to me. "Are they massing for an attack?"

"Could be," I said. "Or maybe they're leaving?"

Xerxes snorted. "We aren't that lucky."

But despite the movements of thousands of men, the Goths did not press our walls. As the final stragglers entered Witiges' camps, I heard the first resounding horn from the southwest, faded yet discernible atop the southeastern edge of the Aurelian Walls.

"Romans arriving," Xerxes said, his eyes widening.

"Await confirmation." I was unwilling to believe anything other than ambush.

Yet when Samur galloped back to Rome's southern gates, our world trembled. I rushed to the Asinarian Gate, finding my brother helmetless and beaming as he demanded the gates to open.

"Varus!" he called, waiving his arm in a wild loop. "You'll never believe this!"

Minutes later, Belisarius galloped below, climbing the walls as he looked down upon Samur. "What news?"

"Look, Lord!" Samur grinned. "We are saved!"

Roman horns blared again. The pace of the newcomer's march increased, with rumbling thunder suggesting that many were mounted. Belisarius and I stood wordless for an hour, watching the Roman procession come into view, the Imperial Chi-Rho mixing with banners of Belisarius' wolf. And then, squinting, I discerned the figure of a woman, dark-haired and bedecked in a sapphire dress, cantering before the army. She rose a hand, and her bodyguard separated from the main Roman column as they closed their distance to the Asinarian Gate.

"Theodora?" I questioned, my eyes fixed upon the figure.

"No," Belisarius replied. He seemed to know the leader of his rescue, yet gave no voice to her identity for several minutes.

At last, she and her guard arrived at the base of the walls, and like Samur, I wanted to laugh—both from the absurdity of our rescuer, as much as from giddiness that fortune, at last, smiled upon us.

"Strategos!" Antonina shouted, her chest heaving with the effort of her ride. "You have petitioned Constantinople, and Constantinople answers!"

Guards along the gate fell to their knees, thanking God for deliverance. I would be a liar if I said I did not join them, shouting aimlessly toward the heavens. Yet I stole a glance toward Belisarius as celebration swelled throughout the nearby expanse of wall. Belisarius did not cheer.

Yet in his silence, he smiled, looking down upon an exultant Antonina as hundreds of Romans filed in behind her. At last, clasping his hands together, he gave the order.

"Open the gates!"

ARIMINIUM

Until her arrival, I had heard little of Antonina since leaving her in my apartments in Constantinople. Occasionally, Mariya received reports of household happenings: that one of our servants had become pregnant or absconded from Constantinople, or that purchases of grain or fruit had been made to offset consumption. Inane activities that I affirmed with a grunt but no further thought.

What I had not realized was that Antonina had received all our pleas for aid. She trekked daily to the Imperial Palace, petitioning whatever minister, priest, or even the lowly clerks that were willing to grant an audience. Occasionally, Antonina was granted entry into the Empress' private chambers, yet still—perhaps due to being Belisarius' estranged wife—she had little success in garnering the funds or permission needed to raise a relief force to send to Italy. Until her departure, Justinian did not permit Antonina into his presence, communicating only through written letters filtered past the Emperor's scribes via Theodora.

Her strategy changed after the Feast of Salona and the subsequent return of Constantinianus from Dyrrachium to Constantinople. As one of the few survivors of Indulf's massacre, Constantinianus was disgraced, with many of Constantinople's patricians believing the young officer had abandoned Mundus or had even been complicit in his death. Yet even Justinian understood the desperate need to rebuild the fallen Thracian Army, with Constantinianus as one of the few trained officers remaining in his employ. Antonina sought out Constantinianus and gained him entry to the Imperial court, and while I cannot know the contents of Theodora's schemes, the result was that the Empress, my oath keeper, secured Justinian's permission to raise a new army for the twin purposes of supporting Belisarius and retaking the Dalmatian provinces and towns that Mundus had nearly grasped.

Together, Theodora and Antonina recruited from those provinces less affected by the veiled sun, the subsequent famine, and the recurring threat of war. At Narses' suggestion, they raised three thousand Isaurian spearmen, two thousand younger Thracians, and a further thousand Heruli—all of whom were inexperienced, yet capable of wielding sword and spear in the name of the Emperor. The Thracians and Herulians gathered in Moesia to prepare for Constantinianus' thrust northward, while Antonina and Constantinianus guided their Isaurians first onto one of a hundred Roman transports, and later into the vaunted harbors of Ostia.

It required a full afternoon to parade Antonina's forces through Rome's southern gates, and two days thereafter to unpack their equipment and supplies. Nevertheless, it was apparent from the moment she passed through the Asinarian Gate that Antonina's host had turned the tide in the Great Siege of Rome.

"Lord Varus," Antonina greeted me as she entered Rome. Belisarius stood beside me, dumbstruck. "I thank you for keeping my husband safe this past year."

I offered a nod. "It is my honor, Lady."

Antonina smiled. "My daughter is with the baggage train. I would like to present her to my husband and speak with him privately. Would you arrange quarters where we might sleep and Joannina consort with friends? She misses Zenobia so."

I saluted and informed her that rooms in the Domus Augustana would be readied for her use. Happy, Antonina called for her baggage train, summoning her young daughter, who appeared awed at the enormity of the Roman walls. She did not recognize Belisarius at first, yet Antonina navigated any awkwardness.

"You remember your father!" Antonina teased. "Now, as Lord Varus has kindly allowed, we shall speak with him of the Emperor's will."

Belisarius shot me a bewildered glance but nodded. His horse was summoned, and Joannina placed upon the saddle with him before the three of them trotted toward the Domus. As before, the last I saw of Belisarius that day was a broad smile, albeit with few words.

"Well, that was unexpected." Samur chuckled. "It looks like Belisarius will take Antonina back."

"I would wager so," I replied. "I don't think he ever wished for a different outcome. See that they are not disturbed, and I will organize her army."

Where Antonina displayed calm confidence, Constantinianus was all grins and bravado. "I took your advice, Varus!"

"None too soon, either!"

The wave of news regarding the arrival of this second army consumed Rome. Constantinianus informed me of the Emperor's demands for the new Thracian Army, as well as the provisions of food and other staples to amplify Rome's stores. Within days, additional grain, fruit, cheese, and salted mutton were allocated to euphoric and grasping masses. Belisarius saw none of this—for three days, he and Antonina remained locked in Belisarius' wing of the Domus Augustana, allowing their daughter to seek playmates with Mariya's wards. Any thought of surrender evaporated, for even though we remained grossly outnumbered by Witiges' army and too under-manned to securely occupy Rome's maze of streets and battlements, belief in Belisarius soared. At that time, if the general had commanded it, the entire army would have marched out of Rome's walls and charge headlong into Witiges' veterans without a second thought.

Not all were pleased to witness Antonina's return, however. I brooked no unflattering talk within my own household, yet outside my own walls I was powerless; graffiti depicting Antonina as a base slattern and Belisarius a cuckold soon appeared on the walls of many Roman buildings. At first, they were ignored and cleaned, yet later, when select Roman civilians gathered in the forum and declared Antonina a whore, action was taken—not by me but by Gouboulgoudou, who seized the two loudest offenders and summarily hanged them for sowing mistrust in the army's leadership.

After that, the graffiti became less frequent and the grumblings rarer—particularly after further donations of food and full rations were distributed to even the poorest of Rome's denizens. And, craven though it may sound, it did not hurt Antonina's reputation that I asked Pope Vigilius himself to distribute this new bounty, which he did, noting Antonina's donation as well as the blessing of Christ upon a long-blighted city.

After Belisarius emerged from his sequester with Antonina, it was as if years had been erased from the ledger of his life. Though tired, his smile was unceasing as he paced about the Domus, joining my family and Liberius for a meal. Generally peckish at meals, Belisarius gorged on Antonina's offerings, unpacking his plans to end the siege between bites. Yet one element nearly brought me to choke, its impossibility almost ridiculous to consider.

"We take Ariminium," he explained.

At first I did not understand, and then did not believe my ears. "Lord, Ariminium is but two days' ride to Ravenna," I protested. "There is little chance we could send a war band that far north, let alone seize a fortified settlement. Not with a massive army at our gates."

"Antonina tells me that our dromons are well-positioned throughout the Adriatic and can assault Ariminium by sea," Belisarius countered. "And Witiges would never expect it, not with so many other cities in closer striking distance."

Though I muttered skepticism, Liberius was clearly intrigued by Belisarius' gambit. "Ariminium has extensive docks, and it would paralyze Witiges if it could be taken."

"If!" I blurted out.

Belisarius beamed, seizing another crust of bread and oil from Antonina. "We send two thousand armored horsemen, take the city before it can mount a defense, and wait. Witiges will have to lift the siege, and even if we cannot hold Ariminium, we could evacuate all of our men into ships without difficulty."

It was lunacy, but he was right that it also held one critical benefit—even if we only threatened Ariminium, Witiges would have to respond. And given the arrival of Antonina and Constantinianus, Witiges might overreact. In that overreaction, we could end Rome's siege.

"Who will lead this attack, Lord?" I asked.

"Bessas," Belisarius answered. "I need you with me, and Bessas has had few duties since holding Hadrian's Mausoleum. He will set out within three days."

Liberius smirked. "I am pleased to see you returned to us, Strategos."

"As am I," Belisarius answered, nodding.

Though the assignment was ambitious, Bessas took it up at a frenetic pace. Ultimately, he absorbed all our remaining cataphracts and a thousand fresh Isaurians, with each man guiding two horses on the winding trek to their coastal target. As with our prior sallies, Bessas dispatched from Rome's southern gates and followed a vast arc, sweeping outside of Witiges' army as he turned northward toward Picenum and Umbria. It was a dangerous route, one that made it impossible for Roman scouts and messengers to safely traverse Gothic territory to reach Bessas, yet it was the only path to Ariminium.

In Rome, we had no way of knowing whether Bessas had succeeded or failed. All we could do was muster by our towers and wait and watch. For two weeks, our days progressed much the same as the three hundred previous, albeit with a sense of cautious hope that our deliverance would come. Yet Bessas sent no messengers, nor did any beacon of fire or banners signal the expedition's progress. Instead, our only insight came suddenly, with no prior warning, and with limited opportunity to respond.

Just as quickly as the Gothic army had spread amongst the hills of Latium, they marched northward. First went the vanguard, and later the Gothic king and his most seasoned warriors. Each camp was emptied of men and goods, revealing few horses and no oxen remaining in the camp. Instead, equipment and food were gathered into packs and carried by emaciated men, following the king and his chieftains.

"They truly were in worse condition than us," Sembrouthes marveled. "Poor bastards."

"Better them than us," Shimon said, a rare note of viciousness in his tone.

Within a day, half of Witiges' army disappeared northward. With them traveled Totila and Indulf, the latter of whom yielded a mock salute as he passed within two hundred paces of the Pincian Gate. Belisarius allowed the gesture to go unanswered—in the moment, at least. His course changed that evening when, after summoning me to his rooms, he condemned the bulk of Witiges' followers to slaughter.

"Ready the men to attack at dawn," Belisarius said. "Vandals in front, with Huns and Heruli on the flanks. Do not pursue beyond the Milvian Bridge, but destroy any who oppose you."

And we did. A year of boredom, of suffering, and of anger were unleashed upon Witiges' rearguard, and they crumpled against our fury. With that spectacle of carnage, the Great Siege of Rome was lifted.

MORS VINCIT OMNIA

Many today question Belisarius' victories. That fact rests upon Procopius' haughty shoulders, for I have seen how his words warp the truth to appease the fickle attentions of his benefactor. Some have the audacity to claim that Belisarius' life was exaggerated, that he was more myth than man. For them, I have only contempt, for they speak of what they do not know. What must be understood is, of all other men who ever drew breath, none more than Belisarius was asked to accomplish so much with so little.

True, his household bucellarii swelled in number and prowess over the years. Also true is the raw talent of the Imperial foederati—Huns, Herulians, Vandals, Goths, and many others—that allowed Belisarius to experiment and adapt with each new foe and terrain. Yet even commanding such a roster of heroes, Belisarius was never granted the luxury of plenty. Always outnumbered, lacking in food and supplies, and ordered to fulfill impossible demands with few or no reinforcements, no other man that I know of, not even from all the stories Justin imparted to me and my brother, could have withstood the torrent of adverse fate for as long as my lord. And for that, I spit upon any who speaks of Belisarius with contempt. They know nothing.

A less celebrated stroke of brilliance in Belisarius' Italian campaign were the actions he took to lift the Siege of Rome. Though his mission was hazardous, Bessas succeeded in reaching a poorly guarded

Ariminium, where he seized its walls and imprisoned its ruling chieftain. As Belisarius guessed, Witiges immediately decamped his army and rushed to recapture Ariminium to relieve pressure on his capital in Ravenna, where he faced both Belisarius' veteran cavalry as well as the swelling mass of Valerian's dromons that stalked the upper Adriatic. In a single maneuver, Witiges was forced to retreat, abandoning thousands of his younger, poorly armored, and inexperienced spearmen to fend for themselves as they followed their king northward. Any other stragglers, including those too ill to march, or any camp followers or servants, were largely left behind.

Samur and I avenged our losses at the Milvian Bridge many times over. Waiting until the Gothic column massed beside the Tiber, our twin flanks loosed arrows from horseback, causing the Goths to clump into a mass for protection. Immobile and scared, the Goths were pitiful beneath Gunderic's onslaught, with groups of ten and twenty at a time tossing aside their weapons and pleading for Belisarius' mercy. Others mobbed the bridge, shoving their way onto its narrow steps as we rained missiles over their heads. At least a hundred Goths fell into the frigid waters and, weighted by armor and woolen clothing, were sucked into its murky depths. For days afterward, fishermen along the river plucked bloated Gothic bodies from those waters.

The fighting ended within an hour, and with no loss of life on Belisarius' end. A full thousand Goths fell beneath our advance, with two thousand others disarmed and captured for a return to Rome. In this, he was merciful—most warlords would have slaughtered their enemies after a lengthy siege, while Belisarius ordered only enslavement. Most of those captured were either very young men or camp followers, used for laundry or cooking or tilling the field, and few were hardened warriors. With those who showed evident prowess on the battlefield, we smashed the two smallest fingers of their dominant hand, ensuring they would not raise a weapon against the Empire for many years to come.

Since I gained my liberty from Justin, I had abhorred the notion of possessing my own slaves. I did not begrudge any who participated in that practice—it was an ancient and lucrative rite, and a natural spoil of war earned by Rome's armies. Nevertheless, I abstained, preferring instead to accept my plunder in the form of coin, or of grain, or of other valuables looted from a conquered enemy. This time, however, was different.

Those too injured to travel to Rome were slain with the swift thrust of a dagger. All others were bunched into groups of fifty and paraded back to the Pincian Gate, with ample warning that attempts to escape would be resolved swiftly and mercilessly. Two men, rare captured warriors, did separate from their group and sprint eastward, yet they had little chance of success against our Hunnic and Herulian cavalry. Sindual dispatched both men with his bow. One arrow connected with a man's skull, piercing brains and sending him motionless to the ground. A second arrow hit the other man in the chest and pierced his rib cage, destroying a lung.

"Forgive me!" the man cried to Sindual as I passed. "I will not run, I promise!"

A third and final arrow silenced his cries. In this, at least, Sindual afforded the man the dignity of not bleeding slowly into Latium's grasses, praying that he would perish before scavengers discovered his helpless body.

Back in the forum, rolling cheers amplified at the sight of humbled Goths. Chains were summoned to link together ten adults at a time, slave collars fastened about their necks. Along with any plunder looted from Witiges' baggage train, those men and few women were consigned as loot for Belisarius' army—forces that had been deprived of prospects for enrichment in the past year. Every group of ten was assigned at least one slave for sale, with centurions and higher ranks receiving proportionally greater shares of wealth—most of whom sold their slaves to merchants, pocketed the coins, and distributed new wealth to their suddenly wealthier men.

I did not envy the fates of those hungry, tired, filthy prisoners, for while some were destined to serve in the hospitable climes of Carthage, Septem, Alexandria, or Constantinople, many would be sold to the mines of Arabia or condemned to yield their labor to Justinian's various construction projects. Such lives were brief and miserable, with rations little better than starvation and injury, and illness running rampant.

As I did not intend to participate in that trade of flesh, I satisfied myself with my ample share of Gothic goods allocated to me as Belisarius' second-in-command. Yet as I passed through the forum with my guards and Shimon, a young and beardless man called to me, pleading for a moment of my time as he stood amongst a hundred of his defeated and listless kinsmen.

"Tribune!" he yelled, his voice hoarse and body covered in grime. "Tribune Varus!"

"Ignore him," Sembrouthes muttered, but my curiosity got the better of me. I drew closer, cautioned by Sembrouthes for a second time. "If you won't heed me, at least check him for weapons."

In this, I listened to good sense. Sembrouthes seemed almost disappointed as he discovered no concealed blades, and grudgingly permitted the interloper to approach me.

The man seemed familiar, although this familiarity only brewed mistrust in my heart. "You are bold to seek a Roman officer after your defeat. What would you ask of me?"

His eyes widened, his voice cracking from fear, yet his words a perfect Latin. "My name is Triarius, and I served you in Septem."

Stepping closer, my sense of recognition grew, although I could not place the lad. "Many Goths served me in Septem. Most betrayed me in Salona, despite taking an oath to serve the Emperor."

"It was Indulf, Lord!" Triarius insisted, a tear trailing from his face and cutting through mud-caked cheeks. "He threatened to kill my family if I did not follow him. I've six younger siblings and no father, and they all depend upon me for food and coin."

These claims were unsurprising, and consistent with what I had observed of Indulf. "You have my sympathies, Triarius, although you ask for an unnamed favor after raising arms against me. What do you ask, and why should I care?"

"Take me as your slave," Triarius begged. "I saw how well you treated your servants in Septem. I can cook and clean and scrape your night-soil. I'm lettered, and I'm even a fair healer, if you need one."

"Leave him here," Sembrouthes recommended, yet drew silent as I raised a hand.

"I keep no slaves," I told him. "And I already have the best healer in the Empire."

Triarius fell to his knees. From that angle, his youth was more apparent, his skin unblemished by disease and face possessed of a childlike chubbiness only recently hollowed from lack of food. "Please, Lord. You owe me nothing, even after Septem, although I would follow you without question. I will do whatever you ask. Please, do not let them sell me away from Italy."

He was pathetic. Weeping and exhausted, the discarded servant of a dishonorable master. And though I had become a great lord that would inevitably be rewarded for services in Italy, I already possessed a small army of household servants. A half dozen caretakers of the children, led by Jamila. Three cooks, and three times again as many servants to aid in food preparation, on top of a handful of scullions to perform mundane chores. Stewards to ration our larder, and ten to manage the Domus' many braziers, torches, and tapers, day and night. Others, many unknown to me, to trail Mariya and oversee her personal wants, on top of a legion of launderers for clothing and plenty more to scrub and clean the floors. Couriers to ferry messages to Belisarius and the other officers, doorkeepers, tutors, scribes, a blacksmith, tailors, cupbearers, and even musicians to entertain Mariya and the children at meals. Some were tied to service of the Domus, but most had sworn loyalty to me personally, though most of their names escape me after so many years. Dozens relied upon me for their wages and board, and the thought of another nameless servant had little appeal.

Yet from what I could tell, the lad's predicament was no fault of his own. If I refused, he would suffer either as another man's slave or as a penniless vagrant who occupied poorer neighborhoods on the

Aventine, always on the verge of starvation. Perhaps it due to my sympathy for one so unfortunate, and my own great fortune to have been cared for as a slave in the Imperial Palace, that I relented.

"I will take you as a slave, as a portion of my bounty," I declared. "But you will work as a kitchen scullion until you can be trusted with other duties. If you bring disquiet to my household, you will be sent to the Ghassanid mines without delay."

Triarius brightened. "Understood, Lord!"

I left Shimon to pluck Triarius from the forum. Later, after a thorough scrubbing and a simple yet filling meal, I administered the oath of a master to his slave, which Triarius accepted with glee. It was the first time I had condemned another to bondage, and though it left me uneasy, I believed it the correct decision that would please God. Mariya was far easier to convince, for she was overjoyed at the additional aid, as well as the influx of silver that would cover a full year of our household expenses, alongside any refitting or repair of the Herulian foederati. Still, my wife sought more.

"Theodora owes you land," Mariya chided me one evening after surveying Triarius in the kitchens. "You've given her everything, including the right to be called Roman. But she hasn't compensated you for any of this."

"She's kept me out of imprisonment," I countered. "What would you ask of the Empress?"

"Land!" Mariya repeated. "Cassiodorus controls Pella now, but there are thousands of towns in southern Italy that all lack masters. By giving you control of a region, she and Justinian gain a trusted governor and you a more dependable vein of income."

She was correct, though the prospect of beseeching the Empress for such a favor was counter to my nature. "I will write to her and explain," I promised.

"That's all I ask." Mariya smiled and planted a kiss upon my cheek. "With Witiges giving up on Rome, this war can't continue forever. It's time that you let others fight Justinian's wars."

Again, she was correct, although this time every morsel of my soul agreed with her. With Belisarius holding Antonina once again in his good graces, I believed that he would be of a similar mind, even as Ravenna remained as our final, and elusive, goal. The prospect of concluding war with the Ostrogoths on favorable terms, and disposed to comfortable peace, was tantalizingly close. And unlike in the aftermath of my expedition to Septem, I now felt no guilt at the prospect of resigning my status within the army. My body ached, and I yearned for the peace of having little to do besides be a father to my children and a mentor to those foundlings whom Mariya gave comfort to.

That first month free from the restrictions of siege passed with a frenetic anxiety borne from yet another development in the war. At the end of that first month, Belisarius embraced his wife and child and led his army along the Via Flaminia, leaving Liberius and me to rebuild Rome's walls, roads, aqueducts, and trade routes. Even with Constantinianus' reinforcements, the marching army numbered no more than six thousand, with Bessas leading a further two and hundreds of others scattered throughout Rome and Italy. Besides a detachment of five hundred veteran Cappadocians, I relied upon Principius' thousand-strong city watch, although violent crime remained at a lull now that food was more plentiful.

Again, Witiges' actions defied reason. Rather than face Belisarius in the battlefield, he marched his army clear of Ariminium, affirming Bessas' control of the town and its port. Later, Gouboulgoudou told of how Belisarius ordered each man within his army to light three campfires within a day's march from Witiges' camp, so as to make Roman numbers appear far greater than any that could actually be mustered. Thus, bloodlessly, Belisarius ended the brief siege of Ariminium.

In response, Witiges broke his army into segments, including fifteen thousand Goths to Auximum, ten thousand to Urbinum, and ten thousand to Ravenna. As a result, though Witiges ceded all southern Italy to Belisarius, the mid-Italian provinces of Picenum and Tuscia would resist all but a concerted fight.

But temporarily, such concerns were set aside within four months after Rome's liberation. Overstretched from Ariminium, Belisarius returned with the bulk of his army to Rome, awaiting reinforcements promised by Constantinople. Constantinianus, likewise, gathered his Isaurians and departed for Barium, eager to open a second front against Witiges' Dalmatian provinces.

"Mundus will be proud," Constantinianus declared. "Just as he did, I will lead the Thracians to crush the Goths."

Offering an outstretched arm, I clasped him firmly about the forearm. "I have no doubt. And you'll make all our lives easier as a result."

The shuffle of men and beasts throughout Rome's gates and roads instilled renewed vigor in the once-vibrant city. The loss of Constantinianus produced worry amongst Belisarius' officers that we would be deprived of sorely needed warriors, yet by rendering Witiges confused and defensive, we gained respite as we awaited permanent reinforcements.

In the meantime, as the army drilled and the local populace emerged from winter, all appeared well. Even I was caught in the fervor, believing my destiny fulfilled after an extensive struggle. Fool that I was, even then, for believing that the world would halt its progress because I was contented.

Belisarius' return to Rome was somehow more jubilant than his rout against Witiges' retreating army. Laden with spoils from yet another baggage train, Belisarius was also followed by a hundred wagons from prominent traders of Picenum's towns, all of which suffered from the loss of exchange with the Eternal City. Some were Romans, but most were Goths, and we soon confronted many wine-soaked circumstances where drunken Goths and Romans brawled in the late-night hours of one popina or another.

At first, the city watch maintained a record of all free Goths that gained entry to the city, yet the sheer magnitude of traffic overwhelmed our spymasters. Instead, all free Goths were disarmed, ordered to swear an oath to God that they would serve Justinian loyally, and then permitted to move freely. The only exception were known sycophants of Witiges or Theodahad before him. Such creatures were few, yet five men were placed in irons and tossed into dungeons that had once sworn blood oaths to one or both Gothic kings. In this, Belisarius was unsympathetic.

Our coffers swelled from trade, both from taxes paid by merchants to do business in the forum, as well from the exchange of goods and slaves from the port of Ostia. On the military front, Belisarius ordered bandae of horsemen to raid deep into Witiges' territory, while detachments of warriors and engineers refitted friendly ports on the Adriatic to serve as points of disembarkation and repair for our dromon fleet. Overall, however, we spent the planting season preparing for Belisarius' northward thrust, praying that the war would soon be ended and peace returned to our lives.

After the fields were tilled and seeds sown, another feast was prepared to celebrate our change in fortune. Rather than the Colosseum, Belisarius requested the feast held in the halls adjoining the Domus Augustana, allowing Mariya and Antonina to guide their collective armies of servants toward the lavishness that such an occasion warranted. Along with a hundred senior officers, Belisarius invited all Roman patricians and families of note, swelling our anticipated guests to over five hundred of the wealthiest and most authoritative people living in Italy.

For me, the entire event was unnecessary. "Many in Italy still struggle with hunger. What example does it show to gorge on food we do not need?"

Mariya rolled her eyes playfully. "You're starting to sound like Father Petrus. The reason behind such a party is that Justinian hopes to rule these people when the war ends, but he cannot do that without acknowledging the power these senators and patricians possess."

Logically I understood, having witnessed plenty of such events under Justin. However, that did little to alleviate my discomfort. "And by stuffing these pampered nobles with food and fogging their minds with wine, their loyalty will be assured?"

"Don't be so embittered, Varus!" Mariya giggled. "I am not so different from them, though I come from the east. Do you think so little of me?"

"Never," I replied immediately. "But these Romans—"

"Will love celebrating Belisarius' victory, and your own," Mariya interrupted. "You need not worry over this. I shall prepare everything for you."

I promised Mariya to enjoy myself, yet the celebration was everything I had come to despise. The whole thing dripped with excess; servants and slaves carried morsels of soft cheese and decadent jams, baked fish, tender cutlets of beef, and even goblets of shaved ice flavored with lemons that adorned the islands opposite Neapolis. Course after course was ferried from the Domus' kitchens, and I spotted many of my servants straining under the weight of their trays, drawing all manner of disdain from their social superiors. In particular, I noticed Triarius mopping up the vomit of an overindulgent senator's wife, absorbing her curses with a passive acceptance I had once known in my childhood. I summoned others to aid Triarius before pulling him aside.

"Don't let them bother you, Triarius," I said. "And if any confrontation becomes violent, seek me immediately."

Triarius relaxed. "Thank you, dominus. But I truly am fine. This position saved me from a far more terrible fate."

Dominus. The word chilled me. Revolted me. Gazing into the crowd, I found Samur huddled near Perenus and his Hunnic chieftains, and I wondered whether he would share in my qualms. I doubted it, yet picturing Samur's broken body from so many years ago only worsened the queasiness in my gut.

"Go to the kitchens and clean yourself off," I suggested to Triarius. "Take however much time you need before returning."

He skipped away, seemingly pleased at being dismissed. After, I returned to the party, bedecked in the polished iron scales and pure white cloak that denoted me as an excubitor.

I preferred conversing with other soldiers, yet Mariya frequently pulled me aside, planting me before some Roman senator or another. Where I fumbled through the idle chatter with such nobles, Mariya navigated each encounter effortlessly, planting compliments upon a senator's lavish estate or a patrician woman's immaculately applied kohl and jewels. In each conversation, Mariya never failed to mention my exploits as a tribune, garnering many a toast as we spoke with no fewer than two hundred Roman citizens over the course of three hours.

Many hours after dusk, I found myself drunk. Not sloppily drunk, but loosened enough that I no longer felt awkward speaking with Mariya's invited company, yet also hazy enough to struggle to call up the right words from time to time. None minded, and many appeared far more inebriated than me, although Mariya retained her sobriety.

"I'll relax soon," she promised to me in a whisper and with a wink. "But someone needs to use this opportunity to advance the prospects of Zenobia and Alexander."

Another hour passed. Perhaps fifty guests departed, although most remained in the Domus, draining cups of wine and sampling an array of fruits that, months prior, the starving men of Rome would have killed over. Many expensively clad nobles plunged jeweled fingers down their throats, prompting regurgitation into deep silver bowls before continuing to consume the Domus' fare. My senses blurred as fatigue and drink set in, yet I forced my throbbing feet onward, following Mariya throughout the hall.

Until, finally, Belisarius gathered our remaining guests for a toast to the Emperor and Empress, as well as the steadfast army that brought about Rome's liberation.

"One more hour and we'll be done, I promise," Mariya whispered to me. "It's all planned. After a tribute of wine, we'll petition each senator for aid and then close for the evening."

"As you say," I mumbled, my body desiring nothing more than to sink into the sort of cushioned chair preferred by Procopius and other clerks.

Alas, it was not to be. At least two dozen servants emerged from a separate entrance, bearing trays of silver goblets that I recognized from Belisarius' prior feast in the Colosseum. Each man was bedecked in a gray tunic and black cloak, muted uniforms against a backdrop of sapphire, emerald, ruby, gold, and silver. I reached for one of the goblets yet received a polite deferral.

"Your goblet will be gold, Lord," the man explained. "For senior men."

A minute later, Triarius appeared from the servants' entrance, ferrying four gold goblets encrusted with all manner of precious gems. From Liberius' tales, I wondered whether these cups were the same as those used by Roman emperors from centuries prior, a display of bottomless wealth. Triarius differed from the others in that his tunic was ruffled, even torn along his hip, while gleaming sweat covered his face. Nevertheless, he rushed toward Belisarius, offering a goblet first to the strategos and second to Antonina. Belisarius grasped Antonina's free hand and guided her to the center of the hall, grinning as he weaved through the press of drunken guests.

Triarius next reached me. "For you, Lord," he said, panting.

"Trouble?" I asked, nodding to the cut tunic.

"Nothing at all." Triarius smiled. "Just clumsiness."

He turned away and walked five paces back to the servants' entrance. Mariya, however, nudged me, demanding he return. "You only took one for yourself?!"

"Sorry," I mumbled, handing her mine. "Triarius!"

Triarius froze and then turned as he offered the goblet. "Apologies, Lord."

His shoulders hunched as his face reddened, likely expecting a rebuke. I only chuckled. "The fault is mine. Go and relax for a time."

By then, I was so inebriated that the thought of further wine repulsed me. Mariya, however, tugged on my arm, urging me toward Belisarius.

"Stop complaining!" she teased, stealing a sip as she dragged me toward the hall's center.

I found Belisarius giddy but far steadier on his feet than me. "Enjoying yourself, Varus?"

"Too much, I believe," I muttered.

Separately, Antonina and Mariya engaged in their own conversation. Belisarius requested a servant to hold his and Antonina's goblet as he called for the attention of all present, finally offering a toast that would permit the evening's conclusion.

"Romans!" Belisarius boomed, met by a deafening cheer. "From here on, all the world will understand that our people have risen again!"

Though I was uncomfortable amongst such company, Belisarius' words did not fail to enflame my passion. We had succeeded! Or nearly had, at least. Ravenna and Mediolanum remained in Gothic hands, yet after the trials of Tauris and Dara, of Carthage and of Rome, those remaining targets seemed minor by comparison. Belisarius, the greatest Roman general in living memory, had fulfilled the dreams of so many, despite possessing so little.

"I will not keep you long from your celebration," he continued. "But know this. I made an oath to all of Rome that we would prevail. And now, today, the Empire is Roman in more than name!"

I cheered with the others, my eyes fixed upon Belisarius as I swayed on my feet. It is difficult for me to recall, but I believed I heard the voice of Liberius calling out to me, although I shrugged the intervention off as Belisarius seized his goblet, lifting it to the air.

"We drink to those who sacrificed so that Rome might live again," Belisarius boomed. "And all those who will make it powerful once more! And I know..."

A scream pierced through the crowd's din, halting Belisarius' speech. He frowned, turning in the direction of the shout. He only found Antonina, her mouth agape and crouched on the floor.

Over Mariya's twitching body.

"Poison!" someone yelled—Liberius, pushing away a gawking senator on his way to my side. "Varus, poison!"

Limbs thrashed feebly, as if controlled by some unseen specter. Mariya's lips, usually so lovely, were lined with hints of white froth. Mariya gagged, causing veins along her neck to protrude from beneath soft skin.

Drink muddled my thoughts. I am ashamed to admit that I stared upon my suffering wife for several seconds, unmoving. Eventually, an overwhelming urge to vomit curdled my guts. Turning my head aside, I disgorged a stream of deep red and wiped my mouth. Only then did my wits return.

"Bring me Rosamund, now!"

Liberius shook my collar. "Where is she?"

"In the servants' quarters!" I yelled, stammering as Mariya's convulsions worsened.

Liberius sprinted away as Belisarius ordered the crowd to disburse. Many guests screamed; some voiced worry that they, too, had ingested a toxin, tipping their wine onto the floor. Yet only Mariya was stricken. Antonina sank to the floor to sit beside Mariya, whose golden cup had spilled its contents onto the tiled floor.

I rushed to her, sat myself at her head. "No!" I moaned. She shivered as I lifted her head onto my lap. "God, please!"

I waited for an eternity. Twice, Mariya cried. It was a screech of pain as she rasped for breath, the veins about her neck widening to the size of serpents that wriggled toward Mariya's head. Her long fingernails dug into her neck as she choked on spittle, and I could only thrust a finger into her mouth to clear it away.

Eventually, Rosamund arrived, hastily dressed and bearing her box of herbs, unguents, and potions. "Do something!" I begged.

Rosamund swallowed hard, sucking a stream of fetid air. "How long has it been? When did she sicken?"

"Five minutes now, perhaps?" Belisarius replied.

Numb, I nodded. "I watched her sip from a goblet a few minutes before our toast. I hadn't consumed any."

"Nor did Antonina or I," Belisarius concurred. "It must be poison."

Rosamund's eyes widened. She withdrew a dagger and sliced a thin arc into Mariya's dress, revealing the skin about her collar and chest. "Hold her arms," Rosamund ordered, and Antonina and I obeyed.

Mariya's mouth continued to fill with fluid. She attempted to speak, but choked, her gaping mouth desperate for air that would not come.

"Be strong, my love," I said. "Save your words as Rosamund cares for you."

After inspecting Mariya's skin, Rosamund scooped a portion of Mariya's spittle into a clay jar, where she mixed it with some unknown concoction of ground roots. What the result was, exactly, I cannot say, but it displeased her. Swallowing hard, she turned her gaze to me.

"Varus—"

"Help her, God damn you!" I screamed.

"*Varus*," Rosamund said again, a tear streaming down her cheek. "There's nothing I can do."

I choked again. Turning my head, I vomited upon a nearby carpet, the bile brushing against Belisarius' boots. Pain throbbed in my throat and forehead as I sputtered and wept, phlegm and tears falling onto my trousers.

"No!" I yelled. "Do something! I know you can!"

Rosamund shook her head, weeping as well. "Varus, I would give anything to save Mariya, but it is not possible. Her fate rests with the gods now."

The gods. I wanted to scream in rage, demand that Rosamund redouble her efforts and try. Or perhaps I did yell those indignities— my memory of those moments is marked by shadows. All I know is that, after vomiting a second time, I lay down and gripped Mariya's face, touching her forehead against my own.

"Please!!"

"What can we do?" The question came, calmly, from Belisarius, over my head and to Rosamund.

"Lift her from the floor and place her on something more comfortable," Rosamund answered. "But we will receive our answer soon."

Many stooped down to help, for I was in no state to care for my wife. I remember Belisarius and Liberius gathering aid from Gunderic, Perenus, and Xerxes. As for me, I was raised to my feet by Samur and remained moaning and crying as he hauled me onward and behind Mariya. In the sleeping quarters of the Domus, they placed Mariya upon a bed and me in an adjoining bench, while Antonina sat next to me.

"Speak to her, Varus," Antonina whispered to me, cradling my hand as she lay a hand upon my back. "She needs to hear your voice."

I sobbed and nodded, rising from the bench and leaning over the bed. I am not certain how many were present—perhaps ten, perhaps a hundred. I had no eyes for them. Only for her.

"Mariya…" I began, stopping to blow my nose into my shirt. "The day that I met you in Justin's court was the happiest of my life."

Antonina lifted my hand, wrapping my fingers around Mariya's own. Whether from impulse or recognition, Mariya squeezed, and I continued.

"I don't know why you escaped with me, but I thank God that you did," I wept. "I'm so sorry, Mariya."

Her eyes opened. Just a sliver, but enough for her pupils to lock upon my own. She coughed, spittle forming on the edges of her lips. "Varus?"

"Yes, my love," I answered. "I'm here."

Mariya's eyes seemed to sober. "My body hurts."

"I know, my love," I said, suppressing a third bout of nausea as I heard her struggle to speak. "Just lay still, and all will be well."

Mariya shook her head, her long black hair rustling against the bed. "I don't want to die. Not yet."

"You won't!"

"Varus…" she gurgled, then slipped back into a convulsion.

It took Mariya an hour to die. I refused to be parted from her for a further hour afterward, striking any who attempted to pry her prone form from my grasp. Eventually, however, my body numbed, and I surrendered to my bench, watching others lift my wife into the hallway.

I screamed. Whether only in my mind or for all to hear, I am uncertain. But I screamed. And I wanted to die.

FLECTERE SI NEQUEO SUPEROS, ACHERONTA MOVEBO

Some amongst the ancients claim that death is glorious, or at least the beginning of a greater journey. They are all bastards, for they speak honeyed lies.

Many of my memories are joyful. Others cause great pain. Some so much that they render me disconsolate, rendered aloof by melancholy. Of them all, Mariya's death is the deepest private hell I can muster. A piece of my soul was cleaved away, leaving me incomplete. Leaving a void. I confess, writing this gives me no joy. There is no moral to be derived from the poison that consumed my wife. There is nothing gained from the event. Only hatred. Only rage. Only despair, wrapped about what remains of me like a sodden cloak, an unshakeable weight.

I considered writing little of what transpired. The weakness in me near demanded I skim over details. At moments, I believed it enough that you know that Mariya died—perhaps that she did so painfully, but little else. What would you gain from knowledge that true evil exists in this world?

But, alas, I promised at the onset to tell the truth, as much as I recall. Most alive today could not recall Mariya's name, nor even that a Ghassanid princess lived and loved in the Empire. After I am gone, it will be the same with me, and hundreds of others whose histories exist only in my mind, remembered if at all in the few tawdry lines that Procopius deigned to commit to posterity. Yet Mariya saw much and meant a great deal to many, and was struck down for no justifiable reason. And so I commit Mariya's memory to you, in hopes that you understand. War is evil. It spares nothing and no one. And inevitably, it is the innocent who suffer.

Most of what followed Mariya's death I know only as it was recounted to me later by many others. Antonina and Samur lingered with me throughout the night and into the morning, departing only after I collapsed into an exhausted heap. I dreamed nightmares of all the men I had slain, including the death rattle of Marcian. After fitful starts, I rose alone, vomited onto the floor, and attempted to exit into the rest of the Domus. However, Gunderic and Xerxes kept me penned in my room.

"Antonina and the servants are tending to the children," Xerxes explained. "You don't want to scare them in the state you are in."

"Their mother is dead," I droned. It was not even a counterargument to his insistence; it was merely a phrase that I still only half believed.

After departing from me, I learned later, Belisarius led the most vicious manhunt that Rome had seen in hundreds of years. The body of a servant was discovered tucked away in a hidden corner of the Domus—the man who was intended to act as wine server during Mariya's party. Eventually, however, Belisarius had to rest and turn some of his attentions to the continuance of war. At that point, Perenus insisted upon conducting all inquisitions.

Like Belisarius, Perenus scoured every cobwebbed nook of the Domus, regardless of whether such sites had been thoroughly searched by Belisarius' bucellarii. Likewise, Perenus' investigators sought out every living soul that had petitioned Belisarius or myself in the month that preceded Mariya's death. All servants were sequestered and questioned, some for hours, and their fearful answers pointed toward a single culprit.

Triarius. Two thorough searches of the Domus grounds revealed nothing of the man, not even his slave clothing. Belisarius ordered all gates closed, and that no horse should be lent or sold to any man not bearing the Emperor's sigil on gold leaf. I remained ignorant of all developments, cooped inside my chamber, and fed a steady diet of sour wine that Gunderic smuggled through Belisarius' bucellarii. I did not see my children—Antonina begged me to allow her time to explain to them what had come to pass, relieving me of such duties. Though it shames me now to admit, I was grateful for that reprieve.

Perenus, however, was unrelenting in his attentions. "We'll find him, Varus. From what I've learned, Triarius was spotted leaving alone. He has no friends here and must be on foot."

Triarius. That motherless, bastard Goth. I had plucked him from starvation, showing pity on a man I viewed as weak. My kindness was returned with blood.

"Good," I mumbled, only half listening.

"I'll tear apart Rome, one hill at a time," he swore, doubly solemn and ignoring my misery. "The entire army won't rest until this is finished, Varus. You don't need to worry about anything."

"Why worry?" I grumbled. "She's already dead."

Perenus grimaced. "I'm here for you, brother. I know what the feeling is like… what you're going through."

"It's not the same." As soon as I growled the words, I was immediately embarrassed by them.

"It's not, of course." Perenus straightened. "But if you need something, just say it. I promise I will succeed for you."

After that, three days passed with no developments. An occasional visitor deposited food or clothing, checked on my well-being. Yet I never saw Rosamund. Instead, it was Agathias who attended to my health. He frequently begged a private audience, but Gunderic demanded he scurry away until more time could pass. More often, Father Petrus stayed with me for most daylight hours, offering prayers but not chastising me when I declined. Instead, we sat in silence, the older man's hand occasionally squeezing my shoulder.

"She never wanted this," I muttered, recoiling from the stench of my own bile-infused breath.

Petrus turned, confused. "Varus?"

"Mariya wanted to retire to Pella in peace," I mumbled. "I took that from her. If I had been more tactful with Cassiodorus or just resigned from the army..."

"You are not the criminal here," Petrus replied, his voice unwavering. "Do not speak as one. Poison is a coward's weapon. Mariya loved you, and I never saw her happier than the times you shared in Rome. Siege or no."

Morose, I nodded. I did not agree, but I lacked the strength to argue. Petrus had not been present when Mariya wept as she learned of the price of Rosamund's freedom from the Brazen Bull—that moment when her dream, and the wealth to achieve it, evaporated like dust with a single snap of Cassiodorus' fingers. Petrus did not hear the defeat in Mariya's voice, nor my pathetic attempts to reassure her that I would make everything right again. That I would fix our predicament. That at least we had each other, safe. We sat, Petrus prayed, and awaited any developments from outside command.

When news came at last, it jolted me to alertness. "We found Triarius," Perenus declared excitedly. "Samur rooted him out first and is with him now. He was hiding in a mill, just a day's ride to the north."

Triarius. The name was like an acid, churning in my guts and poisoning my mind. In an instant, days of drunken stupor were wiped clean, my senses never sharper. I was ready to punish, to kill, in some macabre hope that the sacrifice of blood might bring Mariya back to me. To fill this aching void in my gut. To do something, anything, to make the days make sense again.

"Escaping to Witiges," I seethed. "Take me."

"Belisarius said—"

"Take me!" I yelled. "Show me where that bastard still breathes."

I had no ears for Petrus, nor Liberius, nor any who would stop me. Instead, I mounted Boreas and rode with Perenus and fifty Herulian foederati that very night, not bothering to sleep as moonlight guided my steps along the Via Flaminia. It was dangerous, not only for the potential to trip over hidden detritus, but also because we rode closer to Gothic lands—that undetermined boundary where Belisarius' authority waned and Witiges' began. My limbs ached, my stomach roiled, my head pounded, yet I cared for nothing. If it killed me, I would find Triarius before I slept again.

The mill would have been difficult to spot had a hundred Huns not guarded its outcrop. Aigan saluted and granted me entry, while Perenus and the Herulians took position in a broad circle outside of the mill's walls. The mill's interior was a solid stone structure, built two or three hundred years prior, possessing a cavernous underground storage, three bedrooms, and a larger workroom. It was there that we discovered Triarius chained to the wall, with Samur and Belisarius seated nearby.

"You shouldn't be here, Varus," Belisarius said. Still, he offered me a seat.

My eyes remained fixed upon Triarius, my former slave bruised and quivering as he shied from my approach. "With respect, Lord, please leave."

Belisarius' eyes ran over me, taking in the state of my body. Though I saw in him a great lord, well-groomed and adorned in fine armor, Belisarius saw before him a man who was filthy, scraggly, likely reeking of bile and other foul humors. I was disgusting, beyond the foulness of a simple camp spearman. No, I had become repulsive, motivated only by suffering. Yet Belisarius did not recoil, though I saw a flicker of aversion in his eyes. And in that instant, I realized I had become a disappointment, and I wanted to weep. I had failed Mariya and Belisarius. I was not fit to even stand in the presence of my children, half orphaned, out of fear that I would traumatize rather than soothe their fears.

"You're certain?" Belisarius asked. "Your vengeance is mine, Varus."

"Thank you, but I'm certain," I answered. "Samur, please stay."

Why Samur? I still debate the reasons to this day. Samur was my blood, and though Perenus, Gunderic, and Belisarius had all sworn oaths to avenge me, Samur alone had special cause to tear Triarius apart for what he had done to his sister-in-law. On my weaker days,

I reason that I desired to give Samur his own vengeance and honor his ties to me. Perhaps that is true. But when I am more honest with myself, a darker rationale emerges. I chose Samur because I knew he would butcher Triarius without hesitation, or even a command. Samur, more than any of the others, held a viciousness that could not be matched, and doubly so out of devotion to family. I did not simply want a killer. I wanted a torturer. Someone who knew what he was doing and would not speak of it with dishonor later on.

Samur scowled at Triarius but awaited Belisarius' departure before speaking. "This monkey pissed himself when I found him. He says he'll tell you everything."

Spying a nearby table, I unbuckled my sword belt and dropped it upon its dusty planks. Then, I paced toward Triarius, tears filling the man's face as I approached.

"Lord..."

"Bastard!" I yelled, driving my gloved fist into his gut.

He coughed, gasping for air as he leaned upon the twin chains that pinned his arms against the wall. Struggling to speak, he mouthed a word before coughing again, his bulging eyes watching as I drew a bench closer to his body.

"Speak," I growled. "Tell me why."

"Lord, I didn't want to betray you—"

Samur smacked Triarius across the face, warping his nose into a bloody horror. "Enough blubbering. Tell us facts, or I'll cut off your balls and stuff them in your mouth. Believe me, I'll do it while singing."

Triarius' limbs shook as his gaze fixed upon Samur, bubbling blood dripping from his nose. "I will, I promise!"

"Then speak!" I yelled.

"The hemlock wasn't meant for your wife, Lord." Triarius sniffled. "Only for you and Belisarius. B-But I couldn't take chances, and poisoned every cup."

Samur nodded. "It was poison, then. But why would you admit to it now?"

Triarius turned back to my brother, struggling to resist weeping. "You've caught me. I'm dead already. If I tell you what you want to know, will you still torture me?"

The burning desire to smash Triarius' teeth into his brain nearly overtook my restraint, although I continued to sit. "Tell me who gave you the order, and we will be merciful."

Triarius sighed. "Thank you, Lord. You were always good to me in Septem."

Another smack from Samur, this time just above the man's eye. "To the point!"

"Indulf!" Triarius yelped. "I told you true in the forum. Indulf threatened to kill my family if I did not serve him. When Witiges gave the order to abandon the siege, Indulf granted me the opportunity to clear my family's debt to him. Find a way to kill Belisarius, or at least you, and they would be free."

"And you crafted the plot to poison us?" I asked.

"No, Lord." Triarius gagged and spat a glob of bloody phlegm before continuing. "He told me that you would accept me into your service, and that I should poison you. Hemlock was merely the easiest poison to acquire without arousing suspicion."

"And you failed," I hissed.

"Yes, Lord," he answered. "And for that, I'm heartily sorry to you, and to God."

I stood, and Triarius flinched. I patted my lack of a sword belt for effect, allowing Triarius to relax and attempt further speech. "Lord, if I may…"

Again, I smashed a fist into his gut, sending him straining against his chains in a struggle for air. As he regained his footing, I drew Aetius' dagger, squaring its honed point against his stomach.

"Please!" he gasped.

I buried the dagger in Triarius' intestines all the way to its hand guard. He choked and gurgled, arching his back from the pain. I withdrew the dagger, cleaned its blade against Triarius' filthy trousers, and set it on the table. Blood poured from Triarius' mouth and nose as his eyes met mine.

"Wander in hell for all eternity," I whispered into his ear.

With both fists, I bashed his body. Ribs. Throat. Cheeks. Abdomen. And, many times, his face. He moaned through it all, a sickly mewing noise, before Samur joined my assault. We beat the young man into a twitching pulp—still alive but no longer human. Pieces of skull shone through cuts on his head, and only sips of air made their way through a shattered neck.

"End him," I asked Samur.

"Gladly." My brother drew his sword and thrust it through Triarius' heart, stopping the man's torment for good. He, as I had, cleaned his blade, then sheathed it.

"Tell none of what you heard here," I said, buckling my sword belt back about my waist. "Not yet."

"More traitors?" Samur asked.

"Unlikely," I replied. "But I can't know for sure. I swear to God and all who hear me, I will kill Indulf."

Drawing his dagger, Samur cut a faint line along his palm, warm blood lining the skin— a blood pact, common amongst the Huns, and still unfamiliar amongst the Greeks. "Your oath is mine, Varus. That bastard will scream for a thousand lifetimes for this."

Belisarius did not ask me what had transpired in the mill. I heard later that Triarius' corpse was burned without ceremony, although I care little for the details. He was a murderer, and he suffered for that sin, although he was little else than an instrument for another. And while he still lived, what remained of my family was not safe.

The next day, I finally bathed myself of nearly a week of sweat, vomit, and Triarius' blood. After, I paced to the children's quarters, guided by Antonina and Jamila. Most of the foundlings had been moved elsewhere for the day; only Zenobia, Alexander, and Tiberius remained to greet me. Though Alexander was too young to understand, Zenobia, my brave Zenobia, cried fat tears when she saw my approach. I embraced them both, pressing their little bodies into my chest as I crouched to meet them. To this day, I have never witnessed Zenobia cry with such abandon.

Tiberius' mouth wavered, though he attempted to remain standing straight. I beckoned him close, wrapping him in my arms with the other two. "It is okay to be sad, Tiberius. Mariya loved you as one of our children, as do I."

At that, Tiberius bawled, yielding further outbursts from Zenobia and Alexander. "Why would someone hurt her? Why?!" Tiberius cried.

I had no answers. All I could offer was my presence, which felt woefully inadequate. Mariya made caring for the children appear effortless; alone, I was befuddled, worried, and stumbling for how to provide comfort. All I knew to do was sit with them for the day, eventually sharing a meal, and allowing their tears to soak into my clothing.

Outside of my children, Sembrouthes was the most inconsolable. "My little Mariya..." he moaned. "I failed her."

"No, my friend," I said, clasping the back of his neck. "There's nothing that any of us could do."

For the only time I could recall, Sembrouthes appeared disheveled, his yellow tunic spotted with grime and stained along its hem. "The poor children..."

"They need you now, more than ever," I insisted. "As do I."

"I'll write to her brother and explain," Sembrouthes offered, ever dutiful. "I just... can't believe it."

Two days after the mill, as I prepared Mariya's funeral rites, Shimon announced a visitor. In prior times, such arrivals would be unremarkable, but this was the first petitioner that Gunderic and Xerxes had allowed into my presence since Mariya's death. I bade the guest enter and encountered a man bedecked in expensive silk robes, denoting his status as a Roman patrician.

"What can I do for you, citizen?" I asked.

"I do not wish to add to your grief, excubitor," he said. "My name is Calogerus, and I witnessed the death of the Ghassanid princess. I was told she was your wife."

"She was," I affirmed, regretting allowing the audience.

"My condolences, truly," Calogerus said. "But I was curious as to why your healer took so few steps to purge your wife of the toxin."

I paused to compose myself. "Citizen, this is a painful topic for me," I replied curtly. "I would appreciate avoiding unnecessary gossip at this time."

He bowed his head. "I only mean to provide you with knowledge. Though I wear the patrician's robes, I was once a medicus to King Theodoric in my youth. I saved his life after a fall from his horse, and he rose me to these fine robes. In my time at court, I became familiar to all known poisons, and the one used during your wife's murder was as common as they come."

My eyes narrowed. "What do you mean?"

"An earthy scent, although difficult to see in the liquid," the patrician healer explained. "Difficult to miss, although easy to misinterpret for one unfamiliar with poison as your wife. I was drunk, I admit, although I gained a closer view of General Belisarius' cup as your wife was carried away."

"Earthy?" I asked.

"A classic sign of hemlock," Calogerus said. "The slayer of Socrates and many highborn ladies and men since."

Hemlock. Only Samur and I had heard Triarius' confession, and hearing the word repeated chilled my blood. Immediately, I recognized Calogerus as no fool.

"You're certain it was hemlock?" I asked, not revealing my prior knowledge of the poison.

"As certain as one can be in a drunken stupor," he added modestly. "And while hemlock poisoning is usually fatal, steps taken early can improve the chances for survival. The most inexperienced acolyte to the healing arts knows this."

I froze. It was as if his voice had turned me into one of the statues that lined so many Roman palaces and thoroughfares. In my mind, I had viewed the scene of Mariya's death ten thousand times, ending with Rosamund's pronouncement that all was lost. My chest hurt as

I considered the patrician healer's argument, for although I knew the plant that had killed Mariya, I understood pitifully little about how it caused death or could be treated.

"Explain."

He nodded. "For example, aiding in the victim's regurgitation is essential to yielding a chance of surviving hemlock and many other poisons. A common treatment is to force the powder from cooled coals down their throats with sips of water, and await the black vomit that follows shortly thereafter. It is an unpleasant business, and not always successful, but can make a difference."

"You've seen this practice yourself?" I asked. "It isn't some theory of a single physician?"

Calogerus sighed. "Poisonings are so common in Rome that they might as well be a sport. For hemlock and other poisons, I have used this technique many times. If caught within the first minutes of encountering the toxin, survival is the norm."

A hint of suspicion crept into my thoughts. "If you know this, why did you not intervene?"

"I regret not being more aggressive to aid your wife," Calogerus admitted. "But I had consumed too much drink, and your healer has a fearsome reputation. I presumed she would refuse aid and act appropriately, by then it was too late."

The impertinent portion of my soul wanted to chide the man's failure to act, though his excuse was reasonable. Besides, I dared not turn the man away or make him an enemy when he had come to me out of condolences and a desire to help. "It was not your responsibility anyway, Calogerus. I understand."

He continued for several minutes more, expounding on his prior experiences with poison and the various other interventions that had been used with degrees of success. I nodded through it all but paid little attention, my thoughts turned toward Rosamund. Soon, he dismissed himself, and although I offered a purse of ten silver coins for his information, he declined.

"I do not wish you to think of me as an opportunist in your time of grief, Lord," Calogerus said. "I truly am grateful for your sacrifice to Rome. All I wanted was to inform you of what I saw and what I know."

I saw no other visitors for the remainder of that day. The following morning marked Mariya's funeral rites, for which I was poorly prepared and overtly dreading. Gunderic snuck a full wineskin into the Domus an hour beforehand, gulping a mouthful before handing the bag to me.

"No shame in mourning a dead wife, Varus," Gunderic told me. "I was married once. Beautiful woman, long legs and big arms."

I allowed an extended stream of wine to swirl into my stomach. "You never told me that."

"Never found the right time to bring it up." Gunderic shrugged. "She died in childbirth. The babe lived a day longer than she did. I loved her, just like I love children, and I wept like a child for days. Any man who doesn't in such hardship isn't truly a man."

Though Antonina had previously cautioned me to avoid drunkenness, indulging with Gunderic slaked the throbbing pain in my guts. My skin flushed with warmth, and the thought of confronting so many others far less uncomfortable. By the time Shimon arrived to prepare my armor, the full effect of the wine left me comfortably numb, and I donned the raiment of an excubitor without comment.

From the hallway outside my rooms, Antonina guided me to the children. All of the children, including Mariya's foundlings, were dressed and washed, surrounded by a dozen of Mariya's closest attendants, with the faces of Zenobia and Tiberius blotchy and tear-stained. I lifted Alexander into my arms as he squirmed and yelled.

"I want Mater!" Alexander whined. "Where's Mater?!"

"You can't!" Zenobia yelled, face steaming with tears. "She's dead! They killed her!"

Alexander shuddered, wailing from his sister's rebuke rather than the confusing knowledge that Mariya had departed from this world. I admit, the ferocity of Zenobia's anger rooted me to the spot, my limbs heavy from the ponderous weight of Mariya's death. Privately,

I knew that I had caused this. I had placed Mariya in danger, and she perished for it. My children... my tiny children... would never know their mother beyond the precious few memories of tender years that would fade all too quickly.

"Oh, child!" Jamila cried, scooping up the weeping boy.

"Mater..." Alexander sobbed. "Please..."

"Hush, now," Jamila cooed, burying Alexander's face into her stola. "You stay close to me, Alexander. Whatever you need, whatever time of day, we will solve it together."

Alexander's clumsy words were muffled against Jamila's linen, though it was plain the boy was still wailing for a mother who could not respond. Helpless to give him what he wanted, Jamila tugged Zenobia close and squeezed her, weeping herself, and all I could do was stand listless, empty. A void. Unworthy of life. If all the devils of the world had materialized before me, I would have traded my life for Mariya's without hesitation. It should have been me.

Eventually, I shrugged life into my limbs but still could not meet Zenobia's gaze. Instead, I beckoned to Jamila, who attempted to straighten but nearly tripped as Alexander clung tightly to her hem. "Keep Alexander here," I told her. "There is no benefit for him to attend. If you wish to join me, another servant can keep watch over the boy."

"I will care for him Lord," Jamila stuttered, the kohl lining her eyes now blotched and streaking from tears. "He needs me."

Numb, I nodded. "You have my thanks, Jamila. I will need your help with the children in the months ahead."

With Zenobia and Tiberius in tow, I followed Antonina through the Domus. The dragon pendant along my neck seemed heavier as we departed the building and reached open air, and I occasionally brushed my fingers against its smooth gold for what small relief could be garnered. Outside the Domus, Perenus led a hundred Herulians as my personal guard, forming twin columns that blocked either side of the road. We trudged toward the forum, encountering more of Belisarius' soldiers with each turn in the street, many who muttered condolences that I cannot recall.

The Pantheon, which served as the site of our ritual, had been prepared the evening before. There would be no pyre—as the princess of a staunch Imperial ally, Mariya had earned the privilege to be buried with long-dead Roman elite. Through my service as a tribune in Belisarius' army, along with lavish bribes to many clerks and even two priests, her body would be secured within Augustus' Mausoleum along the Campus Martius. It was inaptly named—many within the Roman elite found their ashes or bones interred within Augustus' monument—yet it remained a beautiful building despite its sack a century prior.

Hundreds of mourners lined both the exterior and the circular interior of the Pantheon. Many were my brothers in the army—Xerxes and Fulcaris, Conon, Thurimuth, and Martinus, Sinnion and Aigan, Principius and Wisimar, and most other men not dispatched to Ariminium or cities to the south. Nearer the dais, Sembrouthes and a dozen Aksumites stood silent vigil, with my bodyguard standing near Mariya's head, dutiful still, yet with a frown marking his usually impassive face. Even many of the older children in Mariya's care were present, with Cours serving as their nominal leader. None, I noticed, were willing to look upon Mariya's body.

Perenus filtered his Herulians throughout the onlooking mass and bade me forward, and I took both children into each arm. At the Pantheon's center, immediately under its fabled oculus, lay Mariya. Her body was wrapped in the same crimson robes that she had favored since childhood, the silk glimmering against the fading light from the oculus' opening. Her face, arms, and hands were laced with gold, and a layer of kohl expertly applied to her eyes as powder brought blush to her cheeks. She appeared a goddess—perhaps she was and I did not know it.

"Mater," Zenobia wailed.

I lifted my daughter into my arms as Samur rushed forward and grabbed Tiberius. Together, we paced forward, a painful knot in my throat as I forced myself closer to the body, grateful to

Gunderic, for that wine had dulled my senses.

Fewer people stood in the inner circle of mourners. Belisarius and Antonina stood together, Belisarius melancholy but silent while Antonina sobbed. Liberius likewise stood by, stony-faced as he nodded at me to take my place beside him. Father Petrus stood closest to Mariya, covered in black except for a simple cross that dangled from his neck. Last was Rosamund, who stood alone, red-faced and inconsolable.

The patrician healer's words stung harder then. Rosamund had proven her capacity to heal the broken and the dying a thousand times over, never consumed by fear or anxiety or any hesitation as she labored over her patients. Yet, when it was Mariya who fell, all that skill was for naught—and for what reason, I dreaded to know.

With Samur and the children, I took my place by Liberius, who placed a hand upon my shoulder and whispered into my ear. "I am so sorry, Varus."

I nodded, fearful of surrendering to my grief. We stood no more than five paces from Mariya's body, the light from the oculus illuminating her slender limbs and softly braided hair. Petrus offered a slow nod and waited a moment longer before beginning the ceremony.

"A gift for you, for what consolation it brings," Liberius said.

"Not now, Lord," I muttered, uncaring for the games that my former dominus Justin and his colleagues had inflicted upon me.

"Not that," Liberius promised. "Give me your hand."

I complied, and he placed a small lock of hair that had been tied by silken ribbons. "Mariya's attendants thought you would like to keep this."

Careful not to disturb Zenobia, I raised the lock to my face. Hints of Mariya's perfume lingered, and I pressed it against my cheek before depositing it safely within a pouch along my belt, where it brushed against Theodora's signet ring. "Thank you, Lord. I will not forget this."

"You deserve more in this life than what you have received," he replied. "Just know that whatever comes, we are with you, always."

Petrus administered his sermon. Though I thanked him for bearing the responsibility of lifting Mariya's soul unto heaven, in truth, I did not listen much. Rather, I hugged Zenobia and glanced occasionally toward the many who stood vigil in honor of Mariya's memory—a woman who stood loyal to the Emperor in the darkest days of the Nika Riots, who maintained grace amidst the Siege of Rome, and who had cared for thousands of crippled veterans and orphaned children in her brief time in this life. Only then did I understand the place of respect that Mariya held amongst my brothers, for as Petrus administered his final "Amen," hundreds of Roman warriors all pronounced the victory cry that bellowed over many a battlefield.

"Roma Victrix! Roma Victrix!"

Petrus shuddered as many saluted Mariya, grumpy from the interruption of the religious procession, though unwilling to halt the chant. Their voices echoed across the Pantheon's expanse, soaring through the oculus and toward the heavens. Zenobia wept into my shoulder, and I gently wiped her face.

"Your mother loved you dearly, anaticula," I whispered. "Everyone present knows this. They honor her now. From this day, you must remember always what you and your brother meant to her."

Zenobia nodded but buried her face once more into my armor. Still cradling Zenobia, I stepped forward to the raised platform, with Samur close behind. Careful not to disturb Zenobia, I bent over and planted a kiss upon Mariya's cheek, her chilled flesh the only evidence of her demise.

"Wait for me," I whispered. "Please, my love, wait for me."

The ceremony ended soon thereafter, and most departed the Pantheon's warmth. Belisarius lingered with me for a time, and I accepted the condolences of those who remained. Again, I offered silent thanks for Gunderic's wine, relieved as the line of well-wishers disappeared into Rome's streets. Yet among my final memories of Mariya's funeral was one of Rosamund, her face covered in tears, muffled moans escaping futile attempts to cover her mouth with her shirt. Then, the patrician healer's words again echoed in my mind.

The most inexperienced acolyte to the healing arts knows this.

Mourning and drunk, I was then convinced that Rosamund had allowed Mariya to die. Call it grief or paranoia, or even a pragmatism to heed the warning of one who stood to gain nothing by accusing Rosamund of carelessness, but I blamed her. I saw her face, and I believed.

What came next soon spun out of control.

JUDGMENT

After depositing the children back to Mariya's attendants, I pulled Samur into one of the Domus' private rooms. Though visibly exhausted, he obeyed. We locked the doors and ventured to the center of the room, where I leaned close to his ear.

"Rosamund let Mariya die," I whispered furiously. "A medicus at the party came to call upon me. He said he smelled hemlock and did not understand why Rosamund conceded Mariya's care so quickly."

Samur frowned. "Rosamund wouldn't do that!"

"Then why not at least try to save Mariya?!" I hissed. "You've seen her save so many lives, including your own. This poison can be treated by a novice, let alone one as adept as Rosamund."

Samur sighed and paced to a nearby bench. He ran a hand through his matted hair, leaning heavily upon an arm as he considered my words. "The physician, he explicitly said hemlock? You told no one else about what we heard at the mill?"

"I am certain, and I did not," I replied. "Could anyone else have known?"

Samur was adamant. "Not from me, and Belisarius kept any eavesdroppers too far away to hear Triarius' explanation."

"Then what does it all mean?" I cried. "Why would Rosamund not treat Mariya's poison, even if she was flustered?"

"I don't know," Samur replied. "But we need a third to reason through this with us."

Through a courier, we summoned Perenus. He, too, initially resisted any impeachment of Rosamund's behavior, although cooled his hesitancy when told of the detail of hemlock.

"In Lazica, poisons like hemlock are used almost regularly in the royal families," Perenus muttered. "When I was a boy, my cousins and I were all told to vomit if our stomachs felt off, and to replace any losses with water. I've seen the powdered coals your medicus mentioned used before."

"But why would she do this?!" I barked. "Years of unquestioned loyalty, and now Rosamund might have allowed my wife to needlessly die?!"

Perenus and Samur glanced anxiously at one another, with neither daring an explanation. "We need this medicus," Perenus requested. "Let's think through this with clear heads."

Though I knew little more of Calogerus than his name, it was simple to find him by reputation. Again, a courier was dispatched to seek him out, and he arrived at the Domus an hour later. Bobbing his head in recognition of my fellow officers, Calogerus reintroduced himself and addressed all questions that Perenus and Samur could muster. Most of all, however, we pried him on his knowledge of hemlock.

"As I said, I could smell the earthiness in the cups a pace away," Calogerus explained. "Like musty dirt. Princess Mariya would have been unfamiliar with that taste and may have believed it characteristic of the evening's wine."

"How would Rosamund have identified the hemlock, absent any cups?" Samur asked skeptically.

"The spilt liquid was all about Mariya's body and would have been present upon her breath," Calogerus replied, unflappable in his confidence. "And even if she was not careful to detect such signs, Mariya's sudden collapse would direct any healer toward poison."

Perenus frowned, yet nodded. "And the treatment for all poisons is similar?"

"Not universally," Calogerus replied. "Unfortunately, there

is much we do not know of many poisons. But for most, ample regurgitation is key. Even if the victim pleads to be allowed to sleep, forcing them to expel the contents of their stomach is crucial."

Samur and Perenus muttered to one another in Heruli, the words of which were too faint for me to detect beyond their accent. However, they appeared to agree, and Samur asked a final question.

"If Mariya might have lived simply by vomiting the poison free of her body, why would an experienced healer not seek that cure?"

At that, Calogerus had no ready-made reply. "Lords, I have asked myself this question a hundred times over the past week. The only reasonable answer I could configure is that she, for whatever reason, would not know of hemlock, or at least how to treat such fast-acting poisons."

I groaned, realizing that our conversation had yielded no further insight into my suspicions. Despite it all, I could not, I *would not*, act upon so grave an accusation without greater proof.

"Citizen, I thank you again for your time..."

"One moment, Varus," Perenus interjected. "I wonder, might good Calogerus be willing to question Rosamund's apprentice?"

Calogerus nodded, and though I did not yet understand, I allowed them to seek the young healer and clerk into our gathering. As Agathias resided in the Domus, he appeared but minutes later, his brow laced with sweat.

"Lord?" Agathias asked. "I've been hoping to speak with you."

I nodded. "Later. For now, citizen Calogerus is here to aid in a sensitive manner."

Agathias squirmed under the volley of questions the three other men sought answers for. Yet in his brief testimony, Agathias affirmed that he had been present at the party, following Rosamund as she was summoned to provide aid to Mariya.

"Though you did not tend to Mariya, what did you assume had happened?" Perenus asked.

"Impossible to say for sure," Agathias replied.

Perenus was unmoved. "Your best guess?"

"Poison, Lord," Agathias answered, his eyes darting across his four observers.

"Did Rosamund train you in treating poisons and venoms?" Calogerus asked.

"Of course." Agathias nodded. "Soldiers mistakenly eat poisoned mushrooms, or come into contact with poisonous flowers, or receive the bites of snakes and other creatures."

"Excellent," Calogerus replied. "And did you know of the poison that afflicted Mariya?"

"Citizen, I..." Agathias stammered, searching for the appropriate response. "Rosamund would know far better than I. She has a talent that a hundred others could not replace."

His response was intended to assuage me, yet only fielded further suspicion. "Agathias, none here accuse you of anything. You have been nothing less than a loyal friend. But I need you to answer our questions honestly and fully."

Agathias nodded, his hands trembling. "Lord, that's why I wanted to speak with you that night, although the others wouldn't let me near the sickroom."

Agathias stuttered again, yet Samur urged him onward. "Go on, Agathias."

"Mariya's wine smelled musty, and... and as soon as I approached, I believed it to be tainted," Agathias admitted, wide-eyed and fidgeting. "It was not subtle, Lord."

Calogerus leaned forward, his face grim. "What was not subtle, Agathias?"

"The earthiness," Agathias repeated. "Like dirt, but even less pleasing. Rosamund had shown me what might cause such a smell, in fact, and how to treat it."

"And what caused it?" I asked, my voice cracking. In that moment, I wanted anything but the answer I feared would spill from Agathias' lips.

"Hemlock, Lord," Agathias said. "Known to Greeks for thousands of years."

But Calogerus was not yet finished. "And your teacher, Rosamund, had taught you of this before? Have you seen it used?"

Agathias nodded. "That's why I wanted to help Mariya. I did not understand why we were not forcing Mariya to vomit. Rosamund has several powders that help expel venom."

Calogerus plucked at a satchel he carried to the Domus and produced a stoppered glass vial. After removing wax from the opening, Calogerus allowed a fine powder to fall into his hand before offering it to Agathias. "Is this one of those powders?"

Agathias examined it, raising the gray-black mixture to his nose. "Coal ash. Yes, I have seen this used before."

It was too much. I rose from my chair, exited the room, and disappeared into my sleeping quarters. Besides meals, I allowed no servants or visitors into my presence, staring blankly at the columns along the walls and tiles covering the floor. At some point, well after dark, my body succumbed to sleep, yet I awoke again before dawn's breaking.

I should have summoned Samur and Perenus, or at least heeded Liberius' guidance. Any reasonable person would have. But I had no interest in following good sense with a clear head. I was disgusted, and I wanted someone to suffer for Mariya's death. Triarius' torture had done little to quench my thirst for revenge, and Indulf was too far away for me to commit his soul to hell.

Worse, however, was the sadness I felt. Rosamund had betrayed me, I was certain. I just did not know why. And two days after Agathias' inquiry, I intended to find out.

In the evening of a particularly stifling summer day, I prepared a table and benches and ordered a servant to bring Rosamund into my presence. The order took two hours to fulfill, and the unexplainable duration only added to my frustrations. At last, late into the evening, a knock sounded at my door.

"Enter," I barked.

"You sent for me?" Rosamund slipped through the doorway. "Something ails you?"

"I did," I answered curtly.

Rosamund sat opposite me. Poor sleep and an inadequate diet hollowed her cheeks, making her skin appear sallow. Her clouded eye's various scars were more pronounced, while her usually tidy hair hung in lank knots about her shoulders. She bore none of the defiance that made her famous in Belisarius' army, nor any of the confidence.

"Varus?" Rosamund stuttered again, adopting a Heruli accent. "Something bothers you?"

I wanted to be tactful. To remain calm and to avoid prejudgment. But, as Godilas knew of me so many years ago, when anger gripped my mind, prudence was the first virtue I abandoned.

"I want to know why you did not attempt to save Mariya."

"Varus!" Rosamund exclaimed. "I told you, it was too late. To inflict anything upon her would only cause suffering... cruelty."

"But she suffered anyway!" I pounded the table, cracking one of its legs. "I sat with her for hours. I watch her twitch and moan and choke her last words. And you did nothing!"

"Varus!" Rosamund whimpered. "If I would have thought—"

"Two others wanted to purge Mariya with coal ash," I interrupted. "One of them was Agathias, who you trained in the treatment of poisons. Both men identified the poison as hemlock."

Rosamund's lip quivered, her eyes widening as they welled. More than ever, she appeared drained of the ferocity that defied Roman conventions, that cursed Cassiodorus as she was condemned to the Brazen Bull.

"There's no way to be certain it was hemlock," Rosamund muttered.

I seethed. "An earthy, musty scent. Agathias sensed it. But even if you were not certain, purging a poison victim is the common practice, yes?"

"It is," Rosamund mumbled. "Varus—"

"Mariya died, and you did nothing!" I yelled again. "Worse, you prevented any other from saving her life!"

"I didn't—"

"You did!" I exclaimed. "That is clear enough. What I do *not* understand is why you would do this."

Rosamund slumped in her chair. Tears trickled down her cheeks, her chest rising and falling as she gazed upon me. Some part of me wanted to console her, to reassure her that all would be well, to worry not. Yet that part of me was now too small to overrule my anger. I craved answers, no matter the cost.

"I've loved you for as long as I can remember." Rosamund did not meet my eyes as she spoke. "I tried to convince myself, and you, that I did not. But I was foolish to think otherwise. I love you, Varus, and I would never do anything to hurt you."

It was an answer that infuriated me. Images of our tryst in the Colosseum, of the dozens of times we spent alone aboard ships, or of our one night coupled together in Constantinople's barracks. Hundreds of nights spent away from my family, my skin brushing against hers, trusting her beyond measure. She loved me but did not say so.

Mariya knew this, even when I did not. And, God forgive me, but my ignorance had cost Mariya her life.

Still, a glimmer of doubt demanded that I proceed cautiously. Again, I ignored that voice of reason.

"You let Mariya die," I spat. "Indulf organized her death, and Triarius fulfilled it, but you are just as complicit."

"Varus, no!" Rosamund wept. "No, no, no!"

I rose, slamming my chair against the wall. It shattered into three pieces as I brushed past her, avoiding her outstretched arms, deaf to her pleas. Throwing the door open, I escaped to the hallway, hailing a nearby guard.

"Rosamund does not leave this room!" I yelled. "Not until I command otherwise!"

THE DARK PATH

My condemnation reached the army's command staff within a day. By the end of the week, lurid tales of Rosamund's imprisonment circulated in every popina in Rome.

None dared oppose me, although Belisarius urged caution. "This is truly the path you wish to take?" he asked. "Rosamund's guilt is that apparent?"

"Even Agathias speaks against her," I replied. "Samur and Perenus concur. Rosamund was like family to me, but she betrayed my trust when it was needed most."

Later, I spoke with Liberius. He did not disagree with Rosamund's guilt, but he questioned the extent of my condemnation. "It certainly is odd that her treatment of Mariya was so insufficient, but whether this was due to malice or merely being overwhelmed in the moment... that, to me, is less clear."

I had to confide the truth to him. "She admitted her love for me and desired to act upon it over the past year."

"Foolish love does not a murderer make," Liberius countered after a moment. "But you know her better than I. If you believe her capable of destroying someone's life for selfish reasons, then act as you must."

No fewer than ten men advised me on this matter, none of whom was invited to do so. Priests demanded that I punish Rosamund for witchcraft and paganism, while Roman lawyers apprised me of countless punishments that her purported crimes qualified for. Procopius, however, was most explicit of all, shaking a handful of pamphlets on ancient Roman law, military law, and the novel codex of Justinian.

"The punishment for a servant who rises against their master is burning," he declaimed. "Lashed to a post in a public square as a warning to all others who would raise a hand against their superior."

Images of the Brazen Bull flooded my mind's eye, the stench of burning fat and keening screams filling the Bovis Forum of Constantinople once again searing my senses. A horrid death, full of suffering, pain that reverberated through the ages and for the rest of time.

And, in my rage, fortified by excessive wine and solitude, I found it a fitting punishment. Few would have protested, and none would have stopped me. If anything, many in power would laud Rosamund burning at the stake, noting that I had finally heeded the good sense to cast heretics aside.

But in moments of sobriety, doubt lingered. Rosamund had wronged me—of this, I was certain. Yet Liberius' words caused me to question Rosamund's intent. And so, though I was unable to forgive, I opted for mercy.

Two weeks after Rosamund's sequester, I ordered a horse saddled and prepared for an extensive journey, its handler to await me at the Appian Gate. The following morning, I awoke, and Shimon and Sembrouthes aided me in donning my armor as an excubitor. Then, I marched to Rosamund's quarters, where I deposited fresh clothing just inside her door.

"Put these on," I ordered. "We're leaving."

Rosamund complied and emerged dressed, her skin cleaned from a basin of water that a servant had provided, but otherwise appearing as vulnerable as before. Behind me, she walked slowly, surrounded by a half dozen Aksumites, until we reached the Domus' exit.

"Varus—"

"Silence," I ordered.

"...are you going to kill me?"

"Not another word!"

Horses awaited all of us, and once mounted, I guided her through Rome's streets, veering toward the Appian Gate to Rome's south. We passed thousands of citizens, most of whom ignored us, but some of whom yelled curses. *Pagan. Witch. Heretic. Whore.* All seemed to brush past Rosamund as she maintained her silence with icy indifference. We continued, past the forum and the Colosseum and hundreds of other monuments, keeping a leisurely pace that cost us nearly an hour to reach our destination. When we did, I dismounted and hailed the prepared mount to approach. Lastly, I ordered the gate opened, its sentries straining against levers that turned chains and opened a narrow portal from Rome to the outside world. It was early in the morning, too early for trade, yet only just.

I strode for Rosamund and grabbed her by the wrist. "Follow."

Rosamund darted her gaze about frantically, yet found no allies. She had no choice but to quicken her pace to keep up with my own, and did nothing to resist. At the gate, I gestured for the mount to be brought beside me, aware that no fewer than a hundred soldiers stood vigil over my actions.

"Rosamund of the Gepids." I glared at her, releasing her wrist from my grip. "Until this day, you have been my oath sworn servant. You have failed that oath. Some would have me take your life as repayment, but I would spare you that suffering."

Rosamund nodded, eyes welling once more. "Thank you, Varus."

"But I release you from your oath to me nonetheless," I declared. "You are exiled from these lands."

She whimpered. "Exile? This is my home! Where would I go?!"

"Wherever you desire," I answered. "But know that if you remain with our army, a sentence of death will come into effect. Instead, I bid you leave with this mount, three months' rations, your weapons and armor, and enough silver to see you back to the forests of Moesia."

Rosamund shook her head, even as two guards advanced to force her atop her new mount. "Varus, please!! I love you! Give me another choice, another chance!"

For a heartbeat, I wanted to. "Goodbye, Rosamund."

From within the saddle, Rosamund grasped for my cloak, catching its hem. "Varus, as the gods judge my actions, I did not do this."

Sad eyes, wide and tinged with yellow, pleaded with me. It was the same mournful look that had greeted me in Moesia, lifetimes ago. When a different set of accusations had been levied upon me and my comrades in Archelaus' army.

"Varus..." she all but whispered. "After everything, do you really believe I am capable of killing... of *hurting* you in this way?"

Another flicker of doubt. An ember, threatening to spread to conflagration. It would be so easy to answer Rosamund's pleas. I wanted to. Desperately, I wanted to. After all, if I believed Rosamund undeniably guilty, why had I allowed her to live at all?

But grief held fast to my heart. I believed that ember a weakness and stomped it out with a snarl. "Goodbye, Rosamund!"

Tugging my cloak free, I pointed through the open gate. Rosamund sighed, seized the reins, and cracked hard. Her horse galloped forth, bringing her silver hair to trail with the wind. A hundred paces from the walls, she paused, turned back, and stared at me.

"Should we go get her, Lord?" the gate centurion asked.

I yearned to. More than ever. "No. Just close the gates. We have work to do."

Did I make a mistake? In my heart, I think not. Yet over the years, a new flicker of doubt has tainted the surety of a younger man, making room for the possibility that Rosamund had simply made a grievous error—a terrible error, one driven by distraction at treating the woman who had been her friend and my wife, one that rendered Rosamund unable to act dispassionately. If I am wrong, I pray that God grant me forgiveness. And grant it to Rosamund as well, regardless of what transgressions followed this dark episode.

So many had died in the name of Justinian. For Rome. For a dream, the costs of which were unbearable. And may God have mercy on the millions of souls destroyed by our hubris—what follows is a tale unrivaled in suffering. We could not know the trials ahead. At that moment, all we knew was that we had Belisarius, who looked northward toward Witiges and his holdout of Ravenna. Shaken, we still believed in our cause. And so, we would continue down a dark road whose destination would damn us all.

Our tale, and the tale of Belisarius, was far from over.

AUTHOR'S NOTE

As with the preceding novels of the Last of the Romans, *The Eternal City* is a work of fiction. Events are reordered, and characters are molded or invented for the sake of storytelling. At times, the names of cities are converted to modern spelling conventions out of familiarity for the modern English-speaking reader. My intention is to provide a period-realistic world for you to explore, while condensing the dense complexity that comprised East Roman and tribal societies.

By the conclusion of the Vandal War, Justinian had engaged in a lengthy period of de-paganism across the Empire. This was widely successful in major cities and suppressed public pagan practices in most provinces, although paganism was stickier in the frontier regions. This did little to pacify religious dissent across the Empire, however. Some Christian dissent came in the form of Arianism — an interpretation of Christianity where Jesus was created by the Father and subsequently subordinate to the Father. Fostered by Arius (early fourth century AD), Arianism had taken root amongst the Vandals and Goths.

More immediately concerning Justinian were those Christians who rejected the Council of Chalcedon in 451 AD. Chalcedonian Christianity, whose adherents attest to Dyophysitism, where Jesus is understood to consist of two natures, divine and human, that coexist in the person of Jesus Christ, had become dominant throughout the Eastern Empire, albeit slowly and incompletely. Oriental Orthodox churches, not to be confused with the later Eastern Orthodoxy, generally rejected the interpretation of the Council of Chalcedon, with major centers in Alexandria and Antioch.

Jacob Baradaeus, formally known as Jacob bar Addai, was a major figure in the early non-Chalcedonian Oriental Orthodox Church, and a leading figure of Monophysitism. Theodora, who was a non-Chalcedonian and had spent considerable time in Egypt during her youth, became aware of Jacob and invited him to Constantinople. Jacob was hesitant to accept the invitation, though eventually did, and was received with honor by the Empress. Jacob was never interested in the Imperial court and would have understood that Justinian disfavored him—as Justinian was an adherent to Chalcedonian Christianity. Theodora used her power to protect the Monophysites, though frequently was incapable of doing so during the worst periods of religious persecution of Jacob's adherents. There would be many meetings and councils to heal the rift between the Chalcedonians and non-Chalcedonians, although Monophysitism remained out of favor for much of Justinian's life and those of his successors. The persecutions led by Cassiodorus in this book are fictional, although they are inspired by the persecutions conducted during Justinian's reign, and possibly with Justinian's blessing.

The Brazen Bull is an ancient and excruciating torture device—much of its use is speculative, as accounts are written centuries after the fact, although its recurring discussion makes its existence seem likely in the Roman world. Hollow, the bull was fashioned from bronze and placed above a furnace that could be stoked with a bellows. Those guilty of crimes deemed heinous were stuffed into the bull's side and slowly roasted alive. The Romans allegedly used the Brazen Bull on early Christians, such as Saint Eustace and Saint Antipas. There is record that Constantinople's Bovis Forum, or Forum of the Ox, was occasionally a center for public torture and execution, and included a Brazen Bull imported from Pergamum. Janin argues that same bull might have been used against Saint Antipas. The Brazen Bull in the Bovis Forum is difficult to track through history, although appears to have been used against the usurper Phocas in 610 AD and possibly against traitors against Justinian II in the early eighth century.

The Eternal City marks a considerable change in the stature and ambitions of Justinian's Empire. In history, Justinian reveled in the acquisition of Carthage and the Vandal kingdom—though that considerable success did nothing to slake his suspicion of Belisarius, regardless of the Triumph that the victorious general was awarded upon return to Constantinople. Regardless, the influx of wealth and the excitement from quick victory spoiled the Imperial government and population alike. They wanted more, and circumstance afforded Justinian the perfect opportunity to seize an even greater prize—Italy.

It might be difficult for contemporary readers to understand both the importance of Amalasuntha to Justinian's and Belisarius' futures, as well as why her death empowered Justinian with the justification to launch another expensive and dangerous expedition. The historical record of Amalasuntha's life is refreshingly vivid. She was born into Gothic nobility as the youngest surviving daughter of Theodoric the Great, who had briefly united the Visigoths (much of Hispania) and Ostrogoths (Italy, Sicily, Illyria, and portions of adjacent provinces) under a single monarch. Theodoric's death plunged both Gothic kingdoms into instability, though as we witnessed in *The Pillars of Herakles*, the Visigoths recovered and asserted their independence under the warlord-turned-king Theudis. For Italy, the situation was murkier, and unresolved for years due to the ascension of Amalasuntha's son Athalaric, who was only ten years old when he succeeded his respected grandfather to the Ostrogoth throne.

Theodoric had been a reformer and more of a Latinophile than other tribes that had invaded and settled Roman territory. Amalasuntha shared those traits—continuing Theodoric's preservation of Roman churches and monuments, preferring Roman cities over Gothic villages, and sponsoring learning, Roman bureaucracy, and sustaining other ancient Roman institutions. This preference for Roman culture even extended to the education of Athalaric—earning the ire of more culturally conservative Gothic chieftains.

As regent, Amalasuntha initially warded off those chieftains based on her bloodline—the Amal lineage was deeply respected to the point of near reverence, with Jordanes indicating a claimed descent from Gapt, a Germanic tribal deity of war, and Theodoric's father Theodemir regained Ostrogoth independence from the Huns after Attila's death. Over time, however, Amalasuntha eventually permitted Athalaric's Latin education to be complemented with military training with leading Gothic families.

Alas, Athalaric lacked the opportunity to lead independently. At roughly eighteen, Athalaric perished, with records mixed on whether his death was from alcoholism (exceedingly common in Gothic warrior culture), or complications from diabetes, or both. Regardless of the cause, Athalaric's death left a considerable void in Ostrogoth leadership—one that Amalasuntha moved quickly to fill.

Shrewdly, Amalasuntha addressed potential rivals by asking her cousin Theodahad to co-rule, albeit in a silent and less assertive manner. Likewise, Amalasuntha empowered a council of leading chieftains to publicly provide guidance on the leadership of the kingdom. However, Amalasuntha retained dominance in court, with the council more of a puppet institution to assuage conservative elements of Gothic society that were unwilling to outright support a queen, especially one notorious for her embrace of Roman culture and language.

Amalasuntha's death at Lake Bolsena is a turning point in Late Antiquity. Prior to her death, Amalasuntha had engaged in a public friendship with Justinian. Missives were frequently exchanged, and some writers even indicate that Amalasuntha was considering reverting direct control of Ostrogoth holdings to Justinian. To the proud Gothic chieftains, most of whom had served under the wildly successful Theodoric, this was unthinkable. Past Gothic kings had ruled with the quasi-legal "assent" of the emperor in Constantinople, but were entirely sovereign from the Eastern Empire.

What is certain is that Amalasuntha was killed suddenly, though the identity of the killer is muddied. Various Gothic chieftains are implicated over time, while Theodahad is raised early on as a likely killer, although this seems contrary to his bookish and nonconfrontational character—indeed, much of Theodahad's rule appears lethargic and reluctant. Some even accuse leaders in Constantinople of engineering a casus belli to invade the Ostrogothic kingdom.

Regardless, Justinian publicly argued that the death of his friend, and one he had conferred protection over, was reason to send his best general to reclaim the Roman cities. Amalasuntha was survived by her daughter, Matasuntha, who would later become an important secondary player in Constantinople's politics in her own right. In the short term, Theodahad was crowned sole monarch of the Ostrogoths, although there appears to be significant disagreement and dissatisfaction with his crowning.

The invasion of Italy was planned in two wings similar to what is described in *The Eternal City*. Belisarius led a seaborne wing, landing in Syracuse and pacifying Sicily before spreading northward onto the mainland. Likewise, Mundus was charged with a landward invasion, intended to purge the Goths from Dalmatia and eventually pressure Ravenna from the north. Of these, both met early success—Mundus captured Salona, while Belisarius swept across Sicily within a single campaign. From there, however, Mundus and Belisarius' fates diverge.

By the onset of the Gothic War, historical Mundus had experienced a successful multi-decade career as a soldier. Notably, Mundus' warriors were instrumental in clearing the Nika Riots and saving Justinian's throne. This earned Mundus his formal independent command, to which Mundus was initially wildly successful. However, his son was slain when fighting a contingent of Goths under Gripas, to which a despondent Mundus launched a vicious counterattack near Salona. While victorious, Mundus was eventually killed. Lacking their leader, the Imperial Army's progress at Salona was halted and even reversed, while further Gothic attacks depleted their manpower.

While the events of the Feast of Salona are my creation, the betrayal of Indulf had immense, systemic effects upon the nature of the Gothic War. A longtime warrior and trusted guard of Belisarius, Indulf had maintained secret correspondence with Gothic leadership. With Belisarius distracted elsewhere, Indulf was able to move freely along the Goth–Roman line of contact and gained the trust of Gothic leadership to the point where they equipped him with an army of hardened veterans. Then, sailing for Dalmatia, Indulf greeted his former compatriots, who believed Indulf was still a trusted ally. Initially unopposed, Indulf slaughtered entire settlements and their sizeable garrisons, and thoroughly defeated a hastily assembled relief force. In a matter of weeks, Indulf had undone everything that Mundus had achieved. Worse, the annihilation of Mundus' forces left Belisarius isolated and alone beyond the sea, reliant upon arduous resupply from Greece, Egypt, or the freshly conquered Carthage.

Belisarius also faced initial successes followed by critical setbacks. My depiction of Belisarius' capture of Panormus follows his historical experience, where the Roman armies dashed across Sicily and captured all major settlements save the well-guarded and thickly walled Panormus. In perhaps one of his more ingenious feats, Belisarius recognized that the sea walls were shorter than landward walls. With several Imperial ships, Belisarius engineered a pulley system where smaller launch boats could be lifted up along a reinforced mast. Staffed with expert bowmen, the defenders of Panormus soon found themselves exposed to Imperial archers that held the advantage of height from sea, which rendered the sea walls indefensible. Panormus surrendered shortly thereafter.

This victory is astounding not only because of the engineering marvel constructed impromptu, but equally because that ingenuity afforded Belisarius a victory under critically important conditions— his army was intact, largely unhurt, caught the Goths unawares, yet secured the entire Italian island. An impending invasion of the mainland appeared imminent.

Alas, Belisarius, too, was struck by misfortune. While he had left Carthage pacified, much of the hinterlands in Numidia and farther Mauretania experienced a power vacuum with the fall of the Vandal kingdom. Many Mauri tribes rose against Solomon, who had been appointed as regional military commander. He is recorded by Procopius as a capable Imperial commander and enjoyed many bloody victories over the Mauri tribes.

Despite an intense campaign of fortification development, however, Solomon had not been able to quell Mauri uprisings and eventually suffered a severe mutiny within the Imperial ranks. Eventually, mutineers drove Solomon out of Carthage altogether, and he fled for Sicily to beseech Belisarius for aid. In the meantime, mutineers and Mauri tribes coalesced under a certain Stotzas, who had fought with the Imperial armies but desired to construct an independent African state. Records of Stotzas are scant, although based upon his actions, Stotzas appears to be both cunning and diplomatic and capable of quickly assembling a large army from a cosmopolitan force rather quickly. Procopius writes that near ten thousand men besieged Carthage, which after Solomon's departure had been left with a paltry force to defend its walls.

With Carthage's fall imminent, Belisarius delayed the invasion of Italy and returned to Carthage. Only a relatively small force could join him, as sea expeditions usually required months of planning and coordination, and few boats were immediately available. Still, Belisarius traveled to Carthage, which upon his arrival was actively experiencing attack.

Yet as Belisarius' banners were raised over Carthage's ramparts, the besieging army collapsed in disarray, fearful of Belisarius' arrival. Belisarius gathered his warriors and Carthage's remaining fighters and gave chase to the mutineer Mauri army, catching them after several days at Membresa, along the Bagradas River. There, and with inferior numbers, Belisarius nevertheless systematically dismantled the less fearful remnants of Stotzas' army. Utterly routed, Stotzas nevertheless survived and would cause trouble for the Romans for many years to come.

In the immediate term, relative peace surrounded Carthage.

Solomon was recalled to Constantinople, while Germanus was installed as the military prefect of the region. Later, that post would be taken by Troglita, who would earn considerable honors for his leadership in the province. That story is for another book, however.

After departing Carthage once more, Belisarius set to the task of invading Italy in the following spring. Ostrogoth resistance had been surprisingly sluggish—the Goths were famed warriors, both numerous and fearless, and experienced in-fighting against Imperial tactics. There was scant resistance as Belisarius first seized Regium and spread through Calabria, where a determined resistance might have bottled the invading Imperials into narrow junctures of the Italian boot.

Quickly, Belisarius advanced northward, encountering his first major resistance at Neapolis (modern Naples). The Goths were heavily outnumbered, and no relief force was mounted, yet the garrison was inspired to resist by two orators. Setting the siege lines, Belisarius warned Neapolis that it would be difficult to restrain his men if they resisted for a lengthy period. However, he also addressed his men formally, imploring them to continue his policy of mercy, order, and discipline—no looting, murder, rape, or violent crime against the populace, who would be the Emperor's subjects. Fragments of that speech are still available and have become popularized by Edward Gibbon: *The gold and silver are the just rewards of your valour, but spare the inhabitants, they are Christians, they are suppliants, they are now your fellow subjects. Restore the children to their parents, the wives to their husbands; and shew them by your generosity, of what friends they have obstinately deprived themselves.*

Unfortunately, Neapolis stubbornly held out for three weeks, with no relief army arriving from Theodahad. Like Panormus, Belisarius resolved this siege through creativity. One of his Isaurian warriors discovered a hidden aqueduct that had fallen into partial disrepair that led directly into the city. Belisarius' engineers widened the entrance while soldiers sang, shouted, and banged their shields together to give cover to the engineers' digging and carving. A small force entered Neapolis through the aqueduct, quickly overrunning the unsuspecting sentries and opening the gates to Belisarius' broader army. Neapolis was brutally sacked and soon repopulated and rebuilt by Belisarius' engineers.

Still, Belisarius persisted northward. Traveling along the Via Appia, Belisarius reached Rome's gates by December 536—just a month after seizing Neapolis. Rome's inhabitants had heard of Neapolis' sack and were unmotivated by the roughly four thousand Gothic warriors stationed to defend Rome against attack. The population emphatically and decisively supported Belisarius' seizure of the city, which occurred on 9 December 536 as Belisarius entered the Asinarian Gate. Generally peaceful, the Gothic garrison escaped northward through the Flaminian Gate, not contesting the Roman conquest of the Eternal City. In a single stroke, the Imperial equivalent of Manifest Destiny had been fulfilled—the return of the Roman mother city to Imperial control.

Naturally, these developments, and Theodahad's inaction, infuriated the Gothic military leadership. Theodahad was deposed and later slain, replaced by Witiges. Witiges married Matasuntha—the only surviving child of Amalasuntha, and therefore one of the last legitimate strings of the Amal Dynasty, and quickly adopted a vigorous, if quixotically reckless demeanor. Witiges was the opposite of Theodahad in nearly all areas—warlike instead of bookish, entrenched in conservative Gothic warrior culture, direct comrades with the chieftains, and prone to action with limited delay. Witiges' initial vanguard arrived at Rome in February 537, though the yearlong siege of Rome does not formally begin until early March as the vast bulk of the Gothic army surrounded the Eternal City's landward walls and roads.

Exact numbers of both armies are difficult to acquire. Belisarius is estimated to have taken five thousand experienced veterans into Rome and conscripted a few thousand locals that would have been of unreliable quality. Reinforcements would arrive to bolster Belisarius' position, albeit gradually. These numbers are laughably small—in peacetime, Rome's garrison via the Praetorian Guard is occasionally estimated at 24,000 men. The Aurelian Walls—the famed shell of ancient Rome, and still visible today—were roughly twenty kilometers in length and interspersed with 380 fighting towers, one every thirty meters. If Belisarius left no men in reserve or to station buildings inside of Rome—which he did, proving pivotal during the worst of the fighting—the most favorable math indicates roughly one Imperial soldier per three meters of wall length, not accounting for casualties, illness, or other issues. By any account, Belisarius was hideously understaffed—a continuing challenge spawning from his relationship with Justinian during the Vandal War and the Iberian War.

In contrast, Witiges' numbers are even more unreliable. Peterson estimates Witiges commanded twenty-five to thirty thousand experienced warriors, although likely this would have been supplemented by a significant number of militia, volunteers, camp followers, and others. Roughly two weeks after the siege lines were formed, Witiges launched the first major assault against Rome, one of the most vicious and populous of the ancient world. Belisarius stationed his headquarters to the north along the Pincian Gate, while trusted officers were each entrusted with command of major gates that linked Rome to various roads.

Witiges' initial attack was along the Salarian Gate—adjacent to Belisarius' command post—and involved the use of four massive siege towers to allow Gothic warriors to storm the walls. Procopius describes the sight of the advancing wood-and-iron structures as terrifying to the Roman defenders. Belisarius, however, laughed at the sight, commanded his warriors to keep silent, and then gradually focused his bowmen upon the oxen that hauled the Gothic towers toward the Aurelian Walls. Shortly thereafter, with the oxen dead, the towers sat useless and well apart from their targets. Belisarius is individually attributed as striking three Gothic riders from his own bow—substantially raising Imperial morale at that auspicious omen.

Near-simultaneous attacks were launched across the length of the Aurelian Walls. One of the earliest trouble points was Hadrian's Mausoleum (the modern Castel Saint Angelo, to the northwest along the Aurelian Walls). Fierce Gothic assaults nearly overran the Romans atop the tower. Fighting became so desperate that the Roman defenders were described as throwing marble statues from the Mausoleum down upon the Gothic defenders, shattering ladders and causing many Gothic casualties. Eventually, the Mausoleum stabilized, though other areas of the Aurelian Walls deteriorated.

The worst of the fighting emerged at the Vivarium, along the Praenestine Gate, where Romans had kept animals for hunts, entertainment, and other purposes. Led by Bessas and Peranius (my "Perenus"), the Romans held out against immense pressure but could not halt the destruction of the Praenestine Gate's enclosure forever. Peranius sent to Belisarius for aid—the general arrived personally with a small force of his most trusted warriors just as the Goths broke through the gate. Then, streaming forward, Belisarius and Peranius counterattacked, scattering the Gothic assault. That sortie also gave Belisarius the opportunity to destroy many of the Gothic siege engines with torches. With that, the great assault concluded, preventing Witiges from striking a quick victory.

The siege would last a full year. Conditions worsened, including the usual challenges of illness, city violence, and the general inability or unwillingness of the court in Constantinople to reinforce Belisarius with sufficient numbers. Most of all, however, the effects of the "Year Without Summer" had ruined harvests throughout the Mediterranean, contributing to acute famines. Belisarius was acutely aware of the dangers that famine and discord could bring and took pains to improve city security by constantly rotating sentry guards and regularly changing locks on gates, for example, as well as bolstering food supply.

One particular innovation includes the "water mills," which Belisarius designed amidst the siege to facilitate the grinding of wheat into flour. The water mills operated by floating a mill on a vessel that was anchored on two different points along the Tiber River. Water intake cranked the mill, which subsequently afforded mechanical capability to grind flour. Versions of these mills are still used today around the world.

Worsening matters for the besieged and besiegers alike was a sudden and intense period of climatic cooling that began in 536 and continued to affect climatic conditions through 540 and possibly even longer. The likely cause is volcanism, though this would have been unknown to residents of Europe at the time. Many scholars commented on this episode: The Roman statesman Cassiodorus (not to be confused with my Cassiodorus) describes a near bluish sun, whose rays were so weak that they cast no shadows from buildings or people. Procopius is even more poetic in his description, noting that "...during this year, a most dread portent took place. For the sun gave forth its light without brightness... and it seemed exceedingly like the sun in eclipse, for the beams it shed were not clear..."

Frosts consumed harvests in normally temperate areas, while snow fell during summer months, causing widespread crop failure. Naturally, this fostered conditions for famine and considerable commentary from religious communities of the time. The event's effects were widespread, ranging in written record from Britain to China and possibly indirect records in North America as well. Ström (1961) even posits that Viking myths of Fimbulwinter and Ragnarök might have been fashioned based upon Scandinavian experiences during this time. Regardless, what appeared in the skies appeared like a hazy veil of dust and would contribute to mass fatality events in the coming years.

Eventually, despite considerable hardship, Belisarius triumphed at the Siege of Rome. Military innovations, notably the use of swift Hunnic horse archers, aided Belisarius in overcoming his deficiency in numbers against Witiges. Eventually, reinforcements would trickle toward the city and empower Belisarius' expedition with enough manpower to threaten Ariminium. Witiges was forced to lift the siege to protect Ariminium, which was perilously close to the Ostrogoth capital at Ravenna, as well as due to the debilitating conditions in his camp. Both sides suffered greatly—much of Rome's outlying infrastructure was devastated by the siege, while thousands died from famine and violence. Ultimately, Belisarius' victory would turn the tide of war squarely in Imperial favor, at least for the time being.

The concluding events of *The Eternal City* center around poison. Many a Roman senator, merchant, and even emperor fell victim to one of hundreds of poisons available to the Imperial world. Of these, hemlock is among the more fabled. Hemlock, or *Conium maculatum*, is highly toxic, with parts such as the hollow stems deadly to humans for three years or more after the plant has died. Indeed, all parts of the hemlock plant are poisonous to most mammals and possess a distinct musty, alkaloid odor. It had been used to poison condemned prisoners in ancient Greece, though it became famous after Socrates consumed a hemlock infusion after being found guilty of corrupting the minds of Athenian youth in 399 BC.

Hemlock and countless other poisons found their way to the Roman court, where local physicians developed various countermeasures and treatments for poisoning. It is impossible to say how many emperors, senators, and other notable citizens fell victim to a noxious plant or attenuated venom, although a glance at the causes of death suggest poisoning as an ever-present threat.

The Eternal City was a challenge to write, but a labor of love. As always, I owe considerable thanks to many for bringing this series to life. Blair Thornburgh of The Author Studio provided the developmental and line edits—I am grateful for her technical abilities as much as her knowledge and diligence to realism for the time period! Crystal Watanabe of Pikko's House provided the copyediting, proofreading, and formatting, and crafted beautiful interiors. The creative Dusan Markovic illustrated the book's cover. Daniel Kogosov "Zalezsky" crafted the stunning maps used for this novel. I am grateful to them, as well as my readers, for their patience and support in bringing this novel to life.

If you enjoyed *The Eternal City*, please consider leaving a review on Amazon and Goodreads. I am so thankful for your time in this—

ratings and reviews are what allow the series to continue! For the Gothic War has only just begun. Ahead lies the still-formidable armies of the Goths, hungering to strike against Belisarius' exhausted army. Likewise, an even more forbidding foe stalks upon the horizon, prepared to claim the lives of millions throughout the known world.

Despite it all, Belisarius and Varus still have wars to fight in Justinian's name.

Printed in Great Britain
by Amazon

43356532R00456